Elvi Rhodes was born and educated in Yorkshire, and now lives in Sussex. Her bestselling novels include: *Opal, Doctor Rose, Ruth Appleby, The Golden Girls, Madeleine, The House of Bonneau, Cara's Land, The Rainbow Through the Rain, The Bright One, The Mountain, Portrait of Chloe, Spring Music, Midsummer Meeting* and *The Birthday Party*. A collection of stories, *Summer Promise and Other Stories*, is also published by Corgi Books.

D1545671

Also by Elvi Rhodes

DOCTOR ROSE
THE GOLDEN GIRLS
THE HOUSE OF BONNEAU
MADELEINE
OPAL
RUTH APPLEBY
CARA'S LAND
SUMMER PROMISE AND OTHER STORIES
THE RAINBOW THROUGH THE RAIN
THE BRIGHT ONE
THE MOUNTAIN
PORTRAIT OF CHLOE
SPRING MUSIC
MIDSUMMER MEETING

and published by Corgi Books

THE MOUNTAIN
and
OPAL

Elvi Rhodes

CORGI BOOKS

THE MOUNTAIN AND OPAL
A CORGI BOOK : 9780552149822

This edition first published by Corgi Books 2002
Copyright © Elvi Rhodes 2001

3 5 7 9 10 8 6 4

including
THE MOUNTAIN
Originally published in Great Britain by Bantam Press,
a division of Transworld Publishers
Copyright © Elvi Rhodes 1995
Corgi edition published 1996
Set in 10/11¼ pt Linotype New Baskerville by
Kestrel Data, Exeter, Devon.

OPAL
Originally published in Great Britain by
Century Publishing Co. Ltd
Copyright © Elvi Rhodes 1984
Corgi edition published 1984
Set in 10/12 pt Monotype Plantin by
Kestrel Data, Exeter, Devon.

Corgi Books are published by Transworld Publishers,
61–63 Uxbridge Road, London W5 5SA,
a division of The Random House Group Ltd.

Addresses for Random House Group Ltd companies outside the UK
can be found at: www.randomhouse.co.uk
The Random House Group Ltd Reg. No. 954009.

Printed and bound in Great Britain by
Cox & Wyman Ltd, Reading, Berkshire.

The Random House Group Limited makes every effort to ensure that the
papers used in its books are made from trees that have been legally
sourced from well-managed and credibly certified forests. Our paper
procurement policy can be found at:
www.randomhouse.co.uk/paper.htm.

THE MOUNTAIN

This book is for Anthony,
with much love

Acknowledgements

I owe a great debt of gratitude to W. R. (Bill) Mitchell who, I daresay, knows more about the Settle-Carlisle Railway and the area in which it still runs than anyone in the world. His many books have been an inspection and a mainstay in the writing of my novel. If I've got any facts wrong it's my error, not his.

I also, as always, thank my son Anthony for all his help in my research, and on this occasion I include my daughter-in-law, Margaret, who built me a detailed plaster model of the Ribblehead area at the time in which my story is set.

1

Jake Tempest (well-named, those who knew him said, for that's what he could be when he was roused) picked up his bag, swinging it aloft with ease. It was not a large bag, considering it contained his life, or as much of it, past, present and future, as he was prepared to carry around with him. It all fitted into the canvas knapsack. He liked to travel light.

In what was a gesture of thanks he rested his hand on Oggy's shoulder. Bill Ogden, the old man's name was, but everyone on the canal called him Oggy. They couldn't shake hands because the old man needed both his to bring the barge in close enough to the canal bank for Jake to jump off.

'Thanks, Oggy,' Jake said. 'It's been a real help.'

'Nay, Skipton to Gargrave's no great distance,' Oggy protested.

'It is when you're walking the rest of the way,' Jake said. 'Every little helps.'

'Aye well! If you'd nobbut come wi' me I could take thee all t'way to Liverpool. Tha could hop on one o' them big ships and sail for America, shake dust o' Skipton off thi feet proper, seeing that's what tha has a mind to do!'

Jake smiled, shook his head.

'I reckon I'll take it in easy stages, Oggy. Get a job, make a bit o' brass. It wouldn't do to land in America, and not a penny to my name. So you can wish me luck, finding work.'

The barge was within a yard of the bank now,

dead easy for Jake, who was long-legged and agile, to jump.

'You'll be all right,' Oggy said.

With a final wave of his hand Jake leapt from the barge, then fitted his bag more easily on his shoulder and walked away along the towpath.

Oggy watched him for a minute, saw him halt his stride to say something to the big horse which was towing the boat, and to run his hand along its neck, before moving on. Then he turned his attention back to the boat, manœuvring it into position to go through the locks.

The canal would turn west now. Soon they would have to go through the long Foulbridge tunnel which cut through the Pennines. He hated the tunnel, but when they came out into the daylight again they'd be in Lancashire. There'd be someone on this side, a young lad most likely, who'd lead the horse over the top, and someone a bit older to help him leg the barge through the tunnel. There always was. It was a way of earning a few coppers in hard times.

He spoke to his dog, a brown, rough-haired terrier type, now lying comfortably on the cargo of wool waste. He often spoke out loud to his dog.

'Well, Kipper, there'll be no difficulty in yon Jake Tempest finding hisself a job, an' that's for sure.'

He'd known Jake Tempest since he was a little lad. Everyone on the canal knew him. And he'd always been bonny, but now that he was grown he was as handsome a man as you'd find in a day's march. His round, childish features had firmed, so that the fine bones of his cheeks, nose and jaw shaped his face. He had thick black hair which curled over his collar, giving him a gipsyish look. They said his father had been a bit of a gipsy, though Oggy had never seen him. He'd not stayed around long.

But there was nothing of the gipsy about the lad's

eyes. They'd come straight from his mother. Bright blue, and always with a lively look in them. Oggy remembered Lily Tempest's eyes.

Yes, her son was a well-favoured man, and young with it, not more than three-and-twenty, Oggy thought enviously. Oh, he'd get on all right!

'I wonder what made him take agen Skipton?' Oggy enquired of Kipper. 'Happen a woman, I wouldn't wonder.'

If you didn't count Lily Tempest, women were the cause of most trouble in life, he reckoned. He'd certainly never have one aboard. He preferred a dog.

Jake quickly left the towpath and joined the turnpike road, turning north towards Settle, which was no more than a dozen miles from Skipton, though in all his life he'd never been there. He'd travelled much greater distances, but always on the canal. In fact he'd almost been born on the canal, on his grandfather's boat, and would have been except that his mother had left it in something of a hurry to go into hospital for his premature birth. She'd brought him back on board when he was ten days old, and for the next twelve years he'd been reared in the boat's cramped and confined living quarters.

He remembered every detail now. The short bedhole at the side of the cabin where he slept, his mother sleeping in a similar one on the other side, and his grandfather elsewhere on the barge – on deck in the summer. There'd been a highly decorated stove in the centre, with its cooking pots, and the kettle always on the boil behind the polished brass fireguard. There were tiny cupboards everywhere, narrow shelves with ornaments on lace doyleys, cushions which his mother crocheted in her spare moments. He had loved it all. They'd been happy, his mother, himself and his grandfather.

For a long time he'd thought his grandfather was

his father, until his mother told him otherwise. He'd always called him 'Pop', a sort of nickname, just as she had.

'No, love,' she'd said. 'Not that he hasn't always been the best of fathers to you.'

She'd taken both his hands in hers, looked straight at him with sad eyes.

'Your dad disappeared before you were born. I've always meant to tell you, but the time was never right. He walked off the boat one day in Leeds, and I've not seen hair nor hide of him since. But at least he married me when he knew you were on the way. I'll say that for him. So you're not a bastard.'

He'd not known what she'd meant.

'It's a child whose father didn't marry his mother, but you're not one, so that's all right.'

She'd always answered his questions truthfully.

'Don't think too badly of him,' she'd added. 'He just wasn't cut out to be a husband and a dad.'

'What did he look like?' Jake had asked.

She'd paused a minute, bringing him to mind.

'He was the best-looking man I ever saw. You're very like him – or you will be when you're older. But not in his ways. You'll make something of yourself, you will.'

'I'll never leave you,' Jake had said.

'Nor I you, love!'

So what had he made of himself, he wondered, as he walked along the road on this August morning in the year 1870.

He could still neither read nor write, though he was good at numbers. He got that from his grandfather, who'd taught him how to add up and subtract and multiply, until one day he said: 'Well, I've given thee what I know, young Jake, but now you've outstripped me. From now on, if you want to go further, you'll ha' to get another teacher.'

But there'd been no other teachers. The boat was seldom in one place long enough for Jake to get more than a few days' schooling at a time. And since he'd been with strangers, whose ways were not his ways, he'd not made much of it.

Oh well, he thought, no matter now. He'd like to be able to read and write, but there were other things in life. He knew more about nature than most boys. He knew where to find the first flowers, which of the plants growing near to the canal were safe to eat and which weren't, where the birds nested, how to foretell the weather. He knew practical things, too. He could catch, skin and cook a rabbit or a hedgehog, catch fish, and from an early age, under his grandfather's eye, he'd been able to take the barge through the locks.

When he was twelve years old life on the canal came to an abrupt end. His grandfather, whose only fault was that when he had money in his pocket he imbibed a drop too much, one night stopped off in Skipton and took on a skinful. On the way back to the boat, weaving his way along the towpath, he stumbled, fell in the water, and drowned.

'Whatever shall we do, Ma?' Jake asked after the funeral.

'I don't know,' Lily Tempest admitted. 'We can't stay on the canal, that's for sure. Oh, I can steer the boat, do the locks and all that, but I couldn't manage the cargoes. Wood, lime, gravel. It's a job for a strong man.'

'I could do it,' Jake suggested. 'I'm strong.'

'Of course you are, love,' she said. 'But you're only twelve years old, and still growing. It wouldn't do.'

'Will Dad ever come back?' Jake asked. 'If he knew about Grandad, wouldn't he come back?'

She'd smiled at that, shook her head.

'I doubt there's any likelihood of that, love. And we

haven't the slightest idea where he is. He could be anywhere in the land; or across the sea for that matter. No point in considering it, Jake. No, I'll sell the barge for what I can get. It's a decent boat, but you can bet your boots I'll not get what it's worth!'

'Why not?' he wanted to know.

'Because I'm in a hurry to sell, and because I'm a woman. I'll be offered less than if I was a man. It's the way of the world.'

It turned out exactly as she said.

'They took advantage of me,' she said. 'But never mind, love. At least I was paid on the nail, so there's a bit of cash, and I'll get a job, earn something.'

'What will you do?' he'd asked.

'There's textile mills in Keighley and Skipton,' she'd said. 'I'll get something, don't worry.'

'But Mam, you don't know anything about mills!' he'd objected.

'You're right, lad! It'll be like a foreign country to me. But I can learn. Don't fret!'

She made everything seem an adventure. When she found a menial job in the mill, and then two rooms in a house in the cheaper part of the town, she spoke as if it was exciting.

'We'll do very well here, love,' she said. 'Won't it be nice to have more space. I can show off all my ornaments!'

He had liked the cabin; it was cosy and warm. It had been a while before he'd got used to the house.

'And you shall have the bedroom,' his mother insisted. 'You're growing up; it's only right. In any case it makes sense because I have to be away to work early in the morning. No point in waking you.'

She had spent some of the money from the sale of the boat in furnishing the two rooms. All the furniture was bought cheaply, from secondhand shops, and there wasn't much of it: a bed, a sofa on which she slept, a chair or two, a table for which she made a fancy cloth from a remnant she'd bought in the market. And yet, each item as it arrived became a cause for a small celebration; buns from the baker, a fish supper, a bottle of dandelion-and-burdock.

It was the picture, however, which was the crown of all her purchases. He remembered as clearly as if it was yesterday the Saturday afternoon she came home with it. She burst in through the door, cheeks flushed, eyes shining.

'Oh, Jake! Oh, I've been so extravagant! But look what I've bought!'

She took it out of her basket and unwrapped it with the utmost care, as if it was the most delicate thing in the world.

'Just look!' she repeated. 'Isn't it lovely?'

She handed him the picture, a watercolour, framed in oak.

He took the picture from her and looked at it.

'It's a mountain!' she said.

It hadn't looked like a mountain to him. He knew how a mountain should look, he had seen pictures: triangular in shape, pointed at the top, purple in colour and with snow covering the summit. The one in his mother's picture was green and rounded, no angles, no sharp points, no snow. In shape it was like a picture he had once seen of a whale rising from the ocean.

'It doesn't look like a mountain,' he said hesitantly.

'Oh, but it *is*,' she insisted. 'It's just that it's a green mountain, an extra-high fell. Oh Jake, I *know* it was extravagant, but I shall never regret it!'

She hadn't. She had hung it on a nail on the wall by the fireplace, and every day he caught her looking at it. It was one of the few things he had brought with him from the past, in his bag, mainly to remind him of her.

* * *

It was getting warmer now. Pendle Hill, away to the west and over the Lancashire border, was a hazy blue in the distance. The sun, high in a cloudless sky, burned on Jake's back. He had a murderous thirst on him that only a pint of ale could slake, but thankfully there were signs of a village in the distance. He could see a cluster of houses, thin smoke spiralling from a chimney; and where there was a village there would be an alehouse.

He reached it twenty minutes later. Long Preston.

It was dark in the bar. The only window was small, set deep into the thick wall, and because the sun was so high very little light entered. After the brightness of the day outside it took him several seconds to adjust his eyes to the gloom. When he did so he saw an elderly man sitting on a bench. He nodded to him as he sat down on the bench opposite, loosing his bag from his shoulder and setting it down beside him.

A woman emerged from a door at the back of the room, a small child clinging to her skirt.

'A pint of your best,' Jake said. 'If you please!'

She made no acknowledgement, but within the minute the glass was on the table in front of him, brimful of the rich, brown liquid, crowned by a creamy collar of froth. He drank deeply, half the glass at one go, then wiped his mouth on the back of his hand.

'Good ale! And well kept!' He set down the glass and nodded his approval at the woman.

'It's my father you have to thank for that,' she said. 'I only serve it.'

And with no pleasure at all, her voice and manner said.

'Best beer for miles around,' the old man said.

Ostentatiously, he drained his glass to the last drop before putting it down.

'Then allow me to refill your glass,' Jake said. He

16

signalled to the woman to do so. 'And mine as well, while you're at it,' he told her, drinking down the rest of his beer.

She collected the glasses and took them away. There was a fierceness in the way she did it, resentment in every line of her body as she moved.

Jake raised his eyebrows at the old man.

'Crossed in love,' the man said cheerfully. 'Her man upped and left her three months ago. Went to sea. Since when, she hates all men. And you'll not escape, though she's nobbut just set eyes on you!'

Jake shrugged. He felt the same way about women as she did about men, but he'd not go into it, not with a stranger; not with anyone for that matter.

'No skin off my nose,' he said. 'Just as long as the beer's good.'

He glanced at the woman as she returned with the beer. She was comely enough. Her hair was thick and glossy, the colour of the corn in the fields outside. Her skin was creamy, her figure rounded in all the right places. So why had her man left her?

But her generation of women were not all they seemed, not what they promised. He'd discovered that the hard way. For all her good looks, she was probably no better than the rest of them.

She served the beer, and left them. The two men raised their glasses and drank.

'Corn's ripening well, I noticed,' Jake said.

'Aye, 'tis,' the old man agreed. 'Another week or two like this and we'll be ready to harvest. And if t'weather holds longer there'll be a second crop of hay. Beasts can do wi' that in the winter.'

They sat in silence for a while, then Jake said, 'Well, I'd best be on my way. No time to waste.'

'Where are you bound for?' the man asked.

'Settle, to start with. I reckoned I might get a job on the railway.'

'Aye, well, there's lots do. Folks have come from all over the place: Wales, Cornwall, Northumberland.'

'So I heard,' Jake said.

'The wages are better, you see. But the work's hard. They say every payday some leave, which is why they can set new men on. But I reckon you've not come far?'

'Only from Skipton.'

He had lived there for six years after he and his mother had left the canal. He had worked at what jobs he could get, not helped by his lack of education. Sometimes on the canal, sometimes in the building trade, which he learnt as he went along. His mother insisted on keeping her job in the mill, though many was the time he implored her to give it up.

'It's too hard,' he said. 'The hours are too long. I'm sure we could manage on what I earn.'

That was doubtful, and he knew it. Building work wasn't regular; when the weather was bad he was laid off. As for the canal, well, the railways were taking the cargoes more and more. He couldn't rely on steady work.

'We're all right as we are,' his mother said. 'You save what you can. Put a bit by in the bank. You never know when you might need money.'

He'd done as she'd suggested, but how many times since then had he regretted that he hadn't been more insistent that she should pack in her job, especially in that last bitter cold winter of 1866. Because, owing to the weather, he'd been laid off, she'd insisted on going to the mill when she had a heavy cold on her. In no time at all it had turned to pneumonia, and in the middle of a February night, even before he could get the doctor to her, she had died.

He had never felt so alone, so bereft, as on that day he'd followed her coffin to the churchyard. There were no other mourners, except for a neighbour. They had no relatives, and had kept themselves to themselves.

Afterwards, he couldn't settle in Skipton. He deeply resented the fact that his mother had been taken from him at only thirty-six. When the spring came he moved down the valley to Keighley, and then, later, to Bradford. He didn't like either of them, they were noisy and dirty, so he came back to Skipton. It was there that he had met Vinnie. It was Vinnie who had brought him back to life.

He rose to his feet now, slung his bag over his shoulder again, and left the inn. He was conscious that the woman watched him go, though she didn't bother to answer his word of farewell.

It was hotter than ever on the road. The sun was at its zenith. Furthermore, the strong ale had made him sleepy. His limbs, his eyes, every part of him, weighed heavily. More than anything in the world he wanted to find a patch of shade, lie down in it and lose himself.

A mile further on, the village well behind him, he found what he was looking for. An ash tree grew close to the hedge which bordered the road, and on the other side of the hedge was a pasture. Through a convenient gap he went into the field, then lay down at the edge, in the shade of the tree, and, using his pack as a pillow, fell instantly asleep.

He dreamed he was with Lavinia, and everything was as once it had been. They were happy together, planning for the future when they would be man and wife. He had never been so happy.

'I've never been so happy, Vinnie love,' he said.

'Me neither,' she said.

He had taken her in his arms and was about to kiss her when, suddenly, he was wakened by the sound of a cart on the road. It took him time to bring himself back into the world, to relinquish Vinnie and face the reality that she was gone. She had left him without so much as a note or a message. It was left to others to inform him that she had gone off, presumably in the early hours of one morning, with the waiter from the Cow and Calf. Everyone seemed to know with whom, though no-one knew where.

'But you must have some idea,' he'd insisted to her mother. 'She's your daughter.'

'That doesn't mean she tells me anything!' her mother said tearfully. 'She was talking about Morecambe the other day, how she'd like to go there. Happen that's where they've gone.'

Each day that followed he had waited for a line from her, an apology, an explanation. At first he knew he would have taken her back, forgiven her everything, but as the days went by his heart hardened.

'I've waited long enough,' he said to her mother. 'From now on she's out of my life and out of my mind – and I'm leaving Skipton!'

But she had not been out of his mind, he thought now, jumping to his feet. And if she had gone to Morecambe she would have travelled in this very direction. But I am not going after her, he told himself. I'll not go after any woman, ever again. The devil take them all!

Back on the road he looked ahead and saw the cart, the noise of whose iron-clad wheels had wakened him. If he put on a spurt he could catch up with it, cadge a lift. He began to run, and the driver of the cart heard him, pulled on the rein and spoke to the horse.

'Whoa there!'

'Can you give me a lift?' Jake asked.

'Depends where you're going!'

'Settle. At least to begin with.'

'Then you're in luck, lad. I'm going through to Giggleswick. Jump on!'

Jake took his place beside the driver. There was very little space; the cart was piled high behind him, everything covered by a tarpaulin. The driver flicked his whip and the horse moved forward at a steady gait.

'What are you carrying?' Jake asked.

'Household effects,' the driver answered. 'A young couple flitting from Keighley to Giggleswick. They took the train on account of the lass is seven months gone. I'm to meet up wi' 'em at the house.'

'You know Settle?' Jake enquired.

'A bit. You live there, do you?'

'No. I've never been there. I'm looking for a place to stay. You don't happen to know anyone?'

'I don't. But there's inns. The Golden Lion; the Spread Eagle.'

'I can't afford that sort of place,' Jake told him. He still had some of the money he'd saved, but he'd have to go carefully. 'A night or two's lodgings is what I want. There's bound to be something. I'll ask around.'

'You do that!'

They fell silent for a while. The road was rising now. The horse walked slowly, straining at the weight.

'I'll jump off for the hill,' Jake offered.

'I daresay she'd be pleased at that, would Polly,' the driver said as Jake got down. 'She's getting old, like me. A bit short of breath – though it's not a heavy load, as loads go.'

The country was altogether more hilly now, especially to the east and northwards towards Settle. The limestone escarpments of the hills were dazzling white in the bright sunshine. Jake watched a kestrel, its tail spread, hover ahead of them, motionless in the air, then drop with lightning accuracy to scoop up a mouse crouching at the side of the road.

A little more than an hour later they drove into Settle. At first sight it seemed, to Jake, smaller than Skipton – perhaps because the road through was narrower, and meandered. It was certainly more hilly, the cobbled streets rising sharply from the road, the market square itself on a slope. But it was every bit as busy as Skipton. And some fine buildings, he said to the driver.

'If you think this is busy, wait until you see it tomorrow!' the driver said. 'Tomorrow's market day. You'll find it hard to get a place to put your foot down then! I'll drop you here, in the market place, shall I?'

'That'll do fine,' Jake said. 'And thanks for the ride.'

He watched the cart go down the street, then stood and looked around him, wondering what would be his next move. Best to look around, get his bearings, and surely he'd find a teashop on the way. He could do with a cup of strong, sweet tea and a currant teacake. He wasn't in the mood for more ale just yet. That could come later.

He found a teashop without difficulty, and was served with a surprisingly good brew and a currant teacake as light as air, thickly spread with fresh butter.

'I'm looking for lodgings,' he told the waitress. 'You don't know anywhere, do you?'

'Permanent?' she asked.

'Oh, I don't think so. A night or two to begin with, then I'll see.'

He was in no mood to settle anywhere permanently. He had no real idea where he wanted to be, except that it was not in Skipton. It was only a chance remark made by a man in Skipton, to the effect that there were jobs in Ribblesdale to be had for the asking, which had brought him to where he was now; that, and the fact that the area had been so close to his doorstep for most of his life, and he'd never set foot in it.

'Only temporary,' he added. 'I don't rightly know where I'm bound for.'

The waitress stood there, her head on one side as

she considered the request. With no emotion, Jake observed that her hair was dark, almost black, and fell in wispy curls over her broad, smooth forehead, almost into her eyes; that her skin was clear, her cheeks pink with health. All this he noted, and brushed aside.

'Well,' she said, looking at him directly, 'I just might be able to help.'

She'd be more than delighted to do so, she thought. He was a corker! Moreover, he had a nice voice, and that was something she could never resist.

'My aunt sometimes takes a lodger or two, only temporary of course. She might well fit you in.'

'That would be fine,' Jake said. 'Where does she live?'

'Wait a minute,' the waitress said.

She left him, and went across to the other waitress who was leaning against the counter.

'Mary, will you cover my tables for a few minutes? I'll not be long.'

Mary nodded. 'What are you up to now, Sally Roland?' she asked.

'Tell you later.'

She hurried back to Jake.

'I can take you to my aunt's if you like,' she said. 'It's quite near.'

She took off her cap and apron and accompanied him out of the café, walking close beside him as they crossed the road and climbed the hill. He was a bit of all right, this one; better than anything she'd come across in Settle. She'd not yet told him she lived with her aunt, and had done for two boring years since her mother had packed her off from Leeds. He'd learn that when she'd fixed him up.

As they turned a corner she bumped against him. He had to put out a hand to steady her.

'Ooops!' she said. 'I must take more water with it! Here we are.'

She hoped he wouldn't leave Settle too soon; and if it depended on her, he wouldn't.

Her aunt opened the door.

'Why, Sally, what are you doing home at this time of the afternoon?' she asked. 'Is something wrong?'

'Not a bit of it,' Sally replied. 'Mr . . . ?'

'Jake Tempest.'

She liked that. A strong name. He looked a strong man; masterful, she wouldn't wonder.

'Mr Tempest is looking for a room, Auntie. Just for a night or two. I reckoned you might fix him up.'

'But Sally you know—'

'I must get back,' Sally interrupted. 'I don't want the sack, do I?' With a parting smile in Jake's direction, she hurried away.

Jane Sutherland watched her niece as she ran back down the hill. Now what's she up to? she asked herself. And then, as if I didn't know!

'Come in, Mr Tempest,' she said to Jake. 'Though I'm not sure I can do anything for you. You see . . .' (and as that little minx knew well) '. . . I only have the one spare bedroom, and that's taken for the moment by Mr Armitage.'

'Then I'll not trouble you,' Jake said swiftly. He turned to go. Why had the silly girl brought him here?

'But wait a minute,' Mrs Sutherland said. 'There's two beds in the room, and if Mr Armitage doesn't object . . .'

And an extra one-and-sixpence a night, she reminded herself.

'. . . And I don't suppose he will, seeing he's moving on himself the day after tomorrow.'

'I wouldn't want to disturb him,' Jake said. He was not sure he wanted to share with a stranger.

'Well, he's in his room now, so we can ask him!' Mrs Sutherland's tone was brightly confident. 'He's a very nice man. You'll find him interesting too. Knows about all sorts of things.'

Mr Armitage, summoned from his room, looked long and quizzically at Jake before delivering his verdict.

'I'll be pleased to share the room,' he said at last. 'I daresay Mrs Sutherland will make me a small reduction.'

'We'll have to see,' Mrs Sutherland said reluctantly.

'And I hope you don't snore, Mr Tempest,' Mr Armitage said. 'I shall certainly waken you if you do. I need my beauty sleep!'

'Well then, that's settled,' Mrs Sutherland said. 'Supper at seven o'clock. I'm making a nice meat-and-potato pie and me and Sally will sit down with you. You'll find this a friendly house, Mr Tempest.' And my niece will make certain of that, she thought.

Mr Armitage took Jake up to the bedroom, where the latter unpacked a few things, including his framed picture. He propped it up on a narrow shelf near his bed.

'My mother bought it,' he said in answer to Mr Armitage's enquiring glance. 'She always called it the mountain, but I was never sure.'

'Then you can be,' Mr Armitage said. 'It's a mountain, and what's more, I know it! It's called Whernside and it's not all that many miles from here.'

He picked up the painting and scrutinized it.

'It's a nice little study. Your mother made a good choice. You might make a bit if you were to sell it.'

'I don't have that in mind,' Jake said.

When, later, they went downstairs to supper, Sally was already there. She had changed into a flowered-cotton frock, and piled her luxuriant hair on top of her head, but loosely, so that it threatened to fall down at any moment. It was difficult not to look at it, though it vied for attention with the locket hanging on a silver chain which encircled her slender white throat, nestling in the cleft between her round-as-apple breasts.

'You're as pretty as a picture!' Mr Armitage said with appreciation. 'Isn't she just as pretty as a picture, Mr Tempest?'

Sally, her blue eyes wide, her red mouth smiling, looked to Jake for his reply.

'Very nice,' Jake said evenly.

If Sally was disappointed she didn't show it. She felt confident of melting his ice, of weakening the resolve she saw in his face.

Mrs Sutherland dished out the steaming pie, spooning the rich gravy over the potatoes.

'Now eat it while it's hot,' she said. 'I know it's been a warm day, but I've always found gentlemen like something hot, whatever the weather.'

'You're right, Auntie,' Sally said. 'And not only the gentlemen!' She attacked her food with gusto, clearly savouring every bite.

And well she might, Jake thought. It was the best food he had tasted in many a week. He gratefully accepted the second helping Mrs Sutherland offered.

'You'll need to walk that lot off,' Sally said. 'Lucky it's a nice evening. I could do with some fresh air myself.'

The look she gave him was a bold invitation. He answered it with an equally direct look.

'I'm going to turn in early,' he said. 'It's been a long day.'

Sally's mouth continued to smile, but her eyes flashed anger. She wasn't used to this.

'But I'd be delighted to accompany you, Miss Sally,' Mr Armitage put in quickly.

'You're a real gentleman, Mr Armitage – and there aren't many of them about. But do you know, I realize I'm quite tired too,' Sally said sweetly. 'I think I'll follow Mr Tempest's example!'

As Jake lay on his bed, the light still filtering in through the thin curtains at the window, he was aware of Sally Roland on the other side of the thin wall. He also realized that she meant him to be aware. Sounds – a drawer opening and closing, shoes being dropped, a long sigh and a clear expression of relief as, he thought, she removed her stays. The bed, close up against the dividing wall, creaked as she bounced into it, and as she rolled over she bumped into the wall.

For a brief moment it felt almost as if she was in his bed, as if he had only to put out a hand to touch her, to touch her warm flesh where the locket lay. Against his will, his body responded. He closed his eyes, then opened them again quickly, and leapt out of bed.

Damn the stupid bitch! She was nothing but a whore. And if he marched in and took her now, as she was clearly inviting him to do, it would not be the first whore he had taken in the last few years. But not for a long time now. Not since the day he had met Vinnie, and with her he had never made love completely.

'Save it for when we're married,' she'd said.

And he had. And perhaps he shouldn't have. Perhaps if he'd shown her that he was a man, he'd have kept her. She wouldn't have turned to that rat of a waiter. The thought of Vinnie came between him and the woman tossing about on the bed in the next room. Was she going to come between him and every woman he'd ever meet?

He was saved from further thought by the return of Armitage from his walk.

'I daresay it might rain,' Armitage said. 'It's in the air.'

'I've decided I'll move on tomorrow,' Jake said. 'I've a notion to see this Whernside. I can put off looking for a job for a week or two.'

'But you'll get a job over that way,' Armitage said. 'They're well on with the railway at Ribblehead. And

27

if you're going, I reckon I'll leave with you, walk with you as far as Horton and set you on your way. I've no reason for staying on here.'

'I'd appreciate that,' Jake said.

'Good. Now remember what I said. Don't keep me awake with your snoring!'

The boot was on the other foot. It was Jake who was kept awake half the night, and not by sounds from the next room, which had promptly ceased the moment Mr Armitage returned. No, it was the older man's talking. He talked until the short summer night was almost over and the dawn began to lighten the room again. And Mrs Sutherland was right. He certainly knew about a lot of things. Nature, art, landscape, literature. There was no end to it.

'My wife – God rest her soul – used to tell me I'd talk a glass eye to sleep,' Mr Armitage said amiably. He glanced across at Jake in the other bed.

'And my word, I think I've talked you to sleep!'

When they went down to breakfast, Sally had already left for work.

'Market day,' Mrs Sutherland explained. 'They have early customers in the café.'

She was surprised when both men told her they had decided to move on. Surprised, but not unduly put out. She took things as they came. It was the best way. Sally, though, was going to be furious. She'd really set her cap at the young one. Nevertheless, she passed on her niece's message, speaking to both men. It was intended for Mr Tempest, but she could hardly single him out.

'Sally said if you'd like to drop in for a cup of tea while you're in the market, she'd be pleased to give you special attention. But since you're making a start, I reckon you'll not have time for that.'

'Oh, I don't know,' Mr Armitage said. 'I daresay we might manage it!'

'But I thought . . .' Jake demurred.

'We've time enough,' Mr Armitage said. 'You'd not want to leave Settle without seeing the market, and then a nice cup of tea would see us on our way.'

Jake gave in. He liked markets, it wasn't that. He didn't want to see the girl again. In spite of the fact that he didn't even like her, last night she'd aroused feelings in him which he thought had gone for good; feelings he didn't want ever again.

The market place was thronged: rabbits, hens, puppies, a goat or two; eggs, butter; pots and pans; cures for backache, toothache, ingrowing toenails and warts. Stalls of every kind. There was scarcely room to set foot. At a point where they found themselves exactly opposite to the café Mr Armitage said: 'Well then, let's get that cup of tea, and be on our way.'

It was as if Sally had been waiting for them. She saw them the minute they came in at the door, rushed them to a table, served them with a fresh brew and thick slices of fruit cake. It was not until then that she noticed that they had what looked like all their worldly goods with them.

'We're leaving,' Mr Armitage said, following her glance. 'Got to move on!'

Sally's face fell. Though last night had come to nothing, due entirely, she told herself, to Mr Armitage's early return, she was not one to give up easily. She'd felt sure she would conquer Jake Tempest today, and now he was walking away. But she wouldn't write him off. He was far too attractive to let go.

'Well,' she said, speaking directly to Jake, 'it's a pity you're going so soon. I could have shown you the delights of Settle. But you'll come back, I'm sure of it. Everyone comes back to Settle.'

The invitation was in her eyes as well as in her words. Resist me if you can, they said.

2

The morning was more than half gone before the two men walked out of Settle.

'I had hoped to have made an earlier start, Mr Armitage,' Jake said. 'Though I suppose it doesn't matter.'

'Of course it doesn't! We have the whole day and the whole world in front of us. Never let time be your master. And call me Armitage,' the older man said.

It was another fine morning, not as hot as the previous day, and therefore all the pleasanter for walking. Jake remarked on it.

'It's not always like this,' Armitage said. 'And it can change in a minute. Not three weeks ago we had one of the worst thunderstorms in living memory as I was walking into Settle. Hailstones as big as pigeons' eggs! Broke the windows. Houses flooded. No traffic possible on the roads. I was soaked to the skin.'

'It looks nothing like that today,' Jake said.

'I agree! But you never can tell in these parts.'

In fact the river, on their left as they walked northwards through the dale, was full, and flowing fast.

'It's a pretty river,' Jake remarked.

'A beautiful river,' Armitage confirmed. 'The Romans thought so when they were here. They called it "Bellissima", meaning "Very beautiful". But it's seen hard times. Robert Bruce scared the living daylights out of the people in Ribblesdale with his bloody raids. And you can hear the folks hereabouts talk as if it all happened yesterday. Some of 'em are still not sure about the Scots.'

'How do you happen to know all these things?' Jake enquired. 'I never met a man who knew so much!'

'Reading. Practically everything I know I've got from reading. I always carry a couple of books in my knapsack. I hope you do the same?'

There was a short silence.

'I can't read,' Jake confessed. It shamed him. Was it somehow his own fault? Had there been a point somewhere in the past when, if he'd made a better effort, he could have mastered it?

'Good heavens!' Armitage was so astonished that he stopped in his tracks and turned to face Jake square on. 'You don't have the appearance of a man who can't read, not in the least!'

He looked intently at Jake. Put aside the fact that the young man was handsome, not badly spoken and, from the way that Sally Roland had done her best to seduce him, attractive to the opposite sex, he also looked intelligent. You could see it in the eyes; clear, alert, comprehending, though at this moment not too comfortable.

'My dear boy,' he commiserated, 'why, you're missing out on the best of life if you can't read.'

'So it seems,' Jake said, though that had not occurred to him before meeting Armitage.

'Well, I wish I had the chance to teach you,' Armitage said. 'The fact is, I'm a here-today-and-gone-tomorrow person, not reliable. But try to do something about it, boy. You don't know what you're missing.'

I wonder what *he* does for a living, Jake thought. In his own way he seems as rootless as I am. He had offered no explanation.

'I'm footloose and fancy free,' Armitage said, answering Jake's unspoken question. 'I have very little money – a pittance I inherited from my mother – but my way of life doesn't need much money. As long as I can afford a stout pair of boots, a few books, paper to write on, and the price of a cheap bed, that's enough. In fact, I bless the day I gave up earning a living.'

'How *did* you earn a living?'

'I was a teacher.'

Of course! It fitted him like a glove. It wasn't only that he *had* all the knowledge, he knew how to impart it.

'And though I say it myself, I was a good teacher,' Armitage added. 'But it tied me down. I've never liked being tied down. And I've always preferred seeking after knowledge. There's no end to it. All the same, I'd like to have had a stab at teaching you to read. I've only ever taught small boys.'

They walked in companionable silence for a while but when, to the right, a high, strangely shaped hill appeared on the horizon, Armitage could not contain himself. He leapt in the air, and shouted:

'There it is! There's my mountain! Pen-y-ghent. A Welsh name, meaning 'Hill of winds', though I never did discover how it got a Welsh name. Oh, but it's magnificent! Don't you agree it's magnificent?'

'Very impressive,' Jake said. It was a strange shape, like a crouching lion.

'Like a sphinx,' Armitage said. 'You've seen pictures of the Sphinx, haven't you? And am I not right? Well, when we reach Horton, and we're not far off now, I'm going to leave you, and I'm going to walk over my mountain and down into Littondale.'

'It looks a stiff climb,' Jake said.

'Oh, not so bad! Not as high as Whernside, which is *your* mountain. But when it comes to mountains it all depends on the weather, and today it's good.'

That was an understatement. The day was

perfection. Sunny, but with an ever-present breeze which at the moment was only strong enough to nudge cottonwool clouds across a high, blue sky. In the pastures the newly shorn sheep were sharp white against the emerald green of the grass, and in the cornfields – fewer in number than the pastures, for this was sheep country, not arable – the grain was almost ready for harvesting.

'It's very good,' he acknowledged.

He felt, for a rare moment, though he knew it would not last, in harmony with the world and with the landscape through which he was walking. At peace with himself. It was a while since he had felt so.

'Well, here we are. This is Horton!' Armitage said presently. 'There's a good inn at the other end of the village. I suggest we take some refreshment before we part company.'

They walked to the point where the river made a right turn under a narrow roadbridge, and to the side of the bridge, settled in a hollow beside the road, stood the inn. Jake, ducking his head, followed Armitage through the doorway.

They were offered lamb chops, with the local cheese to follow. They ate with hearty appetites. Armitage cleared his plate, drained his tankard, patted his stomach appreciatively, then stood up.

'Well, that's it! I'll be on my way, young man! What about you?'

Jake rose to his feet and they walked out together.

'Thank you for your company,' Armitage said. 'I've enjoyed it. And I suppose I should thank you for listening to me. I seem to have talked a lot. But once a teacher, always a teacher!'

'I've learned a lot,' Jake said. 'Thank you.'

'But not as much as you will when you learn to read.'

'I hope we'll meet again,' Jake said.

'If God wills it, then we will!'

33

They shook hands, and parted, Armitage to the east, Jake continuing on the road northward. It was true, Armitage reflected as he began his climb, that he had enjoyed the young man's company, but he was not sorry now to be on his own. He was a loner, always had been. When you were walking the hills there was nothing to compare with solitude.

A curlew circled in the clear air above him, uttering its strange, mournful cry; then it dived to the ground ahead of him, so close that he could see its long, downcurved bill, its white rump. A bird of the moorlands, of open spaces; he felt at home with it.

Jake, in a way, was sorry to part from Armitage, but in another way he too was glad to be on his own again. Listening to Armitage, his head had been crammed with facts, with no time to sort them into any order. He wondered if he would ever see the man again. He hoped he might, but it seemed unlikely. They had not exchanged addresses because neither of them had an address.

The road was undulating here, rising and falling, though never dramatically. The river, which had crossed the road under the bridge at Horton, was on his right now, flowing a little less turbulently through meadows which stretched a fair way until the hills began to rise in the east. The sound of sheep still accompanied him. 'When sheep aren't eating, they're bleating,' Armitage had said.

It surprised Jake a little that there was no traffic on the road, not a solitary cart, not even a pony and trap, nor another person walking. He had the world to himself.

He thought about Vinnie. He didn't want to, but he couldn't help himself. She was in and out of his mind the livelong day. Wasn't she the reason he was taking this lonely journey?

Like a mirage in the sunlight, the vision of her

danced before him, there in the middle of the road as if she was flesh and blood, her red hair piled in curls, her green eyes dancing, though now filled with mockery. If only she'd come to him, if only she'd told him; if they'd had it out between them, he could have borne it. It was the deceit, the thought that she'd been planning this treachery even while she was in his arms, which he couldn't stomach. It ate at him like a worm at his vitals.

Sunk in his thoughts, he didn't notice time passing until it came to him that the narrow road, though not the pastures to the east, was in shadow. He raised his head and looked around him. To his left now was a great hill, and beyond that another, behind the summits of which the sun had dipped. Armitage, he thought, would have known their names, but he had no idea himself. It did seem to him, though, that by now he must be nearing Ribblehead where, so Armitage had told him, the road split, and he would have to choose his direction.

And then suddenly – he had breasted a rise in the road and taken a bend without noticing either – he saw it. He saw what he had walked all these miles for when he might have remained in Settle. It was there before him, to the north. The mountain! Not sharp-pointed, not snow-capped, but with broad slopes leading up to the wide, rounded summit. It appeared to him as though it was rising from the depths of the ocean, that one day it might, should it ever wish to do so, rise even further. Such was its power. It dominated the landscape, though, on this bright summer's day, with a benign dominance.

He could not understand his emotion on seeing it, and it didn't matter that he couldn't. Feelings of awe, wonder, satisfaction, of a goal reached (though two days ago he had had no such goal in mind) fought with each other, filled his heart and his mind.

He set his knapsack on the wall which bordered the road, and delved into it for the painting. His hands shook a little as he took it out. He looked at the painting, and from it to the scene in front of him. They were one and the same, there was no doubt about it. Indeed, the picture could have been painted from this exact viewpoint, and the colouring, too, was right. In both the picture and the real thing the afternoon sun caught the green of the fellside and tinged the tops where the green faded into browns and greys, blues and purples. Oh, what would his mother have thought? What would he have given for her to see it?

Immersed in the scene, he didn't hear the footsteps of the man approaching him along the road. Not until the fellow called out a greeting, and was almost past, was Jake aware of him.

'Wait a minute!' he called out.

The man stopped.

'What's the name of that mountain?' Jake demanded. Armitage had said the picture was Whernside, and in his heart Jake knew they were one and the same, but he had to be sure.

'Yon's Whernside,' the man said. 'I reckon you must be a stranger not to know that!'

'I am,' Jake agreed.

'Where are you bound for, then?'

Where am I bound for? Jake asked himself. In Settle he had decided, on a whim, to find the mountain of his mother's painting, and now he had found it, though he had yet to climb it, and that he knew he must do.

'I'm not sure where I'm bound for in the end,' he told the man.

'I thought happen you were after a job on the new railway,' the man said. 'There's a lot of building going on at Ribblehead, and you're not far off.'

'Then I might do that,' Jake said.

'You'll come to Salt Lake City on your left, and not long after you'll be at Batty Green. Can't miss it! You'll see the huts. Someone'll tell you where to apply for a job. Were you thinking of working on the viaduct?'

'I hadn't thought,' Jake said. 'I'll see what happens. Thanks for the information.'

Soon afterwards, on rising ground on his left, he passed a group of huts which he assumed was Salt Lake City. There was little sign of life there, just a woman with a small child clinging to her skirts. They waved as he went past, and Jake returned the greeting. And then, at a point where the road north came to a sudden halt, dividing into east and west directions, he was at Batty Green.

It was a sight which, long after he had been and gone; had arrived, stayed, and finally left, would remain with him. When the wide expanse of moorland had been reclaimed by jealous nature, he would remember the alien sight it had presented on that August afternoon.

Huts!

In the flat foreground, in the middle ground where the land began gently to rise, and on the higher ground at the far side of the moor, towards the beginnings of the lower slopes of the mountain, there were groups of huts, some large groups, some no more than two or three buildings. The huts were mostly, but not all, of a similar size, and the same low, rectangular shape. Many were whitewashed against the glare of the sun, so that they had the appearance of a crop of mushrooms which had sprung up overnight in a great green field.

He stood there, at the junction of the road, staring, and then realized he was not just seeing buildings, but that from the primitive chimneys which rose from the centre of each hut, smoke spiralled into the air, and that around the nearer huts, in and out of the doorways, people were moving: mostly women and children, he noticed, and realized that the men would still be at work.

Close to the huts, dogs, hens, pigs, giving an air of permanent domesticity, foraged around for pickings.

There were tracks everywhere, flattened into the grass, churned into the mud, running in all directions, criss-crossing. Tracks along which sturdy horses pulled strange-looking carts, the like of which he had never seen before; along which men wheeled barrows, carried hods and picks and shovels; called out to each other.

Jake took a deep breath, crossed the road, and stepped into the scene.

He stopped the first man he met, a man pushing a barrow over a footbridge which spanned a narrow stream. There were small streams everywhere.

'Where do I go to ask for a job?' Jake asked.

The man set down his barrow, and pointed.

'You see that four-wheeled hut, over there? The contractor's hut. You'll find the agent there.'

'Thanks!'

The hut was no more than five minutes' walk away, over ground which, though there had been no rain for several days, was soggy beneath Jake's feet, springing with water, so that he had to take care where he trod. Four or five rough wooden steps led up to an open door in one end of the hut. Jake climbed the steps and knocked on the door. A voice growled to him to come in.

The hut was dark inside, lit only by a square window with four small panes of glass, set high in one of the two long walls. The atmosphere was stuffy, for the window was tightly shut and the stove, though not burning fiercely, was lit, with a kettle boiling on top.

What air entered through the doorway failed to reach the far end of the hut where the owner of the voice sat behind a wooden table. A brown-and-white dog, half spaniel, the other half indeterminate, lay on the floor beside the table. It raised its head at the sight of Jake, but did not get up. The man at the table studied Jake.

'I don't know you, do I?'

'I've just arrived,' Jake said.

'I thought so,' the agent said. 'I know most of the men, even though they do come and go. I've a memory for faces. What are you after?'

'A job,' Jake answered.

'Oh yes? And what sort of job?'

'Whatever's on offer. I don't mind.'

The man leaned back in his chair. There was a glint in his eye.

'I see! Well on this contract we've got carpenters, brickmakers and bricklayers, masons, engineers, clerks, stokers, saddlers, miners, labourers and navvies. And a dozen others I could mention if I had the time. So which of these various trades are you skilled in, if any?'

'Well . . .' Jake hesitated, trying to recall something in the long list to which he could lay claim.

'Where do you come from?' the man barked.

'Skipton.'

'Married?'

'No. No living relatives.'

'So, footloose and fancy free! And what did you do in Skipton?'

'Mostly in the building trade. Labouring; a bit of bricklaying. There's plenty of building going on in Skipton.'

'So why did you leave?' the man snapped.

'Personal reasons,' Jake said shortly.

Woman trouble, the man thought. He looked like

39

a man who might have the women after him. But it's not my business.

'Do you drink?' he demanded.

'Moderately.'

'You'd be wise to keep it that way. It's the curse of this place, drink is. It's where most of the wages go. If I'd any sense I'd be a publican! So what do you reckon you can do?'

'I wondered if there was an opening on the viaduct?' Jake said.

'It's mostly very skilled work,' the man said. 'They're laying the foundations and it's not child's play, I can tell you. Twenty-five feet those shafts go down to bedrock, and then six feet of concrete on top before we can start on the piers.'

'But there must be some labourers, some navvies?' Jake prompted.

'That's true, but at this moment it's skilled men we want on the viaduct. We've got all the labourers we need. Of course, come payday some will leave. It's always the way, the minute they lay hands on the money. The work's too hard, the hours too long, it's an isolated place. But it's not yet payday, so they'll stick it out.'

'So is there somewhere else I could be set on?' Jake enquired. 'I don't much mind where I go.' He didn't yet know whether he would stick it. He'd have to see.

'There's the tunnel,' the agent said thoughtfully. 'They can always do with more men on the tunnel.'

And always would, he thought, because it was a rotten job; working in the dark, or at best by candle-light; falling rocks, not enough air, and what air there was, foul. Worst of all, though, the incessant struggle to dig a way under and through the mountain for a distance of a mile and a half. But he'd not go into all that. If this man took the job, he'd find out himself soon enough.

'Where is it, the tunnel?' Jake asked.

'About two-and-a-half miles from here, up on Blea Moor. They're tunnelling under the mountain.'

It was that which decided Jake. To be working on the mountain, actually inside the mountain! They could keep the viaduct!

'If there's a job for me there, I'll take it,' he said without hesitation.

'Then report there in the morning,' the man said. 'Ask for Isaac Hargreaves.'

'Thanks,' Jake said. 'I'll do that. And can you tell me where I can get a bed for the night?'

'Let's see. If you're going to try for the tunnel, you'd be best looking for a place close by it. Jerusalem, say – or Nazareth.'

'Jerusalem? Nazareth?'

'Shanty towns – or the beginnings of them. Not many huts at Nazareth, as yet; but there will be.'

While the agent was speaking, there was a knock on the door and a man entered. He was tall, powerfully built, dressed in dark trousers and unbuttoned waistcoat, his shirtsleeves rolled up over muscular arms. He wore a black, brimmed hat, and in his mouth a clay pipe was clamped.

'Ah, Seymour!' the man behind the table greeted him. 'You're just the man I want. This young fellow here . . .' He turned to Jake. 'What did you say your name was?'

'Jake Tempest.'

'Right. He's going to try for a job in the tunnel and he'll need somewhere to stay. Your wife takes in a lodger or two, doesn't she?'

'That's right,' Seymour said. 'We live at Nazareth,' he told Jake. 'I'll point you the way.'

He had a short conversation with the agent, then went outside with Jake.

'Keep ahead,' he said, 'the mountain on your left.

In fact, follow the tramway, then you can't go wrong. It goes up to the tunnel.'

He pointed towards the lowest part of the valley, where men were working on the viaduct. Jake glimpsed the tramway, where a light engine pulled trucks.

'Tramway?' Jake queried. 'Any chance of a ride?'

Seymour shook his head.

'I doubt it. Supposed to be for goods only. But if you keep clear of the bog it's not a bad walk. You'll come first to Sebastopol and Inkerman, and about three-quarters of a mile on you'll reach Jericho. Nazareth is the same distance again. Anyone there will tell you which my hut is.'

'I'll be off then,' Jake said.

'Right! And you can tell my wife I'll be late home. We're working while the daylight lasts.'

Jake struck out towards the viaduct area, picking his way. If it was all going to be like this he'd need some stouter boots. He wondered what the people here did for shops. His question was partly answered as he passed through Sebastopol and Inkerman – he didn't know which was which – and observed a pedlar going from hut to hut, and a cart delivering milk.

As the ground rose, there were fewer huts, fewer carts, horses, people. But for the noise of the tramway, it was almost tranquil. Flowers grew abundantly in the grass, cropped short by the ubiquitous sheep: buttercups, daisies, Herb Robert, the small, bright yellow tormentil carpeted the ground; and in the strange circular hollows, completely symmetrical, which he had noticed all along his walk, and which he knew to be shakeholes, meadow cranesbill abounded.

He stopped, and watched a hare dodging around in a particularly large hollow, in and out of the ferns. If it saw him, it gave no heed.

Presently he came to another settlement. He spoke

to a woman sitting at the door of a hut peeling vegetables.

'Is this Jericho?'

'It is,' she said. 'Who would you be wanting?'

'Nazareth,' Jake said.

'A bit further up,' the woman said.

Nazareth, when he reached it, surprised him. There were fewer than a dozen huts, built on both sides of the tramway, which passed through the middle of the settlement, presumably on its way to the tunnel. The huts were uniform in size and appearance, freshly whitewashed, tidy around the outside, one or two with lace curtains at the small windows. It was quite different from Sebastopol and Inkerman, even from Jericho: cleaner, tidier, civilized.

A girl sat on the grass outside one of the huts, weaving a daisy chain. She looked up as Jake's shadow fell on her.

'Hello,' he said. 'I'm looking for the Seymours' hut. Do you know which it is?'

'Over there,' she said. 'The other side of the tramway track. The middle one.'

He knocked on the door.

'Come in please!'

It was a woman's voice, but low-pitched. He stepped into the hut.

The woman stood behind the table, her hands deep in a bowl of dough. She stopped her kneading for only a brief moment while she looked at him.

'Yes?'

'Mrs Seymour?'

'That's right.'

She was tall, so that she had to stoop over the baking bowl, but while she regarded Jake she stood to her full height. Her eyes, meeting his directly as if in appraisal, were brown, flecked with yellow: cool, but not hostile. Her hair was brown also, but deep with colour, like the leaves of a copper beech. Or even more, like a chestnut newly escaped from its husk, Jake thought. Rich and glossy. Her face was pale, her dress was black, and she wore a white apron. So why, he thought, did this combination of sombre hues result in an impression of someone alive with colour?

'Your husband sent me,' he said. 'I'm looking for lodgings, hoping to get a job on the railway.'

She finished kneading, turned the dough over in the bowl, smooth side uppermost, covered it with a cloth and set it closer to the stove to rise.

'You would have to share,' she said. 'I don't have much room. This is the living-room, and it's exactly as you see. The room at one end is mine and my husband's, and the one at the other end I let to lodgers.'

'How many would I share with?' Jake asked. He didn't like the sound of it.

'One only, at the moment, though there are three beds in the room, so it could be two. Would you like to look? The other man is out at work. He works in the tunnel.'

He followed her into the room. There were three narrow beds set close together, one chest of drawers, a shelf over the head of each bed, and various hooks on the wall. There was no room for a chair. It was, however, clean and fresh-looking, with colourful checked blankets on the beds.

'How much do you charge?' he asked.

He thought the sum she asked was on the high side, and she read that in his face.

'It's the usual,' she said. 'And if you get a job you'll earn good wages, as much as eight shillings a day if you're lucky – depending on what you do. Why else do you think men come from all over England to this benighted spot?'

'I suppose so,' Jake said. He had not discussed

money with the agent, and was agreeably surprised at the wages.

'All found,' Mrs Seymour added. 'I do your washing, and I'll feed you well. Ask anyone.'

'Well then, if you'll have me,' Jake said.

'This will be your bed,' she said. 'Mr Mahoney has the one against the wall. You must sort out the drawer space with him.'

'Thank you. I'd like a wash,' Jake said.

'The men wash in the back. It's only yards away. If you choose the right place it can be quite private. It saves carrying the water.'

'Mr Seymour said I was to tell you he'd be late home. They're working while the light lasts.'

A slight frown line creased Mrs Seymour's forehead. She knew what it meant. When they'd worked as long as the light allowed, the next step would be the alehouse. There was no shortage of alehouses.

'Then we'll not wait till he comes for our dinner,' she said. 'It'll be ready in an hour.'

Jake found the spot in the beck he reckoned his landlady had intended. A steep outcrop of bank overhung the stream, so that he was able to strip off his clothes and bathe without fear of being over-looked. The water was fast-flowing and icy cold, and stung sharply against his flesh; but when it was over, and he was dressed again, he felt invigorated: a new man, all his fatigue washed away.

Back in the hut, the air was filled with the delicious smell of mutton stew. He realized how sharply hungry he was. Another man sat at the table, waiting. He was small and dark, with a black beard and an untidy moustache.

'This is Patrick Mahoney,' Mrs Seymour said. 'Your room mate.'

'Pleased to meet you,' the man said.

Even aside from his name, there was no need to

announce his nationality. His soft voice, his accent said it all.

'I'm from Cork,' he added.

'And since you're both here, I'll serve the dinner,' Mrs Seymour said. 'It's a hot meal on a hot day,' she apologized as she filled the plates with the thick stew, topped with dumplings.

Soon after the meal was over the Irishman went out.

'Will you be coming with me, then?' he invited Jake. 'It's a few beers I'm after.'

'Thank you, I won't,' Jake said. 'I reckon I'll turn in early. It's been quite a day.'

'Suit yourself.'

'And I have a pile of ironing,' Mrs Seymour said. 'So if you've finished at the table, I'll get on with it.'

It was a dismissal, Jake thought; not unkind, but quite brisk.

'Then I'll say goodnight, Mrs Seymour.'

In the bedroom, he lay on the bed, listening to the soothing sound of the beck. What would tomorrow bring, he wondered. Would he get a job? And, just before he fell asleep, where was Vinnie? What was she doing?

Some time afterwards – it was pitch dark – he was wakened by the sound of someone coming into the hut, singing; and then his landlady's voice asking for silence. He had thought the singer must be the Irishman but, his eyes now used to the darkness, he saw that Patrick Mahoney was in his own bed. He had slept so deeply that he hadn't heard him return.

' 'Tis Himself!' Mahoney mumbled. 'One over the eight! But at least he sounds cheerful with it.'

3

It had taken a long time for Jake to get to sleep again after Seymour's return. At first it had been Seymour who had kept him awake. He paid no heed to his wife's pleas to be quiet, but continued to laugh and sing and talk. Although the two bedrooms were separated by the living-room, the walls were thin, the doors flimsy – the huts were, after all, only temporary – and there was no shutting out the sounds. Fortunately, when Seymour came to the end of his song and lowered his voice to talk, his words were indistinct. Only his cajoling tones came through, and from his wife there was silence. Minutes later, and abruptly, Seymour too fell silent.

The interruption, though perhaps no longer than twenty minutes, left Jake wide awake. He tossed and turned, flung off the blanket because he was too hot, then gave up the effort to find sleep, and lay on his back. The night was less dark than it had been and the square of sky, seen through the window, hinted at a rising moon, but the silence of the night was intense. All that disturbed it was the beck, which sounded faster and more furious than it had in the daytime. Thank heaven, Jake thought, that the Irishman didn't snore. He was sleeping as peacefully as a baby.

Eventually, though not before the sky was already lightening with the new day, Jake turned on his side, pulled the blanket around his shoulders, and at last fell asleep.

When he wakened the room was bright, Mahoney's

47

bed was empty, and there was a smell of bacon in the air. He jumped out of bed, pulled on his shirt and trousers, and went into the living-room. Mrs Seymour was clearing dirty dishes from the table. She looked up and smiled at him.

'Good morning! I hope you slept well, Mr Tempest?'

'It seems as if in the end I slept too well,' Jake said. 'You've finished breakfast!'

'The men have,' Mrs Seymour said. 'They left a while ago. They make an early start, especially Will. He has a two-mile walk to work.'

She moved across to the stove, where thick rashers of bacon were cooking in a black iron frying pan.

'I can only give you one egg with your bacon,' she said. 'The hens aren't laying well, but there's fried potato.'

'It smells good,' Jake said. 'I'm sorry to give you the trouble of cooking a second breakfast just for me.'

'Oh, it's not just for you,' she said. 'It's for the both of us!' She moved aside the sizzling bacon, tilted the pan, and dropped two eggs into the pool of fat. 'I always wait for mine until the men have gone to work. It's my bit of peace.'

'Then I'm sorry to disturb you,' Jake apologized.

'That's all right,' Beth Seymour said. 'How do you like your egg?'

'Turned over, fried on both sides,' Jake said.

'A ruin of a good egg,' she said. 'But if that's what you want!'

She dished up the food and put the plates on the table, then she paused before sitting down.

'I hope you'll not find me rude, Mr Tempest. What I meant when I said it was my time of peace was that I always read when I'm having my breakfast. I don't get much chance otherwise. And I'm nearly at the end of the book. I want to finish it. Do you think that's very rude?'

'No,' Jake said. 'Don't mind me.'

'Thanks.'

She took a book from a shelf, sat down at the table and opened it.

Nothing more passed between them. Jake watched her, fascinated, though not so much by the fact that she was reading, but because, while seeming never to move her eyes from the book, she ate at a steady pace through the contents on her plate. Then she stretched out a hand and, without looking, took a slice of dry bread and mopped up every vestige of fat. Simultaneously with the last mouthful she reached the end of the book, giving a deep sigh as she closed it.

Then she came quickly back to earth.

'Why, Mr Tempest, you've only half-finished!' she cried. 'Is everything all right?'

'Delicious!' Jake said quickly. 'My mother always complained I was a slow eater.'

It was untrue, but he could hardly tell her that he'd been busy watching her instead of getting on with his bacon.

'You'll have another cup of tea?'

He hesitated. It was time he left. He was going after a job, wasn't he?

'Well . . . if *you're* having one.'

He observed her again as she went to the stove and poured water from the kettle into the large brown teapot. She wore a blue cotton blouse this morning, with the sleeves rolled up high, showing her strong arms as she manoeuvred the heavy kettle. Strong arms, but not coarse; rounded and shapely, with fine skin, lightly freckled; slender wrists. Her hands looked capable, an unusual mix of square, practical-looking palms and long, tapering, artistic fingers.

'What were you reading?' Jake asked.

'*Wuthering Heights* by Miss Emily Brontë. Of course it's not the first time I've read it. It was given to me

49

by a woman I worked for before I was married. Oh, it's so romantic, isn't it?'

She seemed not to notice that he didn't reply.

'I could read all day,' she confided. 'The same lady who gave me this book was a member of a circulating library. She would lend me any books I cared to read. I've read all Mr Charles Dickens. I cried like a child when he died earlier this year. I do truly mourn him!'

She brought the teapot back to the table and poured two cups, then she picked up the book, and ran her hand over the cover as if it was a live and cherished thing, before replacing it on the shelf.

'Do you read much, Mr Tempest?' she asked.

'No,' he said.

He changed the subject.

'I should be away. I have to see a man name of Isaac Hargreaves. I'm hoping he'll have a job for me.'

This time yesterday he hadn't been all that sure whether he wanted a job hereabouts, or whether he'd move on somewhere else. Now, he thought he'd be disappointed if he didn't get one.

'I expect he will have,' Beth said. 'I don't know him. He probably lives up at Tunnel Huts. They're always wanting men in the tunnel.'

It was her turn to observe him as he sipped his tea. He couldn't be in that much of a hurry, the way he was making it last. She didn't mind. As soon as he'd gone she'd set to, and it would be all go until the men came home in the evening.

He was good to look at, a cut above a lot of the men who worked on the railway. But no doubt, if he stayed, he'd fall into their ways, he'd soon be as rough as the rest. She'd not been here long, but she'd already seen it happen; to her Will for instance. She saw the change in him, much though she loved him.

'Which way do I go?' Jake asked.

'It's simple. Follow the beck, which means you'll

keep the cutting on your left. Where the beck crosses the cutting – they've built an aqueduct there – you'll see the mouth of the tunnel. It's not more than three-quarters of a mile, all told. The Tunnel Huts settlement is right by it. You'd perhaps have been better looking for lodgings there. No distance to walk at all.'

'I reckon I'll be all right here,' Jake said, smiling. 'Better not to live right on top of the job.'

'That makes sense,' Beth agreed.

'Then I'll be off.' He pushed his cup away. 'I'll just put on a clean shirt, and I'll be away.'

'Hand me your dirty one,' Beth said. 'And anything else that needs washing.'

'Thanks. Shall I fetch you some water before I go?'

'It's all right,' Beth said. 'I do the washing in the beck. It's the best way. Good luck!'

He walked out of the hut into another fine, warm morning. A group of children, including the girl he had spoken to yesterday, were playing a skipping game; two dogs lay stretched out in the sun and the sound of a baby crying came from one of the huts. Down by the beck, a woman washing clothes called out to him.

'Good morning! You're new here!'

'Good morning,' Jake said. 'Yes I am.'

Again there were no men around. The answer to that was quickly made plain. They were all working on the line, or in the deep cutting at the approach to the tunnel. Steep, rocky hillsides climbed up on either side of the narrow strip of land along which, when it was levelled, the railway would run until it plunged into the darkness of the tunnel, inside and through the mountain itself.

He stopped to survey the slope of the land. It rose steeply in front of him, yet they would have to keep the line as level as possible if the engines were to haul the trains at any sort of speed, and this was to be a fast line, fifty miles an hour. But Armitage, that fount of all knowledge, had told him that the maximum gradient they could allow, even though the ground climbed all the way from Settle to Blea Moor, was one in a hundred.

'And that's as steep a gradient as you'll find any-where in the country,' he'd said. 'No wonder they call it the Long Drag! Which means,' he'd added, 'they'll have to sink some pretty deep shafts from the top of the tunnel, to get down to near-level ground.'

Jake missed Armitage. He could have done with him right now. There were so many things he'd like to know, all of which Armitage would no doubt have learned from reading the newspapers. Also Armitage could have told him something about the book Mrs Seymour had been reading.

Mrs Seymour herself, Jake reckoned, probably knew a lot. She had a lively air about her. Not that he had any intention of asking her questions. Rather than ask a woman, he would keep his ignorance to himself. There were ways of finding out things if he kept his eyes and his ears open.

There was a hut on a piece of levelled ground at the end of the cutting, and to that, walking now along a narrow path at the base of the rock, he made his way. As he reached it a man came through the doorway.

'Excuse me,' Jake said. 'I'm looking for Mr Isaac Hargreaves.'

'Then you've struck lucky,' the man said. 'I'm him! What would you be wanting?'

He was a tall, lanky man with a narrow white face. Black bushy eyebrows met over the bridge of his nose and curled upwards at the ends, in exactly the same manner as did his luxuriant dark moustache. His voice was harsh, rasping. Somehow it went well with his face.

I'd not want to get on the wrong side of him, Jake thought.

'A job,' Jake said.

'What sort of job?' Hargreaves demanded. 'We've got mainly miners, bricklayers and labourers in the tunnel. Which of those jobs can you do?'

'I'm not a miner,' Jake admitted. 'But I can do labouring, or a bit of bricklaying.'

'You can, can you? And where've you worked before?'

'Skipton. But I don't carry references.'

Why had it never occurred to him to do so, he wondered. Because he'd left in a huff, that was why. 'But I can give you names.'

'You needn't bother,' Hargreaves said. 'I don't go much on references. Pack o' lies more often than not. Are you as strong as you look?'

'Stronger,' Jake said.

'You'll need to be. It's hard graft in the tunnel, and tunnel's what I'm offering you.'

'Then I'll take it!'

'Have you got lodgings?'

'In Nazareth, with a Mrs Seymour. There's a Patrick Mahoney lodges there, works in the tunnel.'

Hargreaves spat on the ground, though whether by need, or habit, or to express his opinion of the Irish, or of Mahoney in particular, it was impossible to tell.

'Six shillings a day,' he said.

'I was told it might be as much as eight shillings,' Jake said. He thought he had the measure of this man. Stand up to him or he'd walk all over you.

'Well you were told wrong,' Hargreaves said. 'Happen seven shillings a day when you're worth it, if I find out you can lay bricks well. Right now, how do I know you can do it at all?'

'You can try me. But if I lay bricks satisfactorily, I'll look for eight shillings. Anyway, I've heard the

53

Midland Railway Company are generous employers on the Settle–Carlisle.'

He had heard nothing of the sort. All he knew of the Midland, and again it was Armitage who had told him, was that they desperately wanted this line to bridge the gap between Settle and Carlisle in order to give them access to Scotland. They'd gone to parliament for permission to build it.

Hargreaves grunted.

'Generous is not the word I'd use. They have to pay over the odds to get men to work here. Mind you, what they *do* do is look after your welfare. Before they've done there'll be more amenities on Batty Green and Blea Moor than ever you saw in Skipton. Come on, then. I'm going to take you up to number one shaft. They're short of men there.'

He set off at a brisk pace in the direction of the tramway which climbed up the steep side of the moor. Jake followed, a pace behind.

'Jump on,' Hargreaves said. 'It's not encouraged but it'll save time.'

The tramway was carrying containers of building supplies.

'Before we had the tramway, all this stuff had to be pulled up the slope by donkeys, poor devils,' Hargreaves said.

They jumped off again at the entrance to number one shaft. The ground was piled with stone and rubble which had been dug and hauled up out of the mountain. A winding engine, which worked the metal cage-like contraptions which brought up the rubble and took down men and supplies, stood empty at the entrance to the shaft. Another engine stood a few yards away. Hargreaves climbed into the empty contraption and Jake followed him.

'What's the other engine for?' he asked.

'It pumps water out of the mountain, when

necessary, and blows air to the men down there – always necessary. Have you never been down a mine?'

'Never!' Jake said. He had never fancied it.

'Oh, well. It's a bit like that at the moment. You'll soon get used to it.'

They were descending slowly, deep into the ground. The cage jerked and swayed in a disconcerting manner.

'How far down?' Jake asked.

Hargreaves shrugged. 'Maybe ninety yards, give or take a bit.'

Jake was thankful when the cage came to a halt on solid ground.

'Out you get!' Hargreaves said.

Two things struck Jake simultaneously. One was the noise: pickaxes, hammers, chisels, spades; men talking, one man singing in a sweet, true tenor voice. And every single sound hit against the black limestone and grit walls of the inside of the mountain and bounced back again, doubling itself.

The other thing was the lighting, the only source of which was candles. They were balanced on jutting rocks, in crevices, wherever there was space enough to take a candlestick. The glow from each one of them penetrated only a short way before it was swallowed up in the thick blackness, and its role taken up by the next one. Jake had never experienced such darkness nor seen so many small sources of light.

'A pity man can't see in the dark,' Hargreaves said, following Jake's gaze. 'It costs upwards of fifty pounds a month to light this tunnel. A fellow would be rich on that!'

At the spot where they stood, at the bottom of the shaft, the tunnel was brick-lined, and the arches completed. As far as Jake could see, it was so in both directions for a distance of several yards, though not all the arches were completely bricked and the ground was not properly levelled.

'Follow me,' Hargreaves said.

He took Jake several yards down the tunnel and introduced him to a man laying bricks.

'Tempest starts as a labourer,' he said. 'You'll know where he's needed most. He'll be on day shift to start with.' He turned to Jake. 'Might as well start at once, now that you're here. This is Bill Thornton. Below ground you answer to him. He'll tell you what you need to know.'

He walked away. Jake's last sight of him was as the cage ascended, bearing him away from the darkness to the daylight.

The rest of the day was unlike any other Jake had spent in his life. Bill Thornton quickly set him on clearing rubble and sending it up the shaft. Each time he sent the container on its way aloft, he wished he was the man at the top, receiving it and piling the contents onto the spoil heap. Would he get a turn at that, he wondered. He hoped so.

The darkness confused him, and the candles, casting flickering shadows, dazzled him. He found himself stumbling over the rough ground. At one point he tripped over a lump of rock and fell heavily, tearing his trouser leg and hurting his knee.

'You'll get used to the dark,' Thornton said shortly. 'You'll develop cat's eyes, like the rest of us. Even so, you'll always have to watch out. If you get injured, let me tell you, if you're off work, you'll earn nowt. There's a Settle and Carlisle Sick Fund, but what a man gets from that won't keep him in beer and tobacco, and since you've hardly been here ten minutes, you'd get nowt anyway.'

'I'm not planning to go on the sick fund,' Jake said. His knee hurt quite badly, but he would say no more about it. He'd not risk losing his job on the first day.

It was a little later, moving a few yards down the tunnel, that he heard Patrick Mahoney's voice. Though he couldn't yet see him, he was presumably hidden in the gloom some yards away, there was no mistaking the accent. He walked towards the sound, and Mahoney spotted him first.

'Why, 'tis yourself!' he said. 'So they put you on number one shaft. Are you all right, then?'

'I am,' Jake said. His knee was hurting like hell, but never mind that.

Presently a whistle blew, and everyone stopped working on the instant and began to move towards the shaft.

'Dinner time,' Mahoney said.

Three at a time, they climbed into the cage and were raised to the surface. Jake blinked, and held up his hand to shade his eyes as he stepped into the strong sunlight. Most of the other men were already sprawled out on the grass a few yards away from the shaft entrance, and it was not until he saw them take out their tins, unwrap their bundles, open their water bottles, that he realized he had brought no provisions at all with him. He had not given it a thought.

Patrick Mahoney, sitting on the ground beside him, opened his jock tin to reveal a thick beef sandwich, a piece of cheese, a slab of fruitcake. Suddenly, Jake was ravenously hungry.

'You've not brought your jock?' Mahoney asked.

'No. I didn't think of it. I suppose I reckoned if I got a job I'd be told to start tomorrow.'

'Herself must have thought the same. She'd not be letting you leave the house without your food. She's a good provider, Mrs Seymour.'

Jake tried not to look at Mahoney's food. He could feel the saliva gathering in his mouth.

'Well, you'd best be sharing mine,' Mahoney offered.

He took out his knife and meticulously divided everything into two.

'I can't do that,' Jake protested.

'And you can't work the rest of the day on an empty stomach,' Mahoney said. 'Come on, let's be having you. There's enough for the both of us. The trick is to eat it slowly. I found that out a long time ago.'

No food, Jake reckoned, had ever tasted so good, and no water so refreshing as that he drank from the Irishman's bottle.

'Meself, I'd rather it was a pint of ale,' Mahoney said, 'but we're not allowed to drink on the job.'

Jake, his hunger eased, lay back on the short-cropped grass and squinted up at the blue sky, then closed his eyes. He was on the point of falling asleep when another whistle sounded. The men rose slowly to their feet and went back to work, down into the darkness. Jake had not noticed it in the morning but, after the sweetness of the high hill, the air in the tunnel smelt foul. Fresh air, he knew, was regularly blown into the tunnel, but it was clearly not enough. There was also another smell which, though he had noticed it earlier, he could not identify.

'Gunpowder,' Mahoney informed him. 'The miners were using it this morning, before you arrived. It's the only way to blast some of the rock. Nasty stuff, gunpowder!'

The afternoon passed slowly, though he was kept hard at work on the same job. There seemed no end to the amount of rubble to be moved. He said so to Thornton.

'And every bit of it needed,' Thornton answered. 'What we take up out of the tunnel will be used to help build up embankments further along the line, or happen on the foundations of the bridges and viaducts.'

Jake was thankful when the time came to knock off.

He was used to manual labour, but nothing as hard as this. His back was breaking and his knee grew more painful by the minute. Also, it had bled. There was a damp, sticky patch on his trouser leg.

When at last they emerged from the tunnel, like animals coming out of their holes, he thought, the men on the next shift were grouped at the entrance, waiting to descend.

'We work around the clock,' Thornton explained. 'Every day except Sunday. You might say it's a rush job, except it can't really be hurried. It's bloody hard work, and bloody slow. If we open up three or four yards a week we've done well.'

A few yards from the entrance to the shaft the two men parted company.

'I live at Tunnel Huts,' Thornton said. 'Very handy!'

A short distance down the track Patrick Mahoney, whom Jake had not seen as they came off the shift, caught up with him.

'And how did your first day go?' Mahoney enquired.

'All right, I suppose, Mr Mahoney,' Jake said. It was the most he could say. He had hardly *enjoyed* it, it hadn't been what he expected; but then, what did I expect? he asked himself.

'The name is Pat,' Mahoney said. 'No formalities. Except, of course, to the bosses. Watch out for Thornton, he can be awkward.'

'I thought he seemed all right,' Jake said.

'Ah well, perhaps 'tis so. Perhaps 'tis because you're not Irish. The Irish are not popular on this railway. I don't know why. But then, did the English and the Irish ever get on?'

Jake didn't answer. He had met with the same feeling in Skipton, but he'd never taken sides, he wanted no part in it.

'You're limping,' Patrick observed.

'I fell. Gave my knee a bit of a knock. It'll be

all right once I can get back and attend to it.'

At a point where they should have turned left to reach the Seymour hut, Patrick said: 'I'll be loving you and leaving you for now. I'm going down to Batty Green. Tell Mrs Seymour I might be a bit late for supper, but perhaps she'll be kind enough to save a bite for me.'

He gave no further explanation. Perhaps he has a woman on Batty Green, Jake thought. But when he passed the message on to Beth Seymour, she smiled.

'His glass of ale holds more attraction than food. It's the same with most of the men, and you can't blame them. They do hard, backbreaking jobs, in all kinds of weather, and they deserve their pint. The only trouble is, they never stop at one or two. They lose count, don't know when to call a halt.'

She was sitting on the grass outside the hut, peeling a mound of potatoes. She had undone the buttons on the high neck of her blouse, against the day's heat. Around the long column of her throat she wore a necklace of red glass beads which glowed like rubies in the light from the sun. The sun also picked out the lights in her brown hair, turning them to flecks of gold.

'Do you not drink, Mr Tempest?' she enquired.

'Oh yes! At the moment it's too far to go. If you don't object, the name's Jake.'

'It's a nice name,' she acknowledged. 'There's water in the jug in the house if you fancy a cold drink.'

'Thanks!'

What he did fancy was a good wash, better still a bath. He felt dirty from tip to toe and, despite the fact that it had been cold in the tunnel, sweaty. He was not sure, however, that it was a good time to bathe. There were too many people around the huts now, and he would be in full view. But a wash he must have, and he must see to his knee.

It was not until he started to move towards the hut that Beth Seymour noticed his torn trousers, and the bloodstain over his knee.

'Good heavens!' she cried. 'Whatever have you done to yourself?'

'It's nothing much. It'll be as right as rain when I've bathed it,' Jake said.

He went past her and into the hut, where he drank two full mugs of water. Then he went into the bedroom in search of his towel and some soap. It was obvious that in his absence it had been swept and tidied, both beds neatly made. A clean-washed vest and socks, a newly ironed shirt, lay on the bed. He felt ashamed that he'd left his part of the room in such a mess, but that was one of the things living alone did to you. You didn't care.

As he looked around the room he realized what was missing. He had not hung up his picture of the mountain. It still lay on the chest of drawers where he had left it last night. He would see to that when he'd cleaned himself up.

He gathered up his spare pair of trousers, his clean underwear and shirt, and made his way to the beck.

'I'll have a look at your knee when you come back,' Beth called after him. 'It might need a bandage!'

The ice-cold water of the beck – he was to learn that however hot the sun, however long it shone, the water on the moor, in the beck and in the many small streams which sprang from the ground, was always cold – refreshed his body while sharply stinging his knee. But there was no great damage: an inch-long cut, and some grazing around it, but his trousers had prevented the gravel embedding itself in his flesh. It would heal soon enough.

He dried himself, and dressed, then washed his blood-soaked trousers in the beck. When he got back to the hut his landlady had gone inside. He held up the wet trousers.

'Where can I hang them?'

'There's a line at the back,' she said.

When he came inside again she said, 'If you'll sit down and roll up your trouser leg, I'll take a look at your knee.'

'There's no need . . .' Jake protested.

'Better to be on the safe side,' she advised. 'It's a dirty place, the tunnel, or so I'd think. If you've got a cut you should have it covered. You wouldn't want it to get worse.'

Her tone was cool, matter-of-fact, as if he was a child. He sat on the chair and, kneeling in front of him, she rolled up his trouser leg. When she saw the cut and the grazing she gave an involuntary gasp.

'Why, it's quite nasty! It must have been really painful. I reckon it needs some disinfectant and a bandage.'

The stinging of the icy beck water was nothing compared to the pain of the disinfectant, which she dabbed on his knee abundantly. Then she covered it with a folded square of cotton, and started to bandage it. She was deft and sure, and at the same time gentle. Those practical-looking hands, Jake thought, as he watched her tying the bandage, had not lied.

She tied the last knot, cut off the ends of the bandage, then, lifting her head, leaned back and smiled up at him.

'There! That's better!' she said.

'Thank you. Thank you very much!'

A shadow blocked the light from the doorway. Jake turned his head and saw William Seymour standing there.

'I see my wife's making you feel at home!' Seymour said.

Beth Seymour rose to her feet, still smiling.

'Jake had a slight accident at work, in the tunnel. I was putting a bandage on. You're early, Will. I didn't expect you so soon.'

He grunted.

'Nevertheless, I'm pleased to see you,' she said. 'Supper won't be long.'

Jake rose to his feet.

'Thank you very much, Mrs Seymour,' he said. 'It's much more comfortable.' He turned to her husband. 'Your wife's a clever nurse.'

'Oh, she's clever at lots of things,' Will Seymour said. 'You'll find that out.'

'Well if you'll excuse me, I have a few things to do,' Jake said. 'Oh, by the way, may I hang a small picture on the bedroom wall? And if I may, could you give me a nail and lend me a hammer?'

Will Seymour rummaged in a box, then handed Jake the hammer and nail. Beth Seymour was busy at the stove.

4

'Remember, both of you,' Beth said as she served breakfast to Jake and Patrick – Will had left earlier – 'I'll not be in when you get home today. I'll leave you a meal, but it will be cold.'

'And where would you be going, Mrs Seymour?' Patrick enquired pleasantly.

Beth stood with her hands on her hips, gazing at him.

'Patrick Mahoney, where do you think I'd be going?' she demanded. 'Where do I go every Saturday afternoon?'

'Oh, it's Saturday, is it?' Patrick asked. 'Do I ever know the day of the week, working under the ground like a mole? And then, aren't Saturdays and Sundays all the same to us? Doesn't the Company like us to work our shifts through the weekend, no interruptions to the work?'

Jake ate his breakfast while looking from one to the other of them. They did a lot of sparring, but it was all good-natured.

'So you're taking the market tramway down to Batty Green to spend your man's hard-earned money,' Patrick said. 'Is that the size of it?'

'You know it is,' Beth answered.

Every Saturday afternoon the empty trucks made a special journey from Tunnel Huts to Batty Green, stopping at the different shanty towns to pick up those who wanted to make the trip, which in practice was all the women and, if the weather was halfway decent, the children as well. It was an uncomfortable journey, everyone jammed together, standing in open trucks which swayed perilously on the downhill run; but it was even worse on the return journey, everyone laden with shopping baskets, possibly livestock, a hen or a rabbit. And there were always those on the homeward journey who had taken more than a drop too much and were boisterous, abusive, or just plain sick, however the drink took them.

'I wouldn't miss it for the world,' Beth said. 'It's a nice change.' In spite of which way it goes, she thought; by which she meant that some Saturdays Will would return with her, help to carry the baskets, but on other Saturdays he would be persuaded by his mates to stay on in the inn, arriving home any old time. Thankfully, the long walk back in the cold, pitch darkness did something towards sobering him up before he reached the hut.

'You need to watch out,' Beth frequently warned him. 'A man could be drowned falling into one of those shakeholes, if he happened to be drunk, and if it just happened to have water in the bottom!'

A few months ago a man *had* been drowned, in just such conditions. It struck fear into the hearts of the wives, but it seemed not to bother the men one bit.

She'd never in her life seen anything like the shakeholes, and no-one knew how they'd happened. Lost in the mists of time, they said. They were scattered over the moor at irregular intervals, circular holes in the ground, ranging in size from no more than a couple of feet across, and shallow, to wide enough and deep enough to swallow a house. The trouble was that since the grass grew to the very edge, or over the edge, you didn't always see the near ones.

'You should carry a lantern,' she advised.

His reply was always the same. 'I don't need a lantern. I can see well enough.'

'Are you going to buy anything special?' Jake asked now.

Beth thought for a minute.

'Not that I know of. But there *will* be something, and I'll recognize it when I see it. I shall buy the newspapers of course. Anything I can find to read.'

He had not yet admitted that he couldn't read, although he'd been living there two months now. He'd have to come out with it, though. He was running out of excuses for not borrowing any of the few books his landlady offered him, or reading the *Craven Herald* and the *Lancaster Guardian* which she brought back every Saturday from Batty Green. Both Patrick Mahoney and Will Seymour could read, though the former only haltingly, stumbling over the long words. Jake felt himself the odd man out. His inability to read had never bothered him much until he'd met Armitage, and now there was Beth Seymour.

'To be truthful, we don't want for much up here, do we?' Beth said. 'Burgoyne & Cocks bring provisions from Settle up to Jericho and Tunnel Huts, and some of what *they* don't sell, the pedlars bring right to the door at least once a week.'

'Mr Burgoyne and Mr Cocks must be making a small fortune,' Patrick Mahoney said.

'I daresay,' Beth agreed. 'But where would we be without them? They're like manna from heaven! No, what I go to Batty Green for every Saturday afternoon is the change of scene. To get away from you lot!'

The fact that traders came from Settle, and up the steep hill from Ingleton, and set up what was almost a market, was a bonus. And it was there that she found the items which made the hut more of a home: a vase, a cushion, a tablecloth, a calendar.

Mahoney rose from the table.

'Time we were off,' he said. 'Don't bother to do me

a meal. I'll be going down to Batty Green myself. I'll get a bite there.'

'Very well. And what about you, Jake?' Beth asked.

'I might do the same thing. I'll see how the spirit moves me!'

His knee, which for a week or two had prevented him undertaking the five-mile return trip to Batty Green, was now quite better. All that remained of his fall was a scar.

'Well, I'll make something for all of us when we get back later,' Beth promised.

Or for those of us who do get back, she thought. If Patrick Mahoney met up with his fellow countrymen, he'd make a long night of it, probably take the Sunday off work. It wouldn't be the first time. It was in the lap of the gods what Will would do. He didn't work Sundays, and often stayed in bed until noon.

As for Jake Tempest, she never quite knew. He'd been lodging with her for two months now and she felt she knew him not much better than she had in the first week. He'd volunteered little of his past life, except that when she had admired the painting of the mountain which he'd hung on the bedroom wall, he'd spoken of his mother. She wondered why, at twenty-three, he wasn't married; why some woman hadn't captured him. Yet, though he kept himself to himself, he wasn't unfriendly. He was always polite, and helpful. It was just that he kept this distance between them when she would have liked to get to know him better.

She went to the door and saw the two men off to work.

'I might see you both on Batty Green!' she said.

She watched Patrick and Jake stride out across the moor, then turned back into the house. She made her own breakfast, then took down her book from the shelf. She was re-reading *Pride and Prejudice* by Miss

Jane Austen, which she had bought herself before she and Will came north, while they were living in Surrey. In those early days of their marriage, Will had taken pride in her love of books, had encouraged it. Now he seemed to resent it.

'You always have your head stuck in a book,' he complained. 'That's no comfort for a man at the end of a hard day's work.'

So now, to save argument, she only read when he was out of the house. In the evenings, if he was not down at Batty Green with his pals, they sat opposite each other, she with her mending or knitting, he falling asleep.

But this time at breakfast was her own. There was no-one to stop her, or even to complain. With a sigh of contentment she found her place in the book and simultaneously lifted a forkful of breakfast to her mouth.

She loved this book. She felt she knew every character intimately, and though she admitted that Darcy was devastatingly attractive, old Mr Bennet was her clear favourite. The story spoke to her of a life of which she knew nothing at all; balls, parties, high-born people. It was, in a way, a fairy story. She devoured every word as avidly as she devoured her breakfast.

Breakfast over, she reluctantly replaced the book, then fed the hens, did some washing and hung it out to dry. After dinner, with her shopping bags and baskets over her arm, she set off to walk down the hill to Jericho, where she would pick up the market tram. When she arrived, a group of women and children were already standing by the track. It being a fine day, no-one had elected to stay at home.

By now she knew most of the women, and was on good terms with them. Jericho was mostly families. The single men, and the more available women, tended to live on Batty Green, closer to whatever entertainment was on offer. The Jericho women were, on the whole, decent, hardworking souls who had accompanied their husbands to this outlandish spot so that, for the time it took to build the railway, they could be sure of money in their purses, the wherewithal to feed and clothe their families. For that, and because it would only be temporary, they were prepared to tolerate the isolation and, above all, the terrible vagaries of the weather.

'Good afternoon, Mrs Seymour,' a woman called out. 'Another nice day!'

'It's been a nice week, Mrs Hobson,' Beth said.

'It won't keep up,' Mrs Hobson said. 'We're halfway through October and up here the winter starts early in November. You weren't here last winter, were you?'

'We came in April,' Beth said. 'It was still cold. There was plenty of snow on the tops.'

For weeks she had been unable to get warm, except in bed, cuddling up to Will. It was so different from her home, where, though there could be snow, the winters were short and reasonably mild. She had left behind trees everywhere, trees coming into leaf, or even in blossom. The daffodils had been almost over, but tulips and wallflowers were bursting their buds. Here on Blea Moor, there were no trees. She badly missed them. The flowers came later than in Surrey and grew close to the ground, sheltering from the wind which blew day and night.

'Then you've got the worst to come,' Mrs Hobson said. She did not believe in looking on the bright side. It led to disappointment.

'You get used to it.' The new speaker was a small, neat woman, carrying a baby, and with three more children in tow. She spoke with good humour.

'But you're north-country bred, Mrs Drake,' Mrs Hobson pointed out. 'You come from Northumberland.'

'I suppose that helps,' Mrs Drake acknowledged. 'Up there, we reckon folk are soft in the south – no offence meant of course!'

The tram was in sight now, descending the hill, the trucks, still mostly empty, swaying alarmingly. They would be steadier, Beth consoled herself, when they had the weight of people in them.

The women sorted out their children, gathered them together, and everyone climbed into the trucks.

'Let me take the baby, Mrs Drake, while you see to the other children,' Beth said.

She could perhaps more usefully have offered to deal with the older children, but she wanted to feel the baby in her arms. Three years she and Will had been married, and never a sign of a child. Every month she hoped, and every month her hopes were dashed. And she wanted not just one child, but several; four, five, six. She herself was the youngest of six children. All her brothers and sisters were dear to her, though there was not one who hadn't protested when she'd announced she was going to marry Will Seymour.

'It won't work,' her eldest sister had said.

'Susan is right,' her brother Tom had said. 'It won't work!'

'It's all very well for the rest of you to talk,' Beth had protested. 'You're already married, all of you.'

She didn't ask them why it wouldn't work. She didn't want to hear. Nevertheless they told her, all of them, separately and together.

Tom summed it up.

'He's just not your type. You're chalk and cheese!'

She had wavered when Tom spoke, but not for long. Though she loved Tom more than anyone in the family since her parents had died, she loved Will more.

'I'm sorry you don't like him, but I love him and I'm going to marry him. So it's no use saying any more.'

And she still loved him. She had found out that he was moody, but she could bear his bad moods because his good ones were magic to her. She couldn't understand why she hadn't conceived. She wanted to consult the doctor, but Will would have none of that.

'Do you think I don't want a child?' he demanded whenever she pressed him. 'Of course I do! Every man does. But if the Lord chooses you to be barren, then I shall bear it, and so must you. It isn't as if I reproached you!'

Mrs Drake handed over the baby. He was well wrapped up in a wool shawl and bonnet, but when Beth held him in her arms he freed his hands and pulled at her bodice. She held out a finger and he grabbed it, fastening his own small fingers around it in a firm grip.

'He'll do well,' Mrs Hobson remarked, watching him. 'He'll hang on to whatever comes his way.'

'I'd sooner not bring all the children,' Mrs Drake said, 'but I do it as much for their sake as for mine. They get fed up, being around the house all day. They'd be better if they could go to school.'

'They say they might start a school,' Mrs Hobson said. 'But if they do, it'll be on Batty Green because that's where most people live.'

'Then it'll be no use to us,' Mrs Drake said. 'It's a two-mile walk, in all weathers. Snow all winter, and even in the summer it's boggy underfoot. The bairns wouldn't be safe.'

'It's a shame,' Beth said. 'When they get to a certain age, children need school.'

'And their poor mothers need them to go to school!' Mrs Drake spoke with feeling.

'I heard you were a teacher,' Mrs Hobson said to Beth. 'Is that right then?'

'Yes and no,' Beth said. 'I worked for a lady, a Mrs Carmichael, who ran a small private school. I helped

71

her with the children, but I couldn't claim to be a proper teacher.'

The tram set off with a jerk, then wound its way down the hillside, stopping at Inkerman, Sebastopol and Belgravia. It was now completely full. When they'd first come to Ribblehead Beth had wanted to live in Belgravia. It was a cut above the other shanty towns. The huts were not quite so close together, and some of them had porches, which not only looked nice, but were a protection against the weather. Belgravia would also have been handier for Will's work on the viaduct. Unfortunately there hadn't been a free hut.

When they reached Batty Green everyone climbed out. Beth, who had kept the baby throughout the journey, reluctantly handed him back to his mother.

'He's lovely,' she said.

'You should have one of your own,' Mrs Drake said. 'I reckon you have a way with you. But you can't have this one, even though he was a bit of an afterthought. There's six years between him and the next one. I don't know why. Nature's very mysterious, and that's a fact!'

'I'll look out for you on the way back,' Beth said as they parted company.

For a moment she stood still and looked around her. The place was thronged. She reckoned everyone from Tunnel Huts to Salt Lake City, on the Settle Road, was here, as well as those who had travelled from Settle and Ingleton to serve them. There were hawkers, cheapjacks, a stall for household goods, another offering boots and shoes; greengrocers, dairy produce, bakers' goods. There were also horses, carts, donkeys, hens, rabbits. Everything except a bookstall, Beth thought. Sometimes she was lucky enough to find a book on the secondhand stall.

Where should she start?

The answer was easy. First of all she must buy the

two weekly newspapers before the newsvendor sold out. She handed over threepence and put the papers safely in the bottom of a shopping bag. She would like to read them this very minute, cover to cover, but they must be saved, and read at leisure. She must make them last.

The arrangement with Will was that they would find each other somewhere in the crowd. Unless overtime was called for, and it often was, he finished work at one o'clock on Saturdays, so he should be around by now. Except, she thought, that the minute they downed tools, he and his mates would make the inn their first stop, and he might well still be there. More likely than not.

She was surprised therefore, and almost jumped out of her skin, when she felt his hand on her shoulder, heard his voice in her ear.

'I've been looking for you. I saw the tram come in.'

'I went to buy the newspapers before they sold out. Where shall we go next?'

He shrugged. 'Up to you, lass!'

'So we'll go to the bakers. I'd like to buy a nice cake for Sunday tea.'

'*You* can bake a cake,' Will protested. 'Better than any of this bought stuff.'

'I know I can. I just thought I'd like something I hadn't made. Something fancy!'

There was a wonderful display of cakes, fancy bread and pastries. Beth spent several minutes considering it, trying to decide what to buy.

'Can I help you?' the assistant asked.

Beth looked up into the face of a very pretty girl; black hair, a flawless complexion and bright eyes.

'I'm sorry,' Beth said. 'There's so much choice!'

'Then make up your mind, love,' Will urged. 'Can't you see the young lady's busy?'

The assistant treated him to a beaming smile.

In the end, Beth chose an iced sponge cake, with buttercream through the middle and walnuts on top, four custard tarts, and a fruit malt loaf. The assistant wrapped them carefully.

'They won't be easy to carry,' Beth whispered to her husband, 'especially the custard tarts.'

Will smiled at the girl.

'Do you think we might leave them here until we're ready to go home? We've other things to shop for, and there's such a crush.'

'Certainly, sir! You can come back any time you like.' There was the faintest, but decisive, emphasis on the word 'you'.

'My word, she's a bit of all right!' Will said to Beth as they moved away.

'So I noticed,' Beth said. 'I'm sorry if I cramped your style. All the same, I'll make certain I go back with you when we collect them.'

They moved around slowly, inspecting each stall in turn. Beth bought a green glass vase, which would look well on the dresser, a new white handkerchief for Will, and a shoulder of lamb which was going cheap because it was nearing the end of the day. And then, to her great delight, on the secondhand stall she found a book of poems: *Sonnets* by William Shakespeare. It was small, not more than three inches across, bound in brown leather with gold decoration on the spine, and it had clearly been much used. She caught her breath with pleasure at the sight of it. She opened it at random, and began to read: 'Shall I compare thee to a summer's day? Thou art more lovely and more temperate.'

She read the words in a half whisper. Oh, it was wonderful; she had to have this book! But it was marked at a shilling, and that much she could not possibly spend.

'Oh, come on!' Will grumbled. 'Surely you don't need another book?'

'But I do, Will! I do! Do you think he would take ninepence?'

'Just *ask* him! Either leave it be, or ask him.'

'Will you take ninepence for this?' she asked the stallholder.

'The binding alone's worth a shilling, lady,' he protested.

'It's very worn,' Beth said. 'And I'm afraid ninepence is all I can afford.'

He pondered.

'Go on then,' he said reluctantly. 'Though I'm a fool to meself and I'll never make a decent living.'

He wrapped the book in a scrap of paper, and she tucked it into her pocket so that nothing in her basket would soil it.

'Let's be moving,' Will said. 'We can't spend all afternoon here. We must go and collect the cake and things.'

'But it's not time for the return tram,' Beth said. 'We've an hour yet!'

Without answering, Will strode off towards the bakery stall. Beth hurried after him. In fact, she was too happy with the purchase of the book to mind much about anything else.

They stood in front of the bakery stall, waiting their turn. The same girl was serving, though now at the other end of the counter. She really was attractive, Beth thought, but in a bold sort of way.

The girl finished serving and moved towards them. She raised her head, looked straight over Beth's shoulder, and cried out in surprise.

'Why, it's Jake Tempest, I do declare!'

Beth and Will spun around, and there he was.

'Don't say you've forgotten Sally Roland!' the girl said. 'I wouldn't believe you if you did!'

Will grinned at Jake.

'You're a dark horse!' he said. 'So introduce us to your friend!'

'I'll introduce myself,' Sally said. She could see Jake Tempest's reluctance and she wasn't letting him get away with it a second time. 'I'm Sally Roland. I live in Settle, with my aunt. Mr Tempest stayed in the same house. We got on very well!'

'I hope your aunt is well,' Jake said non-committally. He hadn't seen her as he approached the stall, or he'd have made off at once.

'In the best of health,' Sally replied. 'So, are you working on the railway here?'

'Not here,' Jake said hurriedly. 'Further up. I'm seldom here.'

Damn the woman! He wanted nothing to do with her. Yet who could deny her attraction? It was so obvious. And apparently so to all the customers waiting to be served. They were drinking in every word.

'Well, we must change that, mustn't we?' Sally said pleasantly.

Beth nudged Will.

'We should pick up our things and make a move,' she said. 'We're holding things up.'

'No hurry!' Will said.

'I'll walk with you, carry some of your parcels,' Jake said hastily. If he had wanted something from the stall, he no longer remembered what it was. All he wanted now was to be off.

'It's interesting you should find a friend here,' Beth said as they moved away.

'Not a friend, exactly. I lodged one night in her aunt's house before I came on here.'

'Oh!' Beth said. 'I thought you knew each other quite well!'

'I'd say you've got a foot in the door there!' Will said, grinning. 'Who knows what could happen if you

76

played your cards right? She's a corker, and no mistake.' He seemed unusually cheered by Jake's encounter with the girl.

Beth gave her husband a sharp look. Personally, she had thought the girl was common, not at all right for Jake Tempest, but she'd keep quiet. It was none of her business.

'Then as Jake's here to give you a hand with your baskets,' Will said, 'I'll leave you for a while and wet my whistle. I'm as dry as a bone!'

'Oh, but—' Beth began.

He didn't wait to hear her objections.

'I'll meet you at the tramway, ride home with you.'

Beth stared after him, then turned to Jake.

'I'm sorry! There's no need for you to be carrying my parcels.'

'It's no trouble,' Jake said. 'But we've three-quarters of an hour before the tram leaves. What would you like to do? Or have you not finished your shopping?'

'I've quite finished,' Beth answered him. 'Do you think we could walk over and see what they're doing on the viaduct? Although Will works on it, I know next to nothing.'

'Me too,' Jake admitted. 'I'd like to take a look.'

They left the vicinity of the stalls, crossed the dirt track, and walked westwards. In the wide valley over which the viaduct would be built the ground was flat, cropped short by sheep and horses, trodden down by feet. But it was uneven, and made more so by its bogginess. It was difficult to know where to walk.

'I'll go first, pick out the firmest bits,' Jake offered. 'You try to follow in my footsteps.'

It was not easy for her. He had a long stride and was not hampered by skirts around his ankles. More than once she was marooned on what seemed to be the only dry bit of land around, and he had to turn around and take her hand, helping her across as best he could.

Nearer to the viaduct, wooden planks had been laid down to make an easier passage.

There were large heaps of stones and rubble at intervals along the ground, stacks of wood in varying lengths, and piles of bricks. The bricks, Beth knew because that much Will had told her, were made at the brickworks erected no more than half a mile away along the valley, made from the clay which lay under the peat, and mixed with ground shale. Jake picked a brick from a heap.

'They're good and strong,' he said. He knew a bit about bricks.

'Will said they make thousands a day,' Beth told him.

'They'll need them,' Jake said. 'They're wanted in the tunnel as well as on the viaduct.'

The building of the viaduct, which they had now reached, was still in the early stages. Much of the work, so far, had been in digging and lining the deep foundations. Twenty-four great arches, built on massive piers, fashioned from black marble, would eventually carry the new railway line eighteen feet above the valley beneath. So far, only three piers were beginning to rise, and they still had a long way to go before they reached the springing, where the arch would start to turn.

'I wonder how long it will take,' Jake said.

'Will reckons a few years yet,' Beth replied.

'And does he plan to stay to the end?'

'Oh, I think so! What about you?'

'It's too early to decide,' Jake said.

They walked forward, past the line of the viaduct. Beyond them, to the west, the view was dominated by Ingleborough, etched black against the late afternoon sun.

'That's much more my idea of a mountain,' Jake said. 'Evenly sloping sides, climbing to a peak at the top – except that in this case it looks as though the top has been sliced off.'

'And so neatly done,' Beth said. 'From here it looks completely flat.'

'It will be even more like a mountain when there's snow on it,' Jake remarked.

Beth laughed.

'You won't have to wait long for that! Six weeks, or even less. Anyway, shouldn't we be moving? I wouldn't want to miss the tram – and Will will be waiting for me.'

Will was not waiting, nor had he turned up when the tram was due to leave. Beth looked across the green – the crowd had thinned by now – hoping to see him hurrying towards her. In her heart she knew it was a forlorn hope. He had undoubtedly fallen in with his friends and there would be no telling what time he'd reach home. Nor was Patrick on the tram, but then she didn't expect that.

'He's no doubt been held up,' she said to Jake. 'He'll be very disappointed.'

He wouldn't be at all, but she had to say something, make some excuse for him, however lame. Jake made no reply.

The tram chugged slowly up the hill.

'It's best to stay on until Tunnel Huts,' Beth remarked. 'Then we can walk down the hill instead of up.'

Jake took most of the parcels. How could she have managed without him, she wondered. When they were inside the hut she made a pot of tea, buttered two currant teacakes, and the two of them sat down at the table. It was peaceful. Jake Tempest was a peaceful man to be with – though did that make him sound dull, she wondered. He was far from that.

She picked up the book of sonnets from the table, fingered through it.

'Do you like poetry?' she asked.

'I don't know much,' Jake admitted. 'In fact hardly any.'

She turned to her favourite sonnet, and began to read aloud: 'Shall I compare thee to a summer's day? Thou art more lovely, and more temperate.'

Then, suddenly, she put the book down and pushed it across the table towards Jake. She had a sudden notion to hear him read. He had a good voice, deep and clear.

'You read it!'

His face reddened. His eyes met hers, and there was panic in them. She couldn't understand it.

'What's wrong?'

'I can't,' he said.

'Then read something else. Anything!' She thought his objection was to the particular sonnet, that perhaps it was too personal, too intimate.

'You don't understand. I can't read! I can't read at all!'

She stared at him in disbelief; not that it was unusual for a person to be unable to read, but because it seemed wrong for him. He was intelligent enough.

'I'm sorry,' she said. 'I didn't realize. Would you like me to read the rest out loud?'

He nodded. She read the sonnet through to the end. They looked at each other without speaking. Then Jake said, in a quiet voice:

'I'd like to be able to read. I'd like to read what you've just read – out loud.'

'Then you shall,' Beth said. 'One day you shall. I shall teach you to read.'

5

It was long past dark when Will Seymour arrived home, steady enough on his feet, but with a carefulness in his speech which signalled that he was not totally sober. Jake saw the flash of anxiety and annoyance in Beth's face as her husband came into the room, and then it was gone, and only a slight tightness in her voice when she returned his greeting betrayed her feelings.

'I've kept your supper hot, Will. Sit down and I'll serve you.'

Is she being polite for my sake? Jake wondered. He would make his excuses and go to bed as soon as he could; but not immediately; that would be too obvious.

'So you didn't wait for me?' Will grumbled.

Beth had put the pan back on the stove and was stirring the contents.

'We did for quite a while,' she said evenly, not turning around. 'But we were hungry. Don't worry, this will be ready in a minute or two. It's not long since we finished.'

Will sat down heavily, his elbows on the table. He gave Jake a cold stare.

'Well at least my wife didn't lack for company,' he said.

'No. And I was glad of Jake on the way home,' Beth said pleasantly. 'I don't know how I'd have managed everything otherwise.'

'Was it my fault if the tram left early?' Will demanded. 'I was there at the right time.'

Beth didn't reply. It was patently untrue, the kind of excuse a small boy would make, and that was so often the way he behaved now. He used not to be like that. It was this place, the strain of his job, which had changed him. She had learnt to deal with him by showing the patience she would have given to a child. She would not make things more difficult for either of them by arguing.

She filled his plate with stew, and set it before him. He ate without speaking. It was an uncomfortable silence. Will himself, when he had cleared his plate, was the one to break it.

'So what *did* you do to pass the time?'

'Oh, I had lots of jobs to do,' Beth said. 'When I'd done them, I read.'

Jake said nothing, thankful that the question had not been put to him. What Beth had *not* said was that she had read aloud, to him. Sitting opposite him at the table, she'd read, quietly, yet with the passion they merited, several of the poems from her newly acquired collection. He had watched as well as listened; observed the way the light from the lamp burnished her hair, noted the expressions on her face as she spoke the lines, for all the world as if she were living them.

For Jake there had been something about the evening which had made it unlike any other he had ever known. And if anyone had told him that an evening spent listening to someone reading poetry would be charged with magic, he would have laughed out loud.

'I suppose you didn't see Patrick on your travels?' Beth asked her husband.

'Neither hair nor hide of him. If you ask me, we'll not see him tonight.'

'I daresay you're right,' Beth said. 'Poor Patrick! He seems to live another life from the rest of us.'

'Poor Patrick my foot!' Will said. 'He's typical of the Irish – born to trouble, they are.'

'But not always of their own making,' Beth suggested. 'You heard about it yourself, we read it in the newspaper, how Irishmen in Settle were threatened, told they had to leave the town. But after the fight, when it came to court, it wasn't the Irish who were found guilty, it was the English!'

'Then why are the Irish always at the centre of any fight?' Will demanded. 'Tell me that!'

'Because they're picked on, that's why!' Beth said sharply. She had meant to stay calm, and here she was, flaring up.

'Nonsense! You're too soft,' Will said.

Yet wasn't it one of the reasons he had always loved her, because she was tolerant, saw the best in everyone, including in him? She had not changed from that; she was the same tender, loving woman she had always been. It was he who had changed, and he knew it.

Why? he asked himself. Why do I pick on her? Why do I go against her all the time?

She was the last person in the world to deserve such treatment, yet he seemed not to be able to help himself. He felt churned up inside, always at war with his own person, and therefore with everyone else.

It had not been like this in Surrey. They had lived in near-tranquillity there, content with their small-holding, both of them working on it; they never made much money but he knew now, looking back, they had been happy.

If they were not now, the blame was his. He would do better.

He rose to his feet and went around to the other side of the table where Beth was sitting. Suddenly he had urgent need of her, he wanted to show her his love, to atone for his churlishness. He placed his hands on her shoulders and bent to kiss the back of her neck.

'Please, Will!' Beth's face flamed.

'Not in front of the lodger, eh?' Will said, smiling. 'Well, I'm sure he'll understand.'

'I'm just off to bed,' Jake said quietly. 'I said I'd go in to work in the morning, Sunday or no Sunday.'

'And so are we,' Will said. 'Going to bed, I mean.' He pulled Beth to her feet, and put his arm around her.

'I'm sorry I was so bad-tempered,' Will said when they were in the bedroom. 'I don't know what comes over me. You don't deserve it.'

'That isn't what matters,' Beth said. 'What matters is that I don't understand it. You've changed, Will. I don't want you to change. I loved you the way you were. Can't you tell me why?'

'I hardly know myself. Perhaps we should never have left Surrey.'

He had wanted to leave Surrey because, although they were happy with each other, Beth's family did not approve of him, and they made that plain. He was not, in their eyes, successful, and never would be.

And then there had been the other cloud in their sky, that Beth did not have children. He had tried to come to terms with that, but it had not been easy, and he was not sure that he had done so. A man wanted sons to follow after him. It was the most natural thing in the world.

'We agreed it would be a good thing to leave,' Beth reminded him. 'We agreed a change of scene, of work, would do us good.'

They had agreed, but she had only paid lip service. It wasn't what she'd wanted, but Will saw the chance of good money, a way to succeed in a new place. It hadn't worked.

'Is it the job?' she asked now.

'Partly.'

The job was hard going, harder than anything he'd

ever done in his life. Also, he hadn't envisaged himself being forever a labourer, but by now he had been forced to accept that that was what he was, and would be all the time he worked on the line. His skills lay in tilling the land, in husbandry, in looking after a few animals. They were of no use to him in building a railway.

'Should we leave?' Beth asked uncertainly. 'Should we try somewhere else?' Where they would go, what they would do, she couldn't imagine, but she would try anything to make Will happy.

'No!' Will said firmly. 'We'll stay where we are. I'll stick it out. I won't be beaten!'

It was because so many of the men had found the job so hard, the land inhospitable, yet resolved to stick it out, Beth thought, that they drank so much. Will had never been a heavy drinker until they had come here, and now drink was changing his character. She watched its effects every day, but could do nothing. It was a subject which Will would never discuss. To mention it at all threw him into a rage.

Jake went to bed, though not, for a long time, to sleep. Long after he had heard the Seymours go to their room he lay on his back staring into the darkness, his thoughts ranging far and wide.

He thought of his mother, then of Vinnie; from Vinnie, by no logical route, to Armitage. Where was *he*? From Armitage it was a reasonable step to Sally Roland, and today's encounter with her. In spite of the fact that he had no liking for the girl, the memory of her blatant sexual charms disturbed him against his will. He pushed the thought of her away, turning over on his side to escape her. But it was when his thoughts turned to Beth Seymour that he really clamped them down, refused to give them form or shape. Would it have been better if he'd found lodgings at Tunnel Huts? Was it too late to do so?

But now wasn't she going to teach him to read? And there was more than one reason why he would not lightly give that up.

When Jake wakened next morning he saw that Patrick Mahoney's bed was empty, hadn't been slept in. He yawned, then rose, glanced at the painting of the mountain, as he did every morning, picked up his towel and left the hut for his morning wash in the beck, closing the door quietly behind him. No point in disturbing anyone, he was quite capable of making his own breakfast and packing up something to eat at midday.

There was a keen nip in the air as he went across to the beck, and when he slipped off his shoes and walked into the shallow water near the bank he gasped at the coldness of it. If he had been half asleep before, he was suddenly wide awake now. He washed quickly, and hurried back to the hut.

When he opened the door the smell of bacon met him, and the sight of Beth at the stove.

'Won't be a minute! Nearly ready!' She spoke quietly. Jake guessed Will was still asleep.

'You shouldn't have got up,' Jake said. 'I can manage.'

'I know. But I was awake,' she said. She had not slept well. Will's lovemaking, which had started gently, had in the end been rough, demanding. When it was over, and he was immediately deep into sleep, she was left bruised in body and confused in mind. It seemed on his part no more than hunger and lust, which left her unsatisfied. He no longer spoke of the child he had also wanted; and what would a child be like, she wondered, conceived in such circumstances? But she *did* love Will, she was sure of that.

'I heard you leave the house,' she said to Jake. 'It's really no trouble.'

She flipped the egg over, fried it on the second side,

slipped it onto the plate, and served him. Then she poured him tea, and a cup for herself, and sat down at the table.

'Is it cold out?' she asked.

'Yes,' Jake said. 'And the water's like ice.'

'Before long it will be frozen over in the mornings. You'll have to bring water in at night, and wash in the bedroom.'

'It'll be warmer,' Jake said, mopping up his plate with a piece of bread. 'And by the way, Patrick didn't come in.'

'I thought he hadn't. I'd have heard him,' Beth said. 'I hope he's all right.'

'I expect he will be.' In the short time he had been there, Jake had developed quite an affection for the Irishman. 'Time I was off,' he said.

'I've packed your jock tin. When I go down to Batty Green this afternoon I'll see if I can find out about Patrick.'

'Batty Green?'

'There's a Mission service. There won't be many more outdoors this year with the weather getting colder, but they say they'll have finished building the Mission hut in a few weeks now, then we'll be under cover.'

'It's a long way to go,' Jake said.

'But worth it. You should try it.'

'I don't think it's in my line,' Jake admitted.

When he had left for work, Beth took down her book and started on another chapter. Will might well be another hour or two before he rose. By reading slowly, and carefully rationing herself to a very few pages each day, she still had the last two chapters left. What she would do after she reached the end she dreaded to think. There were the newspapers, of course, but that was not the same. Nevertheless, she steeled herself to close the book with the last chapter

saved for another day. And now she had the sonnets.
Perhaps she would learn some by heart.

She thought about how she would teach Jake
to read. She had very little experience even with
children's reading – that had not been one of her
duties at Mrs Carmichael's – and none at all with a
grown man. How would she set about it?

Will came in from the bedroom.

'I'm ready for my breakfast,' he said.

'It won't be long. Patrick didn't turn up.'

Will shrugged. 'It doesn't surprise me.'

'I thought I'd make some enquiries when I went
down to the Mission this afternoon,' Beth said.

'You'd be better doing nothing of the kind. Leave
it be. It's not the first time he's done this.'

'I know,' Beth acknowledged. 'I just have a feeling . . .'

'If you *must* go all the way to Batty Green, be content
with your hymn singing. Leave the man to stew in his
own juice.'

Beth said no more. Will's brief, gentler mood, when
they'd first gone into the bedroom last night and had
actually talked to each other, had passed. She would
do what seemed best to her.

Walking down to Batty Green, she caught up with
Mrs Drake and her two eldest children, and fell into
step beside them until the children skipped ahead.

'I left the baby and the little one with their dad,'
Mrs Drake said. 'These two like to come, and at least
they learn something more than I can teach them.'

'How old are the children?' Beth asked.

'Emily's eight, Tom's seven and Ada is six. They
should all be at school, and if I'd had my way they
would have been. I didn't want to come here, you
know. It's like living on the edge of the world. But
you have to follow your husband, don't you? And he
has to go where the work is.'

Her words about the children fanned a spark in Beth's mind, a spark which Mrs Drake herself had ignited yesterday when they had spoken on the same subject, and had been kept alight by Jake's admission that he couldn't read. Could *she* teach these children – not just Emily, Tom and Ada, but a few more from Jericho and Nazareth, even two or three from Tunnel Huts? She would have to keep it to a small group, she couldn't manage a large one. In fact, she didn't know that she could do it at all. She would have to give it more thought. And there was Will. What would he have to say? Quite a lot, no doubt.

'A nice crowd gathered,' Mrs Drake observed as they neared Batty Green. 'Though mostly women and children, as usual.'

There was a scattering of men; a few dogs wound in and out among the crowd, and hens pecked away at the ground on the fringes of the grass. On a raised knoll an upturned beer crate had been placed for the Missioner, and nearby a man with a concertina was practising hymns.

'I daresay some folks are curious to set eyes on the new Missioner,' Mrs Drake said. 'I am meself.'

'New Missioner?' Beth queried. 'What's happened to Mr Tiplady?'

James Tiplady was the man appointed by the Bradford City Mission and the Midland Railway Company to look after the spiritual needs of the workers and their families on this section of the line. He was an extremely popular young man, much respected. Beth felt a pang of disappointment that he was gone.

'Nothing's happened to him,' Mrs Drake said. 'He's just gone back to Bradford for a few days. This fellow's to take his place in the meantime.'

The Missioner came out of Mr Tiplady's hut and crossed towards the crowd, who gave way for him as he walked to the hillock and climbed onto the beer crate. He was a tall, fair-haired, lively-looking man. And he had a nice smile, Beth thought.

'We're going to start with "All things Bright and Beautiful",' he announced in a loud, clear voice, 'because it's a beautiful day. We don't have enough hymn books, but it doesn't matter because you all know it. So sing up everyone!

'Now,' he said when that was over, 'I'm going to read you the story of a small boy called Samuel, and how God called to him, though at first he didn't think it *was* God.'

He found the place in the bible, then suddenly, as if the thought had just struck him, he raised his head and looked around the people in front of him.

'I have a better idea,' he said. 'Why not one of you? Raise a hand, anyone who will volunteer to read the passage!'

Not a hand was raised.

'Oh, come on! I don't believe this!' the Missioner said. 'Someone out there must have the courage!'

Mrs Drake nudged Beth.

'You can read, Mrs Seymour! Go on, have a go!'

Shall I, Beth wondered? It was a lovely story, one of her favourites.

'Come along! A lady would read this very well.'

'He could charm the ducks off the water!' Mrs Drake said. 'I wish I was a good reader. I'd be up there quick as a flash!'

In a sudden rush of enthusiasm, hardly knowing what she was doing, Beth raised her hand.

'Ah! A brave lady!' the Missioner said. 'Please come forward!'

She did so. The Missioner stepped down from his box, helped her onto it, and handed her his bible.

'Here you are,' he said. 'First book of Samuel, chapter three, verse one.'

For a second, before she began to read, Beth raised

her eyes and looked at the crowd in front of her. What am I doing? she thought. I must be mad! Then she lowered her eyes to the book and began to read. And as always when she read, she was quickly transported into the story.

When the reading was over they had a hymn, then prayers, then another hymn.

'I really enjoyed that,' Mrs Drake said when the service was over. 'I do like a good sing. It fills the lungs.'

As the crowd began to disperse, the Missioner sought out Beth.

'That was a brave thing to do, and you did it well,' he said. 'Do you live on Batty Green?'

'No,' Beth answered. 'I live in Nazareth. It's further up, near to the tunnel.'

'I don't know it,' he admitted. 'Do you have any special difficulties there?'

'We do,' she said. Then in a rush – she hadn't meant to talk about it, any more than she had meant to read the bible in front of all those people – she told him about the lack of schooling for the children.

'I know we're getting a school on Batty Green,' she said. 'But that won't be any use to *our* children. They desperately need something not only to occupy them, but to educate them. They can't even learn to read, or to count.'

'But you read very well,' he said firmly. 'Why can't you teach them? A few children together, including your own.'

'I have no children,' Beth said. 'I'm like Hannah, waiting a long time for the Lord to send her Samuel.'

'And in the end He did,' the Missioner reminded her. 'But in the meantime, couldn't you do something for these other children? We should always use what gifts we have.'

91

'I'll think about it,' Beth promised.

'Write and tell me what you think,' he said. 'The City Mission at Bradford will find me. Mr Tiplady will be back here soon, and I know he'll be interested, but I'd also like to hear what you decide. And if there's anything I can do to help . . .'

'I really will think about it,' Beth repeated.

'Remember what you read today,' the Missioner advised. 'Don't ignore the call!'

'Right now I want to look for my lodger,' Beth said. 'He didn't come home last night. Not that it's the first time, but as I was coming down here . . .'

She broke off, and they both turned their heads at the sound of fierce shouting across the Green. A group of men was leaving the alehouse, or more likely they were being thrown out, since a fight was already in progress.

'Trouble!' the Missioner said.

He set off at a run towards the scene, Beth following close behind. The last thing she wanted was to witness a fight, but she couldn't stand aside, any more than the Missioner could.

She was horrified by what she saw. This was certainly no fair fight, one man matched against another, though even that she would have hated. Here, a single man was the target and he was being assailed by two others while a circle of onlookers, most of whom had poured out of the alehouse at the prospect of an exciting spectacle, stood around shouting encouragement, cheering and booing. Such was the confusion that it took Beth a second or two to recognize the man at the centre of the fight.

'It's Patrick!' she cried. 'It's Patrick Mahoney! Somebody do something or they'll kill him!'

He had no chance at all. He was hemmed in by the two men, who rained blows upon him from all sides, to his head, his body and his arms. And then he was tripped and fell face down, and one of the three, a big man, kicked him in the side, then jumped on his back and repeatedly bashed his face into the ground. Patrick's screams died away. He was silent, but still the man on his back kept at him.

With no thought for her safety, or what action she could possibly take, Beth started to run forward. The Missioner grasped her by the arm and tried to pull her back.

'No!' he ordered. 'Leave it to me! There's nothing *you* can do!'

She ignored him, broke away from him and ran to confront the smaller of the two men. Possessed of a strength which her intense fury gave her, her fists flailing, she pummelled him hard, and then, in a moment of inspiration, she raised her leg and kneed him in the groin.

'Take that, you brute!' she yelled.

He turned away with a howl of anguish. For a moment she was horrified by what she had done, though not repentant. He deserved it. She began to walk towards Patrick, and as she walked a sharp stone flew through the air and caught her a stinging blow on the back of the head.

'And you take that!' the man shouted. 'You bloody cow!'

She put her hand to the back of her head, and when she brought it away it was smeared with blood. But there was no time to think about it now. She would say nothing. In any case, she was probably more angry than hurt.

The Missioner, with a superhuman effort, had dragged the bigger of the two men off Patrick.

'Get back!' he shouted. 'Can't you see the man's unconscious? Do you want to finish him off?'

'Irish pig!' the man said. 'It's no more than he deserves, and the rest of his lot! I'd be glad to do it!'

'And be hanged for murder?' the Missioner said. 'I'd see to it that you were, make no mistake!'

The man spat on Patrick's prone body, and left. By now the crowd had joined in a free-for-all, fists flying, blows landing without discrimination on whoever happened to be in the way.

Beth went on her knees beside Patrick. Troubled that, face down, he was unable to breathe, she turned him onto his back. She gave a loud cry when she saw him, turned dizzy and sick with shock at the sight of his injuries.

The Irishman's face was covered in blood and mud. Blood oozed from a cut above his swollen right eye, trickled from his battered nose. The skin around his cheekbone was livid; his lips were split and bleeding, as were his gums where two front teeth had been knocked out.

'He's coming to!' the Missioner said, kneeling down beside her.

He examined the injured man carefully.

'I want to make sure you can be moved,' he told Patrick. 'I'll try not to hurt you.'

Patrick gave no sign that he had heard. The Missioner turned to Beth.

'I'm no doctor, but I doubt he's broken any bones. We'd better get him into Mr Tiplady's hut and see what we can do.' He looked up at the people standing around. 'Two or three of you help me to carry him.'

When Mr Tiplady's housekeeper came to the door she gave a scream at the sight of the bloodstained figure.

'Why, whatever's the matter?' she cried. 'What in the world has happened to the poor man? Bring him in at once!'

'A fight,' the Missioner said. 'We'll lay him on the sofa and then attend to him.'

'You must give me time to spread it with a sheet,

and a towel or two,' she said firmly. 'I have to answer to Mr Tiplady for the condition of that sofa.'

'Then do it quickly,' the Missioner instructed.

The housekeeper covered the sofa and Patrick was lowered onto it, then she brought bowls of water and she and Beth between them started to bathe his wounds.

'Just look at his hands, poor thing!' the housekeeper said. 'His knuckles are all bruised and bleeding.'

While she tended to his hands, Beth saw to his face, gently wiping away the congealed blood, staunching the cuts which were still bleeding. He stank of liquor, but perhaps it was as well that he was full of alcohol, Beth thought. It might act as an anaesthetic against his pain.

'Should we send someone for the doctor?' the housekeeper asked.

The Missioner considered.

'I don't think we need to,' he said in the end. 'In the time it would take someone to get down to Ingleton and bring the doctor back, I think we'll find he's rather better. He's a little improved already.'

'He is,' Beth agreed, though that was partly because she had cleaned the dirt off. All the same his injuries were nasty. He must be in pain.

Patrick now tried to smile his thanks, but his mouth was too stiff and swollen. Then he attempted to sit up, but fell back immediately, too dizzy to move.

'Oh, Patrick,' Beth said ruefully, 'how in the world am I going to get you home?'

'I can manage that,' the Missioner said. 'I have my horse. If I can borrow a light cart I daresay we can make him comfortable in the back. I reckon the sooner he's in his own bed, the better.'

'He's going to have a cup of tea first,' the housekeeper said. 'We all are. And while I'm making it,' she said to the Missioner, 'someone in the contractor's hut might tell you where you can borrow a cart.'

The Missioner untethered his horse and led it the short distance to the contractor's hut, from which he returned fifteen minutes later with the horse hitched between the shafts of a light, high-sided cart. The housekeeper had found a narrow mattress and a pillow which, when they were fixed in the cart, made a comfortable enough bed for Patrick. Beth tucked a rug around him.

'We'll soon be home,' she said. 'Try to sleep.' She wondered how he had got himself into all this, but now wasn't the time to ask him.

The Missioner helped her onto the front of the cart, then jumped up himself and took the reins.

'How far is it?' he enquired.

'Between two and three miles. Not all rough going, but you'll have to watch out for the boggy places or you'll get a wheel stuck.'

'Perhaps I should have borrowed a bog cart,' he said. The bog cart, instead of having wheels, was fixed onto a drum-like, revolving cylinder, far less likely to sink into the marshy ground.

'I think we'll be all right,' Beth said. 'We're a light enough load.'

'And I'll take it slowly,' the Missioner promised.

Though he drove slowly, and the horse picked its way carefully, it was a bumpy journey over the rough track. Beth twisted around a great deal of the time, keeping an eye on Patrick, who now lay with his eyes closed, breathing stertorously, and from time to time uttering a low moan, though that was more a result of the pain of his injuries rising to the surface, Beth thought, than the roughness of the ride.

'Thankfully,' she said to the Missioner, 'I think he's on the verge of sleep most of the time. I do wonder, though, whether we should have sent for Doctor Stokes.'

'Then if you are still uneasy when he's been put to bed, I will ride down to Ingleton and ask the doctor to call, though I daresay it will be tomorrow before he does so.'

'Of course,' Beth agreed. 'It would be dark by the time you reached Ingleton. Except for a grave emergency I wouldn't expect the doctor to ride so far out on the moor at night.'

When the cart drew up at the Seymours' hut, Will appeared in the doorway.

'What's this?' he said sharply. 'My wife being driven home in style? Are you not well then, that you can't manage on your own two feet?'

'I'm quite well, thank you, Will,' Beth said. 'This is not for my benefit. It's poor Patrick. He's been badly beaten up. He's lying in the back of the cart and we'll need your help to get him to his bed.'

Will turned his attention to the Missioner.

'And who might you be?'

'I'm Alan Crossland. I'm the Missioner here while Mr Tiplady's away.'

'He went to Patrick's rescue,' Beth explained, 'then kindly borrowed a cart to bring him home. Otherwise I don't know what we'd have done!'

'Left him where he was,' Will said. 'Some drunken brawl he was in, I don't doubt.'

'I'm afraid so,' the Missioner admitted.

'Never mind that now,' Beth interrupted. 'We must take Patrick in. It's turning cold and he should be in bed. I don't think he can walk, though.'

'Why not?' Will demanded. 'Has he broken both legs?'

Beth gave him a sharp look. His remark was totally unnecessary.

'Not either leg,' the Missioner said. 'But when he tries to stand, he keels over. I think the cause might be a blow to his head.'

97

'Then he should be in hospital, not here,' Will grumbled.

'I'm hoping he'll be all right after a good rest,' the Missioner said. 'All the same, I *will* ride down to Ingleton when I leave here, and inform the doctor. In the meantime, Mr Seymour, will you help me to carry him into the house?'

'Is Jake not home?' Beth asked. 'He could give a hand.'

'He's not,' Will said.

But as they were lifting Patrick out of the cart, Jake appeared.

'Good heavens above!' he called out. 'What's happened? Here, let me give a hand!'

When Patrick had been carried inside it was Beth and Jake who, between them, put him to bed. He was drowsy, and seemed hardly to know what was happening to him. Although his cuts had almost stopped bleeding, new bruises had appeared on his face and hands, and both his ears were purple and swollen.

'The fight didn't last long,' Beth told Jake. 'You wouldn't think he'd be so badly knocked about – but there were two of them onto him. Anyway I'm not going to bathe him again yet. We'll let him sleep.'

It was when she bent over the bed to tuck in the bedclothes around Patrick's shoulders that Jake saw the matted hair, sticky with blood, on the back of her head.

'You're hurt!' he cried out. 'The back of your head! What happened?'

'It's nothing. A man threw a stone at me. If you knew what I'd done to him,' she added primly, 'you might say I deserved it!'

'I can't believe that,' Jake said. 'Are you quite sure you're all right?' He looked at her anxiously. 'You look pale.'

'I'm quite all right,' Beth assured him.

The truth was, her limbs were shaking and she didn't know how to control them. She would be glad to sit down, but she couldn't let the Missioner go without offering him refreshment. So when she went back into the living-room and saw that Will had at least put the kettle on she was grateful.

'You'll take a bite to eat, and a cup of tea?' she invited the Missioner.

'Or something stronger?' Will suggested.

The Missioner waved away Will's offer.

'Tea will be fine.'

'You've signed the pledge, I suppose,' Will said in a sour voice.

The Missioner shook his head.

'Though James Tiplady has told me more than once that drink is the biggest problem of the men building this line. It worries him a great deal.'

'And it'll take more than him to cure it!' Will said. 'What do you expect? Hard, dangerous work, a hellish climate in a godforsaken country; no comforts – most of the men don't bring their wives. Drink's the only thing.'

'It will be better when the Mission hut is finished,' the Missioner said. 'It won't only be used for services. We'll be able to have concerts, recitals, readings; something for everyone.' Though I suppose as usual, he thought, it'll be the women and children who'll attend. It will take more than a concert to keep the men out of the inn.

'I must say, Mr Seymour,' he said, 'your wife is a remarkably courageous woman.'

'My wife is too impulsive,' Will said. 'She rushes into things which are none of her concern.'

'We must be thankful that some people do,' the Missioner said. He drained his cup, and stood up. 'I must go now.' He turned to Beth. 'I'll return the cart and then ride down to Ingleton and have a word with the doctor.'

'Thank you,' Beth said. 'Thank you for all your help, Mr Crossland.'

'And don't let all this make you forget about the reading business,' he said. 'It's very important. If there's any way I can help, let me know.'

He jumped onto the cart and set off down the hill.

'Reading business?' Will said when they went back into the hut. 'What does he mean?'

Beth was annoyed that the Missioner had mentioned the subject. Except where Jake was concerned, she had not yet decided what she would do; and if she did decide in favour of teaching the children, she wanted to tell Will in her own time, seizing the right opportunity. With him in his present mood, now was definitely not the moment.

'Nothing, really.' She spoke in an offhand manner, busying herself with making a meal.

'How can it be nothing if he said it was very important?' Will persisted. 'Whatever it is, I've a right to know. I am your husband, in case you've forgotten the fact!'

'Don't be silly, Will!' Beth said mildly. 'You know perfectly well I keep nothing from you.'

That was not totally true, she thought uncomfortably. She had said nothing to Will about teaching Jake to read. In fact, she had thought of not mentioning it at all if she could manage to do it in secret. It would only cause trouble. Will was so insanely possessive these days.

'Come on then,' Will said impatiently. 'What's it about?'

'Oh, it's just that I was wondering whether I'd try to teach a few children to read. There's no hope of them getting any schooling here, so it would be good for them, and an interest for me.'

'And I suppose when you'd settled everything the way you wanted it you'd have graciously informed me.'

'It's not like that at all,' Beth said. 'Of course I'd have consulted you first. I just haven't had time, that's all. The subject only came up this afternoon.'

'You can put it out of your mind, then,' Will ordered. 'You're a married woman, with a husband to look after and a house to run. You don't need any other interest. As far as that goes, you don't need lodgers. I'm quite capable of providing for both of us.'

He glowered at Jake.

'I'll go and take a look at Patrick,' Jake offered. He was not going to be drawn into this. It would be easier for Beth if he wasn't.

'And that's another thing,' Will said when Jake had left. 'You had no business to bring Patrick Mahoney back here. This isn't a hospital and you're not a nursemaid!'

It was too much for Beth. She'd tried to keep her temper, but she'd try no longer. She banged down the pan she was holding, and turned on her husband.

'This is Patrick Mahoney's home,' she said furiously. 'While he pays his way and behaves properly, he has every right to be here. If you think I'm going to turn him out when he's in trouble, then you can think again, Will Seymour. As for teaching the children to read, I wasn't sure what I'd do, but now you've made up my mind for me! I shall do it, and nothing you say can stop me!'

She was amazed at herself, and in her heart a little frightened. She had never, ever before spoken to Will like this.

'You'll do what I say,' Will thundered. 'I'm your husband and you'll obey me!'

'I'll obey you when you're reasonable,' Beth

retorted. 'I will *not* obey you when anyone can see you're totally wrong!'

He took a step towards her, and raised his hand. She faced him defiantly. She knew he was going to hit her, but there was no way she would retreat. The flat of his hand caught her on her cheek, and the weight of it sent her stumbling backwards against the table. Will dropped his hand and looked at her, horrified. What had he done? What had come over him? He saw the exact marks of his fingers, red on her cheek, and thought he would never forget them as long as he lived.

Jake rushed into the room.

Beth and Will were staring at each other as if frozen to the spot, Beth with her hand to her face, her eyes bright with tears. It was crystal clear what had happened.

Jake rounded on Will.

'How dare you strike your wife! Don't you know what she's been through today?'

'Keep out of this,' Will snarled. 'It's none of your affair!'

'If you so much as lay a finger on her again, I'll make it my affair!' Jake was white with anger.

'Please Jake!' Beth pleaded. 'Please don't make things worse!'

Will turned to Beth.

'I didn't mean it! I don't know what came over me!' He took a step towards her.

'Don't touch me!' she cried. 'Don't touch me!'

Without another word, he turned and ran out of the hut, slamming the door behind him.

6

The sound of the door slamming reverberated in Beth's ears; its ferocity shook the glass in the window frames. In her heart, below her anger, there was fear and consternation; she wanted to run after Will, to bring him back, to heal the awful wound which had so suddenly opened between them; but anger was uppermost and her body was incapable of taking the step. She cradled her cheek in her hand, still smarting from the blow. He had never before laid a finger on her. What had she done to provoke him to this?

She had forgotten Jake's presence until he spoke.

'Are you all right?'

'I shouldn't have let him go. I should have stopped him.'

'Do you want me to go after him?' Jake asked.

'No. It could only make things worse.'

'Whatever you say. I'm sorry if I've already done that.'

'And when he comes back, it might be kinder if you weren't here,' she said nervously.

'I couldn't have stood aside, Beth!'

Jake's voice was calmer than his thoughts. He was not concerned with being kinder to Will, far from it. He could willingly have wiped the floor with him, and knew he would have done so had the man gone an inch further, but for the moment he would do whatever was best for Beth.

'Sit down,' he said. 'I'll get you a drink. And I don't

mean a cup of tea. I'll pour you some of that whisky Will offered the Missioner.'

When Jake gave her the whisky, she gulped it, and promptly spluttered and choked.

'Oh! It's so strong!'

Jake smiled. 'You're meant to sip it slowly.' But the *contretemps* with the whisky had lightened the atmosphere just a little.

'Perhaps you should go to bed now,' he suggested. 'If you drink the rest of the whisky I poured you it will help you to sleep.'

'Oh, no!' Beth said quickly. 'I couldn't possibly. No, I shall wait until Will returns. Though please don't think you have to keep me company at all.'

'I'll stay for a while if you don't mind,' Jake said. 'I'm not at all sleepy.'

They sat in silence for a while, a silence both awkward, and at the same time intimate. There could never be the same distance between them again.

'I couldn't help but hear that you were arguing about teaching the children to read,' Jake said presently. 'I didn't try to listen but I couldn't help hearing.'

'Don't apologize,' Beth said. 'You could hardly fail to hear. It's I who should be sorry, not you.'

'If it's going to make for further difficulties, and I think it will, then you should give up the idea of teaching me,' Jake said.

Beth studied him intently.

'Do you want to learn to read? Really *want* to?'

'Of course I do,' Jake said. 'I want to very much.'

'Then you shall,' Beth said. 'You must leave me to work out how, and when, but teach you I will. What's more, if their parents want it, I shall teach those children. I'm quite determined and I know it's right. My husband will have to get used to it, which I'm sure he will.'

'There's something else I must ask you,' Jake said. However difficult it was, it had to be said.

'Yes?'

'Would it be better if I left Nazareth? If I found lodgings at Tunnel Huts? Perhaps you and Will would be better on your own?'

His question took Beth by surprise, and her reaction to it even more so. It had not dawned upon her, until now, how much his presence in the house meant to her, how much she would miss him if he left. She preferred not to think about why this was so, but it was the truth; and perhaps, she thought, that was the very reason why she should agree to his suggestion. She pushed the thought away from her.

'Oh no!' she said quickly. 'There isn't the slightest reason for you to leave here – unless it's your wish, of course. Besides . . .' she searched around for a reason to give for wanting him to remain '. . . besides, we wouldn't be on our own, would we? There's Patrick. I might really be glad of your help with Patrick. I'm not at all sure how he's going to be.'

It was a flimsy excuse. There was no reason to suppose that Patrick would not be perfectly fit in a very short time, nor that she would not be able to deal with him until he was.

'I'd be glad to do that,' Jake said. 'But if the time comes when . . .'

'If it does I will let you know,' Beth promised. 'You know, Will is a good man, really. His bark is worse than his bite. What you saw tonight was not the real Will, not the man I love. I think the job is getting him down. Working on the viaduct is not easy. It's not work he's used to.'

'I suppose not,' Jake said.

And working every day in the tunnel was no bed of roses, he thought. There were many times when he envied Will, and all those others who worked in the open air instead of in the black bowels of the earth. But he had chosen the tunnel, he had accepted the challenge, and he wouldn't go back on it.

He changed the subject.

'Do you know how Patrick came to be in the fight?' he asked. 'I know he's wayward, he's a law unto himself, but I wouldn't have put him down as a fighting man. He's easygoing.'

'I know nothing,' Beth said. 'It was all so quick, everything happening at once. But I do remember the worst of the two men who were setting about him, the one Mr Crossland went for. I shan't ever forget him. And if anything happens to Patrick . . .' she broke off.

'Nothing will,' Jake said. 'He'll be all right.'

'I know,' she said. 'But if anything did, I'd track that man down and I'd see that he was punished, even if it meant I had to testify in court.'

'Don't worry,' Jake said. 'It won't come to that. If the man thinks he's hurt Patrick badly, he'll probably leave the neighbourhood. What about the one who hurt you?'

'I couldn't remember him,' Beth admitted. 'I went at him so hard, I didn't even look at his face.'

The time crept by until it was almost midnight.

'You really should go to bed,' Jake said.

'No. I'll wait a little longer,' Beth said. 'But you should go. You've an early start in the morning.'

'I daresay you're right,' Jake agreed. 'I'll go. But call me if you need me.'

An hour later, most of which time Beth had spent looking out of the window watching for him, Will had not returned. It was a dark night and he had no lantern with him, nor had he been wearing a coat, and by now the ground was white over with frost, and he had had a cold on him for the last two days. She moved the lamp from the table into the window, so that he

106

should see it. There were no lights left in the huts in Nazareth; everyone went to bed early, on a Sunday night especially.

She picked up her book of poems but it was impossible to concentrate. They made no sense. She poked the fire in the stove into a blaze, walked restlessly around the room. In the end she could bear it no longer. She must go and search for him, though where she didn't know, other than down the rough track towards Batty Green; or perhaps higher up, towards the tunnel.

She put on her cloak, lit the lantern, and left.

It had been Jake's firm intention to stay awake until he heard Will Seymour return, but after his long day in the tunnel, nature took over and he fell asleep. When he wakened, he thought it was Patrick, moaning a little in his sleep, who had roused him, and then, coming to slowly, he realized that he had heard the outer door being closed. He waited for voices and for footsteps, but there were none. No-one had come in; someone had gone out – and it must be Beth.

He sprang out of bed and ran into the living-room, saw the lamp set in the window, saw that her cloak was gone from the hook by the door and the lantern from its usual place on the shelf. He looked out of the window, but there was no sign of her. The night was as black as ink, no moon, no stars. He must go after her! He left the hut – if there was a spare lantern he had no idea where it was – and hurried down the track.

So which way shall I go? Beth asked herself. And could she do any good at all, searching for Will like this? But she had to, she couldn't have sat quietly at home waiting, not after the manner in which he'd rushed out of the house, the wild look he'd had on him.

He would be more likely to go down the hill towards Batty Green than uphill towards the tunnel, she thought. It was the way he normally went; on the other hand, he hadn't been normal. Even so, she'd take the downhill track.

Against the velvet darkness of the night the light from the lantern did not reach far ahead, but hopefully it was far enough to keep her from walking into a boggy patch of land. She made for the tramway track. If she walked as near as possible to that she should be reasonably safe. Her eyes were already getting used to the darkness. Over to her right she could now distinguish the great mass of Whernside, brooding over the moor.

Jake, though Beth did not know it, was not far behind. Guided by the glow from her lantern, he had spotted her quickly but, he decided, he would not catch up with her. He would remain a short distance behind, but close enough to see that she came to no harm. When she met up with Will, it would do no good for him to be on the scene. When that happened, and once he could be sure that everything was all right, that she was safe, he would make his way back to the hut and be in his bed before they arrived home.

The moor, Beth thought as she walked, was a frightening place at night. Where could Will be? Was she even looking in the right direction? Supposing he had hurt himself? Supposing he had stumbled and fallen, as she herself almost had on the uneven ground a moment ago – would she even see him unless he was directly on the track?

She began to call his name.

'Will! Will, where are you? Where are you, Will?'

Her voice cut through the darkness. Jake, hearing her cry, wanted to catch up with her, to comfort her. He began to hurry towards her, but before he had taken more than a few steps there was an answering sound; not words, but a groan. Though faint, it was unmistakable.

Beth stood still, frozen to the spot, frightened by the sound. Just supposing it was not Will? In that case who might it be, what would happen? She called out again.

'Will! Is that you, Will? Where are you?'

The answering cry was again faint, but now she knew it came from her left, away from the tramlines. There was still no telling whether or not it was Will.

'I'm coming!' she called. 'Hold on! I'm coming!'

She moved in what she hoped was the direction of the voice, though no further sound came. Jake, keeping her lantern in sight, moved behind her. Every few yards she called again, straining her ears for an answer, but none came. The ground was more difficult now, wet and boggy, with tussocky grass which, in the darkness, made it difficult to proceed.

'Will!' she cried. 'Are you there? Where are you? Please answer!'

She swung the lantern around in an arc, but could see no-one, though she was sure the voice had come from this direction. Then as she swung the lantern yet again she saw, with horror and dismay, that she was in an area of shakeholes. As far as the light reached, there they were, all around her, waiting to entrap her. It was a miracle they had not done so. She had no doubt now that that was what had happened to the owner of the voice. And she was convinced that it was Will.

'Please answer, Will!' she cried again as loudly as she could. 'Please call out! I'm trying to find you!'

This time there was a reply, a definite call, but too faint to tell for sure where it came from, though it seemed to be straight ahead.

'I hear you,' she shouted. 'Keep calling. I'm coming to find you!'

Gingerly picking her way – it was impossible to hurry across the treacherous ground – she moved forward in the direction of the voice, which she was now sure was Will's. When she found him it was clear why he had fallen into the shakehole. Tall grass grew all around its rim, concealing its size and depth. Had she not been moving cautiously, she might well have fallen into it herself.

It was not safe to stand too close. Carefully, she lowered herself to the ground and lay face down, then inched forward until she could see over the edge. She held her lantern at arm's length, shining its light into the depths of the hole. Then she saw him.

It was Will all right, lying ten feet down, in six inches of water. He lay on his side, with one leg bent up towards his body. Only because he was against the side of the hole, where the ground sloped upwards a little, was he able to keep his face clear of the water.

'Oh, Will,' Beth cried. 'Oh dear, dear Will!'

'Hurt my back,' he said. 'Can't move.' His words were indistinct, as if he had no strength in him.

'Oh Will, how am I going to get you out?' Beth said. 'I'll have to fetch help!'

'Be quick,' he mumbled. 'Very cold. Very cold.'

'I know, my love. I'll be as quick as ever I can. I'll knock someone up in Jericho. Oh Will, hang on, my love. I won't be long. But I'm sorry, I'll have to take the lantern. It's not safe otherwise.'

She did not hear Jake coming up behind her. When she rose to her feet and turned around and saw the figure of a man, though not who it was, she screamed.

'It's all right!' Jake said. 'It's me!'

'Oh! Oh Jake! Oh, I'm so glad . . .'

It was not the moment to ask how he came to be there, only to thank God that he was.

'He's down in the bottom,' she said. 'He's lying in the water. Oh Jake, what shall we do?'

'Give me the lantern,' Jake said.

He took the lantern and peered down the hole, and then around all sides of it.

'We're coming!' he shouted. 'Hang on!'

He turned to Beth.

'We must get him out, and as quickly as possible. He must be very, very cold.'

'How can we move him?' Beth cried. 'How can we get him up? He's hurt his back, I don't know how badly.'

'We'll find a way. We must.'

Jake swung the lantern again, carefully studying the inside of the dark hole.

'The ground slopes a little on the side where he's lying,' he said. 'That's how he's keeping his head above water. I want you to light my way with the lantern while I get down there and lift him out.'

'Oh Jake, I don't see how you can!' Beth protested. 'Shouldn't one of us go to Jericho and get more help?'

Jake shook his head.

'It will take too long and there's no time to waste. He's lying in ice-cold water. We must get him out as quickly as possible.'

He called down the shakehole. 'It's Jake. I'm coming! Don't go to sleep, Will! Stay awake!'

If he lost consciousness he would be a dead weight, impossible for one man to carry or drag up the steep slope.

It was not too difficult to descend, and to his great relief Jake found a narrow ledge not far above the place where Will's head rested. If he could get him onto the ledge, he thought, it would get him out of the water and give them both a short breathing space while he worked out the rest, how to get from there to the top. If he couldn't do it, then they would have to stay on the ledge while Beth went for help. But that was a last resort; the night was bitter.

'You're going to be all right,' he said to Will. 'I'm going to turn you on your back then I'm going to put my arms under your armpits and pull you up onto the ledge.'

Will gave a loud cry of pain as Jake began to move him.

'I'm sorry to hurt you,' Jake said. 'I'll be as careful as I can.' But Will Seymour was a heavy man and it was only possible to get him onto the ledge by giving a tremendous heave.

Will could not contain his shouts of pain as he was moved. But at least he was now fully conscious, Jake thought, and would be able to follow instructions, though what those should be he hardly knew himself. It seemed an insurmountable task. Should he, after all, have gone for help instead of attempting the rescue himself? But he knew it would have been too great a risk. If Will had lost consciousness he might well have slid into the water. Which, though shallow, was enough to drown a man if he turned face down.

'We can't do it!' Will said faintly. 'It's impossible.'

'We can do it!' Jake's voice was firm. 'Though I'll need your help, as much as you can possibly give me. It isn't a sheer drop on this side, it's a slope; steep, but still a slope, with one or two near-level shelves. I'm going to continue to hold you under the arms, and I'm going up backwards, dragging you with me. It'll be painful for you, but it could work. And if it doesn't, we'll try something else.'

But what else? How could he carry Will, even on his back, and at the same time climb the slope? And had Will enough strength left, in that case, to cling onto him?

'We're coming up!' he called to Beth. 'Make sure you lie flat on the ground, and don't lean over too far with the lantern. I'll need the shallowest slope and any ledges, and it won't be easy for me to see them because I'm coming up on my back. I want you to guide me when you can.'

'I'll do that,' Beth said. She was trembling with fear. 'Oh, Jake! Oh, Will!'

Jake dug his heels into the ground as well as he could, and thanked heaven that it was soft, then with every ounce of strength in his body he began to prise himself up, dragging Will with him, stopping every few inches to catch his breath and renew his strength.

Afterwards, he found out that it had taken no more than a quarter of an hour to reach the top, and safety, but it had been the longest fifteen minutes of his life. The moments when he thought they would not make it, that the two of them would slide back into the water, had each one been an eternity.

'And now I *shall* have to go to Jericho and get help to carry him back,' Jake said to Beth when they were safe on top again. 'If we were to attempt to do it on our own we might do great harm to his back.'

He laid Will, who was shivering violently, on the ground. Beth wrapped him in her cloak then sat on the ground beside him and cradled his head in her lap. His face was contorted with pain. She took his hands in hers and rubbed them, trying to bring him warmth, then she stroked his face.

'Oh Will, love, I wish I could do more,' she said. 'But don't worry, we'll have you home soon.'

Jake took off his jacket and put it around her shoulders.

'Oh no!' she said. 'You need it yourself.'

'I can keep warm by walking,' Jake said. 'You'll freeze to death, sitting here. But I *will* have to take the lantern, because we're off the track. Otherwise it will take me twice as long.'

'Of course you must.'

'I'll be as quick as I can,' he promised.

Will fell asleep almost as soon as Jake had left. He was icy to the touch and Beth wondered whether it was wise to allow him to sleep when he was so cold. Nevertheless, she decided to let him do so. At least he would feel his pain less, though she could tell from the spasms which contorted his face that the pain was haunting his dreams.

Sitting there in the darkness, she wondered how long it would be before help arrived. She tried everything she could to make the time pass more quickly, though she could concentrate on nothing for long. She made herself think about the book she had been reading earlier in the day; she thought about the Missioner, then about Patrick Mahoney. Was Patrick all right? He was alone.

What she refused to dwell on – she resolutely pushed it away whenever it came into her mind – was her quarrel with Will, and the fact that he had struck her. It was her fault, it must be. She had driven him too far.

And now she was growing sleepy herself. Though she knew she must not allow herself to drop off, only the fact that her feet were so cold, and that the weight of Will's head on her lap was uncomfortable, kept her awake until, suddenly, she saw the lights of lanterns bobbing in the distance and, as they came nearer, heard the sound of voices.

There were three men with Jake. They had brought blankets, a can of hot soup, and a door on which to carry Will. Gently, Beth wakened Will, and made him drink some soup. Then the men wrapped him in the blankets, laid him carefully on the door, and began to carry him home. Beth put on her cloak and, taking Jake's arm, followed them.

It was not until Will had been carried into the hut and laid on his own bed that Beth remembered Patrick again. She looked at Jake.

'Patrick?' she queried.

'I've looked in on him. He's all right,' Jake assured

her. 'In fact, he's asleep. He looks as though he hasn't moved since we put him to bed.'

'Thank goodness for that!' Beth said.

Jake was not so sure. It seemed not quite normal that Patrick should sleep so deeply. Even through all the disturbances of Will's homecoming, with so many people walking about the house in the middle of the night, he had not stirred. But at the moment Will Seymour was the more urgent matter.

In spite of the fact that his soaking wet clothes had been replaced by dry ones, his bed heated by a stone hot-water bottle, plus a brick which Beth had heated and wrapped in a piece of flannel, and that blankets were piled upon him, he remained cold. He had stopped complaining about his back, indeed he was now too lethargic to complain about anything.

'I don't like it,' Beth worried. 'He seems so unresponsive.'

'I think we must rouse him,' Jake said. 'I think we must force some hot drinks down him.'

'I reckon he needs the doctor,' one of the men from Jericho said.

'The doctor is coming tomorrow, to see Patrick Mahoney,' Beth said. 'But I don't know when. I can't be sure he'll come early. I wish I could.'

'It's three o'clock in the morning, there's not much to be done now,' the man said. 'What I will do is walk down to Ingleton before I start work, and tell the doctor it's urgent. I work on the viaduct, so I go in that direction.'

'I'd be greatly obliged if you'd do that,' Beth said. 'And thank you, all three of you, for what you've done.'

'We'd best get off, then,' the man said. 'Not long 'til morning.'

'You had better go to bed, Jake,' Beth said when the men had left. 'Get some sleep in what's left of the night, before you have to be up again for work. I'll sit with Will.' They were standing together by Will's bedside.

'I could stay with you,' Jake offered. 'We could take it in turns to catnap.'

'No!' Beth was emphatic. 'You've done enough.'

'Then promise you'll call me if you need me,' he said.

'I promise!' She stretched out her hand and touched his. 'Jake, I can never thank you enough. You've saved my husband's life.'

Have I, Jake asked himself as he went to bed. Had Will's life, in fact, been saved? He was not so sure.

When Jake had gone, Beth continued to sit by Will. She took each of his hands in turn in her own and chafed them gently, trying to bring back the warmth, but with little success. Then she took off her long skirt and climbed into bed beside him, curling her body against his cold one, trying to give him all the warmth that was in her.

Jake rose early next morning, but when he went into the living-room Beth was already there. She had stoked up the stove, and the kettle was singing.

'How is he?' Jake asked. 'Is he warm again? And what about you?'

Her face was pale, with dark shadows of fatigue around her eyes and fine lines of worry marking her smooth forehead.

'Will's not only warm again,' she said. 'Now he's burning hot. He has a fever on him.'

'I'm sorry to hear that,' Jake said. But he was not surprised, not after what the man had gone through. And they still didn't know how long he had lain in the shakehole.

'And you?' he repeated. 'How are you?'

The kettle was boiling; he made the tea.

'I'm all right,' Beth said. 'I just hope the doctor comes soon.'

She was surprised that she felt as wide awake as she did. She had slept little, trying to remain as still as possible in case her movements should disturb Will, or cause more pain to his back. By the time morning came the heat from his body had been more than she could bear; she had had to get up.

'What about Patrick?' she asked Jake. 'Poor Patrick, I keep forgetting him.'

'I think he's all right,' Jake said, but there was doubt in his voice. 'His cuts have bled a bit during the night.'

'Then I'll go and bathe them in a minute,' Beth said.

'No,' Jake said. 'I'll do that. You have enough on your plate. He was awake a few minutes ago, so when I've drunk my tea I'll see to him.'

The truth was that he was worried not so much about Patrick's cuts and bruises, which would heal with time, as about the fact that he seemed confused. His words were slurred, and nothing he said made much sense.

He saw to Patrick, who, even before Jake had finished bathing him, fell into another sleep. When Jake left him Beth had gone back into her bedroom. He knocked on the door and she called to him to enter.

'I'm off to work now,' he said. 'Are you sure you'll be all right? Would you like me to stay?' He stood at the foot of the bed, looking at Will. He didn't like what he saw. The man's face was flushed a dusky red; his breathing was short and rasping.

'I'll be fine,' Beth said. 'You must go to work.'

It was a fine, bright day as he walked up to the tunnel, the morning sun shining on the face of Whernside. There was still an early morning nip in the air. It was the kind of day when he would have liked to have stayed on top, not gone down into the darkness of the tunnel. In any case, he was not happy about leaving Beth with the two sick men.

7

Before taking his place in the queue to go down into the tunnel, Jake sought out Mr Hargreaves.

'I'm reporting for Patrick Mahoney,' he said. 'He can't come to work today. He's poorly.'

'Poorly?' Hargreaves queried. 'So what's the matter with him?'

Jake hesitated.

'Well, not exactly poorly . . .'

'Then what?'

'He's been in a bit of an accident,' Jake said. 'He's a bit cut up, a bit fuzzy in the head. Not fit to work in the tunnel. He should be all right in a day or two.'

Hargreaves gave Jake a long, hard look. 'Has he been in a fight? Is that it?' he asked suspiciously.

'Don't ask me,' Jake said. 'I wasn't there. I don't know the details.'

'No doubt he was drunk,' Hargreaves said.

'I know nothing about that. As I said, I wasn't there. But he's not suffering from a hangover. He's poorly. The doctor's coming up to see him.' If only it was as simple as a hangover, he thought.

'It had better not be a hangover,' Hargreaves was sharp and sour. 'We have a reputation here, on the tunnel job, of turning up regularly on a Monday morning in a fit condition to work. Never mind the other sites; we're different.'

'Yes, sir,' Jake said. 'Well, if Patrick isn't here himself tomorrow, which he might well be, I'll be sure to let you know what the doctor says.'

'Do that,' Hargreaves said. 'And remind Mahoney, no work no pay. No help at all if he's brought it on himself.'

'I'll tell him,' Jake said. He wouldn't, of course.

He walked away, climbed into the cage, and was lowered down the shaft into the tunnel. The tunnel was progressing at a steady rate, so that when he reached the bottom he had a longer walk underground to where he was working. He was still on general labouring jobs, endlessly moving stones up to the surface, from where they would be taken away to build up embankments on other parts of the line, nothing being wasted. He had been promised that when there was an opening he would be given a trial on the bricklaying, and he looked forward to that. He would feel then that he was really helping to build the tunnel, that there would be a part of it he could look at when it was finished, and say, 'I built that!'

It came into his mind that Patrick was a bricklayer, and that perhaps if Patrick was off work for a little while Mr Hargreaves might allow him to step into that job. Then he quickly put away the thought as a strong feeling of guilt swept over him.

To Beth's great relief, Doctor Stokes arrived at ten o'clock in the morning. He was a short, stocky man, well matched to his broad-backed horse.

'I gather the patient was injured in a brawl?' he said. 'That's what the Missioner told me.'

'Oh no!' Beth began. 'It wasn't . . .' Then she recollected herself. She was so concerned about Will that she had forgotten for the moment that it was not her husband the doctor was here to see, but Patrick Mahoney.

'So where is he, then?' the doctor asked. 'Let's be seeing him.'

'I'm sorry. This way, Doctor.'

She led him into Patrick's bedroom.

Patrick lay on his back, his usually pleasant features disfigured and distorted by his injuries, his hands, outside the bedclothes, purple-bruised and swollen against the white counterpane. His eyes were open, and staring, though at what it was impossible to tell.

Doctor Stokes turned to Beth.

'I thought you said he hadn't been in a fight?'

'I didn't mean Mr Mahoney. Of course *he* has. It's obvious isn't it? It's my husband who wasn't in a fight.'

The doctor stared at her.

'This is somewhat confusing, Mrs Seymour. What has your husband to do with it?'

Beth explained.

'In fact, Doctor,' she finished, 'I'm very anxious you should look at him when you've finished with Mr Mahoney.'

The doctor bent over Patrick.

'Well man, you've made a real mess of your face,' he said. 'But that will heal, given time. I'll give your landlady some crystals and she'll dissolve them in water and bathe your face – and your hands. How do you feel in yourself?'

Patrick seemed to reply, but his words were jumbled, making no sense. It was not even certain whether he was speaking to the doctor, or rambling to himself. Whatever it was, it seemed to distress him until, on the instant, he closed his eyes and was asleep again.

Gently, the doctor ran his fingers over Patrick's head, exploring the scalp under the matted hair. Then he raised the man's eyelids and looked closely into each eye. Patrick gave no sign that he felt any of it. This done, the doctor looked at Patrick intently for several seconds, then he straightened up and walked out of the room, Beth following him.

'What do you think, Doctor?' she asked. His careful, silent examination of Patrick had unnerved her.

Because her attention had been on Will, where Patrick was concerned she had thought only of his cuts and bruises, nothing more. Now she felt sure there was more. It showed in the doctor's manner.

'He's had a blow to the head. A considerable blow, I'd say, as if he'd been kicked. There's a nasty swelling. Did he lose consciousness?'

'For a short time,' Beth said.

'I thought so. The man's concussed, though how badly it's impossible to tell as yet.'

'Oh no!'

Beth felt stricken with guilt. Since the moment Patrick had been brought home and she had helped to settle him in bed, she had not been near him; moreover, she had given him no more than a passing thought.

'I'm very sorry,' she said. 'You see, it was the other things happening. So what are we to do, what can *I* do? Ought he to be in hospital?'

'I think not. For the time being he's better off where he is,' the doctor said. 'The journey to the hospital would do him no good at all. So unless he gets worse . . .' He left the sentence unfinished. 'But are you able to look after him, that's the question.'

'I hope so,' Beth said. 'He's my lodger, and he has no family of his own.'

'There's not a lot you can do,' Doctor Stokes admitted. 'Just keep an eye on him, keep him quiet. He could recover quite soon.' Or not, he thought. 'And now I'll take a look at your husband.'

His face was grave as he examined Will, listened intently to his chest. He turned to Beth. 'You say he hurt his back.'

'Yes. It's been giving him a great deal of pain,' Beth said. 'In the lower part.'

The doctor turned down the bedclothes and tested the movement and feeling in Will's leg. Though he did not open his eyes, or speak a word, Will winced with pain when his left leg was touched.

'At least the feeling's there,' the doctor said. 'That's a good sign. But I'm afraid we'll have to inflict more pain because there's no way we can leave him lying so flat. Your husband has double pneumonia, Mrs Seymour. I'll need a few more pillows or cushions to prop him up.'

'I'll get them at once,' Beth said. 'But won't it hurt his back, to be raised so?'

'It will,' the doctor admitted. 'But the pneumonia is what matters now. We must do everything we can for that! Did he have a cold on him before he went out?'

'He'd had one for several days. He hadn't thought it was serious.'

The doctor studied Will again, then left the bedroom, motioning Beth to follow him.

'I have to tell you, Mrs Seymour, that your husband is very ill. Also, that he will get worse before he's better. He has a high fever, and such is the nature of the illness that over the next few days it will mount to a crisis. If he survives the crisis, he will recover. We must pray that he does so.'

The room spun around Beth. She grabbed at the nearest chair, and felt Doctor Stokes pushing her head down between her knees. Then her head cleared, and she sat up.

She's a pretty thing, Doctor Stokes thought, but now she was white with anxiety; and with good reason, more than she realizes.

'Do you know how long he was in the shakehole, in the water?' he asked.

'I don't. He doesn't seem able to tell me anything. I think he set out to go to Batty Green. It could have happened on his way there, or not until his way back.'

'So he could have been in the water half an hour, or as much as three hours?'

'Oh Doctor, he could! And it's all my fault!' Beth cried out in anguish. 'If he dies, I'll have killed him!'

Doctor Stokes put his hand on her shoulder.

'Then we shall have to make quite sure he doesn't die, my dear. And if you nurse him well, it will be you who has saved him. You can do more than I can.'

'It's all my fault,' Beth repeated. She was not to be comforted.

'And why is it your fault?'

'I provoked him,' she said. 'We quarrelled. He ran out of the house. It's all my fault!'

'No!' Doctor Stokes said. 'It is not your fault. All married couples quarrel. You can't take the blame for everything, so dry your eyes. And tell me, are you going to be able to look after two men? Do you know anyone who could help you?'

'I don't,' Beth said. 'I have a lodger, but he works in the tunnel during the day, though I know he'd keep an eye on Patrick at night.'

'Well, that's a help. It's your husband who'll need the most attention.'

'But I'll manage,' Beth said. 'There's no two ways about it. I'll manage! I'll do all that's needful.'

'I'm sure you will,' the doctor agreed. 'But you must also contrive to look after yourself. Take rest whenever you get the chance, and see that you eat well. You must keep up your strength or you'll be no good to anyone.'

'I will,' Beth promised.

'Then I'll be here tomorrow.'

Beth saw him to the door, and watched while he mounted his horse and rode away. Then she squared her shoulders, took a deep breath of the clear air, and went back into the house, back to Will. He had slipped sideways from the pillows and was no longer propped up. As carefully as she could, fearful of hurting his back, she righted him. The heat came off his body as if from glowing coals. When she touched his face, his skin was hot and dry, his lips blackened and cracked.

She fetched water and bathed his face, trying to cool him down. Throughout it all his eyes remained closed, his breath short and rasping. Sharp fear swept through her. Whatever the doctor might say, it was her fault. It had been that last sentence, 'Don't touch me' which had sent him out of the house, perhaps to his death.

'Will,' she begged. 'Will, come back to me! Please open your eyes! Please look at me! Say you forgive me.'

It was impossible to tell whether he had even heard her.

Tears ran down her face and splashed into the basin of water as she carried it back into the living-room.

When a knock came at the door she snatched up a towel and hastily dried her eyes.

Mrs Drake stood on the doorstep.

'I've come to see if there's anything I can do. My husband was one of the men who helped to carry Mr Seymour back, though of course you weren't to know that. He was the one who went down to the doctor this morning.'

'Oh, please do come in,' Beth said. 'I can't thank your husband and the other men enough. We could never have managed without them.'

Mrs Drake, stepping into the house, waved the thanks aside.

'There's half-a-dozen others in Jericho who'd have done the same. And I daresay in Nazareth for that matter. It just so happened that your lodger knocked on our door first.'

'Even so, what they did was wonderful.'

'So how is your husband?' Mrs Drake asked. 'My man said he didn't look too good.' Her husband had said more than that. He'd said he wouldn't take bets on Will Seymour's recovery.

'He's not good,' Beth acknowledged. 'He has double pneumonia. The doctor says there's not a lot to be done, apart from nursing.'

'Well, I'm here to offer help,' Mrs Drake said. 'Whatever you need.'

'But you have your children to look after,' Beth said. 'How can you spare the time?'

'Don't let that worry you, pet. I can make arrangements about them. People are very neighbourly. You find that out when there's trouble.'

'So it seems!' Just the sight of Mrs Drake, small, plump, homely, lifted a little of the weight from Beth, made the world seem less dark. 'And I'm grateful. You see, it's not only Will. I have Patrick to look after.'

'Patrick?'

Beth explained.

'My other lodger, Jake Tempest – it was he who got Will out of the shakehole – will help with Patrick when he can, but he works in the tunnel, at present on the day shift, so he doesn't have much time to spare. He has to get his sleep.'

'And you look as though you could do with a good night's sleep,' Mrs Drake said. She had quickly observed Beth's tearstained face, the droop of her shoulders.

'I didn't get much last night,' Beth admitted. 'But it doesn't matter. Anyway, I wouldn't want to leave Will.'

Mrs Drake nodded.

'I'm sure he mustn't be left, but you can't do it all, pet. Now, if you'll pardon me taking the liberty, I'll make us both a cup of tea; I could do with one, and you look as though you could. And while I'm doing that, why don't you go back to your husband. I'll give you the nod when the tea's ready, then you and I can have a chat.'

Ten minutes later she put her head around the bedroom door.

'I've poured,' she whispered. 'Will I bring it in here, or not?'

Beth glanced at Will.

'What do you think of him? He seems to be fast asleep.'

Mrs Drake crossed to the bedside. The poor man looked terrible, and that was a fact. It was a look she had seen before, when her father had had pneumonia, but she wouldn't say anything about that, or its outcome, to Beth Seymour. Anyway, this man was young and presumably strong. Her father had been pushing sixty. Gently, she laid a hand on Will's forehead.

'He's certainly got a high fever,' she said. 'I think we should moisten his poor lips again before we have our tea, then perhaps we can leave him be for a few minutes.'

While they drank their tea, Mrs Drake put forward her suggestions for helping out. Her soft yet firm north-country voice, her fund of common sense, were balm to Beth's troubled spirit. She recognized that in Elsie Drake she had found what she had always had until she'd come to live here, and what she'd sorely missed: a friend of her own sex.

'In the first place I'll take all the washing, including the bedding,' Mrs Drake said. 'You've no time to bother with that.'

'It's extremely good of you . . .' Beth began.

'Not a bit of it,' Mrs Drake said. 'It can go in with mine. And I'll come for two hours every afternoon to let you get a bit of rest. Also, if you want any messages done, my Jack will do them. He has to go down to Batty Green every day to work, so it'll be no trouble.'

'It's unbelievably kind of you,' Beth said. 'I wish there was some way I could repay you.'

'Oh, I'm sure there will be one of these days, but for now don't even think about it, hinny.'

'I'd be grateful if you'd take a look at Patrick while you're here,' Beth said. 'Would you mind?'

'Not a bit!'

He was sleeping deeply, snoring a little.

'My goodness, he's a bit of a mess!' Mrs Drake said.

'He should have his face bathed again, but it seems a pity to disturb him.'

'Quite right! Never disturb a sleeping patient. Well, I hope he won't give you too much trouble. You've got enough on your plate.'

'I'd better get back to Will,' Beth said.

'And I'll be off, but I'll be back at two o'clock sharp.'

Back in her own bedroom Beth found Will less tranquil. He was half awake now, tossing around, and had thrown off his bedcovers. Quickly, she drew them up again around his shoulders, but when she tried to tuck them in he lashed out at her, trying to push her away. She was amazed at his strength, but observing the dusky redness of his face and the glassy brightness of his wide-open eyes, she realized that his strength came from his fever.

'Hush, love! Lie quiet.'

She spoke softly, and as calmly as she could, though there was no calm in her. She stroked his burning, dry hand with her own cool one, and in the end she had the relief of seeing his eyes close and his limbs quieten down.

She fetched her mending basket, and sat on the chair by his bedside. She darned socks and sewed on buttons, but it was impossible to concentrate; too many thoughts were chasing around in her head. After a short time she laid the work aside.

She thought, for the first time since the doctor had

left, of what her position would be, because of Will's illness. There had been no time to consider it until now.

There would be no money at all coming in from him, nor indeed from Patrick. She had a little saved, though not much, and she doubted if Patrick had a penny piece to his name. It was the pattern with most of the men who worked for the Company; they earned good money and spent it as fast as they got it. Indeed, many of them ran out of money long before the next payday was due, in which case they subbed from the Company, and were thus always in debt. She didn't know that Will did so. He never told her how much he earned, or what he spent it on. He gave her her housekeeping money, and that was it. But Patrick, she suspected, was another matter. She would not be surprised to learn that he owed the Company.

What would she do when the money ran out? But wasn't it wrong of her to think about that now, with Will lying so desperately ill? Never mind the money, Will was all that mattered!

Even more resolutely did she push away the thought which had flashed into her mind for a brief second, the question which asked, 'What will you do if he dies?' She would not answer that.

The wedding-present clock which had pride of place on the dresser was striking two as Mrs Drake knocked at the door.

'Oh, I'm so pleased to see you, Mrs Drake!' Beth said.

'Call me Elsie. How is he? How are they both?'

'Patrick is sleeping. Will is much the same. He's calm at this moment but he has these restless fits, and he's as hot as fire.'

'Well, you can leave him to me for a bit,' Elsie Drake said. 'I'll see to him. And I've brought a couple of lemons. I thought you might not have any, and there's nothing better than home-made lemonade for a fever. Well sweetened to restore strength. It wouldn't do Patrick Mahoney any harm either.'

'I'll make it,' Beth said.

'No you won't! I'll do what's needful. You lie on the sofa here and do your best to get a couple of hours' sleep. Don't worry, they'll both be looked after.'

'I know they will, Elsie,' Beth said. And she would have no difficulty in sleeping. She was dog-tired.

'I'll waken you at four o'clock with a cup of tea,' Elsie Drake promised. 'And you're not to make a single move before then, otherwise I might as well not be here.'

'But what if . . . ?'

'If you're needed, I'll fetch you. And that's a promise!'

Beth lay on the sofa, a cushion under her head and a rug spread over her, and was asleep within minutes. Afterwards she wondered, guiltily, how she could have slept, knowing Will's desperate state.

It was half-past four when she opened her eyes. Elsie stood in front of her, a cup of tea in her hand.

'I hadn't the heart to waken you earlier,' she said. 'You were well away.'

Beth sat up quickly.

'How is he?'

'About the same, I'd say.'

'And Patrick?'

'Sleeping. So you can concentrate on your husband.'

In fact, Elsie thought, Will was, if anything, worse, but she wouldn't say so. There was nothing more to be done about it.

'Doctor Stokes warned you he'd be worse before he was better,' she said as cheerfully as she could. 'So you mustn't be alarmed if that happens. The doctor will be here tomorrow, and if you need me at all, send

129

Jake Tempest down to fetch me. I'll come at once.'

When Elsie Drake had left, Beth went first to look at Patrick. He was still asleep. Was it natural to sleep so much? she wondered.

She went to Will, gently laid her fingers against his cheek. It was burning.

'I'm going to bathe your face again with cool water,' she said. 'Then I'll give you another drink of lemonade.'

He made no reply, his eyes remained closed as she bathed his face. Has he missed me? she wondered. Did he even know I wasn't here, that it was someone else?

'Now drink your lemonade, love,' she said, holding the cup to his lips.

He turned his face away, silently refusing it.

'Come on, Will,' she said. 'You've got to drink if you want to get better.'

Did he want to get better? He seemed beyond caring about anything.

'Oh, Will darling, please try!' she begged. 'For my sake!'

With the minimum co-operation on Will's part, she managed to get some lemonade down him, though as much ran over his chin as into his mouth. She needed a feeding cup with a spout. Now, he seemed exhausted again.

'I'll straighten your pillows,' she said. 'Then I'll leave you in peace.'

He said nothing, but she saw the anxious look in his eyes, and he stretched out a hand and grabbed her wrist, his hot fingers burning her skin.

'Oh, I'll not leave you, love!' she assured him. 'I'll sit right here beside you while you try to sleep.'

She was too anxious to read, or to occupy herself with mending or knitting. Instead she sat, hands clasping and unclasping, trying to control the thoughts which whirled around in her head. It was wicked, she knew it was, to think that Will might die, yet however often she pushed it away, the thought came back, strong, unbidden, and with it a yawning, black future; as dank, as dark, as cold as the deepest shakehole. She had been no more than sixteen when her brother had first brought Will home, and from that first hour he had filled her life. However difficult he had become, she could not envisage a life without him.

And I mustn't do so now, she admonished herself. I must be positive. She would will him to recover and to live. Whatever strength was in her, she would give to him. He would feel it flow from her, fill him. She would save him. 'Please God!' she prayed. 'Please God!' She had no more words, but if God was any good at all, if He was all-knowing, He would know what she wanted.

It was a relief when she heard the door open, and Jake's tread in the house. When he came into the bedroom she put her finger to her lips.

'He's just fallen asleep,' she whispered.

Even in sleep, the shocking sound of the sick man's breathing filled the house. It spoke of pain, Jake thought, with every indrawn breath.

'How is he?' he asked quietly. 'What did the doctor say?'

She motioned him to go into the living-room, and followed him. She gave him the doctor's verdict.

'He says we must expect him to get worse until the crisis comes. After that . . .'

Her voice failed her. She turned away, trying to hide the tears which had sprung into her eyes and threatened to fall.

Jake stood by the table watching her, her head bent, one hand raised to cover her eyes. Her hair was escaping from its coil on the top of her head, falling untidily around her neck. Compassion welled in him. He wanted to take the step forward which separated them, to hold her close against him and let her cry on his shoulder; but he could not do that.

'I'm sorry,' he said.

Beth took a deep breath, then lifted her head to face him.

'Doctor Stokes was worried about Patrick, too. I mustn't forget Patrick. He has concussion. He's been beaten about the head.'

'And what's the treatment?'

'Nothing really. Keep him quiet, let him rest. The doctor will be here again tomorrow.'

'Then I'll go in and see him,' Jake said. 'After that I'm here to do anything you want doing.'

'I'm sorry your tea's not ready,' Beth apologized. 'It wasn't possible today.'

'It's no matter,' Jake said. 'I can make a meal for both of us. Since she had no daughters my mother saw to it that I knew how to cook. Simple things, nothing fancy.'

'Thank you,' Beth said. 'That's very kind. Everyone's kind. Mrs Drake came. She was wonderful. She's going to come each afternoon for two hours, to give me some rest. Did you know it was her husband who helped to carry Will home, and went to see the doctor this morning?'

'Yes, I knew. I saw Mrs Drake when I knocked them up. I'm glad she's coming. She's a nice woman.'

'I must go back to Will,' Beth said.

He was awake.

'I'm going to give you another drink of lemonade, love,' she said. 'The more we get down you, the better.'

She tried to hold his head steady while she gave it to him, but the liquid still dribbled out of his mouth. He seemed too weak to deal with it. She set the cup down, then, hearing Jake back in the living-room, she went to speak to him.

'I'm sorry to ask you before you've even had your tea, but would you go down to Mrs Drake's and see if you can borrow a feeding cup?'

'Right away,' Jake said.

Mrs Drake opened the door to him with one child in her arms and another standing close behind her. Two more children sat at the table, drawing. She welcomed Jake warmly. He explained his mission.

'Come in,' she said. 'I've got just the thing.'

From the cupboard she brought out a white china cup, shaped like a small teapot, but without a lid. It had a fine, curved spout.

'I used this when my dad was bad,' she said. 'I'm surprised Beth doesn't have one.'

'Perhaps she's never had to deal with illness,' Jake said.

'Poor lass! Well, she's got plenty on her plate now,' Mrs Drake said. 'It's as well she's got you.'

'And you.'

'Now, will you stay and have a bite with us?' she invited. 'It'll be ready in a minute, and there's plenty.'

'Thank you, I'd better get back. Besides, if I make a meal it might persuade Beth to eat.'

'You're right,' Mrs Drake agreed. 'Well, just wait a minute, I want to get a few things together.'

She bustled around, and finally put a filled basket on the table.

'There you are! I was going to bring this with me tomorrow, but if you'll carry it, so much the better.'

When Beth unpacked the basket she found a loaf of newly baked bread, six eggs, a jar of lemon curd, a pat of butter and an apple tart.

She looked up at Jake with the first smile he had seen on her since Sunday.

'Oh Jake, it's wonderful! Not so much for what's in

the basket, as for the fact that she thought of it at all!'

'I know. I think you've found a true friend there, Beth.'

When Doctor Stokes came next day he examined Will carefully, then stood by the bed, not speaking, his face grave.

'How is he, Doctor? Please tell me!' Beth begged.

He shook his head.

'I'd be deceiving you if I said anything other than that your husband is still critically ill. I'd do you no service. He has pneumonia in both lungs, and there's little I can do for him. As I said before, it comes down to good nursing, and God's will.'

'But he's young! He's strong! Surely that counts for something?'

'It should,' the doctor agreed. 'Pneumonia is called "the old man's friend", but I've seen time and time again how fiercely it can strike the young.'

'Then what more can I do? Please tell me,' Beth implored.

'Watch over him. Get every drop of fluid down him you possibly can. See that he's moved as often as possible; it's harmful for him to stay in the same position all the time. But you must get someone to help you with that, even more for his sake than for yours. It won't be easy on him.'

'I'll do all that,' Beth promised. 'But what else? Surely there must be something else I can do?'

'If you believe in God,' Doctor Stokes said, 'then pray. It can do no harm. It might even work where all else fails.'

He looked in on Patrick.

'His cuts and bruises are healing,' he pronounced. 'Otherwise he seems much the same.'

'He was rational for a short time last evening,' Beth said. 'But he has no memory of what happened. He was puzzled as to why he was here.'

Doctor Stokes nodded.

'That's not unusual. He might never remember what happened before he was concussed. And it could all be a long job. Keep an eye on him, but concentrate on your husband. If nursing Mr Mahoney in addition proves too much for you, then let me know, and I'll see what can be done.'

Afterwards, looking back on it, Beth wondered how she had come through the week which followed. And if it had not been for Jake and Elsie Drake, she thought, she could not have done so.

It was they who between them moved the sofa from the living-room into the bedroom so that Beth would be able to lie down, and perhaps snatch some sleep, during the nights.

'While I'm here in the daytime you can rest in the armchair in the living-room,' Elsie said.

Between them, Jake and Elsie took on every household chore. Jake fetched the water, cleaned out and stoked the stove, made most of the meals; gave an eye to Patrick when he could. Elsie did every bit of washing and ironing, and most of the housework. And they both, in turn, and in accordance with the doctor's orders, helped to move Will at regular intervals, doing it with the utmost care and compassion.

'I shall never be able to repay either of you; never, ever,' Beth said.

As for what Beth did, aside from sitting hour after slow hour with Will, watching his fight against the consuming fever, hearing his noisy breathing, she prayed. She prayed as she had never prayed in her life before. She importuned God, she railed at Him, she begged Him. She bargained with Him: 'Spare Will and I'll work for you for ever. I'll always be on your side!' But they were the kind of bargains she had made with God when she'd asked Him to send her a child. They hadn't worked then.

On the Friday evening – it was the fifth day of Will's illness and he showed no sign of recovery, quite the reverse – Jake said, 'I know you must be needing things from Batty Green. I could go down tomorrow afternoon, if you like.'

'I don't like to trouble you,' Beth said.

'It's no trouble,' Jake assured her. 'In any case, I need new boots. The bad weather will be here any time now, and what I have aren't strong enough to stand it.'

'Well it's true there are things I need,' Beth said. 'Flour, salt, butter, meat, for a start. So yes, I'd be grateful.'

'Then make a list,' Jake said.

When Beth had written the list she took her purse from the dresser drawer and counted its contents. There was Jake's money to come, of course, but there would be nothing from Patrick and Will, and perhaps not for some time. And there would be the doctor's bill. Doctor Stokes had refrained from forecasting how long Will, if he survived the crisis, would be incapacitated. 'We must take a day at a time,' he'd said. She knew it would be several weeks. It was too soon to break into her small savings so there was nothing else for it, she must start at once to make economies.

She went back to the table and studied the list again. Jake watched her as she struck off one item after another.

'I really don't need all these things,' Beth said lightly. 'I don't know what I was thinking of!'

'If you don't mind me saying so . . .' Jake hesitated; he had already discovered that Beth Seymour was a proud woman. '. . . Well, I was thinking, it's possible the Company owes your husband a bit since last payday. I know you can't get down to see anyone, but I could ask the contractor, if you like. If they wouldn't let me have it, then the clerk could bring it up here to you.' It was not an easy area to speak about to her. There was also the possibility that Will Seymour owed money to the Company; there might be little, if anything, to come.

'I'd appreciate that,' Beth said. 'It would be best if the clerk could bring the money here to me. In fact, I'd like a word with him.'

That was not strictly true; she just didn't want Jake to know how short of money she might be.

'I'll try to arrange that,' Jake said. 'And I was thinking, now that Patrick's off work, I could pay a bit of his money each week, say ten or fifteen shillings, and he could pay it back to me when he's earning again.'

'Oh no!' Beth began.

'It would be between him and me,' Jake interrupted. 'I can't trouble him with explanations now, he wouldn't take it in, but if I could I'm sure it's what he'd want.'

'No!' Beth repeated. 'It's good of you, but Patrick is *not* your responsibility. I'll manage without his money until he gets better.'

'He's not really your responsibility.'

'Oh yes he is! He's my lodger. This is his home, and as far as I know he has no other, so I'll stand by him as long as it's necessary.'

'Well, if you change your mind . . .'

'If I do, I'll tell you,' Beth promised.

8

'You'll have to hurry, Jake, or you'll miss the tramway.'

Beth's voice was tight with anxiety. She didn't want him to go, she didn't want to be left alone, but he had to. They needed the supplies he had undertaken to bring back, aside from the fact that he was going to buy much-needed new boots.

She would not have Elsie Drake's company this afternoon. Elsie's husband was working, so that she herself would have to go down to Batty Green to buy in, *and* take the children. Saturday was the one day when neighbours were not free to help; they were all flocking in the same direction and would all return burdened.

'I'm just leaving,' Jake replied. 'And I won't hang around for the tram back. I'll walk it. I'll be as quick as I can.'

'Your time's your own, Jake,' Beth reminded him.

All the same, she would be glad to see him back. She was so nervous. She wanted to be with Will every minute of the time, of course she did, but sitting there, watching him grow steadily worse, was frightening beyond anything she had ever known. Thankfully, the doctor was due at any time. He rode up from Ingleton every day and, though he said little, it was a comfort to know that he was keeping a watch over Will.

'You won't forget the newspapers, will you?' she asked Jake. They were now an extravagance, a luxury she could not afford, but she was prepared to make do with less food for herself in order to have something to read.

'They're on the list,' Jake reminded her. 'I won't forget.'

He hurried down to Jericho and caught the tram by the skin of his teeth. Elsie Drake was already aboard with her children, and he went and stood by her.

'How is he today?' she asked.

Jake shrugged.

'No better. No better at all! Worse, if anything.'

'Poor man! He can't go on like this, can he? It's not humanly possible. And poor Beth, too. It's a miracle the way she's coping.'

'It's with your help,' Jake said. 'I don't know what she'd do without it. All the same, I reckon she's near the end of her tether.'

He had watched Beth every day for the past week, reluctantly left her every morning to go to his work, hurried back at the end of the shift. He had seen her grow paler, the shadows under her eyes deepen. She moved around the house as if she was trapped inside a bad dream which was sapping her strength.

'I worry about her,' he said to Elsie.

He worried, too, about Will Seymour, and about Patrick, but most of the time about Beth.

Elsie looked up at him. It was not just his words, but the note of his voice, which startled her.

There's a man in love, she thought, if ever I saw one! But did he know it? And did Beth Seymour know it, or was her whole mind centred on Will? As well if neither of them did; it was not the time for complications, it was not the time for Jake Tempest to have to leave. Right now, and who knew for how long, Beth needed him. That much was certain.

The tram shuddered to a stop at Batty Green. Jake helped Elsie out with the children before they parted company.

'See you on the way back!' Elsie called.

'I'm walking!'

Batty Green was, as always on a Saturday, crowded. Jake pushed his way through the throng towards the newspaper seller, and from there to the stall where he hoped to find the boots he was looking for. Most Saturdays, he'd been told, a shoemaker from Settle set up shop on Batty Green, and did a good trade.

Sally Roland, standing behind Burgoyne & Cocks's stall and not at the moment serving, looked across, though quite at random and with no particular interest, towards the shoemaker's stall. She gasped at the sight of Jake standing there, looking intently at boots while waiting his turn. Her employer did not know it – he had thought she was being unusually obliging – but she had volunteered to work Saturdays on Batty Green in the hope that she might set eyes on Jake Tempest. She had not been able to get him out of her mind, which was unusual for her since her motto was 'love 'em and leave 'em'. He had presented a challenge which she would not ignore.

She turned to the other woman serving on the stall.

'Call of nature,' she said quickly. 'Be back in a minute!'

And it *was* a call of nature, she thought, as she picked her way towards Jake. Nothing had ever called more clearly to her than the nature of this lovely man. He looked even better than she'd remembered, which was unusual. She'd found the reality seldom lived up to the dream, but in his case it did. He was taller, his shoulders broader, his legs longer, his features more finely cut.

He didn't see her as she moved quickly towards him. She took him by surprise, thrusting her arm through his. He felt the softness and warmth of her even before he turned his head and found her blue eyes looking up into his, her red mouth curved in a smile.

'Surprise, surprise!'

She clung tightly to his arm and moved closer to him, so that there wasn't a hair's breadth between them.

'Good afternoon, Miss Roland,' Jake said.

'I hope you're pleased to see me!'

He wasn't especially pleased to see her, but neither, he realized to his surprise, was he entirely displeased. She was certainly the brightest thing he had set eyes on this past week. She wore a blue wool costume – the day was chilly – buttoned up to her throat, but still showing every curve of her body, and above its neckline a frilly white ruff framed her face. On her head, in accordance with a rule laid down by her employers for anyone who was serving or selling food, she wore a white mobcap with black ribbons. If it was meant to cover her hair, it failed. Her black curls sprang from underneath it, corkscrewing down her neck, falling over her broad, white forehead. She was a pleasant sight, Jake acknowledged.

'Miss Roland, is it?' she pouted. 'We're very formal today! And you haven't said you're pleased to see me!'

'Of course I am,' Jake said politely. 'You're looking very well.'

'Is that all?'

She knew she was being too forward, but she judged it was the only way with this man. He escaped too easily, and she didn't intend to let him escape again if she could help it.

'You look charming,' Jake said. It was no less than the truth.

'Then you can treat me to a cup of tea,' Sally said. 'One of the huts is serving tea. Did you know that?'

'No, I didn't. But I'm in a hurry. I have to get back. I also have to buy some boots. I'm sorry!'

She gave no sign that she was annoyed by his

coolness, and when he made a move to free himself, she clung to him more tightly than ever.

'Oh, it won't take but a minute! And I'm cold, and quite desperate for a hot cup of tea!'

She began to pull him gently, but with persistence, in the direction of the tea hut. 'I promise we won't be long,' she said.

The hut was presumably a family home on other days of the week, but now the main room had been almost cleared, and set up with a large table in the middle and one or two at the sides. It was quite busy, but they found a small table and Jake ordered tea.

'And a piece of gingerbread,' Sally begged. 'I just love gingerbread!'

When, without thinking, he laid his hand on the table, she covered it with her own. It was at this moment that Elsie Drake walked in with her brood, and they took their places at the centre table. The moment she sat down she saw Jake, hand-in-hand with a girl she knew she'd seen before somewhere.

Jake looked up, and felt himself redden at the sight of Elsie's frank stare, though she was not to know that it was annoyance, not guilt, which made him do so. He snatched his hand away from Sally's, and gulped down the rest of his tea.

'I'm sorry. I definitely must go. I have to get back.'

'Why the rush?' Sally asked. 'We could have a good time together.' She laid her hand on his sleeve.

Jake shook his head. The sight of Elsie Drake had brought Beth back into his mind. She was, he knew, worried and frightened, waiting for his return. He could have shaken this pretty little flirt by his side for keeping him even for five minutes, though in fairness, he reminded himself, she couldn't know the circumstances. He must have seemed as rude to her as she was irritating to him.

Nevertheless, he stood up.

'I'm sorry, I must go.'

He spoke to Elsie Drake as they passed her.

'I'm on my way back,' he told her.

'But Jake, I thought we were going to choose some boots for you?' Sally said in a clear voice.

He said nothing, but walked out of the hut, Sally following. He had not yet done Beth's shopping. He would have to walk back with Sally, since most of the things on the list were to be found on Burgoyne & Cocks's stall.

'I'll leave the boots for now,' he said. 'I don't have the time.'

'That's sensible,' Sally agreed. 'You'll do far better, coming to Settle for your boots. Eli Drummond only brings a small selection up here. *And* he charges more.'

'Settle's a long way on Shanks's pony,' Jake said. 'I'll take my luck here another time.'

'Oh, you don't need to walk it,' Sally said quickly. 'There's always some cart or other going in either direction. Or you could come back with me on a Saturday night, stay at my aunt's, and fit yourself up with boots on the Sunday. Eli would open up for you.'

Jake strode up the moorland track as fast as the slope and the weight of the shopping would allow him. He was annoyed that he had wasted time dallying with Sally Roland over tea when he had intended to hurry back to Beth. Nor had he bought his new boots, which he was going to need before long. It would be November next week, and here, on the high moor, the bad weather would come early. It would be boggy, even snow-covered, underfoot. The brightness had already gone from this late October day. Not many weeks now before he would be coming home from work in the dark.

He reached Nazareth. From a short distance away

he saw a man leave the Seymours' hut, mount his horse, then come towards him down the track. It could only be the doctor. He raised a hand to halt him.

'Excuse me stopping you, Doctor. I saw you leaving the Seymours' hut. I'm one of their lodgers, Jake Tempest. I wonder if you'll tell me how you find Mr Seymour? I'm very worried about him.'

'And with good reason,' Doctor Stokes said. 'Mr Seymour is a very sick man.' He didn't usually give bulletins to someone who wasn't close family, but this man seemed genuinely concerned. Also, Mrs Seymour had told him what a great help her lodger had been to her.

'I think the crisis must come tonight, or tomorrow,' he said. 'He can't go on much longer.'

'What can I do?' Jake asked.

'You can support Mrs Seymour,' the doctor said. 'She's going to need all the help she can get. She shouldn't be left alone at this stage. I haven't told her in so many words, and nor should you, but it's likely that her husband will die.'

'I'll be there,' Jake said. 'I won't leave her.'

'Good man. I'll be back tomorrow, then.'

When Jake went into the hut, Beth's face lit with relief at the sight of him.

'Oh Jake, I'm so glad to see you! Will . . .'

'I spoke with the doctor just now,' Jake interrupted. 'He told me. But at least—' He broke off. How could he say it? How could he say, as he almost had, that at least, if the doctor was right, by tomorrow Will could have turned the corner? They both knew that, just as easily, Will could have died.

They faced each other, saying nothing for fear of saying the wrong thing. It was Beth who spoke first, with words that were nothing to do with what was in her heart.

'Did you get everything?'

'Everything on your list.'

'And your boots? Did you get those?'

'No, I . . . didn't see what I wanted. I'll have to try next week.'

'I'm sorry. Did you see Elsie?'

'I travelled down with her.'

He would say nothing about seeing her in the tearoom, though he was aware that she might do so. Not that it mattered, it was easily explained, but now was not the time. He felt annoyed with himself that he should feel guilty, then put it out of his mind.

'I must go back to Will,' Beth said.

Jake nodded agreement.

'I'll look in on Patrick, and then I'll make a meal.'

Beth shook her head.

'Not for me. For you and Patrick – but I couldn't.'

Patrick was awake, and looked better than he had all week. He spoke hesitantly, but his words made sense.

'The doctor came to see me. Have I been badly then?'

'Since last Sunday,' Jake told him. 'You were in a fight. You were injured. Don't you remember?'

Patrick's face creased with the effort to do so.

'I don't remember a fight. What was it about?'

'That's what we'd like to know. Don't you recall being in the inn?'

Patrick scratched his head.

'Not at all, at all. Haven't I all these things in my head, and going round and round, or maybe they're just dreams. But nothing about a fight.'

'Well, don't worry about it now,' Jake said. 'It might come back to you later, but it's no matter if it doesn't. Just get well!'

'Oh, I will,' Patrick agreed. 'I am well. Just a bit tired for the moment. But is Beth all right? She came in with the doctor. She looked peaky.'

'Will is seriously ill with pneumonia. I'll tell you more later. Why don't you go to sleep now, and when you waken I'll have your tea ready.'

Patrick gave a deep sigh. He was tired again. He couldn't be bothered with all this. He closed his eyes, and was asleep almost before Jake reached the bedroom door.

For Beth, though the week through which she had just lived seemed like a year, the hours through which she sat at Will's bedside following the doctor's visit were an eternity. Time ceased to exist.

She was aware that from time to time Jake brought cups of tea, which she sipped briefly, then set aside; that when it was dark, he lit candles in the bedroom, two at the head of the bed and another on the table next to the sofa. For several stretches of time he sat with her, neither of them speaking, and at one point she was dimly aware that Elsie Drake came into the room, stayed a while, then left. But all these happenings were outside the world in which she was living.

That world was confined to herself and Will, to the small area of the bed in which he lay propped up against the pillows, and the sofa on which she sat, watching for any sign, hearing no sound but his breathing.

Not until afterwards did she realize that she had sat there for more than six hours, and that at some time after midnight – one of the few things which came through to her was the clock in the living-room striking twelve – she had fallen asleep.

It was three o'clock in the morning when she wakened with a start. She was aware at once that something was different, that something had happened. To begin with, the sound of Will's breathing no longer dominated the room. Also, the candles at the head of his bed had burned low. In her half-awake state the two differences came together and made one. She gave a loud cry.

'He's dead! He's dead!'

She would have flung herself on his body had not Jake seized her from behind and led her, shrieking, from the bedroom. He was saying something, but she didn't want to hear it.

'Why didn't you waken me?' she cried. 'Why did you let me sleep? How *could* you?'

He turned her around to face him, held her by the shoulders and shook her.

'Beth! Beth, listen! Will is *not* dead! He passed through the crisis and now he's asleep. He's going to be all right! Do you understand?'

Beth stared at him for a second, and then his words sank in, and when they did she burst into tears, a flood, a torrent, her whole body shaking, all the hours and days of strain and fright pouring out of her.

Jake folded her in strong arms and held her close against him, stroking her back. Not thinking about it, hardly knowing what he was doing, except that he wanted to comfort her, he kissed her on the top of her head. Then he put a finger under her chin, raised her head – her face was wet with tears – and kissed her full on the mouth, hard and long. He was filled with desire for her; with his mind and his body, he wanted her.

She was compliant in his arms, so soft and yielding. Then she stirred, and he realized that she was returning his kiss with a passion which matched his own.

'Oh Beth!' he said. 'Oh Beth!'

Perhaps it was the sound of his voice which brought her to her senses. She pushed him violently away and stared up at him in shocked confusion.

He dropped his arms to his side, stepped back.

'I'm sorry! I'm sorry! Oh Beth, I meant only to comfort you!'

That was how it had started out, but not, for him, how it was now. Now he knew – and how had he not recognized it before? – that he was in love with her, with this woman whose husband had all but died, and who lay asleep, and still so ill, only a few feet away from them.

With an effort, Beth calmed herself, spoke quietly.

'It's all right, Jake. It was the heat of the moment for both of us, nothing more. We'll forget it.'

Oh no, Jake thought, I won't ever forget it! It had happened in the heat of the moment all right, but for him that moment was one of blinding truth. It would never leave him.

'I'm going back to Will,' Beth said. 'And you should go to bed now, get a few hours' sleep. Oh, Jake, how shall I ever thank you for all you've done for me?'

She reached up and kissed him gently, on the cheek; a kiss which a sister or a friend might have given.

Jake said nothing. He could not trust himself to speak.

'Good night, Jake,' Beth said. 'I must go to my husband.'

She went into the bedroom, and closed the door behind her. The sound of the door closing pierced Jake to the heart. It was a symbol of where he stood. She was where she belonged, and he was forever outside that door. He sat down at the table and buried his head in his hands. It was almost four in the morning and his life seemed as dark as the night outside. What would he do? How could he stay here, seeing her every day, watching her go through that bedroom door and close it behind her?

The windows were squares of daylight before he rose from the table and went to his bed, resolved on only one thing, that he would leave Nazareth. He would tell Beth before the new day was over, and he would tell her why. To declare his love, hopeless though it was, would be his one and only indulgence.

Doctor Stokes was at Nazareth early on Sunday morning. Beth, looking out of the window, saw him riding up the hill and rushed outside to greet him. He was as jubilant as she was at her news. He was also surprised. He had not expected to find Will Seymour alive, but that he would keep to himself.

'Then let's have a look at your good man!' he said, following Beth into the house.

'Yes,' he said when he had examined Will, 'yes, he has turned the corner. And you can take the credit, my dear. Your nursing has done more than I could ever have done.'

'I can't take all the credit,' Beth said. 'Not by any means. I couldn't have done it without the help Mrs Drake and Jake gave me.'

'That's as may be,' the doctor said. 'I grant you've been fortunate there, and I hope that's going to continue. Your husband has turned the corner, he's on the right road, but there's a long way to go yet. A slow recovery is best in the end, and that's what you must aim for. Don't let him rush at it.'

'Oh, I won't!' Beth promised.

'Good, nourishing food: calves' foot jelly, beef tea, gruel, broth. A glass of ruby port every midday wouldn't go amiss, as soon as he can take it.'

'I'll see he gets all that,' Beth said. Somehow she would.

'And in a day or two, when he's stronger, I shall want to take a look at his back. Has he complained much?'

'He's hardly spoken,' Beth said. 'He's been too ill to talk. But I can tell that it's been paining him. I see it in his face.'

'Well, we must see what can be done,' the doctor said. 'And now while I'm here I'll take a look at your lodger, see how he's getting on.'

He found Patrick awake, and lucid, though his speech was hesitant.

'I'd like to get up, Doctor,' he said.

'You can do so tomorrow,' Doctor Stokes said. 'But don't rush at things, take it easy.'

'When can I be going back to me work?' Patrick asked. 'I'm needing the money, so.'

'I don't doubt it,' the doctor agreed. 'You work in the tunnel, don't you?'

'That's right.'

'Then we'll consider it in another week. It's too soon to say.'

Elsie Drake arrived within minutes of the doctor's departure. She had hurried from Jericho full of apprehension. When she'd left Nazareth late last night she wouldn't have given a row of pins for Will Seymour's chances, but now the minute she came face-to-face with Beth, she knew everything was all right. It didn't need words to tell her. Beth's shining eyes did that. She opened her arms wide, and Beth rushed into them.

'Oh, Elsie. Isn't it wonderful!'

Elsie nodded. It was all she could do. There was a lump in her throat the size of a hen's egg, and it wouldn't let the words get out.

'Well,' she said when her voice returned, 'what he'll need now is a nice blanket bath, and his bedding and nightshirt changed. He'll have been in a right sweat. I'll give you a hand.'

Between them the two women did all that was necessary, but though they were as gentle as they could be, Will winced with pain when he was moved.

'I'm sorry, Will love,' Beth apologized.

He nodded his head briefly; he was too weak to talk.

'You'll feel all the better for it,' Elsie said, smoothing the last crease out of the counterpane. 'I daresay you'll fall into a good sleep now, a natural sleep.'

When Elsie had gone, Jake was left alone in the

living-room with Beth. Will had, as Elsie had forecast, fallen into a deep sleep.

'Please come and sit down, Beth,' Jake said. 'I have to talk to you.'

She was ready to sit down. She suddenly realized that she had had practically no sleep – nor, for that matter, had Jake.

'What is it Jake? I'm terribly tired.'

'I'm sorry. You must be.' Now that the time was here, he didn't know how to begin.

'What is it, Jake?'

He plunged in.

'I'm going to leave Nazareth.'

She stared at him, uncomprehending.

'Leave Nazareth?'

'I must, Beth! I have to.'

'But why? I don't understand. You've said nothing of this before. I thought you were happy.'

'I was.' But had he been? Hadn't there been this longing, undefined, unacknowledged, almost from the first?

'Then what? Is it the job? Is it the tunnel?'

'Oh Beth, it's none of that! Don't you know what I'm talking about? Don't you know that I'm in love with you? Surely you felt that, just a few hours ago? I thought then, just for a minute, that you felt the same way about me.'

She stared at him.

'But Jake, it wasn't like that! It was the relief of it all. Who else would I turn to but you? Not just because you were there, but because it was *you*. Whatever else happened was in the heat of the moment. You know that.'

'No!' he contradicted. 'For you it was, though I didn't think so at the time. For me it was real. I thought for the moment it was the same for you, but I was wrong.'

151

'It couldn't be, could it?' Beth said quietly. 'I'm a married woman. I love my husband. I thought he'd died, and suddenly he was alive again.'

'And I discovered I could love a married woman,' Jake said. 'And I know I'll go on loving you. So you see why I have to leave?'

Beth jumped to her feet, walked to the window, and looked out.

'I can't bear it!' she said.

Her voice was muffled, he could tell she was crying and he longed to go and comfort her, but it was impossible. He gripped the table, willing himself not to move, not to go near her.

She turned around and faced him.

'What will I do without you, Jake? Especially now. You're my best friend and I need you. I can't love you as I love Will, but I love you as a friend. I truly do. Won't that suffice?'

'You don't know what you're asking,' Jake said roughly.

'I think I do. And I'm still asking it, Jake. Please don't leave me! Not while Will is ill. I beg you!'

They looked at each other, long and hard, each searching the other's heart. Jake was the first to speak.

'Then I'll stay until Will is on his feet again.'

It had not occurred to either of them, and did not until much later, so that it was never part of either Beth's request or Jake's decision, that without him there would be no money at all coming into the house. What they had asked, and given, though painful to both of them, was too deep for that.

'Beth!'

It was a faint cry from the bedroom, the first time for several days that Will had had the strength to call out.

'I'm coming!' Beth cried.

152

A few minutes later Jake tapped at the bedroom door.

'I'm going for a walk,' he called softly.

He had to get out of the house. The room was full of emotion, it hung in the air, almost tangible. He had to have time and space to clear his thoughts. He had to be able to breathe.

Beth looked out of the bedroom window and watched him leave, his shoulders hunched, his hat pulled down, his coat collar turned up against the cold. He walked away with long strides; thankfully, Beth thought, not out of her life – or at least not yet. She could not have borne it.

9

Over the next two weeks Will's chest improved remarkably.

'It's no more than I'd expect, now that the worst is over,' Doctor Stokes told Beth. 'He's a strong young man. What we have to look out for now is his back.'

'It's giving him a lot of pain,' Beth admitted.

'He'll need rest. And massage would help. I don't suppose you know how to do that?'

'I've no experience,' Beth said. 'But perhaps if someone would show me . . .'

'You have to know what you're doing, but there's a woman living in Jericho who's gifted that way. If she'd give your husband one or two treatments, then perhaps you could learn something.'

'I'd certainly like to.'

There was more than one reason why Beth would prefer to do it herself. First and foremost, she wanted to help Will. She could not shake off the guilt which his condition aroused in her, reminding herself constantly that if she had not driven him into leaving the house on that night he would not be in his present pain. When he vented his ill-temper on her, when he grumbled, as he did much of the time now that he was getting better, she bit back the retort which sprang to her lips, stifled the resentment she too often felt, telling herself that it was no more than she deserved.

Also, by now she was desperately short of money. How could she afford to pay for treatment? During the first week of her husband's illness the wages clerk had brought what was owing to Will: a sum of three pounds, seven shillings and sixpence. There would be nothing more until Will could resume work. All she possessed was what remained of her meagre savings, and Jake's regular money. There was nothing yet from Patrick, and there was still the doctor's bill to come. She dreaded that.

Doctor Stokes, reading her thoughts, as he so often did on similar occasions with his patients, said: 'There's no point in me continuing to come, Mrs Seymour. Rest, and good food, is the quickest way to get your man back to work, though I can't say how soon that might be. In any case, November is a treacherous month. He mustn't venture out too soon.'

'I'll see he doesn't,' Beth promised. 'And you'll let me have your bill?'

'In due course,' the doctor said. 'In due course.' He would delay it as long as he was able. 'Your friend, Mrs Drake, will no doubt know the woman I mentioned.'

'I'll speak to her today,' Beth said. 'And what about Patrick Mahoney?'

'I'll take a look at him before I leave,' Doctor Stokes said.

Patrick was lying in his bed. He sat up quickly as the doctor came into the bedroom.

'So how are you?' Doctor Stokes asked.

'Sure, I am much better. 'Tis just my headaches. But I want to go back to work on Monday.'

Doctor Stokes was dubious. You could never be totally sure with a patient who'd suffered a head injury. It wasn't straightforward, you couldn't see into the head. He would have been happier if the Irishman hadn't worked in the tunnel. It was not the place for a man with his problems. However, there was nothing he could do about that.

'Very well,' he said reluctantly. 'But don't overdo it. And come to see me if need be.'

In the afternoon Elsie Drake came, as she still did most days, though sometimes now with her youngest child, Joe.

'You don't mind, do you?' she'd asked the first time she'd done this. 'The other three are all right, but it's not always easy to find somewhere to leave the baby.'

'Of course not!' Beth had told her. 'Anyway, he's a good little soul. I like having him here!'

Now, she held out her arms to Joe, who came readily to her. Beth held him close, enjoying the feel of the child in her arms, his softness and warmth, the sweet smell of his skin and hair.

'The doctor says Will needs massage,' she told Elsie. 'He says there's a woman in Jericho who does it.'

'That's right. Phoebe Grange. They say she's excellent. Not trained, but with a natural gift.'

'Do you think she'd charge much?'

Elsie looked up at the anxious note in Beth's voice.

'I don't know. I shouldn't think so. I expect you're finding things a bit difficult, aren't you?'

'Very difficult.' She hesitated. 'To tell you the truth, I don't know how much longer I can manage.'

It was a relief to tell someone. She couldn't bother Will with it; how the good food she was providing and the extras like the bottle of port she had managed to buy were eating away at the money. It would only make him worse-tempered. She was too proud to tell Jake, and there was no point in saying anything to Patrick. But Elsie was a friend. She couldn't help, but at least she would sympathize without spreading it around.

'I wish I could think of a way of earning some money, but I can't. There's nothing I can do,' she said. 'Or at any rate nothing that people want.'

'Oh, but you're wrong there!' Elsie said quickly. 'You can read. You talked about teaching the children to read. There's a skill not all that many folks have.'

Beth looked doubtful.

'It's true I intended to give it a try. It got pushed aside by Will's trouble. It was never my intention, though, to make money from it. I don't know that I'd like that.'

'Stuff and nonsense, Beth!' Elsie protested. 'Not that you'd make a fortune, of course, but I'm sure people would be only too pleased to pay what they could. I would, for one!'

Joe had grown suddenly heavy in Beth's arms as he fell asleep against her shoulder. She sat down in the nearest chair, easing the child's weight against her.

'Oh Elsie, how could I take money for teaching your children to read!' she said. 'Think of all you've done for me!'

'That's different,' Elsie said. 'That's no more than one neighbour helping another. You'd do the same for me!'

'But you *did* it!' Beth argued. 'Where would I have been without you?'

'Well, if you're going to teach my children to read then I'd want to pay my whack,' Elsie's mouth set in a stubborn line. 'For a start, it might cause awkwardness with others if I didn't. I reckon everyone has to be the same.'

'In fact,' Beth said, 'even aside from the money, I'd quite like to do it. It would give me something else to think about.'

Her days now consisted entirely of the demands of the household and of Will's and Patrick's illnesses. It was not that she was unsympathetic to either of them, but she would dearly like to turn her mind in another direction.

'Of course I'd have to see what Will thought,' she said. 'I doubt he'd like it.'

'Put the plain facts before him,' Elsie advised. 'Men

157

have their theories, and that's all very well, but sometimes they have to be made to look at the facts.'

Beth sighed. It had never been easy to make Will do anything he didn't want to do, and it was getting increasingly difficult, but Elsie was right. Somehow, though she didn't look forward to it, she'd have to make him face the situation, if only because things couldn't continue as they were.

'I'd best be off,' Elsie said. 'Think over what we've said. I'm sure you'd get half-a-dozen children, more if you wanted. For a start, Phoebe Grange has a couple who ought to be at school if there was anywhere for them to go.'

Beth watched Elsie set off down the path towards Jericho, then she went back into the house and closed the door. It was a chilly day, with a sneaky wind.

I *will* do it, she thought! I'll do it for the money, and I'll do it for myself! Moreover, she would tackle Will that very afternoon. There was nothing to be gained from putting it off, and in any case she'd like to have it settled before Jake came in from work.

When she looked in on Will he was asleep, though stirring a little, as if ready for waking. She returned to the living-room and prepared a tray of tea, and when she took it into the bedroom he was awake. He lay flatter now that his chest was so much better, but she saw his grimace of pain as he moved awkwardly in the bed.

'I've brought us both some tea,' she said. 'Can you manage with an ordinary cup, or would you like your feeding cup?'

'I don't want the feeder,' Will snapped. 'I'm tired of being treated like a baby.'

'I'm not treating you like a baby,' Beth said patiently. 'I just want to do what's most comfortable for you, Will love.'

'If that's what you want, then help me to sit up, so

I can drink like a man. And another thing, I'm sick of drinking tea! When am I going to get a glass of ale?'

Beth didn't answer. She was too busy trying to help him into a better position. He cried out in pain as she did so.

'Not like that, stupid!'

The words cut her like a whip, but she contained her anger, telling herself that it was the pain which made him like this.

'I'm sorry if I hurt you,' she said quietly. 'I'm doing my best.'

He grunted, then with Beth's help he eased himself onto his side, propped himself on one elbow, and with sharp impatience took the cup from her. He was filled with frustration and anger, careless of what he was doing, so that when he raised it to his lips he spilt half of it. The hot liquid soaked the sleeve of his nightshirt and slopped over his hand. He gave an angry cry.

'Now look what you've made me do!'

'I did not—'

She swallowed the rest of the sentence, fetched a towel and a clean nightshirt, and with great care helped him to change.

'Now you can lie down to ease your back, and I'm going to pour you some fresh tea into the feeding cup so that you can drink it in comfort. It doesn't matter how it looks because there's no-one but me here to see you.'

She sat beside him while he drank the tea.

'Doctor Stokes says it would do you a lot of good – for your back I mean – if you had some massage treatment. There's a woman in Jericho – Elsie knows her – who's apparently good at it.'

'And how can we afford to pay for such treatments?' Will asked. 'I'm not daft, so don't think I am. I know there's nothing coming in except for your fancy lodger, and I'm not having *him* paying for me!'

Beth took a deep breath. His attitude was exactly what she'd expected it to be, but she'd have to drum some sense into him. Finding the right words was not easy.

'What I want above everything, Will, is for you to be better—'

'Do you think I don't?' he interrupted. 'Do you think I enjoy being a useless lump?'

'Of course you don't. I know that. And if the doctor says massage might quicken your recovery, help your pain, then somehow or other you must have it.'

'So you can wave a magic wand, can you?' His voice was heavy with sarcasm.

'Not a magic wand,' Beth said. 'But I know a way I can make a bit of money.'

'So what is it?' He was all suspicion. 'I warn you, I'll not take charity from anyone, and I forbid you to borrow money.'

'I've no intention of doing either of those things.' Somehow she kept her voice calm and even, though inside she was shaking.

'You remember I had the idea of teaching some of the local children to read? I know I hadn't thought of doing it for money, but in fact I could. Oh, I know I wouldn't earn much, but it would make a difference, not only to pay for your treatment, but to help to keep us going. And the sooner you're better, the sooner you'll be back at work and earning your wages again. We'll be back to normal.'

She faltered. There was nothing more to say. And deep inside her she recognized, with great surprise, that to go back to what had been normal was not any more what she wanted. She wanted more, something extra, though she didn't know what, and in Will's present frame of mind it was certainly not to be mentioned.

Will's face was as dark as thunder, and in his eyes

she saw the hurt he was feeling. Why couldn't he understand that she wanted to help? Why did he make demands on her, yet feel diminished when she tried to do something?

'I don't like it,' he said presently.

'I know you don't, Will. I didn't expect you to. But admit that it makes sense. And what alternative is there?'

She waited. It seemed an age before he spoke, as if he had dismissed the whole thing, then he said: 'Have it your own way, then!'

It was a grudging permission, given without the slightest encouragement, but at least it was permission.

'Think on, only until I'm earning again,' he added. 'You'll stop it at once, then.'

Beth didn't answer. How did he think she could break off halfway through teaching the children to read, just to satisfy his pride? But she'd face that problem when it arose. In the meantime she'd move quickly, before he changed his mind.

'Then, first things first, I'll go down to Jericho tomorrow morning and see about your massage. The sooner the better. Then I must go to Batty Green to see Mr Tiplady about some books.'

It was Mr Crossland, the regular Missioner's stand-in, who had offered help with the project, but it would be only polite to ask through Mr Tiplady.

'And who's going to look after me while you're gallivanting here, there and everywhere?' Will grumbled. 'What happens to me when you're off teaching these children?'

'I promise you won't be neglected,' Beth assured him. 'For a start, I needn't go anywhere to teach the children. They can come here.'

'A houseful of noisy kids isn't going to help me to get better,' Will said.

Beth caught her breath. She wanted to shout at him,

to scream. He was clearly going to make her fight every inch of the way, but fight she would, and she'd win. She'd try not to show her frustration, and she certainly wouldn't give in. She was going to do this, she'd not go back on it.

'Well, it'll have to be one thing or the other,' she said reasonably. 'Either I go to them, or they come to me. But you can make the choice, Will. Whatever you say.'

She would rather by far go to the children. She longed to get out of the house. She admitted to herself, and was ashamed of the fact, that she would be glad to get away from Will for a few hours a day. Of course, he wouldn't let her. She could guess which choice he would make, and she'd have to abide by it.

'I can't start until I get some suitable books,' she said. 'So I must see Mr Tiplady as soon as I can.'

Will turned his head aside and closed his eyes. The subject was closed. I would have liked a glimmer of encouragement, Beth thought; just a glimmer. But since there was none to be had, she'd be thankful for the least possible discussion. Silence was preferable to grumbles.

'Do you want anything?' she asked Will.

His eyes remained closed, he didn't answer, though she knew he was awake.

'Then I'll make a start on the supper,' she said.

Jake would be home in less than an hour. The thought lightened her heart. Almost without noticing it happening – and she would not allow herself to acknowledge it for fear she might feel she must bring it to an end – his return from work had become for her the high point of each day.

She dreaded the day when he would leave, though it had not been mentioned again since he had declared his love for her. Why could they not be just the very best of friends? Special friends. She pushed away the question of what the situation did to Jake, so great was her need of him.

When he came into the house he brought something of the outside world with him, enlarging her world, which seemed otherwise to be bounded by two sick men. He would talk about the happenings of the day; it didn't matter that they were trivial rather than dramatic. His anecdotes about the men with whom he worked were such that she almost felt she knew them. Most of all, she never needed to look at Jake to judge what sort of a mood he was in, what his temper was. He was unfailingly pleased to see her, and she him.

She peeled onions, carrots, a turnip, and added them to the stock in the large pan. There was precious little meat in the stew. Yesterday the butcher's old horse had dragged a small cart up the hill, all the way from Ingleton to the huts, as it did twice a week, but she had only been able to afford a bit of scrag end and two pennyworth of bones. The butcher, though, had been generous with the bones. There was quite a bit of meat left on them, so it would be a tasty meal and, as well as seeing to Will, she would ensure that Jake got his share of what meat there was. After all, he was paying his way, and he did the hardest job of any of them.

But never mind, she thought, her spirits lifting, when she started to earn a bit from teaching the children, they'd celebrate with mutton chops!

When Jake came into the house Beth was standing at the stove with her back to him. He paused in the doorway, watching her. Though she was busy at her task, her head bent, her hands occupied, there was, as always, a stillness about her which never failed to attract him. It was not the stillness of inaction, but rather of an inner strength which had no need of fuss. She inhabited her own world with confidence. Seeing her, he had an almost overwhelming urge to put his

163

arms around her, to turn her around to face him, to enter her world.

He had opened the door quietly, so that she had not heard him, but now the cold blast of air reached her and she turned around.

'Jake! You're home!'

There was a world of welcome in her voice and in her face. What wouldn't I give, Jake thought, to have the right to this welcome every day of my life; for the brightness of her face and the shine in her eyes to be exclusively mine?

'I'm sorry if I startled you,' he said.

'I was deep in thought.' She had been thinking of him, though she wouldn't tell him that. 'It's blowing cold, isn't it?'

Jake turned and closed the door.

'It's straight from the north, and nothing in the way to stop it. It wouldn't surprise me if we had snow! What sort of a day have you had?'

'The doctor came,' Beth said. She told him what Doctor Stokes had suggested about the massage treatment. 'So I'm going to look into it tomorrow morning. But there's also something else.' Eagerly, she told him about her plan to teach reading.

'You sound excited,' Jake said.

'Oh I am!' she admitted. 'And of course when I start to teach the children, I'll also start to teach you. I haven't forgotten my promise.' She was fearful of what Will would say about that, but she wouldn't be put off. She would do it.

Before Jake could answer, Patrick came in from the bedroom. He was fully dressed, his hair combed, and he looked more cheerful than Beth had seen him for a long time, more like his old self. Except – the thought struck her suddenly – that he had lost weight. She chided herself that she had not noticed this before. Almost all her concern had been for Will.

'My word, Patrick, you're looking better!' Jake said.

'Oh I am, I am!' Patrick said quickly. 'Hasn't the doctor given me the sack, and I'm going back to work on Monday morning!'

He felt better than he had at any time since the fight, about which, tease at his brain though he might, he could still remember nothing. But no matter, he was cured. Providing his headaches didn't come back he was as good as new.

'That's good news!' Jake said. He hoped he sounded more sure of it than he felt. At this moment the Irishman sounded fine, but in Jake's experience he could change his mood in an instant. Since the fight you never knew where you were with him.

'And there'll be a job for me to go back to,' Patrick said. 'Isn't that so?'

'Of course!' Jake replied.

In fact, during Patrick's absence he had been promoted into his job, and he had enjoyed the bricklaying, as well as earning more. Would he now have to go back to the labouring? But the tunnel was coming on fast, so perhaps there'd be bricklaying for both of them. He said nothing of this to Patrick.

'I'll have a wash,' he said to Beth, 'then I'll lend you a hand.'

He fetched soap and his towel and went outside. He still washed in the stream, though not for much longer, he thought now, as the icy water tingled on his skin. Winter was too close.

On the following morning, after Jake had left for work, Beth saw to Will, then said: 'I'd like to get down to Jericho as soon as I can to see Mrs Grange. If she'll agree to come, then the sooner the better. Will you be all right?'

'I'll have to be, won't I?' Will said. 'Too bad if I need anything!'

'Patrick's here,' Beth pointed out. 'I'm sure he'll see to you if need be.'

'I don't want that mad Irishman looking after me,' Will grumbled. 'For all we know he's not right in his head!'

'Oh, I'm sure he is,' Beth said. 'He's going back to work on Monday.'

It was the wrong thing to say. She realized that as soon as the words were out of her mouth, and the expression on Will's face confirmed it.

'I suppose you think I don't want to get back?' he said fiercely.

It was what he wanted most in the world, and not only for the money. There was no sense of purpose in his days now, lying here like a clod, afraid even to turn over for the pain it gave him. He missed his work-mates, longed for the easy banter that flew between them on the job, for the drinking in the inn when the day's work was over. He needed men's company, and Beth didn't seem to understand that. At the beginning of his illness, when he was too ill to benefit from it, his mates had walked up the hill to visit him. Now when he needed their company, no-one had been near him for more than a week.

'Do you think I enjoy lying here?' he persisted.

'I know you don't, Will,' Beth said. 'That's why I'm anxious to get Mrs Grange here as soon as ever I can. I'll be back as quickly as I can, and with any luck she might come with me.'

Beth called first at Elsie's hut. The baby was asleep in its wooden cradle which stood near the hearth. The three other children sat on the floor, mildly bickering among themselves.

'Sit down and I'll make a cup of tea,' Elsie said. She turned to the children. 'Either go and play in the bedroom, or shut up!' she ordered. 'I can't hear myself speak. I'm sorry,' she apologized to Beth. 'They get fast what to do, and it's too cold for them to be out on the moor.'

'I can't stay,' Beth said. 'I've left Will.'

'A cup of tea won't take a minute,' Elsie argued. 'The kettle's on the boil. So did you put it to Will about the reading lessons? What did he say?'

'He agreed,' Beth answered. 'Well, no, that's not quite true. He didn't agree. He didn't like it at all, but he said I could go ahead. But more urgent, he did agree to the massage, and it's my belief that once he feels a bit better, the easier he'll be to deal with. So if you'll tell me where Mrs Grange lives I'll go and have a word with her.'

'Drink your tea, then I'll walk across with you,' Elsie offered.

Phoebe Grange was not at all what Beth had expected. For no good reason – as she admitted to herself when she thought about it afterwards – she had expected, when her knock at the door was answered, to see a comfortable, motherly-looking sort of woman, a penny-plain lady with strong, capable hands dedicated to healing the sick. Mrs Grange was twopence-coloured and, from the top of her golden hair, which was rolled into at least a score of rag curlers, by way of her flowered sateen dressing-gown, to the thin soles of her pink, pom-pommed mules, as fancy as anything Beth had ever seen.

She stood with one slender hand on the doorknob, the other raised to her face, her long, delicate fingers resting against her smooth cheek. The fact that it was eleven o'clock in the morning and she was clearly not long out of bed took nothing away from her gaudy appearance. She was like an exotic butterfly.

She held the door no more than half open, but behind her Beth glimpsed two children. The younger, a girl of about six years, wore only a vest, which came

167

halfway down her thighs. The boy, a year or two older, wore trousers, but no shirt.

Elsie spoke first.

'I hope we haven't come at an awkward time, Phoebe, but Doctor Stokes recommended you to Mrs Seymour here.'

'Then you'd better come in,' Phoebe Grange said. She turned to the children. 'Go and get dressed before you catch your deaths.' She yawned. 'We've only just got up,' she added unnecessarily.

'So Doctor Stokes recommended me, did he? Well, I *am* going up in the world! I get plenty of recommendations for one thing and another but not usually from the doctor! So it can't be what I think.' There was a glint in her eye as she looked at Beth. 'So what can I do for you? You look fit enough to me.'

'Oh, it's not me, it's my husband,' Beth said. She explained about Will. 'Perhaps if you could give him two or three treatments, then maybe I could learn to do it. You see, I'll be honest with you, I couldn't afford many.'

Mrs Grange raised her finely arched eyebrows.

'So you plan to learn my skills and take my customers, do you?'

'Oh no! Nothing's further from my mind,' Beth assured her. 'It's like I said—'

Mrs Grange's mouth curved into an enchanting smile, revealing a row of pearly-white teeth.

'Don't worry! I didn't mean it. I doubt you could do it, not unless you're a natural. Oh, you could learn the movements, but you have to have the gift. I have the gift. My mother had it, and her mother before her.'

She sounded supremely confident without being in the least boastful.

'Well, I'll see what I can do. Where do you live? Shall I come this afternoon?'

'That would be wonderful,' Beth said. 'I live in Nazareth.' She hesitated. 'You haven't told me how much you charge, Mrs Grange.'

'Call me Phoebe. It's more friendly. We'll talk about money later. First off, I'll need to see what I can do. I can't help everyone, you know.'

'What did she mean about recommendations not usually being from doctors?' Beth asked Elsie as they walked away.

Elsie laughed.

'She's the one some women go to when they find they're pregnant once too often. Me, I wouldn't touch that with a bargepole, and I don't suppose you would either!'

'It doesn't seem as though I'll ever need to,' Beth said bleakly. Sometimes she thought the world was peopled with women who had more babies than they wanted. She didn't understand why some cruel fate had decided that she, who had looked forward to and would have welcomed half-a-dozen children, should be barren.

When she told Will that Phoebe Grange was coming to give him a treatment that afternoon he frowned.

'I don't know that I want some old woman mauling me about,' he grumbled. 'What good can she do?'

Beth opened her mouth to put him right, then thought better of it. He had a surprise coming to him, but let him find out for himself.

At half-past two, without waiting for her knock to be answered, Phoebe Grange walked into the hut, entering like a summer breeze, cheering up the dull November day; a scented breeze at that, since she moved in a cloud of spicy, musky perfume. Without waiting to be asked she took off her cape, revealing a bright green blouse, lavishly trimmed with braid and fringing, which closely moulded her curving bosom and neat waist. When she removed her bonnet her hair, elaborately coiffured, shone like gold. All those rag curlers, Beth thought, had not been in vain.

'To work,' Phoebe Grange said briskly. 'Take me to your husband!'

When she followed Beth into the bedroom Will's eyes opened wide. He clutched the sheet and pulled it up around his chin.

'So, Mr Seymour,' Phoebe said, standing by the bed, smiling down at him, 'I gather you're in a bit of pain?'

Will nodded. He opened his mouth to explain, but no sound came. Phoebe took hold of the sheet and without ceremony pulled it down as far as his knees.

'I'm going to roll you over onto your side,' she said. 'And we'll have to have your nightshirt off first, otherwise I can't get at you, can I?'

Beth stepped forward to give a hand.

'Can't you just roll it up?' Will's voice was no more than a whisper.

'We'd best have it off,' Phoebe said firmly. 'I need to find just where the trouble is or there's no point, is there? And don't be embarrassed, Mr Seymour. You're not the first man I've seen mother-naked, not by a long chalk.'

She ran practised fingers up and down the full length of his spine. His head was turned away from her but, standing by the other side of the bed, Beth saw the colour spread over his face and down his neck. Even his ears glowed red. Poor Will, she thought! She had never seen him embarrassed before. He had always made himself out to be a ladies' man, more so than she'd appreciated sometimes.

Phoebe bent over the bed, her expression intent, her fingers probing into Will's back until, suddenly, he gave an involuntary jerk and a loud cry.

'Ah! Good! Found it! There's the trouble!' Phoebe sounded as pleased as Punch at Will's yell of agony. 'Now we know where we are! No! Don't hold yourself stiff, Mr Seymour. I can do much more if you just let go; don't fight me.'

Beth turned away to hide a smile she couldn't quite suppress. Poor Will! At this moment he couldn't have fought a day-old kitten. She had never seen him so powerless, so subjugated to someone else's will, and a woman's at that.

She composed herself, and turned back again to watch what Phoebe Grange was doing.

'I think you'd be most use, Mrs Seymour, if you were to go and put the kettle on,' Phoebe said. 'I'll be finished in fifteen minutes and I'm sure we could all do with a cup of tea then.'

It was a clear dismissal. I'm not to be allowed to learn her secrets, Beth thought.

To the accompaniment, from the bedroom, of sharp cries and groans from Will and encouraging noises from Phoebe Grange, Beth set about preparing the tea. Patrick hurried in from his bedroom and stood open-mouthed.

'What in the name of all the saints is she doing to the poor man?' he demanded.

'Making him better,' she said. 'At least I hope so.'

'Then I'll be going out for a walk,' Patrick said. 'I would not like her to be starting on me!'

'Don't go too far,' Beth warned. 'It's cold.'

For fifteen minutes the sounds came from the bedroom, then gradually subsided. When all was quiet again Phoebe Grange came into the living-room.

'My word, I'm ready for that cup of tea!' she said. 'And so is your man. The poor fellow's quite exhausted! But men are such babies, aren't they?'

'I haven't looked after a sick man before,' Beth confessed. 'They seem so strong when they're well. At least Will does.'

'They're all alike,' Phoebe said dismissively. 'But we

wouldn't like to be without them, would we?' She winked at Beth.

'So what can I do for him?' Beth asked.

'Nothing really. You haven't the knowledge, so you could make matters worse, and you wouldn't want that, would you?'

'Of course not,' Beth agreed. But how am I going to pay her? she asked herself.

'I'll need to come every day for at least a week,' Phoebe said. 'And if it's the money you're worried about, then you can pay me a little bit at a time. I don't do it for the money, though God knows I need it, same as we all do, especially when we have kids.'

'There's something I might be able to help with where your children are concerned,' Beth said. 'I'm thinking of starting a reading class – reading *and* writing probably.' She explained what she had in mind. 'I'd have to charge,' she said. 'Especially while Will's not in work. But perhaps in your case we could do a deal.'

'Sounds all right to me,' Phoebe said. 'I don't hold with too much book learning, but the Lord knows I'd be glad to get my two from under my feet a bit. I've other fish to fry.'

'I have to wait until I get the books,' Beth said. 'Then we'll make arrangements.'

When Phoebe had left, Beth went in to Will.

'Are you feeling better? Did she do you good?' she asked.

'She half killed me!' Will moaned. 'I daresay my back's black-and-blue.'

'I'm sorry, love. But did she do you some good?'

'She might have,' he admitted. 'When's she coming again?'

'Tomorrow. And every day for a week.'

Will said nothing to that, but Beth reckoned his face brightened at the thought.

Next morning, to Will's annoyance, Beth went down to Batty Green to seek out the Missioner.

'You're never at home,' Will grumbled.

She said nothing. To answer back was to start another argument and she had no stomach for it. She had too much on her mind.

She found Mr Tiplady at home, and explained the situation to him, including the fact that until Will was earning again she would have to charge for the lessons.

'Mr Crossland said he felt sure the Bradford City Mission would help,' she said. 'I thought if *you* were to write to him it would be best – if you approve, that is.'

'I approve most heartily,' Mr Tiplady said. 'It will be a wonderful thing for the children, *and* for their parents. As I daresay you know, we'll be opening a school here in the spring, but of course that won't be much use to anyone as far away as Jericho and Nazareth. So you tell me what you'll need and I'll write to Mr Crossland today.'

'I need first readers,' Beth said. 'I could do with about nine if they're to have a book each. And I had thought I might try to teach them to write at the same time. I don't quite know how that would work out, and I'd need slates and slate pencils.'

'And a blackboard and easel,' Mr Tiplady said.

'I suppose so.' It sounded a great deal. 'I couldn't pay for these things all at once,' she said.

'We'll think about that later,' Mr Tiplady assured her. 'And the moment I hear from Mr Crossland I'll walk up and let you know.'

From Batty Green back to Nazareth Beth walked on air. In spite of the dullness of the day, of the wind in her face, never had the distance seemed so short, or the going so easy.

In the afternoon, and every afternoon for the rest of the week, Phoebe Grange came to treat Will, and each day, though he complained to Beth after Phoebe had left at the torture she had put him through, he was a little better.

'We'll soon have you on your feet,' Phoebe said as she left Will on the Sunday afternoon.

On Monday morning Patrick went to work. Jake accompanied him, and Beth watched out of the window as the two men walked away over the moor towards the tunnel.

Things are looking up, she thought. Things are definitely looking up.

10

At the end of that first day of Patrick's return to work he and Jake were in the first cage up the shaft to the surface. Getting out, they stood for a moment with the others, greedily breathing in the fresh moorland air. It was what all the men did when they came up out of the tunnel, especially those who were not miners by trade, not used to working underground. But half-a-dozen deep breaths and they were restored, all except Patrick Mahoney, who continued to gulp in the air as if he could never get enough of it.

'So how did it go, your first day back?' Jake asked as the two of them set off to walk back to Nazareth.

Patrick shook his head, said nothing.

I don't need to ask, Jake thought. He was well aware that for Patrick it had not gone well. They had worked close together on the same side of the tunnel, each with their own labourer – to Jake's relief he had been kept on as a bricklayer – and to Jake, it had seemed an average sort of day, neither worse nor better than any other.

'First day back,' he said now. 'You'll soon get used to it again.'

It was not that Patrick had expressed his un-happiness in so many words, but he had been uncharacteristically silent, he who had the Irish gift of the gab, who always had something to say for himself.

'That I will not,' he replied. 'I will never get used to it again!'

How could he explain what the ring of the miners'

sledgehammers as they battered with such force against the hard rock did to his head? How could he describe, and to whom could he confess, the terror which swept through his body, so that his insides seemed turned to water, at the roar of the explosions in neighbouring parts of the tunnel where they were using gunpowder? And you never knew when the explosion was going to come. You waited for it, apprehensive, not knowing, and when it did come you wanted to throw yourself down on the ground and bury your head in your hands to shut out the noise.

You couldn't do that, of course. You had to keep the panic inside yourself. If you didn't, if you were the cause of spreading it, you'd be out on your ear. He hoped no-one had noticed him, though the foreman had never been far off, always on the prowl.

Jake had noticed. He had observed a number of things. When the other men had taken up a song, or whistled a tune, Patrick, though he was known to be a fine tenor, hadn't joined in. He hadn't laughed at the jokes which flew back and forth, though formerly he would have been the first to crack one. And after one of the explosions Jake had seen rivers of sweat running down his ashen face. He was also aware that these signs had not gone unnoticed by the foreman.

Deliberately, as they walked now down Blea Moor, picking their way around the bog, he changed the conversation, turning his head to where, on the right, the great mass of Whernside was silhouetted against the darkening sky.

'I never did climb the mountain,' he said. 'It was one of the first things I meant to do when I came here, and now I reckon it'll have to wait until the spring.'

The days were getting shorter. Already he was going to work in the dark, and soon night would fall before they came up from the tunnel. He would see daylight only at the weekend.

'I wouldn't mind going on the night shift before long,' he said to Patrick. 'I'd still be going to and from work in the dark, but at least there'd be a few hours of daylight to enjoy – when I wasn't sleeping.'

Patrick didn't answer. He hoped that Jake's shift wouldn't be changed, not unless his own was changed to match. If anything had kept him on an even keel today it had been the close proximity of Jake. Jake had looked after him with great care through his illness, and today he had realized that he still needed him. Not for ever, of course – he would pull himself together – but for now.

He seems a thousand miles away, Jake thought. They were almost at Nazareth now, and walked the rest of the way to the Seymours' hut in silence.

Entering, they met head-on with Phoebe Grange, who was on the point of leaving. She nodded briefly to Patrick, whom she had seen on a previous occasion, and turned her full attention to Jake, giving him the benefit of her charming smile.

'I haven't met this gentleman before,' she said to Beth. Not for one second would she have forgotten such an attractive man, even though at the moment he was in his working clothes and his face was liberally smudged with dirt.

'Mr Jake Tempest, Mrs Phoebe Grange,' Beth said. She deeply envied Phoebe's self-confidence. 'Mr Tempest lodges with us. Mrs Grange has been giving Will a treatment. She's just leaving.'

Phoebe held out her hand. Jake extended his, painfully aware that it was exceedingly grubby from his day's work, ashamed when he saw his dirty fingermarks on her gloves, to which she paid no heed at all.

He was totally unprepared, on a November day in Nazareth, for the sight of anything as exotic as this woman. With her fashionable clothes, her feathered and flowered tiny hat tipped forward on her golden curls, her voluptuous figure, she would have drawn immediate attention in Settle or Skipton, even in Bradford or up-to-date Leeds.

'I'm later than usual today,' Phoebe said. 'But ten minutes earlier and I'd have missed you.' Her eyes were on Jake. They told him she would have regretted that.

Beth broke in.

'So I'll see you tomorrow, Phoebe. I'm glad you're pleased with Will.'

Phoebe nodded.

'He's doing very well. As I promised, we'll have him up tomorrow. And by the way, I might be a little late again!'

Her parting smile included them all. When Beth had closed the door behind her she looked at the two men, who stood rooted to the spot.

'A sight for sore eyes!' Patrick said with awe.

Jake pulled himself together, grinned at Patrick.

'Well at least she's cheered you up,' he said.

'I must get on with my chores,' Beth said. 'I've no time to waste.'

Jake looked up at the edge in her voice.

'I'll give you a hand,' he said gently. 'I'll fetch the water first, then I'm yours to command.'

He always would be. No bird of bright plumage could compare to Beth Seymour.

When Jake and Patrick returned from work next day it was to find Will sitting in his armchair in the living-room, Phoebe Grange and Beth hovering around him.

'Well, this *is* a surprise!' Jake said. 'It's good to see you up. How do you feel?'

'I feel all right,' Will said. 'From now on I'll be up every day.'

He spoke defiantly because defiance was what he

felt. He was full of anger against the pain in his back. It thwarted him at every turn. He wanted to be fit and well, and back at his job, but almost every movement he made was a reminder that this was still a way off. Dressing – he had refused to sit in the living-room in his nightshirt – and walking through from the bedroom, even with the help of a woman on each side of him, had called for a major effort. He was as exhausted after it as if he had climbed Whernside. Now, the sight of Jake and the Irishman coming in from a day doing man's work, earning money, did nothing to soothe his feelings.

'You'll be up a bit each day only if you behave yourself!' Phoebe said. 'And I said a *bit*, not all day. And remember, you're to wait until I'm here to help you!'

The severity of her words was softened by her merry smile, and the pressure of her hand on his shoulder as she stood beside the chair. She was a woman-and-a-half, this one! She had done him good from the moment she'd first walked into the bedroom, dressed to the nines, even before she'd laid a finger on his body. And did she know, Will wondered, what her massage did to him, apart from easing the pain in his back? Did she guess at his feelings as her warm hands moved across his body with such delicate yet firm strokes? Did she know that she made him feel a man again, with a man's desires so strong that he wanted to pull her into the bed with him?

He suspected she did. There was something in her look, something in the occasional slap she gave him, ostensibly part of the treatment but really reproving him for what he had neither said nor done but only thought about. She could read a man's thoughts, he was sure of it.

But now, though she kept the pressure of her hand on his shoulder, she was smiling at Jake Tempest, who stood in the middle of the room, tall, strong and healthy, effortlessly dominating the space simply by his presence.

'I'll do whatever you tell me to, Phoebe,' Will said. 'Anything!'

'That's what I like to hear,' she said. 'And I think it's time you went back to bed. You've been up long enough. Mustn't overdo it on your first day! Perhaps you'll give a hand, Mr Tempest?'

'Certainly,' Jake agreed.

'My wife can do that,' Will objected. He wanted no favours from Jake Tempest.

'Of course I can,' Beth said.

'No need, Beth,' Phoebe said, 'since Mr Tempest is here. He's a big, strong man.' She looked directly at Jake, her voice and her eyes full of approval.

Between them they raised a reluctant Will to his feet and led him back to bed. If she *can* read a man's mind, Will thought, she'll know I'm not liking this. And what about Tempest, what was *he* thinking as Phoebe stood close by him, the two of them looking down on him as he lay helpless in bed?

'I'll be off now,' Phoebe said. 'I'll be back tomorrow afternoon.'

Was she speaking to him, Will asked himself, or to Jake Tempest?

Jake followed her out of the room; Beth saw her to the door.

'How do you think Will's doing?' Beth asked.

'He's doing well, I'm pleased with him,' Phoebe said, 'though he'll need a few more treatments before he's fit to go out, let alone return to his job.'

'I want him to have whatever he needs,' Beth said. 'But you still haven't told me what you charge.'

'Oh, don't worry about that at the moment,' Phoebe said. 'Didn't we agree you'd teach my kids to read. We'll see how it works out.'

Beth saw Phoebe out, watched her walk away, then turned back to Jake.

'Phoebe's so clever. There's nothing I can do for Will that she can't do better.'

'I wouldn't say that.'

He wanted to tell her that just by being herself she was a hundred times better than Phoebe Grange, attractive though that lady undoubtedly was, but it was yet another of the things he couldn't say to her. He recognized the kind of woman Phoebe Grange was. Once upon a time he would have fallen for it.

'Where's Patrick?' Beth asked.

'Gone to lie down. He has a headache.'

'Has it been a bad day?'

'No. Just average for work. But he doesn't seem to be settling in too well.'

Patrick had been as nervous as a cat all day, right from the moment at the start of the day when they'd gone down the shaft into the tunnel. The cage had swayed, which was not uncommon, they were used to it, but Patrick was clearly frightened. He clutched fiercely at the man standing next to him, all but knocking him off balance.

'What the hell do you think you're doing?' the man demanded.

'I didn't do nothing! You pushed into me!' Patrick said.

'You're a fool and a liar, Mahoney,' the man said. 'I did no such thing!'

Patrick put up his fists. There was a wild look in his eyes.

'No man calls me a liar and gets away with it!' he cried.

Jake had gripped Patrick by the arm and physically restrained him. Fighting while in the cage, or anywhere in the tunnel, was a sackable offence, and there

181

was no shortage of witnesses to the fact that Patrick had started it.

'Calm down!' Jake said. 'Let it go!'

The cage reached the bottom of the shaft, and the man whom Patrick had threatened got out and walked away, saving the situation, though, it seemed, only for the moment. As he walked off he called out over his shoulder, 'I'll see you on top, Mahoney, when we come off the shift. Don't think I won't!'

Halfway through the morning Jake had gone along the tunnel to seek him out.

'Let it go, will you? You know Patrick Mahoney's not himself. He's been ill.'

'He's a menace,' the man said. 'He shouldn't be working in the tunnel. But I'm not spoiling for a fight. It's up to him, not me.'

The strange thing was that by dinnertime, when they ascended the shaft, the cage totally steady on this occasion, Patrick seemed to have forgotten all about the morning's incident. He faced the other man with a blank expression and apparently no remembrance of it.

'Is he going to be all right?' Beth asked anxiously.

'I wish I knew! Not if he goes on like this.' He would do all he could to protect Patrick. He liked him; there wasn't a nicer man alive when he was in his right mind, but there was only so much he could do. The rules were strict, perhaps more so in the tunnel and on the viaduct than on other parts of the line.

'At any rate, Will seems better,' he said to Beth.

'Oh, he is, thanks to Phoebe!' And better in health than in temper, Beth thought.

The next day two things happened.

The first was that, early in the afternoon, an official from the Company rode up from Batty Green to see Will. Beth opened the door to him.

'Mrs Seymour?'

'That's right.'

'My name's John Pennington. I'm from the Company. I've come to enquire about your husband, to see him, in fact.'

Beth's heart lurched. A *frisson* of fear went through her. Though his words were polite enough, there was something in the man's voice which told her that this was no ordinary social call. Moreover, it was one she had been expecting and dreading for a week or two now. She could guess what it was about.

'Please come in,' she said. 'Take a seat. My husband's in bed, he was just taking a nap. Can I help, Mr Pennington?'

John Pennington took a seat at the table, observing the worried look on the face of the young woman who sat down opposite him. This was a part of the job he did not like, but he had no option, it was one of the duties he was paid for.

Beth waited.

'Well, Mrs Seymour,' Pennington said, 'I've been asked to see your husband, to enquire how he is and, not to put too fine a point on it, when we may expect him to be back at work. So I'll need to speak to him; but before I ask you to wake him, perhaps you can put me in the picture.'

It was often easier to get a straight story from the wife. Nervous she might be, but she didn't try to pull the wool over one's eyes, to bluff him, as the man sometimes did. He'd not make a judgement, though, until he'd seen Seymour for himself.

'So how is your husband?' he enquired.

'Oh, he's much better in himself!' Beth spoke with all the cheerfulness and confidence she could muster. 'He's made a very good recovery from the pneumonia. It's just his back, now. You see, he injured it when he fell down the shakehole.'

'I see. And what does the doctor say? When did he last see him?'

'Oh, Doctor Stokes is very pleased with him! He doesn't need to see him much now. He recommended some massage, and Will's having that every day. It's doing a lot of good.'

'That must be costing a bit,' Mr Pennington said.

'I can manage it,' Beth said quickly. 'I have an arrangement with the lady who does it. Anything to get Will better as soon as possible. He can't wait to get back to work.'

'And the fact is, Mrs Seymour, we can't wait to have him back. At least, we can't wait much longer.'

'He's not being paid,' Beth said quickly.

'I know. It's not just that. There's also the question of this hut.'

'I've been paying the rent. At least . . .' She faltered. 'Until the last week or two. But I'll make up the arrears as soon as I can!'

'And it's not only that, Mrs Seymour,' Pennington said. 'You see, these huts are only for the occupation of someone working on the line. And if your husband isn't going to be fit to work . . . I'm sure you understand.'

'Oh, but he is!' Beth urged. 'Quite soon! He just needs a little longer!'

'It's a question of how much longer, Mrs Seymour. The Company's a reasonable and fair one – I'm sure you'll agree – but it's not a charitable institution.'

Beth flushed, tried not to show her anger.

'Mr Pennington, the last thing my husband has ever wanted is charity! He's a proud man and a hard worker, as I'm sure anyone will tell you.'

He nodded.

'I don't dispute that. The question is, will he be *able* to work, especially on the viaduct? And when? If it's not to be soon, then we'll need to replace him, and whoever takes his place will need somewhere to live. It's what the huts are for, and we don't have any spare for people not employed by the Company. That's the brutal truth, Mrs Seymour.'

However just it was, he hated what he was saying. He felt personally guilty for the deep anxiety in the woman's face.

'You realize I have two lodgers?' Beth said. 'They have to live somewhere, have to be looked after.'

Pennington nodded.

'I shall bear that in mind. But I don't have to tell you that it's not as difficult for a single man to get lodgings in some other hut, thus releasing this for a family. If it should come to that,' he added. 'If it comes to it.'

Silence fell. What else can I say, was the question in both their minds. John Pennington was the first to speak.

'And now, I'm afraid, I have to see your husband for myself.'

'Of course.'

Beth rose to go into the bedroom to Will, but at the same moment he called out.

'Who's there? Who is it?'

'I'm just coming,' Beth called back.

She turned to Mr Pennington.

'You've told me everything and I've taken note of it. I'll explain it all to Will later. Can I ask you not to upset him more than you need?'

'Of course.'

A minute later he stood beside Will's bed.

'So how are you, Mr Seymour? How are you getting on?'

'Very well,' Will said. 'Very well indeed! If you'd called later this afternoon you'd have seen me up, walking around.'

'Is that so?' Pennington turned to Beth.

'Oh yes, it is!' she confirmed. 'And he'll be up each day from now on.'

Pennington chatted with Will for a few minutes, then rose to his feet, made his farewells, and followed Beth back into the living-room.

'I've made up my mind, Mrs Seymour,' he said. 'Of course the final decision isn't up to me, it's for the Company to say, but what I shall suggest is that we do nothing until the end of the year. It's the middle of November now, so it allows a few weeks.'

'Thank you. Thank you very much.'

'And I hope your husband continues to improve.'

When he had left she sat down; she had to, her legs were trembling. What will we do if we lose our home? she asked herself. Where will we go? One thing was certain, in spite of what she had said to Mr Pennington she would not speak to Will of that possibility. He had no need of a spur to goad him into recovery. To get back to work was what he wanted most in the world. The question was, and she knew it had been in her heart long before Mr Pennington's visit, *would* he recover? Would Will ever again be fit enough to do his job? But it was a question she must keep locked inside her.

'Beth! What are you doing? Come here!'

Will's voice was firm and strong, and for once he sounded reasonably happy. Beth took a deep breath and went into the bedroom.

'Well, that was all right, wasn't it?' Will said. 'It was good of him to pay me a visit.'

'Very civil,' Beth said steadily.

'I reckon so. When is Phoebe coming?'

'She'll be another hour yet.'

'She does me a lot of good, you know.'

'I do know.'

What was more important than ever now was that Will should have as many treatments as he needed.

Somehow, somewhere, she would find the money. Could she, she wondered, confide in Phoebe Grange, tell her it was vital that Will should be cured, and soon? She didn't know Phoebe well, or how discreet she was. And did she herself wish to hear, if that was what Phoebe had to tell her, that a complete cure was impossible?

'Well, what about a cup of tea while we're waiting?' Beth was glad to have Will, with his mundane request, break in on her uneasy thoughts.

Fifteen minutes later when they were drinking the tea, there was another knock at the door.

'It'll be Phoebe!' Will sounded pleased.

'I don't think so, Will.' Phoebe would have walked straight in. She didn't stand on ceremony.

When Beth answered the door James Tiplady, the Missioner, stood there. His horse, the same strong Fell pony which had brought Patrick Mahoney back on that awful Saturday afternoon, was tethered near by.

'Good afternoon, Mrs Seymour,' he said pleasantly. 'May I come in? I've got something for you!'

He deposited the bundle he was carrying on the table, opened it up, and took out nine books, nine slates and a box of slate pencils.

'There!' he said proudly. 'How will *that* do? And don't think the blackboard and easel have been forgotten. I couldn't manage them on my old horse, but I've persuaded the fellow in charge of the tramway to bring them up. He'll deliver them to you tomorrow.'

Beth cried out with excitement.

'Oh, Mr Tiplady, this is wonderful!' She picked up a book and examined it. '*My First Reader*. It's *exactly* what I wanted! And illustrated, too!' Her face clouded. 'The only thing is,' she said hesitantly, 'that though I did ask for nine of everything, I'm no longer sure that

I can afford so many. Nor am I sure that I'll get nine pupils.'

'Oh, you'll have no difficulty in getting the pupils!' James Tiplady was full of confidence. 'And there's even less difficulty about paying. Everything you see here, plus the blackboard and easel, is a gift from the Bradford City Mission.'

Beth stared at him.

'I can't believe it!'

'Well it's true. According to Mr Crossland, the people at the Mission are most interested in what you're going to do. And I think you'll find if you have other needs for the job, they'll meet them.'

'But that's most tremendously generous,' Beth said.

James Tiplady nodded agreement.

'Yes. The people of Bradford *are* generous. And how is your husband?'

'He's improving, but it's slow work,' Beth replied. She had a sudden urge to tell him about Mr Pennington's visit, and the worries it had caused her. Perhaps he could do something? Perhaps he would put in a good word with the Company?

She decided against it. After the wonderful gift he had just brought her it was too much to ask for more, though if the worst came to the worst, she thought, Mr Tiplady was someone she could turn to.

'Shall I have a word with him?' James Tiplady asked.

She showed him into the bedroom. Will was civil to him, but no more. She felt ashamed of his lack of response to the Missioner's friendliness. She was relieved when Mr Tiplady left after ten minutes' one-sided conversation.

'Why did he come?' Will asked. 'Why did you ask him in? You know I'm not one for parsons.'

'As a matter of fact,' Beth said, 'he didn't come to see you. He came to see me. He brought me the reading books and the slates.'

188

'Oh, *that*! You're determined on that nonsense, aren't you?'

'I am,' Beth kept her voice steady. She would not let it be the subject of another argument.

'Well just remember, the day I'm back at work is the day you give it up!'

She was saved from replying by the sounds of the door opening, and Phoebe's quick step in the house. She stood in the bedroom doorway, radiant in yet another colourful outfit, blue and green with touches of red. She cheered up the drab day. Like a bird of paradise or a summer butterfly, Beth thought. Certainly she cheered up Will. For the first time that day a smile spread across his face.

'So, Will, are you ready for me?'

The bantering note in Phoebe's voice sparked off a reply from Will.

'I'm always ready for you!'

'Shall I give you a hand?' Beth offered.

'Ta, love,' Phoebe said, 'but I think we can manage, eh Will?'

'Then I'll leave you to it,' Beth said.

For the next half-hour grunts and groans, interspersed with laughter, came from the bedroom. Phoebe was still smiling when she came back into the living-room.

'You certainly do him good, and in more ways than one,' Beth said. 'It's the first time I've heard Will laugh in weeks.'

'Poor man! It's not easy to laugh in his situation,' Phoebe said.

'I know. He's desperate to get back to work. He's a frustrated man.'

'And I daresay you're just as desperate for him to do so?'

'As a matter of fact, yes,' Beth admitted. 'Though I wouldn't want him to overdo himself.'

She made a sudden decision, and as a result told Phoebe about Mr Pennington's visit. 'So when do you think . . . ?' she concluded.

Phoebe shook her head.

'I don't know. Not yet, love. When I do know I'll tell you. Now shall we go and get that husband of yours out of bed – though to my mind, if his back would let him, he'd sooner get the two of us *into* bed!' Phoebe laughed heartily at the thought. 'He's a frustrated man in that direction all right! I'll have to do something about it before he goes off pop!'

Beth blushed. Phoebe always spoke so openly, but though there was usually a *double entendre* in her words, there was also an honest vulgarity which robbed them of offence. More often, what she said left Beth feeling that if there was a fault it was her own, that she was a prude.

Once again, Phoebe was still there when Jake came in from work. This time he came alone.

'Why, Mr Tempest, fancy seeing you!' Phoebe said. 'We do keep running into each other, don't we? Now if you like I could give you a nice massage, take all the weariness of the day's work out of you!' Her tone was teasing, though with just enough undercurrent to make it clear that she was ready if he was.

'Thank you, Mrs Grange,' Jake said. 'Actually, I'm feeling fine.'

'Some other time,' she conceded. 'Or place!'

'Where's Patrick?' Beth broke in. 'Is he all right?'

'He's gone down to Batty Green.' Jake's tone was even, but the look on his face warned Beth not to ask any more questions.

Will picked up the look, not intended for him.

'If he's in trouble, he needn't come here. And if he comes back drunk, he'll not be let in!'

'Oh, I don't think you need worry,' Jake said. 'As it happens, when I've tidied up and had a quick bite,

I'm going down there myself. I'll meet up with him and see he's all right.'

You're worried about him, Beth thought. There's more to it than you're letting on. But she wouldn't ask, not while Will was in the room. Patrick was like a red rag to a bull to him. As for Jake, sometimes she thought Will hated him. She couldn't understand why. It hadn't been like that in the beginning.

'Now, Will, time you were back in bed!' Phoebe said.

Between them, the two women saw him back to his bed.

'You're certainly walking better today,' Phoebe said. 'We'll have you up longer tomorrow, walk you around the house a bit.'

Since Jake had gone to his room she did not linger, but as soon as she had left, Jake reappeared.

'Is there something more about Patrick?' Beth asked.

Jake hesitated, then said, 'He hasn't been himself all day. He's been behaving strangely, talking wildly. He's been picking quarrels with the other men, threats flying through the air from both sides. Now he's marched off to Batty Green in a nasty, pugnacious mood. I don't like it. I'm worried what might happen.'

'What will you do?'

'Go after him. He wouldn't hear of me going with him but he can't stop me following.'

'What about your supper? It'll be another half-hour.'

'I'd rather not wait. I'll take a sandwich, eat it on the way,' Jake said. 'It's dead certain Patrick will have gone to the alehouse, and if he has a drop too much, goodness knows what sort of trouble he'll get into! And if he's in a fight, and the foreman hears about it, he'll lose his job as sure as God made little apples. If that happens, he'll not get another anywhere on the line.'

'Patrick's a changed man,' Beth said unhappily. 'He was the mildest of men when he first came here.'

Jake, as he had expected, discovered Patrick in the alehouse. It was crowded to the door but there was no difficulty in finding him.

It was his voice which gave him away, his fine tenor voice singing 'The Minstrel Boy'. A small man sat beside him, accompanying him on the concertina, and a group of men stood around, listening.

'Thy songs were made for the brave and free, They shall never sound in slavery!'

There was a moment's silence when the song ended before the applause broke out.

'Give us another!' a man cried. 'Give us "Sally Gardens"!'

Patrick and the accordionist duly obliged, and then with another and another. The Irishman sang of his homeland, of its history, of its people. Jake, standing on the edge of the group, watched and listened in amazement. This was not the Patrick he had known today. There was no belligerence, no quarrel, no turmoil in this man. How could it happen, this lightning change of mood?

When Patrick finally stopped singing, the pints of ale lined up beside him, and beside the accordionist. Both men grinned with pleasure.

'Thirsty work!' Patrick acknowledged.

When he was drinking his third pint – in no time at all – Jake pushed through towards him.

'That was grand,' he said. 'I'm leaving now. It's getting late. Shall we walk back together?'

Whatever Patrick said, Jake decided, he would go along with. He would stay by his side. There was no way he was going to leave him here, drinking. It was a relief, therefore, when Patrick said, 'I'm ready!'

The November moon was all but hidden in the heavy mist. Lights in the huts around the Batty

Green area penetrated the damp darkness for a short distance, but once they had left the settlement behind it became difficult to see more than a yard or two ahead.

'We'll stick by the tram track. That's the safest way to avoid the shakeholes,' Jake said.

Carefully though they picked their way, there was no escaping the bog. Time after time one then the other sank ankle-deep into the mud, yet it was the same clay which, on a dry day, hardened to such an extent that the men working on it could break it only with a pickaxe.

'A hell of a climate,' Jake said.

' 'Tis indeed,' Patrick agreed. 'And I'm thinking I'll be leaving it for a better.'

'Leave?' Jake was astonished. 'But why? Where would you go?'

'Where else but back to Ireland?' Patrick said. 'As to why . . . I've come to it that I can't manage my life here. I can't think straight for long. At this minute, sure, I'm fine, but the devil gets into me before I know it. It's not me, you know. 'Tis the devil himself. There's no holding him!'

'You'll improve,' Jake assured him. 'You'll get better.'

Patrick shook his head.

'The devil is powerful here. I'd be safer from him back in Ireland with my own folk. I have a mother and sisters in Cork. Did I ever tell you that? They'd look after me.'

Perhaps he was right, Jake thought. It was too hard a life, working in the tunnel, for all but the strongest.

'When would you go?' he asked.

'One day soon. A day when God seemed on my side, when He would walk with me.'

'I would miss you,' Jake said.

They were almost at Nazareth now. The small shanty

town was dark as they walked into it, the only light was that which shone ahead of them from the Seymours' hut.

When Jake had left, Beth made the meal and took Will's plate into the bedroom.

'This is the last time I have my supper in bed,' Will said. 'From now on I'll be up for it, see if I'm not!'

'Good!' Beth said. 'I hope you will be.'

'Phoebe's doing me the world of good,' he said. 'She's a remarkable woman, that one.'

'She certainly is,' Beth agreed. 'Now you eat your supper before it goes cold, and I'll go and get mine.'

What she longed for most of all at this moment was an hour's peace and quiet. The day had seemed one long bustle, one happening after another. She was eager to look at the readers Mr Tiplady had brought, which she'd not had time to examine in any detail. She wanted to work out her plan of campaign, decide which parents she might approach, and how she would set about teaching the children.

Book in one hand, she ate her meal, hardly tasting her food. When she had finished eating she began to make notes. There was so much to think about, to decide. Seldom had an evening passed so quickly.

Immersed in what she was doing, she didn't at first hear Will call out. It was the demanding note in his voice which told her that he'd done so more than once.

'I'm coming!' she called. Reluctantly, she put down her notes and went into the bedroom.

She could hardly believe the sight of Will. He was a stranger, sitting up in bed, his face flushed, his eyes glittering, for all the world as if he had a fever.

'What ever is it, Will?' she asked. 'What's wrong?'

'Come to bed!' His voice was hoarse. 'Come to bed at once.'

'To bed? Why, is it late? The men aren't back.' She wanted to be there when they returned. She wanted to know about Patrick.

'Damn the men!' Will shouted. 'It's me you're married to. I'm ordering you to come to bed!'

'Very well,' Beth said quietly. 'If it's what you want.' She didn't understand his mood, but clearly she must try to placate him.

She crossed the room and began to make up her bed on the sofa.

'Not there!' Will shouted. 'You've slept on the bloody sofa for the last time. You're my wife and I'm your husband and you'll sleep in my bed or I'll know the reason why.'

A chill fear crept into Beth, but she would not show it. 'But you *do* know the reason why,' she spoke as calmly as she could. 'I sleep on the sofa because of your back. I don't want to do anything to hurt you.'

'I'll decide that,' he said. 'I'll show you what hurt is,' Will said. 'You've never known that, have you, but by God you will!'

Ice-cold waves ran down her body. She stood rooted.

'Come here!' Will commanded. His voice was hoarse and angry. There were round, crimson spots of colour on his cheekbones.

This is a nightmare, Beth thought. It's not real. She felt sapped of strength, unable to do anything of her own accord. With halting steps she approached the bed and when she was within arm's length he leaned forward and jerked her towards him.

'No!' she cried. 'No, Will! What are you doing?'

He had finished with words. As he grasped her she felt his breath hot on her face, rasping in her ears. He fumbled with the top button of her blouse, but when it wouldn't yield to his clumsy fingers he took hold of the material with impatient hands and tore the

195

garment from her as if it had been no more than tissue paper. She was astonished at the strength in him.

He pulled her further onto the bed, pushed her on her back and pinned her there. Then he lifted her skirt, tore off her undergarments and came down on top of her.

It was when the searing pain and the deep, deep humiliation of what he was doing to her became more than her flesh and spirit could stand, that the whole world blotted out in a merciful blackness.

When it was all over, and he lay asleep and still, as if he was unaware of what had happened, she crept out of the bed. She tasted the blood on her lips, where he had bitten through the skin, and felt it trickling down her chin. Her body was an enormous, throbbing bruise.

She staggered into the living-room. All she knew, and the need consumed her, was that she must wash herself. She must scrub herself from head to foot. No matter how much it might hurt. She must scrub away the deep disgust.

Not seeing clearly, she tripped, and fell to the floor. She did so at the same moment as Jake, followed by Patrick Mahoney, came into the house. She lay there before him, unable to move, looking up at him like a frightened animal.

11

For a second, Jake stared at Beth in horror and disbelief, then he dropped to his knees beside her, enfolded her in his arms and held her close.

'My darling! My darling! What is it? What's happened?'

No words came from Beth. She gave a small whimper, like a frightened child seeking comfort, and finding it in his arms. She could think no further than to stay there for ever. Jake, sensing her deepest need, continued to hold her against him, murmuring endearments.

'You're safe now,' he said gently. 'I'm here. Hush now!'

But as he continued to hold her, as she looked up at him, he saw more clearly the state of her; her bleeding lips, a bruise on her neck, and another, red and purple against the white skin of her breast; her clothes torn from neck to hem. There was no doubt in his mind as to what it was she had suffered.

Anger flooded him, anger so fierce, so strong, that his body trembled with it. How could this have happened? Had someone broken into the hut and attacked her? But as fast as that idea came into his mind, he dismissed it. It wasn't so. In a way, it would have been preferable to know that the act had been perpetrated by a frenzied stranger. As it was . . .

'Who did this to you, Beth?'

He tried to keep his voice calm, not to alarm her further, but Beth heard the anger in it, felt the trembling in his body. She didn't answer him. In the silence while Jake waited for her reply they could hear Will's deep snores from the bedroom.

'It was him. It was Will, wasn't it?'

Beth nodded.

Beside himself, Jake gripped her hard.

'I'll kill him!' he said. 'I'll beat him to a pulp and then I'll kill him!'

His voice went into Beth like a steel blade. She pulled herself away from him.

'No!' she protested. 'No! I can't bear any more! Please don't do anything, Jake. Go to bed. Leave me.'

'How can I?' Jake demanded. 'How can I leave you like this?'

'You must,' Beth begged. 'It will be worse for me if you don't, if he finds you and Patrick here.'

He had forgotten that Patrick was there. The Irishman had stood by silently, saying nothing.

'Please!' Beth implored.

Jake considered for a moment. It went against his every instinct to leave her like this, but perhaps she was right – and it was her choice.

'Very well,' he said reluctantly. 'I'll do so, but only because you ask it. It's not what I want to do, and I'm not sure it's right. In any case, I must bathe your face first.'

Without being asked, and without a word, Patrick fetched a basin of water and a cloth. Gently, with the utmost tenderness, Jake bathed Beth's face, and the bruises on her neck and chest. Only by the greatest effort did he contain his anger as he did so. And when Beth winced with pain at the cold water on the sore places, the pain shot through him also.

It was not until the bathing was over that Beth realized to what extent her clothes were torn and how immodestly she was exposed to the two men. Hastily she tried to pull the two halves of her blouse over her breasts. Without a word, Jake fetched her cloak from its hook by the door, and wrapped it around her.

'You must keep warm,' he said, as if that was the only purpose of the cloak.

'Thank you,' Beth said. 'Please go now. Please leave me.'

'Promise me you won't go back into that bedroom,' Jake said.

Beth shuddered.

'I can promise that.'

'And you'll call me if you want me? I'll leave my door open.'

'I will.'

He kissed her gently on the forehead, then left her, Patrick preceding him into their bedroom.

When the men had gone, Beth sat for several minutes wrapped in her cloak, her head leaning back against the chair. She was weary beyond belief, unutterably tired, but then, rising above the weariness, the strong, irresistible desire to wash herself, to cleanse herself thoroughly from top to toe, rose in her. There could not be even the beginnings of sleep, for which she longed, until she had done that.

She stirred the fire into life, then fetched clean water and put the bowl on the table. She would have liked to have plunged into the fast-running waters of the beck where it was deepest, or failing that to have filled the tin bath, but the first was impossible, and as for the bath, she had neither strength enough to carry it in from where it hung on its nail outside, nor water enough to fill it. The bowl would have to do.

She took off her cloak and the rest of her clothes, then systematically she washed every inch of her body, lathering the flannel well with the red carbolic soap.

When she came to the washing of the most private parts of her body, the secret places which until tonight she had yielded to Will in such love, and which now she never would again as long as she lived, she held her breath against crying out with the stinging pain of it. Yet the very act of washing, of using the strong, coarse soap, cleansed her in more than a physical way. The greater the pain, she told herself, the more I am cleansed. For it was not sexual love, or an excess of it, or anything at all to do with love, which had happened to her. It was violence. She was washing away violence.

When it was done she dressed herself in clean clothes which she had ironed that afternoon and left on the clothes-horse to air. Then she put on her cloak, picked up the bowl of water from the table, and went out of the hut. There she flung the tin bowl and its contents as far as it would go. Never again would she have it in her house. The bowl bounced against an outcrop of stone, the sound reverberating in the still night.

Back in the hut she picked up, with the firetongs, the garments she had been wearing earlier, and fed them to the fire. When they had been reduced to blackened shreds she took the poker and beat the shreds into ashes.

That done, and the last vestige of her torn and stained garments destroyed, she wrapped her cloak further around her, sat down in the armchair, and prepared for sleep. She turned the lamp low, but did not put it out. She knew that, for the moment, she couldn't bear to be in the dark.

Weary though she was, sleep was slow to come. She tried to pray, but the familiar prayers she normally said – thanks for the day past, hope of blessings for the day to come – she could not bring herself to utter. Where had God been when she needed Him? There were too many questions in her head.

'What shall I do?' she asked herself. 'What shall I do when tomorrow comes? How shall I live?'

In the men's bedroom Patrick and Jake prepared for bed quietly. It was a time when, usually, they talked, but what was on their minds now was not for discussion.

'Do you think anything will happen?' Patrick ventured anxiously. 'Do you want me to stay awake? I can, you know.' He was yawning heavily.

'No,' Jake said. 'You get your sleep. If I'm needed I'll waken all right.' He had, in fact, no intention of falling asleep until he was sure Beth was settled.

Though she moved quietly, he heard the sounds as she washed herself. Then when he heard the outer door open he was startled, and jumped out of bed to go after her, but was relieved to hear her come in again before he could do so. With his whole heart he longed to go in to her, to take her in his arms and comfort her.

When he wakened in the morning his first feeling was one of guilt that he should have slept at all. Quickly, he went into the living-room.

Beth was asleep, fallen sideways in the armchair, her head on a cushion. She was pale. Her eyelids were swollen and there were dark circles beneath her eyes. Her lips, though no longer bleeding, were still bruised and swollen. Looking down at her as she slept, he knew he had never loved her more; also that there was little he could do to help her. He went back to his bedroom, where Patrick was stirring.

'She's asleep,' he said. 'You get off to work. I'll stay until she wakens. No use two of us being absent.'

But when he had dressed, and went back into the living-room, Beth was awake.

'I'll stay with you,' he offered. 'I'd like to.'

'No,' Beth said. 'I'd rather you went to work. I have to face Will and it will be better if I do it alone.'

'But what if . . .'

'I'll be quite safe,' Beth interrupted. 'He wouldn't touch me. If he tried I would run out of the house, go to Elsie. He can't run after me.'

'You promise?'

'I promise.'

'When I get home from work,' Jake said, 'I want to talk to you.'

Jake and Patrick had not been gone long when Will called from the bedroom.

'Beth! Beth, come here!'

She was washing the breakfast dishes. Slowly, she straightened up, took a towel and dried her hands, meticulously attending to each finger in order to prolong the act. She didn't know how to face him.

'Beth! Beth!'

There was no escape. She put down the towel and walked slowly to the bedroom, standing in the doorway, not wanting to set foot inside the room.

Will was sitting up in bed. He looked at her, then stared at her. She knew what he was seeing, she had seen it in the mirror. He was seeing the swollen mouth, the bruises, the deadness of her eyes. She continued to stand there, not speaking, observing the red tide creep up his face, seeing the mounting horror in his eyes as he saw what he had done.

'I'll get your breakfast,' Beth said, turning away. The words came awkwardly because of the stiffness of her mouth.

'No, Beth! No! Come here!'

Without answering, she left the bedroom and began to lay his breakfast tray. When she took it in to him and placed it on his bedside table he stretched out a hand to touch her. She stepped back quickly, out of his reach.

'Beth, I'm sorry! I'm sorry! What else can I say?'

She felt no emotion as she saw the tears spring in his eyes.

'What can I say?' he repeated. 'Beth, please say you forgive me!'

'Don't say anything.' She was amazed at the flat calm of her voice. 'There's nothing to be said. And don't ask me to forgive you. It's not possible.'

'Please, Beth,' he pleaded. 'I don't know how it happened. It'll never happen again. Can't we make a fresh start?'

'Yes,' Beth said. 'We must make a fresh start, that's for sure. But don't expect it ever to be the same. It won't be. I'll look after you. I'll make your meals and keep your house. But I will never share your bed again. Never!'

'Beth! Don't be hard on me! I didn't mean it!'

'But *I* mean this. I mean every word of it. If you so much as lay a finger on me I shall go to the police. Now please get on with your breakfast. I want to clear away. I have things to do.'

She fought back the tears until she was in the living-room, but then she could do so no longer. Sitting at the table, she buried her head in her hands and let them flow.

How can I go on? she asked herself. Day by day to the end of my life? Yet what else could she do, where else could she go? What alternative had any woman to a bad marriage unless she was rich, and therefore independent? But there must be a way, there must be something. There must be someone who could advise her.

She thought of Mr Tiplady. He was a minister of God, wasn't he? There to help people. He would listen to her, treat her kindly. But in the end, she thought, he would remind me of my marriage vows, 'for better or for worse'. Well, she didn't need to be reminded.

She dried her eyes. That's it, she thought. The crying is over. I have to go on. The mainspring of her life, her marriage, was broken beyond repair, but there were other things, even in her small world, and she would concentrate on those.

The sight of the children's readers, still piled on the table, gave her the first ray of hope. The sooner she started on that job, the better. She would begin by going down this very morning to see Elsie.

And then she remembered the state of her face. How could she let herself be seen by anyone, looking the way she did? How could she explain it? For she had no intention of telling the truth. She was too deeply ashamed, even though common sense told her the shame was not hers. It couldn't be helped that Jake and Patrick knew, but she could trust them to tell no-one, nor would she allow them ever to speak of it to her.

Any idea that she may have had of not showing herself until her face was healed came to nothing half an hour later when there was a knock at the door and Elsie Drake walked in, carrying the baby, and with the three other children at her heels.

'It's freezing cold out there!' she said, closing the door firmly behind her. 'If it doesn't snow before the day's out my name's not Elsie Drake! I reckon we—'

She stopped short, catching sight of Beth's face.

'Why, what in the world . . . ?'

'I tripped over the rug and fell against the corner of the table,' Beth said quickly. 'So clumsy of me!'

Elsie continued to stare at her. It didn't ring true. How could falling against the table give her that mouth, and the bruise on her neck? Also, she was ghastly pale.

'Fell against the table?'

'That's right.'

Beth's look was defiant. It was plain that Elsie didn't believe her, but it was all she was going to get.

Elsie read the look. It said, 'Ask me no questions

and you'll get no lies!' Even though she'd just told a whopper.

'Well, I never!' she said. 'Now, a bit of zinc ointment's what you need. I use zinc ointment for just about everything from a sore finger to a broken leg.'

'I don't have any,' Beth said. 'I'll get some next time I go down to Batty Green – if I'm not completely better before then.'

'Which brings me to what I came for,' Elsie said. 'I wondered if you'd mind the children while *I* went down to Batty Green. There's a few things I need – and I'll bring you some zinc ointment, or anything else you want. I don't want to take the children in case it starts snowing.'

'I'd be glad to look after them,' Beth said. 'You know that.'

Elsie Drake looked at Beth closely.

'Are you sure you're all right? You look washed out.'

'Quite all right, thank you, Elsie. I'm a bit tired. I didn't sleep well, that's all.'

'Well it takes it out of you, not sleeping. Don't I know it with four kids!' If that was Beth's story, she'd let her stick with it, but when did falling over a rug give that look in the eyes?

'I wanted to see you,' Beth said. 'The reading books have arrived for the children. I reckon I'll be ready to start on Monday, if I can get the children together.'

'You can have my three any day,' Elsie said. 'And I reckon the same will go for Phoebe's.'

Phoebe! I'd totally forgotten Phoebe, Beth thought, and she'll be here this afternoon. She'd managed to deceive Elsie about her appearance, or at least to stop her asking further questions, but would she be able to do the same with Phoebe? Phoebe Grange was a woman of the world; candid, outspoken, pulled no punches. And if Phoebe guessed the truth, how far would she spread it?

'I reckon Mrs Parker would let her two come,' Elsie said, breaking into Beth's thoughts. 'That would be seven to start with – and a lucky number at that!'

'I think I could manage seven,' Beth said. 'And we'll have to decide just where I'll teach the children: here, or in one of your houses. With winter almost on us we have to think of the weather.'

She would like, very much indeed, to be able to hold the classes in some house other than her own, for the simple reason that it would take her away from Will for a spell. Will, though, was the reason why that would be difficult to do. He was still unable to get around without help, so how could she leave him for even a few hours each day?

'I've brought a bottle for the baby in case he gets fractious, though I don't suppose he will,' Elsie said.

Beth held out her arms.

'Give him to me then. I'm sure he'll be no trouble at all.'

The feel of the baby in her arms, held close against her breast, was balm to Beth's spirit.

'I'll be off then,' Elsie said. 'I'll try not to be long.'

'No need to hurry,' Beth assured her. She was glad of the children's company. Apart from welcoming them for their own sakes, they would be an effective barrier between herself and Will.

When he heard the door close behind Elsie Drake, Will called out again.

'Beth! Beth!'

Beth went reluctantly, standing in the doorway with the baby in her arms. She looked at Will without speaking.

'What's happening?' he asked.

'I'm looking after Elsie's children while she goes to Batty Green.'

He looked a sorry sight. He had not had a wash and he needed a shave. The bed was unmade, in the same state as when she had run away from it last night. She knew she should do something about these things, it was her duty, but she could not. She couldn't bear to go near him, let alone to touch his flesh with hers. She was aware that a little later Phoebe would arrive and she would not expect to see Will in his present state, but there was nothing she could bring herself to do about it.

The baby fell asleep, growing suddenly heavy in Beth's arms. She left the bedroom and laid the child on the armchair, blocking him in with another chair so that he couldn't roll off.

'Now you three,' she said to the other children, 'come and sit to the table. I have something to show you.'

She gave them each a slate, a slate pencil and a reader, then found the place for them in the books and pointed to the picture.

'What's that?'

They all knew the answer.

'A cat!' they said in unison.

'And you see that, underneath the picture. A word. What does *that* say?'

Only Emily could answer.

'It says "cat", Mrs Seymour.'

'Indeed it does. Did you know, or did you guess?'

'I guessed,' Emily admitted.

'Then you guessed well. It's always worth while having a guess.'

It was terrible, Beth thought, that at eight years old Emily could only guess at the word. But I shall change all that, she told herself – and the thought gave her the first lift of the day.

'Well now, I want you to do something you'll be able to show your mother when she gets back from Batty

Green. I want you each to draw a cat on your slate. You can copy the picture in the book, or you can draw any cat you like.'

It was clearly seven-year-old Tom who had the artistic talent. He drew a large, fearsome-looking cat with long whiskers while Emily and Ada painstakingly copied the cat from the book.

'Very good,' Beth said when they had finished. 'Now, can any of you write words?'

'No, Mrs Seymour,' they chorused.

'Well, you're going to,' Beth said. 'Look at the book and just draw the word "cat" under your picture. Watch me first.'

On a slate of her own she showed them, carefully forming each letter in turn. Again, Tom got the hang of it quickly but the girls' efforts were less sure.

'That's splendid,' Beth said. 'You've all written and read your first word. Now, if you turn your slates over to the other side we'll do something even better. I want you to draw a picture of yourself. If you like you can go and look in the mirror, and then draw what you see.'

'I can't do it,' Ada said.

'Then I'll help you. Bring your slate and stand by me and I'll draw you. Let's see . . . you have a round face, long, curly hair with a ribbon bow, and big eyes. A beautiful blue, but I can't put the colour in with a slate pencil.'

And I am no portrait artist, Beth thought as she drew on Ada's slate. But Ada seemed satisfied.

'Now *you* can draw in your dress,' Beth said. 'It's got stripes so that's easy.'

The drawing of the self-portraits took a long time, and much squeaking of slate pencils, which set Beth's teeth on edge.

'Now this is the exciting bit,' she said. 'I'm going to show you how to write your own name. Copy what I do on my slate and put it under the picture on yours. And be thankful your mother gave you all short names!'

The time flew by. Tom, carried away, wrote his name several times, all around his portrait.

'That's very good,' Beth said. 'They're all very good. Another day I'll show you how to write your last names. People who can't write their names have to put a cross, but you'll be able to sign your own names for the rest of your lives.'

They were still at it when Elsie returned. They shouted at her as she came in at the door.

'Look what we've done! Just look!'

Elsie gazed at the slates in astonishment. 'I wouldn't have believed it!' she said. 'It's wonderful. And so quick!'

'I don't suppose every lesson will go as well, but we've made a good start,' Beth admitted. 'And the baby has slept through it all.'

'Well, we'd best get off,' Elsie said. 'It's started to snow. Here's your zinc ointment.'

When Elsie and the children had left, Beth took Will's dinner tray and left it on his bedside table. She did not stay and talk with him, as she sometimes did, while he ate it, but left immediately.

Later in the afternoon there was a knock at the door and Phoebe walked in. She stopped dead halfway across the room.

'What in the world . . . ?'

'I tripped over the rug and fell against the corner of the table,' Beth said. The lie came more easily the second time, though she doubted, from the look on Phoebe's face, whether it was any more convincing than it had been for Elsie.

'Well, you certainly fell hard,' Phoebe said. 'And how's Will?'

'About the same. He'll be pleased to see you. Will

you excuse me if I leave you to it? There's something I have to do urgently.'

'Of course,' Phoebe said.

In the bedroom, Phoebe stared at the state of the bed, and of Will himself. He was slumped down in the bed, his hair unkempt, his chin and jowls blue with a day's growth of beard. The bedclothes were every which way, and on the table close to him lay the congealed remains of his dinner, of which he seemed to have eaten very little.

Something had gone badly wrong. Beth Seymour had always been meticulous in her care of her husband, and of his surroundings. Phoebe had never seen him like this.

And it has something to do, she thought, with the state of Beth's face. Not for a minute had she believed the tale of falling against the table. So what had he done that his wife was not going near him? More worldly, more experienced with men than either Elsie Drake or Beth, Phoebe guessed what he had done. Hadn't something like it happened in her own life? Didn't she have a child whose father she had never seen again, to prove it?

She had been well aware, when she had been treating him, of Will's desires, and of his frustrations. She'd perhaps added to them. She had had a certain sympathy with him, but she could never condone what she now felt sure he had done to his wife. If a woman gave herself willingly, in marriage or out of it, that was one thing. She understood that well enough. If she was taken by force it was quite another. However, she concluded, I'm here to treat his back, not to sort out his marriage.

'So!' she said. 'You've decided to grow a beard?'

'It looks like it,' Will grunted.

'Or have you changed your mind? Would you like me to shave you?'

'Beth usually helps me,' Will said. 'She's been too busy. Did she say anything?' His tone was nervous.

'What about? Oh, you mean her face? Only that she'd tripped over the rug and fallen against the table. Dangerous things rugs can be.'

So at least Beth had not given him away, Will thought. He was not to be further humiliated.

'Well, since Beth's busy I'll clean you up and tidy your bed before I give you your massage,' Phoebe said.

If you hadn't massaged me the way you did, Will thought, if you hadn't played on my feelings, none of this might have happened. But, he soon found out, it was to be different this afternoon. Her hands moved over his body in a brief, competent and impersonal manner.

'I'll get you out of bed on my own today,' Phoebe said when she had finished. 'I think you're mending fast. The sooner you get back to work the better. For today I'll walk you round the bedroom and the living-room, and you can try a bit of it on your own. I reckon you're not quite as helpless as I thought you were.'

Will gave her a quick look. Was she getting at something? But he wasn't going to ask.

She was correct in her estimate of his walking. He managed it much better than he had hitherto. When, in the living-room, Phoebe suddenly said, 'Now you do the next bit on your own,' he did so, though clinging onto the furniture for support.

Beth sat at the table, poring over her books, not even pretending to watch Will. Passing close by her he put out a hand and would have used her shoulder for support, but she twisted away and went to do something at the other side of the room.

So I was right, Phoebe thought. This is a pretty kettle of fish.

'Sit in here for a minute,' she said to Will. 'I'll make

your bed before you get back into it.' She spoke pleasantly, though all three of them knew it was not her job to do it. Beth followed her into the bedroom.

'I'll do it,' Beth said. 'It's up to me.'

They faced each other across the bed, met each other's eyes.

'I can see you're busy with your books,' Phoebe said mildly. 'I don't mind doing it this once. And while I'm at it, shall I change the sheets?'

Without a word, Beth went to the drawer and took out fresh sheets and pillowcases.

'I must tell you, and I reckon you'll be glad to hear it, your husband's improving fast,' Phoebe said. 'But now he needs to be got out of bed twice a day, and walked around the house. And he should stay up for longer. He needs to get his muscles in trim if he's to get back to work.'

'I'll see to it,' Beth said quietly. 'Not today, but I will from tomorrow.'

She would too. Tomorrow she would make a fresh start. She would look after him as well as she was able, neglecting none of his needs except one; but sleep with him she would not. That was over. She would share the bedroom, sleeping on the sofa. She had no wish for others to know the state of her marriage. It was strange that she had no fear that Will would molest her again.

'Oh, Will,' she cried in her heart, 'what has it come to that I use the word "molest" about my husband?'

'Then I'll leave you to it, and thank you,' she said to Phoebe.

Phoebe changed the bedding, found Will a clean nightshirt, then brought him back and helped him into bed. He tried to catch hold of her hand but she pulled away from him.

'Don't think I've no sympathy, and don't think I don't understand,' she said. 'I know. I'm not daft. But if ever I hear or see that Beth has fallen over the hearthrug and bashed into the table again, there'll be trouble. She's too good for that, and you know it.'

'I didn't mean . . .' Will began.

'We'll not discuss it further,' Phoebe said. 'I'll see you tomorrow.' She patted his hand briefly and was gone.

12

When Jake and Patrick emerged from the candlelit
tunnel in the early evening of the November day,
expecting to meet the darkness of the moor, it was
to discover a white world. Snow covered everything;
every hillock, every depression, every tuft of winter
vegetation. As yet there was no great depth to it, and
for the moment it had stopped falling. The air was
still and frosty, without wind, so that there were none
of the deep drifts in which a man could easily lose his
way. The moon was rising, too, and later on the moor
would be as light as day. Already there was no need
of the lanterns the men carried.

'Did I not say 'twould snow?' Patrick demanded.
'Did I not tell ye so?'

Snow was another of the things he disliked in this
alien country. At home on the west coast of Ireland,
where – so clever men said – the Gulf Stream came
all the way from America, without getting cold, to
warm the waters offshore, there was scarcely any snow.

'Didn't I foretell it?' he repeated.

'You certainly did,' Jake said. 'And I agreed with
you.'

Jake was used to snow. Here in the North of
England, and especially on the high moor and on the
fells, it came early and stayed long. It would not be as
bad in the valleys. There they could hope for days,
even weeks, when it might melt away, filling the
streams and rivers; but here, once it fell to any depth,
it would remain until the late spring.

At the moment the snow was of little consequence to him. His mind was, and had been all day long, on Beth. He had not wanted to leave her and he was anxious to be back, therefore he set off at a good pace, which Patrick found difficulty in matching.

'Will ye slow down!' he begged.

Jake did so.

'I'm sorry,' he said. 'I'm in a hurry to be back.'

It was not that he thought that anything worse would have happened to Beth; if that had been in his mind he would never have left her, no matter what she'd said. It was simply that he wanted to be with her, to comfort her in whatever way he could.

'No, *I'm* sorry,' Patrick said.

He'd almost forgotten. Things went in and out of his mind so quickly these days. Sometimes they never came back at all. But now he remembered the sight of Beth when they'd come back from Batty Green last night, and her face when he'd fetched the water for Jake to bathe it.

'If 'twas not that the man is half-crippled already,' he said in an angry growl, 'I would take him out and tear him limb from limb, so I would!'

Jake said nothing. When he thought of Will Seymour his rage knew no bounds. If I started on him at all, he thought, I would kill him. And what good would that be to Beth, her husband dead and me in prison, or worse?

But he would take her away from him. On that he was determined. Plans had run through his head all day long as he had laid the bricks in the tunnel, and before the day was over he would put them to her.

When they reached the hut Phoebe Grange was on the point of leaving. There was no sign of Will, so presumably he was back in bed.

'Why, Mr Tempest!' Phoebe exclaimed, 'I haven't

seen you for a day or two. How are you? You're looking fine!' She made no attempt to conceal her admiration.

'I'm very well, thank you.'

Jake's tone was terse. Given any encouragement, Phoebe Grange would linger to chat. He didn't want that. He wanted to be with Beth who, pale and subdued, stood behind Phoebe, every bit as anxious for her to leave.

'That's good! Is it still snowing?'

'Not at the moment,' Jake said. 'Though that isn't to say it won't come down heavily any minute.'

'Oh well, a few flakes of snow won't hurt me,' Phoebe said. 'I'm warm-blooded!'

Patrick brushed past her to the bedroom, and Jake followed. It was the quickest way to get rid of Phoebe. When he heard the door close behind her he returned to the living-room and went towards Beth. He would have taken her in his arms, but she turned away.

'Supper's on,' she said quietly, standing at the table with her back to him. 'It will be ready as soon as you are.'

Jake took the one step it needed to bring him close to her. He put his hands on her shoulders but she was rigid under them, steadfastly facing the other way.

'Don't turn your back on me, Beth,' he said quietly.

With gentle force he turned her around so that she was facing him.

It was the expression in her eyes which hurt him. Her face was already healing, though it would be some days before it would be back to normal, but as for her eyes, it was as if the light which had once glowed so brightly behind them had been extinguished. They were dull, empty, almost colourless.

'Beth, I've got to talk to you.'

He kept his voice low, glancing at the bedroom door, not knowing whether Will was awake or asleep.

Beth followed his glance.

'He's asleep,' she said. 'He always sleeps after his treatment. But it makes no difference, there's nothing to be said.'

'Oh yes there is!' Jake contradicted. 'And you must listen to me.'

'Whatever it is, I don't want to hear it,' Beth said.

'You're going to.'

Her body was facing his, but she turned her head away. She didn't want to listen to him or to anyone else. She wanted to be left alone. Couldn't he understand that?

'Beth, you must leave him! You can't stay here. Come away with me. I'm not sure where we'd go, what we'd do, but there'd be something. I could get a job further up the line, on another contract. Appleby, even Carlisle. They wouldn't know us there. It would be a fresh start.' The thoughts and plans which had whirled around in his head all day long poured out of him. Beth turned to face him again, shook her head, interrupted him.

'Please stop!'

'I won't stop,' Jake said. 'Not until I've said what I have to say. I love you, Beth. I'd look after you, I'd make you happy. I'd never harm a hair on your head, or let any hurt come to you.'

'Please stop!' she repeated. 'It's impossible.'

'It's not impossible,' Jake urged. 'We can do it.'

'No!'

'Why not? Don't say you don't love me, because I wouldn't believe you. But even if you do say so it doesn't matter. I've enough love for both of us; and one day you will, I know you will.'

'No!' Beth said. 'I'm married to Will. I made promises . . .'

'And what about *his* promises?' Jake demanded. ' "With my body I thee worship." Didn't he promise that? Is that what he did?'

Beth felt the blood drain away from her face. She thought she would faint.

'For pity's sake stop it!' she cried. 'Do you think I don't know?'

He was caught by the agony in her voice. He had wanted to bring her comfort and instead he had caused her anguish. He dropped his hands to his sides. He had never felt so helpless.

'I'm sorry,' he said. 'I've been clumsy. I've said it the wrong way; I've chosen the wrong moment.'

'Please, Jake!' Her voice was softer. 'There isn't a right moment for what you've just said to me. It can't be done.'

'Then promise you'll remember it, and if you change your mind . . .'

'I won't change my mind.'

Nor, Beth thought, would he ever know how near she had come to losing herself in the shelter of his arms, to going with him wherever he wanted to take her.

'It might be best if *you* went,' she said. 'It might make it easier for all of us.'

Jake shook his head.

'Not as things stand. I couldn't leave you like this. I have to stay, but I won't trouble you. I'll be here if you need me, if you change your mind.'

'I shan't do that,' Beth said. 'Go and get ready for supper.'

He collected a jug of water, took it into the bedroom and poured it into the bowl. When he had washed he changed out of his dirty working clothes into clean ones.

'I'm hungry!' Patrick said. 'It smells good.'

They sat at the table, Patrick eating heartily, Jake and Beth trying to give the appearance of doing so. Beth had taken a tray in to Will, wakened him, and waited until he began to eat it. From now on she must

218

do everything that was to be part of her normal life; a new kind of normal life, but she had to go forward. She would not look back. There was a deadness inside her, but perhaps it would change, and if it didn't, no-one would know.

'I had a piece of news,' Jake said.

In view of what he had had to say to Beth, he had put it aside. Now that she had turned him down he had to give it. Patrick and Beth looked up at him.

'I'm going on to nights,' Jake announced. 'Starting next Monday.'

Astonished, Patrick stopped eating, his fork halfway to his mouth.

'No-one said anything to me about changing on to nights. 'Twas never mentioned.'

'It's not the whole shift,' Jake said. 'Just a few, mostly brickies.'

'Not me, then?'

'No.'

'But who will I work with?' Patrick asked anxiously.

'I suppose with whoever takes my shift,' Jake said. 'Don't worry. You'll be all right.'

Patrick's reaction to the news was exactly what Jake had feared. Without telling the Irishman, when the foreman had sent for him to tell him of the change-over, Jake had at once asked if Patrick couldn't also change, so that they could continue to work together. The foreman had refused outright.

'He's a liability on the day shift,' he said. 'He'd be worse on nights.'

'But I'll be there to look after him,' Jake promised. 'I'll see he's all right.'

'You won't have time,' the foreman said, 'because the other thing is that I'm putting you in charge of a small group of bricklayers. You won't have time to wet-nurse Mahoney. You'll have enough with your own job and supervising the others. And since it's promotion, and more money, I take it you'll not refuse it. Even if you do, you can't have Mahoney.'

Jake had said nothing of this to Patrick. Time enough when it had to come out. It had all, to Jake, been of less importance today than Beth.

Patrick put down his fork, pushed his plate away. What would he do? How would he manage? Jake was his rock and stay. Jake understood how he was, noticed quickly when he was in difficulty.

'Then I shall leave,' he said. 'I'll go home to Ireland.'

'Don't say that,' Jake begged. 'Give it time. I'll still be here. Beth will be here.'

'No, I'll go home,' Patrick said. 'I had it in mind anyway. Didn't I tell you so, and wasn't it only yesterday?'

He rose to his feet and went to the bedroom. He had a headache coming on. Jake stood up to follow him but Beth put out a hand and drew him back.

'Not just yet, Jake. Let him be alone.'

'He thinks I've let him down,' Jake said.

'Well, you haven't. It's better for him to go home, we both know that.'

They were quiet for a while, hardly speaking. How can everything change so much in just twenty-four hours? Beth asked herself.

After a while, Jake broke the silence.

'So I'll be here during the day,' he said. 'Part of the time I'll be in bed, and for the rest I'll try not to get under your feet.' I would rather be here at night, he thought. I want to be here to protect her if need be.

'I shall have the children here,' Beth said. 'I start on the lessons next week. And it might be easier for *you* to start learning when you're here during the day – though I'm sure you wouldn't want to mix in with the children.'

Whatever he decided, it wouldn't be easy with Will

around, as he would be more and more. But she wouldn't let him stop her. She'd promised Jake to teach him to read, and she'd not break her promise.

If the weather was halfway decent, Jake thought, he'd take some of the walks he'd promised himself and never got around to, but if the snow really came down that wouldn't be possible. He would have to get out, though. How would he sit for so many hours in the same room as Beth, feeling as he did about her? And how would he endure Will?

A week later Patrick Mahoney left, quietly and without fuss, his few belongings carried on his back. He was ready to quit the house when Jake came in from the night shift.

'I'll walk down to Batty Green with you,' Jake said. 'Or a bit further if you like?'

'I'll be glad of your company so far,' Patrick said. 'I'm hoping to get a lift on a cart from Batty Green – if not to Settle, then to Ingleton.' It was not a long way from Ribblesdale to the west coast of England, and from there he'd get the boat home. It would be good to be home. His mother would be glad to see him.

'Neither of you is setting foot outside this door without a good breakfast inside you,' Beth said firmly. 'So you can both sit at the table and I'll serve you.'

At Batty Green the two men went into the alehouse and had a last pint of beer together. Patrick, Jake thought, would have stayed for another and another, but he dissuaded him. In any case, there was a cart almost ready to leave for Settle.

'I'll never forget you!' Patrick said.

'Nor I you,' Jake replied.

He stood there, waving, until the cart was out of sight, then he went back into the alehouse.

Will, so much improved was he, had started to get up towards the end of the morning, to stay up for his dinner and return to bed for his treatment, which Phoebe gave him after she had made him walk around the hut. He could have managed without so many treatments now, she said, but as the children were there five days a week for their lessons, and she usually came to collect them afterwards, she said she might as well do it.

'At this rate,' she said to Will, 'we'll have you back to work after Christmas – weather permitting.'

'It can't come too soon,' Will said. 'I'm fed up, stuck in here!'

He had never wanted the children in the house, and now that they were there he didn't like it. He didn't like the attention they had from Beth.

'You wait on them hand and foot!' he grumbled. He was sitting in the most comfortable armchair, close to the warmth of the stove, a cup of tea at his elbow.

'Is there anything you want?' Beth asked patiently.

'No,' he admitted. 'Not at the moment.'

'Well, then! And when there is something, I'm right here.'

She knew very well – they both did – that he couldn't fault the care she gave him, the way she kept his house, made his meals, attended to his person. She was pleasant, she was civil, she was ever-helpful, but he would have given up a large slice of that in exchange for the warmth which existed between her and the children. He listened to the greetings when they arrived in the morning, to their laughing and chattering throughout the day, to their quips and jokes, occasionally to their tears. Beth was in the middle of it all, enthusiastic, interested.

'Are you saying I neglect you for the children?' she asked when he grumbled about it.

'I'm not saying that. You just seem to be having a good time with them, and I'm out of it.'

'That's because you keep yourself out of it. You

won't take any interest, you won't even learn their names,' Beth said. 'So what do you expect?'

'I never wanted you to do it,' Will said.

'We need the money,' Beth said. 'It isn't much, but it does help. You know that's why I started it. You ought to be pleased that I find it rewarding in other ways also.'

He was not yet up when Patrick left for the last time, and Patrick did not go in to him to say goodbye.

'Good riddance!' Will said when Beth told him the Irishman had gone. 'The sooner we get rid of the other one, the better!'

'We'll not be getting rid of him,' Beth said. 'Not if we want to pay the rent and eat.'

'The minute I'm back at work, he goes!' Will threatened.

'Perhaps you're right,' Beth said in a calm voice. 'Perhaps that would be best. We'll discuss it at the time.'

Did it occur to Will, she wondered, to ask himself why Jake stayed at all when he was so rudely treated by the man of the house? Apparently it didn't.

And then the hut door opened and in came the children, all seven of them, and all in the care of eight-year-old Emily Drake, who shepherded them every morning. It was only because it was dark by the time they left in the afternoon that one of the mothers came to take them home.

A blast of cold air blew into the hut as they streamed through the door. But, thought Beth, welcoming them with a wide smile, they bring enough warmth to heat the whole house.

'Wipe your feet on the mat,' she said. 'But before you take off your caps and coats I want to show you something.'

'What is it, Mrs Seymour?' Emily asked.

'Turn around, all of you,' Beth instructed, 'and look

223

at the wall by the door. What do you see that's new?'

Tom saw it first.

'Hooks, Mrs Seymour. They weren't there yesterday!'

'Quite right!' Beth said. 'Mr Tempest kindly put them up, and at just the right height for you to hang your outdoor clothes. Tell me how many there are. Start by the door and count along the row.'

'Seven, Mrs Seymour,' Emily said.

'That's correct. Now you can each choose a hook, hang up your things, then come to the table and I'll tell you what we're going to do.'

At the table she gave them each a strip of paper and a wax crayon.

'Now first of all you're going to print your name on the paper, just your Christian name, and in your very best printing, then we'll fix them up over the hooks so you'll each have your very own. Don't rush. Do it carefully.'

Tom Drake was, as usual, the first to finish.

'I've done! I've done!' he cried.

'And so you should have,' Beth said. 'Yours is an easy name.'

'I haven't finished mine,' Clarissa Grange said.

'And I can't remember how to do mine,' her brother admitted.

'Well, Clarissa's is the longest name and Aubrey's is the most difficult,' Beth acknowledged. 'I'll give you a hand.'

Trust Phoebe Grange to give her children fancy names, she thought. It's quite in character.

'Jane and Bertie, you can do yours, can't you?' she asked. Jane and Bertie Parker, children of Elsie Drake's neighbour, had learnt to write their names before they came to the class, though not to read. But they were apt pupils, there'd be few difficulties with them.

'Shall I draw a pattern around mine while I'm waiting?' Tom asked.

'If you like,' Beth said.

In a way, Tom would be the most difficult pupil simply because he was the brightest. He had known no more than the others on the first day but, in addition to his artistic talent, he soaked up knowledge like a sponge. It wouldn't be easy to keep him occupied.

He was a handsome boy, she thought. He had a face a painter would want to put on canvas; oval, fine yet strong-featured, clear, olive-skinned. He had an exotic, foreign look about him – not the least bit like either of his parents. As she studied him, thinking that he was the kind of son she would like to have, he looked up from his drawing and caught her eye. His own were dark, and sparkling with intelligence. They exchanged smiles.

Beth was surprised, too, by the rapidity with which Jake was learning to read and write, though why she should be surprised she didn't know. He was an intelligent man. It was just that, like the children around the table, he'd not until now had a chance. Now he worked every spare minute at it. When he came in from the night shift he washed, changed his clothes, ate his breakfast, and was ready to start when the children arrived.

'You don't have to sit with the children,' Beth said. 'I'll give you separate lessons.'

'It's all right,' he said. 'I'm happy to do that. After all, we're at the same stage at the moment – at least me and Tom are.'

'Well, it's good for them to see a grown-up learning,' Beth said.

After an hour or so Jake would close his book and take his things into the bedroom. He had to get his sleep, he pointed out. Beth was aware that he timed his day so that he would not still be having his lesson when she broke off to help Will to get up, and that he would be out of sight when Will took his place in the living-room. So he slept, or worked at his reading and writing in the bedroom, until halfway through the afternoon when Will went back to bed for a spell. Thus the two of them managed to meet each other only for supper, after which Jake usually went down to the alehouse at Batty Green until it was time for him to go to work.

He grew to enjoy the company at Batty Green, though he had to keep a watch on how much he drank. If he turned up the worse for it he'd be barred from working in the tunnel, let alone being in charge of other men. What he hated about going to Batty Green was leaving Beth with Will.

Weekends were the worst times for him. The children, whose weekday presence made the hours go quickly, did not come in at the weekend, and as Saturday was Jake's night off it meant that he was at Nazareth from the time of his return from work on Saturday morning until he went back on Sunday night. Will, who was improving with every day, was up most of the time. There was no getting away from him. It was not that there were open quarrels between the two men, but Will was truculent, sniping. Jake, for Beth's sake, held himself in check against the jibes.

On a Saturday morning in mid-December Will was at his most awkward. He had breakfasted in bed and risen soon afterwards – he was capable now of getting up without Beth's help. When he came into the living-room, Beth and Jake were at the table eating breakfast. Jake, between mouthfuls, was reading aloud from the book which lay open in front of him.

'Very good!' Beth said. 'You really are coming on, Jake. I'm going to write to Mr Crossland to ask him for a couple of more advanced readers. You and Tom are both ready for them.'

'Quite a cosy little scene,' Will said. There was a wealth of ill-feeling in his voice.

Beth looked up.

'Come and sit down, Will. I'll pour you another cup of tea.'

'Oh, I wouldn't want to interrupt,' Will said.

Jake rose, pushed back his chair.

'I've finished.'

'Don't go,' Will said. 'Read to us! What is it then? The cat sat on the mat? The cup is on the table? Oh no, table's a long word, isn't it? But never mind. With all the attention my wife gives you you'll soon be able to read long words.'

Jake picked up the book and snapped it shut.

'Jake is doing exceptionally well,' Beth said steadily. 'He can be proud of himself.'

'Hooray!' Will said, clapping his hands.

Jake went into his bedroom and gave vent to his anger by flinging the book from one side of the room to the other, where it fell on the floor behind the bed. He didn't mind the taunts to himself – they were childish and deserved to be ignored – but he couldn't bear it that Beth had to suffer the indignity of them. Once again he wondered whether he should leave, find other lodgings. That shouldn't be too difficult. Yet not only did he not want to leave Beth, he didn't want to cut himself off from the new world which even his elementary reading had opened up for him. He was greedy for more. He wanted to take it in in great gulps.

Presently he went back into the living-room. Beth was busy cutting out letters which the children would assemble into words on Monday morning; Will sat, unoccupied, in his chair. Jake broke the silence between them.

'I won't be in for my dinner. I'm going down to Batty Green.'

'Oh!' Beth said. 'I thought . . . but you will be back for supper?'

'I'm not sure,' Jake said. 'If I'm not, don't bother to save me any.'

'We won't!' Will said.

As Jake emerged from the warmth of the hut, the cold was biting, the air frosty under a clear sky. The gain was that with the temperature so low, the snow, where it had been trodden, lay as hard as iron underfoot. It was possible to stride out, and this Jake did, pulling his hat down over his ears, muffling his neck and chin in his scarf. It was the wrong time of the day for the tram to Batty Green, but it didn't matter. He needed exercise, the more vigorous the better. Even more he needed, for a while, to put a distance between himself and Nazareth.

The snow was kind to the moor, forgave what men had done to it. It softened and blurred the mean-looking huts, the pieces of machinery, the spoil-heaps of rubble which had been taken out of the tunnel and the cutting. Since it had stopped falling, blotting out the landscape, the men were back at work in the cutting and on the viaduct. There was no time to be lost. On his right as he walked, the white peak of Whernside stood magnificent and strong against the sky. The sight of it put his frets and troubles into perspective. There was nothing, he thought, that the mountain had not seen in its long history.

Reaching Batty Green his first stop was at the café. The keen air had made him hungry and he ordered meat-and-potato pie. When he had followed that with a plate of jam roly-poly and washed it down with a mug of tea, he left, and walked around the Saturday market. It was disappointing that, though there was money in his pocket, there was nothing he wanted to buy. He hesitated at Burgoyne & Cocks's stall, wondering whether he would buy biscuits to give to the children on Monday, but in the end he decided against it. Even so small a thing could be taken the wrong way by Will Seymour.

Sally Roland, he noted, was not serving on the stall. He wondered why.

When he walked into the alehouse he had the answer. There she was, drinking port-and-lemon in the company of a man whom Jake recognized as a regular.

When Sally saw Jake she smiled, and called out to him in a ringing voice.

'Why, just look what the cold's brought in! If it isn't the handsome stranger himself!'

She moved up on the bench to make room for him, and when he sat down she leaned close to him, her body soft and warm against his, her heady perfume assailing his nostrils. Jake made no attempt to move away from her. Suddenly, surprising him, her warmth was what he needed.

'What would you like to drink?' he asked her.

'Well,' she said, 'by rights I should be going – in fact I shouldn't be here in the first place!' She laughed merrily at the thought. 'I escaped from the stall at the insistence of this gentleman here. He thought I looked in need of something and he was quite right. I've been slaving away all morning. I'm quite worn out!'

'You don't look it,' Jake said.

She looked as fresh as a daisy and as pretty as a rose. Though she wasn't his style, he told himself, there was no denying that she was attractive, and not least because she was so full of life, exuding vitality from every pore.

'So what's it to be?' he asked.

'Well, since you're so pressing,' Sally said, 'I'll have another port. It warms you up, port does; and it's cruelly cold behind that stall.'

They sat a long time, Sally with a third glass of port, Jake with as many pints of ale. Why not, Jake thought? It was warm, the company was congenial – though the man who had originally brought Sally into the inn had wandered off.

'He knows when he's outclassed,' Sally said. With one finger she delicately stroked the back of Jake's hand, and when she looked up at him her eyes were as soft as velvet, the pupils wide and dark. There was a moment of silence between them and then it was broken by a man who came into the inn and made straight for Sally. Jake recognized him as an assistant who worked on the stall.

'If it's all the same to you, miss, and if it wouldn't be interrupting anything, it's about time you got back to work! We'll be packing up soon. If you don't come we'll be off to Settle and you'll be left behind here.'

Sally Roland sighed.

'What's the world coming to when a girl can't have a few minutes to talk to an old friend?'

'A few hours more like,' the man said. 'Well I've told you, we'll be off soon!' He turned and marched out.

'I'd better go,' Sally said mournfully. 'He can be awfully mean. He might tell on me. Not that I'd mind being left here – if the conditions were right, that is.'

Jake went with her to the door, watched her walk across to the stall. She'd passed a bit of time, and pleasantly too. He felt grateful to her. He went back to his seat and ordered more beer. There was nothing to hurry back for.

The following Friday there was a hitch with the bricklaying in the tunnel, which made it necessary for Jake and two of his men to go in to work on Saturday afternoon to make up for it. It was late in the evening when he reached home. He was not sorry to have been away. Will had been at his most unpleasant all week and Jake doubted if today would have been any different.

'There's a letter for you, Jake,' Beth said as soon as he entered. 'Elsie Drake brought it. She said a young woman at Batty Green asked her to deliver it to you.'

She knew who the young woman was since Elsie had lost no time in telling her.

'It was that hussy from the bakery stall,' Elsie had said. 'No better than she should be, I'd say. I'd advise him to steer clear of that one! I was in two minds whether I'd deliver it.' But she *had* agreed to do so, if only because she hoped to learn later what was in it.

Jake opened the letter. He looked at it long and hard. There was no way he could read it. What made it worse was that it was in Sally's scrawling handwriting, not in clear print as in the reading book.

'What is it?' Beth asked. 'Not bad news, I hope?'

'I don't know,' Jake confessed. 'I can't read it. Only the odd word here and there.'

'Oh Jake! Do you want me to read it for you?' Beth offered.

He handed her the letter. There was nothing else he could do. She read it aloud in her soft clear voice: 'Dear Jake, Am pleased to tell you Mr Armitage is coming here for Christmas and he would like to see you. My aunt says to tell you you will be welcome. You can have a lift on the cart from Batty Green on Christmas Eve. Yours truly, Sally.'

Will listened with interest.

'What a good idea!' he said.

As she handed the letter back to Jake Beth's heart plummeted with disappointment. She wanted him to be in Nazareth for Christmas. She would not enjoy it without him.

'What shall you do?' she asked.

'I'll have to think about it,' Jake said.

13

On Monday Jake had still not decided what he would do about Sally Roland's invitation; how he would answer it, which he must do soon. Of course he wanted to see Armitage, there was no doubt about that, but, equally, he didn't wish to be away from Beth at Christmas. Yet what right had he to be with her? None at all. And would his presence help the situation between man and wife, or would it simply make matters worse?

Monday was not an encouraging day. When Jake arrived home from work Will was, unusually, already at the table, drumming his fingers while he waited for breakfast which Beth was preparing at the stove. The aroma of frying bacon filled the room.

'He's here!' Will called out with ill grace as Jake entered. 'Perhaps we can eat! I'm starving.'

'It won't be more than a few minutes,' Beth promised. 'Good morning, Jake! Did you have a good night?'

'Very good,' Jake replied. 'Everything went well. I'll just wash my hands and face. I won't be long.'

When he returned his breakfast was already on the table. Will had started on his.

'A fellow at work gave me the piece of rope I've been wanting,' Jake said towards the end of a meal which had drifted into silence because it seemed there was no topic on which Will could be pleasant. 'It's all I needed to finish off the sledge.' He had been making the sledge for a couple of weeks now.

'I thought it might be a good idea to go down to Jericho and bring the children back on it. It won't take them all, but the four smallest could ride. It isn't easy for them, walking in the snow.'

'Rubbish!' Will said. 'Pampering them, that's what it is. When I was a child we walked in the snow.'

'We also sledged,' Beth said. 'And we didn't often have snow like they have it here. I approve of the idea, Jake, though it won't be easy, pulling four up the steep bits.'

'Oh, our hero won't baulk at that!' Will said nastily. 'Showing off his strength!'

Jake gritted his teeth.

'I had thought,' he said to Will, 'that I could take you on the sledge down to Batty Green – if you can face the cold, that is. You could have a drink, it would make a change.'

'And you'd pull me back, would you?' Will said truculently.

'That's right.' He could manage that. Will had lost a lot of weight during his illness.

'No thank you,' Will said. 'When I go down to Batty Green it'll be on my own two legs, not carted around like a baby!'

Jake shrugged.

'Please yourself.'

He rose from the table and went into his bedroom, where he was working on the sledge. In better weather he would have been able to work outside, but now his bedroom was his refuge. He was not welcome in the living-room. Fifteen minutes later he had fixed the rope, and was ready to leave to collect the children.

'Like a bloody Saint Bernard dog!' Will grumbled as Jake left. 'Anyway, why do we have to have the kids in this weather, coming in with snow on their boots, dripping all over the floor? Why can't they stay at home?'

Beth, who had been standing in the doorway watching Jake set off on the new sledge down the hill towards Jericho, thinking how much she'd like to be on it, closed the door with a bang and whirled around to confront her husband.

'When did you ever care about the state of the floor, Will Seymour?' she demanded. 'When did you ever have to do anything about it? And why are you so horrid to everyone? To the children, to me, to Jake Tempest. You never have a pleasant word. So why?'

'If you can't see the answer to that, you must be bloody blind!'

'Well I can't! So tell me! And I don't like your language.'

They faced each other, two angry people. Will gripped the arms of his chair. Why am I like this? he asked himself. Why is it I resent the children? And why do I hate Jake Tempest – which I do?

'Tell me! Tell me why!' Beth persisted.

He knew the answer. He'd spent more time thinking about it than he'd ever been given credit for, but it was so difficult to admit it in words.

'Tell me!' Beth repeated.

'Very well, I will! It's because you belong to *them*. You belong to those kids and to that man.'

There was more to it in the case of Jake Tempest. Jake knew what had happened on that night. Oh, he might not have been told, he didn't suspect Beth of that, but he knew all right. He would always know. And every day he stands in judgement of me, Will thought bitterly.

'You don't belong to me any more,' he said.

'I look after you,' Beth said. 'I do everything I can for you.'

'I know. But it's not what I want, not all I want. You don't belong to me.'

234

'I don't belong to anyone,' Beth said. Her voice was tight.

'You used to! You were mine once! You were all mine!'

Beth heard the anguish in his tone, but she could not say what he wanted to hear.

'I belong to myself,' she said.

Nor was that what she wanted. Desperately, she desired to belong to someone. It was unbearably lonely not to. During the day she had the children, and she was happy with them, but at the end of the day they went back to their homes and parents, where they *really* belonged. As for Jake – well, it was better not to think about Jake. She simply thanked God that he was there.

'Beth,' Will said suddenly. 'Can't we go back to where we were? I'll try to do better, I really will.'

Beth shook her head.

'We can't do that. We can't go back.'

'Why can't we?'

'You know why!'

'Then can't we make a fresh start? Can't we begin again?'

'I don't know,' Beth said. How can we, she thought. But how could they continue to live like this? It was slowly eating away the life from both of them. In the silence which followed they continued to look at each other, trying to find the right words. It was Beth who spoke first.

'You're right! We have to make a fresh start. We can and we must. We can't go on as we are, nor can we mend everything at once. But at the very least we could try being decent to each other! *And* to the rest of the world.'

'I'll do that!' Will said eagerly. 'Oh, Beth, I'll do anything! But being agreeable to each other is not all I want, and you know it. We are man and wife.'

'It's all I can give you,' Beth said. 'At least for now.'

He didn't hide his disappointment; he couldn't.

'It *is* a start.' It was Beth who was pleading now.

'Very well,' Will said, though reluctantly. 'I'll try to be patient.' He didn't know how he would manage it, but he would try.

'It's almost Christmas,' Beth said. 'Season of peace and goodwill. At least let's get through Christmas decently.'

'And who knows what the New Year will bring?' Will felt suddenly hopeful. He wanted to put his arms around her, but he knew he mustn't attempt it. He must go slowly; he would win her back, but it could only be little by little.

He stretched out his hand and took hold of her wrist, pulling her closer to his chair. Beth, though she tried not to, flinched at his touch, but she steeled herself not to jerk her arm away.

Then, to her relief, she heard the children shouting outside the hut, and in the same instant the door burst open and they trooped in, Jake with them. Will's hand was still on Beth's arm as she stood beside him. She knew at once that Jake had taken in the scene. When he looked at her, and she returned his look, she saw disbelief in his eyes.

It was seeing Will's hand on Beth's arm, and the pleased look on Will's face, as though he had won a prize, and the fact that Beth stood there, not attempting to escape, which decided Jake to accept Sally Roland's invitation. The rest of the day confirmed him in his decision. Though there was embarrassment in Beth's manner, he sensed a difference in her relationship with Will. It was notable also that Will treated both him and the children with unusual civility. Why would he do that? Why the sudden change?

Before he went to work at the end of the day, when the children had left and Will was back in bed, Jake said: 'I've made up my mind, Beth, I *will* go to Settle for Christmas.'

'Oh, Jake!' Beth looked at him in consternation. 'I'm disappointed. I'd hoped we'd have a good Christmas here.'

'I daresay you will,' Jake said. 'But I don't think you need me.'

'Oh, but you're wrong,' Beth said. 'As for the rest, as for anything else . . .' she hesitated, 'it's not what you think.'

For one brief moment Jake's self-control deserted him.

'Oh Beth, how *can* you? How *can* you?'

'I've told you, it's not what you think,' Beth repeated. 'It's just that . . . I have to make an effort.'

'Don't try to explain,' Jake said. 'You don't have to. If things are . . . improving . . . then I suppose I have to be pleased for you.'

He was not being honest with himself. He was not pleased. How could she do it? How could she let Will touch her? He thought of the night he had seen her lying on the floor, bruised and bleeding, her clothes torn from her body. This new thing, whatever it was, would not work and, in his heart, did he want it to? One thing for sure, however; he didn't understand women. It seemed to him he never had.

On Christmas Eve Beth gave the children a party. She had baked mincepies and gingerbread men, and in the afternoon Elsie and Phoebe joined them and everyone played games; Nuts in May, Kneel on the Carpet, Blind Man's Buff. Jake agreed to be 'blind man' and Beth tied a scarf around his eyes so that he could see nothing as he clumsily tried to catch the children. It was Phoebe Grange he caught, and there was no difficulty in guessing who she was, both from the feel of her and her scent.

'No trouble in catching *her*,' Elsie muttered to Beth. 'Every move he made, she stood in front of him!'

Will could not take part in the games, but he watched. It seemed to Jake that he watched Beth the whole time, his eyes hungrily following her every move, though he kept himself in check and said nothing untoward.

This is no place for me, Jake thought. Let me get away. He would go down at once to Batty Green, and if Sally wasn't ready to leave, then he'd wait in the alehouse until she was.

As soon as the game ended he said: 'I'll have to go. I mustn't miss the cart.'

'We'll all have to go soon,' Elsie Drake said. 'It's almost dark already.'

'The children can borrow the sledge over Christmas, if they want to,' Jake said.

'Can I be the driver?' Tom asked.

'I suppose so,' Jake agreed.

Tom was certainly the most skilled at it. He knew which way and how far to bend when taking a corner. He knew which leg to put out, and when. He was as skilled with the sledge as with everything else he did, yet, surprisingly, not one of the other children resented his superior skills. He was far too popular for that.

Jake stood in the doorway.

'Well then,' he said, 'I'm off! Merry Christmas everybody!'

It was Beth's eyes he sought, as she stood at the back of the room. In them he saw the longing he felt in his own heart. Why am I going, he asked himself? Why am I leaving her? I'm a fool!

When he reached Batty Green Sally was not yet free.

'I'll not be more than a half-hour,' she said. 'We've nearly sold up. You wait at the Welcome Home and I'll join you there.'

It was the better part of an hour before she appeared. Once, he left his seat and went to the door to look for her. The short December day had already given way to night. Lanterns and flares lit the area around the green and Burgoyne & Cocks's stall was still at work, with a straggle of last-minute customers waiting to be served. Jake returned to his place.

'I might as well have another tot of rum while I'm waiting,' he said to the landlord. It would be his fourth, and the landlord, full of seasonal goodwill, was doling out generous measures. But what did it matter, Jake asked himself. He was not driving the cart.

Sally came at last, fresh and bright, no sign on her that she had been at work from early morning.

'Here I am!' she announced cheerfully. 'I hope you're going to buy me a nip of something before we set off. I need something to keep the cold out. It's perishing out there!'

'Then come close to the fire and get warm before we leave,' Jake suggested.

He ordered a drink for her, and for the driver of the cart who had followed her in.

'But we mustn't linger,' the driver said. 'The horses are rarin' to go, and I'll not be sorry to see my own bed, I can tell you.'

By the time they left Ribblehead and set out on the road to Settle the moon was rising, though what gave even more light than the moon was the covering of snow. It shrouded everything; fields, barns, hedges, near and distant hills. Pen-y-ghent brooded like a huge white animal over the broad valley beneath. Leafless trees stood out stark and black against the whiteness.

When he had last travelled this road, Jake thought, on his way to look for a job on the railway, the fields, even the high slopes of the fells, had been dotted with sheep, shining white in the sunshine. Now they had been brought down and were just discernible, concentrated near the farm buildings, close at hand for feeding and where an eye could be kept on the pregnant ewes.

'Have you thought,' Jake asked Sally, 'that in the south, where it's coats warmer than here, they'll be birthing their first new lambs at Christmas? We shall have to wait until the beginning of April, when the new grass comes through.'

Sally yawned. 'No I haven't,' she admitted. 'I don't give a lot of thought to sheep.'

'It's a whole new world down south,' Jake said.

'It's a world I'd like to see,' Sally said. 'I'd like to go to London. Things happen in London. Nothing ever happens here.' But something would over Christmas if she had her way.

She pulled up the rug which she was sharing with Jake, and underneath it she cuddled closer to him, settling her head against his shoulder.

'Oooh, I *am* cold!' she said. 'My poor hands are numb. Can't you warm them?'

Jake took her hands in his, first one and then the other, and began to chafe them.

'Mmmm!' Sally murmured. 'That's better!'

'Here,' the driver said, 'we'll have a little drink. Keep us all warm!' He took a flask from his pocket and handed it around.

'I shall be tight!' Sally giggled.

It was almost midnight when they reached Settle. Sally had fallen fast asleep, leaning heavily against Jake. The driver stopped the horses at the end of the narrow street which led to Sally's aunt's house. Mrs Sutherland was at the door to greet them.

'I thought you were never coming!' she said.

When they stepped into the house Jake looked around, expecting to see Armitage. There was no sign of him.

'Has Mr Armitage gone to bed?' he enquired.

'Mr Armitage?' Mrs Sutherland said. 'What—?'

Sally interrupted quickly.

'Oh, Aunt Jane, don't say he hasn't shown up!'

'Shown up?' Mrs Sutherland looked nonplussed.

'Anyway, we need a nice cup of cocoa,' Sally said. 'I'll help you to make it.' She grabbed her aunt's arm and dragged her into the kitchen.

'What's all this about Mr Armitage?' Mrs Sutherland demanded. 'Who said he was coming?'

'Why, surely *you* did, Aunt Jane?' Sally was wide-eyed.

'I said no such thing, and you know it! What are you up to, Sally Roland?'

'But I was sure you said Mr Armitage was coming here for Christmas! Oh dear, I expect you said it would be nice *if* he came.'

'As far as *I* remember – and since I'm not yet in my dotage I remember quite well – Mr Armitage's name has never passed my lips. All you said to me was that Mr Tempest was at a loose end and wondered if he could come for Christmas.'

'Oh, I *have* got it wrong!' Sally was the picture of contrition. 'Auntie, please don't give me away. Can't we leave it that he just hasn't turned up? Who knows, he might do so.'

'And why would he do that, without a word of warning?' Mrs Sutherland asked.

'Well . . . well, because it's the kind of thing Mr Armitage might do. Oh, please don't say anything. Jake will be so cross if he thinks I've made such a stupid mistake!'

'Mistake, is it?' Mrs Sutherland said. 'You could have fooled me! But since he's here, and there's no getting back to Ribblehead until after Christmas, I'll keep quiet – though for his sake, not for yours. I wouldn't want to make him feel uncomfortable.'

All the same, she thought as she poured the cocoa, and since it was Christmas Eve added a tot of rum to each cup, someone should warn him. But how could *she* do it? The silly girl was her niece, her sister's child. She was fond of her sister.

The minute he had finished his cocoa Jake stood up.

'If you'll excuse me, I'll be off to bed. It's a pity about Mr Armitage. Perhaps he'll arrive tomorrow.' There was something strange about it, he thought, but he was too tired to work it out now. Also, he had drunk too much.

Mrs Sutherland took a candlestick from the sideboard, lit the candle and handed it to Jake. 'The same room, Mr Tempest. Sleep well!'

Sally yawned, stretched her arms wide.

'I must go to bed too,' she said. 'I'm dead beat. Merry Christmas, all!'

She preceded Jake up the narrow staircase and at the door of her room she turned around and faced him, holding her candle so that its soft light lit up her face beneath her cloud of dark hair, adding even more brightness to her eyes.

'Is it good night then, Jake?' she said softly. 'Suddenly, I'm not tired.'

'I am,' Jake said. 'Good night, Sally.' He brushed past her and went into his room.

Five minutes later he had blown out his candle and was in bed. He lay on his back and watched where the moonlight crept around the gaps at the sides of the window blind, lighting up a corner of the wall. For a moment he was wide awake, his thoughts as clear as crystal. He thought of Blea Moor under the snow, of the hut at Nazareth and, beyond and above all, of Beth Seymour. Heart, soul and body he longed for her. Why had he been such a fool as to leave her to come to Settle, even for Armitage?

Hers was the last face he saw, superimposed over everything, her eyes looking directly into his, before he was suddenly pitched and drowned in an ocean-deep sleep.

At first, less than an hour later, he was scarcely aware of it when Sally climbed into his bed. The feel of her soft, naked flesh, the curves and hollows of her body against his, had the quality of a dream, a dream in which she led him, guiding his movements, and he simply obeyed. It was not until her hands began to explore his own body, at first slowly and then with increasing urgency, and always with expertise, that he emerged from the dream into reality.

It was too late. He had awakened with a desire, the strength of which consumed him. His whole body, joined with hers, impelled him, goaded him, towards one end. He was hardly conscious of her except as, at one and the same time, fuelling his need with her own swift crescendo and, finally, in a burst of a thousand shafts of light, fulfilling it.

'Beth!' he cried out. 'Beth!'

Sally, lost in her own fulfilment, did not hear him, or perhaps didn't care. She had got what she came for.

Jake left Settle immediately after breakfast on Boxing Day.

'Must you go so soon?' Sally asked. She was still half asleep and would have liked to have stayed in bed, preferably in Jake's bed. But there would be other times. She was certain of that.

'Yes, I must,' Jake replied. 'I have to work tonight, and since there's no cart going to Ribblehead today, I need an early start.'

On a visit to the inn on Christmas Day he had managed to arrange a lift as far as Horton, but from there, the greater part of the journey, he would have to walk. He was not sorry to be leaving. He would have liked to have done so on Christmas Day itself, but out of politeness to Mrs Sutherland, to whom he could not offer a reasonable explanation for such a premature departure, he stayed.

No mention was made between himself and Sally as to what had occurred on Christmas Eve. It might almost not have happened except that, throughout Christmas Day, Sally exhibited a new-found proprietorial manner towards him – a hand on his arm, a turn of speech – which did not go unnoticed by her aunt. But when she went to his bedroom door that night, she found it locked.

'Jake!' she called softly. 'Jake, it's me!'

There was no answer. No matter, Sally thought. There was no way he could hold out against her for ever.

As Jake walked the long road to Ribblehead, thoughts raced around in his mind. He thought of Sally Roland, and what had happened between them on Christmas Eve. The memory didn't perturb him unduly, much of it still seemed dreamlike. Nor was it, he reckoned, an isolated experience for her. She was no novice, he could swear that. It was no more than an episode in which he had given her what she wanted. Or rather, he thought, she had taken it.

He dismissed Sally from his mind and thought about Armitage. For what mysterious reason had he not shown up? The memories of Armitage crowded in as he tramped the road they had walked together. I liked him, he thought, I wouldn't have reckoned he'd have let me down.

And where was Patrick Mahoney? Hopefully he was in Ireland, safe with his family.

Most of all, though, Jake thought about Beth, and his thoughts quickened his step. He had surprisingly little feeling of having been unfaithful to her, for whatever had happened to his body, no other woman had for a single second entered his mind. It had been

Beth, all Beth. His one vivid memory was of how he had called out to her. In his own way, in his heart, he had been faithful to her.

It was dark before he reached Ribblehead, and when he walked over Blea Moor the snow had started to fall again. When he reached Nazareth and saw the light in the hut it was like coming home. Never mind that nothing would be ideal, that he was returning to a situation he had been glad to leave only two days earlier; Beth would be there.

In the week after Christmas Mr Pennington, the Company representative, called again.

'I'm glad to see you looking so much better, Mr Seymour,' he said. 'What we want to know now is just when you'll be back to work. It's been a long time . . .'

'And don't think I'm not aware of that,' Will interrupted.

'The Company's been very patient,' Mr Pennington said, 'but there is a limit, and it's my duty to tell you that we're fast approaching it.'

Beth felt sick with fear at his words. To her mind, though he was greatly improved, Will was not yet fit to return to work; but if he didn't, would they lose the house?

'As a matter of fact, I'm fit enough right now,' Will said. 'And eager to go!'

'But with the weather taking such a turn since Christmas,' Beth interrupted, 'I've heard all work's at a standstill, except in the tunnel.'

Elsie Drake's husband, and Phoebe's husband who worked in the cutting, had both been laid off. Since Boxing Day there had been another foot of snow, and strong winds had caused drifts too deep to dig through. Even in the tunnel, Jake said, the snow had blown down the shafts. And to get to and from the tunnel was a hazard in itself.

'That's true,' Mr Pennington conceded. 'But the minute the weather improves . . .'

'Then you'll see me back on the job,' Will promised.

'We'll leave it at that, then,' Mr Pennington said. 'I trust you'll not let me down.'

'I'll not do that,' Will spoke with confidence.

'You'd think he'd have something better to do than come here in this weather,' Beth said when Mr Pennington had left.

The fresh snow had taken its toll of everything. It was impossible for the children to get to and from Nazareth, even with the help of Jake's sledge. Once or twice Beth had managed, with difficulty, to get to Jericho, but aside from that the reading lessons had come to a standstill. Jake had benefited from that, since Beth had been able to spend extra time with him. He had forged ahead with both reading and writing.

But no lessons for the children meant no money from them, and there was very little left in Beth's purse. That was balanced, in a way, by the fact that there was hardly any food to be bought. It was a week now since supplies had come from Settle or Ingleton.

'It's a good thing I laid in all I could afford to,' Beth said anxiously. 'I don't know what we'd do otherwise. In any case, what we have won't last long.'

The worst thing, she thought, would be if she ran out of flour.

'As long as I have flour,' she said, 'I can make some sort of bread. There won't be much nourishment in it, but it'll help to fill us. And the potatoes are nearly finished, and what few *are* left are going bad.'

There had been no milk for several days. She wished she had done the same as some others on the moor, and kept a goat. When the spring came, if ever it did, she would consider that.

It was mid-February before the weather improved

and the desperately needed supplies came through to Ribblehead. News that there was food to be had spread like wildfire.

'I'll take the sledge down to Batty Green,' Jake offered. 'I can bring back goods on that.'

'Bring back anything you can lay hands on,' Beth said. 'Spend what money we have. If there's one thing we've learned it's that food is of more use than coins in a purse.'

Jake went first to Burgoyne & Cocks's stall, joining the throng of people waiting to be served. When at last it came to his turn Sally Roland stepped forward to attend to him. He had been observing her while he waited. She looked pale and tired, she had very little chat for the customers, which wasn't like her. But no wonder, he thought; there were so many of them, impatiently pressing to be served.

She attended to his purchases, handed him his change, then said: 'I've got to see you! I'll be in the Welcome in half an hour. I'll sneak off. Mind you're there!'

'What is it?' Jake asked. 'Is something wrong?'

'You can see I'm too busy to talk now,' Sally said. 'I'll see you later.'

He was waiting when she came in.

'You look cold,' Jake said. 'What would you like to drink? A hot toddy?'

Sally shuddered.

'Lemonade, nothing more. My stomach won't take it.'

'I'm sorry to hear it,' Jake said. 'What caused that?'

She gave him a hard look.

'You did!' she said. 'You caused it. I'm pregnant!'

Jake stared at her in horror.

'Don't look at me like that,' she said. 'It takes two to make a baby. And you helped to make this one all right. We hit the jackpot first time!'

'Are you quite sure?' he said. 'Couldn't you be mistaken?'

'Of course I'm sure!' Sally snapped. 'You'd be sure if you were sick every morning and felt like death the rest of the day!'

'I'm sorry!' He couldn't think of words to say.

'I'm sure you are,' Sally said. 'So am I. But sorry won't mend it and there's only one thing will. You'll have to marry me. I'll be forced to tell Aunt Jane any day now, and if I tell her I'm in the family way and there's no husband in sight, she'll turn me out of the house, lock, stock and barrel! You wouldn't want your bairn to be born in the workhouse, would you?'

14

At the end of February Will Seymour was able to return to his job, as were all the men working on the viaduct. The weather was still cold, though not quite so bitter, and the wind, ever-present at Ribblehead, though it had hardly abated in strength, had changed to a thaw wind from the west. It was now possible to clear the area around the viaduct of the deepest snow so that work could begin again – greatly to the relief of the men, who had been too long without wages.

To Will, there were several new faces, but that didn't surprise him. On every part of the line men came and went, finding the work too hard and the weather impossible to bear. He was pleased, therefore, to find that Joseph Clark, whom he had known from the beginning, was still there.

'My word,' Will said, 'it's come on by leaps and bounds since I was last here!' He nodded towards the viaduct.

'How long is it you've been away, then?' Joseph asked.

'Four months. You couldn't see anything above the ground then. Everything was in the foundations.'

'Sure, foundations are what count in life,' Joseph said soberly. 'Without strong foundations, what can stand against the enemy?'

Joseph, Will noted, had not lost his turn of phrase which made his utterances sound as though they were straight from the scriptures.

'The enemy in this case being the weather,' Will said. 'Well, you're right there, Joseph!'

Now, the piers of the first few arches, built from huge blocks of black limestone, had risen as far as the 'springing', the point at which the arches would begin to curve.

'I reckon Mr Farrer must have made a fortune from all the limestone on his land,' Joseph said. 'A gold mine under his feet!'

At the point where the arches turned, limestone gave way to bricks, made from local shale and clay at the brickworks which had been set up close by on Batty Green.

'They reckon the brickworks can turn out twenty thousand bricks a day if need be,' Joseph said. 'And they *will* be needed before the viaduct and the tunnel are done.'

The wooden scaffolding which had surrounded the piers while they were being built had been dismantled, moved along the line of the viaduct to support new piers. These first few, merging into their arches, now stood silhouetted against the winter sky; tall, independent, strong, and seemingly indestructible. Will felt a lump rise in his throat as he gazed up at them. Dear God, how he had missed all this! No-one would know the half of how he felt. But now he was back where he belonged! From now on everything would get better.

The thought of Sally's pregnancy pressed down on Jake like a heavy black cloud, a cloud which would not go away, which would at any moment break on his head and drown him. He knew what he must do, he had known from the moment she'd broken the news. Without loving her, and while loving another woman, he must marry Sally Roland. It was the right thing, the only thing, payment for a brief pleasure which he could hardly recall. There was no escaping it and he didn't intend to try to.

In the week since it had happened he had relived that scene in the inn a hundred times.

'You'll have to marry me!' she'd repeated, almost in hysterics. 'I'm not bearing a bastard child – and you know it's yours, you can't deny it!'

'I'm not denying it. I will marry you.' He'd spoken quietly, hoping she'd do the same.

'You promise? God's honour?'

'I promise!'

She'd relaxed immediately, and at once begun to make plans.

'I'll tell my aunt the minute I get home. First off there's the date – it'll have to be soon! And then all the other arrangements.'

She'd prattled away fifty to the dozen. In his numbed state he'd hardly heard any of it. She could arrange what she liked and he'd go through with it because he had to.

That had been a week ago, a week in which, whenever he thought about it, which was most of the time, he envisaged a hopeless, loveless future stretching before him – for he doubted that Sally, in spite of her eagerness to be married, had any more love for him than he had for her. And now it was Saturday again, and she would be at Batty Green, and he must see her. There was no avoiding it. It wouldn't be fair to her and also, if he were to do so, it was inevitable that she would seek him out at Nazareth.

This he could not allow to happen for the simple reason that he had not yet told Beth. For the whole week he had, insofar as it was possible while living in the same house, avoided her. He had spent hours in his room, ostensibly at his reading practice. He had taken long walks, in spite of the weather. He had jumped at the offer to work a few hours' overtime in the tunnel. What he had not been able to avoid was sitting down to meals with Beth and Will, though he had never felt less like eating.

Now, he pushed away his dinner plate and rose from the table. Beth broke off eating and looked up at him.

'Why, Jake, you've hardly touched your dinner! Is it not to your liking?'

'It's fine,' Jake said. 'I'm not very hungry.'

'You've been picking at your food all week,' Beth said. 'Is there anything wrong? Do you not feel well, is that it?'

It was the perfect moment to tell her. Will was at work, the children didn't come on a Saturday, her concern was obvious, but he couldn't bring himself to do it. How could he possibly begin to say the words?

'I'm all right,' he said. 'A bit tired. It's been a hard week.'

That at least was true. With the beginnings of the thaw the snow on the hills had begun to melt, overflowing the streams which ran down the moor. Most of the week they had been working in several inches of water in the tunnel.

'I've one or two things to do,' he said, 'and then I'm going down to Batty Green.' He would tell her the minute he returned, when he'd seen Sally again. He promised himself he'd put it off no longer.

He went into his bedroom, closed the door behind him, sat on the bed and put his head in his hands. What a mess he was in! What a mess!

Sunk in his thoughts he hardly noticed time passing, nor did he hear the knock at the door of the hut. It was only Beth's tap on his bedroom door, and her voice calling out, which roused him.

'Jake! There's a visitor for you!'

The surprise in her voice might have warned him, but it didn't. When he walked into the living-room, there, standing by the table, a broad smile on her pretty face, was Sally Roland.

'I thought I'd pay you a visit!' she said brightly. 'I've never been to Nazareth, never seen where you live. So the boss gave me an hour off for good behaviour, I cadged a lift on a cart, and here I am! Oh Jake, I've got such a lot to tell you!'

Beth, standing between them, looked as stupefied as she felt. Sally, seeing her expression, gave a peal of laughter.

'He's not told you! I can tell he hasn't! Jake, you are a naughty boy not to have told your landlady!'

'Told me?' Beth queried.

'Why, that we're to be married,' Sally announced. 'There! What do you think of that?' There was a smile of pure triumph on her face.

Beth stared at Sally. It was impossible. She didn't believe it. Yet there was no doubting Sally's utter certainty. Beth switched her look to Jake. He was staring at her, and the expression on his face confirmed everything Sally had said. But there was no triumph in him. He was the picture of abject misery, his eyes pleading with her as his gaze was locked in hers. She felt the blood drain from her face, felt herself go cold.

For a moment Sally did not exist. She and Jake were the only two people in the room.

'Why?'

Beth's lips framed the word, but no sound came. She started to tremble, and desperately hoped it didn't show. She put out a hand to the table, to steady herself.

But what right have I to feel like this? she asked herself. I have no right at all. I'm a married woman. Jake is a free man. There is no way we can mean anything to each other.

Yet that was manifestly not true. He meant the world to her, and she knew that she did to him. Nevertheless, she told herself firmly, he is free to marry whoever he chooses, and I am not.

But why Sally Roland? She knew at once that this girl would never make Jake happy, nor he her.

Stop it, she told herself. It isn't your business. She took a deep breath and forced herself to speak.

'Congratulations! And now I'm sure you must have a great deal to discuss so I'll leave you to it. If you'll excuse me, I have jobs to do in my bedroom.' She was amazed at the steadiness of her voice.

She went into her bedroom, closing the door firmly behind her, and lay on the bed, face down on the pillow, her hands tightly clenched.

'I can't stay,' Sally said. 'I've got to get back to the stall. I thought you'd come back with me, and then when I've finished work we can meet in the Welcome Home. I've so much to tell you!'

'I can't come now,' Jake said. 'I've things to do. I'll be down by the time you finish.'

He had to speak to Beth. There was no way he could leave the house without seeing her alone.

'There'll be a tramway down quite soon,' he said. 'You catch that and I'll follow.'

Beth heard the outer door open and close, and then there were no more voices. They have both left, she thought. She was mercifully alone, and now she could let the tears flow. At first she didn't hear Jake when he knocked on her bedroom door.

He knocked again, urgently.

'Beth! Please! I must talk to you!'

There was a moment's silence before she came to the door. She looked him straight in the face, then walked past him into the living-room, sat in the armchair, leaning her head against the sheepskin which draped the back of it. Her face was as white as the sheepskin but her eyes, though red-rimmed, were now dry.

'Why?' she said. 'Tell me why.'

'She's having a baby.'

'And you . . .' It was difficult to speak. 'You're the father?'

'Yes. But there's more to it, Beth . . . It was the only time . . . Never before, nor since.'

He wanted to tell her that it was she, and only she, who had been in his mind. Sally Roland had had nothing to do with it.

'I don't want to hear any more,' Beth's voice was quiet, but firm. 'I hope . . . I hope you will be happy.'

'You know I won't!' Jake cried. 'How can I be happy without you – or you without me?'

'You mustn't say these things,' Beth said wearily. 'I'm a married woman and you are about to be a married man.' And a father, she thought; and *she* is to have your child, and I am never to have a child. She wished he would go away. Suddenly, she was unbearably tired.

'When will you leave?' she forced herself to ask.

'I'm going down to Batty Green shortly,' Jake said.

'I don't mean that. When will you move out?' She wanted it to be soon; she couldn't bear to go on seeing him every day.

'I don't know. I haven't thought about that,' Jake confessed.

'It will have to be before you're married.' There was no way he could spend even one night under her roof, married to Sally Roland. Surely he understood that?

'I understand,' Jake said, reading her thoughts. But did she realize what it had been like for him all this time, seeing her go into the bedroom with Will, and even more so now that they were on better terms? 'I understand that only too well,' he said.

'I know you do,' Beth acknowledged. 'So the sooner you go, the better for both of us.'

'I don't know where,' Jake said, thinking out loud.

'The Company might rent you a hut,' Beth suggested. 'Or perhaps someone at work might know of something. If you'll allow me to ask her, Elsie Drake might help. There's no spare room in her house, but she knows a lot of people.'

How can I do this? she thought. How can I sit here, calmly discussing how he can most conveniently go out of my life? She was not calm inside. She felt sick – sick in her stomach and sick at heart.

'Then please ask Elsie,' Jake said. 'I'd be grateful.'

In the event, she saw Elsie Drake on Monday morning when she brought her children and Phoebe Grange's.

'Well, that's a right turn-up for the book!' Elsie said. 'I'm astonished – though having a slight acquaintance with Sally Roland I shouldn't be. She's been after him quite a while. I fancy she knows how to play her cards, that one!'

Beth, settling the children to their work, said nothing.

'Have you thought of having them here?' Elsie asked. 'You'd get twice the price for the same room, with the two of them.'

'It's out of the question,' Beth said sharply. 'Will wouldn't countenance it. Especially now that he's back at work. He never wanted lodgers.'

'Well, I'll ask around,' Elsie said.

The answer came later that same day when Phoebe Grange arrived to collect the children.

'I hear your lodger's wanting a new berth – a double berth at that! Well here's one who'll be more than willing to accommodate him – and his new wife of course, when he gets her. And I've got the room.'

'What will your husband say?' Beth asked. She did not like the thought of Jake living in Phoebe's house. But it has nothing to do with me, she reminded herself.

'Oh, he's easy enough!' Phoebe said. 'He'll not mind. When would Jake want to come?'

'*If* he decides on it,' Beth said. 'And that's up to him . . .'

'I'd make him very comfortable!' Phoebe interrupted.

'I'm sure you would. *If* he decides on it, then I daresay the sooner the better, though you'll have to ask him. He's taken two days off work to go to Settle. He'll not be back until tomorrow night.'

'Making arrangements for the wedding, I expect,' Phoebe said.

'I daresay,' Beth's voice was stony.

It was decided between them that Jake and Sally should be married in Settle on a Saturday in March. Sally, half-serious, put forward the idea that they should have a gipsy wedding. It was little more, as far as she knew, than jumping hand-in-hand over a broom laid on the ground, or some said laid on a fire.

'It would be fun,' she giggled. 'Though what if my skirt touched the broom and gave me away?'

'What do you mean?'

'If the bride's skirt touches the broom as she jumps, it shows she's not a virgin.'

'We're not marrying over the brush,' Jake said firmly. 'Since we're doing this for the sake of the child, I want to be sure it's legal.'

'The gipsies reckon it's legal,' Sally said.

'We're not gipsies. We'll be married in front of the registrar!'

Though Jake was adamant about this, in every other detail – what she should wear, what he should wear, the choice of the wedding ring, where they should spend the two-day honeymoon she insisted on (she chose Skipton as being the liveliest place they could afford) – Sally had her own way. Though Jake did his best for her sake to show interest, his heart was not in it. Only when he thought of the child did his hopes rise a little. The child was to be the salvation of this unsought marriage.

Accepting the fact that Jake must be close to his work, Sally agreed to lodge with Phoebe Grange. 'For the time being,' she said. 'Though we *will* want our own place sooner or later.'

She had given up her job with Burgoyne & Cocks a week before the wedding, and after their short stay in Skipton, stopping only briefly to see Aunt Jane in Settle, she returned with Jake to Jericho, where she settled down to being a married lady.

What came as a shock and a surprise to Sally was Jake's total ineptitude in the marriage bed, especially in view of their lovemaking on Christmas Eve. True, she had taken the initiative then, and she did so now, but with no success whatever. In the end, it was always he who turned away from her, leaving her angry, humiliated, frustrated.

'You're no man!' she stormed. 'You're worse than useless!'

'I'm sorry,' he said in a quiet voice.

He had not willingly humiliated her. He could not help it that he had no desire for her and that, in the end, her very presence in his bed, the warmth and voluptuousness of her body, were anathema to him. When he turned away from her it was with relief.

'It's very strange,' Phoebe said to Elsie Drake. 'I mean, I can't help noticing what goes on – or in this case what *doesn't* go on! After all, I live in the same house, and we all know how thin the walls are!'

'You are awful, Phoebe,' Elsie protested. 'I daresay it's because she's pregnant. You know how strange women can be when they're pregnant.' It was inconceivable to either woman that the failure could be on Jake's part.

'Oh, I do!' Phoebe agreed. 'With my first I was always craving for kippers! Any time of day or night I fancied kippers, and actually I hate the things. But I never went off bed. After all, it's the one time you can have as much as you want without worrying you'll end up in the family way.'

'That's true,' Elsie said. To her way of thinking, Phoebe had a one-track mind. And she must know something I don't know, she thought, or how would she have only two children?

'No,' Phoebe mused, 'there's more to it, but I can't fathom what it is.'

When Phoebe took the children to the Seymours' hut the next day, Beth said: 'I'll only be able to have them for the morning tomorrow. In the afternoon Mr Tiplady's having a party, and I'm invited. I'm to meet Miss Herbert, the new schoolteacher at Batty Green. She comes from Nottingham. You know they've opened the school there?'

'I've heard,' Phoebe said. 'But she'll do no better with the children than you have with our little lot. It's a miracle how they've come on – and especially young Tom Drake. He's a genius, that little lad!'

'He's certainly remarkably gifted,' Beth agreed. 'He'll go far, given the chance.' She would always be proud, she thought, that she had given him his first chance by teaching him to read and write.

'And now Jake Tempest can read, there's no holding him, either. Never his head out of a book, even if he's read it twice before. And he helps my two a lot. He's a good teacher.'

'Shortage of books is the trouble now,' Beth said. 'I'm going to have a word with Mr Tiplady and Miss Herbert, see if something can't be done about it.'

How wonderful it would be, she thought, if she could discuss with Jake the books they'd read. She knew of no-one with whom she could talk about such things. Will, though he was able to read, wasn't interested. But she mustn't complain about Will, even to herself. Since he was back at work he was a changed man.

On the following Saturday afternoon Sally said to Jake: 'I want you to take me down to Batty Green this afternoon. I'm bored here. I want to see a bit of life!'

She had stayed in bed until after eleven o'clock, eaten a substantial breakfast, then spent the time since in trying on dresses and doing her hair. She was quite pleased with her reflection in the mirror and didn't see why someone other than the deadly dull inhabitants of Jericho shouldn't have the pleasure of seeing her.

'Of course I'll take you,' Jake agreed. 'As for being bored, why don't you find something to do? Why don't you make a start on making baby clothes, for instance?'

Sally pulled a face.

'I hate sewing. I'm no good at it.'

'It will have to be done, sooner or later,' Jake said. 'Perhaps we'll find some material this afternoon.'

'Don't rush me,' Sally protested. 'I'll do it when I have to – or more likely I'll get someone else to do it for me. Some women are quite clever at that sort of thing. I'm not.'

'Be ready in twenty minutes,' Jake said. 'We'll catch the tramway.'

'What I *would* like,' Sally said persuasively, 'is a new dress! I haven't a thing fit to wear. I suppose you *do* want your wife to be smart?'

'You always look good,' Jake said truthfully. 'And what's the use of buying a new dress now? It wouldn't fit you for more than a few weeks. But after the baby's born, *then* I'll buy you a new dress!'

'Oh the baby!' Sally said petulantly. 'I'm sick of hearing about the baby. It's all you can talk about.'

Jake bit back a sharp retort. With his failure in bed

added to the fact that she was carrying the baby, she had every right to be difficult.

They caught the tramway. At Batty Green they went first to Burgoyne & Cocks's stall where Sally, from her exalted position as a married woman, was condescendingly gracious to her former colleagues. Then, when they had walked around a little while, Sally wanted to go into the Welcome.

'I'm tired,' she complained. 'I want to sit down. And I'm thirsty.'

'What about the tearoom?' Jake suggested.

'I don't want the tearoom. I might see a few old friends in the Welcome. You don't grudge me that, surely?'

'Of course not!' Jake said. But when she chose to drink gin instead of the lemonade he suggested, he remonstrated.

'Gin is bad for the baby.'

'Oh, not the baby again!' she said. 'Always the baby! Well if you won't buy me a proper drink I know plenty who will!'

He ordered the gin, which she drank in one gulp then promptly asked the waiter, who was still at the table, for another. 'A large one!' she ordered.

After that Jake angrily refused to buy any more. While she was picking a quarrel with him he pulled her to her feet, took hold of her arm, and escorted her out of the inn.

'You're next door to drunk,' he said. 'We'll walk around until your head's cleared and then we'll catch the tramway home.'

It was while they were walking across Batty Green, he holding her arm, that they came face to face with Will and Beth Seymour.

Jake raised his hat.

'Good afternoon, Beth, Will.'

'Good afternoon, Jake, Mrs Tempest,' Beth said.

Will raised his hat to Sally while eyeing her with appreciation. She was a looker all right, he'd always thought so when he'd seen her on the stall, and now there was a becoming flush on her cheeks and a sparkle in her eyes. What did she see in a sobersides like Tempest? But then what did the rest of the women see in him? There was no accounting for women's tastes.

'You're looking very well, Mrs Tempest,' he said.

She flashed him a smile.

'Please call me Sally! I'm feeling very well. On top form!'

She spoke with slow deliberation, rather too carefully. Beth gave her a quick look, and then looked from Sally to Jake.

'My wife is rather tired,' Jake said. 'We're just going to get the tramway back to Jericho.'

'My wife,' Beth thought. Did he have to say that? Did he have to rub it in? And his wife was without doubt intoxicated.

'My husband and I still have some shopping to do,' she said, slipping her arm through Will's.

She was lovelier than ever. Jake's heart ached at the sight of her. Her hand on Will's arm gave him a swift stab of jealousy.

'Then we mustn't keep you,' Jake said politely. He raised his hat again and the two couples walked away in opposite directions.

'She's a toffee-nosed bitch!' Sally said.

'Stop it!' Jake snapped. 'I won't have such language!'

'Could it be that you have your eye on her?' Sally teased. 'Could it be that *she* could make a man of you? But if you have, you're wasting your time! I can't see that husband of hers letting her out of his sight. He looks at her as though he could eat her.'

'You're talking a load of nonsense,' Jake said. But he had observed Will Seymour's attitude towards Beth. It made him sick.

It was not until late that night that the encounter with Jake and Sally was mentioned in the Seymour home, though all evening Jake had been in Beth's thoughts.

'She's a bonny lass, that Sally Tempest,' Will said. 'He's on to a good thing there. When is the baby due?'

'How should I know?'

Will looked up in surprise at the sharpness of her voice.

'Women usually do know these things,' he said mildly.

'Well I don't. It's not my concern.'

Of course she knew. Hadn't she calculated almost to the day when Sally would have her baby? Jake's baby. Hadn't she imagined what it would be like, carrying it all those months in her body; feeling it move against her, giving birth, feeding it, clothing it. There were days when she was tormented by such thoughts, and having met with Jake and Sally face to face, today was the worst of them.

In spite of herself, her eyes filled with tears, which brimmed over and ran in slow drops down her face.

Will looked at her in consternation.

'Oh, love! I've upset you! It's the baby, isn't it?'

Beth nodded. It was more than the baby, but there was no way she could tell him that. He stepped towards her and put his arms around her, and for once she didn't push him away, but accepted the comfort he offered her.

'It was stupid of me,' Will said. 'I should have had more sense. I know how much you want a child, and believe me, love, so do I.'

He stroked her hair gently, and for a while there was a silence between them, which he was the first to break.

'Couldn't we . . . ? Couldn't we try again?' He was quiet, hesitant. There was something in him at this moment of the Will Seymour she had first known.

'Surely,' he pleaded, 'I've not to spend the rest of my life without your forgiveness for one mistake, however terrible? And I know it was terrible.'

She felt a sudden overwhelming pity for him. He had been punished enough, and wasn't she at the same time also punishing herself? The time had come to put Jake out of her life. He was lost to her, and she must face that, let him go. And perhaps, she thought, if I forgive Will, God will also forgive me, and send me a child.

'Please take me back,' Will urged.

'I will try,' Beth said.

Without a word she took his hand and led him to the bedroom.

It was no good. From the moment Will began to make love to her, from the moment his hands moved over her body, she felt herself stiffen. She felt sick, there was an ice-cold sweat on her face. She tried with all her strength not to show her feelings, her terrible anathema, and then it seemed that she succeeded, for Will, seemingly oblivious of her rigidity, went through with the act to the very end. When it was over and he lay on his back with his eyes closed, she got out of bed, crawled into the living-room, and was sick.

'I must say,' Phoebe said casually to Sally one Monday, 'you seem to be having an easy pregnancy.'

She was getting ready to take the children to Nazareth, picking up Elsie's brood on the way. Sally was still at the littered breakfast table – and it will still be littered when I get back, Phoebe thought. Madam won't lift a finger to clear it.

'I mean,' she continued, 'not a bit like mine. I was sick from beginning to end with my two – *and* I had indigestion, strange fancies, swollen ankles, the lot! You seem to escape everything!'

'Would you rather I was wretched?' Sally demanded.

She wished they would all shut up about her pregnancy. She was fed up hearing about it.

'Not at all,' Phoebe said pleasantly. 'I just thought . . .'

Another thought struck her. She was not sure where it came from. She left the sentence unfinished.

'I'm off,' she said. 'Elsie will be waiting.'

'I've had a strange thought,' she said a few minutes later to Elsie. 'Strange – but I'm sure it's true!'

'What?' Elsie asked.

'Sally Tempest. I don't think she's pregnant at all. I reckon it's been lurking in the back of my mind for some time, and this morning I was sure it was true!'

'Not pregnant?' Elsie said. 'Then why would she pretend she was? What would she gain from that?'

'A husband,' Phoebe said. 'I'll lay any bet that's why he married her. He's certainly not in love with her, that's as plain as a pikestaff!'

'You could be right,' Elsie said thoughtfully. Come to think of it, there had been a number of signs, small things which didn't quite fit. Nevertheless, it was strange.

'What shall you do?' she asked.

'Tackle her with it. I shall tell her that if she doesn't tell him, I will.'

'It's not our business,' Elsie pointed out. 'In any case, he'll find out in the end.'

In the middle of the morning Jake came in from work.

'You're late,' Sally said. She was still sitting at the table.

'I did a couple of hours' overtime,' Jake said. 'We can do with the money. As soon as I've had my breakfast I suggest you get dressed and we'll go for a walk. It's a lovely day. The fresh air will do you good – and the baby.'

Sally leapt to her feet, made a wide, impatient

sweep of her arm and knocked a cup and a plate to the floor.

'Damn the baby!' she shouted. 'Damn and blast the bloody baby!'

Jake stared at her.

'Whatever do you mean? Are you ill? Has something happened?'

'I'm not ill. More to the point I'm not pregnant! There *is* no baby!'

'No baby?' What could she mean? He didn't believe what he was hearing.

'There never was a baby. If it's anything to do with me, there never will be.'

'But you said . . .'

'I pretended. It wasn't difficult, you were as green as grass. If I hadn't said I was expecting you wouldn't have married me, would you?'

'No,' he admitted. 'I wouldn't.'

'It was what I wanted. I wanted to be married and I wanted to be married to you. Little did I know! I was a fool. I can see that now.'

And I am trapped, Jake thought. Now and for ever I'm trapped.

He turned swiftly and walked out of the house.

That same afternoon Phoebe was standing at the table, ironing, while Sally was sprawled in the armchair.

'Aren't you worried that Jake hasn't been home for his dinner?' Phoebe asked. 'He doesn't usually miss a meal.'

'He'll be all right,' Sally said calmly. 'If you must know, we quarrelled. He stamped out in a mad hig.'

'Quarrelled?'

'I'm sure you're dying to know what about. Well, I'll tell you. It'll come out sooner or later.'

Phoebe put the iron down, the better to listen.

'I think you'd more or less guessed I wasn't

266

pregnant. Well it's true, I'm not! I told him and he wasn't best pleased, so off he went! But he'll be back.'

Phoebe opened her mouth to speak, and at the same moment Elsie Drake, the children following her, came in at the door. Elsie could tell at once there was something going on, she could feel it in the air, even if Phoebe hadn't given her a meaningful look.

'Am I . . . am I interrupting something?' she asked tentatively.

'I'm sure Phoebe'll be pleased to tell you all about it,' Sally said.

Once again, before Phoebe could speak, the door opened and Jake came in. The three women stared at him.

'Have you heard the news?' he asked. His voice was tight with anxiety.

Phoebe found her voice.

'News?' Surely he wasn't going to mention Sally in this way?

'It's very bad. Smallpox! There's smallpox at Sebastopol.'

Sebastopol was the next settlement down the tramway from Jericho, not far from Batty Green.

'Smallpox?' Elsie said.

The three women stared at him in horror.

'A woman and her two children. Real bad, they say. They've taken them into the hospital at Batty Green. It could spread like wildfire! They say there's a suspected case at Batty Green.'

'What are we going to do?' Sally asked, shuddering. If you got the smallpox and you didn't die of it, it left you horribly disfigured. 'What are we going to do?' she repeated.

'First and foremost,' Jake said, 'you must none of you go near Sebastopol, or to Batty Green. And above all, you mustn't take the children there.'

15

Within the week everyone, in every settlement from Batty Green to Tunnel Huts, had heard the news that a third child of the woman from Sebastopol had gone down with smallpox and that the mother and all three children had died of the disease.

Terror gripped the population of Ribblehead and many, especially single men who did not find it too difficult to move on, packed their bags and fled.

'I'd like to do just that,' Elsie Drake said to Beth, 'but with four children where would we go – and who would have us when they knew where we came from? But you and Will could leave.'

Beth shook her head.

'Will wouldn't hear of it! He says if we're fated to catch it, we'll catch it, and if not we won't.'

'And what about you? What do you think?'

'I shall stay with Will,' Beth said. 'It's my duty. All the same, I think we should take every precaution, keep close to home, not mix with other people. And I reckon it would be wise, with our menfolk meeting with others at work, if we abandoned the children's reading classes for the time being. Just to be on the safe side.'

'I suppose you're right,' Elsie said. 'They'll miss it, though. Especially Tom. He won't know what to do with himself.'

'I shall miss Tom,' Beth admitted. 'He's a wonderful pupil. In fact, one of these days I know he'll outstrip me. But I'll tell you what I'll do. I'll lend him a couple of my own books in the hope that they'll keep him going until all this is over.'

Not for the first time since that awful day when Jake had brought the news, fear gripped Elsie's heart.

'Oh Beth, when *will* it be over?' she said. 'And what's to come before it is?'

Beth put her arm around Elsie's shoulders.

'I don't know, love. We must hope and pray.'

Thus, each and every family tried to keep itself to itself, within the confines of its own house. It was not entirely possible. Shopping had to be done, food to be bought, the men had to go to work and mix with others. And then there were a few, like Will Seymour, who seemed untouched by fear, who went about as always, mixed where they pleased.

But in spite of the precautions most people took, and probably because the infection had already begun to spread before anyone was aware of its existence, the disease went through the settlements like wildfire. Not one shanty town was spared. In Jericho a father of three was taken; in Nazareth a young woman, pregnant with her first child.

'They're building two huts at Batty Green just for the smallpox cases,' Jack Drake said one day when he came home from work. 'I reckon it won't be enough. I reckon they'll have to build more.'

Elsie looked at her children, three of them sitting at the table, Baby Joe asleep in the cradle. What more could she do to keep them safe? She would do anything in the world, she would give her life if need be, but what *could* she do? She had never felt so helpless.

'The people on this railway line have had more than their fair share of sickness and death, accidents and suffering since it started,' she said. 'And the innocent pay just as much as the careless and the guilty. What about that little girl thrown off the tramway when the engine was derailed? She only came to see her aunt at Sebastopol. She was killed before she'd begun her visit! And the man killed in the tunnel, and two at the viaduct? What about them?'

'Hush, love!' Jack said. He saw the older children watching and listening open-mouthed. 'Accidents will happen.'

'Far too many, if you ask me. If you want to know, I've begun to hate the railway. And now why does God have to send the smallpox?'

'More likely the devil sent it,' her husband said. 'We must pray to God that we escape it.'

Jake returned from work a day or two later with the news that there were two more cases at Tunnel Huts. Sally shuddered with horror at the thought.

'How do I know *you're* not bringing it home with you?' she accused him.

As far as she could, though it was next door to impossible, she held herself aloof from everyone in the house, constantly washing herself, laundering her clothes, cleaning the bedroom.

'They reckon we should whitewash the inside of the hut,' she said to Phoebe. 'It keeps the infection away. So why don't we?'

Phoebe shrugged.

'What has to be, will be. I reckon those who are most frightened of it will catch it first!'

'You only say that because you know I'm terrified,' Sally said. 'Well I admit it! Anyway, I'm going to whitewash our bedroom, or rather, I shall get Jake to do it.'

It would be safer, she thought, if she were to spend most of her time in there. Nothing could free her from sleeping in the same bed as Jake, though mercifully not at the same time, since he was still on the night shift and slept during the day. In any case he now made no move at all to be intimate with her. They were like strangers, forced to inhabit the same place.

'Go ahead,' Phoebe said. 'Though if you don't mind a bit of plain speaking I can think of better things to do in a bedroom!'

'You would!' Sally retorted. 'It's all you *do* think about!'

'And if you don't think about it a bit more, you stand to lose your man!' Phoebe warned her. 'Why would anyone be such a fool as to lose Jake Tempest?'

'Mind your own business!' Sally snapped. What did Phoebe know about it, anyway? And she'd certainly got the wrong end of the stick this time.

When she asked Jake about whitewashing the bedroom, he said: 'Since Phoebe agrees, all right. She's the landlady.'

'Don't I know it,' Sally grumbled. 'She thinks that gives her the right to say anything she likes to me. Oh, why can't we leave here? Why can't we move right away? I tell you, it's not safe!'

Jake made no reply. There was nothing to be said. Although in his worst moments he thought he would flee to the far side of the world, though not because of the smallpox, there was no way he would leave the area with Sally in tow. It was bad enough that he was tied to her, but while he remained here he had his job, his workmates and most of all, though she was unattainable, there was Beth. To know that she was nearby was enough to keep him at Ribblehead. Further than that his thoughts wouldn't reach.

During the rest of that spring, and into the early summer, the smallpox epidemic did not abate. Day after day the sad processions left the shanty towns and the hospital, making their slow way to the church at Chapel-le-dale where the vicar was kept busy reciting the funeral rites over the victims as they were interred in the small burial ground.

'They say,' Will Seymour said to Beth, 'that the

churchyard won't hold any more. The vicar's asked the Earl to let him have a bit more land, otherwise there'll be nowhere to bury the dead.'

The hospital at Batty Green had been doubled in size, and every known measure to contain the disease had been put into operation, but still the epidemic continued, until one day in early June, when the weary doctor to whom every awful day for several weeks had merged into the next awful day, so that all time seemed the same, looked up from the records he was penning after his round in the hospital, and spoke to the matron.

'Do you realize, Mrs Halifax, that we have some empty beds, and that the last death from smallpox was a fortnight ago?'

'I do indeed, Doctor,' Mrs Halifax said.

'Can we dare to think it's over at last?' he said slowly.

'I think we can. Almost over. The Lord's name be praised!'

'I could wish the Lord had acted sooner,' the doctor said.

'It seems our ordeal is behind us,' Mrs Halifax said.

The doctor shook his head.

'For some the worst is to come. They have to face life without their loved ones; children, fathers, mothers. However far they go back to their homes, they'll never forget the Settle–Carlisle railway.'

'I think we could start the reading classes again, don't you?' Beth said to Elsie Drake.

'I'd be glad of it,' Elsie said. 'My lot are fast what to do with themselves, and I know Phoebe feels the same about hers.'

Beth was glad to see the children back. With no lodger to look after, and Will out at work all day, and having been confined to Nazareth, time had hung heavily on her hands. At Mr Tiplady's party she had made friends with Miss Herbert who had given her much useful advice, and had lent her more equipment. Now that the smallpox was over, she would be free to go down to Batty Green, and to meet up again with the schoolteacher.

On the children's first day back at Nazareth she quickly discovered that they had fallen behind with their reading, which was no more than she expected. They needed constant stimulation. Not so Tom, of course. He stood before her now with shining eyes.

'I finished both the books you lent me,' he said. 'Then I'd nothing to do, so I wrote two stories.'

Beth prickled with excitement as he handed them to her. 'I'll read them as soon as I can,' she promised.

When she had settled the children down with lists of words they were to copy and learn, she started to read. From first word to last she was engrossed, and when she had finished she called to Tom to come and stand beside her.

'Are these the first stories you've written?' she asked.

'Yes, Mrs Seymour,' Tom said.

'And did anyone help you?' It was a silly question, she thought. Who was there to help him?

'Oh no!' Tom said. 'I did them on my own. I didn't show them to anyone else.'

'Well, I reckon they're very, very good,' Beth said. 'There are one or two mistakes, and I'll point them out to you, but nothing important. Thank you for letting me read them. I enjoyed them very much.'

He went crimson with pleasure.

'I'd like to be an author when I grow up,' he said. 'I'd like to write books.'

'And I don't have the slightest doubt that one day you will,' Beth assured him. 'Now wouldn't it be a nice idea, when you got home, if you were to read these aloud to your mother? Show her what you can do.'

And I must speak to Elsie myself, Beth decided. This child's gifts are too precious to be wasted.

'He really needs more education than I can give him,' she said later that day to Elsie. 'He's hungry for it. Will you let me speak to Miss Herbert and Mr Tiplady about him?'

'Well of course – if Jack agrees, that is.' She couldn't think how she came to have such a clever son. There was no-one in the family like that.

'I'm proud of him,' she admitted to Beth. 'Of course I am. But I'm glad he's a nice boy, a loving boy, as well as a clever one.'

'He's certainly that,' Beth assured her.

'What could the teacher and the Missioner do for him?' Elsie asked. 'Would they give him more lessons?'

'I don't know,' Beth said. 'What Tom needs is to go to a good school, a really top-class school where he'll be stretched. And it's possible Mr Tiplady might be able to arrange that. There are scholarships, and I'm sure he could win one, so you'd not have to pay.'

Elsie looked at Beth in dismay.

'You mean he'd have to leave home?'

'In term time,' Beth said. 'He'd come home for the holidays.'

Elsie shook her head.

'I don't think me and Jack would like that. We want him with us.'

'But it would be a wonderful chance for Tom,' Beth said.

'Well, I don't know,' Elsie said doubtfully. 'But I'll talk to Jack when he comes home.'

'Will it be all right if I walk across tomorrow evening, see what you both think?' Beth asked.

'Of course. But we'll say nothing to Tom for the moment.'

The next morning Beth suggested to Tom that instead of joining in with the lesson he might like to

274

try to write another story. He jumped at the chance, and for the rest of the morning his head was bent over the table while he wrote, oblivious to anything else happening in the room. He ate his dinnertime sandwich while still writing, and by the end of the afternoon he had finished the story.

'Will you mind leaving it so that I can read it when you've gone?' Beth said. 'I mustn't keep you any longer. Your mother, and Mrs Grange, will be expecting you all home.'

In the summer weather there was no need for them to be accompanied by an adult. It was enough that Emily was in charge, mainly to ensure that they kept away from the shakeholes and to see that they didn't loiter. Beth stood at the door and waved them off and when they were out of sight she brought a stool out and sat down in the afternoon sun to read the story.

It was wonderful. He had a way with words and a natural rhythm in his sentences, and his main character, a boy of his own age, leapt off the page with reality.

She was still reading when Will came home, not pleased that his tea was not on the table.

'I'm sorry,' Beth said. 'I was carried away – and if you read that while I'm making the tea, you'll see why! I *must* do something for that boy!'

Will regarded her thoughtfully.

'It's not up to you, Beth. He's not your lad.'

'I know that!' Beth said.

'I'm going to the beck to have a good wash,' Will said. 'I'll be back in quarter of an hour.'

'I'll have your tea ready,' Beth said.

Will did not approve of her going to Jericho to talk to the Drakes about Tom, and flatly refused to accompany her.

'Leave people to bring up their own children,' he said. 'They know what's best.'

'I'm not sure that they do,' Beth said. 'I don't think that they recognize Tom's potential.'

It turned out she was wrong.

'We've thought it over,' Jack Drake said. 'Elsie's not totally sure, but I am. We should let the lad have his chance. We've got a good lad and we mustn't stand in the way of his future.' There was pride in his voice. 'So if there's anything you can do . . .'

'You'll not regret it,' Beth said. 'I'm certain of that. And he has a bright future.'

Next morning she was up early, served Will with his usual hearty breakfast, which he ate with relish. He scraped his plate clean, grunted with satisfaction, and rose from the table. As he turned, he winced.

'What is it?' Beth asked.

'Nothing much. A stiff neck; it hurts when I move it. It'll wear off.'

'Then you must wear a neckerchief,' Beth advised. 'The best thing for a stiff neck is warmth.' She searched in a drawer and brought out a clean neckerchief, red with white spots. She was about to hand it to him when she changed her mind.

'Come here,' she said. 'I'll tie it on for you!'

He stood there while she fixed it for him, adjusting the folds, carefully tying the knot. The feel of her cool fingers against his neck was balm to his spirit. He raised his hands and touched her shoulders and for once she did not flinch, or try to move away. After a second or two she stepped back and surveyed him.

'You'll do nicely,' she said. 'The neckerchief suits you. And if your neck isn't any better by the time you get back home I'll rub it with some camphorated oil.'

'That'll do the trick,' he said. 'You always did have healing hands.'

'When I've done a few jobs,' Beth said, 'I'm going down to Batty Green to see Miss Herbert and Mr

Tiplady about Tom. No point in letting the grass grow under my feet.'

'I've told you, love, you shouldn't interfere,' Will said. 'It's nothing to do with you. We should keep out of other people's business.'

'I don't agree,' Beth said. 'Not in this case. And I'm doing it for Tom's sake. It might not come to anything, but I mean to try.'

Will shook his head. There was no moving her when she set her mind to something, but he would say no more. Suddenly, this morning, they had had an easier relationship and he would do nothing in the world to upset that.

'I'm also hoping to get a nice bit of calves' liver while I'm down there,' Beth said. 'I'll have a good tea for you to come home to.'

'I'll be off then,' Will said.

Greatly daring, he leaned forward and kissed her lightly on the cheek. She did not return his kiss, nor did she rebuff him. When he left the hut she stood in the doorway and watched him walk – jauntily, and with a spring in his step – away down the moor.

As he walked Will breathed deeply, filling his lungs with the clear, moorland air. It was a perfect day, warm in the sun, but with a fresh breeze which rippled through the long grass away from the track and sent fleecy clouds scudding across the sky. He felt truly alive and full of hope. Things were going to change between himself and Beth. He could feel it in his bones. He began to sing, his clear, strong baritone startling a hare, which bounded away from him in long leaps. He sang all the way to the viaduct, not even ceasing when he passed people on Batty Green, not the least put out when they stared at him. It was a day for singing, and hadn't he something to sing about, whether the rest of the world had or not?

When he reached the pier on which he was working

he climbed the scaffolding to the top, twenty-five feet from the ground. He was still singing. Except for the stiffness in his neck, he climbed with ease. In spite of his long weeks in bed, he was in fine fettle again, his muscles strong, his body ready to do what he demanded of it.

His mate, Alf Reddy, was already at the top.

'You sound happy enough!' Alf said.

'And so I am,' Will said. He couldn't tell the other man what had made him happy; simply the fact that Beth had tied his neckerchief and had allowed him to kiss her cheek without turning away. It was such a small thing – but not to him. To him it was the start of something new, he was sure of it.

'Well, you'll not have much breath to spare for singing in this wind,' Alf said.

They were working on a king pier. Every sixth pier was a king, very much thicker than the other piers and designed so that if the arches, which would be built on them, were to collapse, only six would fall.

'I don't mind the wind,' Will shouted. They had to shout at each other, and even then they couldn't hear what was said. The wind carried their voices away. Though it might be no more than moderate on the ground, at this height it came in strong gusts.

'We should finish this one today,' Alf shouted.

They had reached the springing, where the arch would eventually be turned. The scaffolding would be taken down and erected again further along the line. It was said by some that there would be eighteen arches in the end, some said twenty-four. No-one seemed to know for certain.

Will paused for a moment to look around him before starting work. He did this every day, seeing the world from his vantage point high on the scaffolding. To the west was Ingleborough, rising up to a top as flat as a table. To the right of that he had a view of the narrow road from Ingleton up which, at this moment, a team of six great horses pulling a car heavy-laden with timber climbed the steep slope to Ribblehead. There were few buildings on the west side of the viaduct since the land was more than usually boggy.

He watched the horses for a while, admiring their strength. He felt that his own strength echoed theirs. Then he clambered around to the other side of the scaffolding from which he could view Batty Green with its huts, brickworks, stables, machinery, inns, people and, dominating everything, Whernside. It was only fractionally higher than Ingleborough, not as tidily shaped, but to Will it was all-powerful.

He was still staring at the scene when Alf called out to him.

'Well, are we going to start work today or not?'

'I'm coming! Anyway, don't nag. Rome wasn't built in a day!' Will spoke with good humour, smiling, as befitted this perfect day.

The smile was still on his face as he turned towards Alf, and as he tripped over a piece of scaffolding, lost his balance and plummeted to the ground. There was no scream, no sound at all from him as he fell as swift as a stone through the air.

When Will had left the house Beth completed her chores as quickly as she could, then changed into the new summer dress she had finished making only two days earlier – green-and-white, narrow-striped cotton with a white collar and cuffs and a deep band of tucking above the hem – dressed her hair carefully, bit at her lips and pinched her cheeks to make the colour come. She wanted to look her best for the occasion, if only for Tom's sake. Then she put Tom's three stories in her basket and set off down the moor.

Sheep, with fast-growing lambs still staying close, cropped at the lush green grass, flowers sprang underfoot. Beth breathed deeply, savouring the mountain air. It was a perfect day and she looked forward to the mission she was about to undertake.

When she arrived at the school, Miss Herbert saw her at once, and listened with interest while Beth told her about Tom Drake.

'I've brought the first three stories he's written,' she said. 'The first two he wrote at home with no prompting, the third he wrote in class but without help from me. It's only in the last few months he's learned to read and write.'

Miss Herbert examined the stories with interest.

'They're extremely good,' she said. 'Here's a child who'd be worth helping; but except in the very best of weather – and even then it's a long way for a nine-year-old – he'd not be able to do the journey to and from Jericho every day. In any case, I'd say he's streets ahead of my pupils. He'd need special teaching.'

'I thought so too,' Beth said. 'Then would you agree that I should speak to Mr Tiplady about the possibility of a boarding school?'

'If he were my child, that's what I'd do,' Miss Herbert said.

And if he were mine I'd leave no stone unturned, Beth thought. Nor will I, though he's not mine.

Mr Tiplady was equally interested, and even more impressed than Miss Herbert by the stories.

'And you say he's good at other things also?' he asked.

'At everything he touches,' Beth said.

'Then we must do something for him. It would be unChristian to let such talent go to waste. Will you leave it to me to make enquiries?'

'Gladly,' Beth assured him.

'Of course I shall call on him, and on his parents,' Mr Tiplady said. 'I must make sure what *they* want.'

'I know they'll be grateful,' Beth said.

She rose to go. Mr Tiplady saw her to the door. As she stood on the step making her farewells, the covered wagon, which was the ambulance, came tearing across the green from the direction of the hospital, the driver whipping up the horse to go even faster, while the man at his side violently rang a handbell. Those in the path of the ambulance scattered to right and left.

'Whatever—' Beth began.

'From the speed he's driving almost certainly an accident,' Mr Tiplady said. 'And in the direction of the viaduct. I must follow at once, see what I can do. Please excuse me!'

He ran into the street and set off in pursuit of the ambulance, as did several people who had been standing around.

Beth gasped in horror. The viaduct! Will! But even if the viaduct was the scene of the accident, why should it mean Will? There were dozens of men working on and around the viaduct. So she told herself as she ran with the crowd towards the scene.

The ambulance was there, also a police constable trying to control the crowd.

'Stand back there!' he shouted, waving his truncheon.

Beth, who attempted to run forward to where, several yards away, a man was being lifted onto a stretcher, was barred by the policeman's outstretched arm.

'I saw it happen!' a woman next to her in the crowd said. 'I was right here when he fell. From the highest bit of the scaffolding it was. I reckon it was a sudden gust of wind blew him!'

She paused for effect, then started again.

'His hat fell off, floated down on its own. It was slower than the man, tossed about by the wind. He came down fast, being heavy I suppose. He was wearing a red neckerchief. You could see it as he fell!'

She paused again, searching her mind for more revelations, but before they emerged Beth had already broken out of the crowd, dodged under the constable's arm, and was streaking across the space which separated her from the ambulance. The ground was boggy, the thick black mud covered her feet, but because she ran so fast she avoided being sucked in.

'A red neckerchief!' The words screamed in her ears. But didn't half the men in the area wear red neckerchieves? It didn't have to be Will.

She ran as fast as a hare, no-one could stop her. When she reached the scene the stretcher was being carried towards the ambulance, the body on it covered by a blanket. She tweaked back the blanket.

'It's Will! It's Will!'

'Stand aside, lady,' one of the stretcher bearers said. 'You're stopping us!'

'But it's Will!' she cried. 'It's my husband! He's dead, isn't he?'

'He's not dead, lady, but the sooner we get him to the hospital, the better. If he's your husband you can go in the ambulance.'

While the ambulance bumped and bounced over the uneven ground, she sat close to Will. He was unconscious, but breathing.

'Will,' she implored. 'Open your eyes! Look at me! Speak to me!'

'He can't hear you, lady! He's not conscious,' the ambulance man said.

She wiped the blood from his face with her inadequately small handkerchief until the man passed her a towel. Not until they reached the hospital and she was walking beside the stretcher, into the hut, did she notice that her new dress was soaked in blood.

Will died two hours later. Though she continued to call his name, begging him to speak to her, to open his eyes and look at her, he did not do so. He remained unconscious until the end.

Someone led her away, seated her in a chair, drew a screen around her; someone gave her tea which she could not drink. She remembered afterwards that at one point Mr Tiplady came in and spoke to her – and went.

She had no idea how long after it was – it could have been one hour or several – that the screen was pulled aside again and Jake was standing there. He held her by the hands, pulled her to her feet, and took her in his arms. When she came to her senses and looked at him, really looked at him, there was blood on him too.

Will Seymour was buried three days later, on a hot June day, not a puff of wind or a cloud in the sky. A surprising number of people walked behind the cart which bore the coffin the two miles to the churchyard at Chapel-le-dale; people from Nazareth and Jericho, drinking pals from the Welcome Home, workmates. The discovery that he had been popular raised Beth, for a minute or two, from her lethargy.

When it was over, Elsie Drake went back home with her to help serve the funeral tea, most of which she had also provided and made, since Beth could not bring herself to do it.

'I don't want a funeral tea!' she said.

'You've got to have one, love,' Elsie said. 'It wouldn't be respectful to Will, otherwise. What would people think?'

'It's barbaric!' Beth protested. 'Burying someone, then sitting down to eat and drink.'

'You're wrong there, love,' Elsie looked at Beth with compassion. 'It has healing qualities, the meal has. I don't quite understand why, but it helps to bring you back to normal. We have to go on, you know, choose how! But what I suggest is that you go to bed. There's no more to be done and it's been a hard day. I shan't be long before I turn in meself. I'll sleep in the other bedroom so as not to disturb you.'

'There's no need for you to stay the night.' Beth's protest was half-hearted.

'Oh yes there is!' Elsie contradicted. 'Just for tonight. Tomorrow I'll have to get back to Jack and the children.'

And what will I do tomorrow? Beth asked herself. No husband, no income. Will I even have a home?

But now she was too tired to think about it. All she wanted now was to sleep and sleep.

16

Beth's worries about keeping her home were solved within a week of Will's funeral.

It was a terrible week in which she could not summon enough strength even to leave the hut. The energy which had seen her through the funeral had quickly evaporated, leaving a dreadful lassitude. She cooked no meals; she didn't want to eat, and who else was there to worry about? She read nothing, not even the newspaper which Elsie brought her and which contained the report of Will's accident and death: she did no housework, went to bed early while the sun was still shining and stayed there until late next morning. Today, the sixth day, she was still in bed when Elsie paid her daily visit around noontime.

'I've brought you some broth,' Elsie said. 'You've got to eat whether you feel like it or not. It'll do you no good to starve. And as a matter of fact, you've got to bestir yourself, get up and get going.'

'Why?' Beth asked.

'I'll tell you why,' Elsie said sternly. 'Though it's not something I ever thought I'd have to say to you, of all people. It's because your house is getting mucky, you haven't washed a pot or dusted a shelf, and because you yourself are not too clean. Will you take a look in the mirror? When did you last put a comb through your hair?'

Beth made a movement with her hand as if she would like to push Elsie out of the bedroom.

'I can't be bothered,' she said.

'You've got to be bothered,' Elsie said. 'Oh, don't think I'm not sorry for you. Of course I am. Why do you think I come every day? And Phoebe, and Jake? Jake Tempest is sick with worry about you.'

Jake had been to see her twice since the funeral. She had nothing to say to him, she had nothing to say to anyone. He had spoken very little; just sat with her, held her hand, left quite soon because she clearly didn't want him there.

'So today I'm going to stay here while you get up, have a top-to toe wash, and put on some clean clothes. Then I'm going to help you put the house to rights. I'm not going to do it *for* you, I'm just going to give you a hand.'

'You can't,' Beth protested. 'You've got the children to think of.'

Elsie shook her head.

'No I haven't! Phoebe's taken the baby and she'll keep an eye on the others from time to time. Emily's looking after Tom and Ada, so they'll be all right.'

Elsie noticed the first flicker of interest in Beth's face at the mention of Tom's name. She seized on it at once.

'Tom did say he might walk over with the girls, later this afternoon.' It was pure invention, but it might work.

Beth sat up in bed, took a deep breath. Tom! She had been visiting Mr Tiplady on Tom's behalf when the ambulance had rushed by. From that moment to this she had not given him a thought. She had not even passed on to Elsie and Jack what Mr Tiplady had said of Tom's chances.

'It wouldn't be nice for Tom to see his teacher looking as you do at this minute,' Elsie persisted. 'Tom thinks a lot of you!'

'I'm sorry,' Beth said quietly. 'I'm sorry about all this, Elsie. You're quite right. I'll get up at once.'

'No need to be sorry, love,' Elsie said more gently. 'I only want what's best for you, we all do. I'll go and heat the water and bring the bathtub in. You can have a nice bath and wash your hair before anybody comes.'

Beth got out of the bed, then she turned her head and looked at it, and it was the sight of the bed which caused a great wave of guilt to sweep over her. I have not been a good wife to Will, she thought. I didn't try hard enough. Whatever he did, I should have tried harder.

It was this, she suddenly recognized, which she had been suppressing since the moment of Will's death. She had allowed no thoughts at all into her mind, pushing everything away, lying around in a near stupor instead of facing her true feelings. And even though she now recognized her feelings as guilt, added to anger for Will's sake that this should have happened to him in the prime of his life and after all he had gone through, she knew that in facing her emotions she would somehow come to deal with them.

She stripped the bed down to the bare mattress, in what felt like a stripping of herself, then she went into the living-room and stepped into the bath which Elsie had prepared for her.

'And while you're having your bath,' Elsie said, 'I'm going to make a start on the bedroom.'

When Beth was newly dressed in fresh clothes, her still-damp hair tied neatly back, the two women worked together throughout the afternoon until the hut was clean from stem to stern. Elsie looked around with satisfaction.

'I think we've earned ourselves a cup of tea and a slice of cake,' she said. 'And it so happens I brought some cake with me. Now confess it, love, you do feel better, don't you?'

'I admit it,' Beth said. 'Tired, but better.'

'And things will improve each day.'

Elsie said the words more from hope than from experience. She wasn't sure she believed them. She didn't know how she would face life if anything happened to her Jack.

'Tom didn't come,' Beth said when Elsie was about to leave.

'So he didn't,' Elsie said, sounding surprised. 'Happen he'll do so tomorrow.'

'I'll start the classes again soon,' Beth promised. 'Except that . . .' Her voice trailed away.

'What?'

'Oh, Elsie, how do I know how long I'll be able to stay here? Even if I can scrape up the rent money, which I doubt, will they let me keep the hut? Won't they want it for someone who works on the railway?'

'Meet that when it comes,' Elsie advised. 'In the meantime, if I were you I'd keep quiet. Say nothing until they do.'

Beth didn't have long to wait. Halfway through the next morning Mr Pennington called. When she opened the door and saw him standing there her first thought was one of thankfulness that the house, and she herself, were clean; her second one of frightening apprehension.

When his preliminary condolences were over he said: 'I've brought you some money – wages due to your late husband. It will tide you over for a bit. Four pounds six shillings.'

Beth took the money from him.

'Thank you.'

'And next we come to the question of the hut.'

Beth stood silent. She could think of nothing to say.

'Now as you know, Mrs Seymour, the Company's policy is to rent the huts only to someone who works on the line . . .'

'But Mr Pennington . . . !'

He held up his hand.

'Hear me out. We have two men, brothers, who've been working on number two contract, and now they've asked to work here, on number one. They're married men, but their wives aren't with them and they need lodgings. You've been a good tenant, Mrs Seymour. You keep things nice.' He glanced around with approval. 'And I fancy you keep a good table.'

'Oh I do, I do! I'd be pleased to look after them if you'd give me the chance!'

'Then we'll give it a trial, shall we? Their names are Alan and Charlie Miller. They'll be working in the cutting, south of the tunnel, so Nazareth will be handy for them. They could come tomorrow if that suits.'

'It suits me very well,' Beth said eagerly. 'I wonder . . . do you know what rent I should charge them?'

'That's up to you,' Mr Pennington said. 'As long as you pay your rent to the Company and keep a good house. Why not charge what you charged that other lodger you had? Tempest, wasn't it? What happened to him?'

'He got married. He and his wife lodge in Jericho.'

'Jericho?'

'With Mrs Grange.'

Did she imagine it, or did his eyes light up at the mention of Phoebe Grange?

Alan and Charlie Miller arrived next day, in the early evening after work. When Beth opened the door to them she thought for a moment that she was seeing double. Though they were not twins – later they told her that there was a year between them – they were as alike as two peas in a pod, both tall, strongly built, with bright blue eyes in faces deeply tanned from working in the open air, and when they simultaneously doffed their hats in a polite greeting, they both revealed thick blond hair.

'Please come in!' Beth said.

She liked the look of them, and over the next few

minutes it seemed they liked everything they saw, especially the room they would share.

'I reckon we'll be very comfortable here,' Alan Miller said.

'Very comfortable,' his brother echoed.

Beth quickly discovered that Charlie Miller echoed everything his elder brother said, always agreeing, never venturing his own opinion first.

'I'll cook you a good breakfast,' Beth said, 'make you sandwiches for your midday break, and give you a good meal when you get home from work.'

'That sounds very satisfactory,' Alan said.

'Very satisfactory,' Charlie repeated.

'And we won't be here at weekends, not unless we're working overtime,' Alan said. 'We only live in Skipton, so we can get home to our wives at the weekend.'

This time Charlie merely nodded in agreement. Beth wondered if, when he was in his own home, he repeated his wife's words or actually used his own. But he was amiable enough, they both were. She foresaw no trouble with them, they would be a source of both income and company in this lonely place.

'Well, I've been making a meal,' she said. 'It'll be on the table in half an hour if you'd like to be settling yourselves in, in the meantime.'

When they had eaten, both of them leaned back in their chairs, wide smiles of appreciation on their faces.

'That was very tasty, Mrs Seymour,' Alan said.

'Very tasty!' Charlie agreed.

'And now, if you don't mind,' the elder brother said, 'we thought we'd take a walk down to the Welcome Home.'

Oh no, Beth thought. Not drinking men! What would she do if they came reeling home? What if they did so every night? When she heard Alan's next words she realized her thoughts must have shown in her face.

'Oh, we'll not be long, Mrs Seymour! Two pints and that's our lot. We have a wife and two little ones apiece to provide for. It doesn't run to much drinking!'

When they had left, she cleared away, then started to lay the table. There was a knock on the door and when she answered it, Jake stood there.

'Come in,' Beth said.

He did so. They stood facing each other. He wanted to take her in his arms, to hold her close, never to let her go. He couldn't do it. What had he to offer her? She was free but now he was bound, that was the terrible irony of it.

'I wanted to see how you were,' he said. 'Are you all right?'

'All right,' he thought. What a feeble way of putting it! Of course she wasn't all right, and nor was he, and would they ever be?

'I'm fine,' Beth said. 'I have two new lodgers, did you hear?'

'Elsie told me,' Jake said. 'So where are they?'

'They've gone down to the Welcome.'

He gave her a sharp look. 'Then I'll stay 'til they return,' he said.

Beth smiled.

'It's kind of you, but you needn't. They'll be all right. They can't afford to drink much. And – admit it – it's livelier at the Welcome than it is here. They need it at the end of a day's hard work.'

All I need, Jake thought, is to be found within these four walls.

'But do stay a bit,' Beth invited. 'That is if you have the time.'

'Oh, Beth, you know I have the time for you! Always and for ever!'

'But you can't have,' Beth said gently. 'You have Sally.'

'Sally means nothing to me, nor I to her,' Jake said.

291

'Nevertheless,' Beth said, 'you *are* married to her, she is your wife.'

For several seconds they looked at each other without speaking. If he were to take me now, Beth thought, if he were only to put out a hand and touch me, I would be powerless.

'I was wondering,' Jake ventured, 'whether I might have more reading lessons?'

Beth shook her head.

'No. You don't need more lessons. You read as well as I do now. All we need is more books.'

Then, with a great effort, she said, 'Perhaps you shouldn't come here at all.'

'I can't promise that,' Jake replied. 'Please don't ask me to.'

He stayed with her until the brothers returned, which was not late, nor were they in the least the worse for wear, simply pleasant and affable. For twenty minutes the three men talked together about their work, while Beth sat and listened.

'It must be hellish in the tunnel,' Alan said. 'Give me the open air any time, no matter what the weather's like!'

'I've grown used to the tunnel,' Jake said. 'It's hard, but you can see it taking shape day by day. I'll stay with it until it's finished. I wouldn't want to work anywhere else.'

He looked forward, these days, to going to work; and when he had finished his shift, no matter how tired he was he didn't want to go home. The strenuous physical labour and the difficult conditions challenged him, suited his mood.

The following day Elsie Drake came to Nazareth, bringing a letter she and Jack had received that morning from Mr Tiplady.

'He's coming to see us tomorrow evening about our Tom,' she said. 'Me and Jack wondered if you'd be there. We'd be glad if you would; you know more about these things than we do.'

'Of course I will,' Beth promised. 'Oh, isn't it exciting?'

Elsie looked dubious.

'I'm not so sure,' she said. 'We'll have to see.'

The purpose of Mr Tiplady's visit was to tell them that he had the highest possible hopes of getting a place for Tom in a good boarding school.

'It's in York,' he said.

'York!' Elsie was dismayed. 'But that's a long way away!'

'Not really,' Mr Tiplady said. 'Trains run to York from almost everywhere in the country these days. It's not a long journey from Settle. He'll be home for holidays, probably even for half-terms – and you might be able to go and visit.'

'That's true enough,' Jack Drake said. 'We mustn't stand in his way, love. We've agreed on that.'

'And the school has agreed that I may have the entrance examination papers and he can take the exam in my house, with me acting as invigilator,' Mr Tiplady said.

'We'll need money for books, and new clothes – uniform and such like,' Elsie said. She knew in her heart she was searching around for reasons why he couldn't go. She was ashamed of herself for doing so, but she couldn't help it.

'If he gets the scholarship it will cover his books,' the Missioner said. 'And I'll try to find a source of money for the uniform.'

'No need for that!' Jack Drake was firm. 'We can manage that ourselves. Never let it be said we couldn't clothe our own children!'

A day or two later, early in July, Tom walked down to Batty Green, by himself, and took the examination in Mr Tiplady's home. After that he walked around the stalls, mingling with the crowds, and bought himself a glass of ginger beer with the penny his mother had given him, before making his way home.

Elsie, who had kept an almost constant watch for him, saw him walking up the hill and hurried to the door to greet him.

'Well, love, how did it go?' she asked.

'Quite well, I think,' Tom said. 'It wasn't difficult.'

'Your dad'll be pleased to hear that when he gets home from work,' Elsie said.

A week later Alan and Charlie Miller brought home the news that there was a new outbreak of smallpox at Batty Green.

'They say several cases, and pretty bad. It's all hands aloft at the hospital,' Alan said. 'We thought it was all over, otherwise our wives would never have let us come. Anyway, it means we mustn't go home until it's over. It wouldn't be fair.'

'Have you been in contact with anyone who might have it?' Beth asked. They went down to Batty Green at least twice a week, sat in the crowded Welcome Inn.

'How can we tell?' Alan asked. 'You don't know until it happens, and by then it's too late. But we shall stay away from the Welcome, that's for sure!'

Next morning Beth went early to Jericho to give the news to Elsie Drake.

'I know,' Elsie said. 'Jack told me.'

'Then once again I reckon we must stop the classes,' Beth said. 'Just to be on the safe side.'

'Oh, I agree!' Elsie said. 'Shall I let Phoebe know, or will you call?'

Beth hesitated. If she called on Phoebe now, like as not Jake would be there. She longed to see him, longed even to be in the same room with him, and knew she must not.

'You tell Phoebe,' she said.

'Very well,' Elsie agreed. 'I've heard they're desperately short of help at the hospital. Have you heard that?'

'I can well believe it,' Beth said.

On the way home, and for the rest of the afternoon as she went about her tasks in the hut, she thought about this. It would be women they needed; women to help with the nursing, to take on the cleaning and the laundry: there were so many jobs to be done. Almost every man in the area was employed on the railway and what women there were – by no means as numerous as the men – were wives, and usually mothers, who couldn't possibly risk working in the hospital. But I am not, she thought. I am neither a wife nor a mother. Come to that, of what great use am I in the world?

She had the Miller brothers to look after, of course, but what was the most important thing; what ought she to be doing?

When they came home at the end of the day, she asked them.

'What shall I do? There are so many hours in the day when I'm not occupied. I could help in the hospital, but what would you two do? How would you manage?'

She left them to discuss it with each other while she did other jobs. When she came back to them, Alan said:

'What if you brought the infection back here? We have to think of our wives and children. We can't take too many risks. We don't mind looking after ourselves for a week or two, it's just the infection.'

'I wouldn't come home,' Beth said. 'I would ask if I could sleep in the hospital. I daresay they'd be glad of that.'

So it was agreed, and the next day she presented herself at the hospital.

Elsie, when she called in and told her on her way down the moor, thought she was out of her mind.

'I shall be worried sick about you!' she said. 'Have you thought what risks you're running?'

'I've thought about it all night,' Beth admitted. 'I won't say I'm not the least bit worried, because I am. But I still think I ought to do it – if they'll have me, that is.'

'Well, I can see there's no changing your mind,' Elsie said.

'I'll see you all when it's over,' Beth said. 'And will you do me a favour? Will you tell Jake, tell him not to worry, and he's not to come to the hospital.'

'I'll tell him,' Elsie promised.

She opened her arms to Beth and the two women embraced. It was something they had never done before. When they looked at each other before parting there were tears in Elsie's eyes.

Beth was warmly welcomed at the hospital. 'Though I've no experience other than nursing my husband through his illness,' she explained.

'You're another pair of hands,' the matron said. 'We need all the help we can get. And the fact that you're willing to live in makes you even more valuable. But you have considered the possible danger, Mrs Seymour?'

'I have.'

'Well then, I'll be glad to have you, and the sooner you can start, the better.'

'I can start tomorrow,' Beth said.

'There are some things you can do to help yourself, to lessen the risk,' Matron said. 'Keep yourself clean. Take baths as often as you can, wash your hair and keep it covered. We disinfect everything we possibly can. Hygiene is the answer. It's the lack of hygiene in the shanty towns which allows infections to spread, but people won't believe that until it's too late.'

How tired Matron looks, Beth thought. But then, she'd hardly had time to pull round from the first wave of smallpox before the second one was upon them – and the second one seemed likely to be worse than the first.

Beth had never worked so hard in her life, never known that she was capable of doing so. As the days went by she discovered that under the direction of the other nurses, who were more experienced but far too few in number, she could do most of the tasks set her. Mostly they needed willingness, care, common sense.

All day long she washed patients, fed them, changed their clothing and their bedding, dressed their sores, fetched and carried bedpans. When the washing of bed linen was more than the two laundry maids – young and frightened – could cope with, she also took a hand with that.

Every day new cases came in, until the hospital was full to overflowing, and then beds only became free when patients either recovered and went home, or died. It seemed to Beth that far too many died. Not all the care and attention in the world could save them.

On Beth's sixth day in hospital Matron sent for her.

'I'm sorry, Nurse, to give you this further burden,' she apologized. 'It's something I'd rather have kept you from for a while longer, but we're desperately short-staffed. I'm asking you to help Nurse Proctor deal with two patients who have died this morning. It has to be done as soon as possible.'

Beth felt herself stiffen. I can't do it! I can't do that! she thought.

'Nurse Proctor will show you what has to be done, but I have to impress two things upon you. One is that the body of a person who has died of smallpox is extremely infectious, and you must take every possible care of yourself. The other is that you must go about this task quietly and soberly, treating the body of every victim, whoever and in whatever state they are, with decency and reverence.'

To behave so, Beth found, when for the first time she carried out the task with Nurse Proctor, came naturally. What she was not prepared for was the rush of pity which threatened to overwhelm her as the two of them dealt with the body of a young man in his twenties. As they sewed him into a blanket soaked in disinfectant, which acted as his shroud, she worked through a mist of tears. When the undertaker came with the coffin, liberally lined with sawdust doused with more disinfectant, she helped to lift the body in, and watched while the undertaker immediately sealed it with putty.

'And it won't be any easier with the next one,' Nurse Proctor said quietly. 'It's a little girl, four years old.'

Two days later, worse was to happen.

In the morning a young man, Adam Beck, was admitted. Beth knew him by sight, since he lived at Jericho, a few doors away from Phoebe Grange. He was desperately ill, barely conscious, and with a raging fever.

'I don't give much for his chances,' Nurse Proctor said, when they had done all they could for him.

In the afternoon there was another admittance. Beth was elsewhere when the patient was taken onto the ward. It was Nurse Proctor who told her.

'It's another one from Jericho. They must be in for it there! A child this time.'

Beth went cold. Six children she knew in Jericho. It could be any one of them. Or perhaps not, she told herself. There were others. But she had to know.

'Excuse me!' she said – and hurried off to the ward.

She knew which bed it would be. It had been made ready only that morning after its former occupant had gone home. Praying – incoherently – she approached the bed. Her prayers were not answered. The boy lying there was Tom Drake.

His face was flushed crimson with the fever, his eyes, when he opened them, were too bright. He moved his head uneasily from side to side. He seemed at first barely conscious, but when he saw Beth he recognized her and gave her a faint smile.

'Hello, Tom!' Beth said. 'How are you feeling?'

'My back aches, Mrs Seymour,' Tom said. 'And my head hurts something terrible. Please do something to stop it!'

'Of course I will!' Beth promised. 'I'll bathe it with nice, cool water for a start. You'll be my special patient, Tom love!'

She had already seen enough of the disease to recognize when there was a mild case or when it was serious. She knew just by looking at him that Tom was very ill indeed. She stayed with him a few minutes longer, then went to see the sister in charge of the ward.

'The little boy in the end bed, Sister . . .' she began.

'Tom Drake,' Sister Kenny interrupted. 'He's a very sick child.'

'I know him,' Beth told her. She explained the circumstances. 'I wonder whether, if I have any spare time, you'll allow me to spend it with him? I realize his mother won't be able to visit him because of the rest of the family – there are three more little ones. He'll miss her so much.'

The only access relatives had to the two smallpox wards was that on certain days and for a strictly limited period they were allowed to look through the window at their loved one. Even this was discouraged. It was best to keep well away from the area.

'I don't know about that, Nurse Seymour,' Sister said. 'You know how busy we are. You have your own duties . . .'

'Oh I know!' Beth said. 'I'll not neglect a single one. I just thought . . .'

Sister Kenny held up a hand to stop Beth.

'. . . And when those are completed it's your further duty to take what rest you can. You have to keep well for the sake of all the patients. We don't have time for special nursing.'

'It's just that . . .' Beth began. How could she explain what she felt about Tom? 'He's a very special little boy.' She felt as if she was pleading for her own child, the one she would never have, but then she thought of Elsie, and what her anguish must be. She wanted also to do it for Elsie.

'All children are special,' Sister Kenny said. 'Nevertheless, I take your point. So you may give him what extra attention you can, while not neglecting your other duties, and I will trust you not to overstretch yourself. Indeed, Nurse, that's an order, and I shall watch to see that it's carried out!'

'Thank you! Thank you very much!' Beth said.

Sister Kenny did watch, and saw that Nurse Seymour was doing far more than her strength allowed, but she did not interfere, not even when the night nurse reported that Nurse Seymour had come down to the ward in the middle of the night to sit with Tom.

'Don't stop her,' she told the night nurse. 'It can't last long, he's too desperately ill, poor child.'

Beth herself was aware that Tom could not go on much longer. He hardly knew her. Fever raged in him; his body was covered in spots, now turning into blisters as the disease took its course. She bathed him, changed his bedclothes, and when she had done all the practical things she sat beside the bed, day or night, it didn't matter, held his hand, and prayed. She had never been so weary, so desperately tired, but she knew she would go on to the end. Nothing would stop her.

Then one night – it was two o'clock in the morning – she was snatching some rest when she wakened with a sense of urgency, of being desperately needed. She went at once to the ward and when she saw Tom she knew that that was so.

She sat by the bed, holding his hand. It was not the time now to do anything more for him, to disturb him in any way.

She didn't know how long she sat there or who came and went, but in the end the days and nights of fatigue overcame her, and she dozed, slumped forward over the bed, Tom's hand in hers.

The first daylight creeping in through the window awakened her. At once, before she even raised her head, she knew that something had happened, something was different. Then she felt a hand on her shoulder and heard the night nurse's quiet voice.

'Nurse Seymour! It's all right! Tom's all right!'

Beth lifted her head and looked at him. It was true! Beneath the ravages of the disease, he was different. The fever had left him. He slept naturally, his breathing eased.

On the same day, four hours later, Adam Beck died. Though Beth's heart was sad as she helped Nurse Proctor to prepare the young man's body for the undertaker, she could not help thanking God that it was not Tom she was dealing with.

Sally stared at herself in the mirror which hung on the wall in the bedroom she shared with Jake. Everyone else in the house, including Jake, had gone to Adam Beck's funeral at Chapel-le-dale, except Phoebe's children who were being looked after by Elsie Drake.

Sally had flatly refused to attend the funeral.

'Why should I walk three miles to Chapel-le-dale to bury someone I hardly know?' she'd said to Jake.

'As a mark of respect,' Jake said. 'Everyone goes to a neighbour's funeral.'

'Well I don't,' Sally had said. 'There are too many funerals. It's gloomy.'

No-one could deny that. In this summer of 1871 death had been an all-too-frequent visitor to Ribble-head. No shanty town had escaped him. But Sally's true reason for not attending Adam Beck's funeral was deeper than the one she gave.

She was afraid. She was dreadfully and terribly afraid of the smallpox. She now went nowhere, never leaving the house and spending much of the time isolated in her room. Every day, sometimes several times a day, she looked in the mirror, as she did now.

She saw a beautiful face. She needed no-one to tell her she was beautiful, it was there before her; her flawless skin – though paler than it should be because she lacked fresh air – her sensual, curving mouth, her lustrous hair escaping in tendrils over her forehead. And her eyes, large, limpid, thickly fringed by black lashes.

It was her eyes she saw now in the reflection in the mirror. She stared at her eyes, and what she saw in them was terror. What if, in spite of all her precautions, she caught the smallpox? What if Jake brought it home with him, or one of the children? What if she died? She wasn't ready to die, she was too young. What if she didn't die but was horribly scarred? Looking in the mirror, she saw her face pock-marked.

'I can't stand it!' she cried out loud. 'I can't stand it another minute!'

And then she knew what she must do. It was the only thing. She would run away, leave this awful place for ever, go where she would be safe.

Into a bag she packed only what she needed for the journey. She wanted none of her clothes or other possessions. Who knew whether they would carry infection? She needed money, but she knew where Jake kept his savings because he made no secret of it. She took those, every last penny. He could earn more.

She glanced at the clock. If she hurried she could get a lift from Burgoyne & Cocks to Settle. It would mean setting foot on Batty Green, but there was no help for that.

Quickly, she found a piece of paper and scribbled a note which she left on the table so that Jake would see it the moment he came back.

She glanced at the clock again. She must be quick or they would be back from the funeral.

When Jake returned from the funeral with Phoebe and her husband he was surprised by Sally's absence. These days she never left the house. Then he saw her note, picked it up and began to read it.

'Is anything wrong?' Phoebe asked.

'Not really. It's Sally. She's gone to stay with her aunt in Settle. It's not a bad idea. You know how nervous she is about the smallpox.'

As the days passed with no word from Sally, Jake wondered if he should go to see her in Settle. It was easy to decide against it. She wouldn't welcome him, she would worry that he might somehow carry infection. In any case, he had no desire to see her.

At the end of a fortnight two letters arrived on the same day, one from Settle, the other addressed in Sally's writing, postmarked Bradford. He opened Sally's letter first, read it quickly, then, hardly able to believe what it said, he read it again.

Dear Jake

I will not be coming back, not ever. The truth is I am not married to you and never was. I married Matthew when I was 16 but it all went wrong and my mother packed me off to Settle. I have met up with Matthew again and I know he is my true love. My aunt did not know.

All in all I daresay you will be pleased.

Sally

He stood there, holding the letter in his hand. There was only one thought in his mind, and he was filled with it.

'I'm free!' He said the words out loud.

Eventually he picked up the second letter. It was of no importance to him, all he needed to hear was in the first one. Nevertheless he opened it. It was from Sally's aunt.

I want you to know, (she wrote) I knew nothing of all this. My sister never said. When Sally told me I sent her packing, never to darken my door again. I know you can report her for bigamy but I am begging you not to for my sister's sake even though she deceived me. You are a true gentleman and I hope you won't.

Yours truly
(Mrs) Jane Sutherland

He didn't bother to read it twice. It was not important. 'I am free!' he told himself again.

He left the hut and set off down the moor at a run, towards the hospital.

17

Nurse Proctor, her face gleaming with excitement, came into the ward. Beth was washing a patient.

'There's a man at the door, wants to see you. I was passing through the hall and the bell was ringing like mad. Eliot wasn't there. I don't know why we have a porter, he's never at his post!'

'So who wants to see me?' Beth asked. Who would seek her out at the hospital? She felt stirrings of alarm.

'He says his name's Jake Tempest. I wish it was me he wanted to see!'

Jake! What could he possibly want? Something must be wrong! Elsie – or Phoebe? One of the children? Surely not the smallpox? Please God not that! The thoughts raced around Beth's head.

'He said to tell you it wasn't bad news,' Nurse Proctor said. 'So you've no need to look like that.'

Beth's relief gave way to a slight annoyance that Jake should have presented himself at the hospital about something apparently unimportant when she had specifically asked him not to. All the same, she longed to see him. It was a longing to which she knew she shouldn't give way. He was not for her and that was the end of it.

'I can't see him,' she said. 'I hope you told him that?'

Apart from her own reason for not seeing him, it was not permissible. In the present circumstances of the epidemic no visitors were allowed into the building, nor was any nurse allowed to step outside to meet with one. The rule was strict. Before a nurse was free to leave the hospital, which she could only do in her rare time off, she must change out of her uniform, take a bath liberally laced with disinfectant, wash her hair and put on clean clothes. Even then she was not advised to mix with anyone; simply to take in a change of scene and breathe some fresh air.

'Oh, I told him,' Nurse Proctor said. 'He says he has something to say to you and he won't go away until he's said it. He'll wait outside until you appear. Aren't you the lucky one?'

'Except that I won't appear,' Beth said. 'And there'll be trouble if Matron sees him hanging around. There'll be trouble for you, too, if she finds out you answered the door. What in the world can he be thinking of?' She longed to know.

'You could talk to him through the glass,' Nurse Proctor suggested. 'He could write a note and hold it up to you. Oh, isn't it romantic!'

It was also feasible. It was the way patients and visitors communicated, since it was impossible, even when they shouted, to hear what was said through the thick glass of the windows.

Beth thought for a moment. 'All right, I'll do that. Then will you do me a favour?' she said. 'I'll be at the linen-room window in fifteen minutes. Will you ask Eliot if he'll show Jake Tempest where it is, and tell him to be there?'

'Oh, I will, I will!' Nurse Proctor said. Wasn't this a most welcome break from routine?

A quarter of an hour later Beth went into the linen room, closing the door firmly behind her. Jake was already at the window. She felt a quick surge of delight at the sight of him, and just as quickly squashed it. This was a stupid, mad thing to be doing and the sooner it was over, the better. What in the world would she do if Sister or Matron walked in?

Jake, looking remarkably happy, spoke words to her through the glass. She thought he said . . . it seemed like . . . but of course she must be mistaken. She shook her head vigorously.

'I can't hear,' she mouthed.

Then he smoothed out the piece of paper he was holding and held it flat against the window pane so that the words faced her:

WILL YOU MARRY ME?

She *had* been right. It *was* what he'd said. What could he mean?

She took the sheet of paper she'd brought into the room with her, wrote on it, and held it against the glass.

DON'T BE SILLY! Jake read. YOU ARE MARRIED!

Jake shook his head

'I'm not!' he shouted.

Then he turned his sheet of paper over and held it against the glass. It was Sally's letter. Jake watched the amazement on Beth's face as she read it, but when she came to the end she shook her head again.

'I can't,' she mouthed.

Jake looked at her in disbelief, then wrote again. WHEN ARE YOU OFF DUTY?

TOMORROW. TWO O'CLOCK, Beth wrote back.

I'LL WAIT FOR YOU AT THE GATE. I LOVE YOU!

The door opened and Nurse Proctor rushed in.

'Sister's on the prowl! She's asking for you.'

Beth gave a hasty wave to Jake, and hurried out after Nurse Proctor.

She went through the rest of her day's work as if in a dream, performing the tasks automatically, hardly knowing what she was doing. When night came she went to bed, but slept little. When morning arrived she counted the hours until she should see Jake. Yet though her heart should have been light, it was not. She was apprehensive about what she must say to him.

307

When she left the hospital he was waiting at the gate. He moved quickly towards her and she knew he would have taken her in his arms had she not sharply turned away from him.

'No!' she said. 'Let's walk. Let's get away from the hospital, away from Batty Green.'

She wanted to get out of the sight of the viaduct which, though still no more than half-built, dominated the scene. She was in its presence every day; every time she looked out of the hospital windows it was there. It seemed as though she always saw, standing out from the rest, the very pier from which Will had fallen. She pictured him hurtling through the air, his red neckerchief around his neck.

'Wherever you like,' Jake said. 'How long have you?'

'Two hours. I'm on duty at four o'clock.'

They turned their backs on the viaduct, walked a short way up the turnpike road which led to Dent, and eventually to Hawes, and then, turning right, left the road and began to follow a stream which ran down from the high hills to join the Ribble. The August day was hot, the way was steep. Except for the road which ran through the valley to Settle, every way from Batty Green ran uphill.

In a very short time they had left the bustle of the shanty towns behind. There was nothing now but birds and sheep, and the sound of the stream.

'Let's sit down,' Jake said. 'I have to talk to you. And first of all I want to know what you mean by shaking your head at me.'

Beth said nothing.

'Beth, I love you,' Jake said. 'I'm asking you to marry me.'

'I can't!' It was no more than a whisper, wrung out of her.

Jake grabbed her wrists and pulled her around so that she was facing him.

'What do you mean?' he demanded. 'Look me in the eyes and tell me you don't love me!'

She met his eyes, and remained silent.

'Say it,' he persisted. 'Say "I don't love you".'

'I can't say that. You know I love you.'

'Then why can't you marry me? I don't understand you!'

'It's Will,' Beth said. 'I feel so badly about Will.'

'I understand *that*,' Jake replied. 'It was a nasty shock, the way he died. You wouldn't have wanted that to happen, and nor would I. But—'

'It's not that! I feel guilty,' Beth interrupted. 'I feel guilty all the time.'

'Beth, love, you're not guilty,' Jake said gently. 'It was an accident. Not the first on the railway, and no doubt it won't be the last.'

'That's not what I feel guilty about,' Beth said.

'Then what?'

'I wasn't a good wife to him. I failed him.'

Jake looked at her in astonishment.

'You're talking nonsense, Beth. You were the best of wives. The boot's on the other foot. I don't want to speak ill of the dead, but if there's any guilt, it's Will's. Not to put too fine a point on it, he was a rotten husband!'

'He was not!' Beth said sharply. 'You knew him mostly when he was ill. He wasn't like that really.'

Jake opened his mouth to speak, then closed it again. He had known Will Seymour before his accident. He had been a selfish, grumbling, bullying man. He had never understood how Beth could have married him.

'You never saw him as I did,' Beth said. 'You didn't know him before we came to this place. It changed him.'

Had she forgotten what Will had done to her, Jake asked himself? But if she had, it wasn't in him to remind her.

'What he did to me,' she said, as if she could read his thoughts, 'was my fault. I drove him to it. I didn't love him enough. He was a decent man at heart, and he loved me.'

'Beth, you loved me when Will was alive. You love me now, you can't deny it. And I've loved you since the minute I saw you. We love each other. Fate, or chance, or whatever you like to call it, has spun the wheel so that we're free to marry each other. *We* haven't made that happen. It's meant to be, Beth!'

'I can't,' she said. 'Not yet at any rate. Not the way I feel.'

'What do you mean by "not yet"?' Jake said roughly. 'Do you mean you *will* marry me, but you don't know when? And in that case, when will you know?'

'Please, Jake, don't bully me,' Beth said. She was close to tears.

Jake was immediately contrite. He drew her close, and held her.

'My darling, I would never bully you. It's just that I love you and I want you so much and I can't see how anything can stand in the way of us being together.'

'And I can't marry you until I sort myself out. It wouldn't be a good start. But in any case, I couldn't marry you until Will's been dead a year. I'd still be in mourning.'

'I don't set much store by such rules,' Jake said. 'I wouldn't have thought you did.'

She drew away from him.

'I find that I do. Oh, Jake, there are so many things separating us at the moment. If we're to marry I want us to have the best possible start, nothing coming between us. But in any case, if everything else was plain sailing, I couldn't leave the hospital while the smallpox is on. It wouldn't be fair. I'm needed there.'

'That, at least, I understand,' Jake conceded. It was also what he dreaded. The thought of the risks she ran was never far from his mind. He wanted to pick her up and run with her, take her miles and miles away from the danger she was in.

'I understand that,' he repeated, 'but I'm terrified of the risks you run.'

'Until it's over we're all at risk,' Beth said. 'You don't have to work in the hospital to catch the smallpox. But let's not talk about that now. We don't have much time left. I'll have to turn back soon.'

They set off to walk further up the hill. For a while they walked in silence, then Jake said: 'I won't give up! I won't stop trying to persuade you!'

'Please don't say that,' Beth pleaded. 'We *must* wait. We must see how things turn out. A year isn't so long!'

'It will seem like a lifetime,' Jake said. 'But promise me one thing, Beth. If you're going to make me wait a year, promise we can see each other – and as often as we want to.'

'I promise that,' Beth answered. Would he wait for her, she wondered? Would he tire of waiting?

A year's a long time, Jake thought, but I would wait for her for ever.

The smallpox summer came to an end, though not before thirty victims, in coffins carried shoulder-high over the long track from the shanty towns, had been buried in the churchyard at Chapel-le-dale. It was now full, chock-a-block, not a single space for another coffin to be found there. Had the Earl not graciously given an adjoining piece of land to be consecrated, there would have been nowhere for the Reverend Smith to bury the dead. He, poor man, what with deaths by accident, in childbirth, from fever, as well as by smallpox, had been kept inordinately busy. Two or three funerals a year were more the usual mark.

When the last case had left, this time to return home cured, though scarred, the isolation wards of the hospital were thoroughly cleaned and disinfected, the rooms fumigated. Beth dropped formaldehyde and permanganate of potash into a bowl then escaped quickly, sealing the doors, before the noxious vapours should overcome her. No-one seemed quite to know what would befall her if she did not escape in time, but the warnings were enough to ensure that she fled from the room well before the mixture started to boil.

When it was all over, when every room, every closet had been fumigated, every surface swabbed, when Beth's hands were raw from scrubbing, Matron sent for her.

'I think we can congratulate ourselves that it's all over, Nurse Seymour,' she said. 'And you have played your part. Should you wish to stay on to nurse in the hospital you will be more than welcome.'

'Thank you, Matron,' Beth said. 'I can't really. I have two lodgers who've been shamefully neglected during the epidemic. It's my duty to get back to them.'

She would be glad to leave the hospital. Nursing had come naturally to her and in other circumstances she would have enjoyed it, but the horrors of the smallpox, the constant deaths, especially of the young, were something she would never forget.

Matron nodded.

'As you wish, Nurse. Thank you for what you've done. Should you ever wish to return you'll be very welcome.'

The summer had been wet. Walking anywhere, even from Nazareth to Jericho, was a case of looking out for small patches of dry turf so that one didn't sink ankle-deep in the mud. To go as far as Batty Green, if the tramway happened not to be running, was hazardous, and it was impossible, in the meadows along the river valley, to get the hay in until a sudden and brief dry spell allowed it. But now the rain had come again, turning the rock-like boulder clay, normally so hard that when a man drove his pickaxe into it the shock of the impact went through his entire body, into a cloying, thick soup.

'It's times like this,' Alan Miller said to Beth 'that the bog cart comes into its own. We couldn't do without it. It can go where horses would just sink into the ground.'

'There was a horse last week,' Charlie said, making a rare observation of his own, 'sank up to its middle in the bog. We had to fix ropes round it to pull it out, poor beast!'

'Whoever invented the bog cart was a clever man,' Beth observed. 'But you have to admit, it's a strange-looking object.'

She was glad to be back with the Miller brothers in her own home, living a more normal life, freed from the fear of sudden illness and death, though the memory of Will's death was never far from her. Time and time again she wondered why he had fallen; had he known he was falling to his death as he hurtled to the ground? Had he been afraid, or had he mercifully lost consciousness in the seconds before he hit the ground? All this she wondered about, but she also thanked God that on Will's last day on earth he had set off for work a reasonably happy man, with a spring in his step.

She had started the lessons again. Now she had eight children, including one more boy from Jericho and two extra girls from Tunnel Huts. It was more difficult to teach now because she had absolute beginners together with those who had progressed over several months, though two lengthy interruptions because of the smallpox had been no help at all.

There was no-one of Tom Drake's calibre. In September he had gone off to his new school in York. She missed him greatly. There had been discussion about how he would get to York, he who had travelled no further than Batty Green on his own. His father could not take the time off and Elsie, much though she wanted to be with him to the last minute, was too nervous to contemplate the journey. To add to that, she was pregnant with her fifth child and was far from well. The rocking of the train, it was reckoned, could prove hazardous.

'And supposing we got on the wrong train,' she said nervously. 'Supposing we got lost in York. They say it's a very busy place.'

'You wouldn't do either of those things,' Beth assured her. 'But if you're really not fit to go, why then, I'll take Tom to York and deliver him to his school. Though only if you want me to.'

She longed to do it. It would be almost like accompanying a child of her own. She held her breath for the few seconds it took Elsie to make up her mind.

'Oh, I'd be so grateful!' Elsie said. 'I'd know he was safe in your hands. After all, you travelled all the way from Surrey!'

And safe he had been. Though every mile of the train journey had been exciting – so much to see from the train window, so many stations which had been no more than names until then – they had arrived in York without mishap, and had had time for a cup of tea and a bun in a small café in Stonegate before meeting the school representative at the appointed place, which since it was no more than yards from the Minster was easy enough to find.

The parting had been swift.

'Say goodbye to your mother, Drake,' the schoolmaster said, but before Beth could open her mouth to explain she was not the mother they were off, a crocodile of a dozen small boys in their new uniforms. She had watched them until they were out of sight, and had then made her way back to the station.

That had been in the autumn of 1871. She had

written to Tom, and he to her, and then at Christmas he had come home for a week's holiday, travelling on his own. In his first term away at school he had changed and yet he had not changed. He had a new independence, a self-confidence which had been missing in him before.

'I like it there,' he said to Beth. 'It's interesting. And there's a whole library full of books!'

'That's good,' Beth said. 'That's very good. But some things are improving here, too. There's a new reading room opened at Dent, with newspapers and magazines, though of course Dent is a far step away. And we've had some good penny readings down at Batty Green. You'd have enjoyed those.'

'I know. Though I'd rather read for myself than listen to someone else. And I don't mean I don't like it here. This is my home.' He spoke politely, not wishing to give offence.

A strange home, Beth thought. Strange for all of us. Living in huts in hastily thrown-up shanty towns in the middle of a wild and bleak moor. And the minute the railway is finished, she wondered, will we all be driven away, thrown out? What will happen to us then?

In spite of the vagaries of the weather, the work was proceeding. One day it would be finished, the trains would run from Settle to Carlisle, over the viaducts, through the deep cuttings, into the tunnels through the darkness of the mountains. When that day came there would be no need of this army of men with all their skills.

She saw Jake frequently. She placed no limit on the number of his visits, though she made it plain that he must come when Alan and Charlie Miller were at home. It wouldn't be right if he came when she was alone.

'You mean you don't trust me?' Jake said.

Beth didn't answer. The truth was that she didn't

trust herself. She loved him so much, longed to be with him all the time.

'I daresay you'd be right not to,' Jake said. 'I'm not sure I could keep any promises I might make. Beth, why can't we be married? Why do we have to wait any longer? We're not children.'

'It's children who can't wait,' Beth said. 'I'll marry you in August – and oh, so willingly! But not before.'

He was back on the day shift now, had been for several months. His visits were confined to the evenings and to part of the weekend. With one part of her Beth did not like it that he crossed the pitch darkness of the moor, with its treacherous shakeholes and bogs, to visit her. With another part of her she rejoiced whenever she answered the door to his knock, and saw him standing there.

In the spring, on a clear, crisp Sunday in late March, they set off early to climb Whernside.

'I meant this to be one of the first things I did when I came here,' Jake said to Beth.

They had reached the summit, had scraped the snow from a flat rock from which they now surveyed the scene below them. The line of the railway, cutting along the valley, was no more than a narrow ribbon, carelessly flung down. The shanty towns and huts were like children's bricks. From this viewpoint the high hills, their tops still under deep snow, and the wide sweep of the land, dominated everything, reduced everything.

'It's taken me two years to get up here,' Jake said. 'But if I'd come when I intended I'd have been alone. Now you're with me. It was worth the waiting.'

Three days later Elsie Drake gave birth to her baby. To her great delight it was another girl.

'It was as easy as pie!' Elsie said to Beth as the latter stood by the bedside holding the small new creature in her arms. 'Just slipped out like a pea from a pod!'

'You're a fortunate woman, Elsie,' Beth said quietly.

'Oh, Beth, I'm sorry! I never think, do I?' Elsie was contrite. 'And of course I do know I'm fortunate.'

As she was leaving Jericho Beth met Jake, coming home from work. He was black from head to toe with the dust from the tunnel. He would have taken hold of her, and then remembered the state of him.

'Oh, Jake!' she blurted out. 'You shouldn't marry me! You know I can never give you children! Never!'

The tears were running down her cheeks now. Ignoring the dirt on him, Jake took her in his arms.

'I don't need a horde of children,' he said. 'All I need is you. You and me together, for always. That's all I want.'

'Are you sure, Jake? Are you quite, quite sure?' Beth pleaded.

'Quite certain. Just you – and the sooner the better!'

They were married in August.

Unknown to Jake, and secure in the belief that her wedding *would* take place, Beth had several weeks earlier sent away for a new dress. It was quite perfect – pale blue with white embroidery, and fitted her as if she had been measured by the highest couturier in the land. When she looked at herself in the mirror on the morning of her wedding day she was pleased by what she saw.

Almost all the inhabitants of Jericho and Nazareth joined the bridal party, which went on the tramway to Batty Green. There Jake had hired a pony and trap for himself and Beth, for Elsie who was Beth's matron of honour, and Jack Drake who was Jake's best man. The rest of the company walked, or rode on hired horses, behind them to the church at Chapel-le-dale. After the wedding, before they left, Beth, with Jake beside her, placed her bridal flowers on Will's grave.

Later in the day the pony and trap took the two of them to Settle, where they boarded a train for Skipton.

They were to have a two-day honeymoon and Jake had booked a room in an hotel.

The trap drew up in the main street. While Jake paid the driver, Beth gazed up at the hotel, with its imposing pillared portico. It was quite splendid; she had never in her life stayed anywhere like this.

'Oh, Jake,' she whispered when he rejoined her, 'are you sure this is the right place?'

'Of course it is, love!' he assured her. 'Why? Doesn't it suit you?'

She took his arm.

'Oh, Jake, don't be silly! It looks wonderful! Are you sure we can afford it?'

'Quite sure!' Hadn't he been saving for this for months? 'So as long as it pleases you, we'd better go in!'

They went together to the desk.

'Mr and Mrs Tempest,' Jake said firmly. 'We have a reservation.'

'Certainly, sir,' the clerk said. 'We're expecting you. Now, if you will just sign . . .'

Standing beside her husband, Beth felt a glow of pride as she watched him write her new name.

'The boy here will take you to your room,' the clerk said. 'If there's anything you want you have only to ring!'

There'll be no ringing from them, he thought as he watched them follow the boy towards the stairs. They'll have better things to do. You could always tell honeymoon couples, they stood out a mile. He envied this fellow; she was a tasty bit and no mistake!

The room was a small one, at the rear of the hotel. Its predominant feature was the high double bed, with scarcely room for any other furniture.

It was strange, Beth thought, that though she had been married before and she was by no means a stranger to what was so soon to take place in that bed, and though she knew that she was not the first woman ever in Jake's life, she felt herself to be, at this moment, totally inexperienced.

She turned away from the bed and looked out of the window. A barge, heavy-laden with coal, was being pulled by an old horse which made its slow, deliberate way along the towpath.

Jake came and joined her, putting his arm around her shoulders.

'Not the most romantic of scenes,' he said, 'but it means something to me. I was brought up on that canal. We'll walk around there tomorrow.'

'I'd like that,' Beth said. 'I want to see all the places you know. I want to see the house where you lived with your mother – everything!'

'So you shall,' he promised. 'Tomorrow.'

He drew down the window blind, shutting out the view, then took her by the hand and led her to the bed. She stood before him in silence while, with trembling fingers, he undid the twelve buttons down the front of her bodice and then, deliberately and not hurrying, took off the rest of her clothes until she stood before him naked.

He gazed at her, not holding her, not touching her. Then just as deliberately, she began to undress him. Everything they had worn lay in a heap on the floor.

He picked her up and laid her on the bed.

'We've waited so long,' he murmured. 'It's been so long.'

'But the waiting's over,' Beth said. 'It's over.'

Everything was new, as if they were the first lovers in the world. Yet everything was perfect, as if the act of love had been created only for them.

18

Batty Green was crowded, scarcely room to move, and the stalls were busy. Beth was there with Elsie, both of them doing their weekly shopping. It was a lively scene, though hardly comfortable. Horses, with or without carriages, brewers' drays, milk carts, butchers' carts, carts of every description trundled across the Green without the slightest discipline, splashing up the mud, frightening the lives out of dogs, small children and shoppers on foot.

'My word, it's a very different scene from when I first came here,' Elsie said. 'Just before you arrived, that was. All but three years ago now. Not so many people then – or vehicles taking up the road.'

Beth nodded. 'And scarcely any wives and children.'

She had been one of the few wives who had accompanied her husband. Living more than two hundred miles away, if she hadn't done so they might have been parted for a long time, which was not to be thought of. Most of the wives had arrived later, when the husbands had tested things out, reckoned it was all right for them to come. Some had never arrived, their husbands being all too pleased with their new-found freedom at Ribblehead.

'When you come to think of it,' Elsie said, 'most of the little ones and the babies have been born in the shanty towns. They've known nothing else.'

'It's better than it was,' Beth said. 'At least in some ways.'

There were more shops, more concerts and penny

readings, the Mission was well attended and, the greatest blessing of all to Beth, there was now a public library. She was no longer starved of books, no longer dependent on finding something cheap and suitable on the newsagent's stall. The riches of literature, or a hundred volumes or so and not nearly enough of them novels, were there for the borrowing in the library hut.

'In some ways, though, it's not all that different,' Elsie mused. 'In some ways it's no different. Just as many fights. Just as many drunks staggering around. Some folks never improve, and the more money they earn, the worse they are!'

While they waited their turn in front of Burgoyne & Cocks's stall, Beth gave a fleeting thought to Sally Roland, wondered where she was. No-one, it seemed, had had sight or sound of her since she had walked away. Jake never once spoke of her. It was as if she had never existed.

It was tedious waiting to be served. Beth was unusually tired and there was a niggling pain in her back. She shifted uneasily from foot to foot.

'I'll be glad to get to the library,' she said to Elsie. 'I can have a sit-down there.'

Elsie looked closely at her friend.

'You do look a bit peaky,' she said. 'I'll tell you what – get served here before me, and get to the library. I'll not go with you there, seeing as I can't read and I've a few more things to do. Wait there for me and I'll pick you up. We don't want to miss the tram back, do we?'

Beth sat at the table in the library with a small pile of books in front of her, wondering which she would take. She would like them all but it wasn't allowed. There was Jake to choose for as well as herself. Since he could now read as fluently as she, his head was never out of a book.

She was glancing through *Vanity Fair* by Mr Thackeray – which she had read before but it would be a pleasure to read it again – when the words on the page began to blur, then run into each other, until finally the page and the book and the table spun round in a black vortex in front of her, and then there was nothing.

When she opened her eyes again it was to see an anxious-looking librarian, together with Elsie Drake, standing beside her. Elsie was chafing her hands.

'She's coming to!' Elsie said. 'My word, Beth love, you did give us a scare! I came in at the door just in time to see you keel over.'

'I don't understand,' Beth said. 'I've never done such a thing in my life!'

'Well, lucky for you Doctor Stokes has a surgery at Batty Green this morning. I know he's still here because I've seen his horse tethered. When you feel fit enough I'm taking you across to see him.'

'Oh no! I'm sure that's not necessary,' Beth protested. 'I'm all right now. Or I will be once I'm home.' She felt weak and dithery, but there was no need for a fuss.

'Better safe than sorry,' Elsie said firmly.

Elsie sat in the waiting room while Beth, reluctantly, went in to see Doctor Stokes. In view of what he told her Beth was glad Elsie was not in the room. She could hardly take it in.

'So what's it all about?' Elsie asked when Beth emerged.

'Something and nothing! He says I'm overtired.'

Elsie looked at her keenly.

'You do too much. You should take it easy.'

'I'll try,' Beth promised.

She would not tell Elsie that Doctor Stokes had said he would come to Nazareth in the morning, give her a good going over.

He came as promised. When he had examined Beth and questioned her he gave his verdict.

'I haven't the slightest doubt about it, Mrs Tempest. You're pregnant. I can't be totally sure how far, because you seem vague about dates.'

Beth stared at him, speechless. This was what he had said to her in the surgery yesterday, but she had scarcely taken it in. She couldn't, because it was too good to be true, it couldn't happen to her. How could she believe him? Most of the night she had lain awake, tossing and turning, her head bursting with whirling thoughts. Much though she had longed to tell Jake, and had found the evening in which she had kept silent interminable, she had not allowed herself to do so in case it was a false alarm.

In the middle of the night he had been awakened by her restlessness.

'What is it?' he asked drowsily. 'Why aren't you asleep?'

'I don't know,' she lied. 'It's nothing. I'm just restless.'

He had grunted, turned over, and was immediately asleep again.

'I can't believe it,' she said now to Doctor Stokes. 'I was married to Will for four years. I'm barren!'

'You most certainly are not. Nor were you,' Doctor Stokes assured her. 'The difference is, you have a new husband. I've seen this happen again and again.'

She could say nothing. She was mute, bereft of words. All these years I've thought it was me, my fault, she thought. Will had never reproached her in words, but the silent reproach had been there. More than that, and far worse, had been her own guilt, eating away inside her. She had never felt herself to be a whole woman. She was lacking in what mattered most. And now, suddenly, everything had changed.

Doctor Stokes looked at her keenly. 'One of these

days the world might stop blaming the woman,' he said.

Beth found her voice. 'It doesn't matter any longer, at least not to me it doesn't,' she said quietly. 'But I won't ever forget it. But can't you please tell me when it will be, Doctor? When will I have my baby?'

'As near as I can say, around Christmas. I'll know better as time goes by,' Doctor Stokes said. 'And what better time than Christmas?'

Beth went through the rest of the day in a dream, hardly knowing what she was doing. When it was time for Jake to leave his work, she set off to meet him. Usually, since the cutting where they worked was a shorter distance away than the tunnel, Alan and Charlie Miller arrived home before Jake, but today she could not bear that to happen. She must give her news to Jake the moment she saw him, and she must see him alone.

How perfect the May day was for the bearing of such wonderful news, she thought as she set off. It was as if the weather had conspired with her. Although the breeze was present, there was warmth in the sun and, except on the summit of Whernside, the snow had gone. Flowers were appearing in the short grass and pushing their way through the cracks in the limestone. Larks rose high in the clear sky and a wagtail went to and from its nest in a niche in a stone wall. Soon now curlews would be back for the summer, raising their young in the meadows before the cutting of the hay drove them out. She had always paid attention to the comings and goings of birds, animals, flowers, but never before had they seemed so significant to her. She felt herself part of Nature's plan.

Halfway up the hill she saw Jake in the distance striding towards her. He was so tall, silhouetted against the sky, he walked so proudly. She quickened her step, and at that moment he recognized her and began to run down the hill. She stopped where she was and waited for him, and when he was only a few yards off she ran into his arms.

'Oh Jake! Oh Jake!'

'What is it? What is it?' Jake said. 'Is something wrong?' But that couldn't be the case. Although there were tears in her eyes her face was alight with joy.

'Oh no! Nothing's wrong. Nothing at all! But you're not going to believe me when I tell you because I couldn't believe it myself, but now I know it's true, and it's wonderful!'

He put two fingers over her mouth to stop the flow of words.

'Please tell me, love! What is it that's so wonderful – or am I supposed to guess?'

'You'll never guess! You'll never guess! Would you ever guess that I'm going to have a baby?'

Jake stared at her.

'There! You wouldn't have, would you? Well I am! It's true! I am going to have a baby!' She shouted it out loud, in pure triumph and the wind carried her words across the moor.

'Sit down!' Jake commanded. 'Sit down and tell me slowly.'

They sat on a rock and Beth told him, every detail. He listened in silence, then when she'd finished speaking he took her in his arms.

'Oh, Beth! Beth! This is the happiest day of my life! Of my entire life!'

'And of mine, Jake.'

They continued to sit there in total bliss, Beth with her head on Jake's shoulder, he with his arm around her.

'We must go!' Beth said at last. 'I don't want to, but Alan and Charlie will be home. I haven't given a thought to supper.'

'Who wants supper?' Jake said. 'I'd rather stay here.'

Beth jumped to her feet and held out her hand to him.

'Come along,' she said, smiling. 'We have to eat. What about me? I have to eat for two!'

Jake stood up.

'Of course you have, sweetheart! And I'm going to take the greatest care of you, beginning this minute!' He took her arm and began to lead her down the hill.

'Be careful how you go,' he warned her. 'You mustn't fall!'

She stopped dead, and turned around to face him.

'Stop it, Jake Tempest!' she said. 'I won't have it! I'm perfectly healthy and I don't need to be cosseted.' She spoke firmly, she meant what she said, but she loved his care for her.

'Try to stop me!' Jake said.

'I will,' she said. 'And I'll succeed. Or maybe you'll tire of it. We've seven months to go yet, remember.'

'I'll never tire of caring for you, looking after you,' Jake vowed. 'I couldn't bear it if anything happened to you – or to the baby.'

Beth laughed.

'Jake, love, nothing's going to happen to either of us! Now stop fussing and we'll go home and I'll make the supper. And by the way, I don't want to tell Alan and Charlie just yet, not just yet. I might tell Elsie, since she's my best friend, but no-one else at the moment.'

'I want to tell the world!' Jake said. 'But you can have your own way on this.'

The Millers were not in the hut when Jake and Beth returned.

'They'll have gone down to the beck to wash,' Jake said.

Like all the men who worked on the railway, the brothers came home filthy every day, not as blackened as Jake, from the tunnel, who looked like a miner

326

emerging from the bowels of the earth, but usually thick with mud and dust from the cutting, weary from a day spent on a job which was all pick and shovel, digging out the heavy soil which would then be used for building up embankments on other parts of the line.

Jake went into the hut to fetch his soap and towel, then walked down to the beck to join the brothers, who were standing waist deep in the fast-flowing water.

'My word, you're a mucky sight,' Alan called out. 'You'll dirty the water and no mistake!'

'Then come out, both of you, and let me in!' Jake said.

In fact, the beck ran so swiftly, its water clear and sparkling from the high hills where it had its source, that the dirt of the day's work was swiftly carried away. The only drawback was the temperature of the water, seldom higher than that of the snow on the summits. Jake caught his breath as he waded in.

'You had a rough day, then?' Alan asked him.

'One of the best days of my life, actually!' Jake said, soaping himself vigorously. He longed to tell them the wonderful news.

The brothers stared at him in disbelief.

'Tunnel going well, is it?' Alan asked.

'Very well,' Jake said. In fact that was true. The work there was, for the moment, proceeding well and they were ahead of schedule. All the same, that had nothing to do with the gladness in his heart. His thoughts were not on the tunnel.

'Rather you than me,' Alan said. 'I couldn't stand to work in the tunnel.'

'I couldn't stand it, either,' Charlie said.

'I need to be able to look up and see the sky,' Alan said. 'I've never worked inside, let alone in a tunnel, in all my life.'

In fact, Jake thought, there had been many days in

recent months when his thoughts had run along the same lines. It was true that the tunnel was going well, but there was more to it than that. When he'd started on the job he'd quickly got used to the darkness, to working in flickering candlelight, to the moisture running in rivulets down the walls, to the air below ground, which, no matter what the Company did to freshen it by blowing fresh air down the shaft, remained stale; but now all these things irked him. He started off each day by hating the moment when he must step into the cage and be taken down into the darkness below. He lived for the moment when he was hoisted up again and could stand on the earth's surface. I'm like the Millers, he thought. I want to look up and see the sky, make sure it's there, and I'm not buried for ever in a dark hole.

He thought this as the Millers climbed out of the beck and began to dry themselves while he ducked under the water and began to wash his hair. But today was different. Today Beth had given him her news and the whole world was transformed.

'We'll be off then!' Alan called out. 'Don't be long. Don't keep us waiting for our supper. We're as hungry as hunters, me and Charlie.'

'As hungry as hunters,' Charlie agreed.

Jake completed his toilet, dressed in the clean clothes he had brought down with him, then went back to the hut. When supper was over Alan and Charlie went down to the Welcome, which was a relief to Beth and Jake because now they could talk about what filled both their minds.

Beth stacked the dirty dishes on the table, fetched a bowl of water and began to wash up. Jake watched her from his armchair. Even washing dishes, her sleeves rolled up, her hair none too tidy, she was so pretty, so graceful.

'A boy or a girl?' he said. 'Which?'

'I don't mind in the least,' Beth said pushing the hair out of her eyes. 'I just want a baby!'

'A girl then!' Jake decided. 'I think a girl.'

'Very well,' Beth agreed. 'A girl first – and then a boy.' There was no reason, was there, why they should not have a family as large as Elsie's? They were both still young.

'Remember what I said,' Jake told her. 'You're to look after yourself every minute of the day. Eat well – and rest. You'll have to give up the classes for a start.'

Beth stared at him.

'Give up the classes! Whatever do you mean?'

'Exactly what I say, love. It's hard work. It's not just when the children are here, it's all the time you spend preparing for them. It's gone a long way beyond just teaching three or four children to read.'

'But Jake, I love the work, I enjoy the children. There's no reason at all why I shouldn't do it. And it earns a little money.'

'There's no need for you to earn money,' Jake said swiftly. 'That's my job. Do I keep you short?'

Beth looked at him in astonishment.

'Of course you don't. You're most generous. But I like the idea of a little independence.'

'You don't need it,' Jake said. 'I'm here for you to depend upon.'

'I know,' Beth said. 'And I do depend on you for almost everything. I'm glad to. But everyone must have some small area of independence. It's not the money that's important. It's the classes themselves – what I do in them, what the children do. Surely you understand that, Jake?'

'What I understand is that you're having a child – my child—'

'And mine!'

'Ours. And that you need to save all your strength

for that, not waste it on other people. The other children can do without you; our child can't.'

His face was set in obstinate lines but, watching him, Beth felt her own feelings harden.

'Our child won't ever be neglected, either before she's born or after,' she said. 'She'll always come first. And I have enough health and strength to carry this baby *and* to keep on the classes. So I'm sorry, Jake, if you don't approve, but that's what I'm going to do!'

She took the dishes out of the water and banged them down on the table. She could hardly believe what she was hearing herself say, or the strength of the rebellion she felt inside her. They were quarrelling! It was their very first quarrel – and it was unbearable. Tears filled her eyes and splashed down into the washing-up bowl.

'Oh, Jake!' she cried. 'I didn't mean to be so harsh! I didn't mean it to come out like that! The last thing I ever want is to quarrel with you.'

He jumped up, spun her around and took her in his arms, kissing away the tears. With soapy wet hands she caressed him in return.

'And I didn't mean to be hard with you,' he said. 'It's just that I love you so much. I want to protect every hair of your head.'

'And I want that too,' Beth said. 'But please don't ask me to give up the classes! Not yet. I should hate it.'

'Very well then,' he said reluctantly. 'But later on, and the moment you start to be tired.'

'Later on perhaps,' Beth agreed. 'And I promise to take every care, take no risks. Please believe that, dearest.'

'Come to bed,' Jake said. 'I want to hold you in my arms properly. There's only one way for two people who love each other as much as we do to make up a quarrel.'

'But Jake, it's early! Alan and Charlie aren't home yet.'

'They don't need us to wait up for them. They're big boys now!'

'I must finish the dishes, clear away,' Beth said.

'No you mustn't. Come to bed!'

Elsie was overjoyed at the news of Beth's pregnancy.

'It's wonderful!' she cried. 'You'll make a lovely mother! Oh, I can't tell you how pleased I am!'

The words were not quite out of her mouth when the door opened and Phoebe Grange walked in.

'So what's this you're so pleased about?' she demanded. 'I must say, you look like two cats who've swallowed the cream!'

Beth and Elsie looked at each other.

'Well, I'm not telling the world, because it's too soon,' Beth said. 'But there's no reason why you shouldn't know. I'm expecting!'

Phoebe gave a whistle.

'And we thought . . . I thought . . .'

'And I thought so too,' Beth interrupted. 'I thought it was impossible I should ever have a child. Well it wasn't, and I am!'

What wonderful luck to be having a child by Jake Tempest, Phoebe thought. Especially what luck to experience what went before it. She had, however, though with a reluctant sigh, put the man out of her mind since he had married Beth Seymour. They were such a pair of lovebirds that it was quite sickening; it was a lost cause on her part. She recognized that, and she was never one for pursuing lost causes. They were a waste of her time and talent, and in this place, peopled with frustrated men and too few women, there were opportunities galore. Still, it was a pity about Jake. He was something special, and a man was at his most vulnerable as his wife's pregnancy advanced. It was a pity also, though not for her, that too many wives didn't recognize that.

'Well, I'm very pleased for you,' she said. 'Very pleased indeed. So, shall you be giving up the classes? I do hope not.'

'I shan't,' Beth assured her. 'Not unless and until I have to.' In her heart she saw no reason why she should abandon them even after the baby was born, but that was a point she had no intention of raising. 'It will be business as usual,' she added.

A week later Jake arrived home from work, put down his jock tin on the table, and said: 'Good news! I'm going back on the night shift from the end of this week. I was given the chance and I took it.'

'Well, if it's what you want to do, I'm pleased for you,' Beth said. For her part she wasn't sure. It would be good to have him in the daylight hours, but how would she feel at night without him beside her in their bed?

'It *is* what I wanted,' Jake said. 'Don't you see, if I'm at home days I'll be able to help you with the classes – since you're so keen on them.'

Though they had not argued about the subject again, Beth knew that he was not happy about it. In any case she would be glad of his help. He could read as well as she could and he had a rapport with the children, especially with the boys. Also, he was much better than she was at arithmetic, which she was only too aware the children ought now to be learning; that, and geography, which was also not one of her strong points. The City Mission had some months ago supplied her with a globe of the world, which was a help, and would have been even more of one had she had the slightest idea where to place her finger on foreign countries.

'I'd appreciate that,' she said. 'There's a real need for the children to spread themselves, and we complement each other, you and me. What I can't do, you can, and you're every bit as good a teacher as I am.'

'I enjoy it,' Jake said.

In fact, he enjoyed his work with the children far more than anything he did in the tunnel, though he did take a pride in the building of that, in seeing it progress. They had turned the curve now and sometimes, especially when the day outside was bright, it was possible to discern the light at the northern end. He longed for the day when the gangs from the south would meet up with those tunnelling from the north. When that happened, or soon afterwards, Blea Moor tunnel would be completed, they would have conquered the mountain.

'All the same,' Beth said, breaking into his thoughts, 'we must work out a timetable. You must be sure to get your proper sleep.'

As the spring moved into summer and Beth's pregnancy advanced she remained well, though she began to tire more easily, and when a warm June gave way to an even warmer July, with herself and Jake and all the children crowded into the small hut, the heat began to worry her. Sometimes they took the children outside for lessons, but there were too many distractions in the open and not enough learning. Inside the hut the stove had to be kept going to provide means for cooking, and heating water. Beth, though she would not have thought it possible, was truly thankful when August came, and she could declare a month's holiday for the children.

'Not a moment too soon!' she said to Jake.

It was Saturday evening, Jake's night off from work. They were sitting outside watching the late sun going down over Ingleborough, the air still warm and insect-laden.

'I've had an idea,' Beth said.

'What?' Jake asked sleepily.

'I keep thinking how much easier it would be, both for us and the children, if we had a separate hut, if I ran it like a school . . .'

Jake wakened at once.

'Wait a minute!'

'No, you wait a minute,' Beth said. 'Let me finish! I think it's something the Company might be glad to do for us. It wouldn't cost a lot in their terms – a hut, desks, chairs, a stove for when the weather turns cold. I feel sure the Mission would do something.'

'Beth, stop it!' Jake interrupted. 'You're talking nonsense! Less than five months and you'll have the baby to look after. What's all this rubbish about starting what would turn into a school before you knew where you were?'

'I daresay it would,' Beth agreed. 'Turn into a school. But that's not rubbish. A small school of our own is exactly what we need on this part of the moor. And it's something I could do. We'd close for two or three weeks at Christmas, while I have the baby, but after that there'd be no problem.'

Jake jumped to his feet and stood in front of her.

'Will you just stop it!' he repeated. 'If you've any sense at all you won't start up the classes again at all.'

'Oh, but I must,' Beth disagreed. 'I'm not sitting around doing nothing until Christmas. The busier I am, the quicker the time will pass.'

'You're mad!' Jake stormed. 'I don't understand you! But I tell you this, you will *not* talk any more about getting a hut and starting a school. I absolutely forbid it and I would tell the Company so. They won't let you do such a thing without your husband's approval, and that you don't have. Do you hear me?'

'Quite well,' Beth said. 'There's no need to shout.'

He was right, of course. The Company wouldn't

consider it if Jake was against it. She was beaten, at least for the time being.

'Very well,' she said. 'I give up – for the present. Until after the baby's here.'

'By which time you'll find you have plenty to do,' Jake said.

'But when the holiday's over I want to go on with the classes. I'll be quite sensible, Jake. I'll give up when I'm tired.'

He put out his hands and pulled her up.

'Come here!' he said. 'Do you realize we almost quarrelled again? And we'd better go inside. The sun's gone. It's turning chilly.'

Arm in arm they walked back into the hut.

Beth started the classes again at the beginning of September, but by mid-November she knew the time had come to stop. She was slow and awkward, the child was so heavy. Also, she found it difficult to sleep at night so that in the mornings she was good for nothing.

'I'll have to give up at the end of the month,' she confided to Elsie. 'Jake will be pleased.'

'I should just think so!' Elsie said. 'I'm on his side in this. Start saving your strength. You'll need it when you go into labour. I can vouch for that!'

Beth's labour started on the twenty-third of December, and at ten in the morning of Christmas Eve the baby was born, Phoebe Grange acting as midwife.

'A lovely little girl!' she said. 'And not so little at that! A whopper, in fact.'

She wrapped the baby in a shawl and placed her in Beth's arms.

'You can have her for two minutes,' she said. 'And then I'll clean you both up and the new father can come in. I've found men like to wait until all's shipshape!'

When Phoebe called Jake into the room a little later it was to Beth he gave his immediate attention. She lay flat down in the bed, stretched out, immobile. Her face was pale, and there were dark shadows under her eyes, but the eyes themselves were shining.

'Oh Beth! My darling Beth! Are you all right, love?' Jake cried, bending over her, kissing her gently.

'Of course I am!' Beth said. 'Except that I'm bound up as tight as an Egyptian mummy! I can scarcely move!'

'It's for your own good,' Phoebe said. 'You want to get your figure back, don't you?'

She glanced at Jake. He was looking at Beth with worship in his eyes. What made me think I could ever get near him? Phoebe asked herself. The man's besotted!

'Don't you want to see the baby?' Beth said. 'Your daughter!'

'You can hold her for a minute,' Phoebe said. She took the child out of the crib and placed her in Jake's arms. When he looked at the dark, downy head and the crinkled red face – which was all he could see, for she was more tightly swaddled even than Beth – his eyes filled with tears.

'So what are you going to call her?' Phoebe asked.

'Mary,' Beth answered. 'What else would you call a baby girl born on Christmas Eve?'

'And Lily for her second name,' Jake said. 'My mother's name.'

The baby fell asleep as he was holding her, and a minute later so did Beth. He placed the child gently in the crib and tip-toed out of the room.

Beth was sound asleep when the knock came on the door. Jake rushed to answer it so that she shouldn't be wakened.

Armitage stood in the doorway. Wherever the snow could settle on his person it had done so; on his

336

shoulders, on the top of his fur cap, thickly on his eyebrows, and on his trousers and boots.

Jake stared at him, hardly believing his eyes.

'Well, aren't you going to ask me in?' Armitage asked.

19

'Armitage! Good heavens! Come in! Come in at once – you look frozen!'

Armitage stepped over the threshold. Jake, overcome with joy and surprise at the sight of his friend, enveloped him in a warm embrace.

'This is wonderful!' Jake said. 'The last person in the world I expected to see – and no-one I'd sooner see!'

The two men stood there, beaming at each other. In the warmth of the room the snow was already melting from Armitage's garments, forming small pools on the floor.

'I'm sorry,' Jake said. 'You're wet – and you must be frozen. Take off your coat and things at once. Come to the stove and get warm. You look blue with cold.'

'It's a bit parky out there, I'll not deny it,' Armitage said. He removed his coat, unwound his long scarf, shook the snow from his hat. Then he stretched out his hands, white with cold as the snow itself, to the stove.

'Your boots as well. I'll find you some slippers,' Jake ordered. 'And then something hot inside you. There's soup in the pan. It'll not take me a minute to heat it.'

Though he longed to know the circumstances which had brought Armitage to his door on this cold Christmas Eve, Jake asked no questions until he had served the old man with a bowl of steaming soup, thick with vegetables, and watched him drink it to the last drop. Only when Armitage put down his spoon and leaned back in his chair, breathing a sigh of relief, did Jake frame the first one.

'How did you find me, Armitage? How did you know I was here?'

'Oh, that wasn't difficult,' Armitage explained. 'I spent the last two nights in Settle at Mrs Sutherland's house. She told me she thought you were still working on the railway, so I decided to risk it.'

'You walked from Settle? In this weather?'

Armitage shook his head.

'No, friend. My days for that, at least in the winter, are over. But there seem to be carts going back and forth quite frequently. It wasn't difficult to get a lift. When I got to Batty Green I asked questions in the Welcome Home. They knew you lived in Nazareth. It was God's grace that I knocked on the right door first. So here I am, and mighty glad to be so!'

'And I'm mighty glad to have you,' Jake said.

Now that he had time to observe him, Jake was struck by how much Armitage had aged in the last four years. When he had seen him last he had been a man to whom you wouldn't think of attributing any particular age; it would have seemed irrelevant. Now he was old.

'Mrs Sutherland said if I found you I was to give you her best respects,' Armitage said.

'Did she say anything else?' Surely she would have told him about Sally?

'Nothing,' Armitage replied. 'In fact, she seemed singularly quiet. I didn't get much of her usual entertaining gossip. Why? Was there something to tell?' He had not missed the note of apprehension in Jake's voice.

'Not at the moment,' Jake said. 'It can wait.'

'They did tell me at the Welcome Home that you were married,' Armitage said. Indeed, now that he had thawed out enough to look around him, he realized

339

that everywhere in the room there were signs of a woman's touch; the pictures on the wall, the vase of dried flowers on the sideboard, the patchwork cushions and crocheted antimacassars on the armchairs, this was not what he would have associated with Jake, though of course he had never before seen him in his own domestic setting. All that was missing from the scene was the woman.

'I am indeed,' Jake said.

Armitage heard the warmth and pride in Jake's voice.

'So is your wife perhaps visiting a neighbour?' he asked. 'Will she be back soon? What will she say when she sees me?'

'She'll soon realize that you're the second most wonderful thing that has happened to us this Christmas,' Jake said. 'The first is that my wife's just given birth to our first child, our daughter! At this moment they're both fast asleep.'

A smile spread across Armitage's face, lit his eyes.

'Why, that's splendid, Jake! I'm very pleased for you.' And then, as suddenly as it had come, the smile left him. 'But you won't want me at a time like this, of course you won't. And I wouldn't want to disturb you. So with your permission I'll rest an hour, and then I'll be on my way.'

'And where would you go?' Jake demanded. 'In weather like this, where would you go?'

'Why, I'll go to the Welcome Home,' Armitage said. 'They'll find a bed for me. The landlord seems a decent sort. As for the weather, I've never given much thought to that. I've tramped these dales from west to east, from north to south, in every kind of weather you can think of. A few inches of snow hasn't stopped me.'

But that was when I was younger and stronger, he thought. When he had turned his face towards Settle a few days ago, determined to find Jake Tempest, he had faced the fact that those days were now over, that this was to be his last long walk. All the same, he wouldn't show it. If he really made the effort, he reckoned he could get back to the Welcome.

'So if you can spare the time I'll stay another hour or so, catch up on what you've been doing, then I'll be on my way.'

'Oh no you won't!' Jake said. 'I won't hear of it. And as a matter of fact, as it so happens, there's a bedroom spare. Usually we have two lodgers – brothers, name of Miller – but they've gone home to their families in Skipton for Christmas. They'd not mind you using their room.'

'And what about your wife? A stranger at Christmas – and she with a new baby?'

'You'll be no stranger to Beth,' Jake told him. 'I've talked about you often. She'd be cross with me if I let you go. And I certainly wouldn't want you to leave without seeing the baby. So as soon as you're ready I'll show you your bedroom and you can unpack your things.'

'Not that I have many,' Armitage said. 'You know I travel light – just what I can carry on my back.' But in the last year, no matter how much he threw out whatever he could dispense with, his backpack seemed to grow heavier. He would be glad to cast it aside for twenty-four hours, perhaps for a day or so longer if he was allowed.

When Jake showed him to the bedroom and he saw the bed he could have fallen into it. He was very tired, very tired indeed.

'Did I tell you . . . ?' Jake asked. 'No, of course I didn't, there hasn't been time. Beth taught me to read!'

Armitage straightened up from his unpacking and grabbed Jake by the arm.

'Why, that's wonderful! That's altogether mighty

wonderful! Didn't I tell you it was the one thing you should do?'

'You did,' Jake acknowledged. 'And you were right. It's opened up new worlds to me. More than that, we've taught a few children to read – Beth's done most of that, but I've helped.'

'And so the word spreads,' Armitage said. 'And so it will from them to others. Imagine a world in which everyone, man, woman and child, in every home in every country, could read. What would that do, eh?'

'Four years ago I couldn't have imagined,' Jake admitted. 'But I can now. Anyway, I'll leave you to it!'

When Jake had left the room, Armitage looked down at the bed, at its thick, soft pillows, its honey-combed white counterpane. Never had any bed looked so inviting. He would lie down for ten minutes, just ten minutes, no longer.

When the baby cried he didn't hear her. He was deep in sleep, though fully dressed. At the first sound from the baby Jake went in to Beth, and as he looked at her she opened her eyes, and smiled at him.

'Ah!' she said, 'I've had a lovely sleep. I do feel better!'

'She's crying!' Jake said.

'I know, love. I've still got my hearing!'

'What shall I do?' He was all anxiety.

'Nothing *you* can do,' Beth said. 'Except hand her to me. I daresay she's hungry.'

He took the baby out of the crib and when he held her against his shoulder she immediately stopped crying.

'You hear that?' he cried. 'She's stopped!'

'You're very clever, dear,' Beth said. 'You're going to be the perfect father! I still think you'd better give her to me.'

She wanted to hold her all the time. She wanted never to let her go. If she could, she would have kept her in her own bed but Phoebe, who had turned out to be quite bossy in the circumstances, said it was not allowed.

'Aside from anything else, you'd neither of you get any rest,' she'd said. 'So make the most of your lying-in. It'll all be over far too soon!'

'We have a visitor,' Jake told Beth.

She looked up from the baby.

'I didn't hear anyone. Who is it?'

'Armitage!'

'Armitage?'

'I told you about him. I met him in Settle before I came here. He was the one who told me I should learn to read.'

'Oh, of course I remember, though I've never met him. So where is he now?'

'Fast asleep on Alan Miller's bed. When I told him about you and the baby he was all for going back to the Welcome, but I persuaded him to stay the night. You don't mind, love, do you? I'll look after him.'

'Of course not,' Beth said.

'He looks very tired. I doubt he's well.'

'Then he's welcome to stay three nights, until the Millers' return. And when he's awake, bring him in to see me and the baby.'

Armitage was awakened soon afterwards by Phoebe Grange's arrival on the second of the twice-daily visits she was making to Beth and the baby. She blew into the hut like a strong wind, calling out as she entered, closing the door noisily behind her, marching across to the bedroom.

Armitage opened his eyes, not sure for the moment where he was, then stretched his limbs and swung himself down from the bed. He felt refreshed from his short sleep but he was glad not to be starting the walk back to Batty Green.

'I'm sorry I fell asleep,' he said, joining Jake in the living-room.

'I expect Mrs Grange wakened you,' Jake said. 'She's looking after Beth and the baby. When she's left I'll take you in to see them both. Beth wants to meet you.'

'And I want to meet the lady who taught you to read,' Armitage said.

Later, he shook hands with Beth as she lay in the bed, then peered at the baby in the crib.

'A most handsome child,' he observed. 'And with a look of both of you.'

He believed that was the thing to say. He knew nothing of babies and was secretly pleased that he was not expected to hold it. He had been married – it was a long time ago now, he had almost forgotten what his wife looked like – but there had never been any children.

'You're very welcome to stay until my lodgers return,' Beth told him. 'And if you want to stay in the neighbourhood longer I feel sure we'll find a neighbour who'll put you up.'

She was worried by the look of him. He was older and frailer than Jake had described him to her. It was certainly not right that he should be tramping the country at this time of the year, and with January and February, the very worst months, still to come.

'You're a very kind lady,' Armitage said gratefully. 'We'll see what happens.'

What happened was that two days later the postman, trudging through the snow to the few people in Nazareth and Jericho who ever received letters, delivered one from Alan Miller.

They were not coming back to Ribblehead, Alan wrote, because their wives and families missed them too much and wanted them nearer home. 'So we have got ourselves jobs at the new limeworks near Settle.

344

There is plenty of work to be had and it will be easier to get home . . .' Beth turned the page. 'Hoping this finds you as it leaves us and thank you for your kindness, Alan and Charlie Miller.'

'So!' Beth said, handing the letter back to Jake. 'What a surprise! And I shall miss them. But now Armitage can stay a week or two. I don't want to take on new lodgers until I'm up and about.'

'There's no need to do it at all,' Jake said.

'We'll see!' But in fact, Beth thought, with the baby, and the classes which she fully intended to resume, she wasn't sure she wanted lodgers, not permanently, though Armitage was welcome for a while, until he was fit again.

The winter passed. Ice, snow, frost, rain, gales, and sometimes something of everything at once in the short days and long nights. Occasionally there was fitful sunshine and Whernside stood out against a pale blue sky, though the mountain itself was blanketed in snow. And then, though in January and February the change was imperceptible, when March came the days were seen to grow longer.

Mary thrived; put on weight, was rounder and rosier by the day; gave her first smile, which Phoebe said was nothing more than wind, but Beth knew better. In the early summer she was sitting up of her own accord, while every day out of her rosebud mouth came new sounds and gurgles, among which Jake swore she said 'Dada' while looking straight at him. She was a happy, healthy baby, the delight of her parents' life, the mainspring of their happiness.

It was not so with Armitage. As Mary grew in strength, so Armitage weakened. He never complained, except with exasperation that even a short walk now fatigued him, but from Christmas to May Day Beth, observing him with worried eyes, thought that he must have lost two stones in weight. His clothes

345

hung on him. There were new hollows in his neck and below his cheekbones and his eyes were set deep in dark sockets.

'I don't like the look of him,' Beth said to Jake. 'He didn't look good when he came to us at Christmas, but he's worse now.'

'You're right,' Jake agreed. 'I reckon he should see Doctor Stokes, but he won't hear of it.'

'I'll have another go,' Beth said. 'I'll try to persuade him.'

The change came sooner than she had expected. Two days later, on a Friday morning, she answered a knock on the door and there stood Doctor Stokes.

Beth smiled at him, but spoke hesitantly.

'I didn't send for you, Doctor – though I'm pleased to see you, of course. Has there been some mistake?'

'Oh, no mistake,' he said. 'I was in Nazareth so I thought I'd look in to see how you and Mary were.'

'How kind of you! We're fine. And I'm particularly glad to see you, Doctor. To tell you the truth . . .' She lowered her voice. 'I'm worried about a friend who's staying with us. We couldn't persuade him to visit you, but . . .'

'Then ask me in,' Doctor Stokes said. 'I'd like to set eyes on Mary again, for a start.'

Armitage was sitting by the stove, trying to warm himself, though the room was like a hothouse.

'Doctor Stokes, this is our friend, Mr Armitage,' Beth said.

Armitage, while regarding the doctor with suspicion, extended a hand.

'He came to check on Mary, as he was passing,' Beth explained. 'Wasn't that kind?'

'Very kind.'

Doctor Stokes turned his attention to the baby.

'She seems in fine fettle!' he said after a few minutes.

'Then if you'll excuse me I'll just put her down in her cot,' Beth said. 'She's due for her nap.'

She went away, leaving the two men together.

'I trust you are well, Mr Armitage?' Doctor Stokes said civilly.

'If you must know, I'm not!' Armitage's reply was sudden and fierce. 'I wouldn't have troubled you, I've never had the need to see a doctor, but since you're here . . .'

'Shall we go to your room?' Doctor Stokes suggested. 'I expect you'd rather talk privately.'

Twenty minutes later the two men emerged from Armitage's bedroom. Beth looked up from her sewing, her eyes full of questions.

'It appears,' Armitage said, 'that all is not *quite* in order. But we know where we stand.'

'Not entirely,' the doctor said in a kind voice. 'Not until I've done a few tests. I'll do them as soon as I can, and I'll let you know.'

'Thank you,' Armitage said. But he doesn't need to let me know, he thought. He's as certain as I am. He himself had been certain for some time now. Wasn't that why he had made his way here?

Beth looked from one man to the other, but said nothing. It was clearly not the time. She wished Jake was here. He would know what to say.

'And your husband?' Doctor Stokes asked Beth. 'He's well?'

'Very well. He's on night shift so he would have been here, except that he's gone to Batty Green to buy provisions. I couldn't go. I'm expecting the children any minute now.'

Doctor Stokes nodded.

'I've heard all about your classes. You're doing a wonderful job there, Mrs Tempest. Just don't overtax yourself.'

'Oh I won't, Doctor!' Beth reassured him. 'It's

347

what I keep telling my husband. I'm as strong as a horse.'

'I daresay you are,' the doctor said. 'And I reckon it's better to do too much than too little.'

'If you meet Jake on your way back I'd be glad if you'd tell him that,' Beth said as she showed him to the door.

She stood in the doorway watching as he mounted his horse. They said his old mare knew every inch of the moor, from Ingleton to Dent Head. *She* would never fall down a shakehole, day or night.

Beth wondered what the doctor had said to Armitage, but there would be no time to ask him, even if she had the courage, because she could see the children approaching, uphill from Jericho and down the moor from Tunnel Huts. She had a dozen of them now, four days a week, and could have had twice as many except that there was not enough space. It was difficult to squash even twelve children into the small hut, and though she hated refusing the parents who wanted their children to come to her, Jake was still set against her asking the railway company to provide a hut especially for the purpose.

She stood there until the children from both directions saw her and started to race to reach her first. As they came near, shouting and laughing, she held up her hands to stop them.

'Come in quietly,' she told them. 'The baby's asleep!'

Armitage was sitting by the stove again and as the children streamed into the hut he moved farther back into the shadow, though there was no way he would leave the room when the children were there, especially as Beth had given him permission to stay.

'You don't trouble me in the least,' she'd told him. 'In fact I like to have you there. If there's a question asked to which I don't know the answer – and goodness knows there are plenty of those – well, you always do! It's true what Jake told me. You know something about everything!'

For his part Armitage was amazed at Beth's skill and patience with the children, considering how limited was her training. She was a born teacher, and so, for that matter, was Jake, who had had no training at all. 'When I watch the two of you with the children,' he'd told them, 'I can't believe you've ever done anything else!'

He himself was allowed to help on occasion. In the last twenty minutes of the school day he was permitted to read aloud a story, or tell one out of his own head; something about his travels, or the people he had met. This week he had been reading *Alice's Adventures in Wonderland* and would be reading a further episode this afternoon. He only hoped that he would not be too tired to do so. He never quite knew when the awful fatigue would strike him.

He planned, when *Alice in Wonderland* was finished, to start on *Through the Looking Glass.* He had sent away for the book. Would his strength last, he wondered – especially in view of what the doctor had said to him today – until he had finished that book? There were so many books waiting to be read.

Jake completed what he had to do on Batty Green and then, refreshed by a pint of ale at the Welcome, turned his steps towards home. Passing the viaduct he paused, as always, to look at it. The work was well ahead now and would soon be finished. The arches soared impressively, strong yet elegant, outlined against the summer sky. The whole edifice was like a great monument, and it *was* a monument, Jake thought; a monument to the hundreds of men who had worked on it over the last few years. From the look of it it would last forever.

He felt a stab of envy as he watched the men working high above the ground in the clear air, high enough to look down on the birds which flew in and out through the arches. Oh, he knew the tunnel was every bit as important to the running of the railway as was the viaduct. He had always taken pride in it, and still did, but apart from the inconspicuous opening at each end its life and function were hidden, secret; its strength and symmetry, the toil and skill which had gone into making it, were invisible to the world and in its darkness would never be seen.

There were days, more and more of them recently, when he felt like a mole or a beetle living in the dark. True, the tunnel was open all the way through now – the headings had met within three inches of each other – and a light engine ran regularly through its length bringing supplies. There was no more of men being lowered in a cage down the shaft, but daylight could not penetrate far – though the low-lying fog did. The fog reached everywhere.

In one way the tunnel was less dangerous; now that they were using dynamite instead of gunpowder there were fewer explosions. But he was weary of it. He had been almost four years in the tunnel, one of the longest-serving men there, for they came and went. Perhaps it was time he changed his job? What would it be like, he wondered, to work on the viaduct? He was a skilled man now, in charge of other men. It might be quite easy to find a job other than in the tunnel.

By the time he was back in Nazareth the children were on their last lesson of the morning, ready at any moment to break to eat the packed dinners they had brought with them.

Beth looked up and smiled warmly at him as he came in at the door.

'Right, children,' she said. 'That's all for this morning. Close your books, and as it's bright and sunny we'll eat our dinner out of doors!'

When the children had eaten she gave them twenty minutes to play their games. It was the season for skipping ropes, though the boys scorned this, preferring to kick a ball about. She sat watching with Jake and Armitage on a bench outside the hut, the baby in her arms.

'Was it busy at Batty Green?' she asked Jake.

'As always,' he said. 'I stopped on the way back to take a look at the viaduct. It's coming on famously. I began to wish I worked on the viaduct instead of in the tunnel.'

'Don't say that! Don't ever say that!'

Beth rounded on him, her voice shrill, almost a scream. Jake looked at her in consternation. This outburst was not like his Beth, not at all like her.

'I'm sorry, love!' he said.

She was not easily to be pacified.

'Haven't I already given one husband to the viaduct?' she cried.

'I'm sorry,' Jake repeated. 'It was thoughtless of me. Of course I won't do it!'

'Promise me! Promise me you'll never work on the viaduct!'

'I promise!' Jake said.

She calmed down.

'I know you've begun to dislike working in the tunnel,' she said. 'Don't think I don't notice, or that I don't sympathize. But it won't be all that much longer. Everyone says another year should see the railway finished and running.'

'I daresay that's true,' Jake agreed. And what will we do then, he wondered?

Beth put the same thought into words.

'What will we do then?' she asked.

'What would you like to do?' Armitage chipped

in. 'Think of that first; what would you really like to do?'

The three of them sat in silence for a moment while the children continued to play. Beth was the first to speak.

'I think I know what *I* would like to do. I'd like to have my own school, run it in my own way. Or even better, I'd like for the two of us, Jake and me, to run it. Yes, that would be my choice!'

Armitage nodded.

'I can picture you doing that. I reckon you'd do it well.'

'It's nothing more than a dream,' Beth said, 'and I mustn't sit here dreaming. It's time the children were in. As for you, Jake, you must get your sleep or you'll be fit for nothing when you go to work.'

All the same, she wondered as she called the children and went back indoors with them, what *would* they do when the railway was finished?

20

On a Monday late in August, the postman handed Beth a letter. *B. Armitage, Esq.* the thick white envelope said, in exquisite writing with many flourishes. *Care of Mr J. Tempest.*

She handed the letter to Armitage. What did the B stand for, she wondered? He was extremely secretive about his given name.

'Ah! Splendid!' Armitage said. 'I've been expecting this! It will be from my solicitor.' He had written to him a week ago and had asked for a speedy reply. He wanted no time wasted.

What can Armitage want with a solicitor, Beth asked herself as she watched him open the envelope and read the single sheet it contained.

'Yes, that's all in order,' he said. 'Now all I have to do is go to Skipton next Friday.'

'To Skipton?' Beth queried.

'I have to sign things,' Armitage said. 'Please excuse me while I fetch paper from my room. I must reply at once.'

'What do you suppose he's talking about?' she asked Jake when Armitage had left them. 'And is he fit to travel to Skipton on his own?'

'I don't know why he's going,' Jake admitted. 'He always was a bit eccentric, and no worse for that. But I agree with you, he's not fit enough to travel to Skipton and back on his own. He's an old man, and sick. I'd not be happy to see him do it.'

'Then we must go with him,' Beth declared. 'The

353

class is still on holiday and I'm sure Elsie will look after the baby. And as for you, you must take a day off work.'

'They won't like it,' Jake said. 'But you're right and I'll do so. I'd not be easy in my mind otherwise.'

Armitage, when he came back into the room and they put the idea to him, was delighted.

'I wouldn't have asked you,' he admitted, 'but I'm most grateful. I wasn't looking forward to making the journey alone.'

'But if it's simply a question of signing something,' Jake said, 'couldn't you ask your solicitor to come to Nazareth?'

'Oh I couldn't possibly do that!' Armitage was shocked at the thought. 'Mr Jepson is quite an important man. I couldn't expect him to come all the way to Nazareth for such as me. But if you and Beth will accompany me to Skipton then that will please me mightily. I'll write and tell Mr Jepson to expect us, and we'll make it a day out.'

Beth cleared the breakfast table and Armitage sat down to write. He wrote at length, and Beth wondered how he could find so much to say on what seemed a simple matter.

'There!' he said at last. 'That's done!'

He turned to Jake.

'Shall you be going down to Batty Green?' he asked. 'If so, will you take my letter to the post office? And I thought that I might hire a pony and trap to take us to Settle, and from there we can get the train to Skipton. Will you see to that for me, Jake?'

'I will,' Jake promised. It would cost money to hire the pony and trap, but since the old man seemed keen to do it he would make no protest. It would certainly be more comfortable for his friend than being jolted around on any old cart which happened to be going in that direction.

Elsie was more than willing to look after the baby.

354

'You know I love to have her, and she'll be no trouble at all. I'll come and fetch her on Thursday.'

'Bring Tom with you,' Beth said. 'We haven't seen much of him this holiday.'

'I will,' Elsie said. 'Have you heard the news about Phoebe?'

'What news?' Beth asked. 'Since there are no classes at the moment I haven't seen either her or the children.'

'They're leaving!' Elsie announced.

'Leaving?'

'That's right. Phoebe says Malcolm is fed up with the railway, but I reckon it's Phoebe who's fed up with Jericho. Too quiet for her. She's every inch a town girl.'

'Where will they go?'

'Bradford. Malcolm reckons he'll get work there. It'll certainly suit Phoebe better.'

'I suppose so,' Beth said. 'I must pop round and see her.'

She found Phoebe on her knees, packing a large tin trunk from an assortment of objects scattered around the room.

'I'm sorry to hear you're leaving,' Beth said.

'Thank you,' Phoebe said. 'I can't say I'm sorry, though. Four years and more we've been stuck in this place. I'm ready for a taste of civilization, a few new faces. Oh, I don't mean you, love,' she added. 'You and me have always got on well. And the children will miss you.'

'I'll miss them,' Beth confessed. 'They've done so well. But in Bradford they'll be able to go to a proper school. They'll learn much more.'

Phoebe shrugged.

'I'm not sure they need more school. They can read and write now, do a few sums. What else is there?'

'Quite a lot,' Beth said.

'Oh well, we'll see. I look forward most to when they're earning a penny or two!'

On Friday, since the driver of the pony and trap had declared it impossible to bring it all the way up the rough moorland track to Nazareth, they took the tramway down to Batty Green. It ran more often now. When Jake helped her into the trap, which was waiting for them at the tramway terminus, Beth was reminded of her wedding day, and she knew by the gentle squeeze which Jake gave to her arm as he helped her up that his thoughts matched hers. She had not been to Settle, let alone Skipton, since then.

The drive through Ribblesdale was enchanting, the trees and hedges thick with their summer greenery, the corn in the fields turning to gold. It would be an early harvest this year. They halted at Horton to let the pony drink, and Jake fetched her a glass of lemonade from the inn.

'Do you remember we stopped here when I first walked from Settle?' Jake asked Armitage.

Armitage nodded. 'I remember it well.' He had taken to Jake from the first. He had always known that their paths would continue to cross.

When they boarded the train at Settle station it was stifling hot. Jake opened the windows and Beth sat with her back to the engine so that the smuts should not blow onto her face or, worse still, onto her very best summer dress.

'This is exciting!' she said, smiling across at Armitage.

'For me too,' Armitage replied. 'I've made most of my travels on my own two feet, though I must say, walking is quieter.'

Most nights, when he blew out his candle, he lay on his back and took a walk in his mind. Each night a different walk, always one of which he knew every step.

He climbed the green fells, scrambled down the steep, shaly inclines, walked through flower-filled meadows and by clear streams. His back never ached, his feet were never sore; the sun shone, or in a brief rainstorm there was shelter. And if he was lucky, long before his journey's end came into sight, he fell asleep. He was glad he had done so much in his younger days. How else would he keep going on his memories?

Now he looked out of the window and marvelled at the speed with which the fields, the trees, the sheep and cattle sped by. All of forty miles an hour the train must be doing through the valley. Only the birds which flew past the window travelled faster. It was no time at all before they were in Skipton.

'Mr Jepson's chambers are in the High Street,' Armitage said. 'Jepson, Murthwaite & Jepson. We can walk there.'

'Are you sure?' Jake asked. 'Wouldn't you rather we had a cab?'

'Not at all!' Armitage said. 'I still have the use of my legs, at least for that distance!'

It was not his legs, but his shortness of breath which was troubling him by the time they reached the solicitor's premises, and the fact that Mr Jepson's own office was at the top of a steep flight of stairs was no help. Jake suggested that he and Beth should remain in the waiting room while Armitage conducted his business, but Armitage would have none of that.

'I want you with me,' he said.

He had told them nothing of what his business was, or why it had been necessary for him to take this journey when he would have been better resting at home. Whatever it was, Beth thought, it was clearly of importance to him.

They waited no more than a minute or two in the outer room before Mr Jepson came out of his office to meet them. He was a small thickset man with a round smiling face. He stepped, arm extended, towards Armitage, and shook his hand vigorously. He's not a bit like a solicitor, Beth thought, though true enough she had never met one before.

'Good to see you, Mr Armitage,' Mr Jepson said. 'And this lady and gentleman must be the friends you told me you would bring.'

He nodded happily towards Jake and Beth and when Armitage had introduced them the solicitor led the way to his office, seated himself behind his imposing desk, with the three of them arranged in front of him. There was a question in his eyes as he looked at Armitage.

'Have you . . . ?' he began.

'No,' Armitage said. 'Mr and Mrs Tempest accompanied me here out of the kindness of their hearts. They know nothing more.'

'In that case,' Mr Jepson said, 'they have a pleasant surprise in store.'

Jake and Beth looked at each other, and then from the solicitor to Armitage, who was leaning back in his chair, a satisfied smile on his face.

'The thing is that Mr Jepson has drawn up my will and I am happy to tell you that the two of you are to be my sole beneficiaries!'

Jake stared at Armitage. It was several seconds before he found his voice.

'But this is a total surprise, Armitage! I had no idea!' He looked at Beth for confirmation and, speechless, she nodded her head. She wondered, in fact, if she had heard aright.

'Are you sure about this?' Jake asked Armitage. 'Don't you think . . . ?'

'I'm quite sure,' Armitage said firmly. 'I've thought it all out. I've no kith and kin of my own and you've been exceedingly kind to me. This is my return.'

'Whatever we did for you, it was a pleasure,' Beth

358

said quietly, finding her voice. 'We had no thought of . . .' For a moment words failed her again, then she pulled herself together. 'I just hope – I'm sure Jake does – that it will be a very long time before any of this happens.'

She spoke the truth. She was deeply moved by the old man's gesture, though common sense told her that the amount involved would be small. Armitage was a poor man. He paid his way in the house but he never seemed to be left with two ha'pennies to rub together. All the more reason, though, to appreciate what he was doing.

'Well then!' Mr Jepson said briskly. 'I have drawn up the will exactly as you instructed, Mr Armitage. All that remains is for you to sign it in the presence of two witnesses, who cannot, of course, be the beneficiaries.'

He rang a bell, and from an adjoining room two clerks appeared. It took no time at all for the signing and witnessing to be completed and for the clerks to leave as silently as they had come.

'And now for my further business,' Armitage said to the solicitor. 'Have you made any progress there?'

'I have indeed,' Mr Jepson said with satisfaction. 'In fact I believe that what I've been able to find will suit you down to the ground! *And* the premises are empty. My chief clerk, Mr Feathers, has the keys and he will be pleased to accompany you.'

Armitage turned to Jake and Beth.

'You look confused,' he said. 'And no wonder. It's my fault. I should have told you earlier, but there it is, I didn't! The fact is, I'm interested in renting a property in Skipton.'

'A property? But why . . . ?' Beth began. 'What sort of a property?'

Why did Armitage want to leave them? she wondered. He had seemed happy enough in Nazareth.

What was more, was he well enough to look after himself? She didn't think so, and that was a worry. She had grown so fond of him.

'You shall soon see,' Armitage said. 'So if Mr Feathers is free . . .'

Mr Jepson rang the bell again and the chief clerk appeared; a thin, grey man clutching a bunch of keys in his bony hand.

'At your service!' he said.

Armitage rose to his feet.

'We'll be off then, Mr Jepson. And I'll let you know what I think in a day or two.'

'The property is no more than ten minutes' walk away,' Mr Feathers said to Armitage as they went down the stairs. 'But perhaps you would like me to get a cab?'

'We'll walk,' Armitage said. 'As I told my young friends earlier, I haven't quite lost the use of my legs!'

'As you wish, sir,' Feathers said. 'The property is just beyond the High Street, and therefore quieter. In fact, a prime position for the purpose.'

Beth looked at Jake. Why did Armitage need a dwelling in a quiet, prime position? her expression said. And could he afford it? Jake shrugged his shoulders, equally puzzled.

Feathers led them to the top of the bustling High Street. As they passed the hotel where she and Jake had spent their honeymoon, a thrill of delight, so strong that she thought it must be visible to everyone, shot through Beth's body. She squeezed Jake's arm and he drew her closer in response.

At the top of the hill, where the church faced down the High Street, they branched off to the right. The houses were larger here, with deep windows and solid front doors. They were not the least bit suitable for Armitage, Beth thought, not unless he simply

360

intended to take a room or two in one of them, and they did not look like houses which let off rooms.

Mr Feathers halted.

'Here we are!' he announced. 'The Beeches.'

Behind an elaborate wrought-iron double gate a wide path, flanked on either side by a square of lawn, led to the front door, set in the middle of a square-built house, its golden stone lit by the summer sun.

'There is, of course, a larger garden at the rear,' Mr Feathers said. 'I daresay you would find that useful.'

Whatever for, Beth wondered – but was too constrained to ask.

Mr Feathers selected a key, unlocked the front door and let them in. They stood in a wide hall, doors opening on either side and a well-proportioned staircase rising to the upper floor. Armitage stood in the centre of the hall and looked around him, a quiet smile of satisfaction on his face.

'Capital! Capital! Very suitable, I'd say!'

Beth could contain herself no longer. Armitage had clearly taken leave of his senses.

'*I* must say,' she ventured, 'it doesn't really seem suitable. Isn't it rather large for you, Mr Armitage?' To say nothing of the cost, she thought.

'Bless my soul, I'd not need more than one or two rooms,' Armitage said. 'Small ones at that, and I'd be content at the top of the house. No, the rest would be for you.'

'For us?' Jake said. 'I don't understand. What would we do with a house like this?'

'Why, it would house your school, of course! Don't say you've changed your minds! Don't tell me you no longer want to run a school!'

Beth and Jake stood quite still. I don't believe this is happening, Beth thought. It's a dream and I shall wake up any minute. She struggled to find her voice.

'Of course we do, Mr Armitage! But we couldn't possibly afford a place like this. You know we couldn't!'

Jake turned to Mr Feathers.

'There seems to be some mistake here. I'm afraid we've been wasting your time.' What *was* Armitage thinking of?

Feathers looked anxiously at Armitage.

'I understood, sir . . .'

'And you were right,' Armitage reassured him. 'The mistake I made is that I didn't tell my friends here what I had in mind. I wanted it to be a surprise, you see. Perhaps that was wrong?' He addressed the question to Jake and Beth.

'Not wrong, Armitage,' Jake said gently. 'But not really practical. You see, there's no way Beth and I could afford to rent a place like this. Not until the school – if we were to have one – was up and running and making a profit. And there'd be a deal of money to be paid out before we reached that stage.'

'But it was a kind thought,' Beth put in. 'We appreciate that.'

'Oh, I didn't expect you to rent it!' Armitage said. 'That's *my* contribution. After all, aren't you my heirs now?'

'But we don't want to inherit for a long, long time,' Beth said. 'Do we, Jake?'

'Certainly not,' Jake agreed.

'It's good to know that,' Armitage said. 'It makes me a very happy man. But it doesn't mean that I can't use some of the money on your behalf, and whenever I like. You see . . .' he was suddenly hesitant, diffident, '. . . there's a fair amount of money. My mother left it to me, and then an uncle left me more still. I never spent much – what did I want with money, living my kind of life? And Mr Jepson invested it wisely for me, so that it just grew. So if you don't like this house, or

362

you don't think it's suitable, well then we can look elsewhere.'

'Oh, it's not that. It seems wonderful,' Beth said. 'It's just that . . . Really, I can't believe this is happening!'

'Nor me!' Jake agreed. 'But let me say at once that if, by some chance, we go ahead, then as soon as the school is in profit we'll naturally pay you back every penny.'

'As you wish,' Armitage said.

'Then would it not be a good idea to look over the rest of the house?' Mr Feathers suggested.

They went from room to room. The more Beth saw of the house, the more excited she became, and Jake quickly caught the excitement from her. It was not that there were over-many rooms, just enough to house themselves, Armitage, their family – even though so far it was only one daughter – with two large rooms which would make ideal classrooms; but that the whole house was light and bright and welcoming, with white paint everywhere and large windows through which the sun streamed in. At the rear was the garden Mr Feathers had promised; large and square, roughly grassed over and with trees around its perimeter.

'The garden needs some work on it, of course,' Mr Feathers said. 'Flower beds. Paths.'

'Oh, we wouldn't want it too spick-and-span,' Beth said. 'It's perfect for children to play in!' She saw the whole thing in her mind's eye. 'Don't you agree?' she asked Jake.

'Absolutely,' he said. 'And I could put up a swing from one of the trees.'

When they had toured the whole house, including the two spacious attics from which there was a view over Skipton to distant green hills, they stood again in the entrance hall.

'Well?' Armitage said.

'It's quite perfect!' Beth said.

'I agree,' Jake said.

'You don't think we should look at one or two others?' Armitage asked. 'To make a comparison?'

Beth shook her head.

'No. We'd not find anything better. This house *feels* right. I can tell it at once.'

'The only thing is . . .' Jake said, 'can you really afford to lend us the money, knowing we can't pay it back quickly? And we'd need more. We'd need money to equip it.'

'The other thing is,' Beth said, suddenly serious, 'can we actually run a school? Do we know how? Of course it would be small, and we'd take only young children, but could we do it? And would we get pupils?'

'I think you would,' Armitage said. 'Skipton is a thriving place, with lots of families. And I'm sure you're competent. Think what you've achieved in Nazareth, with so few advantages.'

'Thank you,' Beth said. 'You give me confidence. And I think you're right. I think Jake and I could make a go of it between us.'

'As for the money, I can see to that,' Armitage said. 'But perhaps you'd like to go back to Nazareth and give it further thought?'

Beth and Jake looked at each other.

'I don't think we need to do that,' Jake said.

'In that case, Mr Feathers,' Armitage said, 'we'll return and talk to Mr Jepson!' He would be glad, he thought, not to have to make too many more trips to Skipton. He was quite tired.

Back in the solicitor's office Armitage quickly made arrangements with Mr Jepson about the renting of the house, paid a quarter's rent in advance and signed everything which needed to be signed. 'Just in case,' he said.

It was late afternoon when they took the train back to Settle and dusk was falling when the pony and trap which they had hired at Settle deposited them at Batty Green. To Jake's dismay, the last tram, which would have taken them as far as Jericho, had already left. Armitage was clearly not fit for the climb over the moor.

'I'll take you as far up as the horse can pull the trap,' the owner of the vehicle said reluctantly. 'But it won't be far. The way's too steep and the track's too rough. The trap would tip over in no time at all.'

'Just as far as you can, then,' Jake said.

They were well short of Jericho before it was clear that there was nothing for it but to walk the rest of the way. Jake supported Armitage as best he could, at times half-carrying him. Armitage was white-faced and silent with fatigue, though trying his best not to be a burden.

Reaching Jericho, they stopped at Elsie's hut in order to collect Mary, but also to give Armitage a rest.

'The baby's hard and fast asleep,' Elsie said. 'It's a shame to wake her. Why don't you let me bring her up to you in the morning?'

'I will,' Beth agreed. 'Come early. I've such a lot to tell you, you'll never believe!'

Jack Drake was looking at Armitage with concern. The old man looked all in.

'It wouldn't be a bad idea for *you* to stay here until the morning,' he offered. 'We can make you up a bed.'

'Oh, no!' Armitage protested. 'I must get home! I must!'

'In that case,' Jack said to Jake, 'you and me can carry Mr Armitage between us. You'll not object to that?' he asked Armitage.

'I confess I'd be grateful,' Armitage said. 'I admit I'm very tired.'

Elsie fetched a blanket and put it around his

shoulders, then between them the two men carefully, and with great gentleness, carried the old man from Jericho to Nazareth. Beth went before them so that by the time they reached the hut Armitage's bed was ready. They laid him on it.

'I'm afraid it's been quite a day for you,' Jake said. 'You've done too much.'

Armitage's face lit with a contented smile.

'It's been one of the happiest days of my life. I shall sleep well tonight!'

It was Beth, taking him a cup of tea, who found him in the morning. He was sitting upright against his pillows and at first she thought he was asleep, and wondered if she should let him be, he looked so peaceful; but then she thought there was a stillness about him which was not right.

Gently, she touched his hand. It was colder than a stone in winter, and as she touched him he slid sideways.

'Jake!' she cried. 'Jake! Come quickly!'

21

Jake came running.

Beth, leaning over Armitage, looked up at her husband with frightened eyes.

'He's . . . Oh, Jake!'

Gently, Jake eased her out of the way and felt for the old man's pulse. It was there; irregular, faint, hard to find, but still there.

'He's not dead,' he said. Though he looks it, he thought. His face was as white as snow, his lips a thin blue line, his breath barely discernible.

'We must get the doctor,' Jake said. 'I can run down to Batty Green faster than you, but will you be all right here?'

'Yes,' Beth said.

'He might . . .'

Beth interrupted him.

'He might die. I know. But please go! Quickly!'

'I'll tell Elsie on the way down, ask her to come round.'

Beth shook her head. 'Don't waste time!'

'I won't!' Jake said. 'I have to pass her door. I don't want you to be alone.'

Elsie, breathless, arrived within minutes of Jake's leaving.

'I ran all the way!' she explained. 'Oh dear, he does look bad, poor man!'

They stood on either side of the bed, watching Armitage for the slightest sign of movement. Then there came a moment when he took a great, shuddering breath, then slowly, almost silently, exhaled it – and was still.

'He's gone!' Elsie said.

Beth stood there, rooted, until a cry from Mary who had been asleep in her crib in the next room brought her to her senses.

'You go to Mary,' Elsie ordered. 'I'll see to Mr Armitage as far as I can, though we mustn't do much until the doctor's been. Then I'll make us a cup of tea.'

Minutes later she followed Beth into the living-room, and set the kettle to boil.

'He looks very peaceful now, poor gentleman,' she said. 'And he was a gentleman, wasn't he? You only had to hear him speak to know that.'

Beth nodded agreement.

It seemed a long wait before Doctor Stokes arrived.

'I was out on a case,' he explained. 'Jake had to find me. I'm sorry.'

'He died an hour ago,' Beth said. 'But I doubt you could have done anything. He was never conscious again.'

'It comes as no surprise to me,' Doctor Stokes said. 'Nor would it to him if he was aware of it happening, which I doubt. He knew it was coming, and sooner rather than later. I'd told him that. He wasn't afraid.'

'If only I'd known!' Beth said. 'If only I'd known earlier, perhaps I could have done something for him.'

'You couldn't,' Doctor Stokes said. '*I* couldn't. His heart was worn out. But you gave him exactly what he needed, a comfortable home in which to spend the last months of his life, a place in which to die with dignity.'

'He was always a dignified man,' Jake put in. 'In spite of the fact that he chose to live like a tramp.'

'A gentleman tramp,' Elsie said.

It seemed to Beth, a few days later, as they followed

368

the track to Chapel-le-dale, that she had walked behind more coffins in the time she had lived on the moor than in the rest of her life until then.

'We must write to Mr Jepson,' Jake said when they returned from the funeral. 'We must let him know.'

'We should have done it at once,' Beth said. 'It's just that everything happened so quickly. I'm sure he'll be shocked.'

It gave Jake a swift moment of pride that he was able, with no difficulty, to write the letter himself to the solicitor. Mr Jepson replied by return of post. His letter showed no surprise, and when, at his suggestion, they visited him at his office in Skipton, he expounded on that.

'Mr Armitage told me he had only a short time to live. It was the reason he wanted to put his affairs in order as quickly as possible, to make sure that his money – a not inconsiderable amount, as you will hear in a moment – went where he wished it to go.'

'We knew he wasn't well,' Beth said. 'But he never told us how ill he was.'

'He wouldn't,' Mr Jepson said. 'My late client was a most modest and unselfish man. He would not have wanted to worry you. And now we must get down to business!'

He rang the bell on his desk and Mr Feathers entered.

'Ah, Mr Feathers, I am about to read the late Mr Armitage's will, and then I'm sure there'll be matters to discuss. I wish you to be present.'

'Certainly,' the chief clerk said, bowing respectfully to Jake and Beth before he opened the file in front of his employer.

My goodness, Beth thought with surprise, they're treating us as if we were really important. But when Mr Jepson, in a solemn voice, began to read the will and then mentioned how much money Armitage had left, she was less surprised.

'It is not a fortune of course,' Mr Jepson said, 'but it is a tidy sum.'

'Oh, but it *is* a fortune, Mr Jepson!' Beth said. 'At least to us it is!' She looked at Jake.

'It is indeed,' Jake agreed.

'Over the years Mr Armitage spent very little. He saved his money and it accumulated, with the result you see.' Mr Jepson spoke with approval. He thought highly of clients who did not squander their money but trusted him to invest it wisely on their behalf. Mr Armitage had been an exemplary client in that regard.

'Now we come to the house which Mr Armitage was to rent on your behalf,' he continued. 'Will you still wish to pursue the idea of starting a school, or in the circumstances will you perhaps have other ideas in mind? I need to know because if you do *not* wish to rent The Beeches, the owner must be advised.'

Beth and Jake glanced at one another, but there was no need to consult.

'Our plans are the same,' Jake said.

'Except that we shall put them into practice sooner than we expected,' Beth added. 'There's no point in waiting.'

'Quite right!' Mr Jepson said.

'Do you think . . .' Beth began hesitantly, 'do you think we could look over The Beeches again while we're here in Skipton? There are things neither of us can remember. It was all such a surprise to us at the time.'

'Of course! Mr Feathers will accompany you,' Mr Jepson said. 'Should you have any questions I'm sure he'll be able to answer them. And I will be in touch with you both before long.'

They went over the house, seeing it with different and sharper eyes than on the first occasion.

'It's even better than I thought, though it's certainly shabby,' Beth said. 'We'll need to make a few alterations, some adjustments, do some painting, but there's nothing we can't manage between us.'

On the train journey back to Settle they discussed dates and times.

'Of course there's no way we can open for the September term,' Beth said. 'It's almost September now. It's a pity, that – but we'll open after Christmas. Oh, Jake, it's going to be so exciting! Did you ever think this could happen to us?'

Jake looked across at her, looked into her bright, shining eyes, alight with enthusiasm. But for the presence of other people in the compartment he would have taken her in his arms there and then.

'No, I didn't,' he said.

He gave his notice to the Railway Company at the end of the week, but was persuaded to stay on for another month.

'They weren't surprised that I was leaving,' he told Beth when he arrived home. 'It's beginning to happen with more than me. It won't be long before the railway's finished. People are getting anxious about what they'll do next.'

'I shall miss you,' Elsie said when Beth told her how soon they might be leaving. 'But Jake is right. Before long we'll all be gone. It stands to reason. There'll be no work left for us.'

Beth put her arms around Elsie's shoulders and drew her close.

'Oh, Elsie, I shall miss you so much! You've been such a friend to me. I couldn't have managed without you!'

'Nor I without you, hinny,' Elsie said. 'But I have to admit, I'll be glad to get back to Northumberland. I wouldn't want to live in Jericho forever. Shanty towns are no place to bring up children.'

'I agree,' Beth said. 'I hope my next child will be born in Skipton. A civilized place.'

'Beth! You're not . . . ?' Elsie cried.

Beth laughed.

'No, I'm not expecting! Not yet, anyway. But there's no reason at all why I shouldn't be, soon!' If it had anything to do with Jake and his love for her, she thought, she would be pregnant tomorrow.

'But surely, moving house, starting a school . . .' Elsie said. 'And Mary not yet a year old . . .'

'None of that worries me,' Beth said. 'There's nothing I can't do. Or at least there's nothing Jake and I can't do together.'

Phoebe left, gladly shaking the dust off her heels, and set her face towards Bradford, though the children had been tearful.

'I like it here,' Clarissa wailed. 'I don't want to go.'

'You'll enjoy it in Bradford,' Beth said. 'I'm sure you will.' From what little she had heard of Bradford she was not at all sure, but she tried to speak with conviction. 'You'll have a nice new school.'

'Aubrey and me don't want a new school,' Clarissa said. 'We like coming here.'

'Well, I shall be having a new school also,' Beth said. 'But it will be much too far for you to come all the way from Bradford.'

'All the same,' she said to Jake a day or two later, 'perhaps we should consider whether we'll take a few boarders. Not many, we wouldn't have the room, and not Clarissa and Aubrey, but it would widen the scope and I'd quite enjoy it.'

'We'll think about it,' Jake said. 'We'll not dismiss anything out of hand.'

The going of Phoebe and her family was the first of several farewell scenes and in early November it was the turn of Beth and Jake to leave.

'We shall stay on a bit longer,' Elsie said. 'Jack's been promised work until the spring of next year. They reckon the trains will be running by then; at least, the goods trains. In any case, I don't think we'd want to move further north with the winter before us, though God knows if even Northumberland is as cold and wild as Blea Moor.'

Snow already covered the summit and upper slopes of Whernside on the day Jake and Beth left.

'I shall miss my mountain,' Jake said. 'I'm glad I have my picture of it.'

'It shall have pride of place in our new home,' Beth promised. 'And we'll never forget it, will we? So much has happened to us here.'

On the day before they left Nazareth Jake had walked with her to Chapel-le-dale and they had visited Will's and Armitage's graves. Beth had no bad memories of Will now. The happiness which had been hers in the last two years had wiped out every unhappy memory of the past.

It had been arranged that on removal day their goods and chattels would be taken down to Batty Green on the tramway, and from there by cart to Skipton. Beth and Jake, with Mary, could also have travelled on the cart, but Jake decided against it.

'We'll go on it as far as Settle,' he said. 'After that we'll take the train. We have to remember that we're no longer poor, though I admit it takes some getting used to!'

'It certainly does,' Beth agreed. 'And we mustn't be extravagant. Setting up the school, getting it running, is going to take a lot of money. All the same, I think you're right about the train. I wouldn't fancy being bumped all the way to Skipton and I'm sure Mary wouldn't enjoy it.'

With Jake by her side and Mary in her arms, all of them ready to leave, well wrapped up against the biting snow wind which was blowing across the moor, Beth looked around the empty room.

'Goodbye, little hut,' she said. 'You've served us well.' She turned to Jake. 'I wonder who'll live here next?'

'No-one, I should think,' Jake said. 'They'll be taking down the huts as people leave. They won't be required much longer.'

He picked up the two bags he was to carry, and they left, closing the door behind them. Facing into the wind, the snow-covered mountain ahead of them, they walked towards the tramway.

'I swear,' Beth said as they walked from the railway station and up the length of the High Street towards The Beeches, 'that Skipton is as cold as Nazareth!'

It was almost dark and snow was beginning to fall as they reached the house, but when Jake turned the key in the lock and opened the door it was a different story. Mr Feathers had been true to his word. He had promised to engage a woman who would at least sweep the floors and light fires in the kitchen, in the main bedroom and in the living-room for their arrival, and she had done so. By now she had left, and the fires had burned down to a red glow, but the three rooms, though without curtains at the windows, or rugs on the bare floors, were a pleasant contrast to the weather outside.

'I'll see to Mary, then make something to eat,' Beth said. 'There's nothing more we can do after that until the furniture arrives. Let's hope it won't be long.'

She had brought provisions with her: bread, cheese, a slab of gingerbread, some apples, and candles for light. They sat on the floor near the warmth of the fire, and ate. It was almost two hours later that the cart drew up at the gate. The first thing the driver demanded, before he began to unload, was a bucket of water for his horse.

'It's a fair step from Ribblehead to Skipton for my old Bess,' he said. 'She's a good strong 'un but she gets tired sooner than she used to. Don't we all?'

When he had watered the horse the three of them, by the light of one street lamp, unloaded the furniture and carried it into the house. There wasn't much of it; it looked lost in the high-ceilinged rooms.

'I must see to Mary's cradle first of all,' Beth said to the driver. 'She needs to settle down. Then I'll give you something to eat.'

'Nay, I'll not bother,' the driver said. 'I'd best get down to the inn and stable Bess. After that I'll eat. Though thank you all the same.'

When he had left, by which time Mary was as sound asleep in her cradle as if she was still in the familiar hut in Nazareth, Jake said: 'Let's not do anything more tonight except put the bed up. It's been a long day.'

Lying in bed, in the curve of Jake's arm, Beth looked towards the faint glow which came from the dying embers of the bedroom fire. The rest of the room was in deep shadow. It was as if they were held, the two of them and the baby in her cradle at the side of the bed, in a magic circle of warmth and soft light.

'Oh, Jake,' Beth said quietly, 'I'm so happy! Everything seems so right. Please tell me you feel the same.'

Jake turned her towards him. 'I'll do better than that,' he said. 'I'll *show* you how I feel.'

From the moment they were wakened next morning by Mary's usual habit of delivering a long speech in her own incomprehensible language while she sat upright in her cradle, for Jake and Beth the hours, days and weeks raced by. What had seemed ample time to do all that had to be done before opening their school in the middle of the following January proved not to be so.

'There's so much to do!' Beth said, taking off her cloak and bonnet on coming in from the December cold. 'I wouldn't have believed it possible that there were so many things we hadn't even considered.'

'Which just shows what amateurs we are,' Jake said. 'Also, we made our decisions in such a hurry,' he reminded her. 'If we had taken more time . . .'

'I didn't want to take more time,' Beth said. 'Neither of us did. You're not sorry, are you?'

Jake shook the flakes of snow from his coat and hung it on the row of high hooks in the hall. Beneath the high row a low rack of hooks had been fixed, ready for when the children should start. It was only one of several jobs the carpenter had done in the house. They had found Mr Lomax just a week after they had moved in and he had been working for them ever since, making simple desks, benches, stools, chairs; fitting extra shelves into the cupboards with which the house was already well endowed. Mr Lomax was a real find, Beth and Jake frequently told each other. He was skilled, amenable to doing what was asked of him, and not expensive.

'Of course I'm not sorry,' Jake answered. 'Far from it.'

'But shall we ever be ready in time?' Beth's voice was anxious. 'Only a fortnight to go to Christmas, and the opening two weeks after that.'

'Don't worry, of course we shall,' Jake said. 'What's more, we'll take time to enjoy Christmas. Our first Christmas in our first real home – for I never intended that we should live in a railway hut for ever!'

'And Mary's first birthday,' Beth reminded him. 'But we were happy in our hut, weren't we?'

'Of course we were,' Jake agreed. 'But it wasn't what I wanted for my two princesses.'

Every morning when he wakened, he was glad not to be working in the tunnel. Sometimes he missed the company of the other men, but less and less so as time went by.

They had already advertised the opening of the school in neat, attractive displays in the Skipton paper and in the *Yorkshire Post*. There was no point in making it known further afield since they had agreed that, for some months at least, they would take only day pupils. The house was not yet ready for boarders.

'And let's face it,' Jake said, 'we can never take more than a few.'

The advertisements had brought a dozen enquiries, and the board – 'Beech House School for children aged 5 to 11. Mr and Mrs Jake Tempest' – painted in green and gold by a signwriter and fixed close to the front gate, had yielded a few more. Beth and Jake together had interviewed several children and parents with the result that they would have a certain nine when they opened for the spring term.

'Though it's not nearly enough,' Beth said. 'We need at least twenty to break even, let alone make a profit.'

'There's still time,' Jake pointed out. 'And by the end of the first term we'll get more pupils from recommendations.'

'Perhaps the handbills will achieve something,' Beth said hopefully.

It was why they had been out this morning, to collect from the printer a batch of tastefully designed handbills, setting out what they had to offer. They had distributed them, though in discreet quantities, around the better-class establishments in the town.

'We must wait and see,' Jake said. 'And don't worry. It will be all right eventually, you'll see!'

On Christmas Day, in the afternoon, Mary took her first steps, walking confidently, as if she had done it since the day she was born, until suddenly, after a dozen steps, she lost her balance and fell with a thump to the floor.

'Now stand up, princess,' Jake said, holding out his hands to her. 'Stand up and try again!'

'How Armitage would have loved to see her!' Beth said. 'He was so fond of her.'

After their Christmas dinner they had drunk a toast to Armitage with a glass of port.

'But for him, we wouldn't be here,' Jake said. He looked around the room. 'We'd have none of this. He changed our lives.'

Jake was proved right about the children. In January they enrolled eleven pupils, mostly between the ages of five and eight, but before the summer term was due to start after Easter they knew they were to have twenty-three children.

'And it will be more when the new school year begins in September,' Jake pointed out. 'That's the time children start school, or change schools.'

In April they received a letter from Elsie Drake. The thoughts were hers, but the letter was written by Tom who was home from York for the Easter holiday.

We are still here though not for much longer (Elsie said). But more and more people have left. Most of the work is finished and the huts are coming down. Next week there is to be a special train to take the directors of the Midland Railway all the way from Settle to Carlisle. Just fancy! Whoever would have thought it.

'There were times when I wouldn't have,' Jake said. 'Sometimes I thought the tunnel would never be finished; that it would fall in, or it wouldn't meet in the middle!'

'It seems long ago and far away,' Beth said. 'Another life.'

'Another life,' Jake echoed. 'And in August, if we're to believe the *Craven Pioneer*, the goods trains will be running.'

'And by next year the passenger trains,' Beth said.

'When that happens we will go on the railway,' Jake promised. 'You and me and Mary.'

Epilogue

Although passenger trains ran from Skipton to Carlisle from May 1876, it was more than a year later before Jake was able to fulfil his promise to take Beth and Mary on the train.

The reasons for the delay were twofold.

The first was that Beech House School was so successful that it never seemed possible to find time to go on the railway. There were now forty-eight pupils, most of whom, as Jake had envisaged, had come from recommendations. And there was a waiting list. Beech House School had become sought after.

A young girl, Florence Mason, had been employed to help with the smallest children, though not to teach them. All teaching was firmly in the hands of Jake and Beth.

The second reason for the lengthy delay was to be seen in Beth's arms as she and her family boarded the train in the late summer of 1877. His name was John Armitage Tempest and he had been born – conveniently – in the Easter holiday of that year.

'At four months old, and just having been fed, he will probably sleep all the way,' Beth said with a contented smile. 'He'll not know what he's missing!'

She settled into her upholstered seat – even the third-class carriages on this new route had upholstered seats, and if you travelled from London, and could afford the cost, you could travel in the Pullman coach with an armchair to yourself, comfortable enough to sleep in. Just like in America.

'I wouldn't like the Pullman coach,' Beth said to Jake. 'It's too public. I prefer this compartment, especially if no-one else gets in.'

She sat by the window, holding the baby. Jake sat opposite with Mary on his knee, pointing out to her the landmarks as the train raced through the countryside. They were going as far as Appleby. Carlisle was too far.

'You see that mountain there, which looks like a lion,' he said. 'That's Pen-y-ghent!'

'Not a lion,' Mary contradicted. 'I got a lion in my picture book.'

'But like a lion,' Jake said patiently.

It didn't matter. He was waiting for Ribblehead and the viaduct, for the sight of his own mountain, and Blea Moor.

The train slowed down, and stopped briefly, on the viaduct. Looking out of the window he could, because of the curve of the line, see the back end of the train. He had never thought of the viaduct being built on such a curve.

He looked straight ahead of him now, across Blea Moor.

It stretched into the distance, wild, empty, no sign of life, the grass blowing in the wind.

He lifted Mary high in his arms and pointed a finger.

'Look! That's where you were born! Right across there!'

Mary shook her head emphatically.

'No! No houses. Babies are born in houses.'

Jake smiled.

'And that's my mountain,' he said. 'Like the one in the picture at home.'

'Mountain,' Mary said, vigorously nodding her head.

'At least the mountain hasn't changed,' Jake said to Beth.

'I don't think the moor has changed, not really,'

Beth said. 'People like us changed it for a few years, but I reckon it's gone back to being itself.'

The train started again, with a jerk. Jake stood looking out of the window until Whernside was out of view, then sat back in his seat.

THE END

OPAL

For my daughters-in-law,
Christine and Margaret

Chapter One

Opal, carrying the child in one arm and a canvas bag over the other, came into the house and kicked the door to with her foot, but not quickly enough to keep out the thin cloud of powdery snowflakes which followed her. They settled on the doormat and, though the room was bitterly cold, were quickly melted and absorbed. The child started to cry, a thin, miserable sound.

'I know son. You're cold,' Opal said. 'Just let me set you down and we'll soon get things warmed up.'

She sat him on the black horsehair sofa which was partly covered by a large square of knitted patchwork.

'There!' she said gently. 'Now wait on. I'll be as quick as I can.'

The light had almost gone from the short February day. She found the box of matches on the mantelpiece and lit the gas, standing on tiptoe and stretching out her arm to the bracket, for she was only five feet tall. The gas popped and spluttered, seeming reluctant to settle down to its usual steady hiss. Its soft glow lit the centre of the room, enhancing the ruby-red plush tablecloth, picking out the odd patches of colour in the rag rugs on the stone floor, but not penetrating into the corners of even so small a room. The rugs were made from old clothes cut into strips, or 'tabs'. Everyone's clothes seemed to have been made in dark, serviceable colours, but whenever she had been able

7

to get hold of something brighter, Opal had worked it into the rug in the rough shape of a flower. She loved colour, and nowhere in her life was there enough of it.

'We need a new gas mantle,' she said, kneeling down to be on a level with her small son. His cry had changed to an intermittent whimper.

'Now' she went on 'Mam'll blow on your hands for a minute to warm them, then she'll light the fire.' She cupped his small hands in her own, though hers were scarcely less cold, and blew her warm breath over them, gently chafing his fingers until he was comforted.

'There!' she said. 'Isn't that better?'

She took food from the canvas bag and put it into the oven, which always retained a vestige of heat. Then she pulled down the window blind and drew the heavy chenille curtain against the back of the street door. The door leading to the stairs was similarly curtained, for the house was full of draughts.

'When the wind blows from the north,' she observed, 'when it's blowing straight from the moor, nothing'll keep it out!'

The fire was laid. She took a taper from the jar on the shelf – for not even a match must be wasted – lit it from the gas and put it to the kindling.

'We'll soon have you warmed up,' she promised the child. 'See the smoke curling up the chimney? And the pretty orange flames, though you must never go near them. Now if you sit there and watch you'll see the black coals turn red and then we'll be really warm. But perhaps you'd better keep your coat and scarf on a bit longer.'

She talked to Daniel most of the time when they were alone together but, being not quite two years old, he seldom answered her. In any case he was a quiet child. He was dark, like herself, with large, solemn eyes which watched everything. She wondered what went on in his mind.

'I had hoped your dad might have been home before us, got the fire going,' she said. 'I wonder where he's got to?'

At this time of the year the fire should be lit in the morning and be warming the house all day; but coal cost money and they had none. To be precise, she had twopence in her purse, which had to see her through until Friday morning. It was Wednesday today.

Every Wednesday she visited her mother-in-law, arriving before the midday dinner and leaving in time to have Edgar's tea ready when he came in from work. Though it was now six months since he had worked she kept to the same routine. No need to rub it in that time was no longer important to him. He could have gone with her, enjoyed a good meal, but he seldom did. Perhaps to visit his mother in the middle of the day was to underline his position and Opal did not press him. She enjoyed Sarah Carson's company. Her mother-in-law was a warm, fat, cheerful woman. Her house was warm too because her husband, Percy, was the local baker. Today's overheated kitchen, right next to the bakehouse, had felt like heaven.

Opal heard her husband at the door and went to ease back the curtain. He entered, bringing a gust of cold air and more snowflakes with him. Edgar Carson was not especially tall, but he seemed at once to fill the space in the small room, perhaps because of the breadth of his shoulders and the set of his handsome head, but really more because of some indefinable inner quality. Whatever it was it never failed to quicken Opal's pulse, to enliven her. Even when things were going badly his magnetism for her never lessened. He removed his cap, shaking the snow on to the floor, and revealed tightly-curled, light brown hair in need of cutting.

'My word!' he said. 'It's bitter out there! I'm perished!'

He looked it. The tip of his nose glowed as red as a beacon in his white face and a few snowflakes had caught and stayed, too icy to melt, in his thick, fair moustache and heavy eyebrows.

'It's cold in here,' Opal said. 'I've only just lit the fire. We went early to your mother's – just after you'd left for the Labour Exchange – so as not to have to light it. Why didn't you come home for your dinner, love? We had a lovely steak and kidney pie.'

'They sent me after a job.'

'And?' But she didn't need to ask.

The years immediately after the war had been good ones. Trade had picked up quickly and there had been an air of optimism everywhere. But it didn't last long. Edgar knew he was only one of thousands who'd been laid off in 1922, and prospects for 1923 seemed no brighter. Hope for a new kind of world, which was what had kept him going in the filth of the trenches, for he had hated every minute of being a soldier, had already died in him.

'There were twenty of us after it. There's a lot of weavers out of work, as well you know,' he said defensively.

'Oh I know all right,' Opal said. 'I know!'

She pushed past him to fill the kettle at the scullery tap, and then back again to place it on the hob. Hunger and cold had so numbed him that he seemed not to have the wit to get out of her way.

'Lloyd George promised us a land fit for heroes to live in,' he said. 'We believed him, simple folk like me. Well, he's out of it now, and serve him right I say. But I see nothing better from this lot.'

Opal sighed. 'Politics! Politics won't fill our bellies! See to Daniel, will you love?'

Edgar moved to the sofa and took his son on his lap. There were days when his insides seemed to turn to stone, when his broad shoulders seemed unable to bear the almost physical weight of his depression. Opal, though he knew she tried, didn't understand how a man in his position felt.

'Don't take Daniel's coat off yet,' she said. 'Not until the house has warmed up.'

'All the same, you're wrong about politics,' Edgar said. 'They matter all right. It's Governments decide the way we live, you and me.'

'Don't forget there was a war,' Opal said.

'I'm not likely to,' he said grimly. 'But who caused that lot if it wasn't the politicians? Answer me that!'

'I can't.'

She sighed. He was in bad mood again, working himself up to no purpose. She *did* sympathize with him, ached at his inability to get a job. Yet as the months went by a cold voice inside her too often asked why, whenever there was a job going, it never went to Edgar? His appearance was good. He was a competent workman. But the months of idleness were dulling him, resentment was taking hold. At a time when even good workmen were without jobs he lacked the spark which would have given him the edge in an interview with a prospective employer. She could see all that so plainly, but how could she tell him without hurting him further?

'Kettle's boiling,' Edgar said.

Opal made the tea and set it aside to brew. The longer it stood the more strength they would get from the spoonful of tea. She wondered if life was to go on like this for ever. And to crown it all she was pregnant again, though see had not yet told Edgar, or indeed anyone. People who were better off preached that it was wrong and improvident of the unemployed to have children. Well, she wasn't overjoyed about the child she was carrying, either. She had no idea how they would manage. But what the well-off didn't understand – how could they? – was that sex was the only pleasure left which didn't need money in the purse; that in the warmth and darkness of the bed it blotted out reality. And that while it lasted, the coupling of the poorest man and woman could equal that of the rich.

But at its conclusion the worry always started again. Supposing I've been caught? We should have been more careful, stopped before the climax. 'Always take a towel to bed with you,' the women advised each other. 'Let him come on that!'

Easier said than done, so that after the earliest possible douching, uncomfortably carried out in the kitchen with a bucket of water and an arrangement of rubber tubing, one waited and prayed daily for the menstrual blood to flow again. And if the blood did not flow, then it was the large measure of gin, the raspberry-leaf tea, the repeated jumping off the kitchen table – all advised to bring on an early miscarriage.

Opal had done none of that, nor would she. She was too afraid that if she tampered with Nature, then Nature might take its revenge and give her a deformed child. But she was three months gone now and she would have to tell Edgar, as well as his parents and hers. Also, she had this other matter in mind. Both subjects would have to be broached. But better wait until they'd eaten. Food might raise Edgar's spirits.

'Your mother gave me a couple of meat pasties today,' she said. 'And currant teacakes to finish off with. I don't know where we'd be without your mother. My Mam's well-intentioned enough, and I know she'd help if she were asked, but somehow she doesn't think of the little things like your mother does.'

Perhaps, Opal thought, because her mother had been a servant in a house where there were no shortages, and since her marriage had lived on farms, where basic foods were more easily come by, it had never occurred to her that her daughter might be hungry. And Opal would not have hinted at it. She did not see her mother often and in her heart she knew that she neglected her.

She served the pasties, one each for herself and Edgar.

'I'll give Daniel a bit of mine if he fancies it,' she said. 'But he ate well at his grandma's today.'

She must visit her mother soon. The small sheep farm to which her parents had moved from Grandpa Derwent's place was four miles away across the moors, and it was a bad time for walking, but see her mother she must. She had a favour to ask of her.

'I'd like you to look after Daniel on Saturday,' she said to Edgar. I want to go to Highcliffe. He's a weight to carry and it's too far for him to walk.'

'Whatever do you want to go for in this weather?' Edgar asked. 'There's snow on the ground. It might not clear by the weekend.'

'It might not clear all winter,' Opal said. 'I can't wait until the Spring comes.'

She went to the kettle and poured more water over the tea leaves.

'I can squeeze another cup,' she said. 'There's no sugar. You'll have to manage without.'

'What is there that can't wait, for Heaven's sake?'

Opal sipped her tea. She felt better now. The room was warming up and the food had done her good. She was always ravenous these days.

'Well . . .' she began hesitantly. 'There's two things I have to tell you, love. I reckon you won't like either of them.'

He stared at her. 'Well, what is it then?'

'The first is, I'm three months pregnant. The second is . . . I'm going to open up a house shop!'

'A house shop? What on earth do you mean?'

It was clear, Opal thought, which announcement had upset him the most.

'What else can I mean, Edgar,' she replied patiently, 'than a little shop right here in the house? It's not uncommon. Other people have done it.'

'But why? Why you?'

'Why me?'

And then it was as if the poison of every bad feeling – of frustration, of hunger, of fear for the future – which for Edgar's sake she had striven to hide over the last few months, churned in her stomach, rose chokingly into her throat, and had to be spat out.

'Why me?' she snapped. 'Because I want sugar in my tea and butter on my bread! I want more to live on every Thursday than a twopenny packet of soup! And Daniel's growing out of his clothes and your boots let in the water!' Her voice rose to a shout and Daniel, frightened, began to cry. 'I can think of several other reasons, but will those do to be going on with?'

Edgar's hurt eyes met hers. To her horror she saw the tears rise in them and spill over. She felt as though she had taken a whip to him. But if crying was any good, she thought wearily, she'd have solved all their problems long ago. She never cried nowadays. As for a man doing so, as for Edgar doing so, that was weakness, and frightening. Now even more than ever they needed each other's strength.

She picked up Daniel and held him in her lap, burying her face in the warm nape of his neck. Then eventually she stretched out her hand and took Edgar's.

'I'm sorry, love,' she said. 'I know you want to get work. I know you deserve to have a job. But it might be a long time before you do and we can't go on like this. Twenty-one shillings a week was bad enough for the three of us, but now you've run out of benefit and what the Board of Guardians allows us won't feed a cat. And another thing – I'm sick of Food Vouchers! Some Jack-in-Office telling me what I can buy and what I can't buy! Do you know there's a list as long as my arm of foods I *can't* get on the vouchers because *they* think they're luxuries? Not for the likes of us! No, Edgar, if I can make just a bit extra, a shilling or two a week, it'll make all the difference. I'm going to need new things for the baby, too.'

She was babbling. She knew it. But anything to wipe that look from his face.

Edgar wiped his eyes with the back of his hand. She was always so logical, so right. When they were courting and in the early days of their marriage he had admired her strengths, though they were different from his own. She was a wife who would help a husband to get on, spur his ambitions. He was a man who would work for his family, strive to do all that was expected

15

of him, given the chance. But sometimes now, though she did not know it, Opal's strength seemed to diminish him. Sometimes he longed for a glimpse of some frailty in her which would excuse the weakness he knew in himself.

'You must see it's reasonable,' Opal said more quietly. She saw by the look in his eyes, the all-too-familiar look of defeat, that she had won. She would have her house shop. But the victory itself gave her no pleasure. How much better if the idea has been his!

'We don't have much room here,' Edgar said in a dull voice. 'Where will you put everything?'

'I thought I'd clear the top of the sideboard and set up shop there, and perhaps on a bit of the table. I could empty the sideboard cupboards, too. God knows there's not much in them. You could take the doors off for me and it would be like display shelves.'

'But what about the other shops in the village? Won't they object?'

'No,' she said. 'What little bit of trade I do won't affect them. I'll sell a variety of things so it'll be a very little from each.' In any case she did not care. She had her own family to look out for.

'Where will you get money to buy stock?' Edgar asked. 'You'll need cash on the nail.'

'I know. That's why I want to go to Highcliffe. I'm sure Mam has a bit put by. Her egg money from the market and suchlike. If she'd lend me five pounds I could make a start.'

Edgar sighed. 'Well, you seem to have it all worked out.'

'Oh I have,' Opal agreed. 'And I'll make it pay. You'll see. But you've not said anything to me about the baby!'

'What do you want me to say? These things happen. Of course I'm pleased. We didn't want Daniel to be our only bairn, did we? But it'll be harder for you than for me. Are you sure you'll be able to manage the shop as well?'

It was strange, Opal thought, that it never occurred to him that he might run the shop while she looked after their children and kept house. While he might not forbid her to go ahead with the scheme it would not enter his head to contribute. Running a house shop – selling needles and thread and sweets and groceries was, like housework, cooking, and bringing up children, women's work. It was beside the point that he had nothing else to do except sign on at the Labour Exchange and attend a decreasing number of interviews.

But having told Edgar she felt the project was as good as launched. She was sure she could get the loan. For the first time in many weeks excitement stirred in her and with it came that other, more familiar feeling. It ran like fire through her body and tingled in her breasts. She wanted, needed, to make love now, urgently. If it had not been for Daniel she would have liked to have lain with Edgar on the hearthrug, naked in the light from the fire, now glowing red, instead of in the dark, chilly bedroom. But, though he knew how much she loved him, such desires of the body were not ones which she could put into words to Edgar. It was shaming enough that she, a woman, should have them.

'I'll put Daniel to bed and we'll have an early night,' she said. 'It'll save the gas.'

She began to undress Daniel. There was one thing to be said in favour of being pregnant; you could make love whenever you wanted to. When Daniel was in his nightshift she put him down gently on the rug. Then she began to remove the pins from her hair. It cascaded around her shoulders, thick, jet black, gleaming in the light from the fire. Edgar had always like to see her hair loose. When they were first married he would take out the pins himself, slowly, one by one, watching the hair fall.

She lifted Daniel from the rug and went up to the bedroom, leaving the stairs door open behind her.

The main street of Milton ran down to the railway bridge, and just beyond that to the bridge over the river. The mill which gave the village its reason for being there (for it had not grown from early beginnings like other villages, but had been built all in one go) stood on a strip of land between two bridges. Sir Henry Milton, in the nineteenth century, had carefully calculated the advantages of this position: the soft river water to wash the wool, the railway (in which he was a shareholder) to bear it away; spun, woven and dyed into the finest cloth.

Though the village was dominated by the mill and could not have existed without it, Sir Henry was a philanthropic businessman and had also built a school, a public washhouse, a chapel (in the grounds of which he now rested in his ornate tomb), a cottage hospital and several streets of small, terraced houses for his millhands, with a few larger ones for the managers. It was because he once worked at the mill that Edgar had been able, on his marriage, to rent the house in Acer Street.

This morning groups of men stood on the railway bridge. One of them called out to Opal as she passed.

'Good morning Mrs Carson!'

'Good morning Mr Holroyd. Cold weather we're having!'

They were standing there, she knew, because Saturday was a working day and they had been used to rising early and going to the mill. Though for most of them there was now no work, they felt better getting up, getting out of the house, meeting with their mates.

Beyond the river the cobbled street ended and the track through the woods up to the moor began, rising steeply from the valley. Opal enjoyed the climb. On the top of the moor the air was clear and dry, the sky unusually high for February. She was glad to get away from Milton for a few hours and was looking forward to seeing her family and hearing the news of the farm.

She had not always thought that way. When Edgar Carson had first called at the farm – he was returning over the moors from Ilkley with two friends and enquired if a ham and egg tea could be provided – Opal had answered the door to him. She knew at once that here was the man she had been waiting for to carry her away. And after that first Sunday he had returned often, sometimes with his friends and then, as time went on, more often on his own.

'It's clear what *he's* coming for,' Opal's mother said. 'Plain as a pikestaff!'

'Well, I like him,' Opal said. She loved him, but that was too extravagant a feeling to express out loud, to her mother.

'So do we all,' her mother replied. 'He's an agreeable lad. And he did his bit in the war, there's no denying that.'

'So what have you got against him?' Opal demanded.

'Not against *him*. Not personally. It's just that . . .

well, your Dad and me thought of something better for you. A farmer or a schoolteacher.'

'But not a weaver,' Opal said. 'Well, he'll not always be a weaver. He means to get on. And I don't see any farmers or schoolteachers queueing up for me, do you?'

'There's plenty of time,' Mrs Derwent said. 'Why is it you can never wait for anything?'

Then in the June of 1920 Edgar had come one weekend to give a hand with the haymaking, working all day beside Opal, forking the hay stooks into the cart. The day's toil, the hot sun, the clover-scented, newly-cut grass, were powerful aphrodisiacs for both of them (had they needed such aids). Before nightfall, in the stone barn where they had stacked the new hay, Daniel was conceived. Benjamin and Hannah Derwent said goodbye to their dreams for Opal and in September the couple were married in the tiny Methodist chapel at Highcliffe.

Opal climbed the last short steep rise before the summit of the moor. From now on it was all downhill. The countryside, its contours softened by the deep covering of snow, reminded her of a picture of Switzerland she had once seen on a calender. A mile down the hill she could see the hamlet which was Highcliffe, and on the edge of it her father's farm. The sheep, which in the summer were allowed to roam the hill, were now folded in the small field close to the farmhouse, where they were handy for winter feeding. They huddled together against the cold. In a couple of months from now the fields would be freshly green and the low pastures would be dotted with new lambs.

She began to hurry down the slope, sliding and slipping in the snow. In spite of being pregnant she felt incredibly fit and healthy. She had no morning sickness and wouldn't have now. But she was terribly hungry and hoped that by the time she reached the farm, dinner would be on the table. They didn't know she was coming but there was always enough for an extra person. The way she felt she could eat two men's dinners.

She was not disappointed. When she reached the farm and walked into the big kitchen the warm air was filled with the delicious smell of food. Everyone was there, including her brother Mark and his bride-to-be, Queenie Stone, and Opal's Aunt Garnet. They were at the table, already starting on the meal. Mary jumped up from her chair and rushed to embrace her sister. Only Mary would ever dream of giving such an effusive greeting, but they all looked up from their heaped plates, pleased enough to see her.

'Come and sit down, love,' her mother said. 'Mary, lay another place. You've not brought Daniel nor Edgar, then?'

'No. I thought the weather might turn bad. And Daniel has a bit of a cold.'

As her mother rose to fetch the meat pie which she had returned to the oven to keep hot, Opal thought how thin she was looking. But she sounded well enough. Her voice was strong.

'I'm starving!' Opal said. 'I could eat a huge helping!'

'You always could,' her father said. 'I don't know where you put it. You not the size of two pennorth of copper!'

'Well, you know what they say,' Opal retorted. 'They don't make diamonds as big as bricks.'

'She's like me,' Aunt Garnet mumbled through a mouthful of pie. Aunt Garnet was the middle one of Opal's father's three sisters. The three were named

Pearl, Garnet and Ruby because Grandpa Derwent said they were his jewels. When his first granddaughter was born he expected the tradition to be followed, favouring Diamond or Emerald, but Hannah was against it and Benjamin reckoned it was the mother's privilege to name the baby. In the end, Hannah compromised on Opal. Her own mother said that that was worse because everyone knew that opals were for tears. When it came to her second daughter and last child she chose the name Mary as being the most straightforward she could think of.

'I didn't expect to find you here, Aunt Garnet,' Opal said.

'No you wouldn't,' her aunt replied. 'But as you know, there's less to do on the farm in winter, so I gave myself a holiday. Father wasn't too pleased, of course.'

Aunt Garnet must be in her forties, Opal thought, and Aunt Pearl was older still. Unlike Ruby, they had never married but had remained at home on the dales farm, where Grandfather Derwent treated them like children.

Opal turned to Queenie and Mark, who were seated side by side and were so much in love that they held hands between mouthfuls.

'Have you fixed the date yet?' she asked.

'Saturday the second of June,' Queenie said happily. 'Only sixteen weeks to go! And I have a favour to ask you, Opal. Will you make the wedding hats? Mine and the bridesmaids? You're so clever at it.'

'You can do mine as well,' Aunt Garnet said.

'You're not having a white wedding, then?' Opal enquired.

'No. With Mother gone and Father rather poorly, it seems best not.'

'Well of course I'll do them.'

'Our Opal was always gifted with her needle,' Hannah Derwent said. 'When she was little she didn't really play with dolls like other children do. She just made hats and dresses for them, and always in the latest style.'

'I'll make you a new hat, too, Mother,' Opal said.

'Nay lass,' her mother answered. 'The one I had for your wedding's as good as new. I've hardly worn it since, except to Harvest Thanksgiving and Whitsundays to chapel. It'll do me nicely.'

'You'll have to go with me to buy the material, Queenie,' Opal said. There was no way she could lay out a penny. She would earn a bit in the end, but not much since it was for family.

'Oh we'll arrange all that,' Queenie said. 'Shall we have a trip to Leasfield? Or Leeds or Bradford?'

Queenie's father was a prosperous wool merchant and none of his family was ever short of money, but Queenie was sensitive to other people's needs and perfectly understood Opal's remark.

When the meal was over Opal contrived to get her mother to accompany her upstairs so that they could speak alone.

'I wanted you to know before the others,' Opal said. 'I'm expecting. It'll be in August.'

There was a barely felt pause, a fleeting look of pain on her mother's face, but swiftly followed by a pleased smile.

'Well that's good news, Opal love!' She patted her daughter's hand, the nearest she ever came to a caress. 'It's best for Daniel not to be an only child. But don't have a quiverful as the Good Book says. It's too big a burden. Oh I don't mean that any of you lot were,' she added quickly. 'Nothing like that. But with jobs so hard to come by . . . I suppose Edgar hasn't heard anything yet?'

'No,' Opal said. 'Which brings me to the next thing.'

She explained to her mother what she had in mind about the shop and asked for the loan of five pounds.

'I'll pay it back as soon as I can. A bit at a time, but you'll get it all,' Opal promised.

'Well if you're sure it's what you want to do, you can have the money and welcome,' Mrs Derwent said. She crossed to the walnut chest and took out a small bag from the back of a drawer.

'Here you are love,' she said. 'And ten gold sovereigns, not five. You'll do better with a good start. I don't want it back. It's yours to keep. Only don't you go telling anyone – not your father nor anyone. What's mine is my own and it's up to me what I do with it!'

'Oh Mam! I don't know how to thank you!'

'Then don't! And now we'd best get back downstairs. There's a mountain of washing-up.'

Downstairs, Mary shooed her mother out of the kitchen.

'You go and sit in the parlour and talk weddings with Queenie,' she said.

'Mam's not well,' Mary told Opal when their mother had left the room. 'But she won't rest. That's why Aunt Garnet's here, only Mam doesn't know it.'

'What's wrong with her?' Opal asked. 'I thought she looked thinner. Why didn't you let me know? I'd have come sooner.'

'I was going to if you hadn't come today. I don't know what's wrong and she won't see a doctor. She says it's simply the end of the winter and she'll be better in the spring. Of course we both know that she's never been the same since George was killed. More than six

24

years now, but she doesn't get over it. George was more to her than you and me put together!'

It was not to be wondered at, Opal thought. She, too, had worshipped her brother. A light had gone out for all of them when George had been killed on the Somme. For their mother it had never been rekindled.

'I'm having another baby,' she announced.

'Oh Opal, you're not! Oh you are lucky! I do envy you. Sometimes I think I'll never get married and have babies, yet it's all I ever want.'

Opal laughed. 'What *do* you mean. Of course you will. You're only eighteen. There's all the time in the world.'

'I never meet anyone,' Mary said.

'You will,' Opal assured her. 'Perhaps someone will come knocking on the door, like Edgar did.'

Too soon it was time to leave. Opal would have liked to have stayed longer, wouldn't have minded in the least walking back across the moor in the dark, but Edgar would expect her back and Daniel would no doubt be waiting for his tea.

'I'll walk along the bottom path with you,' her mother said. It was an unusual gesture, and even more strange that she should wave Mary aside, wanting to have Opal to herself. Yet as they walked she had nothing of significance to say. At the end of the level path where Opal must turn to start the walk up to the moor, she took both her daughter's hands in hers.

'You've always been a good lass to me,' she said. 'I don't forget it. Now get on and take care of yourself.'

'And you do the same, Mam,' Opal answered.

She wondered about her mother as she climbed the hill. Was she perhaps trying to say that she was sorry for her concentration on her dead son and the exclusion of her living children? When she reached the top of the hill she turned and looked back. Her mother was still standing there. The two women raised their hands in a final gesture of farewell. But when Opal started on the downward slope her thoughts turned at once to her house shop. She began to plan what she would buty with the ten gold sovereigns in her purse.

On the Monday following her visit to Highcliffe she did the family wash; starching, blueing, mangling, drying, ironing – so that by bedtime everything had been aired off on the clothes horse by the fire and could be put away. On Tuesday she cleaned the living-room, polished the sideboard, scrubbing the table top with coarse salt, blackleading the range until Daniel could see his face in the oven door.

'Why all the fuss?' Edgar enquired. 'If somebody wants a packet of pins in a hurry they won't care a tinker's curse whether the firegrate's clean or not.'

'Oh yes they will,' Opal contradicted. 'They may not realize it, but everything about the surroundings matters when you're trying to sell something.'

Edgar looked at her in astonishment.

'How do you know? You've never sold anything.'

'I just do, that's all. I know I'm right. I wish I had a few flowers to brighten up the place. When I'm rich I shall have fresh flowers every day.'

On Wednesday she made her usual visit to her mother-in-law and gave her the news. Mrs Carson was delighted about the baby. 'It was great sorrow to Percy and me' she said 'that Edgar was the only one.' About the shop she was dubious but resigned, even a little guilty that her son might have brought this upon his family.

'I'm sure our Edgar tries to get work,' she defended him. 'These are hard times we live in. We can't even afford to take a man on in the bakery, or there'd be a job for Edgar there. I just wish we could help you more.'

'No-one's been more helpful than you have,' Opal said. 'You've been a Godsend.'

'I daresay you'll make a go of it,' Mrs Carson said more cheerfully. She could never be downhearted for long. 'Though I'm sorry you won't be able to come here on a Wednesday any more.'

'With Wednesday being half-day closing around here,' Opal said, 'it's a good time for me to be open.'

The next day she was up early. Immediately after breakfast she set off for Shepton, pushing Daniel's empty perambulator. Ridley's was the wholesaler she intended visiting. She had seen the advertisement in the *Argus* and it looked as though they might supply everything she needed. She hoped for as many lines as possible, reckoning that by stocking all the different goods her capital would allow, she might attract more customers. A woman who came for a reel of thread might be tempted by a chocolate bar if it was under her nose. 'You can get it at Opal's' was to be her slogan.

The wholesaler's was situated over a newsagent and tobacconist, in the middle of a row of dismal-looking shops. 'Keenist prices, highest quality' the advertisement had said. Well, that was what she was after. She propped the pram against the wall outside the newsagent's and hoped it would be there when she returned.

'K. Ridley, General Wholesaler' the door on the first landing proclaimed. And below that a notice said 'Please do not ask for Credit since a Refusal may cause

Offence.' She knocked and entered. The warehouse was larger than she had expected. The walls were shelved and crammed with goods from floor to ceiling. The man who greeted her was a wisp of a man; scarcely bigger than she herself.

'Ken Ridley, Esquire, at your service,' he announced.

His voice was inappropriately deep and strong. 'I don't know you, do I?'

'Mrs Opal Carson.'

'So what can I do for a pretty lady like you?' he asked.

Opal explained her errand.

'Well then,' he said. 'You'd best look around and see what takes your fancy! It's all here somewhere!'

It was difficult to know where to start and even more difficult to know when to stop. She chose reels of cotton, reluctantly confining herself to black and white; cards of white linen shirt buttons, pins, sewing and darning needles, knicker elastic, grey darning wool. From the confectionary shelves she selected small items which children could buy with a halfpenny: toffee bars, aniseed balls, sherbert fountains, liquorice chews, fruit gums, dolly mixtures, jelly babies, pear drops and acid drops. And to tempt the mothers with a copper or two to spare and a treat in mind, Fry's cream bars and Rowntree's whipped cream walnuts.

'You'll find sweets a good line,' Mr Ridley advised. 'The less money people have, the more they seem to want to suck sweets. But save enough money for a few packets of groceries. Baking powder, tea. And a few medicinal items for the sudden upset. All obtainable in handy sizes. Daisy headache powders, senna pods, epsom salts, syrup of figs – if you'll pardon me for mentioning them. And Doctor Cassell's tablets.

Magical for shell-shock, nervous debility, stomach pains. Take the one-and-threepenny box and sell them a couple at a time. You'll make a penny or two there.'

'I think I must have reached the limit,' Opal said eventually. She had been trying to add up in her head but had long ago lost count. 'But what I *would* like, even if I have to put something else back on the shelf, is a jar of Fortune's Whispers.'

'Ah!' Mr. Ridley said. 'You're a romantic, like all the ladies!'

'No,' Opal said. 'I'm a realist. It's my intention to allow every customer for the first month to pick out a Fortune's Whisper, free. I'm relying on everyone else to be romantic, you see. To want to see into the future.'

Mr Ridley clapped his hands. 'Well I'll be blowed if you don't take the biscuit,' he chuckled. 'I'll tell you what, I'll do something which is against the rules of a lifetime. You can have the Fortune's Whispers on credit! Pay me when you have given them all away! And while you're at it, pick one for yourself. Go on! Let's see what *your* future's going to be! Come on, dip in. Close your eyes first!'

Opal put her hand into the sweet jar and extracted the small, flat, pastel-coloured sugar sweet, with its message printed on one surface.

'Well, what does it say?' Mr Ridley was all eagerness.

She read the words aloud.

'This could be your lucky day.'

'There you are!' cried Mr Ridley. 'I knew it!'

So did Opal. She felt it in her bones and was at once elated and awed.

Amazingly, the goods came to sixpence short of ten pounds. She would be able to eat.

'And I'll throw in a few little cards which might be

useful,' Mr Ridley said. 'You'll find the customers appreciate them' He gave here three oblong cards, threaded with string to hang on the wall. 'We Aim To Please', 'If You Don't See What You Require, Please Ask', and 'Thank You, Please Call Again'.

Before leaving Shepton she bought a plain teacake filled with boiled ham and spread with mustard, for fourpence, and an Eccles cake for a penny. Walking along the road, pushing the laden pram, she ate them greedily.

On Friday morning when Edgar had left for the Labour Exchange she spread her best tablecloth on top of the sideboard and arranged her stock. She placed an empty Oxo tin on the corner of the sideboard and hoped that no-one would require change. She had a float of one penny. Then she sat back, too excited to engage in any activity, and waited for customers. She had put the word around among the neighbours and there was nothing more she could do.

It was a quarter before midday when the door opened and her first customer appeared – a small boy, the son of a neighbour.

'What can I do for you, Thomas?' she asked.

'Mam says do you sell Oxo cubes?'

'I do,' Opal said. 'How many would you like?'

'One.'

When he had paid her she proffered the jar of Fortune's Whispers. 'There's one for every customer who buys,' she told him. 'A lucky dip. Be sure to tell your friends, won't you? And because you're my very first customer, Thomas, you can choose something from amongst the sweets. Anything you like as long as it costs a halfpenny!'

She was in business.

Chapter Two

Opal cleared the breakfast table quickly, then opened the door and shook the crumbs from the tablecloth to the sparrows waiting in the street. She glanced up at the sky; blue, with fleecy white clouds hurrying before a breeze. A perfect May morning. Earlier she had taken a cup of tea to Edgar but he had not yet come down. Well then, he must fend for himself when he did get up – which she hoped would be soon because she was going out and both Daniel and the shop were to be left in his care.

Each day now she made an early start with the shop so that she could catch the children's custom on their way to school. How, in these hard times, parents could afford to give their children a halfpenny two or three times a week, she just didn't know. But so long as they did, she wanted it to come to her. Mr Ridley had been right; the less money some people had, the more they spent on sweets.

She wished Edgar would get a move on. These last few weeks, except on his signing-on mornings, he'd taken to sleeping late every day, sometimes not coming down until after eleven. It seemed that the harder she tried, the less he co-operated. She went to the bottom of the stairs and called out to him.

'Edgar! It's time you were up! Don't forget I'm going to Queenie's.'

A grunt confirmed that he had heard her, but it was

another quarter of an hour before he shuffled down-stairs, rubbing the sleep from his eyes.

'I don't know how you can loll in bed the way you do,' Opal said.

'You wouldn't,' he replied.

Even after all this time he still wakened at six, forgetting for a moment; then remembering. Why couldn't Opal understand that to rise early only made the day longer. There was no purpose to it. Better to turn over and go to sleep again.

'You know perfectly well I have to take the hats,' Opal said.

'I'd forgotten. What about my breakfast?'

'I've left you some porridge. It's in the pan on the side. Don't use the milk. Daniel needs it.'

She ought to be drinking milk herself, being preg-nant, but most of the half-pint a day which she bought went to Daniel. Perhaps before long she could order extra. She was now making a regular two or three shillings a week profit on the shop. A proportion of this was regularly put aside to invest in more stock, but some she did spend on food. Twice a week she bought fresh herrings, which were cheap and tasty. Every Saturday night she bought 'pie bits' or a rabbit from the butcher, so that they always had a good Sunday dinner. But also, though she had no clear idea why, she was trying to save a few coppers each week, in a toffee tin. One day she would know why she wanted them, and they would be there. Meanwhile the sight of the toffee tin gave her a feeling of security.

'How long will you be gone?' Edgar asked.

'I don't know. It'll be dinner-time before I get to the other side of Leasfield. After dinner I have to set to and do the final bits on the hats. Mary and the other bridesmaid will be there and Mary's taking Aunt Garnet's hat back with her.'

'Aunt Garnet's not back at Highcliffe, is she?' Edgar asked.

'No. But they'll be stopping there on their way to the wedding.'

She wished her aunt could have been at Highcliffe, since her mother was no better. She had walked over to the farm a fortnight ago and had been concerned to see her thinner than ever, and breathless after the slightest exertion.

Opal tried to fasten her jacket and found that it would no longer meet over her increasing girth.

'It's a good thing it's cut to hang straight from the shoulders,' she said. 'I can leave it undone and it'll help to hide me.'

She looked at herself critically in the mirror over the sideboard, adjusting her hat. It was a cream-coloured straw with a deep brim, the crown trimmed with green ribbon finishing in a large bow at the side. However little she had in her purse she tried never to show poverty in her appearance. Her clothes were always clean and well pressed and by clever alterations and small touches here and there she kept in fashion. Never, ever, would she be seen like the other women in Milton, with a shawl over her head to slip to the local shops. And when she went out she always wore gloves.

She gave a final adjustment to her hat and turned to face Edgar.

'Will I do then?' she asked.

'You look grand,' he said. 'Good enough to eat!'

She smiled happily, her good humour restored by his praise.

'What in *my* condition? Well I'll be off then.'

She gathered up her bulky parcels and bent to kiss Daniel.

'Now don't forget Edgar,' she said. 'There's some soup in the pan for your dinner and Daniel's. See that he has his afternoon sleep. I've set out the shop, as you can see. Try not to use paper bags, but if you really must, then use the smallest. Wrapping paper costs money. And don't forget—'

'All right, all right!' Edgar interrupted. 'Are you sure you wouldn't like me to do the washing and blacklead the fireplace in my spare time?'

'Well, if you were me you might have to,' Opal quipped. 'Ta-ta then!'

It was generally supposed that the tram ran from Leasfield to a point quite close to Milton because Sir Henry and his descendants held so much power in both places. Also because when Milton was in full work the Miltonians flocked to Leasfield to spend their wages. In Leasfield there were large shops, two markets, two theatres, three cinemas and countless public houses. Opal took the tram into the centre of the town, then boarded another tram outside the smoke-blackened town hall, destination Barton, where the well-to-do lived.

Queenie's father, Henry Stone, had made his money in wool. His wife had died, leaving Queenie to look after her father and, when the time came, to inherit his wealth. Mr Stone would never have let Mark Derwent come near Queenie if Mark hadn't saved her life, Opal thought, climbing the steps of the large stone house, ringing the bell. He had seen her in difficulties in the river, near Milton, and as her boat capsized he jumped in and rescued her. It was love at first sight for both of them. Queenie would look at no-one else and her father could hardly turn away the man but for whom, his daughter assured him, she might not *be* there.

A maid showed Opal into the large, comfortable sitting-room where Queenie stood with outstretched hands to greet her.

'Opal, how lovely to see you! Oh, how exciting your parcels look! I can hardly wait. But I must, and you must have a cup of tea after your journey. Or better still a glass of sherry. That's it! We'll both be quite wicked and have a glass of sherry! Come over here and sit on the sofa.'

Opal sank into the soft, springy comfort of the sofa, pushing one of the several down-filled cushions into the small of her back. Intent on getting here, she hadn't noticed until now how tired she was.

'There you are!' Queenie said. 'Finest Amontillad' ! It will put new life into you. Now tell me how you are. Oh, I can't wait to be pregnant!' She blushed. 'After I'm married of course.'

'I'm fine,' Opal said. 'And this May weather is perfect for me. Selfishly, I hope we don't have a hot summer.'

'As long as you'll allow me a fine wedding day,' Queenie said.

'You shall have a beautiful wedding day,' Opal promised. 'Now, do you want to take a peek at the hats before dinner?'

'Oh yes please. I can hardly wait. But bring them upstairs and I'll show you the dresses. Mrs Bassett has almost finished them. By the way, how is Edgar?'

'He's a bit low,' Opal replied. 'I suppose it's to be expected and I do feel sorry for him, but sometimes I think he should make an effort to snap out of it.'

'Poor Edgar!' Queenie said sympathetically.

In the bedroom Queenie opened the large mahogany wardrobe and took out her wedding dress, holding it with reverence.

'I know it's extravagant to have crepe georgette when so many people are poor' she apologized. 'But it's the only wedding I'll ever have. I'm not beautiful like you, but I want to look my very best for Mark.'

'It's quite perfect,' Opal assured her. 'And so will you be. This soft lavender with your fair colouring is exactly right. And Mrs Bassett's made a marvellous job of the silver beading.' She touched the georgette lovingly. She had a feeling for fine materials.

'Hasn't she just! She still has to turn up the hem. The last few stitches won't be put in until the day, and I mustn't try it on, once it's finished, until I'm ready to wear it because that might bring bad luck.'

Opal laughed. 'Don't be silly!'

'I know it's silly,' Queenie confessed. 'But I daren't risk it.'

'Well, don't let Mrs Bassett make it too long. Seven inches from the ground is quite long enough. Skirts are getting shorter all the time. Now, here's your hat, my lady!'

She unwrapped the hat carefully and held it out to Queenie. The crown was deep, the brim wide, but narrowing towards the centre and dipping at the sides. The whole shape was covered in fine silk velvet in intermingling, finely-graded shades of pale mauve, deep lilac and cream. Queenie, eyes shining, cried out with pleasure.

'Oh it's beautiful, Opal! It's beautiful! Don't you think it's the loveliest thing you've ever made?'

'I think it might be,' Opal admitted. 'Especially when

I've finished the trimming. I thought I'd use a little of the material left over from your dress to make the band, and embroider it with some of those silver beads. What do you think?'

'I think that would be perfect.'

'And here are the bridesmaids' hats. Lilac straw, trimmed with the rose-coloured velvet we found in Leasfield. They're smaller in the brim than yours because yours must be the most important; but don't you think they'll be pretty with the pale grey dresses?'

'Oh I do, I do Opal! Mary will look lovely with her dark colouring. And even dear Cousin Maud . . .' she giggled '. . . will be enhanced. Oh I'm so grateful to you, dear Opal!'

'There's no need,' Opal said.

It was true. She would do almost anything in the world for Queenie. Although the Stones were well-to-do, Queenie had treated her like a sister from their very first meeting. Her love for Mark had spread out and embraced his whole family. Even Edgar fell under her spell and on the few occasions he was with her he became at once brighter and more cheerful.

'Will your father be well enough to attend the wedding?' she asked.

Queenie's face clouded. 'I don't know. He's not at all well and the doctor has advised him to take things very quietly. It will be sad for me if I have no parents at my wedding. But yours will be there and they are always so nice to me. Even your grandparents are coming, which is wonderful.'

'Which reminds me,' Opal said. 'I have to tell you that I can't come.'

Queenie stared at her.

'*You* not come? But Opal, why?'

'Well,' Opal said, 'I'll be seven months pregnant. I shouldn't really be appearing in public. But the truth is I shan't have a single garment which will fit me. Things are difficult right now. I haven't been able to make anything.'

Tears filled Queenie's eyes.

'Oh Opal, how selfish I've been! I never thought . . . I expect because you always look so smart. But you must let me buy you something. Some nice material.'

'Thank you, Queenie, but I couldn't,' Opal said firmly. 'I really couldn't.'

'Then there must be something in my mother's wardrobe' Queenie said. 'I haven't been able to bear to give away all her things. She wore voluminous clothes so there's sure to be something with plenty of material for you to make over. You couldn't refuse to have something of my mother's.'

'No,' Opal agreed, 'I couldn't refuse that.'

'Then we'll go and choose it before Mary and Maud arrive. No-one else need know.'

'It's a fine day,' Opal remarked. 'I knew it would be.'

She got out of bed slowly. If she moved too fast she might go dizzy again and have to rest, and today there was no time for that. She looked out of the window. In one way they were lucky. Acer Street ran north and south so that, though the street itself with its long rows of dark stone houses on either side was uniformly drab, from the bedroom window it was possible to see beyond the village to the moors on the horizon.

Every morning of her life now, Opal's first act after getting out of bed was to look towards the moors. When she'd married and come to live in Acer Street she had thought she was gaining her freedom. 'In any case we shan't be in Acer Street long,' she'd said to Edgar. 'I just know you'll be a Mill Manager one of these days and then we'll live in Park Road.'

Now it seemed as though she had simply flown into another cage; a smaller one with a heavier lock on the door. She felt trapped by poverty, by Edgar's failure to find work; by Daniel who needed her all the time; by the child she was carrying. Between them they imprisoned her here, and she knew she was born for something better. She was born to go somewhere, be somebody.

'It's time we were up and doing,' she said.

'Why? The wedding's not until two o-clock.' Edgar's voice came muffled from under the bedclothes.

'There's plenty to do,' Opal said. 'We're all to get ready. I've got to set out the shop and then clear it away again before we leave, or the mice will have it.'

Edgar sat up slowly, yawning. Daniel, wide awake, climbed from his cot on to his parents' bed, which he much preferred to his own. Edgar took his son in his arms and ruffled his soft, dark hair.

'You're surely not going to open the shop today, Opal?'

'For an hour or two this morning, of course I am. Whyever not?'

'I would have thought you could have given yourself one day off,' he said. 'It can't make all that much difference.'

'Oh yes it can,' Opal replied. 'That's just where you're wrong. People don't have all that much loyalty. It only needs a shop to be closed one day for them to take their custom elsewhere. I can't afford to risk that.'

'Then I wonder you haven't got someone to look after it while we're at the wedding.'

'I thought about it,' Opal admitted. 'But I'm not keen on neighbours knowing my business. So I'll keep open for most of the morning and if we're not too late back I'll open up again in the evening.'

Edgar said nothing more. He might as well keep his mouth shut, he thought, for all the weight his opinions carried.

After breakfast Opal took the kettle of hot water from the fire to the kitchen, closed the door and, standing at the sink, gave herself a good wash from top to toe. She had treated herself to a small tablet of scented soap especially for this day and she used it lavishly. As she rinsed and dried her swollen stomach, hating the sight of it, she felt the baby kick, and then saw the ripple of its movement across her flesh. She ought, she supposed, to feel pleasure, tenderness, but such feelings did not come as they had when she was pregnant with Daniel.

She dressed, for the time being, in a clean blouse and the navy wrap-around skirt which was all that would fit her. She would not put on her new dress until the last minute for fear of accidents.

She was pleased with the new dress and looked forward to wearing it. In the end, from the late Mrs Stone's wardrobe, she had chosen a long skirt in fine, cream gabardine, with a matching coat. There was so much material in it that she had been able to contrive a dress with plenty of fullness, and from the clippings she had made small flowers which she had appliquéd on to her brown hat.

'I dread to think what it's like up at Highcliffe, with Grandfather and Grandma and the aunts there and everybody getting ready at once,' she said, coming back into the living-room. 'A good thing they had a bath put

40

in. I'd like to live in a house with a bathroom. They say the new council houses in Leasfield have them.'

'If all we lack is a bathroom we shan't do so badly,' Edgar said.

'Well one day we shall have a house with a bathroom, hot and cold water, electric light and a garden,' Opal said pleasantly. 'And it won't be a council house either.'

She made him feel, Edgar thought, that it was his fault that she didn't have these things. That if only *he* was different, then everything would be all right. But they weren't the only people in their present straits, not by a long chalk.

'And what'll you use for rent money?' he asked. 'Shall you use monkey nuts?'

Opal smiled. 'Oh we won't rent the house. We'll buy it,' she teased.

And then suddenly her mood changed. In the act of setting out the shop, the children's sweets well to the fore because with luck they'd be coming in with their Saturday pennies, she paused, and looked at Edgar.

'Can't you see, can't you *see*, Edgar, that the only way I can bear this rotten present is to look forward to the future. Oh I know it's not your fault, love – and I know my dreams are a bit fanciful, but can't you understand that?'

'I try,' he said quietly. 'I do try to understand, but I can't always share your feelings about the future. You leave me behind, Opal. I wasn't born with your imagination.'

'I know,' she spoke gently. 'Mam always said I had too much imagination and I dare say she was right. But sometimes it's what keeps me going, even if I don't believe every bit of it myself. I wish I could give a bit of it to you, love!'

She recognized, with a deep feeling of sadness, that what she missed most in Edgar, what more and more came between them even though she truly loved him, was not their poverty, not his lack of a job, but his refusal, his inability, to share her dreams. That was what mattered. That was what lay at the root of the loneliness she increasingly felt.

Shortly before noon they had a slice or two of bread to keep them going until the wedding reception, at which there would be a spread. They were ready for off when the door opened and a girl of about twelve walked in. It slightly irritated Opal that no-one around here ever knocked before entering, though she knew it was an irrational feeling in one who had set herself up as a shopkeeper.

'Oh Mrs Carson, you do look lovely!' the girl said.

'We're off to a wedding, Milly,' Edgar told her. 'Mrs Carson's brother. In fact we've just shut up shop.'

'Never mind that,' Opal said quickly. 'If there's something you want I'll be pleased to get it out for you.'

'It's me mam,' Milly said. 'She says have you got a Daisy headache powder. Her head's splitting.'

'I'm sorry to hear that, Milly,' Opal said. 'Yes, I always keep them. Tell your mother I hope she'll soon feel better but should she need another powder I'll be back this evening.'

They reached the church in the nick of time. It was not possible to greet anyone for as they settled into their seats the organ music announced the arrival of the bride. How radiant and lovely Queenie looked! How clearly and eagerly she made her responses.

Insofar as she ever addressed God, Opal prayed that marriage would not rob her new sister-in-law of that radiance and eagerness. But marriage changed people.

After the ceremony everyone except the bridal couple and the bridesmaids walked back to the house. Opal fell into step beside her mother. Hannah's pace was slow and her breathing difficult. She took her daughter's arm and though to Opal her mother looked slighter than ever, as if a strong wind on the top of the moor would blow her away, she leaned heavily upon her daughter. Opal, bearing the weight of her own pregnancy, found it difficult to support her mother, though not for the world would she have showed it.

'You should have gone in the motor car,' she said. 'This is quite a hill. In fact, should you have come at all, Mother?'

'Of course I should. I wanted to see Mark married.'

They were the last to arrive at the house. Queenie, standing beside her new husband, her eyes shining, cheeks glowing, embraced them in turn.

'Come and sit down, Mother!' She blushed prettily at her first use of the new title. 'You know, you *are* my mother now!'

'And pleased to be,' Hannah Derwent said. 'You're looking very bonny, isn't she Opal?'

'She looks beautiful!'

'Well it's partly due to Opal if I do. Everyone's been admiring my hat, and the bridesmaids'. In fact, Opal, one of the guests is the sister of a lady who has a milliner's shop. She says you're just the person her sister's looking for.'

Opal glanced down at her figure. 'Not in this state,' she said ruefully.

43

'That's what I told her,' Queenie replied. 'And that you also had another child and a husband to look after.'

'Now that everyone's here,' Mark broke in, 'we can have the toast and then we can all eat. I'm starving!'

'We're to drink champagne,' Queenie said. 'Father insisted, though *he's* not supposed to touch it.'

'Is he feeling better?' Opal asked.

'Not really, though he's determined to get through the reception. He's over there, sitting in the armchair by the screen. Do go and have a word with him, Opal. He enjoys talking to you. He thinks you're much cleverer and more sensible than I am.'

'Rubbish,' Opal said. 'He thinks the sun shines on you.' All the same, she was pleased by Queenie's remark.

She moved to where her grandparents, parents and aunts stood in a tight group. Champagne was handed round and the toast was drunk to the newly-weds.

'Mmm! It's delicious!' Opal cried. 'I've never tasted champagne before!'

'Nor have I, and I'm seventy-three,' her grandfather said. 'And I reckon nothing to it. Here you are, Opal. You can have mine. I'd sooner have a glass of beer any day.'

'Oh, but Father, do you think Opal should? In her condition?' Aunt Pearl said doubtfully. 'Alcohol!'

'Nay, it's more like fizzy lemonade,' her father said. 'What can that do except give you belly-ache?'

'Abraham! Do mind your words!' His wife's quiet whisper was anguished. 'You're not on the farm now. You're in a drawing-room, and a very lovely one it is, too.' She gazed appreciatively at the green flock wallpaper, the rosewood grand piano, the embossed velvet upholstery and the crystal chandelier. 'Fancy our Mark marrying into a home like this!'

Opal laughed. 'He's married Queenie, not the piano!'

As for her grandfather, she thought, though his warm personality made him welcome wherever he went, the background of his farm suited him better than this room. It was a long time now since she had been up to Langstrothdale. Her grandfather was the fourth generation of Derwents to farm there and her own earliest memories were of the dale where she had spent the first five years of her life, before her father had moved to his own farm in the West Riding. It was a small, wild dale which saw the beginnings of the River Wharfe. The river was always the clearest thing in her memories of childhood.

'Do you remember, Grandma, that afternoon when you showed me how to dam a bit of the river with stones?' she asked. Her grandmother, in spite of the hard work of the farm, had always had time to spare for her.

'Aye, I do that,' her grandmother said. 'I mind it well. You enjoyed that bit of power, didn't you? You thought you had it in you to change the whole course of the river!'

So I did, Opal thought. 'I'm going to talk to Mr Stone,' she said. 'I promised Queenie.'

Mr Stone seemed pleased to see her, though she thought how strained and tired he looked.

'Queenie talks a lot about you,' he said. 'She's very fond of you, you know.'

'And I of her,' Opal said. 'I hope she'll be very happy with my brother.'

'Young Mark'll have me to answer to if she's not,'

Mr Stone said. 'But I wouldn't have offered him a job in my Company, let alone give him my daughter, if I hadn't thought highly of him – once I got to know him. I hope you'll come and see them often when they're living here.'

'I will,' Opal promised.

She would have liked to have talked to him longer but other guests came and claimed his attention and she could see that he was weary. She left him and found herself a seat. She was desperate to sit down. Besides, food was being handed round; ham and tongue sandwiches, salmon patties, savoury things on toast – and on the table she could see cream trifles and iced fancies flanking the two-tier wedding cake. She was tremendously hungry. She took several items of food from the tray a waitress offered and settled down to eat in earnest. Daniel was being looked after by his Aunt Mary; Edgar was talking, with unusual animation, to Queenie. When she had eaten her fill she went over to join them.

'We must go soon,' she said. 'If we stay too long Daniel will get too tired, and then he'll be fractious. He's fine now, but it won't last.'

'I understand,' Queenie said. 'We're going to cut the cake now, and then Mark and I must leave.' The colour rose in her face again at the thought of the honeymoon. 'I hope you won't take it amiss, Opal, but I've asked Jane to pack you a basket to take home. It will be waiting in the hall for you and no-one will see it. There's so much food here and if someone doesn't take it it will go to waste. So you'll be doing me a favour.'

'I'm grateful,' Opal said quietly. It would probably feed them through the weekend and beyond. 'It's been a lovely wedding. I hope you have a wonderful honeymoon.'

Queenie and Mark looked at each other, their faces alight with love.

'Oh we shall,' Mark said. 'We shall.'

'Your mother looks none too good,' Edgar said when they were home. After the double tram ride they were hungry again and when Daniel, who had fallen asleep on the tram and had had to be carried home in his father's arms, had been put to bed, and the shop set out afresh, Opal spread some of the contents of Queenie's basket on the table.

'I agree,' she said. 'I'm worried about her. Well, best come and eat.'

'Bits and pieces,' Edgar said. 'Bits and pieces. Not what I call solid food.'

'It's all delicious,' Opal said. 'I'd like to eat like this every day. And drink champagne!'

'You've got ideas above your station,' Edgar said, but not unkindly. Something, perhaps the champagne which he affected not to like, had put him in a good mood.

Only two people came to buy from the shop; a small boy for a sherbert fountain and a woman for a whipped cream walnut. 'As it's Saturday night,' she said. At nine o'clock, though it was still daylight, Opal said, 'It's been a long day. Why don't we go to bed?'

She was nearing the end of the Monday wash when she heard the knock at the door. The whites, having been rubbed, boiled and starched, with a squeeze of Dolly blue in the starch water for added whiteness, were already drying in the sun, on the line which stretched across the street. On Monday mornings the whole length of every street in Milton was strung with laundry, like a village *en fête*. No cart of any kind could pass and even a pedestrian must dodge between sheets and shirts, shifts and blouses.

Opal straightened her body as she heard the knock. Pounding and twisting the peggy stick, in her condition, was painful. Thank goodness Edgar would help her with the mangle.

'See who's at the door, Edgar,' she called out. 'If it's a hawker he's out of luck, poor devil!'

'Why, Sam, whatever brings you here?' she heard Edgar say. Her stomach lurched at the greeting. Sam worked for her father on the farm and in the middle of Monday morning he could only be bringing bad news.

'What is it' she asked, coming to the door. 'What's amiss?'

'It's Mrs Derwent,' the boy said. 'She's been took real bad. The Maister thinks you'd best come.'

Opal grasped Edgar's arm, trying to steady the world which had started to spin. And yet it was no surprise. She had seen it in her mother's face at the wedding, only two days ago. She had felt it in her mother's weight on her arm and heard it in her weakened voice.

'Steady on,' Edgar said. 'Sit down and I'll make you a cup of tea. Sam, you'll have a drink of tea?'

'Nay, I mun get back. Shall I tell the Maister you're coming, then?'

'Yes,' Opal answered. 'I'll be there as quickly as ever I can.'

'You'd best have a few minutes rest before you go,' Edgar advised when Sam had gone. 'It's a tidy walk. Do you want me to come with you, take Daniel to Ma's?'

'No. You stay here and look after him. I'll be all

right. But I might not be back tonight. If there's nursing to be done I shall want to take my share. I won't wait for a cup of tea right now. Fetch my clean nightdress in from the line, will you. Quickly!'

Climbing the hillside, though there was some shade from the trees, was warm work. Sweat ran down Opal's face and around the collar of her blouse, which clung damply to her back. She would have liked to have taken a short rest but there was no time. In spite of the awkwardness of her body she walked quickly. On the top of the moor, away from the trees, it was hotter than ever. The sun, almost at its zenith now, beat down on her head. There was no shade anywhere and the outcroppings of rock seemed to reflect the sun's rays, bouncing them back into the air to heat it still further. But she kept up her pace, trying not to notice her fatigue.

She had neglected her mother. She knew it only too well. 'Dear God,' she prayed. 'Only let my mother live and I'll be better!' But would God make a bargain with someone who most of the time ignored him? The pain in her back was worsening. She wanted more than anything in the world to lie down, but there was no question of doing so.

She was almost at the top of the moor now. The downhill journey would be easier. When she reached the crest of the hill and saw Highcliffe down below she felt a new rush of strength to match her urgency, and started to run. She never knew what tripped her up, perhaps a bramble root, perhaps a stone on the track. She fell to the ground and rolled over and over down the hill until a narrow, shelving plateau stopped her. There, for a second or two, she lay on the ground, her whole body shaking. But there were no bones broken and she must get on. She must hurry, hurry! She got to her feet and started down the hill again as quickly as her trembling legs would take her.

When she reached the farm the door was open. She passed through the empty kitchen and, with great difficulty, for she had neither breath nor strength left, went upstairs to her mother's bedroom. Her father, Aunt Garnet and Mary stood by the bed. It was Mary who turned towards her, the tears streaming down her white face.

'Oh Opal!' she sobbed 'You're too late! It's all over! She died not five minutes ago. You're too late!'

And then her sister and her aunt moved forward quickly as Opal, the pain searing her back and now embracing her belly with hands of red-hot iron, screamed as the world grew dark and she dropped to the floor.

It was almost a month before the doctor declared Opal fit to return to her own home.

'You'll be glad to get back to your husband and your little boy,' he said. 'But go carefully, my dear. You're not completely strong yet.'

In her heart she knew she was not, and never would be, ready to return to Acer Street. Though it contained those she held most dear, Edgar and Daniel, the doctor's words sounded in her ears like a prison sentence. 'I condemn you to penal servitude for life!' If only they could get away! If only they could make a fresh start. But she said nothing of these feelings; not to her father, sunk in his own world of grief; not to Aunt Garnet or to Mary; not to Edgar when he came to visit her.

Her baby daughter, born before Hannah Derwent was in her coffin, had died less than twenty-four hours after the grandmother who never saw her. Aunt Garnet said they would meet in heaven and know each other.

'She was quite perfect,' Mary wept – though whether for the baby or her mother she was not sure. 'Such a darling little girl!'

'But too small to survive,' Aunt Garnet said. 'Our Opal's small herself, so at seven months what chance did the bairn have? And a rough passage into the world at that.'

It had been clear to all except Opal, to whom because of her pain nothing was real except the pain itself, that the child could not live, and the same clergyman who was in the house because of Mrs Derwent's passing, baptized the infant. Opal, rallying for a moment, chose the name Judith. Then the milk which Nature sent so liberally to Opal's breasts turned against her. When the small coffin followed the larger one out of the house, to be buried in the graveyard on the side of the moor, Opal was raging with milk fever, too delirious to know anything. For a while it seemed as though a third funeral must follow.

But as the days went by the fever subsided. She knew that she would recover but her spirits were low and she wondered, lying in the narrow bed which had been hers until she had married, whether she wanted to do so. Edgar came to see her frequently, sometimes bringing Daniel, more often leaving the child with his mother. She did not tell him how she felt but he was aware that something was wrong.

'You must make an effort, love,' he said. 'For my sake and little Daniel's. We want you back'

'I'm being punished for my sins,' Opal said. 'I never wanted the baby and I didn't do enough for my mother. Now I'd give anything to have them back but it's too

51

late. God is just! He's not merciful, but he's just. He gives punishment where it's due.'

'I don't understand about that,' Edgar said helplessly. 'I'm sure you'll feel better when you're a bit stronger. I've been keeping the shop going,' he added, trying to turn the direction of her mind. 'People have been very kind asking after you. And I'm going to see Mr Ridley in a day or two. Perhaps you should think about what I ought to buy from him?'

In the end, though she did not come to it quickly, it was the thought of the shop which aroused Opal from her apathy. Yet even while she thought of it, sitting now in a chair outside the farmhouse in the July sunshine, looking up to the moors which were breaking into their covering of purple heather, she knew that it was not enough. She must do something, anything, to change her life, to change life for all three of them. And then she realized – it came to her quite clearly – where her hope lay.

When Mary came towards her with a cup of tea and piece of fresh curd tart to tempt her appetite she asked, 'Will Queenie be coming at the weekend?'

'I think so. Why?'

'Well, since they'll come over from Leasfield in her father's car, I thought she might take me back to Milton. It's about time I was going.'

'That's a bit sudden,' Mary said. 'Oh I know Doctor Lee said you could, and there's Edgar and little Daniel to think of, so I dare say you're right. But it's been a comfort to me to have you here to look after.'

When Queenie arrived on Saturday afternoon Opal took her at once into the parlour. Queenie's grief for Hannah Derwent had been deep, but simple, and without guilt, so that the tears she had shed had comforted her, as Opal's could not. Opal wished that she could be more like Queenie; uncomplicated, kind and good. But it was not in her.

'Do you remember at your wedding you mentioned a lady with a hat shop?' she asked quickly. 'You said she might be wanting an assistant and her sister liked my hats.'

'Why yes, I remember,' Queenie said.

'Did she engage anyone? Is the job still open?'

'I've no idea,' Queenie said with surprise. 'I don't even know whether it was serious. But Opal, you can't mean . . . You can't possibly do it! You're not yet strong enough. Besides, you've got Edgar and Daniel to look after.'

'Never mind that just now,' Opal said eagerly. 'Will you find out if there *is* a job? And if there is, will you put in a word for me?'

'But I don't . . .' Queenie sounded bewildered.

'Oh *please* Queenie! I beg you! I assure you it's what I need if I'm to stay sane! And the woman won't regret it if she takes me on.'

'I'm sure she won't,' Queenie said. 'But what will Edgar say? And what about Daniel?'

'I'll deal with that,' Opal said hurriedly. 'Don't mention it to Edgar, or to anyone else just yet.'

Edgar would hate it, that was certain. Even after all this time without work he saw himself as the bread-winner, the one responsible for supporting his family. She had no wish to deprive him of this role, but somehow he must be made to see her point of view.

Back in Acer Street, she paused inside the doorway. How small the room looked! How small and shabby; tidy enough but not clean. The fireplace was dull, and behind the lace curtains, which were badly in need of washing, the window was smoke-grimed. True to his promise, Edgar had set out the shop, though not with her order and precision. It looked tatty. She doubted whether she could ever settle here again. One way or another, however long it took, she must get out.

She waited until they had had their tea and she had put Daniel to bed before she broached the subject which was burning inside her. In the end she could think of no subtle way of leading up to it, no tactful manner of introducing it. Her blunt announcement, she thought, sounded like an attack.

'You may as well know, Edgar, I'm thinking of going out to work.'

He stared, not believing his ears.

'What did you say?'

'I'm going out to work,' she repeated. She wished she did not sound so defiant. It was not how she had meant it to be.

'But I don't understand!' He looked confused. 'You're a married woman with a young child. *You* shouldn't be going out to work.'

'I want to. Please Edgar, I really want to!'

She watched the shadow pass over his face.

'You mean you need to. Because I can't keep my wife and family like a man should. That's what you mean, isn't it?'

She could have borne it if he had been angry, shouted at her, shaken her by the shoulders. It would have hurt her less.

She shook her head. 'You're wrong. It's not like . . . But you must admit that it would help?'

'So what makes you think you can get a job?' he asked. 'What can you do? You've no sort of experience.'

'Well I can make hats for one thing. And I can serve in a shop. I've proved that. So I shall look for something which combines the two. Of course I might not find anything.' But she would, she knew she would.

'And what about me and Daniel while you're out working?'

She was irritated by the self-pity in his voice, but even so she tried to speak reassuringly.

'You and Daniel have shown how well you can manage without me. You've looked after him very well. He's the picture of health.' She intended to say nothing about the state of the house. 'And I'm sure his Grandma will be pleased to have him when you have to sign on.'

'I see you've got it all worked out,' Edgar said. 'There's not much left for me to say, is there? I suppose, then, you'll be giving up all this?' He motioned to the house shop, laid out on the table.

'Give it up?' Opal retorted, stung to an anger she could no longer control. 'No, Edgar, we'll not give it up! Why should we? *You* shall run the house shop, Edgar! There's no point at all in giving it up!'

Chapter Three

'So there it is,' Madame Dora said. 'Since he's taking
me to lunch. I can't be out when Mr Hessle comes.
It's his last visit before he retires and he's bringing his
nephew who's taking over from him. I shall want to
meet him. So there's nothing else for it, Opal, you'll
have to deliver the hats to Miss Taylor!'

Miss Taylor, though goodness knew she could be a
nuisance, was one of their best customers. She seldom
set foot in the shop (Opal had never seen her) but about
once every couple of months she telephoned Madame
Dora and asked her to bring a selection of hats up to
the house, and she almost always bought one.

'Sometimes I wonder if I was wise to have the
telephone installed,' Madame Dora said. 'But with a
high-class business like this it's expected. It's not as if
we were a sweets and tobacco or a greengrocer's.'

'I'm sure you 're right, Madame Dora,' Opal agreed.

Her employer liked to be addressed as Madame Dora
though everyone in the locality knew that she was really
Dora Barraclough, widow of the late Asa Barraclough,
pork butcher, who had died of the Spanish flu in 1919.
Indeed, the very premises which now, carpeted in beige
Wilton and tastefully decorated, housed Madame
Dora, High Class Milliner, had once contained Mr
Barraclough, surrounded by sides of pork, legs of ham,
dishes of chitterlings, faggots and, on Fridays at twelve
noon, a leg of succulent hot roast pork which could be

purchased, thinly sliced, by the quarter pound.

Sometimes when she was hungry Madame Dora imagined she could smell that roast pork, taste the crackling. Out of the whole business it was the only thing she had been able to stand. That, and the money her husband made. When he was taken she had genuinely mourned him, but she was glad to be rid of the butcher's shop and to put her inheritance into something more refined.

'Moreover,' Madame Dora said, 'I know Miss Taylor likes to see me personally. But you're more than capable of delivering the hats and you can tell her I'll call myself later this afternoon, even though it's early closing, to help her make a choice.'

'Supposing she wants to try them on while I'm there?' Opal asked.

Madame Dora frowned. She was aware that her assistant was more than able to help Miss Taylor choose a hat, and to trim it for her. She was the best assistant she had ever had in the salon. (Madame Dora never thought of it as a shop.) In fact, what with her instinct for fashion, her skill with a needle and her interest in everything to do with the business, Madame Dora thought that Opal might be a greater talent than herself. But, she comforted herself, clients did prefer the attention of the proprietoress.

'Well, the customer is always right,' she conceded. 'If she does insist, try to sell her the velour. It's expensive – a guinea untrimmed – but she can afford it. Her father was Taylor's treacle toffee, you know.'

'I'll do my best,' Opal promised.

'And before you go, let down the sunblind. The September sun isn't as damaging as the spring sun, but we can't afford to have the hats fade. In fact, I think you'd better bring the velvet toque out of the window. And cover the mauve felt with a sheet of tissue. Mauve's the very devil for fading.'

They waged a constant battle between the need to display the finest hat – though never too many at a time since both ladies agreed that that was common – and the propensity of every material to fade in the light. Sometimes a single, sunny morning was enough to ruin a hat.

Opal took the toque out of the window and placed it on a stand in the shop.

'I don't suppose this shape will ever go out of fashion,' she remarked. 'Not as long as the Queen wears it.'

It was a beautiful hat and she alone had made it, though for herself to wear she preferred something more up-to-date.

'You did a good job on that,' Madame Dora said. She believed in giving praise where praise was due. When she had first set eyes on Opal – tiny, thin, her face white and pinched – she had not been impressed by her. Height was an asset in a shop assistant, as was a fashionable figure to show off clothes and a pretty face to enhance a hat. Opal's figure, since in spite of her slenderness she had well-rounded breasts, was unfashionable. She needed a good, tight bust band to flatten that area. Nor was she, in Madame Dora's eyes, strictly speaking pretty, though she had good cheekbones and fine, dark eyes. Nevertheless, Madame Dora recognized style when she saw it. It transcended many faults.

'I wanted to talk to you, Madame Dora,' Opal said. 'Could you spare me a minute later in the morning?'

'Well, we'll see how busy we are, shall we?'

She knew what it would be about and she was not worried. The labourer was worthy of his hire and she had no objection to giving Opal an extra half-crown a week.

'Right now you'd better be off,' she said. 'Oak House, Nab End Rise. Halfway up the hill.'

It was good to be out in the air on such a fine morning. Though Opal had often delivered hats to back doors she had not up to now been entrusted with an errand which might possibly take her inside a rich customer's home. In her two years' service she had done most tasks, from sweeping the shop floor and cleaning the plate glass window to making and trimming hats for quite important weddings and funerals. She knew how to start with nothing more than a length of millinery wire and finish up with a hat fit for a queen.

The only chore which she had never been allowed to touch was that of totting up the contents of the till and entering them in the ledger. This Madame Dora kept to herself.

'But I know the cost of all the materials,' Opal told Edgar. She talked to him regularly about her job in spite of the fact that he showed little interest. She doubted that he had ever forgiven her for taking it and she felt compassion for him that she had found a job so easily while he was still without.

'I know the cost of the buckram shapes, the linings, ribbons, feathers, flowers,' she told him. 'And I've a fair idea of the rates of the shop with the living quarters over. With the prices Madame Dora charges for hats she must be making a pretty good living.' It seemed to Opal that she deserved a bigger share of it than the ten shillings a week she was paid.

Her wages, though, had been a godsend. With them, plus the few shillings the house shop still made, and Edgar's dole money, they just about managed. There was still no sign of work for Edgar, nor for hundreds of others who formed long queues outside the Labour Exchanges. He seemed now to have settled down to a workless condition as if he had known no other. It worried Opal that he seemed interested in nothing, except for Daniel. Even politics no longer had the power to move him. He had not so much settled down, she thought, as succumbed.

As for any physical expression of love between them, well that almost never happened. Sometimes, aching with her own desire, and wanting also to give him comfort, in bed she tried to draw him into her arms. Too often he turned away from her, leaving her ashamed of her longings.

Resolutely she put Edgar out of her mind as she turned the corner into Nab End Rise. It was a road where people of substance lived in handsome houses set in large, tree-bordered gardens. Opal hesitated outside the large iron gates of Oak House, wondering whether she dare present herself at the front door. But that might be going too far.

'I'm from Madame Dora,' she told the maid who answered the kitchen door. 'Miss Taylor's expecting me.'

'That's right. This way if you please!'

Opal followed the maid along the stone-flagged passage to the other side of a baize-lined door. It was a different world here: a world of deep-pile carpets, gilt-framed paintings, embossed wallpaper, exotic plants in jardinieres. The room into which the maid ushered her was grander still, with green silk curtains and a green and gold Chinese carpet. Miss Taylor, standing in front of the white marble fireplace, was tall, angular, and expensively dressed in a brown frock coat which did nothing for her sallow skin and grey hair.

'I'm sorry Madame Dora couldn't come,' she said. 'She knows what I like.'

'She's disappointed too,' Opal said. 'But such a severe stomach upset.'

It was the fiction they had decided on. It would never do to let Miss Taylor know that she had been passed over for a commercial traveller.

'I hope I may help you,' Opal ventured. 'Madame Dora thought that if you were to try on the hats while I was here I might be able to assist you in your choice.' She could always tell Madame that Miss Taylor had insisted.

'Well, we'll see,' Miss Taylor said doubtfully. Opal wondered why she bought hats so often since she had a face so rugged and individual that there could be few hats which could actually adorn it.

'I suppose you had better come up to my bedroom then,' Miss Taylor said. 'We can't try on hats without a mirror.'

Opal followed her up the wide, curving staircase and into a large room with a dressing table set into the deep bay of a window. Miss Taylor sat herself in front of the mirror and waited for Opal to unpack the hats. They were not what Opal would have selected for Miss Taylor now that she had seen her, but she was here to sell and she must do her best. She was confident that she could change the nature of some of them with judicious trimming and she was glad that she had persuaded Madame Dora to let her bring a few things along. But the artificial flowers were out. Miss Taylor was definitely not the type to be flower trimmed.

She placed each hat in turn on top of Miss Taylor's sparse hair while the lady frowned at her reflection in the glass. Opal knew that the rust-coloured velour was far and away the most suitable, so she saved it until the last.

'You could wear any of them, Madame,' she said politely. 'But I think this is really *you*! I always think it's a pity' she added thoughtfully 'that we only see ourselves in mirrors, because that's not any of us at our best. Something to do with 'reversed image'.' I don't understand it, but it's a fact that we all look nicer than we think.'

She held her breath while Miss Taylor gazed into the glass, frowning. Had she said too much, even though it was true? She was relieved when she saw Miss Taylor's expression soften, watched her lift her head and view her reflection with something like approval.

'I think you should have quite a severe trimming on this one,' Opal advised. 'A stiffish bow, almost self-coloured – I have the very ribbon here – and well to the side to add a little width.' Deftly, she formed the ribbon into intricate folds and held it in position.

'Yes,' Miss Taylor said. 'I think you're right!'

'Would you like me to complete it while I'm here?' Opal asked. 'I could do it quite quickly.'

'Very well then,' Miss Taylor agreed. She seemed amiable enough now. Not at all a bit of a Tartar. 'I dare say you'd like a cup of tea?'

Opal knew by the maid's down-turned mouth as she brought in the tea-tray that she did not approve of this gesture. Certainly Madame Dora had never mentioned tea, and surely she would have done had it happened? The tea was pale gold in colour, delicate in flavour, served in rose-patterned china. It was quite unlike the brew she and Edgar drank every day.

When she had finished the hat Miss Taylor tried it on again. 'Yes,' she said. 'That will do nicely. You're a gifted young lady. But I supposed you'll give it up and marry some man and have hordes of children!'

'I *am* married,' Opal said hesitantly. There was a polite fiction that no young woman in a job was married. She was always addressed as 'Miss Carson'. 'I have a little boy. My husband is unemployed. He couldn't get a job, so I did.'

But it was not as simple as that. Something other than economic necessity had driven her to seek for work and now her job had become all-important to her. She enjoyed leaving the house each morning and going out into the world, even a world no farther away than Madame Dora's.

'What about your little boy?'

'His father looks after him very well. And of course I'm able to do better by him – give him better foods, clothes. Daniel doesn't lose out at all.' She sounded on the defensive and was cross with herself that she should. After all, where Daniel was concerned, she was the loser. She missed him so much, was painfully aware that she had shut herself out from a part of his life and tried to make up for it in the time they were together. She was unreasonably jealous of the close bond she recognized between Daniel and his father.

'Isn't it hard work, going out to a job and running a home?' Miss Taylor asked.

'Yes. I have to be at the salon at eight-thirty in the morning and I don't finish until seven at night.'

She could have added that to save the tramfare she

walked the two miles each way from Madame Dora's to Acer Street, that on her half-day she cleaned the house, looked after the house shop and sometimes, usually taking Daniel with her, went to Ridley's for new stock. Also that on Sundays she did the week's washing, ready for hanging out on the line first thing on Monday morning.

'I think I should have liked to have had a job,' Miss Taylor said. 'But naturally I looked after my parents until they were taken. I don't know what I could have done, though. I'm not cut out for teaching and I could never have worked in a hospital. And what else is there?'

For you, since you're a lady, not much, Opal thought. For me, anything I can get.

'Tell me, Miss Carson,' Miss Taylor said suddenly. 'What does someone like you think of votes for women?'

Opal flushed. 'I only know what *I* think,' she said pertly – and was then aware that she had spoken rudely to a valuable customer. But when Miss Taylor's sharp eyes met her own she saw, with relief, that there was amusement rather than anger in them.

'And what *do* you think?'

'That it's right and proper. That it's unfair that we should have to wait until we're thirty. We should be equal with the men.'

'What you mean is that we should have equal voting rights with the men,' Miss Taylor corrected her. 'I agree with that. But we can never be quite equal with the men. It's not in our nature.'

'I mean,' Opal began, but thought better of it. She knew what she meant; that women should have the same chances as men. She wondered if Miss Taylor would have liked to have been a man with – for those who were lucky – a man's opportunities? For herself she was glad to be a woman, but she wanted the opportunities too.

'Well, thank you. I mustn't detain you any longer.' Miss Taylor spoke briskly, as if conscious that she might have spoken too freely with the milliner's little assistant. Perhaps it was to restore matters to their proper footing that she gave Opal a shilling as she was leaving.

Opal hurried back, from time to time restraining herself from breaking into a run from her joy at being out on so fine a morning. The shilling tip was most generous. She would spend it all on Daniel, perhaps even on a nice toy. She was glad she had sold the velour. It was important that she should please Madame Dora today.

When she reached the salon Mr Hessle had not arrived.

'So tiresome!' Madame Dora grumbled. 'I could have gone to Miss Taylor's after all. Still, I must say you've done very well.'

'As there's no-one in the salon at the moment, could I speak to you now?' Opal asked.

'Very well, Miss Carson. But if it's what I think it is you can save yourself the trouble. You've worked hard this last year and I've already decided to give you an increase of half-a-crown a week from the end of the month. There! Does that suit you?'

Opal hesitated. 'Not quite,' she said slowly.

'Not quite? Well I can assure you, miss, I can't possibly give you more! I consider I'm being most generous!'

'Oh you are, you are!' Opal cried. 'I didn't mean

that. It's just that what I had in mind was something a little different.'

'Something different? In heaven's name what?'

Opal took a deep breath.

'Well . . . if you could agree to it . . . I wondered if I might have . . . what I'd like to have is a small percentage, oh a very small one, of the profits. Instead of a rise, I mean.' She was astonished at her own audacity. She could get the sack for less than this.

'*A percentage of profits?*' Madame Dora sounded as though Opal had spoken in a foreign tongue. 'A percentage of profits? Why, some weeks I hardly make a profit at all – and some weeks nothing!'

'Then on those weeks you would only pay me my ten shillings,' Opal said quickly. 'You would save half-a-crown.'

Her voice was steady, but inside she was trembling. Now that she had come out with the idea it sounded impossible. 'And I mean profits over a certain amount, naturally,' she continued. 'Perhaps over what they are now. That way you couldn't lose. You'd only pay me extra if I earned extra first – and then only a small part of it.'

'What makes you think,' Madame Dora said slowly (though Opal could hear the interest creeping into her voice). 'What makes you think you could increase the profits?'

'I have several ideas,' Opal said eagerly. 'I've given it a lot of thought.'

'What ideas?'

'Well, for instance, I thought that perhaps we . . . I mean you . . . might introduce a few more lines. Not just hats, but other accessories – scarves, gloves, hosiery. Lots of people are wearing the new art silk

66

stockings and since they last no time at all they have to keep buying more. And ladies underwear, or in our case, lingerie, for I know you'd only sell the best. They're beginning to sell it in the big stores. People don't make their own underwear as much as they used to. And no-one around here sells these items – at least not yet.'

'Well,' Madame Dora exclaimed, 'you certainly *have* been thinking about it, haven't you? I'm not sure that I can take it in so quickly!'

'And I thought you might change the name to "Madame Dora's Modes".' Opal said.

'Madama Dora's Modes, eh? Yes. But there's the question of space – that is supposing I were to agree to any of it in thc first place. Have you thought about space?'

'I have—' Opal began.

She was interrupted by the arrival of Mr Hessle. Unlike some of their commercial travellers who crept into the salon as if uncertain of their welcome, his entry was that of a leading actor on to the centre stage. He was a large man, but it was more his air of bonhomie than his size which seemed to fill the shop.

'My dear Madame Dora! Dear lady! I do apologize if I've inconvenienced you in the slightest degree. We were unavoidably detained. Yes, unavoidably detained!'

In the Red Lion, Opal thought, smelling his breath.

'I have to blame my imminent retirement,' he continued. 'I had no idea, no idea at all, that I had so many friends in the trade. And far too many of them, I'm afraid, wanted to toast my future. But I've saved the best to the last, dear lady, and my time from this moment on is all yours. Wednesday afternoon, early closing, all the time in the world for a long, leisurely lunch!'

'I'm looking forward to it, Mr Hessle,' Madame Dora said.

'Capital! And now let me introduce my nephew Mr David Hessle, who will take over from me. David, step forward to meet Madame Dora! And her young lady assistant, Miss Carson.'

David Hessle was tall, all of six feet. He was well dressed in a light grey suit with a striped silk tie. On removing his silver grey trilby he revealed a head of rich, auburn hair. When he shook hands with Opal, with a grip that was firm and pleasant, he smiled directly at her and the smile extended to his grey-green eyes. Opal thought he looked a cut above any commercial traveller she had ever seen.

'Now unless there's anything you're particularly wanting – though we have a nice line in velvet ribbon which I *would* like you to look at – we won't concentrate on business today,' Mr Hessle senior said. 'Mr David will be around again in the second week in October and I know he'll have some new lines to discuss with you. But not today, Madame Dora! Today luncheon awaits!'

Over the top of Madame Dora's head David Hessle caught Opal's eye, and smiled. She wished she was being included in the party.

Opal took the iron from the fire, blew the ash from it, and spat on it to test the heat. Then, to help the iron glide over the cloth, she rubbed the hot sole with a piece of candle fat wrapped in a bit of cotton cloth.

'I shall have to have some stuff for a new work

dress,' she remarked to Edgar. 'This one's getting very shabby.'

She would buy the new black material from the savings in the toffee tin and she would make up the dress to the same pattern – long sleeves, high round neck (with a white collar which had to be washed every day) – only this time it could be a little shorter. Skirts were knee-high in London though no doubt she'd have to be a little more circumspect. She reckoned that wearing a new dress had helped her to get the job with Madame Dora; that and the fact that she'd had her hair bobbed. It hung straight and heavy, with a thick fringe across her forehead and the sides curving on to her cheeks. Edgar hated it.

'You need a new shirt too,' she continued. 'I saw some in Tatham's window; cotton and flannelette, lined across the shoulder, for three-and-eleven three-farthings. You can get them cheaper but cheap clothes don't pay in the end.'

'I can manage,' Edgar said.

'No you can't,' she contradicted. 'It's important to be decently dressesd. How much money is there in the savings tin?'

'I don't know.'

'Then count it.'

She didn't need him to do so. She knew there was thirteen shillings and fourpence, but anything to make him move, take an interest.

Reluctantly, he took the tin from the dresser drawer, spilled the money on to the table, and began to count.

'Thirteen and twopence,' he said.

'That's wrong! There should be thirteen and four-pence.'

He pushed the money away angrily.

'If you know how much there is why do you ask me to count it? And if you must know, I took twopence for a packet of woodbines. I'd none left. A man needs a smoke.'

Opal flushed.

'I'd have bought you extra if you'd said.'

Like most women she bought her husband's cigarettes along with the groceries. In work, the men handed over their unopened wage packets, out of work their dole money. The women handed back the man's pocket money and bought his cigarettes. It was the way things were done and there was simply no reason for the sense of shame Edgar's words had roused in her.

'Anyway,' she said, 'it's enough to buy some dress material *and* a shirt, and some socks for Daniel.'

She had never made a secret of the savings in the tin. They were more or less common property. But what Edgar didn't know, and she was not sure why she had never told him, was that she now had her own bank account with the Yorkshire Penny Bank. There was not much in it but it was growing steadily. The Penny Bank boasted that it would gladly receive any sum, from one penny upwards, and she therefore felt no awkwardness in paying in her small amount each Friday as soon as she drew her wages. She enjoyed looking at the bankbook, watching the balance increase. She had made no withdrawals, nor would she unless for something so extra special that it had not so far even entered her mind.

She put the newly-pressed dress on a hanger and, striding over Daniel who was playing on the floor with a small wooden cart which Edgar had made him, she suspended it from the ceiling clothes dryer to air off. She smiled at Daniel. At four years old he was still a quiet child, undemanding, easygoing. Which was just as well, she thought, for much as she loved him she had little time to spend on him. There was always so much to do. It would be better for Daniel when he could go to school, be with other children of his own age.

'I took some hats to a customer in Nab End Rise this morning,' she told Edgar. 'It was a beautiful house. She gave me a lovely cup of tea and bought an expensive hat.'

'It's not right,' Edgar said.

'What isn't?'

'It's not right that some women can spend all that money on a hat.'

'I dare say it isn't,' Opal said mildly. 'All I know is that if she and her like couldn't, then I wouldn't have a job. It's no use *me* grumbling at the Miss Taylors of this world. I have to be thankful for them. Anyway, she was nice.'

She would like to be one of them. She would like to live in a big house with a garden and have a maid to answer the door. She would even like to be Madame Dora, with a nice little business and living quarters over. Or rather, not Miss Taylor, not Madame Dora, but her own self in a similar position. It was her circumstances she wished to change, not herself.

'Old Mr Hessle came in for the last time today,' she said. 'He brought his nephew, who's to take his place.'

But Edgar wasn't listening. He was staring into the fire. She wondered, fleetingly, if Edgar could ever get a job as a commercial traveller, just supposing she ever heard of one? He was good-looking, reasonably well-spoken, and in his navy blue suit which he now seldom wore, he looked as smart as the next man. On

71

the rare occasions when they went out together she was always proud to be seen with him. What he lacked, what, try as she might, she seemed unable to give him, was confidence in himself. Now David Hessle, she felt sure, had that quality in abundance.

Chapter Four

'It seems to me,' Edgar said, 'that you're none too pleased I've got the job!'

'That's ridiculous,' Opal objected. 'How can you think such a thing?'

But she felt mean that she hadn't shown more pleasure at his news, guilty at the lack of enthusiasm inside herself. Perhaps it was simply that she was so very tired. The week before Whitsuntide was a busy one in the shop and she had been on her feet since early morning.

'Well you're not saying much. Hardly a word. I'd have thought you'd have been as pleased as Punch!'

'I am, I am!' Opal protested. 'It's the shock. It's hardly five minutes since you told me. An insurance agent! I can hardly get it into my head!'

'I was dead lucky to get it,' Edgar said. 'I don't know that I would have but for the Reverend Atkinson putting in a word for me. It so happens that the District Manager is his churchwarden, and Ma knew that, you see.'

'How did you know about the vacancy?' Opal asked. 'Had you written to the Company?'

She thought that unlikely. He had written for nothing in the last two years, saying it was a waste of time and stamps.

'No, it was Ma! She came dashing round here as if her coat tails were on fire! Told me Jonah Ramsden had had a seizure on his way to pay out the insurance on old Grandma Battersby. He fell down in the street with the money on him, Ma said, and as likely as not they'd be paying out on him before the week was out. 'So get into your Sunday suit, and around to Reverend Atkinson to ask him to put in a word for you,' she said. 'And then off into Leasfield with you.'

'But it's more than a week since Mr Ramsden was taken bad,' Opal said. 'He died yesterday. I can't understand why you didn't tell me you'd been after the job!'

He'd had good enough reason for that, Edgar thought. He'd gone off to the interview without any hope whatever. After more than four years hope had died in him. So what was the use of telling Opal? When he didn't get the job it would be simply another failure to chalk up against him. She would never say it, but sometimes he saw it in her eyes. He knew he was a failure.

'Shall you be able to do it?' Opal asked. 'I mean . . . well, you've not done anything like this before.'

'I don't know till I try, do I?'

'Of course not,' she agreed. 'Anyway, if Jonah Ramsden could go it, I'm sure you can.' It was so good to hear hope in his voice. 'I am truly pleased for you, Edgar,' she assured him.

And now – he could still hardly believe it – he was a failure no longer. The slow, terrible, gut-rotting years had ended. From now on everything was going to be all right. And yet, he thought, if he had not gone after the job so quickly, urged on by his mother, he would never have got it. He could not have stood up to the competition once they had seen several other candidates. For him, to be an insurance agent was a step up.

74

'I suppose you'll have to go after new business?'

'I dare say,' he said. 'But people always want a bit of insurance. The worse off they are, the more they need it. Nobody's going to risk being buried by the Parish if a penny a week will pay for the funeral. It stands to reason.'

'I expect it does,' Opal agreed. 'But don't you have to put down money for an insurance agency?'

'Twenty pounds,' Edgar said. 'Ma lent me her savings. I shall pay her back as soon as I get on my feet.'

He could have asked me, Opal thought. But he'd rather take his mother's last penny than ask me. Well, though it said nothing good about the state of their marriage, it had its compensations. Now that she had the arrangement with Madame Dora she had been able to put a bit more by, but she had no wish to dissipate her savings because she had at last decided what they were for. Her goal was now as firmly fixed as the pole-star, though no-one beside herself knew anything about it. Under the top surface of her mind it occupied her thoughts from waking to sleeping. Sometimes it pursued her in sleep, and she had vivid, pleasurable dreams of the future. But she would willingly have given Edgar whatever he needed, if he had come to her.

'So I start next Wednesday, after the Whitsun holiday,' Edgar said. 'They don't want the payments to fall into arrears. I thought you might give me a hand with the books. You're good at figures.'

Where does he think I'll get the time, Opal asked herself.

'I'll make a cup of tea and see to Daniel,' she said, turning to her son.

'And what did *you* do today, love?' she asked.

'I did a drawing,' Daniel said. 'I brought it home to show you. Look! Miss Potter said it was the best in the class.'

Opal studied the drawing with interest. It depicted a street scene, in coloured chalks. Though the houses, the children playing, the horse pulling the coal cart, were all crudely drawn, the picture had great life and vigour.

'Well I think it's nice too,' she said, smiling at him. 'We'll pin it on the wall, shall we, where we can all see it? And now into the scullery and start getting washed while I put the supper on. And don't skip the back of your neck, my lad!'

At five years old he was capable and independent beyond his years and (for which she was truly thankful) with the capacity for enjoying himself for hours on end. He was never as happy as when he had a box of wax crayons and some paper to draw on. That he had talent she was sure, though she didn't know where he got it from. Also, he could now read. He was no trouble and she loved him dearly. He was part of all her dreams for the future.

'We shall have to make some arrangement about Daniel,' she said to Edgar when the child had gone into the scullery.

'I'm sure his Grandma'll have him,' Edgar said. 'It'll only be for a week, until you've worked out your notice.'

Opal, in the act of laying the table, paused and stared at him.

'My notice?'

'You'll be able to give it in tomorrow. The job's certain, you know. From next week on, *I'll* be the breadwinner!'

'But—'

'Oh you can keep on the house shop if you want to. But no more working from morning until night, coming home too tired to lift a teaspoon. No, you'll be back in your rightful place. But don't think I'm not grateful for what you've done, love!'

Opal knew, now, the reason for the disquiet which had stirred her mind at the moment he had given her his great news.

'Edgar,' she said quietly. 'I can't give up my job.'

He leaned across the table and took her hand in what was an almost forgotten, loving manner.

'You're afraid I'll not succeed,' he said gently. 'Well I can't blame you. But I'm going to prove you wrong. I'm going to show you that all I needed was the chance.'

'It's not that!' Opal protested. In her heart she knew she had her doubts about him, but she would never show them. And what sort of a job was it? Where would it lead, compared to what she had in mind?

'It's not that,' she repeated. 'I'm sure you'll do well. It's that I *like* my job. I enjoy every minute of it, even though I do come home tired. I'm good at it, Edgar, and it's what I want to do.'

Edgar's forehead tightened in a frown. His eyes, meeting hers, were hard and puzzled. He doesn't really understand at all, Opal thought.

'We can't talk about it now,' he said. 'We'll discuss it when Daniel's gone to bed.'

'As you wish,' Opal said. 'But you may as well know that I haven't the slightest intention of giving in my notice.'

Edgar jumped up from the table. She saw his neck suffuse with red where it bulged against his collar. He bounded to the window, turning his back on her, his broad shoulders hunched in anger.

'You'll give in your notice,' he shouted. 'You have a working husband now and it's your place to run the home and look after your child!'

She left the table and went into the scullery, to Daniel. Her whole body was shaking but she tried to speak calmly to her son. He was the witness, recently, of far too many quarrels.

'Have you finished, love? Let me see.'

She bent down and kissed his shining face. He smelled deliciously of the Knight's Castile soap which was especially kept for his delicate child's skin.

'Supper and then bed,' she said. 'It's time you were asleep.'

During the meal she and Edgar did not speak, though she kept up a conversation with Daniel. She was thankful when supper was over and she could take the child upstairs. He had his own bedroom now, about the size of a cupboard. She tucked him in and heard him repeat the prayers his grandmother had taught him, then she kissed him goodnight and went downstairs again.

Edgar was standing with his back to the fireplace, his arms tightly folded against his chest, his head lowered as if he was about to charge.

'Now, madam, let's get things straight,' he said grimly.

'Certainly!' Opal flashed back. 'That's what I want, too! For a start, I do look after my child, I do run the home, working or not. How much housework do *you* do, though you're home all day? When do you cook a meal?'

'That's not the point,' Edgar said. 'A woman's place is in the home. Everybody knows that.'

'Well I can assure you, Edgar, I am *not* giving up my job, not for you, not for anyone.' She spoke calmly, but inside she trembled and felt sick.

'Not even for Daniel?' Edgar said. 'I know you've got precious little time for me, but don't you care about Daniel?'

His voice was quieter, too, but it pierced her more than his temper could ever have done. He knew her vulnerability all right. It was the vulnerability of all who carry a child in the womb, bring it helpless and dependent into life. It was a pain of the heart more deeply felt than any bodily pain and she was no more immune to it than any other woman.

Convention had nothing to do with it. She didn't mind what people said, and no-one was going to tell her where her place was. It was what she herself must give up, must be prepared to miss, in the hours of separation from Daniel. That, and the niggling question as to what such a separation might or might not do to her son. She knew the risks, but the fight was for her own identity, for the right to do as she pleased with her own life. In spite of the doubts which remained in her – and perhaps always would – it was a fight she intended to win.

'You're being unfair!' she cried. 'It's not true that I've no time for you, and you know it. But you don't own me. As for Daniel, you're talking as though I have to choose between loving Daniel and going out to work. Well, I don't! I can do both.'

'Not properly,' Edgar insisted. 'You can't do both things well and we all know who'll suffer.'

But for all the strength which had come to him with

the prospect of his new job, he was no match for this small, determined woman; this woman he loved but frequently did not understand. He had lost and he knew it.

'I promise you, Edgar, Daniel won't suffer,' Opal assured him. 'And now I'll go around and see your mother and we'll come to some arrangement. She'll understand.'

'I'm not sure I approve' Mrs Carson said doubtfully. 'Oh, your wages must have been a godsend over the last three years, but now that Edgar's got himself a job . . . Anyway, it's not my approval you're after, is it? Of course Daniel can come here to his dinner every day. And if Edgar's likely to be out on his rounds he can come to his tea as well.'

'He'll love that,' Opal said. 'You know how he enjoys coming here.'

'Aye, well, that's settled then,' Mrs Carson said.

She admired her daughter-in-law – so competent, so ambitious – but she did not always understand her and in this case she couldn't enter into her feelings. But she would do anything for little Daniel. The way things were going he looked like being the only grandchild she'd ever have.

'I'd best be getting back,' Opal said. 'There's some ironing to do.'

'You work too hard,' Mrs Carson said. 'I should have thought you'd have been glad of the chance . . . But there it is. Anyway, I've got a nice apple pasty for you to take back with you. Fresh baked today.'

She wrapped the pasty carefully, taking pleasure in the sight of it. There were few situations that a nice, well-baked apple pasty couldn't improve.

When Opal arrived home Daniel was sitting in the armchair, wrapped in a blanket.

'He's been sick,' Edgar informed her. 'I brought him down and gave him a drink of warm milk.'

His tone of voice said that if she had been in her rightful place this wouldn't have happened. Oh Daniel, she thought ruefully, did it have to be now?

She knelt down by the chair and put her arms around him. 'It must be something you ate, love. Did anyone give you anything at school?'

'Dick Foster gave me some pink sweets,' Daniel confessed.

'Then that's it! Are you better now?'

'Yes.'

There was colour in his cheeks and his eyes were bright enough, the whites clear and blue.

'Well then, back to bed or you'll be too tired for school in the morning.'

'Carry me upstairs,' Daniel demanded.

'A great big boy like you?'

'Well I *was* sick.'

'All right then' she said. 'Just this once. It'll have to be a piggy-back.'

She changed the sheet and tucked him into bed. He flung his arms around her and they hugged each other tightly. Who could possibly say that she did not love her son enough? Then he lay back on the pillow and closed his eyes. She traced the fine arch on his eyebrows with her finger, touched his cool cheek. He was asleep before she left the bedroom.

'Supposing this happens when we're both out at work?' Edgar demanded, 'What then?'

'We'll meet that when it comes,' Opal said. 'It's no

use, Edgar. You're not going to make me change my mind.'

By mid-morning it was really busy in the shop, but in this particular week that was to be expected. Everyone who could possibly afford it wanted something new for Whit Sunday, to wear to church or chapel, and perhaps afterwards to the brass band concert in the park. And if there was not enough money for a complete new outfit, then a new hat, and perhaps new white gloves, must do.

'We're selling a lot of white gloves,' Madame Dora said. 'I wonder if we should get another two dozen pairs when David Hessle comes in? Or is it too late? Will the rush be over? Thank goodness the General Strike's finished. If it had gone on even a day or two longer it could have ruined out Whitsuntide trade!'

'I think the rush is about over,' Opal said. 'But white gloves could sell right through the summer. What we *must* have, though, is more art silk stockings in that new beige shade. No-one wants lisle for best any more. Do you think he might make a special delivery?'

'He might,' Madame Dora said. 'Especially if *you* ask him.'

Opal bent her head over the deep drawer in which she was checking the hosiery stock. She had got on well with David Hessle from the start, but Madame Dora made too much of it. It was nothing more than a pleasant business relationship. How could it be otherwise, even if she were so inclined, which she was not. Though he was single, she was a married woman with a child. But she would not let Madame Dora see her irritation.

Her employer had been good to her, no doubt about

82

that. She had agreed to all her ideas for expansion and had even moved the office and stockroom upstairs into her flat to free more space. They now did a good trade in gloves, scarves, hosiery, artificial flowers and sundry other items to adorn the female form. Lingerie had done well though it was falling off a little at present, this being the season for outward show. Hats, though, continued to be their mainstay. They had many more customers now, and if they were not quite as exclusive as they had been, well, their money was good. And since Opal now had two-and-a-half per cent of the extra profits she wasn't complaining.

'Perhaps you'd better telephone him,' Madame Dora said. 'Order what you think best.'

Her confidence in Opal grew all the time. The takings had doubled in the past two years. And Opal, though she didn't know it, was to have her reward. Not an immediate tangible reward. Madame Dora hoped it would not be reaped for a long time to come. But something for Opal to look forward to, in a manner of speaking. It would also be one in the eye for her sister, Millicent, Madame Dora thought with satisfaction.

'Don't let me forget I'm to see Mr Ratcliffe at twelve noon,' she said. 'I mustn't be late. Solicitors charge you for the time you keep them waiting.'

'I'll remind you,' Opal promised.

'When I get back' Madame Dora said solemnly 'I'll tell you all about it.'

Opal scarcely heard her. She was making a list of items required from David Hessle. It was important to achieve the right balance between having too little stock to meet the demand and thereby missing sales, and having too much when the season was over. She must also try once more to persuade Madame Dora to have a July sale. Sales were the one thing on which she dug in her heels. A discreet discount on an item which had been slow to sell was one thing; sales, with price tickets in the window, were quite another. As for advertising . . . ! Opal wondered if David Hessle might get hold of any special sale items. She completed her list and was about to unhook the telephone receiver when he walked into the salon.

'I was coming this way,' he said. 'I thought I'd call on the off chance.'

'You're just the man we wanted,' Madame Dora said. 'But I'm leaving you to Miss Carson. I have to see my solicitor.'

'What's that about?' David Hessle asked when Madame Dora had left. 'Not trouble, I hope?'

'I don't think so. She's probably changing her will again. She does it to spite her sister. She hates her since their father died last year and left everything in the house to Millicent. Have you any white gloves, sizes six-and-a-half and seven? And art silk hose, beige dawn, sizes eight-and-a-half and nine?'

Their dealing was interrupted several times while Opal broke off to serve customers. Hessle stepped back out of the way and watched her. She was so competent. She had exactly the right balance of deference and friendliness towards the customers, and the skill to guide them, without ever seeming to hurry, to a reasonably quick decision. She was damnably attractive too, but a hard nut to crack.

By the time the last customer had left and he had completed his order book it was five minutes to one.

'Come and have a bite to eat with me,' he said. 'I'm always asking you and you never accept.'

'Well I can't today,' Opal said. 'It's kind of you but,

84

as you see, Madame Dora isn't back and we never close the salon over the dinner hour.'

'Always the ready answer,' he said with good humour.

She thought how attractive he looked. It would have been pleasant to have gone with him.

'Shall you be going to the band concert on Sunday?' he asked.

'It depends on my husband,' Opal said. 'It depends on what he wants to do.'

'Do you always defer to your husband?' David Hessle asked.

'Of course!' But her eyes, meeting David's, were not as demure as her words.

Then minutes after he had left, Madame Dora returned.

'Lock the shop door!' she said. 'Yes, I mean it! And come upstairs. I've got something to tell you.' She had an air of great importance, but her eyes were excited, like a child with a secret to impart. Opal followed her upstairs and took a chair in Madame Dora's private sitting room.

'Now!' Madame Dora said. 'Prepare yourself for a shock! A pleasant one – a *very* pleasant one – but a shock!'

'I'm prepared,' Opal said. What could it possibly be? Was Madame Dora perhaps going to get married again?

'Well I've seen Mr Ratcliffe, and the long and short of it is, Opal – and I'm far too excited to beat about the bush – I've changed my will and I'm leaving the business to you! There!'

'To *me*?' Opal gasped. 'You don't mean it! I can't believe it!' She felt dizzy with the news.

'I don't suppose you can,' Madame Dora said. 'It's not something that happens every day. But it's true. It'll all be yours one day; lock, stock and barrel. Or to be more precise, stock, fixtures, fittings and goodwill. You deserve it and it'll be one in the eye for that greedy pig of a sister of mine!'

The world stopped spinning. Opal was on firm ground again. It was a kind gesture of course, but in practical terms it could mean very little to her. Madame Dora was forty-two and in the best of health. She would live another thirty years or more, by which time Opal was quite certain she would have her own business, far bigger and more important than this one could ever be. It was her goal, it was why she was saving her money. Any inheritance from Madame Dora – who in any case might change her mind half-a-dozen times between now and then – would be of small account by the time she could claim it. Now if it were to happen *soon* . . . She stopped her thoughts in mid-flight, horrified by the direction they had taken.

'Thank you, Madame Dora,' she said. 'I appreciate it very much indeed. But of course I hope you're going to live a very long time yet, to enjoy Madame Dora's Modes to the full.'

'Shall we go to the band concert today?' Opal asked on Sunday. 'It's the Black Dyke Mills. You always like them.'

'I'd have thought you'd have been too tired for traipsing up and down in the park,' Edgar replied.

'A change is as good as a rest,' Opal said briskly. 'Besides, Daniel might enjoy it. If you don't want to go I suppose I could take him.'

'Well I dare say it would help to take my mind off things,' Edgar said.

As the time grew nearer he was increasingly nervy about starting his new job. Though little more had been said about it, Opal could sense that. She would have liked to have talked to him, tried to reassure him, but it was a sensitive area and she had no wish to provoke another quarrel. She had won her point and that was that.

'It would do that,' she agreed. 'But there's no need for you to worry, Edgar. You'll be all right. Especially as the Supervisor's going around with you for the first week. Anyway, do we go to the band concert?'

'I suppose we might as well,' he said.

'Then we must look our best. Wear your Sunday suit, and the tie I bought you.'

She changed into the cream gabardine which she had worn for Queenie's wedding three years ago. She had taken it in to suit her normal, slender figure, shortened the skirt, trimmed it with a new braid, changed the buttons. No-one would recognize it and the material was as good as ever. She had borrowed a hat from the salon, which was allowed since it was good for trade. Daniel had a new suit, as befitted the time of year. They made a smart trio, she thought with satisfaction as they set off.

They took a tram to the park, sitting outside on top at Daniel's request. At the park entrance Edgar tossed twopence into the canvas sheet at the entrance, which entitled them to a printed programme.

'It looks like a good selection,' he said. 'Poet and Peasant, Gondoliers, Il Travatore. And a nice cornet solo. Shall we treat ourselves to chairs and concentrate on the music?'

87

Though the band concerts, which started at Whitsun and took place every Sunday until the middle of September, were supposedly musical occasions, everyone knew that they were also the scene setters for fashion parades. Those who really wanted to concentrate on the music could pay twopence to sit in a deck chair in a roped-off enclosure around the bandstand. The rest strolled, preferably in groups of three or four, up and down the wide avenues of the park. For them the music was a pleasant background to the more important business of seeing and being seen, especially by the opposite sex.

For no reason at all Opal suddenly wondered just how interested David Hessle was in music? For instance, would he sit in the enclosure? Then she dismissed the thought. She had not come here to see David Hessle.

'I think Daniel might get bored, just sitting still,' she said. 'It would be best to walk. But why don't *you* take a seat by the bandstand while I walk around with Daniel. I know you appreciate the music more than I do. I like to see what people are wearing.'

'I'll come with you,' Edgar said. 'Anyway it's a bit chilly to sit still, in spite of the sun. I don't know how some of you women keep warm in such thin dresses.'

'Pride keeps women warm,' Opal informed him.

All the same she was glad she was not wearing the flimsy voile which was everywhere around, pretty though it looked. The crowded avenue with people sauntering up and down looked like a summer flowerbed moving in the breeze. The women's hats – by far the larger number of them of white straw trimmed with flowers – were interspersed by the men's fawn or grey trilbys or their cream-coloured boaters with striped hatbands.

'Your outfit's as smart as any, even though you did wear it to Queenie's wedding' Edgar observed.

A great deal had happened to Queenie since that June afternoon. She and Mark had two little daughters and were now hoping that the new arrival would be the son they both wanted. Mr Stone had died, leaving a fortune to his daughter. But nothing could spoil Queenie's nature. She continued as simple and affectionate as ever, and every day more in love with Mark. She was the only person in the world Opal envied, and not for her possessions.

Daniel tugged at Opal's skirt.

'Can we go to see the ducks?' he asked.

Opal frowned slightly. The pond was out of earshot of the band and, except for children, the area would be deserted. Everything of interest was here.

'Perhaps later,' she said. 'Not just now. Mother and Father want to listen to the music and look at all the people.'

'Perhaps we *should* take him,' Edgar said.

'He can wait a little while. He mustn't think he can have everything the minute he asks for it.'

Edgar looked at her in surprise. 'You've changed your tune,' he said.

And then Opal saw David Hessle. He was walking towards her, and clinging to his arms was a pretty, fair creature. The floating panels of her ninon dress lifted in the breeze, which also caused her to hold down her fine straw hat with a small hand elegantly gloved in white kid. Good quality, eight-and-eleven three farthings, Opal noted automatically. Hessle's gaze was concentrated on his companion and he did not see Opal until he was almost upon her. When he did, there was no doubting the pleasure of his recognition.

'Why, Mrs Carson!' he exclaimed. 'I didn't expect to see *you* here! How pleasant!'

'My husband is very fond of music,' Opal said. 'We come whenever we can, don't we Edgar?'

'Allow me to introduce my cousin, Miss Dolly Simpson,' Hessle said.

They chatted amiably for a minute or two. Opal was aware that David Hessle missed nothing of her appearance, also that he approved. She was pleased that, for once, he had seen her in something other than her black work dress, even though her gabardine was not nearly as glamorous as his companion's flowered ninon.

'We must go,' she said after a little while. 'Daniel wants to see the ducks and we've promised him he shall.'

'If she's his cousin' Edgar said as they walked in the direction of the pond 'I'm the Prince of Wales!'

It was while they were waiting for the tram, close by the park entrance, that the accident happened. The concert was over, everyone rushing home to tea, crowds pouring through the park gates. Opal, standing in the long queue with Edgar and Daniel, saw Madame Dora among them. She was unmistakable in her elegance. Her wide-brimmed, yellow hat had been trimmed by Opal only a few days ago.

'There's Madame Dora!' Opal cried. 'How strange we didn't meet her in the park!' She let go of Daniel and raised her hand, waving to attract her employer's attention.

Eventually Madame Dora saw her. She returned

Opal's wave and started to cross towards her. After-wards, no-one in the crowd seemed to know where the motor car had come from. One minute it was not in sight and the next it had hit Madame Dora when she was no more than three yards from the pavement. For a split second she lay terribly alone, the yellow hat on the ground a few yards away where the breeze had carried it. Then suddenly people gathered around her still figure. Opal, already running from the opposite side of the road, pushed her way to the front of the crowd.

Madame Dora was alive, though unconscious, when the ambulance came. By the time it reached the hospital Opal, travelling with her, clutching the yellow hat as if it might work a miracle, did not need to be told by the ambulanceman that she was dead.

What horrified Opal for a long time to come was the speed with which the thought came into her mind. She pushed it away again, but it was already too late. The words into which it formed itself burned inside her.

'It's all mine! The business is all mine!'

Chapter Five

Opal looked up, frowning, as her new assistant rushed into the stockroom. The girl must learn to conduct herself in a more decorous manner. She was new, of course, and young – not yet twenty. But she would have to be trained.

'Oh Mrs Carson,' the girl began breathlessly.

'Calm down, Miss Browning,' Opal admonished.

'Well there's a great big car just drawn up at the kerb, with a chauffeur and everything, and I think the lady's coming in here! You'd better come, Mrs Carson!'

Opal smiled; not the polite, upcurving of her lips which she offered to customers, but a smile of real pleasure which lit up her face and shone in her eyes.

'That will be my sister-in-law, Mrs Mark Derwent,' she said. 'I'm expecting her.' She rose and hurried to greet Queenie as she entered the shop. Connie Browning was surprised at the warmth of the meeting between the two women. Mrs Carson was such a cool customer, she wouldn't have thought she'd have had it in her.

'You're looking wonderful, Opal dear,' Queenie said.

'You too!' Privately Opal thought, in the kindest possible way, that her sister-in-law's expensive outfit would have benefitted from being more up-to-date, but it was still true that she looked wonderful.

'Come along upstairs,' she said. 'Oh yes, this is my

new assistant, Miss Connie Browning. She's been with us just a fortnight. Miss Browning, do you think you could possibly keep an eye on the shop?' She no longer referred to it as the salon, as in Madame Dora's day. 'If there's the slightest problem, the very slightest, call me down at once.'

She went in front of Queenie along the corridor and up the narrow staircase which led to the living quarters above the shop. She heartily disliked this approach to the flat. It was so cramped and dark. When funds allowed she planned to have it decorated in light and bright colours, with a plain green carpet on the stairs; but for the last two years almost every spare penny had gone into the shop, expanding the range of goods, building up the business.

The living-room which they now entered was furnished almost exactly as it had been when Madame Dora was alive. Beige-covered sofa and armchairs, walnut table, brown curtains. Opal had inherited the contents of the flat along with the business and had lost no time at all in getting rid of almost everything which the Acer Street house had contained. Not that she liked Madame Dora's taste. She would have preferred more colour. But first things first and the shop was the most important. Except for Daniel, of course. He, she was pleased to think, now lacked for nothing.

'How is business?' Queenie asked.

'Very good. Very good indeed. As far as space permits I'm introducing new lines all the time. And the takings are well up on last year, let alone on what they were when Madame Dora had it.'

She had been surprised, and not pleasantly, to find how little money Madame Dora actually made. Her own small, regular share of the extra profits had seemed

93

riches only because she was so used to having nothing. Studying the books after Madame Dora's death, she had at once seen several ways in which profits might be increased. The moment the lawyers had sorted everything out, dealing swiftly with Millicent's vigorous protests over her sister's will, she had started to put her ideas into effect.

'The trouble with Madame Dora was' she said to Queenie 'that she tried to make money by economizing on everything, cutting back everywhere. I believe you have to use money to make money. Invest it in goods and increase the turnover.'

Queenie smiled, shaking her head in wonderment. 'I don't know where you get it from, your business sense, I mean. You sound just like my father used to!'

And look where it got him, Opal thought. Look what his success gave you. A chauffeur-driven limousine, an ermine stole over your shoulders, diamonds and emeralds on your hands. But there was no animosity in her thoughts. Queenie wore her riches with such natural grace, with so little ostentation, as to disarm all criticism.

'I'd be glad to have half your father's business gifts,' Opal said. 'And I envy his training. It's what I lack.'

'Ah, but you have *flair*!' Queenie said. 'I'm sure that's worth even more. But where's Daniel? I expected to see him.'

'He's out with his father,' Opal said. 'Edgar thought he shouldn't be sitting inside on such a fine afternoon so he's taken him on his rounds. I don't really approve, but Daniel was dying to go.'

'It sounds a good idea to me,' Queenie said. 'What's wrong with it.'

'Only that . . .' She did not quite know how to tell

Queenie that she disliked the thought of her son being taken around the poor streets, entering the poverty-stricken homes – probably none too clean – which made up the larger part of Edgar's round. In little more than two short years she had left that behind for ever and as far as her son was concerned she would like him to forget that it had ever existed. She intended life to be very different for Daniel.

'You never know what's going around,' she said. 'Infections and so on. I wouldn't want him to catch something just as he's about to go to a new school.'

'Is he looking forward to going to Bishop Tanner's?' Queenie asked.

Opal was saved from replying by the sound of Daniel's footsteps on the stairs. He came running into the room, followed a moment later by his father. The boy's cheeks were flushed in his otherwise pale, bright-eyed face. Edgar's skin was tanned from being so much in the open air, but in spite of this, Queenie thought, he did not look healthy. It was difficult to say why. He had plenty of flesh on his bones and his decent navy suit sat well enough on his muscular body. It was perhaps something in his demeanour, in his stance. He entered the room quietly, his shoulders hunched, his head down, as if he was not sure that he belonged. And though he had been in work for two years now, it was the previous four years of unemployment which showed in the lines on his face and in the dullness of his eyes. She had seen little of him for some time and she was moved, shocked even, by his appearance. He was twenty-nine and looked at least ten years older. But when he raised his eyes to hers his expression brightened.

'It's such a long time since I saw you,' Queenie said. 'You must tell me about your job.'

'There's nothing to tell,' Edgar said abruptly.

'I can tell you,' Daniel offered. 'We went to a lot of houses today and some of them asked us in. There was an old man in a bed downstairs. He gave me a cough sweet from under his pillow.'

'I hope you didn't eat it,' Opal said sharply. 'It's not fit!'

'It was quite nice,' Daniel said. 'Sort of aniseedy.'

'I told you to watch him, Edgar,' Opal said. 'You know I didn't want him to go in the first place. You never know what he might pick up!'

'He only ate a sweet,' Edgar said. 'It won't kill him. And it gave old Mr Sykes a lot of pleasure. You remember old Sykes in Maud Street? He wouldn't hurt a fly.'

'A sweet from under his pillow! It could be riddled with germs!' Opal protested.

Edgar shrugged his shoulders. He poured himself a cup of tea from the pot on the table and took it to a chair by the window.

'I came to see if Daniel would like to come to stay with us for the last week of the school holidays,' Queenie said, changing the subject. 'But it seems he's going to Grandpa Derwent's at Highcliffe tomorrow. Well, you'll enjoy it on the farm, won't you Daniel? And Aunt Mary will be very pleased to have you for company, I'm sure.'

'Uncle David's taking us in his car,' Daniel said. 'He's got a Ford. It can go at forty miles an hour!'

'Uncle David?'

'He's a friend. A friend of the family,' Opal said. 'I can't think why you've never met him. He's a wholesaler and I buy a lot of my stock from him. He's always been very helpful to me.'

'So he's going to take you all to Highcliffe!' Queenie said. 'Well, that's very kind. It's not an easy place to get to.'

'Almost impossible in the evening,' Opal said. 'And I can't leave the shop during the day.'

'And Father can't go at all,' Daniel said. 'He has to work on Friday nights because that's when people have the money to pay him.'

Miss Browning's voice came from the bottom of the stairs. 'Mrs Derwent's car has come back for her, Mrs Carson.'

'I must be off,' Queenie said. 'Thank you for the tea. I'm glad I managed to see all three of you this time. Couldn't you all come over for the day one Sunday? I know how busy you are, Opal, but surely you could take a day off?'

'I usually do the books and see to the stocks on a Sunday. And a thousand other things. But yes, we'd like to come. And we will, just as soon as I can manage it.'

'And you must let me know how you get on at your new school, Daniel,' Queenie said. 'Are you looking forward to it?'

'No,' Daniel said flatly. 'My friends won't be going. And they'll make me do a lot of arithmetic and spelling and things. I only like to do drawing. I don't suppose they'll do much drawing.'

Opal put her arm around him. 'Of course they'll do drawing,' she said. 'And painting. I especially asked. They do it every Thursday. And, you know, you can't get through life without arithmetic and spelling.'

'Why not?' Daniel demanded.

97

'Well, you'll never be successful,' Opal said. 'You want to be successful, don't you?'

Queenie drew on her gloves and went downstairs, accompanied by Opal, and by Daniel who wanted to inspect her car. Edgar watched them go. If only all women were like Queenie! Gentle and yielding. There wasn't an ounce of hardness in her. Of course she wasn't half as clever as Opal, and no-one worked harder than his wife. She had earned her success. But what she couldn't understand was that not everyone was cut out to be successful. She thought that it was simply a matter of putting your mind to it. Well, even if he had a mind as clear and decisive as Opal's, and he knew he never would have, what was there in his job to put it to?

He had quickly come to hate his job. It was not that he disliked the homes into which he had to enter, though his patch was one of the poorest, but he hated collecting coppers from people who could scarcely scrape them together. And when they could no longer keep up the payments, which happened all too often, he was embarrassed by the meagre surrender value which the Company offered. It was always so much less than had been paid in and sometimes, if they hadn't made enough contributions, it was nothing at all. Oh, he knew all the Company's arguments, and they sounded reasonable enough. Nevertheless they grew richer and richer, and he saw where the money came from.

He was no good at the job. It didn't need Mr Hardaker, the Supervisor, to tell him that. The main idea was to get new customers to replace those who were so frequently lost, and at this he was hopeless. It was bad enough pushing in where new babies had been born, persuading the mother to do her best for the child by taking out insurance she could ill afford, but it was not as bad as intruding on the bereaved, advising them, even in the act of paying out on the deceased, to take proper precautions against their own demise by investing in more insurance. He had been reminded more than once that if he was to keep his job he must do better.

'The trouble with you' Mr Hardaker complained 'is that you're not Company minded! I'm not at all sure that you're cut out for insurance!' It was true enough. But what was he cut out for? Was there anything in the world he was good at? He doubted it.

'Mother says to tell you she'll be down in the shop until closing time,' Daniel said, coming back into the room. 'And she says I can have two custard cream biscuits.'

'Oh! And what does she say I can have?'

Daniel laughed. 'She didn't say. I expect you can have the same as me.'

Never, Edgar thought. I'm not in the same class. Everything for Daniel. He pulled himself up sharply. What was he coming to, to begrudge the boy? He cared for his son with a love at least as deep as Opal's. It hurt him that he couldn't do the things for him that she could. If he'd been capable at all of getting new business, as the Company wanted, he'd have done it for Daniel. But Opal took care of it all. Paints, drawing paper, toys, clothes – anything the child wanted. And now a fine new school, the fees for which, had he been required to contribute, would have taken every penny he earned.

Daniel sat at the table painting. There wouldn't be

another word out of him. Edgar stood and stared out of the window. In the street a September wind blew up the dust. He disliked the autumn because it led so quickly to the winter, and here the winters were long. Before he knew it he would be trudging from house to house in the snow and the sludge.

It was a quiet afternoon in the shop. Summer being only just over and the autumn a fine one, no-one was prepared to buy for the winter. Thankfully, most of the warm-weather stock had been shifted in the July sale. It had been a good sale, Opal thought. The items she had bought in specially – hosiery, gloves, lingerie – from a bankrupt stock in Leeds, had all sold out. The marked-down goods from her own stock had gone well too. Everything had been sold at a profit, if sometimes a small one, and more important for the future, she had many satisfied and appreciative customers. The sales at Madame Dora's – she had had half-a-dozen over the last two years – were now acknowledged to be something special.

'All we need now' Opal said to Connie Browning 'is for the weather to turn cold for a day or two so that people will come in and buy their thick stockings and winter nightdresses. In the meantime I think we should dress the millinery window with hats suitable for wearing to the Harvest Thanksgiving services. Browns, rusts, reds, I think. Autumn colours.'

'Yes, Mrs Carson,' Connie said. 'Shall I empty the window?'

'Good gracious no!' Opal replied. 'Never have the window empty while the shop is open. You can clear it just before you leave and I'll dress it again right away.'

She searched through the millinery drawers, looking for hats which would suit her theme.

'When I first started here,' she remarked, 'I used to make hats starting with nothing more than a length of millinery wire twisted into a ring – building everything up from there.'

That was ages ago, now. It was five years to the week since she had started here, but it seemed twice as long. She had soon known that one day she would have her own business, though she had never expected it to happen the way it had. Sometimes, against her will, she recalled the thought she had had when Madame Dora had told her about the inheritance. 'If it could happen *soon*'. But she had never wished her to die. She had had nothing to do with it, it was pure accident. And every year on Whitsunday she visited the cemetary to place fresh flowers on her late employer's grave.

But I've not come all the way yet, Opal thought. Not by a long chalk. This shop was far from the summit of her ambition, in fact she felt she had already outgrown it. She wanted something much bigger, preferably in Leasfield itself, and she knew she would get it in the end. As well as putting money into this business she was saving hard, still paying her weekly visit to the bank but no longer depositing coppers or the odd shillings as she once had. When the opportunity for expansion came she would reach out and grab it with both hands.

'Who taught you to make hats?'

Opal was aware by the loudness of her assistant's voice that she was repeating the question.

About to say 'Madame Dora taught me' she stopped and considered. In fact Madama Dora had taught her very little. She had provided the tools and a place in which to use them, but in their use Opal had out-stripped her employer in no time at all.

'I suppose you could say I taught myself,' she said. 'But you won't need to learn all that because I've moved away from bespoke hats, except for a few old customers like Miss Taylor. There isn't the profit in it. Ready-to-wear hats are the thing now. One can always change the trimming to put up the price. The special orders I *do* take I can cope with quite easily.'

'By the way, Miss Browning,' she continued, 'I want to get away in good time tomorrow evening. Mr Hessle is kindly taking Daniel and me to my father's. Daniel's going to stay on the farm for the rest of the school holiday.'

A smile spread over Miss Browning's face and her blue eyes sparkled. She really is quite pretty, Opal thought, in a conventional sort of way.

'Oh I do like Mr Hessle,' the girl said. 'He's a real Prince Charming! Ever so handsome. I'll bet he's a right one for the ladies! Why, he even made a pass at me and I've only met him twice, both times here in the shop. He's not backward at coming forward, I must say. Of course he's too old for me. He must be pushing thirty.'

He's twenty-eight, the same as me, Opal thought. But men did not have to worry about age. What did the girl mean by saying he'd made a pass at her?

'That will do, Miss Browning,' she said in a cool voice. 'Now get on and check the glove drawers. I want to know exactly what we have and in what sizes. And please remember for the future that I don't allow gossip. In any case, I'm sure you must have misunderstood Mr Hessle.'

Miss Browning jerked open the glove drawer and

began to count. Oh no I didn't misunderstand, she told herself. Do you ever go to the pictures was what he said to me and I don't need anyone to tell me what he meant. As sure as eggs is eggs, Madame is jealous. But better to tread carefully. Jobs were not all that easy to come by and she quite liked this one.

Later, after Miss Browning had departed on the dot and she had arranged what she thought would be an eye-catching display of hats in the window, Opal locked the shop door, emptied the till and went upstairs.

'Time for bed, love,' she said to Daniel. 'Clear your things away now and I'll poach you an egg for your supper. If I know your Auntie Mary you'll be having a week of late nights. She spoils you.'

Her sister spoiled Daniel by giving him unstintingly of her time. Opal was aware that Mary was never too busy to play with Daniel, or walk up on to the moors, or down to the village for sweets, however much work there was in the house. She does all the things I don't have time for, Opal thought. But it's all very well when you're not a parent. And I give him all the rest. He understands. He knows I love him and that I'm working for him, she consoled herself.

'A bit of spoiling never did anyone any harm,' Edgar said.

'I dare say I shall be back latish tomorrow night,' Opal said. 'Dad will be disappointed if we don't stay for a bit of supper and we can't rush away straight afterwards. But David will see me back safely.'

'I don't see why it couldn't have waited until Saturday morning,' Edgar protested. 'I could have taken Daniel then. We could have made a day of it, walked over the moors. We'd both have enjoyed that.'

'It's too far for Daniel to walk,' Opal answered. 'Besides, I want to see Dad and Mary.'

'Then the three of us could have gone on Sunday,' Edgar persisted.

'In any case,' Opal said finally, 'Daniel wants to go in David's new car. I'm going tomorrow evening to please Daniel.'

There was nothing more to be said. Edgar picked up the newspaper, though he had already read it. It was full of petty crime, social chit-chat, politics – which had once interested him and now no longer did. But there was nothing else to do. Opal had already opened her account books and was engrossed in adding up figures.

'I must go upstairs and finish Daniel's packing,' Opal said to Miss Browning towards the end of the busy Friday. 'We must be ready to leave the minute the shop closes. In fact if we don't have customers in I might just close a few minutes early. Mr Hessle should be here any minute. Ask him to come straight upstairs will you?'

She wondered, as the girl obviously had silly ideas in her head, whether she should wait in the shop until David came. But there was too much to do. Edgar was out working and Daniel could not be trusted to get himself ready entirely without supervision. But how silly she was being! David, she was sure, had scarcely noticed the girl. Notwithstanding, as she packed Daniel's case she kept an ear open for the sound of the shop bell. When she heard it, but David did not appear, she went downstairs again. Most likely it was a late customer. She might be needed, if only to sell her something quickly and get her off the premises.

There was no sign of a customer. Miss Browning was stretching up to a high shelf and David Hessle was standing close beside her.

'I heard the bell several minutes ago,' Opal said. 'I thought it must be a customer.'

'It was,' David said quickly. 'She was leaving as I came in just now.'

'Were you not able to help her, Miss Browning?' Opal asked.

The girl hesitated. 'No. That is . . .'

Of course there had been no customer. The girl's manner gave her away. But how silly of David!

'Very well, Miss Browning, you may go now,' Opal said. 'And by the way, when you can't reach the high shelves, remember there's a step ladder. That's what it's for.'

She knew at once by the swift smile which David could not conceal that she had said the wrong thing. If there was one thing more attractive than another about Miss Browning it was her long, shapely legs beneath her short skirt. What man would not be pleased to watch her climb a step ladder?

'Good night Miss Browning,' Opal said firmly. 'Be on time in the morning. We're hoping for a busy day.'

There was hardly any traffic on the moorland road. On either side, and as far as the eye could see, the heather was still in bloom, a blazing reddish-purple in the light of the setting sun. By the time they reached the farm the daylight had gone, leaving only a strip of dark blue in the western sky. As David drove into the farmyard Mary came out of the house to meet them. Daniel, who had fallen asleep despite all his efforts not to do so, wakened as the car stopped.

'We can't stay long,' Opal said, following her sister into the kitchen. 'It's going to be late as it is when we get back. I have to make an early start on Saturday mornings. It's good of you to have Daniel. I know he'll enjoy himself.'

'It will be a lovely change for me,' Mary said. 'Nothing ever happens here. You don't know how lucky you are, Opal. Anyway, you must have a bite of supper.'

'Where's Grandpa?' Daniel asked.

'In the stables, seeing to Victor.'

'Can I ride Victor tomorrow?'

'Of course you can. Providing you go straight to sleep tonight.'

If she had a son, Mary thought – if ever she did, which seemed unlikely since she was stuck here on the farm without the slightest prospect of marriage – she would like him to be just like Daniel. But even if the chance of marriage came, how could she ever leave her father? He depended upon her entirely. Yet all she had ever wanted was a husband and children, and time was passing. She was already twenty-three. Opal had married at eighteen.

Ben Derwent came in from the stables, washed his hands at the sink and sat to the table.

'You look well, Dad,' Opal said.

He looked much less tired than Mary, but it was she who bore the double burden, that of deputy wife and of daughter. In the five years since his wife's death her father's duties had not changed. Opal knew that she could never have been as unselfish as Mary, she would have had to get out long ago, found her father a housekeeper. But Mary was not like that.

They ate supper; lamb from the farm, salad from

Mary's garden, freshly-baked bread. After supper Opal wanted to leave at once but the two men were immersed in conversation.

'It's gone ten, David,' she reminded him.

She could not think what he could find to talk about with her father, though it was part of David's charm that he could get on well with anyone. Even with Edgar, if Edgar would only let him. But she knew that her husband – though he never said so – hated David Hessle.

She went upstairs to Daniel but he was fast asleep. She kissed him gently, hating to part with him even for a week. She loved him so very much, had such plans for him. At half-past ten David allowed himself to be dragged away. When they left the farm the night was clear and fine, with an early September nip in the air. The wide sky was navy blue, and star-filled. She looked forward to the drive back through the peaceful country-side.

Chapter Six

At first they drove in silence. The moorland road was
narrow, not built for motor traffic. It stretched out
before them like a silver ribbon, in the light of a moon
so brilliant that, in patches here and there, it coaxed
a pale lilac colour from the dark heather. Except for a
rabbit or two, momentarily transfixed in the headlights,
they had the road to themselves. It was as if they were
in some magic country on the edge of the world. Would
she like to be suspended there for ever? Opal asked
herself. She thought not. In spite of having been
brought up on a farm she was not at heart a country-
woman. She preferred the hum and bustle of the town.
She felt more a part of what went on there; the
production of fine clothes in the mills, the buying and
selling. In no time at all her mind was back in the shop.
But with the thought of the shop came the niggling
memory of Miss Browning.

'You seem to have made quite an impression on my
new assistant,' she said, breaking the silence.

David laughed. 'She's an attractive kid. Lively too,
I should think. You've made a good choice there.'

'She's pretty enough,' Opal agreed. 'But immature.
She'll need a lot of training. By the way, she seems to
have ideas about you! I wonder what put them into her
head?'

David did not reply and his silence goaded her into
a remark she regretted as soon as it was uttered.

'I would rather' she said 'that you kept off my assistant. She's young and silly. If you're going to turn her head she'll be no use to me.'

David, without answering, stopped the car by the side of the road and turned off the engine.

'What are you doing?' Opal demanded. 'You know we're in a hurry to get back. Edgar will be worried.'

He was looking straight ahead, his strong, beautiful profile etched in the moonlight. She wondered if he knew how attractive he was, and suspected that he did. But when he turned to face her his eyes were hard, his finely-curved lips unsmiling.

'Let's forget Edgar,' he said roughly. 'And Connie.' (She noted in spite of herself that he called her 'Connie') 'Let's forget everyone except you and me.'

'What do you mean?' She had never before seen him in this mood, so remote from his cheerful, well-mannered self. She felt a frisson of fear, tinged with elation.

'You know quite well what I mean. If you don't, you're not the intelligent woman I took you for – though sometimes I wonder if you're not all intelligence and no heart. But that's not true either. The fact that you're jealous – yes I said jealous – of Connie Browning shows that somewhere under that efficient exterior there is actually feeling.'

'What are you trying to say?' Opal asked.

'I'm trying to say – I *am* saying – that it's you I'm head over heels for. I think I have been ever since the first day I walked into Madame Dora's with my uncle. And now at long last I think you might just care a bit about me. So will you admit it?'

Was it true, what he said? she wondered suddenly. If not, why did his words not surprise her? She was fond of him, there was no doubt of that. She enjoyed his company, looked forward to his visits, missed him if he didn't come. There was a warmth in David, had been from the beginning, that was lacking in the rest of her life, especially in her marriage. There was none, any longer, in Edgar, nor did he want any from her. Whatever she offered, Edgar refused. She realized, then, that she would have liked to have been in love with David. And that even though she was not, she would like to throw discretion to the winds, to take whatever he offered and be thankful for it. But it was impossible.

'I'm married,' she said flatly. 'I'm a married woman with a child.' She was not sure whether she was speaking to David or reminding herself.

'I'm talking about your feelings, not your circumstances,' David said. 'Don't pretend to me that your marriage means a row of pins to you. I've seen you with Edgar, watched you together.'

She turned her head away from his searching look. Was it so plain to the world, the failure of her marriage? Did her hunger for physical satisfaction, which was by now almost entirely denied her, show in her face? Tears came into her eyes and she raised a hand to brush them away. David turned her face to his. His touch was gentle, his eyes compassionate.

'Don't worry,' he assured her. 'It doesn't show. Except to me because I care. Oh Opal, I want to give you so much!'

His arms went around her and his mouth sought hers. She did not resist; she had no desire to do so. In that awkward embrace, in the front of the little car, the longings of weeks and months, years even, rose up in her – though whether they were for David himself or for what Edgar would not, or could not, give her, she didn't know. Nor did it matter. His strong yet gentle fingers caressed her breasts. Wild delights and desires swept through her body. She knew that not far from here was the point of no return.

'Stop!' she cried. 'Stop! It's impossible!'

He held her more tightly, stopping her words with kisses, his hand now caressing her thigh. She felt the hard urgency in his body and the desire equally in her own. Then she jerked her head away from his and twisted and turned in his arms, fighting to free herself.

'We can't David! We can't'

He let her go, and for a moment looked at her as though he did not know where he was, who she was. His face was full of anger.

'We can,' he said. 'I love you. You love me. Don't deny it because I shan't believe you. I felt it in you just now. You can't go back on that. Your marriage doesn't mean anything, you know that. Leave Edgar and come to me. It's as simple as that.'

She looked at him in astonishment.

'You can't be serious, David.'

'I am serious.'

'And what about Daniel?'

'I'll care for Daniel. Edgar can see him whenever he wants to. He'd never be denied that. And I'll care for Daniel as I care for you. He won't suffer, I promise you.'

'And the shop?' Opal asked. 'Oh David, who will patronize a woman who has left her husband, gone to live with another man? Even if I was divorced, and we married, it would never do.'

She was surprised by the astonishment on his face. Surely be understood that?

'The shop?' he said. 'You don't have to bother about the shop. I can support you. I can give you a good life. The kind of life you deserve. Come to me, Opal!'

He took her hands in his, gently now, and in the silence which followed his words, in the pause while he waited for her answer, she could feel his body trembling.

'I can't,' she said at last.

'Why can't you? Why not?'

'I don't love you, David.'

'I don't believe you.'

'And if I did there would still be Daniel.'

It was the truth, she told herself, but in her heart she knew that it was not the whole truth. The truth included Daniel, it included her hopes and plans for the future; it included Edgar, though she was not sure why.

'You don't fool me,' David said slowly. The hardness of his voice stabbed her. 'You're using Daniel. I think you would use anyone to get what you wanted. It's the business, isn't it? You can't give it up. You can't relinquish the power.'

'It has nothing to do with power . . .'

'Oh yes it has. I know you better than you know yourself.'

Right now, she thought, that could be true. In the conflict inside her she hardly recognized herself.

'David, I swear to you . . .'

'Don't,' he said roughly. 'Don't, because you'd be lying. You can't stifle your ambition, can you? You have to be the one with power. Well, long may it serve you!'

'I recognize that I'm ambitious,' Opal said quietly. 'I can't help that. I can't change it.'

He turned on the engine, put the car into gear. 'It's the same old story,' he said bitterly. '*You* can't change, but others must – to fit in with you.'

'Being ambitious doesn't make for an easy life for a woman,' Opal defended herself. 'But right now I'm just desperately sorry and I wish I could comfort you.'

'Well, don't let that worry you,' David retorted. 'I promise you I won't lack for comfort!'

He pressed his foot hard on the accelerator and the car leapt forward, racing along the moorland road. The moon was covered by clouds now, and the roads and moor were a sheet of blackness pierced only by the headlights from the car. Opal put a hand on David's arm.

'Please slow down, David!'

He seemed not to hear her. She sat beside him in terrified silence until – and it seemed a lifetime later – he stopped the car at her door.

Then he said, 'I'm not sure that I can stop loving you, Opal. But the next move, if there's to be one, is yours. And don't expect me to wait for ever, or to behave like a saint while I'm waiting. It's not in me.'

When he had driven away she let herself in through the shop entrance, locked the door behind her and dragged herself wearily upstairs. She was so tired.

As she expected, Edgar was waiting up for her. He had, unusually for him, been drinking. There were several empty beer bottles around the room and the small bottle of brandy which she kept for emergencies was on the table, half empty.

'So you decided to come home?' He spoke with slow, deliberate articulation. 'You actually remembered you had a husband?'

'How could I forget?' Opal said wearily. She was

113

drained of emotion. All she wanted was to be on her own and to sleep.

'Easily enough I daresay. Do you know what time it is? Do you know it's after midnight?'

'We were late leaving,' Opal said shortly. 'Dad kept us talking.'

'I expect that wasn't all that kept you. I'm sure your fancy man wasn't averse to lingering!'

'You're drunk,' Opal said. 'Otherwise you wouldn't talk like that.'

'Yes I'm drunk' Edgar said. 'Why not? What else is there? A sod of a job. A bitch of a wife who doesn't give a damn!'

She felt his words like a slap on the face. They were undeserved. In the last half hour the thought of Edgar had been strong in her mind.

'For God's sake stop it,' she flared. She hated it when he was in a maudlin, self-pitying mood. 'If you don't like it here why don't you get out? Nothing I do suits you. You're no support to me at all. What do *you* ever give *me*?'

She felt weak now; in need of a man's strength, a man's arms about her, not in passion or sexual love but in comfort and security.

'I give you all I've got' Edgar said. 'It's not enough for you. You don't want me or what I can give. You haven't for years.'

'That's not true and you know it,' she said. 'You're the one who holds back. But I repeat, if you're so unhappy why don't you just go? Ours isn't a proper marriage any longer. Perhaps we'd be better apart. Go and live with your mother for a while.'

'You'd like that wouldn't you?' he shouted. 'Me leaving the field clear. Well, there's no way it's going to happen. There's no way I'm leaving Daniel – though God knows I'm not much use to him either!'

He knew too – it was more clear to him because he was slightly drunk – that as long as he lived he could not leave Opal. Though sometimes he almost hated her, he could not envisage life without her.

'I'm very tired,' Opal said. 'I'm going to bed.'

But upstairs she went into Daniel's room. There was no way she could bear to be near Edgar tonight. She was unutterably weary, tired of everything and everybody. Something must change soon. It must, it must.

At five minutes past one on the following Wednesday Opal locked the shop door after Miss Browning and went upstairs to put on her hat and coat. From time to time on a Wednesday afternoon she took the tram into the centre of Leasfield to look at the shops. Leasfield's early closing day was Thursday. It was not so much that she wanted to buy anything, more that she wanted to see what other people were buying. Leasfield was in advance of its neighbours in fashion and by carefully studying the shops there she could often judge what to buy for her own. Sometimes she would buy items in the Leasfield sales and sell them at full price at her own shop. And today, she thought, seeing her pale face in the mirror as she adjusted her hat, the expedition might cheer her up.

She had not seen David since he had left her at the door on Friday night. He was due tomorrow and she both dreaded and looked forward to his visit. By Saturday morning Edgar had seemed his usual self; quiet – but then he was always quiet so it was difficult to judge. They had carried on their normal, sparse conversations as though Friday night had not happened. But she had not returned to his bed and he had not commented on the fact. It was a state of affairs that, in the two-bedroomed flat, could only last until Daniel returned. After that she supposed they would resume their usual condition – miles apart in the same bed.

She took the tram to Leasfield, alighting in the centre of the town, from whence it was no more than a five-minute walk to Miller's fashion store, her venue for the afternoon. As always, she walked slowly and carefully around each department, noting everything of interest. An evening dress in lace, with insets of chiffon in the skirt, caught her eye. The saleswoman moved in on her as she studied it.

'It's the very latest from Paris, Madame,' she said. 'We had it copied. You see the new hemline, just dipping a little at the back?'

'I suppose it had to come,' Opal said. 'Skirts have gone about as high as they can. It's really quite pretty.'

She moved on. She had no room on her premises to stock dresses. It would mean fitting-rooms too. But what she had been wondering about was cosmetics. Most women now had abandoned the paper powder leaves in favour of real face powder, kept in a pretty box with a swansdown puff. Many used lipstick, discreetly applied. Rouge she was not sure about for her class of trade; but why not, if a woman wanted it?

There were several items on the toiletries counter she thought she might be able to sell: lavender water, eau-de-cologne, talcum powder – as well as make-up and the pretty containers to keep it in. Altogether, it need take up no more than a couple of drawers and a shelf or two. She must find out the best wholesaler for such goods.

She climbed the stairs to the balcony tearoom on the next floor, choosing a table with a good view of what went on below. The waitress came at once.

'I'd like a pot of china tea and some buttered toast,' Opal said.

While she waited to be served she watched a constant, if steady, stream of customers at the toiletries counter. They took their time about their purchases but seldom left without buying.

'I've been watching the toiletry counter,' Opal said when the waitress brought her tea. 'Is it always so busy?'

'I don't get much time to watch' the waitress said. 'I suppose it is. They sell what we all want, don't they? Something to make us feel a bit better.'

'That's true,' Opal agreed.

She wished she was near enough to see exactly what the customers chose. She was sure the enterprise would be a good one for her and she wondered why she had not thought of it sooner. She hoped she was not getting slack. She tipped the waitress, paid her bill at the cash desk, and left.

No daylight had penetrated into the store and she had forgotten how bright the day was outside. Perhaps, rather than taking the tram all the way, she would walk the first mile or two. She enjoyed walking and did it too seldom. She had walked about a mile when she saw the building. She could not imagine why she had never seen it before until she realized that the buildings around it had been pulled down, thus rendering the one which remained more conspicuous.

It was three storeys high, solidly fashioned in an ornate, Victorian style with a small, square tower rising from the roof above the main entrance. Along the front, at ground level, were eight, large plate glass windows. It must surely, once, have been a retail store? For what other purpose than to display goods would one need such large windows? Now, though, they were fitted with grimy venetian blinds, as if the building might have been more recently used as a warehouse. The paintwork was shabby and peeling but, as far as she could see, the woodwork and the stone were sound. Surely this building was not to be demolished with the rest?

She walked along the front, trying without success to peer in through the blinds. When she reached the centre door she found a notice fixed behind the glass. 'Enquiries to Davies and King, Estate Agents, Hart Lane, Leasfield.' She knew at once, without the slightest shadow of doubt, without considering anything for or against, that she must see them. She did not even wish to walk around to view the rest of the building from the outside. Only let her get to Davies and King and the rest could come later. Directed by a passer by, she found them easily enough.

'If you'll tell me what it's about,' the clerk in the front office said, 'I'll find out if our Mr King can see you.' He returned two minutes later. 'Luckily,' he said, 'Mr King is available. Please come this way.'

'Please tell me, Mr King,' Opal said without preliminaries 'Was it originally built as a retail store?'

'How observant of you,' Mr King said pleasantly. 'That is exactly what it was. But some years ago now. I understand – it was before I came to the neighbourhood – that it was a nice store, but a little old-fashioned. Didn't move with the times. And then it's just a little too far out of town for a retail business. Almost a mile, you see. They couldn't make it pay.'

'And what is it now?' Opal asked. 'Or what was it before it was empty? It is empty, isn't it?'

'Oh quite. Except of course that most of the shop counters and suchlike are left. No-one ever bothered to move them. It's been such as a warehouse, on and off, for a few years now. All clean stuff, of course. Garments mostly. The last tenants moved out to smaller, more modern premises, when their lease ran out.'

'I notice that some of the buildings around have been pulled down,' Opal said. 'Is that likely to happen to this one?'

'Oh no,' Mr King said. 'I don't think there's any question of that. It was small, back-to-back houses which were pulled down. No loss to anyone. The tenants have been moved into Council houses with baths and gardens and that sort of thing.'

'And what would be the rent of the place?' Opal asked.

'Well now, that depends on how much space you would require,' Mr King said. 'If you would ask your husband to call in and discuss what he has in mind, we could perhaps put a figure on it.'

'My husband isn't the interested party,' Opal said coldly. 'I am. I'd like a price for the whole building, though it's possible that at first I'd only be able to rent one or two floors. Even so, I wouldn't take any of it without an option on the whole.'

She heard the words, like an echo, as she spoke them, but it seemed impossible that they were issuing from her mouth. Had she taken leave of her senses?

Mr King leaned back in his chair, surveying this small, neat woman, with clear bright eyes which met his without blinking.

'I see,' he said doubtfully.

Poor man, he doesn't see at all, Opal thought.

'I can't imagine the rent would be high,' she said. 'The place looks very run down. And naturally I'd like to see the inside. In fact, now, if that would be convenient. I have business committments which prevent me coming to Leasfield often.'

'Perhaps you would tell me what you propose to use the premises *for*?' Mr King said. 'My clients would naturally want to know that.'

'Of course,' Opal said. 'I propose to open a retail store.'

'A *store*? But as I've just told you, my dear lady . . .'

'A fashion store. Ladies' and children's clothing. Millinery, materials, gloves, haberdashery, cosmetics, hosiery and footwear. To start with, that is. I would hope to diversify later.'

'But how . . . ?'

'Leave the how to me, Mr King,' Opal said with more conviction than she felt. 'All I want from you right now is to see over the premises and have a figure for the rent. Of course any structural defects – worn stairs, plumbing and the like – would have to be made good by the owners before I could consider it. But I'm sure that would apply to any tenant. Shall we go?'

Mr King, as if mesmerized, called to his assistant for the keys.

'Could we open a few blinds?' Opal asked. 'It's all rather dark.'

Mr King, who without quite knowing how it had come about realized that he had surrendered his will to this commanding young lady, did as he was asked. Light flooded in.

'That's better,' Opal said. 'Oh dear, it *is* a dirty mess, isn't it? And everything such dark paint. I'd have a great deal to do on this floor before I could even attempt to use it.'

But she had noted that the paint, though grimy, was not flaking, and that the counters which had been left behind would be quite adequate when well polished. There were also plenty of drawers. Opening one or two, she found that they ran smoothly. No damp, she thought.

The staircase which ran through the centre of the building to the two remaining floors was as solid as a rock, though the carpet which covered it was worn, and would have to be thrown out. But no matter. Good oak treads, which these were, were quite adequate. On the first floor the windows were smaller, but more in number, and without blinds, so that everything seemed brighter. As on the ground floor, there were counters and other fittings, and a certain amount of carpet, which she thought might clean up well. This would be the floor for gowns, coats, millinery. One day, perhaps she would sell furs.

'Now Mr King, what about the second floor?'

'That has never been fully developed,' Mr King said, leading the way. 'A certain number of offices and, of course, stock rooms.'

'I see,' Opal said. 'Yes, it is rather makeshift, isn't it?' But she saw no sense of giving overmuch space to offices. Offices were non-productive. If one was to make a business pay, then every foot of space must be calculated to show a profit, and those which could not must be kept to a minimum.

'What's this small staircase here?' she asked.

'That leads to the tower room. A folly, I think you

could call it. Typically Victorian. It leads nowhere and has no especial use.'

It could be my private office, Opal thought.

When they had seen over every inch of the building she demanded that they start again at the beginning, and only when everything had been seen twice did she declare herself satisfied.

'But when I say "satisfied",' she amended, 'I mean that I would be provided that the owner would make the repairs which you have noted down, and that the rent is reasonable. The figure you suggested is undoubtedly too high. Not many people would be interested in such a property, would they? Especially surrounded by derelict land.'

She hoped he would not call her bluff on that one, for the spare land she saw as a real asset. When the time came she would buy it, build on it, expand even further.

'Well, my dear Mrs Carson, *you* are interested for one,' Mr King said smoothly.

'And how many others?' Opal asked. 'Anyway, let me know within the week. You have my telephone number. And in the meantime, thank you for showing me over.'

She left him, and walked to the tram stop. To take a tram was to return to the real world after the fairy-tale world she had inhabited for the last hour. But the real world, the world of rents and rates, of goods and wages – in short, of money – was what she now had to contend with.

She needed David's help. Not only his practical help, though she had marked out in her mind what he could do for her in that area, but his interest as a friend, his opinion as a businessman, his reassurance that she was doing the right thing. How much had she forfeited his friendship since the events of Friday night? She could only put it to the test. At seven o'clock in the evening she telephoned him.

'He's out,' his sister said. 'He came in and went out again. Ther's no telling when he'll be back.'

'I see. Well, when he does come in, will you ask him to telephone me? No matter how late.'

Edgar was also out, which suited her. She had no intention of telling him anything until her plans were more settled. She was certain of his disapproval. When he came in and saw her, sitting at the table, head bent over columns of figures, it was nothing new to him.

'I suppose you had a profitable afternoon in Leasfield?' he said.

'I believe so,' Opal said. 'I think it will turn out to be quite profitable.'

At midnight she decided that David was not going to telephone. She went to bed but, lying in Daniel's narrow bed, found no sleep until it was almost time to get up again. At half-past seven in the morning she went down into the shop to telephone.

'David! I expected to hear from you last night,' she said. 'Can you come over this morning? It's important.'

'It must be for you to ring me at this hour,' he replied. 'What's it about? Is anything wrong?'

'Nothing. I can't tell you about it on the telephone.'

'Very well,' he promised. 'I'll make you my first call.'

Miss Browning arrived at half-past eight, pale and yawning.

'You look half asleep, Miss Browning,' Opal remarked.

'I am,' Connie Browning said. 'Had a late night. Went to the pictures and out to supper afterwards. My Ma didn't half create a fuss when I got home after midnight!'

Her smile, as her wide blue eyes met the direct look from Opal's dark ones, was one of triumph. It was a pity it would be unwise to tell Madam just who had kept her out so late. She'd have liked to have had the pleasure. Bosses were all the same; thought they could rule your life twenty-four hours a day. Well, she was definitely one up now! Come to think of it, Madam looked a bit odd this morning. Sort of excited. Surely *she* couldn't have been living it up?

'Well it's too bad you don't feel at your best,' Opal said briskly. 'I've decided to start stocktaking today. So will you please begin by measuring all the ribbons, then count the hosiery and gloves. Write down the quantities and sizes and put the price per yard or per pair at the side. I will do the extensions.'

The bold look her assistant had given her had not gone unnoticed. It taunted her, as it was meant to; but no matter how strong her suspicions were, and she felt quite sure that the girl had been out with David, there was little she could do about it. She did not care to risk jeopardizing her own friendship with David any further. She was still unsure how matters stood between them. When he arrived, however, an hour later, his manner towards her seemed the same as always. He gave Miss Browning no more than his usual polite greeting, but this did not prevent her from looking like a cat which had found a rich source of cream.

Little fool, Opal thought. She's quite transparent. He won't like that. But she had more on her mind this morning than David's flirtation.

'Will you come into the office?' she said to him.

The second she had closed the door she began to tell him about the empty store, and almost as quickly, he stopped her.

'Wait a minute! Opal, there's no way you can do this! Have you taken leave of your senses?'

'Don't!' she cried. 'Don't say that yet. I asked you to come this morning because I wanted to tell you about it before anyone else. You are, I hope, still my friend? In spite of everything?'

'Yes,' he replied. 'In spite of everything. Perhaps against my better judgement. Do you want to talk about that?'

'No,' she admitted. 'Not now. I just wanted to know. David, will you do something for me? And not form any opinions until you've done it? Keep an open mind?'

'What is it you want?'

'It's not difficult. All I want is for you to go into Leasfield and look at the place. Not with me. In fact, you're not to let on that you know me. This is what I want you to do. Now listen.'

'I still think you're mad,' he said when she had finished.

'But you'll do it for me? And you'll go today?'

'Very well.'

'And you'll come back right away and tell me what happened?'

It was late afternoon when he returned.

'What did you think?' she asked eagerly. 'Tell me at once!'

125

'Well, there's one thing sure,' he said. 'I didn't have to put on an act for the benefit of the estate agent. It's hopeless! Oh, I agree the place is basically sound. But it's far too big, even if you only opened a floor at a time. How would you stock it? How would you manage for staff? You can't possibly consider it, Opal!'

'That's not a decision you have to make,' Opal said quietly. She did not feel the slightest bit discouraged by his words. 'But thank you, David, for doing as I asked. With you turning it down so flatly they might think seriously about my offer. What a pity I can't get half-a-dozen people to do the same thing!'

'I was pretty forthright,' David said. 'I told them I wouldn't touch it with a bargepole – which is the truth – and that I couldn't imagine anyone who would!'

'So I have every hope that they'll accept my offer,' Opal said. 'And if they do, then I shall go ahead and try to raise the money.'

'But *how*?' David asked. 'How can you *possibly*?'

'Well not through you for a start, since you don't have faith in me!'

'Of course I have faith in you! If you'd suggested taking a bigger shop – even twice the size of the one you have – I'd have said go ahead and good luck to you. But a department store! In any case, I haven't any money. All my money is in my warehouse stock.'

'I know,' Opal said. 'But if you do want to help me there is one way you can. Would you let me have long credit on your lines? I've always paid you promptly. Would you trust me a bit further if I managed to raise the money for rent and wages and so on? And could you give me introductions to other wholesalers who

126

might do the same? Or vouch for me if I give your name as reference?'

'I'll do whatever's in my power to help,' David said. 'You know that.'

He felt quite safe in his promise. It would never come to fulfilment. There was no possible way that Opal could raise the money.

Chapter Seven

It was the first time, Opal reflected, that she had ever set eyes on a bank manager. They were creatures beyond her ken and until now her affairs had been so simple as never to need one. Mr Harper was not how she had pictured him on her way to the bank this Friday morning – tall, well-made, venerably greying, avuncular. He was a thin, hungry-looking man, the top of whose head, as Opal noted while he bent over the accounts she had given him, was bald except for a few wispy, black hairs.

'There's no doubt that you've got a good little business here,' he said, looking up. 'And you've built it up in a surprisingly short time. I commend you on your business acumen!'

'Then you'll back me?' Opal said.

He leaned back in his chair, clasping his hands together as if about to lead in prayer, and smiled a slow, gentle smile.

'Alas, my dear Mrs Carson, it's not quite so simple!'

'Why not?' Opal asked. 'You've seen my accounts, verified by the accountant. You've heard my proposals, to which I've given a great deal of thought. It's not a new idea to me, Mr Harper; not something thought up on the spur of the moment. It's something I've dreamed of for a long time. But not only dreamed. I've planned, too.'

'And most interesting your plans *are*,' Mr Harper

conceded. 'Though some of them, I must say, are a little . . .' He struggled for a word. '. . . Well, shall we say *innovative*? Yes, innovative.' Having found the word, he rolled it off his tongue with enjoyment.

'They're all feasible,' Opal assured him.

'But of course there's more to it than that . . .'

'Such as?'

'Well, in the first place I think what you propose would be an unwise move on your part. You're doing very nicely now, Mrs Carson. Why not build on what you've got? It doesn't do to be over-ambitious, you know. A young lady like yourself. A prosperous little business such as you have, easy to handle, not many staff, is much more suitable for the fair sex.'

'Would my ambition be more agreeable if I were a young man?' Opal asked swiftly.

'Now you're putting words into my mouth?' Mr Harper said pleasantly. 'But, naturally, ambition is more to be expected, and indeed more necessary, in a man. Though even a man might hesitate to take on what you have in mind. I suspect your husband would agree with me there.'

'Oh I'm sure he would,' Opal answered. 'But as I've already told you, my husband wouldn't be involved. I would be running the business myself.' And that remark will *not* have helped me, she thought. 'But do you mean you have a different policy towards a *man* who wants a loan?'

'Well . . .'

'Why?'

'It stands to reason, dear lady. Here you are, a young married woman.' He gave her a look which told her she was also attractive in his eyes. 'You have one child. Who is to say – and I hope you will forgive me for being so plain spoken – that you will not be blessed with more children? And what would happen to your business then?'

He spoke with calm confidence, almost with benevolence, as one who has made an unassailable point. Opal's reply was equally confident.

'It would carry on. Being a mother, though I admit there are certain practical matters I would have to sort out, would not stop me any more than being a father would stop a man.'

'More easily said than done,' Mr Harper said. 'Now if you were a widow . . .'

I would be a widow first and a woman second, Opal thought. And I would suddenly be capable of running a business. But she did not say it out loud. Nor did she consider herself as unlikely as any widow to have another child. It was clear, in spite of the polite smile which had not for one moment deserted him, that she had antagonized this man. Well, he antagonized her. He was a patronizing idiot.

'And there is another matter, equally if not more important,' he continued. 'You see, you have no collateral to offer me. The Bank must have security, you know. We owe it to our shareholders.'

'But I've shown you my trading figures,' Opal protested. 'You've seen what I 've done in the time I've had Madame Dora's. Doesn't that count?'

'But surely, Mrs Carson, if you were to move into something bigger, Madame Dora's would have to go? If you failed in your new venture the bank would have nothing at all to realize on!'

Opal rose to her feet. Anger flooded through her so that she could have beaten her fists against this man, wiped the everlasting smile from his face. She was furious with herself, too, that she could not hold back the tears which filled her eyes. It was exactly what he would expect of her. But she managed to keep her voice steady.

'So that's your last word?'

'I'm afraid so, Mrs Carson. Though of course if by some means you *were* to be successful . . .' The tone of his voice said that the possibility was as remote as the farthest star from the earth. 'If at any time you wanted to expand a little, don't hesitate to consult us. We're always ready to listen!'

He held the door open for her, watching her as she marched out of the bank into the street. A pretty little thing. Lively. Quite clever too. He must ask his wife if she ever patronized Madame Dora's.

Opal walked quickly, looking neither to right nor left. She admitted to herself that, angry though he had made her, she was not entirely surprised by the bank manager's attitude. Banking was a man's world. Well, no matter. She was not beaten yet, not by a long chalk.

The shop was empty of customers when she returned, but evidence that there had been some lay strewn around in the form of gloves, hosiery, scarves. She bit back the sharp reprimand which rose to her lips as she saw Miss Browning standing idle amid the disorder. It would be necessary to absent herself from the shop, to leave it in Miss Browning's hands, on more than one occasion in the near future. In the last few days Opal had become curiously unsure of her assistant's temperament. That she was capable of taking charge of the shop for short periods Opal didn't doubt. But there was a boldness about the girl which suggested that she would not be driven.

'You've been busy I see,' Opal said, keeping her tone level.

'Nothing I couldn't handle,' Miss Browning said.

'I'm glad about that. It so happens that over the next few days I might have to leave you in charge for the odd hour or two now and then. I have some business to attend to. Shall you be able to manage?'

'I dare say' Miss Browning answered.

She really must find out what these mysterious absences were about. But if she was persuasive, and she knew exactly how to be persuasive, David Hessle would tell her. He was sure to know because he and Madam were as thick as thieves. Well, perhaps no longer as thick as thieves since she was sure Madam hadn't an idea what he was up to. You'd be out on your ear otherwise, Connie Browning, she told herself. As a matter of fact she quite liked being left on her own. She got to serve the customers, which she enjoyed, and didn't do so often when her employer was around. Also, she could use the telephone when she felt like it, even though David had told her not to 'phone him.

'That's good,' Opal said. 'And now perhaps we should tidy things away while we have the chance.'

By which she means *I* should do it, Miss Browning thought. Correctly.

'It all sounded so mysterious on the telephone,' Queenie said, seating herself, drawing off her gloves. 'And so unlike you to summon one! An important matter to discuss, you said. Oh, Opal, I hope there's nothing wrong! It couldn't be anything to do with Edgar, could it? I mean . . .' She hesitated. 'I mean . . . you and Edgar?'

'Why of course not,' Opal said. Her sister-in-law was more perceptive than she seemed. 'It's got nothing to do with Edgar. Not in the way I think you mean. There's nothing wrong. It's just that I have something of importance to tell you . . .'

'Opal, you're not – you're not *expecting*. Oh, Opal!'

'Of course not, Queenie dear! I've told you before, I've got my little Daniel and I love him dearly – but I've never wanted a large family. I leave that to natural-born mothers like you.'

'Then whatever can it be?' Queenie asked.

If only you would give me the chance to tell you, Opal thought. But one could not rush Queenie. In any case she was far too fond of her to be really impatient.

'I'm about to tell you,' Opal said. 'And if what I have in mind comes off, then it will be the best thing that's happened to me, and to Edgar and Daniel too. But I don't think I can do it at all without your help.'

She sat down beside Queenie and told her what she had in mind. She told it, not in outline as she had done to Mr Harper, but in detail; in colourful scenes which she could so easily picture. And as she talked and Queenie listened, Opal felt the store come alive, as vividly as if she were standing in it, surrounded by her merchandise, thronged by customers. And she thought that if she could not have it she would die of disappointment.

'So you see why I need the money,' she concluded. 'Quite a lot, I'm afraid. Needless to say, however generous you are – and I know you *are* generous – I couldn't do it all on a loan from you. It's my intention to approach, also, an old and very rich customer. She's already agreed to see me.'

'Do I know her?' Queenie asked.

'I don't think so. And I'd rather not tell you who she is without her permission. I thought that if she would act as guarantor for the rent, lighting and so on, and you would lend me the money to start the alterations – which I shall keep to a minimum – and to help with stock – then I could manage the wages out of the profit I made and with what I get for this place. To start with, that is.'

'I must admit, you seem to have it all worked out,' Queenie said. But from the tone of her voice it was impossible, Opal thought anxiously, to tell what she really thought about it.

'Oh I have,' she said. 'I really have. And I'm sure I can do it, only given the chance. You'd get your money back, every penny and with interest. How quickly will depend on how quickly the business takes off. I have to be frank with you and say that I would need to give priority to paying wages and buying stock. It might be five years before you were paid. But you would be paid, I promise you! Oh, Queenie, what do you think? Please put me out of my misery and tell me what you think!'

'Opal dear, you mustn't rush me,' Queenie said gently. 'It's all so new to me. I have to take it in. Could we possibly have a cup of tea, do you think?'

Opal jumped to her feet.

'Of course! How remiss of me, Queenie. I'll put the kettle on at once.'

In the kitchen she set about making the tea. Her hands trembled as she laid the tray, so that she thought she would drop a cup or spill the sugar. When she carried the tray into the living-room her hands shook so much that it was difficult to pour.

'Just look at me!' she said. 'I'm so nervous. But then I'm not used to asking for loans, not even of family!'

She remembered, suddenly, the winter Saturday, all that time ago it seemed now, when she had asked her mother for the loan of five pounds and had been given ten. Was that a good omen?

'Well,' Queenie said thoughtfully, sipping her tea, 'it's no secret that my father left me a lot of money. Anyone who reads the Leasfield Argus knows that. And Mark is doing well in the business, so we never touch my money. Of course, even though the money is my own to do with as I wish, and Mark never questions what I spend, I shall have to consult him. I shall show him your figures and I daresay he'll have some questions to ask. But apart from that . . .' She put down her teacup and stretched out her hand to take Opal's.

'Yes, Opal dear, I'm agreeable to lending you the money!'

For a moment Opal stared at her. She couldn't believe it! It was her dream, and it was beginning to come true! Then she fell to her knees and buried her face in Queenie's lap, not trying on this occasion to keep back the tears.

'Oh Queenie,' she said at last, 'there's just no way I can thank you!'

'I'm your family' Queenie said. 'Why shouldn't I be the first to help? And I remember how much my father thought of you. He said you were a very clever woman. I'm sure he'd have approved of my decision, just as I'm sure Mark will.' She laughed. 'Anyway, if half you say comes true you'll be an enormous success and I'll have done myself a good turn!'

'Please don't go on about it,' Opal begged. Edgar had arrived home shortly after Queenie's departure and she had decided it was now time to tell him what was afoot.

'Mary will he here with Daniel any minute and I don't want it mentioned then. It's Daniel I'm thinking about. He starts his new school on Tuesday and I don't want him to have anything on his mind other than that. Anyway, nothing is settled. Time enough to let everyone know when, and if, it is.'

'I suppose I'm lucky you bothered to tell me,' Edgar complained. 'Perhaps you wouldn't have if you'd not been afraid Queenie or Mark might spill the beans!'

'Don't be silly,' Opal said. 'You're my husband. I'd want to tell you. In any case how could I do anything without your knowing?'

'Easily! You managed to find the property, didn't you? See the bank manager, fix a loan with Queenie and get it approved by Mark, all without me knowing a thing!'

'It all happened so quickly,' Opal protested. 'Anyway, I knew you wouldn't approve. I wanted to take one or two steps first. If they'd all come to nothing, well, that would have been that. Please let's not quarrel. Edgar. Daniel will soon be back and you know how it upsets him when we quarrel.'

'He's going to get a good deal more upset when he learns about this. Have you actually given a single thought to me and Daniel? Do you care in the slightest what it's going to do to us? When you have your precious store, where do I fit in?'

'I'm glad you say "when" and not "if",' Opal said dryly. 'It shows you have faith in my getting it.'

'Oh I'll back you to do that,' Edgar said. 'I'll back you to get anything you set your mind on, no matter what it does to anyone else.'

'That's unfair,' Opal flared. 'I think about Daniel a very great deal, and you know it! Who is sending him to a good school, who is making sure he'll get the best possible education? And what I'm proposing now will ensure a good future for him. One day, when he's ready, it will all be there, waiting for him. As for you, it can do you nothing but good. When I get the business off the ground you can give up that job you hate so much and come in with me. I'd like that, Edgar, I really would. There's bound to be something to suit you.'

'Thank you,' Edgar said. 'I suppose it doesn't occur to you that I might not want that? I hate my job all right but it's my last bit of independence. Everything else is yours.'

Opal sighed. When he was in this kind of mood, and it happened more and more often, there was no pleasing him. All she wanted for herself and Edgar was for them to live in some degree of harmony. She had given up the high hopes of marriage she had started out with. She supposed she might even, in the end, lose her desire for physical love, though her encounter with David had shown her that it was still there in strength, just below the surface. But she would settle now for tranquillity, and just a little warmth. Everyone needed that. She tried hard, but Edgar never responded.

'Perhaps you'll find that Daniel doesn't want the future you've so carefully mapped out for him,' Edgar said bitterly. 'Perhaps he'll have ideas of his own. You won't like that, will you? You like to be the one with the ideas. And another thing, when you've sold Madame Dora's and we have to leave here, where are we going to live? Have you thought of that?'

'Of course I have. I've thought of everything. We'll find somewhere, you'll see!'

It was true that she had thought of it but it had not

loomed large in her mind. There had been – still were – so many other things to consider. If Miss Taylor didn't turn up trumps, then where else could she turn? But if Miss Taylor *did* agree to give her backing then there were a thousand new problems, large and small, to be settled. A place to live was just one of them. If she had only herself to think of a camp bed anywhere in the store would do for her. But Daniel, and, she supposed, Edgar, were dependent on her.

The downstairs door banged and Daniel bounded up the stairs as fast as his short legs would carry him. Mary followed close behind. He flung himself at Opal and she knelt on the floor and held him close.

'Oh, it's so good to have you back!' she cried. 'I'm not sure that I shall ever let you go away from me again, even to Aunt Mary!'

At last she let him go and he turned to his father. Edgar scooped him up in his arms and lifted him high in the air, high enough to touch the ceiling.

'You've put on weight,' he said happily. 'You weigh a ton, lad!'

'He's eaten well,' Mary admitted. 'Everything that was put before him. I can't think why you said he was finicky about his food, Opal.'

'I expect he plays me up,' Opal said indulgently. 'I must say, he does look well.'

'Grandpa taught me to milk Daisy,' Daniel said. 'And I helped to pick the apples. I've made you a picture of the apple picking, Mother. And one for you, Dad, about the sheep. Grandpa says I can go again in the Easter holidays when they've got the new lambs. Can I go, Mother?'

'Hey! You've only just got home,' Opal said. 'It's a

long time to next Easter. There's Christmas to come first.'

'So you'd like to be a farmer, would you?' Edgar asked.

Daniel looked at his father in surprise.

'Oh no! I'm going to be an artist. But I might be an artist and live on a farm. That would be a good idea!'

Edgar, catching Opal's eye, raised his eyebrow. With Daniel's return home he seemed to have recovered his temper. He was usually better when Daniel was around. They both were.

'He's painted scores of pictures,' Mary said. 'I've pinned them up all over the kitchen to remind me of him when he's not there. Oh, Opal, I do envy you being married and having Daniel. If I had your lot in life I'd have nothing left to wish for!'

How unobserving Mary was! She lived in cloud-cuckoo land. But Opal doubted whether she would wish to be the one to wipe that starry-eyed look from her sister's face.

'I enjoyed meeting that nice Mr Hessle,' Mary said. 'Dad liked him too. Shall you bring him again?'

Opal gave her sister a sharp look. Surely Mary couldn't be getting ideas about David? No two people could be less suited to each other. Except – the thought stabbed her – that they were both free. But Mary, so quiet and domesticated, so naïve in her approach to life, could never satisfy a man like David. He was smart, sophisticated, up-to-the-minute. Why, even a chit like Miss Browning would fit him better than Mary. The thought came, uncomfortably, that in some ways Miss Browning and David were two of a pair. Both sharp. But he would never take Miss Browning seriously because she was too common.

When Mary had left it was Daniel's bedtime. It was with great pleasure that Opal bathed him. Mostly, now that he was seven, he did it himself, but occasionally Opal indulged herself and soaped his soft child's body. When he was in bed she sat on the edge of the bed and read to him, though he was capable of doing that for himself too. 'You can have as many stories as you like tonight' she said. 'I'll read until you fall asleep.'

He fell asleep quickly. The week on the farm and the moorland air had done him good, she thought, gazing down at him. He had a healthy colour in his usually pale cheeks. She kissed him gently and left him. Back in the living-room she took a sheet of paper and, sitting at the table, headed it in bold capitals 'THINGS TO BE DONE'.

In the three years since her visit Opal had called upon Miss Taylor many times. Miss Taylor had continued one of her best customers, buying not only hats, but expensive lingerie, gloves, lace-edged handkerchiefs and the like. She had shown an interest in all Opal's ideas for getting the most out of the small business and nowadays would often call in at the shop to see what was new. But today was different. Opal was going to see Miss Taylor; and instead of a box of hats, which she would have borne with confidence, she carried her account books in an attache case.

Should she on this occasion, she wondered, nearing 'The Oaks', present herself at the front door or the back? It was a matter for fine judgement which she was mercifully freed from making since Miss Taylor was in the garden and called out to her.

'Good morning Mrs Carson! I'm just taking a turn around my garden while there are still flowers to see.

A sad, though beautiful time of the year, the autumn. Don't you think so?'

'I suppose that's true,' Opal said. 'Though I've never had a garden to bring it home to me.' She thought of it more as the beginning of a new season for various items of apparel.

'Well, let's go into the house,' Miss Taylor said.

Opal followed her through the front door and into the drawing-room.

'Now,' Miss Taylor said briskly. 'What is it you have to tell me? It all sounded quite mysterious on the telephone.'

She sat upright in her chair while Opal, nervous at first but gaining confidence as Miss Taylor from time to time nodded her understanding, put her case.

'And I've brought my accounts for you to look at,' she said.

Miss Taylor waved them aside.

'I'll look at those later. I haven't any doubt they're all you say or you wouldn't have brought them. There are, however, one or two fundamentally important questions to be asked. For instance, you admit that the building is at the wrong end of the town. Now I'm no businesswoman but it would seem to me that in a case of this sort, position was everything. What do you say to that?'

'I would say that you've put one of the most important points of all,' Opal replied. 'I don't quite agree that position is everything, but it is tremendously important and I've given a great deal of thought to overcoming this particular disadvantage.'

'So what would you do?'

'Well,' Opal said, 'in the first place I would have to make it worthwhile for the customer to come a mile out from the centre of town – which means that my quality must be good, my range wide and my prices keener. I'd need to offer more in every way than the shops in the centre of Leasfield. I would also need to make myself known – customers aren't likely to find me by chance – so I'd need to advertise. I would count money spent on advertising *well* spent. And I have several ideas for bringing customers in. Would you like to hear some of them?'

'I would.'

Opal, for the first time, put into words the notions which had been whirling around in her head since last Wednesday afternoon. It was wonderful to hear them spoken out loud and she was encouraged by the deep, sometimes amused, attention which Miss Taylor gave her.

'Most ingenious,' Miss Taylor said. 'And now another important question for you. Why come to me? Why me particularly? You can be quite frank – indeed you must be.'

Opal hesitated.

'Perhaps' she said 'because the first time I ever came here you treated me like a real person. It wasn't just that you gave me tea, but you asked my opinion on something not to do with trimming a hat.'

'I remember,' Miss Taylor broke in. 'Women's suffrage. Well, we've got the vote now. Let's hope we know how to use it.'

'You've continued to treat me in that way,' Opal said. 'But I'm also asking you because that what I want to do is the kind of thing you might have done yourself, had you been encouraged. Don't think me presumptuous, Miss Taylor, for I don't mean to be – but I think that in some ways you and I are two of a kind.'

The girl was right, Miss Taylor reflected. She had spent her life doing nothing more useful than a few charitable works. She would have liked to have done so much more, and she was sure she had the talent for it. But her parents, perhaps because they had risen so quickly and successfully from trade themselves, had not wanted to see their only child soil her hands with it. How wrong they had been! Why, she might have been running her father's factory now!

'And then' Opal continued 'I came to you because you are a woman. I think a woman is better able to see my point of view.'

'Are those all your reasons?' Miss Taylor asked.

'Not quite. I asked you because I thought you could afford to help me. Because you are rich, and have the money I need.'

Miss Taylor nodded her approval.

'I'm glad you admit that reason. It shows a hard, practical streak, which goodness knows you'll need. And now I have something to ask you. If I were to help you, would you consider taking me as a partner?' Miss Taylor felt herself suddenly fired with enthusiasm. Perhaps it was not too late, after all, to make her mark?

Opal's spirits plumetted. It was not what she had in mind at all. 'Would that be a condition?' she asked.

'Why? Do you dislike the idea?'

'Not for any personal reasons,' Opal said. 'I wouldn't want you to think that. If I had to have a partner I think you would be a good choice. But this is something I want to do on my own. It's important to me.'

'I understand,' Miss Taylor said. She could, she supposed, hold out the partnership as a condition. But would she want to do that?

'But I would consider having you as a sleeping

partner,' Opal said. 'You could be *au fait* with all I did. But . . . I have to say it . . . I would want to keep control. And I would like the option to buy you out in, say, ten years time.'

'Well,' Miss Taylor said. 'I must have a day or two to think things over. It's a big decision. And I would like to see over the premises, though that, I think, I would prefer to do on my own.'

'I would prefer that also,' Opal agreed. 'It would be better still if you didn't mention that you knew me.' She told Miss Taylor about David Hessle's visit on the previous Thursday. 'A similar one from you might work in my favour,' she said.

'Perhaps you might like me to suggest to them that they'd be wise to snap up any offer they receive?' Miss Taylor said with a gleam in her eye. 'And now before you go I think you might like a glass of sherry. I seldom drink it myself but on this occasion I think I shall join you.'

She poured sherry into thin, crystal glasses.

'Where would you live when you'd sold Madame Dora's?' she asked.

'I don't know,' Opal admitted. 'I would have to look for a small house in a suitable position. My son starts school in Leasfield tomorrow.'

'And your husband's work?'

'Is in Milton,' Opal said. 'I dare say he'd manage with the tram. And it's possible that, eventually, he might give up his job and come into the business.'

'Well,' Miss Taylor said, 'I'll be in touch with you quite soon.'

'Mr Hessle called while you were out,' Miss Browning said. 'He said he didn't have time to wait. And of course I couldn't tell him where you were because I didn't know.'

And you would dearly love to, Opal thought, but I'm not going to tell you.

Wouldn't Madame be furious if she knew who he really came to see, Miss Browning thought. Well it might be that she would have to get used to it. The way things were going it couldn't be kept hidden for ever.

Two days later Miss Taylor came into the shop.

'Can we talk privately?' she asked.

'We'll go upstairs,' Opal said. 'Miss Browning, will you take over for a little while, please?'

'I won't waste time,' Miss Taylor said. 'I've thought over everything we discussed and I've been to see the premises, and you'll be pleased to hear that I've decided to help you. I will guarantee the rent, rates, heating and lighting for the first three years. At that point we'll look at the situation again. Mind you, I almost changed my mind when I actually saw the place! There's so much to be done to it. But there again I might be able to give you a little help. You see I have faith in you, Mrs Carson.'

I'm going to faint, Opal thought desperately. I know I'm going to faint! She gripped the arms of her chair and took a deep breath. She was sure that Miss Taylor must hear the loud beating of her heart.

'Oh Miss Taylor! I don't know . . . I can't find words!'

Miss Taylor put out a hand as if she would have touched Opal, but did not quite do so.

'I would like to take you up on your offer to have me as a sleeping partner,' she continued. 'I'm not making it a condition, however. I realize, after thinking about it, that I'm not young enough to be a full partner, even if you had been agreeable. But in the background I could perhaps be helpful, and it would be of great interest to me.'

'Oh Miss Taylor I'll be delighted to have you!' Opal cried. 'I really will. And now all I have to wait for is the agent's reply!'

It came the same afternoon, after the shop was closed. David Hessle had called just before closing time and, to Miss Browning's visible chagrin, had elected to stay with Opal after her assistant had left. A minute later the telephone rang.

Opal unhooked the receiver, held it to her ear and listened. 'Thank you,' she said quietly after a time, and then hung up. Then, turning to David, she rushed into his arms, burying her face in his jacket, sobbing wildly. He held her tightly until the spasm of tears had passed.

'Never mind,' he said 'Something else will turn up.'

Opal stared at him.

'Something else? But don't you understand? I've got it! They've accepted my offer. Oh David, I'm so happy!'

'Then I'm happy for you,' David said quietly. 'It's what you've always wanted, isn't it?'

'Yes,' Opal said. 'I think it is. And do you know what I shall call the store? I shall call it "Opal's". Nothing more. And I shall have my name plastered everywhere so that everyone will know it belongs to me!'

Chapter Eight

Opal gave a last look around the flat. How poky it appeared now that the furniture was out of it! Though she was not happy about the location of their new house – it was in an area of Leasfield which had been acceptable at the turn of the century but was now run down – at least they would have more room. This place, though, was quite suitable for the new owner of Madame Dora's, a woman on her own.

Opal did not think for a moment that Mrs Fletcher, an attractive woman in her thirties, would spend too much time alone. She had concluded in the first few minutes of the lady's visit that she was the mistress of the elderly man who accompanied her. Also that it was doubtful that she had the ability to run so much as a bran tub, let alone a busy shop. But that's not my business, Opal had told herself firmly. The lady wanted it, the gentleman – Opal never knew his name – was pleased to buy it for her, once he had inspected the accounts. Opal had never dreamed it could be so easy.

Connie Browning came into the room.

'I've made some tea. I thought you'd like a cup before you left. I didn't bring it up because there's nowhere to put it. Doesn't it look strange in here without so much as a table or a chair?'

Opal followed the girl downstairs. It had been good of Miss Browning to stay and help her on her half-day. She had wondered, at first, whether she should offer her a position in the new store; but she knew that, good worker though Miss Browning was when the spirit moved her, she did not really want her. Opal was never quite comfortable in Miss Browning's presence – which was absurd considering their respective positions – so it had been a relief when Mrs Fletcher had asked Miss Browning to stay on and the girl had accepted.

'Another cup?' Miss Browning asked presently. 'There's plenty in the pot.'

'I won't, thank you,' Opal said. 'There'll be a lot to do at the other end and I must get there as soon as I can.' She held out her hand. 'Well, goodbye Miss Browning. Thank you for your help over these last months. I hope you get on well with your new employer.'

She gave a last, swift look around and left. You think you've seen the last of me, Madame High-and-Mighty, Connie Browning thought, watching Opal walk with never a backward glance towards the tram-stop. But you haven't, not by a long chalk. You won't be so lah-di-dah when you hear *my* bit of news!

The furniture van was at the door when Opal arrived at number seven, Alma Place. She entered the house behind one of the removal men who was carrying an inverted armchair on his head. Their possessions, seen thus, seemed meagre and shabby. She supposed the neighbours were assessing them. Edgar, standing in the narrow entrance passage, leapt out of the way as the removal man tried to pass him.

'A good thing you've arrived,' he grumbled. '*You* can try telling them where everything goes!'

'But Edgar, I wrote it all down! I made a plan of each room and indicated the positions of the furniture.'

'Oh I know you did. You gave me my instructions

all right, but *they* don't want to bother with them. All they want is to get shot of the stuff. It's mostly dumped in the front-room, except the bedroom stuff. That's piled in our bedroom.'

'That reminds me,' Opal said, following him into what would be the sitting-room when she had had time to sort it out. 'I forgot to tell you. I've ordered a single bed from Cobley's. Has it arrived?'

'A bed?' Edgar queried. 'What's wrong with Daniel's present one? He's had it no more than four years. A bed should last a lifetime.'

'It isn't for Daniel.' Her voice came muffled from inside a tea-chest packed with curtains. 'It's for the spare room.'

'Spare room? What do we want with a spare room? No-one comes to stay.'

She straightened up, moved a step-ladder to the tall window and ascended, curtain in hand.

'Well, they might, now that we have three bedrooms. Mary might come, or Aunt Garnet. Also I'll be working late a lot of time over the next few months. It might be useful if I were to sleep there at such times so as not to disturb you.'

She slid the brass rings on to the pole and let the curtain drop. 'They're still going to be too short,' she said. 'I shall have to do something to lengthen them. Edgar, hand me the other one.'

There was no reply. He was not in the room. Looking out of the window she saw him walking away down the street. She sighed. She had tried to be tactful, but trust Edgar to turn awkward. How could he pretend that a shared bed meant anything any longer? And whose fault was that? Not hers, certainly. He was always the one to turn away. And it was not as if she had suggested that she should occupy the spare room permanently, though in her heart she wondered if it would come to that. Somewhere there was a limit to her feelings.

She climbed down the ladder, fetched the other curtain and hung it unaided. He had most likely gone off to find the nearest public house. Now that he had a little more money to call his own he spent more time in such places. To be fair, he seldom drank too much, and he did not usually go out until Daniel was in bed. He spent a lot of time with Daniel; taking him for walks, playing card games, talking with him. Opal wished that she could do the same.

Daniel was spending the week with Queenie. On first seeing the new house he had disliked it intensely and for this reason she wanted to have everything ship-shape, his own room with his familiar possessions ready and waiting, when he came into it.

'That'll be it then, Missus,' the removal man said, coming into the room.

She paid him and he departed, leaving her in sole possession of her new home. She went from room to room, standing in the middle of each one, trying to decide what she would do with it. She had given herself no more than forty-eight hours to get everything into place. After that she must concentrate entirely on the store.

She had planned the store's opening for Saturday the twenty-third of March. The first Saturday of spring would be an auspicious date. It was less than four months away and almost everything was still to be done. There could be no question of postponing the date since from now, until the first sale took place in the store, she would be earning no money at all. They would have to rely on Edgar's meagre earnings and – but only if it became absolutely necessary – her savings. They must economize in every possible way.

When David Hessle arrived, entering without waiting for his ring at the front door to be answered, he found her in the kitchen, putting away china in a high cupboard. Looking down at him from the top of the step-ladder on which she was precariously balanced, she knew that something was wrong. His face was drawn, his eyes troubled. When he greeted her there was none of the usual pleasure in his voice. She was about to ask him what was wrong but something in her warned her not to. She must let him tell her in his own time.

'I'm sorry I couldn't get here any sooner,' he said. 'I called in at the shop but you'd already left. Connie was expecting Mrs Fletcher any minute. So what can I do to help?'

'You can hand me up all the stuff from the table,' Opal said. 'These cupboards are far too high.'

He would continue to see Connie Browning. There was no getting away from that since Mrs Fletcher intended keeping on the same wholesalers. Oh well, it wasn't important. But in that case, Opal thought uncomfortably, why did the thought niggle her?

'I was so lucky to get this house,' she said. 'I was just about at the end of my tether, with Mrs Fletcher waiting to move in on me. If Miss Taylor's tenants hadn't moved to Huddersfield and she hadn't offered me the house at next to no rent, I don't know what I'd have done.'

He was not listening. And when he dropped a willow-pattern jug he was handing to her, let it fall to the floor where it smashed into a hundred pieces, she forgot her resolve not to question him.

'What is it, David? What's wrong? I know there's something.'

'Come down here,' he said quietly. 'I have something to tell you.'

They sat on kitchen chairs, facing each other.

'Where's Edgar?' David asked.

She shrugged. 'Your guess is as good as mine. Out somewhere. So what is it?'

He sat with his head bent, shoulders drooped. He looked at his hands, examining the long fingers, the well-tended, filbert-shaped nails, as if he was seeing them for the first time. The silence seemed without end. Then he raised his head and looked at her.

'I'm going to be married,' he said.

She stared at him. She must have misheard. Who could he possibly . . . ? But before she could frame the question, she knew.

'I'm going to marry Connie.'

'No! No you can't!' She was already shouting in protest 'Not Connie Browning! You can't!'

'It's fixed,' he said quietly. 'We're to be married in a fortnight's time.'

'But how can you? How can you, David?' The words rose in a scream. She did not understand the wild panic in her. 'She's not right for you. You know that. You'll be miserable for the rest of your life.'

But she knew inside herself that it was not David's future she was thinking of. It was her own. How could she give him up to Connie Browning?

'Come on Opal' he said 'She's not as bad as all that! She's a nice kid really.' He spoke without conviction. 'I know – and so do you – that she'll never be to me what you could have been. But you prefer to continue with your sham of a marriage . . .'

'I've got to,' she said quickly. 'You know that.'

'So why begrudge me someone else?'

'I don't.'

She wondered whether she spoke the truth, whether she wouldn't feel the same whoever he was marrying; her sister Mary, for example.

'It's just that . . . Connie Browning . . . David, it's not reasonable!'

'On the contrary,' he said. 'There's every reason. She's pregnant.'

Slowly, holding on to the chair-back because all the strength had gone from her limbs, she rose. She wanted to say something but the words would not come. Her lips were icy cold, and stiff. Was it possible that even at the time . . . ? She choked back sick memories of his arms around her, his hands on her body. She took a deep breath, squared her shoulders, turned and began to run.

She ran along the passage and out of the house, down the flagged path. David came after her and as she reached the pavement he caught her wrist, swung her round and dragged her back into the house.

'Opal, please! Please don't turn away from me! We can't lose each other. Not you and me. We mean too much to one another.'

'I thought we did,' she said. 'I was mistaken. Let go of me!'

'You were not mistaken,' he said, 'and you know it.'

He pulled her roughly towards him and held her. His kisses, on her lips, on her closed eyes, on her throat, were fierce with longing. At first she was leaden in his embrace, her arms stiff by her side. And then the yearnings, the frustrations, the body's needs, rose up in her again and she responded to him, her hands caressing him, her mouth seeking his, willing to succumb to every demand that his body made of hers.

Then her head cleared. She shivered violently, summoned all her strength, pushed him away from her. These were the demands he had made of Connie Browning. What she herself had a moment ago been so willing to give, her former shop assistant had already given. And carried the proof within her, soon to be seen by all the world.

'No!' she cried. 'No!'

Then she heard the squeak of the gate, recognized Edgar's step on the path, and went swiftly into the kitchen, David following.

'We're here, Edgar!' she called out.

She could hardly believe that the calm voice was hers since, as she mounted the step-ladder, hid her face in the china cupboard, her body was still shaking. She wondered if she might be sick. With an effort that was almost beyond her she spoke again.

'Edgar, somewhere there's a bottle of port and some glasses. Can you find them? We have to drink a toast. David is to be married – to Miss Connie Browning!'

The words were bitter in her mouth. She tasted them like poison on her tongue. But no-one would ever know her feelings.

Standing in the window, Opal saw Miss Taylor's chauffeur-driven car pull up at the gate, and went out at once. It had been Miss Taylor's idea to call for her since they were to go to the store together. Miss Taylor was interested in every detail of the alterations and could hardly wait to inspect them. In the car Opal leaned back in the thickly upholstered, leather-covered seat and wondered if, one day, she might have such a car, with a chauffeur. It was an idle dream and not something for which she longed. It's value would be as an outward sign that she had succeeded in what she'd set out to do.

'I like the date you've set for the opening,' Miss Taylor said enthusiastically. 'There's something symbolic, something hopeful about the first weekend of spring. But shall you have everything ready in time?'

'I hope so,' Opal said. 'But I shall open in any case. I shall make certain that the whole of the ground floor is completed, and as much as possible of the first floor. If everything there is not absolutely ready I'm sure people won't mind. They might even enjoy seeing it take place over a period of time. Who knows? I intend, you see, right from the start to establish a *rapport* with my customers.'

It was a short drive only to the store. Miss Taylor instructed her chauffeur to collect her in an hour. 'But I shall stay on,' Opal said. 'I have a lot to do.'

'You see how it's taking shape,' Opal said as they entered. 'See the floor! Under all that dirt the parquet is in really good condition, and bit by bit we're getting it clean.'

Miss Taylor frowned.

'I see that,' she admitted. 'What is finished looks fine. But there's so much still to do! Acres of walls and ceiling – and this is only one floor. You need an army of people in here, not two women on the floor and a couple of men painting.'

'That's all I can afford,' Opal said, 'I've budgeted most carefully. But don't worry, Miss Taylor. It *will* be done. I myself am going to clean and polish all the old counters and shelves.'

'I'm not at all sure . . .' Miss Taylor began doubtfully.

'Come and see if you approve of my choice of colours,' Opal interrupted. 'I thought this red for the walls would make the whole place look warm and cheerful; and then the ceiling, which is rather beautiful, is to be picked out in red and white. Don't you think it will look very welcoming?'

'Perhaps so,' Miss Taylor said. 'They're not *fashionable* colours, are they? Beige, cream, green . . . they're more usual.'

'I shall *make* them fashionable,' Opal said firmly. The light fittings I shall have painted gold. There's no way for a long time that I can have them gilded, but gold paint will look pretty. A quick effect is what I have to aim for.'

'Well, you seem to have it all worked out' Miss Taylor said. 'Shall we go up to the next floor? What departments do you intend to have there?'

'To begin with, very few,' Opal admitted. 'Most of what I sell will go on the ground floor, until I can expand both the stock and the sales staff. There I'll have dress materials and paper patterns, haberdashery, hosiery, gloves, cosmetics, a sort of general gifts counter, stationery. Children's clothes as soon as I can. Toys also.'

'On this floor,' Opal said as they reached the top of the staircase, 'I shall have my millinery. There'll be a great deal of space for it – too much – but that means that women can sit down and buy a hat in comfort and at leisure. I shall also have underwear here and, as soon as possible, ladies' dresses and coats.'

'Very well then,' Miss Taylor said. 'There is one thing I insist on. This floor must be better carpeted. A nice, grey haircord. I have friends in the carpet trade in Halifax and I shall persuade them to do the whole floor and give you a year's credit!'

'That would be wonderful!' Opal said. 'Especially since here I also want to create an area, however small at first, where customers can have a cup of tea and some light refreshment – or even just a rest in a comfortable chair. If they've taken the trouble to come the extra distance to my store, then they must be rewarded. Of course I'll see to it that they have to walk through several departments to reach such an area! Hopefully they'll spend on the way.' Miss Taylor laughed. 'How many hours have you spent, working this out, I wonder?'

'It hasn't been difficult,' Opal said. 'It all seems to be there in my head, ready and waiting. If it hadn't been for you and my sister-in-law, of course, it would have had to remain in my head. I shall always be grateful to you.'

'Well, you've given me a new interest,' Miss Taylor acknowledged. 'Money of itself isn't interesting. It's what one can do with it. You've shown me that. And how is Mr Hessle getting along with helping you to acquire your stock?'

She can't know the effect that even the sound of his name has on me, Opal thought. How could she. I dare say she's never experienced love, and in that case perhaps she's fortunate. Yet she remained clear-sighted enough to doubt that it was love she felt for David. Passion, yes. Jealousy, with some shame, she admitted to, could not deny. But not love as she had known it for Edgar.

157

'Well enough so far,' she answered levelly. 'But I'm not sure that he'll be as much help to me as I had hoped. He's getting married next week.'

'Getting married? You surprise me.' Miss Taylor looked keenly at Opal.

'He is marrying Miss Connie Browning, my assistant in Madame Dora's. You remember her?'

'Indeed I do. I always thought she was demure, yet bold. An unlikely and powerful combination. Well, we must hope that they'll be very happy together.'

'Come and see my office,' Opal said brightly. 'It's at the very top of the building, in the little square tower you can see from outside. Of course I shan't be spending much time there when the store is open. I shall be amongst the customers. That is where my place will be.'

Christmas came and went. On Christmas Day Opal took time off to be with Daniel, share in his presents, but on Boxing Day she knew she must be back in the store. There was not a day, not an hour, to be wasted from now on. They had been invited to visit David and Connie Hessle but Opal had pleaded pressure of work. She had, out of duty, attended the wedding with Edgar and Daniel, and the reception afterwards in a small hotel in Leasfield. Gnawed by her own feelings she had no compassion in her heart at the unhappiness in David's eyes as he stood with his bride. Connie was radiantly pretty, inordinately pleased. She showed, as yet, no sign of her pregnancy. I shall not be able to bear it when she does, Opal thought. I shall not be able to look at her.

'You could come to the store with me,' she said

to Daniel on Boxing Day. 'Perhaps you would like to come, too, Edgar?'

But Edgar had a chesty cold, a legacy of his time in the army. It was the same every winter.

'No thanks,' he said. 'I have to get right again for tomorrow.'

'Can I take my new paints?' Daniel asked.

Opal laughed. 'It's all you ever think about,' she said indulgently. 'But yes, of course you can.'

In the store she walked around with him, showing him all that had been done. 'You should be interested,' she said. 'One day it will all be yours! Think of that!'

'Can I start painting?' he asked.

'Very well,' she said. 'You can sit at this counter and I shall work nearby. Let's see if you can paint a picture of what the store will be like when it's finished!'

Perhaps, since I shall have more space than I can fill on the first floor, she thought, I could mount a children's art exhibition. Or set up a painting competition for the children of customers? It might bring people in.

Less than three months now and the people would be in this place. The counter she was now polishing with might and main would display – what? Gloves? Fine lace and ribbons? Silk or woollen materials? It was a detail she had not yet decided. What she *was* aware of, every waking moment of her life and often in her dreams, was that in such a short time, when the winter was over and the spring came, her dream would come true.

Chapter Nine

Opal drew back the curtains and looked out on to the street. In the small front gardens of Alma Place a few forsythia shrubs arched their flower-laden branches against the soot-blackened stone of the house, and daffodils poked their heads between the iron railings which divided each small plot from its neighbour. Nature had done well to choose yellow flowers for spring, she thought. If, in fashion, she were to follow Nature's guide in her choice of colours for each season of the year, she would not go far wrong.

'It's a perfect spring day,' she said. 'I knew it would be!'

'It wouldn't dare to be otherwise,' Edgar said from the bed. (She had not, after all, moved into the spare room). 'Not with you organizing everything.'

Opal could not tell whether his words were sarcastic of teasing. His face was expressionless and these days his moods were so variable that it was impossible to understand him. Yet not all that variable; more often black. His few lighter, gentler moods were saved for Daniel.

She did not take up the challenge, if challenge it was. Everything must go well today; nothing must be allowed to spoil the occasion. After all, Edgar *had* agreed to take the morning off work to be present at the opening, and she was grateful for that. In a place like Leasfield, to be seen to have the support of one's husband could do nothing but good. If she could have believed that she actually had it it would have meant a lot to her.

'I must be there really early,' she said. 'There are sure to be last-minute things to attend to.'

In fact, when she and David had left the store last night, well after midnight, everything had been in place; everything except the cash float in the Lamson room (to which, through a network of tubes still mysterious to her, money, hopefully, would speed from the counters) and her own personal flag which would be run up from the tower this morning. She had chosen a rich blue flag with her name emblazoned across it in large red letters. 'OPAL'S'. Nothing more. Nothing more was needed. From today her name would be synonymous with all that was best in department stores.

'Shouldn't you be up?' she asked Edgar. 'And I think I must go and waken Daniel. Be sure you're both there by half-past nine at the latest.'

'Stop fussing,' Edgar said. 'We'll be there on time.'

Inside the double doors of the main entrance to the store an area had been marked off by a yellow satin ribbon at waist height. The size of the area was so arranged that should a great many people attend the opening it could be enlarged by moving the ribbon, and should fewer people than hoped for turn up, the confined space was small enough to make them seem a crowd. At ten minutes to ten it was reported to Opal, in her office in the tower, that a respectable number of people had arrived and that more kept coming. It looked as though it might be necessary to adjust the ribbon.

'I'm desperate that I can't see them arriving from here,' Opal said.

Now that the moment had almost come she felt sick with apprehension, excitement, not a little fear. What if she had overestimated herself; her talents, her capacity, her potential? But she knew she had not. This was the day to which her life had been leading.

'It wouldn't do to show yourself,' Queenie said firmly. 'You're the star. You must appear at the precise moment. We shall all go down before you and set the stage for your appearance.' She put her arms around Opal and kissed her on the cheek. 'Good luck, my dear!'

'Thank you,' Opal said quietly. 'Thank you for everything, all of you here.'

'Well, I think we should go now,' Miss Taylor said briskly. 'Mr Carson, you are to escort me I believe. Then Mr and Mrs Derwent, Miss Mary Derwent, Mr Hessle and Daniel.'

Opal was still not sure whether Daniel should be there, in public. Mothers of young children who did jobs outside the home were frowned upon. But he had wanted to come and she could not deny him. She could never deny him anything.

'I'm sorry your wife couldn't be present, Mr Hessle,' Miss Taylor said. 'So unfortunate to have influenza on an occasion such as this!'

David smiled pleasantly. 'She was sorry too.'

They arranged themselves, and left by the narrow staircase from Opal's office and then went, in a little procession, down the wide staircase and towards the front entrance. Opal gave a last quick look in the mirror. Her face was pale against the grey wool dress. She would have looked better with a touch of rouge on her cheeks, but it was too late now. Her eyes, surprisingly, showed nothing of the hard work and fatigue of the last few months. They were clear and shining. She adjusted the small pink rose which David had given her to wear, and which she had accepted as a token that things were all right between them again, or as right as they ever could be. Then she smoothed down her already immaculate hair, and left.

A ripple of applause greeted her as she walked towards the respectably-sized crowd. Sensing that David was about to introduce her, she raised a hand to stop him.

'Ladies and gentleman,' she said. 'I am Opal. This is my store, and I hope from now on it will be yours. Let me introduce you to my family and friends, and to some of my staff – though I hope that before long *all* my staff will be familiar to you. This is my husband, Mr Edgar Carson . . . my son, Daniel.'

She introduced everyone in turn.

'Mr David Hessle is my Store Manager and my right hand,' she said. 'He will always be there to help you though that will not, I hope, prevent you from seeking me out whenever you wish to do so.'

Six weeks ago it had not seemed possible that David could be working for her. Up to that time she had seen little of him since his marriage, no more than business between them had made necessary. On one of his business calls he had been accompanied by Connie. 'I want to learn as much as I can about David's job,' she'd said, 'so that I can be a help to him.'

'How enterprising of you!' Opal said. 'But will you have time for that once the baby is born?'

She had forced the words out through cold lips. It was unbearable to think of this . . . this *chit* . . . with David's child. By this time – it was the only way – she had laid the blame for the whole affair at Connie Browning's door. She had been too wicked, too subtle for David. Demure and bold, as Miss Taylor had said. He had been well and truly caught.

Caught, as it turned out, was exactly what he had been. When the weeks went by with, on Connie's part, no sign of a swelling stomach, of breasts more than usually burgeoning, let alone morning sickness, fancies for strange foods or a preoccupation with baby clothes, Connie's mother began to have her doubts. When Connie admitted that she was not, and never had been, pregnant, it was her mother who insisted that he be told at once. 'If you leave it too late,' she counselled, 'if you make him a laughing stock in front of all his friends, it could be the end of your marriage! You don't want that do you?'

Connie did not, though her marriage had turned out to be much less exciting than she had expected. Boring even. So her no-longer-interesting condition was presented to David as a mistake on the part of the doctor, a wrong diagnosis for which she could not be blamed. But this time David was not deceived. His resulting anger was of a degree Connie had not thought possible, and since then it seemed that whatever she did was wrong.

Small wonder, Opal thought fleetingly, seeing David standing beside Miss Taylor, that Connie had feigned influenza. Unless obliged to do so the Hessles now went nowhere together. She believed it likely, though David had not spelt it out and it could be wishful thinking on her part, that already they no longer shared the marriage bed. 'Come and work with me,' had been her solution. 'Help me build my new store. It's something we can do together.'

Perhaps he had accepted to spite Connie? Whatever the reason, day by day they worked side by side; planning, discussing, arguing, agreeing. Life was undoubtedly enriched by David's presence, though no word passed between them which might not be heard by the whole world; and he never touched her. Their relationship was entirely platonic.

But David was not in her thoughts now as, smiling, she spoke to the people gathered around her in the store.

'I am here to serve you,' she said. 'It is as simple as that. To give you the best value for your hard-earned money. I know that we don't live in the easiest of times, so I shall always be on the lookout for bargains for you. But I also believe that when times are difficult a little variety, a little luxury, are more than ever needed. I shall run my store so that you will find these too. And if my store is not all that you want it to be, then please let me know. Never be afraid to stop me and speak to me when you see me in the store. Seek me out and tell me what you want.'

She realized, suddenly, that this was the first speech she had ever made in her life and that people were actually listening to her with interest.

'And now since you have been good enough to make the journey here,' she continued, 'there will be a cup of tea for everyone in Opal's café on the first floor – though when we reach our twenty-first year of trading I promise you champagne!

'The cafe is small – like the rest of the store it will grow according to *your* needs – so we shan't be able to serve you all at the same time. May I also remind you that if you *do* make a purchase – but please don't feel obliged to do so, feel free to look around – but if

165

you do buy you will receive a small gift to remind you of your part in this special day in my life – and I hope in the life of Leasfield.'

When the applause had died down, David stepped forward.

'Before I ask Miss Phoebe Taylor, whose family is so well known to most of us, formally to declare Opal's store open, just let me remind you of the offer in our advertisement. If you have made the journey from the centre of Leasfield by tram, then simply hand in your tram ticket at the desk by the cosmetics counter on this floor, and your fare will be refunded. But not only for today, ladies and gentlemen. This refund will be made to you for at least the next three months. It is Opal's way of saying "Thank you for coming".'

He brought Miss Taylor forward to cut the ribbon, but she beckoned to Opal.

'*I'm* not going to make a speech,' she said. 'But in front of all of you I want to present Miss Opal with a memento of this occasion. Opals, some say, are for tears. I'm sure that this day will prove the opposite to be true!'

To Opal's surprise she slipped a pendant on a silver chain over her head. Then she cut the ribbon and the crowd surged through into the store. My store, Opal thought. My dream has come true. She watched the people fanning out this way and that into the various departments. This was her supreme moment. Nothing would ever surpass it.

She stayed near to the entrance for a few minutes, greeting new customers as they came in, introducing herself. The advertising over the last few weeks, culminating in the half-page spread in yesterday's

Leasfield Courier, had paid off, though David had been against such extravagance.

'There's no way you can afford a half page,' he said. 'The cost is prohibitive!'

'On the contrary, there's no way I can afford *not* to,' she had told him. 'Not only once, but for some time to come. Advertising must be a top priority.'

The Courier had not been her only form of advertising. Several boys and girls in and around Leasfield had acquired unexpected riches by the payment of half-a-crown for leaflets pushed through every letter-box in their neighbourhood and posters fastened to every available board. David thought it undignified. Miss Taylor had also looked doubtful.

'As yet I can't afford too much dignity,' Opal said. 'I need every ounce of publicity I can get. In fact I can tell you now that mine will never be one of those companies which goes under in dignified silence because it's too refined to seek publicity! When I need help I shall call for it.'

What she needed to know now was which way of advertising had brought people in. As she moved around the store she would ask them.

There was a short queue of women – no men amongst them – at the desk where the used tram-tickets were being redeemed. The fare from the centre of Leasfield was twopence. Though she felt sure that not everyone who was entitled to it would bother to claim it, she must keep an eye on what was paid out over the next three months and make sure that the amount was offset in some other way, though not necessarily, indeed preferably not, at the customers' expense.

'Good morning ladies!' she said. 'Welcome to Opal's! Now tell me, do the trams run often enough from the town centre, or did you have to wait?'

'They run fairly often,' a woman said. 'But they don't stop near enough. If it was a rainy day we'd get wet walking from the tram-stop, wouldn't we?'

'Then there's a clear case for having the tram-stop moved,' Opal said cheerfully. 'Perhaps you would sign my petition for that? Miss Conran has it right there on the desk. I'm sure all you ladies between you will be much more influential than I!'

That should do the trick, she thought. When she had approached the Tramways Department (she wished to put 'Trams stop at the door' in her advertisements) they had laughed at her. They wouldn't laugh at a hundred or two paying customers, and a petition sent in every week until they did something about it.

She noticed that the nearby cosmetics counter was busy. That had been a good idea. She was convinced that its success would increase, especially as she aimed, by every persuasion she could think of, to encourage women to make the best of themselves. She thought of organizing demonstrations in the store. There was plenty of space for such events. Indeed, filling the space while she did not really have enough departments, or sufficient stock to put in the existing ones, was a major preoccupation with her. It must all seem to be done naturally, as if space was part of her plan. Customers must never suspect that she could not yet afford to fill it.

She saw Queenie and Miss Taylor by the glove counter, and went to join them. Queenie, already with several parcels in Opal's distinctive blue-and-white striped wrapping paper, was completing the purchase of a pair of doeskin gloves while Miss Taylor was trying on beige kid with gauntlets. Opal spoke to the assistant.

168

'Please see that Miss Taylor and Mrs Derwent are always given House discount on their purchases, Miss Feather.'

'I've done that, Mrs Carson,' the woman said. 'Mr Hessle gave me a list of people for House discount.'

'Good! And please remember to call me Miss Opal, won't you? Have you had many customers? What is selling best so far?'

'The doeskin at four-and-eleven are going well,' the woman said. 'But the special line in white fabric at two-and-sixpence is selling like hot cakes. We might run out!'

'Opal, everything's really splendid,' Queenie said enthusiastically. 'Just as I knew it would be. Oh I *do* wish I could help!'

'By the look of your parcels I think you have,' Opal replied. She glanced towards Miss Feather who was rearranging her display, out of earshot, at the other end of the counter. 'Seriously, Queenie, if it hadn't been for you and Miss Taylor this day could never have happened. And Miss Taylor, my pendant is quite beautiful!'

She held the opal up to the light, admiring the ever-changing blues, the iridescent pinks, greens and purples which shot through the large, oval stone.

'There's no way I can ever thank either of you enough. I shall never forget what you've done.'

'But I mean *really* help – like selling something,' Queenie said. 'I always thought I should like to work in a shop.'

'*Store*, if you don't mind!'

'Store then. But first I was needed at home by my parents and now Mark won't let me go out to work. He says my place is with the children.'

'Opal' Miss Taylor interrupted 'I'm suddenly rather tired. Do you think you could possibly have me a pot of tea sent to your office, and tell Gregson to bring my car around to the entrance in about twenty minutes?'

'Oh I'm so sorry, Miss Taylor,' Opal said. 'I'll take you up to my office at once.'

She really did look unwell. Was it fatigue from the excitement of the morning, or had it been coming on for some time? Am I getting so absorbed in my own affairs, Opal wondered, that I can't see anyone else?

'There's no need to go with me,' Miss Taylor said firmly. 'You have plenty to occupy you here. I'll just drink a cup of tea and then go home. Telephone me this evening if you have time.'

'Of course I will!'

As Miss Taylor walked away a tall, stout woman in a fur coat approached Opal.

'I am Mrs James Carstairs,' she announced, 'and I'm taking you up on your word. About supplying what the customer wants.'

'Why certainly,' Opal said. 'What can I do for you?'

'I bought this material to make a blouse,' the woman said. 'Now I find your haberdashery department has neither ribbon nor sewing cotton to match it!'

'Dear me! May I look at the material?'

Opal took the parcel from the woman and opened it out on the counter. 'What an unusual shade of green, isn't it? But very pretty. I think green is going to be fashionable this coming summer.'

'Well, what are you going to do about it?' the woman demanded.

'Why, find you something to match, of course!' Opal said pleasantly. 'I shall try to get it today, but I might not be able to find it until Monday. However, if you'll allow me to take a small snip of the material, and give me your address, I'll see that it's delivered to you.'

'Very well,' Mrs Carstairs said. 'I want three yards of double-sided satin ribbon, three-quarters of an inch wide, and one reel of sewing silk. And I want a perfect match.'

'We'll do our very best, Mrs Carstairs,' Opal promised. 'Now if you haven't yet visited our millinery department on the first floor I think you might find the new season's straws in a shade which would go beautifully with your new blouse. If you have any difficulty, please ask the assistant to call me.'

'What an ungracious woman,' Queenie said. 'I've suddenly decided I'd never make a saleswoman. I'd have been quite rude to her.'

'*You* wouldn't be rude to anyone! But if you really want to help me, here's your chance.'

'What do you mean?'

'Would you be an absolute angel and take this pattern to try to match it with ribbon and thread. There's no-one I can ask right now. I rather think you'll get it at Miller's'

'Why Miller's?' Queenie asked.

'Because I dare say that's where she bought the material in the first place. She certainly didn't buy it here. We don't stock this one.'

'I can't believe it!' Queenie gasped. 'I can't believe anyone would have the cheek! Why didn't you say anything?'

'Because though I'll start by supplying her with cotton and ribbon at no profit at all, I reckon I'll eventually make her a customer. I should say she's well-to-do. It takes a lot of pennies to buy a dyed ermine coat like that.'

'Especially in her size! Oh, Opal, can you imagine how she'll look in green satin?'

Opal pulled a face. 'But are you going to be a darling and match it for me?'

'Of course! And I'll take great pleasure in having it delivered to her by my chauffeur.'

'I shall have to think seriously about deliveries before long,' Opal said. 'All I have at present is a boy with a bicycle. But please excuse me, Queenie, I must go and see Miss Taylor before she leaves, make sure she's all right.'

Miss Taylor had finished her tea and was about to depart by the time Opal, waylaid by another customer, reached her office. She looked pale and cold, in spite of her all-enveloping fur coat.

'You really don't look too well,' Opal said anxiously. 'I do hope you haven't caught a chill. Did you feel a draught, standing in the entrance so long?'

'I never feel draughts,' Miss Taylor answered. 'But I am quite exceptionally tired. I shall go straight to bed with a hot toddy. I'll be as right as rain in the morning, you'll see!'

'I must thank you again for this beautiful pendant,' Opal said. 'I shall treasure it.'

'Well, I thought that the day ought not to go by without some memento, something tangible you could see and touch. You'll always have memories, of course.'

'Always,' Opal said. 'As long as I live.'

There was a tap on the door.

'Ah, here is Gregson!' Miss Taylor seemed glad of the interruption. 'Goodbye for now, Opal. Don't forget to telephone me.'

Opal was about to go back into the store when

Edgar came in, accompanied by Daniel and Mary. She realized, guiltily, that she had seen none of them since the opening, nor had she given them a thought.

'Well then, what do you think, Edgar?' she asked.

'Very good,' he said. 'It's going to be a big success. You've done well.'

'Thank you, Edgar'. She felt genuinely pleased by his approbation. 'There's still a lot of ground to cover. But I'm on the way.'

'You certainly are,' he agreed.

'We came to tell you that we're leaving now,' Mary said. 'We thought we should get back.'

'I'm starving,' Daniel complained. 'I wish you had a proper café with meat and potato pie and jam pudding!'

'We shall have one day, I promise you,' Opal said. 'Do you know, I'd forgotten all about food. How awful of me!'

'Don't worry, Opal,' Mary said. 'I'll make a meal for Edgar and Daniel the moment we get back. Since I'm staying the night I have lots of time. And I think your store is wonderful! I bought myself some handkerchiefs and a new hairbrush.'

Mary thinks it's wonderful, Opal thought, watching them go, but she'd rather have a husband and children than all the stores in the world. Well, I shall show everyone that it's possible to be a good mother *and* a good businesswoman at the same time. I could have been a good wife to Edgar, but he wanted another sort of wife. She was not his kind any more, she thought, though she had been once.

She left the office and went downstairs, meeting David on the way.

'Satisfied?' he asked.

'More than! Very, very happy. Aren't you glad you came in with me, David?'

'I couldn't be otherwise. I still wish that you'd let me have a partnership.'

'We've discussed all that,' Opal said. 'It was never on the cards. I wanted, as I've always wanted, to go it alone.'

'I sold my business to join you,' David reminded her. 'I could have bought the partnership, put money into the store.'

'I appreciate that. But you've not done badly, have you David! Apart from my own, yours is the most important job in the store. It always will be.'

He had sold his business, she knew very well but did not choose to remind him, because having inherited it from his uncle, he had never really liked it. And when Connie started taking an interest he liked it less than ever. He had jumped at the chance of joining Opal's – so much so that she wondered if his own business had not been doing well. But she was glad to have him. She had wanted him all along.

'I must go and speak to more people,' she said. 'We both must. I'll see you at the Staff Meeting.'

The Staff Meeting took place in the café as soon as the store had closed at half-past six.

'I won't keep you long,' Opal said. 'It's Saturday and I'm sure you all have things to do. I chose to open on a Saturday because in Leasfield that's the big spending day and I wanted us to start with a bang. Well, we've done that, and I'm grateful for your part in it. I've learned several things today that will be of use to all of us, but I won't go into them now. I'll save them for the proper Staff Meeting on Tuesday. We shall meet

174

every Tuesday at the close of business and I want you all to feel free to express yourselves, put forward your ideas on anything.

'The only thing I want to tell you right now is this. As you probably know, there's a bill before Parliament to enable shop assistants to have holidays with pay. We don't know that it will ever become law, but I've decided that whether it does or not, every member of my staff is to have a paid holiday, each year, of at least eight days. We shall be the first store in Leasfield to do this. Mr Hessle will start next week drawing up this summer's holiday lists for each department.

'That's all for today. Again, thank you all, very, very much!'

As they filed out she called back one man.

'Mr Burton, will you see to it that what I have just announced gets into the Leasfield Courier? I think it might even be of interest to the Yorkshire Post. See what you can do!'

'I'll give you a lift home,' David said.

'Thank you, but no. It's not far to walk and the fresh air will clear my mind.'

'Are you sure?'

'Quite sure, thank you,' Opal said.

Getting ready for bed, Opal told Edgar the amount of her first day's takings.

'Do you remember' she said 'my first day in the house shop in Acer Street? I had one penny float in an Oxo tin.'

'I remember,' Edgar said.

They climbed into bed and lay back to back.

'That was the beginning of my success,' Opal said drowsily.

175

And the beginning of the end for me, Edgar thought, wide awake in the darkness. Why does every stroke of Opal's success drive us farther apart? Why aren't I capable of sharing it? He had no doubt that he loved her, admired her, looked up to her. But he could not enter into her success any more than he could now, and for many months past, enter into her body. Why? He lay awake, pondering, until another spring day crept into the room.

Chapter Ten

'I don't want to go!' Daniel growled.

His voice, these days, alternated between a deep growl and a high squeak and was at times quite beyond his control. 'I shall hate it! You're cruel to send me!'

Opal faced him with all the patience she could muster. She did not want another scene, not now as they were about to set off. There had been enough of those over the last few weeks, ever since she had broken it to him that he was to go away to boarding school.

Daniel was changing fast; not only physically – he was already taller than she and would soon top his father – but in character also. As a small boy he had been so gentle, so acquiescent. She had felt him so close to her. Now, at thirteen, he was a creature of moods, one minute enthusiastic and responsive, the next dour and truculent, shutting himself up in his room, painting for hours on end. And such weird, incomprehensible paintings too.

'Don't talk nonsense, Daniel!' she said firmly. 'You were just the same when you first went to Bishop Tanner's and that turned out all right, didn't it?'

'Then if it's all right, why do I have to leave?' he demanded. 'I could have stayed on until I was sixteen. Why do I have to go away from home?'

She sighed. 'We've been through all this before. Because it's best for you. Because a public school education will help you in later life. One day you'll thank me for it.'

She turned to her husband.

'Edgar, can't you talk some sense into him?'

It was foolish of her to appeal to Edgar since he disapproved of Daniel going away. But then, if their son's education had depended upon Edgar the child would still have been at the local Council school. However, Edgar would no longer argue with her in front of the boy. For Daniel's sake they had made an agreement not to do so. Their quarrels, now, took place in private. When Daniel was present they were polite to each other. They avoided controversial topics – which meant, in practice, that they spoke little.

'Father doesn't agree with you,' Daniel said. '*He* doesn't believe I should go!'

He stood squarely in front of them, looking angrily from one to the other.

'Don't think I don't know that!' he cried. 'I know what you're both like. You can't hide it from me. You . . .' he shouted fiercely at Opal, his voice rising to a treble '. . . you think you know what's best for everybody and you always get your own way. You, Father, you know she gets away with everything and you let her; even when you don't agree, you let her. You never fight for anything, not even when it's important!'

Edgar met his son's eyes, dark and angry, and was shocked at the accusation in them. He despises me, he thought. He sees me as the failure I am. He felt sick at the discovery. It did not seem so long ago that he and Daniel had been the best of friends. Always in the school holidays, when Opal was all the time tied to the store, they went about together: to museums;

178

to the cinema; to art galleries, for which Daniel had an insatiable appetite, where he would stand enraptured before paintings which Edgar neither liked nor understood, however hard he tried to. And in the last three years, since Opal had bought the car and he had found an unexpected pleasure in driving, they had gone farther afield. Scarborough, Manchester, once to Liverpool to see the big liners which had fascinated them both. He had thought until now that he and Daniel were friends. Was it possible that even while they were being so companionable his son had been contemptuous of him?

Daniel saw the hurt, the puzzlement in his father's eyes, and wished he had not spoken. Nowadays his anger came upon him so quickly that he could not control it, and afterwards he did not know how to make amends.

'After all, York is only forty miles away,' Opal said soothingly. 'You'll be going to Grandpa Derwent's for half-term, and then before you know it you'll be home for the Christmas holidays!'

She was pricked by his accusations against her, but determined not to show it. He did not really mean a word of it. How could he? It was all part of adolescence and she was sure he would settle down at his new school in no time at all. He was extremely fortunate that she had got him into so good a school, but now was not the time for him to appreciate that.

'Come along or we shall be late,' she said. 'Daniel, you can travel in front of the car with your father.'

She, too, had learned to drive, but she seldom did so. Edgar was so much better at it. In fact, she had some figures she wished to study on the way to York. And then she must give serious thought to how many temporary staff they must take on for the Christmas season. It must be as few as possible, yet enough not to miss any sales. She planned to start the Christmas season early this year – by mid-November at the very latest.

The journey passed in near silence, Opal in the back of the car busy with her calculations, Edgar and Daniel side by side, yet with a distance between them which neither could bridge. Arriving at the school they spoke with the Matron, were shown Daniel's dormitory, had coffee with the Housemaster. Daniel, pale and mono-syllabic, trailed behind his parents. When they left, Opal with a hug and a kiss which said she had forgiven and forgotten her son's bad temper, Edgar with a formal handshake, and eyes which pleaded forgive-ness for his guilt, it was Edgar, even more than the abandoned Daniel, who felt that his heart must break.

'Don't run away with the idea that I don't feel anything,' Opal said on the way back. 'I shall miss Daniel every waking moment. It's because I love him so much that I want him to have what's best.'

It was Daniel, though they had different ideas of what was best for him, who united himself and Opal, Edgar thought. But after the boy's outburst today, the revelation of what he thought of his parents if only in a moment's anger, how long could that last? He wouldn't be a child much longer, dependent upon them, needing them. The thought that Daniel saw him as a failure had come even more as a shock to Edgar since in the last few years, though he knew himself to be not much good as a husband, he had done unexpectedly well in his job. He was successful there. He liked it no better, but by hard work and a stroke or two of luck he had had several promotions.

In fact he was now in a position where, given the chance, he could have kept his wife and son in reasonable comfort. Though not including expensive public schools, he thought grimly.

But he knew he could never reach Opal's heights. Her success had been phenomenal, the talk of Leasfield. And she had made it for herself, with her talents and her hard work. He was proud of her, but the gap between them was wider than ever and he could find no way of expressing his admiration. He did not know how to get near her. His sorely needed consolation was that this clever, beautiful woman – every year she grew more lovely – was his. That she was his in little more than name was something neither he nor she was likely to divulge. At least he was grateful for that.

'Drop me off at the stores,' Opal said. 'I have a busy day ahead. Shall you come in and have some lunch?'

'No thank you,' he replied. 'I have a busy day, too.'

Opal had not quite finished what she called her 'walk around' when she was asked by an assistant on lingerie to return to her office to take a telephone call. Each day she went around the whole store, not always at the same time or in the same sequence, but walking through every department. She did not pause everywhere – though she always stopped to have a word with a customer she recognized and by now there were many of those; or she would speak to someone who seemed to be in need of help. It was said by her admirers that she thought nothing of measuring out a yard of elastic, or choosing a hairnet, for a customer waiting to be served.

Usually she would make about half-a-dozen stops,

enquiring about the health of a member of staff or – as at the moment when the message came – examining a line of merchandise. But though she might walk as swift as the wind through some departments, seeming to look neither to right nor to left, it was a fact that nothing escaped her. Soon after she had returned to her office a series of notes, brief but polite, would go forth. 'To Miss Butler, Blouses: Please have an assistant fasten *every* button on the white crepe-de-chine blouse on the model.' 'To Mr Simpson, Leather Goods: There is an address book upside down in your showcase.'

Her secretary, indeed most of her staff, knew that the walk-around must not be interrupted unless the matter was unusually important, so when the message came she immediately put down the camiknickers she was examining.

'They're certainly very pretty, Miss Williams,' she said to the buyer. 'Is this new coffee shade selling well? Are we getting a good mark-up?'

'The mark-up is all right,' Miss Williams assured her. 'And at four-and-eleven for art silk with lace trimming, so is the price. But they've not taken off yet. Customers still go for white or peach shades.'

'Then if we're fairly heavily stocked perhaps we should include them in the next advertisement. The new fashion shade – something like that. I'll talk to you later.'

She left lingerie, trod the grey carpet through gowns, coats, millinery, sportswear, to the door which concealed the staircase to her office. On the other side of that door the luxury ended. The stairs were uncarpeted and her office was sparsely furnished, the only exception being a long, comfortable, chintz-covered sofa.

But there was a practical reason for that. She did not sit on it during the day, nor did she encourage anyone else to do so. It was there because there were times – in the Christmas season, during the January and July sales, at the financial year-end – when she worked so late that there was no point in going home. On those occasions she slept on the sofa.

Her secretary handed her the telephone as she entered.

'It's Miss Taylor's maid. I'm afraid it's bad news.'

Opal took the receiver.

'Miss Opal here. What is it, Jenny? I see, When? What does the doctor . . . ? Yes, I'll come at once.'

'Miss Taylor has had another heart attack,' she said. 'It sounds most serious. Will you get my car around at once, please. Inform Mr Hessle. You can sign any letters which must go today. I might not be back before closing time.'

In the car her thoughts were all of Miss Taylor, dreading what she might find at Oak House. Jenny had sounded genuinely frightened, though it was by no means her mistress's only heart attack in the last few years. The first had occurred five-and-a-half-years ago, the very day after the store's opening, and she had had three or four since then. But since each one had been less severe than the last, and the doctor had declared that if she would take things quietly she would make old bones yet, they had been lulled into security. At least I have, Opal thought. Had Miss Taylor?

The friendship between the two women, though in many ways still formal, ran strong and deep. Opal could not envisage a world without the older woman. She sometimes felt that Miss Taylor understood everything about her, even those things which were left unsaid, and that in understanding, she accepted.

She turned up Nab End Rise and into the drive of Oak House. How green I was when I first came here, she thought. A little shop assistant, delivering hats. It was a lifetime ago – yet it was only nine years, almost to the day. Jenny, who now opened the door, was the same maid who had let her in at the tradesmen's entrance on that occasion, who had grudgingly brought tea and Barmouth biscuits. I'm not sure that she's ever approved of me, Opal thought, walking past her, going up to the bedroom.

She was shocked by Miss Taylor's appearance. It was less than a month since she had seen her last, yet from the change in her it could have been a year. Propped against the pillows she seemed small and shrunken, her skin grey, the area around her mouth darkened by pain. And on her face was the look Opal had seen long ago on that of her own mother at Queenie's wedding; the indefinable aura of death. She knelt beside the bed and took Miss Taylor's hands in her own. The bony fingers were icy cold, as if death had already taken them and waited impatiently for the rest. In spite of her resolve to remain calm, Opal cried out in anguish.

'Miss Taylor! Oh Miss Taylor! You must get better! For my sake you must get better!'

The sick woman's voice was weak. She had difficulty in summoning enough breath to speak. Opal strained to hear her whispered reply.

'Not this time . . . Everything for you, dear child. Made me so happy . . . Enjoy it all.'

As she closed her eyes for the last time the pain left her face. Opal saw her grow young again, younger than

184

she had ever known her; her features clear, her skin unlined. When the last sigh had left her body Opal cried out and flung herself across the bed, and cried out again and again until the maid came running.

'There was no need for you to come back to the store,' David said. 'You should have gone home. It's well after closing time anyway.'

She was sitting on the sofa in her office. David put a glass of brandy into her hand.

'Drink this,' he ordered. 'You look awful. Is there anything I can do if I go to Miss Taylor's now?'

'No. I saw to everything.'

Once she had pulled herself together she had done everything that was necessary: drawn the sheet over her dead friend's face, darkened the room, summoned the doctor, the undertaker. Then she had driven herself back to the store. No other death, not her mother's, not Madame Dora's, so terrible in its suddenness, had left her like this. She felt herself in an unreal world, as if her own spirit had died in her.

'You shouldn't have come back here,' David repeated.

'Where else would I go? Where else?'

At his insistence she gulped down the brandy and handed back the glass. He came and sat beside her, putting his arm around her, drawing her head on to his shoulder for comfort. The touch of his hand as he stroked her hair was all she needed to free the tears which, until now unshed, had felt like a great weight inside her. He let her cry and then with gentle fingers wiped away the tears, kissed her wet cheeks.

At first they held each other with no thought except to give and receive comfort. And then the grief of the

185

moment merged, for both of them, with the sexual longings and needs of barren months. Their love-making was urgent, strong, passionate. She exulted in his fierceness and met it with a ferocity of her own. How had she borne without him for so long? Was anything in life as important as to love and be loved?

When the act was over, when – murmuring endearments, kissing her body gently now – he had helped her to dress, she remembered Miss Taylor. But now, though the sorrow, the loss, the bereavement were still there, the bitter anguish, the feeling of death in herself, had gone. As if, she thought in some confusion, as if the act which could give life had exerted some sort of supremacy over death.

Miss Taylor's words as she lay dying, her announcement that she had left everything to Opal, did not at the time penetrate Opal's consciousness. She was too overwhelmed by her friend's death to take it in. Unlike Madame Dora's death, when to her shame her inheritance had been almost her first thought, it was not until next day that it came back to her. When it did she wept again, knowing that she would have renounced it all to have bought Miss Taylor even one more day of life.

The inheritance, however, turned out to be less than might have been supposed. Miss Taylor's investments (the lawyer said after the funeral) had not done well over the last few years.

'Then she must have made a real sacrifice in putting money into my store?' Opal said.

'I think she did. But it was what she wanted to do. Of course you will, in addition, have Oak House. You will have to decide whether you want to live in it or sell it, though I should warn you that the market for large houses is not good at the present time.'

It took Opal no time at all to decide what to do with the money. She had wanted for some time to expand her small café into a much larger restaurant. There was plenty of space for it. She envisaged a place where business men or families might come for a good lunch, whether or not they were customers of the store. Since they would have to walk through the store to reach the restaurant she felt confident they would soon become customers. It was a scheme she had discussed with Miss Taylor, one which had found her approval.

On the evening of her visit to the lawyer she drew up rough plans for the extension. She would call her architect in the morning.

'What shall I do about Oak House?' she asked Edgar.

He shrugged his shoulders.

'Do whatever you please. I don't see the need of a house that size for the three of us, but it's up to you, isn't it?'

'Well we shan't want to stay in Alma Place for ever,' Opal said. 'We've already been here longer than I intended. Of course I could sell Oak House and buy something smaller, but in a better area than Alma Place.'

They had not moved, partly because all her profits went back into the store, partly because she was always too busy to think about it. Now she would have to make a choice.

'I'll decide later,' she said to Edgar. 'It's coming up to the Christmas season and I'm going to be very busy. Also I want to start work on the new restaurant as soon as possible.'

*　　*　　*

Opal had little doubt that she was pregnant. By the middle of November she had missed a second period, and though she told herself that there might be other causes, her body contradicted her. Already her breasts were filling out, and when, on two consecutive mornings the room spun around as she rose from the bed, and she had to rush to the bathroom to be sick, she knew she could lie to herself no longer.

It was David who had sought out the doctor, a stranger on the other side of Leasfield, in whose consulting room she now sat. On David's advice she had not given her own name. The doctor's examination had been brief, his questions few. She had dressed quickly, and awaited his verdict.

'I am pleased to inform you that you are indeed pregnant, Mrs Derwent,' he said pleasantly.

He was quite sure she was not Mrs Derwent and that he had, somewhere, seen her before. It would come back to him sooner or later. In the meantime he must be careful.

'You seem to be in good health,' he continued. 'Though perhaps you are a little too thin. From now on you must take care of yourself, eat well. Remember that you are eating for two.'

'That is not the problem,' Opal said nervously. How could she tell him? How could she ask what she must? David had assured her that this man would immediately understand, but he gave no sign of doing so.

The doctor noted the way she twisted the gloves in her hands, saw the anxiety in her eyes. He knew well enough why she was here. She was not the first and would not be the last. He watched her struggling for words.

'I . . . you see, Doctor I . . . I can't have this baby! There are reasons why it's impossible.'

There always were. They were depressingly similar. He seemed to remember now that he had seen her photograph in the newspaper at some time. He was taking no chances.

'Please do something to help me!' Opal whispered.

He rose and walked towards the door.

'Mrs Derwent,' he said, 'neither the law, nor the ethics of my profession allow me to do what I think you are asking me. And if they did I would still not do it. Also, unless you are willing to take a grave risk, to submit yourself to pain and danger, I would strongly advise you not to seek out some less skilful means of achieving what you have in mind. And now I bid you good day. Since I can be of no possible use to you there is no fee for your visit.'

He held the door open and waited for her to leave.

In the street, coughing in the damp November fog, Opal's feelings swiftly changed. She was relieved, glad almost, that he had refused her. To rid herself of the child had been David's solution, and in her panic she had agreed. But in her heart she was against it. She was not sure that she could ever have gone through with it. And now it had been decided for her. She began to walk towards the town centre. It would be more sensible in this weather to take the tram, but walking would help her to think.

She was in an impossible situation. She knew for certain, now, that she would make no further attempt to rid herself of the baby, yet it seemed equally impossible that she should have it. Everything was against it.

Edgar must be told. It could not be long before

someone or other noticed the signs and she must not risk him finding out from some other source. But only he and she (and David who already knew) could have any idea that the child was not his. In Edgar lay her only hope. She had never before been afraid of him – what was there to fear? – but now she was. But it was not only fear which ate into her – of what he might do, of what he would say – but a deep aversion to the pain she must cause him.

They had given each other too much pain over the last few years, not by their actions so much as by the coldness which lay between them. She did not, as Edgar seemed to think, ever want to belittle him by her own success. She would have liked to have shared it all with him, but he was unwilling. Looking back, it seemed to her that except for the first two years they had seldom made each other happy. Yet it had not been deliberate on either side. They had never been cruel to each other and she believed she would have continued to love him had he not turned away from her.

The failure of their marriage had been the slow erosion of the bonds which bound them, and in the early days the strongest of those bonds had been sex. Now she must wound Edgar in the sharpest possible way, thrust in the knife where she knew him to be most vulnerable.

By the time she reached the store, almost an hour later, the wet fog had drenched her coat, her hat, her hair. She was not aware of it and wondered why Miss Morton looked at her strangely when she came into the office.

She broke it to Edgar that evening. She was glad that Daniel was away at school, thankful that no-one in the world could witness the pain, anger, disbelief in Edgar's face.

'It happened only once,' she said. 'It will never happen again. There were circumstances . . . Miss Taylor's death . . .'

'You think it makes it better that on the evening Miss Taylor died you went straight from her to him?'

She flinched before the disgust in his voice.

'It wasn't like that. You don't understand . . .'

'You're right! I don't!'

'Edgar, I beg of you! I swear to you that if you'll stand by me now I'll be faithful to you as long as I live. I never wanted to be anything else. I will be a better wife, Edgar. I will, I will! But you must help me.'

'Why must I?' he demanded. 'Do you know what you're asking? You are asking me to take this man's child and watch it grow up in my home – perhaps looking like him, reminding me every day of your betrayal! You're asking me to accept the child in your body – a body I haven't known for a long time – as my own.'

'Who else can I ask?' Opal cried. 'Who else can I turn to?'

He was silent for a while, his head buried in his hands. She could think of nothing more to say to him. At last he looked up.

'If we'd had a loving marriage,' he said slowly, 'if we'd shown each other any warmth and affection over the last few years – if it had happened in such circumstances – I think, though I don't know, that I could have accepted it, forgiven you. But it's not like that. I happen to be the only one who can solve your problem. There's no more to it than that.'

'That's not true!' Opal protested. 'I've offered you

love and affection. You've thrown it back at me. And I care deeply that I've hurt you so.'

'It's too late,' Edgar said flatly. 'And I won't do what you ask. This time I won't be your puppet on a string, dancing to your tune. I've had enough. I'm leaving!'

'You can't!' She was frantic. 'Edgar, you can't leave me!'

'Oh yes I can. Quite easily.'

'But Daniel? What about Daniel? Don't you care about him?'

Edgar lunged towards her, gripped her by the shoulders and began to shake her. She was frightened by the wild look in his eyes.

'I would like to kill you!' he shouted. 'I would really like to kill you!'

Then as suddenly as he had taken hold of her he flung her away from him and she fell to the floor.

'You know I love Daniel!' He was weeping now, deep, tearing sobs, which shocked her. 'I love him more than you've ever known how to. But I'm no use to him. You've seen to that. You're the one who can give him everything. He doesn't need me. When he finishes at his posh school he'll never need me again. But don't you ever dare to say I don't love him!'

It was Edgar who slept in the spare room that night. In the morning, by the time Opal rose, he had already gone. He had taken his clothes, and two photographs from the sideboard, one of herself and the other of Daniel. He had left behind the silver frames in which they normally stood.

Mechanically, as if she was sleep-walking, she dressed, did her hair, applied lipstick. Once she had to break off to be sick. When the time came for her to leave for the store she was ready.

192

'If I may say so,' Miss Morton said, 'you don't look at
all well. Perhaps because you're the only one of us who
hasn't had a holiday. Can I get you anything? A cup
of coffee?'

Opal's inside heaved at the thought. 'No thank you,'
she said.

She stood in front of the board, on her office wall,
which showed a plan of the whole store and the
deployment of staff.

'We must move two extra people into the Toy
Department today,' she said. 'And I think we must
steal a little more space from Sportswear to display
the new Christmas stock of board games and jigsaw
puzzles. Miss Deacon's not going to like it, but games
and toys sell better than sportswear at this time of the
year.'

Thank God for work. It could not solve her problem,
which this morning seemed less than ever soluble
(where had Edgar gone to? What could she do to get
him back, to get him back she must) but while there
were things to attend to in the store other questions
could be pushed to the back of her mind for a few
hours. At least she hoped they could.

'Is Mr Hessle in?' she asked her secretary.

'I think so. Shall I ask him to come up?'

'Yes.' She must tell him about Edgar. 'No, don't
bother. I think I'll do my walk-around early today.
After that I'll see Mr Hessle and then I'll go through
the copy orders. Will you be getting them ready,
please.'

She spent a long time walking around the store,
visiting almost every department, asking questions,
checking sales. Christmas cards were beginning to

move, though the assistant told her that no-one seemed disposed to buy the new nineteen-thirty-five calendars. 'You get the feeling that they think it's bad luck to have them beforehand,' she said.

On Toys she met David. He was talking to an assistant she had not seen before, a pretty young woman with blonde hair to her shoulders, longer than the current fashion.

'I don't know you, do I?' Opal asked.

'This is Miss Nash,' David said. 'She's with us for the Christmas season.'

That explained it. She herself always saw permanent staff before they were engaged, but staff who were to be here for a few weeks only were engaged by David.

'I'm almost through,' she told him. 'Could you meet me in my office in fifteen minutes' time?'

She moved on to a disgruntled Miss Deacon in Sportswear and was pleased to have the lady's complaints interrupted by being called to the telephone.

'You have a visitor,' Miss Morton said. 'Mrs Carson. Your mother-in-law.'

Was it her imagination, or did Miss Morton's voice sound strained?

'How long has she been waiting?'

'Just a few minutes. But I think you'd better come, Miss Opal.'

She had not seen Mrs Carson for many months. There was somehow never enough time for visiting and her mother-in-law seldom came to the store. In any case she would scarcely have recognized the woman who awaited her in her office.

Her grey hair was wild and unkempt under the

old-fashioned hat; her coat unbuttoned as though she had rushed out of the house without bothering about anything. But worse than her clothes was her face – purple-red, blotched and swollen with tears, her eyes sparking anger.

'You may leave us, Miss Morton,' Opal said quickly.

'She needn't bother!' Mrs Carson shouted. 'She knows! Don't you think I won't tell everyone what you've done to my son, because I will! Don't you think you'll get away with it!'

Opal stepped forward, her hand outstretched to her mother-in-law, but the old woman pushed her away.

'My only one!' Her voice was a wail of anguish which cut into Opal. 'And now I'll never see him again! Never as long as I live! You've driven him away. Canada! Already he's on the train to Liverpool, and you drove him to it. I've seen it coming. I knew it would happen!'

She was screaming now, shaking her fist at Opal, when David entered.

'And you!' Mrs Carson yelled at him. 'You're the one! My Edgar didn't tell me that but I know. I've watched you. I've seen you look at her!'

'But it's you,' she shouted, turning back to Opal. 'It's you who've made him suffer. Don't think I haven't seen it all these years. Seen him grieving, eating his heart out because he couldn't keep up with you. May God punish you, Opal Derwent, and he will!'

She spat in Opal's face. The saliva caught her between the eyes, and ran down. The old woman collapsed in a sobbing, shaking heap on the sofa.

She's demented, Opal thought. She's gone mad. And

I'm going to be sick. She felt beads of cold perspiration on her forehead.

'Miss Morton, bring Miss Opal a glass of water,' David called out. 'Quickly, please!'

He took out his handkerchief and wiped Opal's face while Mrs Carson beat her fists against the sofa.

Chapter Eleven

Sleep evaded Opal that night. She who usually fell asleep instantly and knew nothing until the alarm sounded next morning, now stared into the darkness, waiting for the day to come, yet dreading it. If she closed her eyes she saw Mrs Carson's angry face, felt the spittle on her own face. Or she saw Edgar, white-faced and angry, his eyes bewildered by pain. She had not wanted to cause this hurt to anyone. But it was too late; all the repentance in the world could achieve nothing.

In her heart she knew that Edgar would never return. He was slow to move – how often she had been irritated by his inability to make a quick decision – but when he made up his mind he did not change it again. She flung her arms across the empty space where he should be. Why was it, when for so long his presence in their bed had meant little to her, that she could now miss him so?

Her thoughts swung around again to her mother-in-law. Mrs Carson had been so good to her when she needed help most. She had fed them, looked after Daniel to enable Opal to go to work. And now they were enemies. At least I am *her* enemy, Opal thought. I can never think of her as mine.

When she could bear the night no longer she got up and dressed, though it needed an hour or two yet to daylight. She would go to the store early. There was always work to be done and there would be other people. She, who had always valued solitude, longed for human company, could not bear the silence of this house.

She must speak with David today. He *must* help her, though she had no clear idea how. Would he leave Connie and come to her? And did she want that? Perhaps Edgar meant to divorce her, and if he did then perhaps she and David might make a fresh start, if only for the sake of the baby. And then, worst of all, there was Daniel to be told. How could she possibly tell Daniel that his father had gone, let alone that she was pregnant? But he must be told.

In the store she did two hours paperwork, carefully studied the latest issue of Vogue to see what high fashion ideas might be translatable to Opal's, and then began her round of the store. It amazed her that with her private life shattered into pieces she could give such close attention to her work. Thank heaven she could, and thank heaven that at least everything in the store seemed to be going well. She lingered in the fashion departments – always her favourite places – trying to find solace.

'It's a lovely time for fashion, Miss Baxter,' she said to her buyer on Gowns. 'Everything's so much more feminine and graceful than it was in the 'twenties. Don't you agree?'

'Oh I do Miss Opal,' the buyer said. 'Thank heaven those short skirts and that awful close-cropped hair have gone – never to return, I should hope!'

'I like your new stock of evening gowns,' Opal said, sorting through them on the rails. 'High front, back cut lower. Backs, by the way, are going to be lower still. Nice simple lines, cut on the bias. Yes, you've bought well, Miss Baxter. But I think one or two of these might be better with, say, the addition of a flower on the shoulder, or a chiffon handkerchief to tuck into a bracelet. Have a word with Miss Tyler and see what she has on Trimmings, and try something with the models on the stands. I'll be down later to have a look.'

It was the season for evening dresses and now everyone, of every class, wore them, since everyone went to dances. Opal was quite sure that not one of her girls, however junior, would be without a floor-length evening dress. It might lack the elegance of those on sale in the store – the girl would probably have run it up herself – but to go to a dance wearing a short dress would be unthinkable.

'If I may say so, Miss Opal,' Miss Baxter remarked, 'you don't look at all well this morning. I hope you haven't got influenza or anything. It's tricky weather.'

Would to God influenza was all I had, Opal thought. She felt wretched. The sickness now seemed to stay with her until the middle of the day and she felt a deep fatigue, far beyond anything caused by her sleepless night.

'I feel a bit queasy,' she admitted. 'Something I ate, I dare say.'

Work had begun on the new resturant, though there was no way it could be opened before the New Year since there was the matter of enlarging and re-equipping the kitchens. After the January sale has ended was the time she planned, so that the two events would not detract from each other. She tried to have new happenings in the store as often as possible; a fashion parade, a dressmaking expert, an artist to draw children's portraits, free make-up sessions. Always something new, something of interest to women.

Though the store was still a place to find a bargain – she made a practice of buying good bankrupt stock and selling it in special sales at rock bottom prices – the general trend was towards more expensive goods of finer quality. She now had a comfortable, and growing, number of well-to-do account customers.

On the ground floor she met David. He looked tired and drawn, as though he, too, had not slept. He eyed her with concern.

'You don't look too good!'

'So I've just been told. Don't you think, with all these women around, it can only be a short time before one or other of them guesses? I'll see you later. We've got to talk.'

Perhaps everything would seem better when she had talked with David, she thought, clutching at straws.

When she had toured the ground floor departments she walked outside to inspect the window displays. It was raining hard; ice-cold drops, dirt-laden from the smoky air. No-one but she would be mad enough to gaze into shop windows on a day like this. She went back to her office and was going through the copy orders with Miss Morton when the door crashed open and Daniel burst in. She jumped up from her chair, her stomach lurching, fear chilling the flesh on her shoulders and back.

'Why Daniel, what in the world are you doing here? Why aren't you at school? And you're absolutely soaking. Take your coat off at once!'

She turned to her secretary. 'We'll finish the orders later, Miss Morton.'

He stood there in the doorway, rain dripping from his hair, running in rivulets down his face. He made no move to take off his wet coat and she moved towards him to help him.

'Don't touch me!' he said harshly.

She stepped back. It was as though he had struck her on the face. What could he possibly know, and so soon? Mrs Carson could not . . .'

'You drove him away!' he accused her. 'It's your fault! Why couldn't you be an ordinary person? Why can't you be like Auntie Queenie, or Auntie Mary?'

He looked so young, so bitterly unhappy. She wanted to take him in her arms, and could not, because he would not let her. He was no longer the small boy she could comfort. There was suddenly a wide gulf between them. He was looking at her with eyes full of misery and hate.

'How did you know?' she asked. 'Who told you?' And how much, she wanted to add.

'I had a letter from Father this morning. I ran away from school and got the train from York. I expect they'll telephone you. But I'm not going back! He wouldn't have gone if I'd been at home. It's my fault as well because I was angry with him that last time. He doesn't know I love him and now we'll never see him again!'

The words poured out of him as if he had no way of stopping them.

'Daniel, don't! I'm sure he'll come back!'

Her words sounded futile. She had no idea what to say to this child whom she loved so much. And she was afraid to speak, too, not knowing the extent of his knowledge.

'Of course he won't come back!' he cried. 'Here, read this!'

He thrust the letter into her hands. It was damp, and

in places the ink ran down the page, as if he had read it and re-read it while walking in the rain.

'I'm off to Canada,' she read. 'By the time you get this I shall be on one of the liners we saw in Liverpool. There are fine chances for men in Canada. Forgive me, son, and don't ever think I don't love you. Take care of your mother.'

She handed back the letter. So he did not know about the baby. She would not tell him yet. The burden he already carried was too heavy for him to bear. She could not add to it now – though soon she must.

'Blame me if you like,' she said quietly, 'I dare say it is largely my fault, though perhaps not entirely. Things are never as black and white as they seem. But you must not blame yourself in any way. Your father loves you dearly, you know that.'

'You don't understand, do you?' he cried. 'You never understand!' The anguish in his voice, the fact that he could not command his voice so that it wavered uncontrollably, hurt her more, even, than the words themselves.

'I *know* he loves me,' Daniel said. 'I've always known it. It's that I didn't show him how much I loved him. You have to show people or they don't know!'

He dropped down on to the sofa, as if his legs would not hold him any longer, and began to sob. Opal put out a hand and touched him and this time he did not shake her off. Let him cry, she thought. It's healing for the young to cry.

'Did you have any breakfast before you left school?' she asked presently.

'No.'

'Then you must be hungry. I'll send for some sandwiches and some hot coffee. And you *must* take off your wet coat. I don't want you to catch cold.'

'I'm not hungry,' he said. But when the food came he ate it, and immediately looked the better for it.

'Now you must go back to school,' Opal said. 'I'll drive you back myself. I'll telephone Mr Cottrell before we go and make it all right.'

It was a silent drive. Daniel had calmed down, but he was still pale, and clearly deeply troubled. She knew he did not want to return to school. It was as if however angry he was with her, he needed her presence. Well, she needed him too, but it could not be allowed.

'You could come home for half-term next week, instead of going to Highcliffe,' she suggested. 'I'll be busy in the store and you might be a help to me. What do you think?'

He made no reply.

'I'll go round by Highcliffe on my way back from York,' she said. 'I shall have to tell them about your father and these things are better said face to face. I'm glad you came to see me, Daniel, even if you did run away from school. Anyway, I'm sure—'

'Look out!' he yelled suddenly. 'Mother, what are you doing? Didn't you see the man? Don't you know you have to give way to pedestrians at Belisha beacons?'

She sighed. 'I'm sorry, love. I know I'm not a good driver. I don't like driving and that's the truth.'

'You're a terrible driver,' Daniel said. 'You never seem to have your mind on it.'

Opal, as she had promised, called at Highcliffe on the way back to Leasfield. Without preamble she told Mary and her father that Edgar had gone, told them about the letter he had sent to Daniel.

'I can't believe it!' Mary said, horrified. 'Not Edgar!'

203

She clearly blames me, Opal thought. I can hear it in her voice, see it in her face. But she was getting used to that. Even without knowing about the baby it seemed that everyone blamed her.

'It's a bad do, our Opal,' her father said. 'Nothing like this has happened in our family afore.'

What will they say when they know I'm pregnant, she wondered. She could not bring herself to tell them, not yet.

Her father was not well. He sat in front of the fire, coughing and wheezing, an old shawl of her mother's draped around his shoulders.

'He should be in bed but he won't stay there,' Mary complained. 'Which means he'll have bronchitis on and off all winter.'

When Opal left, Mary walked out to the car with her.

'He's not said anything to you yet,' she said. 'But Father's thinking of selling up. It's getting too much for him. The weather up here on the moor is no good to anyone with a bad chest, not in winter.'

'What shall you do?' Opal asked.

'I don't know. Move to something smaller where it's a bit warmer. I shall have to take a job, though goodness knows what I'm fitted for!'

You're fitted for marriage and children, Opal thought, moved by the sadness in her sister's face. Why did it come to me and not to you? You wouldn't have failed at it. You would never find yourself in the mess *I'm* in.

David was waiting in her office when she got back. 'I thought you might have gone,' Opal said. 'I'm glad you haven't.'

'Miss Morton gave me your message. How was Daniel?'

'Better, by the time I left him. Of course he blames me and I suppose he's right about that.'

'Did you tell him . . . ?'

'That I was pregnant?' she said harshly. 'No I did not. He has enough on his plate right now. I'll break that to him in the Christmas holidays, as I will to Mary and Dad. David, what are we going to do?'

'That's what I have to talk to you about,' he said hesitantly. 'Opal, there's something I must tell you and I don't know how to begin.'

Why was he afraid? Anxious – yes – but there was something more. It came to her with absolute certainty that something was terribly wrong.

'Whatever it is,' she said, 'why don't you come straight to the point?' Yet she didn't want to hear it. She knew it must be bad.

'The fact is,' David said, 'Connie is pregnant!'

The silence seemed to go on and on, as if there was nothing left for either of them to say. And what *was* there to say?

'*Really* pregnant this time?' Opal said at last. 'Really and truly pregnant?' Her voice sounded like a stranger's. Hard, sarcastic.

'The baby is due next April. I've been meaning to tell you.'

'So she was pregnant when you and I . . . ?'

'Yes.'

'Well, you have been a busy bee, haven't you?'

Why do I speak so lightly, she thought. He is killing me. He is surely killing me.

'I take it that the baby is yours? Her baby, I mean. We know mine is.'

'Of course it is!' His voice was sharp.

'Why of course?' she asked wildly. 'Not every woman

205

in the world is bearing her own husband's baby. But perhaps Connie is finer material than I? Perhaps I'm a different kind of woman? Is that it?'

'Opal, you're being ridiculous . . . !'

'. . . Perhaps I'm what my mother-in-law said I was? A whore. Is that what you think too?'

'Opal, I'm bitterly sorry . . .' he began.

'I'm sure you're sorry . . .' she interrupted. 'But I'd like to reserve the word "bitter" for my own feelings. And now I have something to say to you, David. Please listen carefully because I don't think I shall be able to say it twice. Only you and I – and Edgar who has gone to the other side of the world because of it – know that the baby I am carrying is yours. When she hears about it Mrs Carson might suspect, but she can't know. So from this moment on the baby is *mine*. Mine entirely; mine alone! Do you understand? You have no part of it, now and for ever. If you have any feeling for this child, which I doubt, then turn it to your own child and leave me to mine. Is that clear?'

It was not her imagination that he looked relieved.

'If that's the way you want it.'

'It is. And I don't doubt that it suits you!'

She longed to punish him, yet what she was doing was setting him free. It could only be that way. She had to free herself, for once and for all, and with what little dignity was left to her.

'Do you want me to leave the store, look for another job?' David asked.

'I would certainly like that, but what good would it be to either of us? As you know perfectly well, I shall need you to take my place when I take time off to have the baby. No-one else can be trained in so short a time. And you would not find it easy to get another job as good as this, though that doesn't worry me. At the moment we're dependant on each other. I wish to God we weren't, but we are. And now will you please get out of my sight!'

When he had left the room she sat for a long time, staring at the pile of papers in front of her, not seeing them. It was impossible even to think any more. She did not hear the knock on the door and was startled when it opened and the night-watchman stood in the doorway.

'Just checking around, Miss Opal,' he said. 'Will you be working much later? It's gone eight o'clock.'

'I'm just going,' she said. 'Thank you, Mr Chambers.'

What was the point of going home, back to a house which was not just empty, but deserted? To another long night in which she would not be able to sleep? She realized, wearily, just how much she had been relying on David's support, counted, somehow, on having him by her side. There was no-one left now from whom she could take strength; Edgar gone, Daniel needing strength from her, Mary against her. And then, putting on her coat, she thought of Queenie. Queenie, who knew nothing of this and must soon learn it. Queenie, who would not sit in judgement, because she judged no-one. Opal went back to her desk and picked up the telephone.

'Why, Opal, how lovely to hear you! I was coming into the store tomorrow, as a matter of fact.' Queenie's voice was like the woman herself; clear, unaffected, warm.

'Queenie, can I come and see you? I mean now? I need to talk to you.'

'Why of course! Is something wrong?'

'Yes. But I can't talk on the telephone. You don't have guests?'

'No. And Mark's in London at the Wool Sales.'

'I'll drive over now,' Opal said. 'Bless you, Queenie!'

She could not, she thought, driving through the dark streets towards Barton, tell even Queenie about David's part in this. For the sake of everyone concerned that was a secret she knew she must bear alone, and bear as long as she lived. There was no-one in the world, save Edgar, with whom she could share that burden – and he would have nothing to do with her.

Queenie must have been watching out for her. She was at the door the moment Opal rang the bell.

'Opal dear, are you frozen?' she said. 'Come in by the fire. Let me take your coat. I've poured you a glass of sherry and you can be drinking it while I say goodnight to the children. I shan't be long.'

What a happy home this is, Opal thought, sitting close to the fire, sipping her drink. Why can't you be like Auntie Queenie, Daniel had said, and no wonder. But she could never be like Queenie. They were cast in different moulds. Queenie knew nothing of the ambition which drove some people so hard, and often so painfully. I didn't ask to be ambitious, Opal thought. It was born in me. And because I'm a woman, and ambition and femininity are ill-assorted, it's told against me. I shall never be what a man looks for in a woman. Yet she knew that even if it were possible she would not be without her ambition. It gave purpose to each day.

'There!' Queenie said, coming into the room. 'All tucked up for the night. Opal, can I get you something to eat? I suspect you've not had supper.'

'No thank you. I'm not hungry.'

Once begun, it was easy to talk to Queenie, so easy that the greatest effort was not to tell her everything. And Queenie was no fool. She had suspected for a long time that matters were not right between Opal and Edgar. But such was her unique gift that she could bring a positive sympathy, a deep feeling of support, to everyone. Her grief for Edgar in his lonely flight did not allow her to condemn Opal. If she wondered why a kind man who loved children, and his own son above all, should leave his newly-pregnant wife, she did not ask out loud, nor would she ever. She did not apportion blame in any direction, though this was not because she stood aside.

She accepts us, Opal thought. She accepts us all, exactly as we are. She doesn't ask us to be different or to measure up to some standard. For the first time since Miss Taylor's death Opal felt comforted. The tears which ran down her face now were tears of release.

'Opal, you must stay the night! It's a nasty wet one for you to drive home. In fact you must come here often in the next few months. I know Mark will want you to.'

Mark would want it, Opal knew, if only because his beloved Queenie did so. Whatever his wife did was good in his sight. The years which had driven herself and Edgar further and further apart had brought her brother and his wife ever closer to each other.

'And now I'm going to prepare some food,' Queenie said. 'I'm quite hungry myself. We'll have an omelette.'

Next morning Opal called Miss Morton into her office first thing. She would need her secretary's help over the next few months.

'I feel I owe you an explanation of the last day or

two,' Opal said. 'You must have wondered what it was all about. Well, it's true that I'm pregnant. It is also true that my husband has gone abroad. His Company wished him to spend a few months in their Toronto office, but we both hope that he will be back long before the baby is born.'

It was a fiction she had decided upon before she fell asleep last night. Leasfield, though it might like to think otherwise, was provincial and narrow. It liked its public figures – of whom she was now undoubtedly one – to lead regular, well-ordered lives, open to public scrutiny. And especially so if they were women. It had been a slight mark against her that she attended no place of worship, professed no religion. If they bought a yard of material from her shop they liked to know that the vendor was upright and honourable.

'Of course Daniel is upset. He's not yet settled into his new school. Adolescence is a difficult time. As for my mother-in-law – well, she is elderly so we must excuse her, but I'm afraid she doesn't quite see things as they are!'

She looked Miss Morton clearly in the eye.

'You can discount anything she may have said in her distress at parting with her son. There is naturally no truth in any of it. In fact I can tell you, though I do so in confidence . . .' She took a deep breath. She could hardly bear to say the words. 'Mr Hessle's wife is happily pregnant and they are both looking forward tremendously to their baby's birth. As I am to mine.

'Of course I don't wish anyone to know just yet that I'm pregnant. You know how people feel about pregnant women showing themselves in public – quite wrongly, I think. When I can no longer disguise my condition I shall take leave of absence until a few months after the baby is born. Mr Hessle will take over from me.'

The January sales had gone particularly well this year, Opal thought with satisfaction. Almost everything cleared, and at a good profit. And now the restaurant was open and beginning to do business. They could seat three hundred people for morning coffee, for a good, three-course lunch, or for afternoon or high tea. The prices were right – a shilling and tenpence for the set lunch, more if one ate *à la carte* – the menus were varied and, above all, the service was efficient and friendly under the new manager, Mr Soames.

Opal had been amazed at the number of women of all ages who were eager to work as waitresses for the low wages paid in the catering trade. She could not pay more than the usual rate, and keep her prices down, but she saw to it that her waitresses had a good nourishing meal each day, and two breaks in the staff rest room where they could put up their feet and look at a magazine.

She had felt better in health since Christmas, less inclined to sickness and with a return of her usual energy, though she tired easily.

'You have to remember you're in your mid-thirties,' the doctor told her. 'You're not a young girl. And you work far too hard. I do think that for the sake of both yourself and the baby you should give up work at Easter.'

The doctor, a woman, came into the store once a week. A room was set aside where she could be consulted by any member of the staff, at no cost to them. Opal believed that many an illness, with its consequent loss of work, was nipped in the bud by this system, and the girls related well to the sympathetic, female physician.

'I suppose I shall have to,' Opal said. 'I'm already beginning to show, and you know what people are like. By Easter I shall be six months pregnant.'

Christmas itself, which they had spent at Highcliffe, had not been easy, though in one surprising way it had been better than she had expected. Daniel had missed his father badly. He had been both consoled and upset by the arrival of a Christmas card, posted in Toronto; consoled because his father had thought of him, upset because he had sent no address. But about the baby he *had* been pleased, partly because he genuinely welcomed the addition to their small family but also, Opal discovered, for another reason.

'If Father could hear the news I just *know* he'd come back!' he said eagerly. 'If only we could contact him. Perhaps Grandma Carson might have had a bit more information than we have. My word, she'll be pleased about the baby! She's always on about having only one grandchild.'

His relationship with his grandmother had remained as unclouded as ever. Whatever she thinks about me, Opal realized, she hasn't passed it on to Daniel.

Her father's illness had been neither better nor worse over the Christmas holiday, but Mary had been worried about the winter still to come.

'He's had an offer for the farm,' she told Opal. 'I want him to accept it. It's really a question of where we would go, what we would do next.'

'I've been thinking about that,' Opal said. 'You know I still haven't made up my mind about Oak House?

What do you say if I keep it on and you and Father come to live there? You can have your own rooms if you wish. There's plenty of space.'

Mary flushed with pleasure.

'Oh, Opal, that would be marvellous! I'm so heartily sick of being stuck in Highcliffe. And Oak House would be so much better for Father. I would have to get a job, though. We couldn't live off you.'

'I've thought of that too,' Opal said. 'I shall need someone to look after the baby when I go back to the store, and Daniel in the school holidays. You're so good with children. Would you like to keep house for me and look after Daniel and the baby? I'd pay you a wage and you'd have a place to live. Besides, I'd like to have you. I know you don't always approve of me, but I'm not really difficult to live with. Anyway, most of the time I'm not there!'

Mary smiled.

'I've envied you, Opal. Perhaps I always will, a bit. But we get on well enough, so if Father agrees it's fine by me. Mind you, I'll bet Grandpa Derwent will be horrified at the thought of Father selling the farm. He thinks land is sacred. He'll hang on to it until he dies – if he ever does.'

'I think Grandpa Derwent is immortal,' Opal said. 'Eighty-four and still ruling his womenfolk with a rod of iron.'

Her father had been happy enough at the thought of moving into Oak House.

'I've had enough of this lot,' he said. 'I don't know that I was ever cut out to be a farmer. It was just something my father expected me to do.'

*   *   *

'When *do* you move house?' the doctor asked.

'Next week.'

She would not be sorry to leave Alma Place. It had not been a happy house.

'Don't you dare to get involved in the moving,' the doctor warned.

Opal left the medical room and went down to the first floor. She was always careful, these days, not to linger on Children's and Babywear, but there were courtesies to be observed and she stopped to speak to the buyer. She had not seen Mrs James Carstairs buying rompers for her grandchild. Mrs Carstairs pounced.

'Ah! I see you're interested in this merchandise!'

'Certainly,' Opal said smoothly. 'I'm interested in everything that's sold in my store.'

'But if what I hear is correct, and my eyes don't deceive me . . .' She stared frankly at Opal's figure. '. . . in this one especially! Come now, don't be coy!'

The buyer moved away. Opal saw her speak to two assistants who were whispering together.

Anger flamed in Opal's face. She clenched her hands around the notepad she was carrying.

'When *I* was in your condition,' Mrs Carstairs said, 'I never went out in public, except perhaps for a walk after dark, and then only when accompanied by my husband. We never flaunted ourselves. But then it's a different world, isn't it?'

'Not different enough,' Opal said. 'I look forward to the day when women don't have to hide what is a perfectly natural condition. When they can go anywhere they please, freely, right up to the last moment of pregnancy.'

'Now *that* is a word we *never* used!' Mrs Carstairs said.

As Opal left the department and continued on her way around the store she felt, uncomfortably, that she was being surreptitiously looked at. She was angry with the convention that caused this, angrier still that she must bow to it. But she must do so. The feelings of her customers – and she was sure that Mrs Carstair's reaction was the usual one – false though she thought them, were important. They were what she had built her business on.

When she returned to her office Miss Morton handed her a copy of the Leasfield Courier.

'I thought you should see this,' she said. 'Under "Gossip of the Day".'

Opal took it from her and read it.

A little bird tells us that a certain well-known business lady – a jewel of a lady it might be said – is in an interesting condition. We congratulate her, and commiserate with her that her husband is not by her side. Are we to assume that before long she will not be 'Open to the Public'?

'Get the editor of the Courier on the 'phone,' Opal said furiously. 'At once. Tell him that if he cares to send a reporter around, Miss Opal has a statement which might be of interest. And ask Mr Hessle if he can spare me a moment right away.'

She saw as little of David as possible these days, though of necessity they met to discuss business. When he came into her office she thought how fit and well he looked. His wife's pregnancy suited him. By this time next month he would be a father.

'Read this' she said 'And then read the statement I propose to give to the Courier.'

The paragraph appeared in the newspaper the next day.

Miss Opal (in private life Mrs Edgar Carson) has informed us that she and her husband are happily expecting a child in June. 'I shall take leave of absence from Easter until a few months after our baby is born,' she told our reporter.

'My store will carry on exactly as usual under the expert hand of my Store Manager, Mr David Hessle.'

Mr & Mrs Hessle are expecting their first child in April. A fruitful year for Opal's Store!

She left on Easter Saturday, at the end of a record day in almost all departments. On a day in June she sent another announcement to the Leasfield Courier.

To Mr and Mrs Edgar Carson (Miss Opal), the precious gift of a daughter, Emmeline.

A bare announcement, she thought, reading it as she lay in bed. It said nothing of the heartache, of her son's unavailing desire for his father's return, or the loneliness of her future. It said nothing, also, of the love which came with the new baby, which surrounded and enfolded it. My daughter shan't be like me, Opal vowed, watching the dark-haired child in her arms. I shall teach my daughter how to love, how to *be* loved.

Chapter Twelve

Afterwards, the summer of nineteen-thirty-five seemed like a dream; a pleasant dream, everyone moving lightly through it, until the moment when the nightmare took over.

Emmeline's birth had been straightforward and easy and from the moment she came into the world she was a good baby, sleeping and feeding well, seldom crying. Against her doctor's advice that she should go into a nursing home for the event, Opal had decided that her child should be born at Oak House. It had been the right decision. The child, though she seldom made her presence heard in the first few weeks, gave the house what it lacked; the feeling of a family home; three generations (Mary and her father were settled in) under the one roof. Not that they could ever be a complete family, Opal thought; children without father, wife without husband. But it was perhaps the nearest they would ever get.

In July, when Daniel came home for the summer holidays and the monthly nurse had departed, Opal rented a house at St Anne's for a month.

'Are you sure you're quite well enough?' Mary asked anxiously. 'It's early days. Emmeline's only six weeks old.'

Her sister had wanted the child to be named Mary. It was Jubilee summer, she pointed out, and it would be a compliment to the Queen as well as to herself.

But the name 'Emmeline' had come into Opal's mind – she had no idea from whence – and she liked it above all others.

'I'm as fit as a fiddle,' Opal said. 'And I've hired the largest car imaginable. We shall be chauffeur-driven, door to door. I can rest as much as I want to in St Anne's. Do you realize that Daniel is fourteen years old and he's never had a seaside holiday?'

'I'm thirty' Mary said 'and I haven't had one since I was six. Do you remember that week in Morecambe? You must have been about ten. George was Daniel's age. We went with Mother and Aunt Garnet because Father couldn't leave the farm.'

'I remember,' Opal said. It had been the long, hot summer of nineteen-eleven. They had stayed in a boarding house in a side street and her mother had shopped every morning for food which the landlady cooked for them. 'We went shrimping.'

'And saw the pierrots every day,' Mary reminded her.

The house in St Annes was on the sea front. Opal sat in the wide bay window, watching the passers-by. Or joined them, pushing Emmeline in the pram, her father by her side leading Floss, the sheep dog who because she was old, her working days over, he had refused to leave with the new owners of the farm. Mary and Daniel frequently took the tram into Blackpool, where Daniel was addicted to the newly-discovered delights of the South Shore Pleasure Beach.

'It's ridiculous,' Mary said. 'He comes off the Big Wheel looking as green as grass, and then insists on going on again the next day!'

'I might go with you one day,' Benjamin said. 'This holiday is doing me good. I feel a different man from when I was up at Highcliffe.'

'I'm glad,' Opal said. 'I feel pretty good myself.'

In fact she felt well enough to be back at work. She found herself thinking more and more about it. The July sales would be over, the autumn season not yet started. August was a quiet little *entre-acte*. Some of her customers would, like herself, be at the seaside. Prices, especially of food, were lower than they had been, so that for those who had jobs the standard of living was higher and a holiday could be afforded. It was more than likely that some of her customers, what she thought of (not meaning to be snobbish) as the lower end of her market, would be in nearby Blackpool. Her better class customers would be in Scarborough or Filey, or in St Annes itself. How much she looked forward to seeing them all again, even Mrs James Carstairs!

Though she had enjoyed it, she was not sorry when the month in St Annes was over and they were back once again in Oak House. She found herself frequently opening the diary in which the date of her return to the store was marked – Tuesday the first of October – and secretly wishing that the days would pass more quickly. But she enjoyed Emmeline, cherishing especially the moments when she held her to the breast and watched her suckle. If her milk would adjust itself she might still be able to keep on the night and early morning feeds. She enjoyed the baby's bathtime, too, though that was gradually being taken over by Mary.

It was good, also, to have Daniel at home for the long school holiday, to observe his tenderness and concern for his sister, whom he adored. But in spite of his new-found happiness Daniel seemed to fret after his father more than ever.

'Why can't we at least *try* to find him?' he asked, not

for the first time. 'We could advertise in a Toronto newspaper. He doesn't even know he's got a daughter. I'm sure if he knew that he'd want to come back!'

Once more Opal fended him off with excuses, but on the day she drove him back to school he took up the subject again. 'Why won't you?' he persisted. 'Why won't you give it a try?'

'If he wants to get in touch with us he knows where we are,' Opal pointed out. 'We must allow him to decide for himself. We mustn't try to force him.'

It hurt her that she must be less than honest with Daniel but honesty, in this case, was not the best policy.

'After all,' she said, 'we can't use little Emmeline as a sort of blackmail. And you must remember that it would be *me* he had to come back to, not just you. It was me he left.'

'And me,' Daniel said unhappily.

He was always at his most miserable when he was returning to school. He did well enough there but he did not enjoy it. He lived for the day when he would be sixteen, at which time, Opal had promised, he might leave York and start a course at the Bradford College of Art. She would have liked him to have come straight into the store with her but it was obvious that he would first have to get art out of his system.

'Not really you,' Opal assured him. 'If anyone could have kept your father it would have been you. Perhaps sometimes we're driven to a moment when our own needs are so demanding that we have to put them first. Your father's need was to get away from me. That had to take precedence even over you.'

But Daniel was not to be comforted. It was not only his father. Going back to school he was being separated from his mother, his aunt, his grandfather, and now from Emmeline, whom he loved more than he had ever thought possible. Sitting beside Opal in the car he was sunk in gloom, and though experience told him that the gloom would lift as the days went by, that was no comfort to him. He did not believe it.

By the last week in September Opal had weaned Emmeline from all except the night and early morning feeds and Mary had taken over the daytime bottle feeding.

'I really do believe, Mary, you'll be glad to see the back of me!' Opal teased. 'You'll be glad to have Emmeline to yourself.'

Mary looked up from the child on her lap. 'I don't mean it to be like that, Opal,' she said. 'It's just wonderful to me that you let me share the children.'

On the morning of the first of October Opal was up early. She had a new dress to wear today, to celebrate her return to the store, chosen from a selection she had had sent up to her. The new autumn colours were subdued, with a tendency to brown which, with her dark hair, did not suit her. But there had been one dress in Autumn Green, a lovely coppery green, dark, yet so much clearer and brighter than the old bottle green. It was perfect for her. She put on her opal pendant and took a last look at herself in the mirror. She had regained her figure quickly. She was absolutely flat.

'I shan't need a coat,' she said to Mary, walking down the stairs into the hall. 'It's quite warm.'

'I'll close the garage doors after you,' Mary said. 'Save you getting out of the car. Now remember Opal, don't work too late on your first day!'

The traffic was heavier than she had expected, as if the whole world was returning to work at the end of the summer. She was thrilled by the thought of the day ahead. She must see David first, get up to date – though she had had reports from him during her absence and all seemed to be going well. On a personal level she did not look forward to meeting him. There was a breach between them which would never be healed though, strangely, she no longer bore him malice for making her pregnant. How could she when she had Emmeline? But then she never thought of her baby as having anything whatever to do with David Hessle. Emmeline was hers and hers alone, as if she had been born of an immaculate conception.

She would do her walk-around early today, renew all her ties. And today was the day of the weekly staff meeting. She had forgotten to tell Mary that she would be a little late home because of that. When the store came in sight on her right, bright and uncommonly clean-looking in the smoky town, she tingled with excitement. She drove along the front of the store, quickly glancing in the windows, and at the far corner made a right turn towards the car park. She had no knowledge of, nor later did she ever remember, the car which came towards her on the opposite side of the road. All she knew, all she ever recalled, was the red film which came over her eyes, a redness in which she seemed to drown, in the second before she lost consciousness.

The surgeon backoned Mary over to the window, turning his back on the patient in the bed and speaking in a low voice.

'Can she hear us?' Mary asked anxiously.

'I can't be sure,' he admitted. 'We don't know how far a patient in a coma is aware of what's going on.

Sometimes we think not at all. At other times it seems as though some outside stimulus, perhaps something to which the patient would, when conscious, have a positive reaction, has a marked effect. But there's so much of which we're ignorant.'

'My sister will get better, won't she?' Mary asked. 'Please be frank with me. There are children . . .'

He looked with compassion at the white-faced woman who looked as though she had not slept for a week. He so often had to answer this question, yet experience never made it any easier.

'I will be frank,' he said. 'She's had an extremely bad accident. Her head injuries are most serious. We've done all we can in theatre. Now it's up to good nursing and Nature. But I should say she's a strong young woman, in good health. If she's a fighter . . .'

'She's a fighter!'

'Then she has a chance.'

'Thank God,' Mary said.

'I would like to keep her in this private wing,' the surgeon said. 'She will need constant supervision for a long time yet, and while we do our best in the general hospital, we're always short-staffed. But it's expensive. Perhaps you would like to think about it, Miss Derwent.'

'I will. My sister isn't without money, though of course I don't know the extent of her finances. But I'm sure she must stay here for the time being.'

'I'll look in on her again later,' he said. 'And of course I'm always on call if I should be needed. I think it might help the patient if members of her family – or close friends – people to whom she relates well in life – could be here as much as possible, at least during the day.'

'Day or night, Mr Talbot,' Mary said. 'I don't suppose my sister knows the difference right now.'

As he left the room, Queenie came in. She put her arms around Mary and kissed her.

'You look all in, Mary.'

'I am rather tired. Emmeline cried a good deal in the night. It's not like her. Perhaps it's because she had to be completely weaned all of a sudden.'

'Would you like me to take her for a few days?' Queenie asked. 'Let you get some rest?'

'No thank you, Queenie. She's used to me. Besides, in a strange way she's a consolation. The same with Daniel. Thank you for fetching him home from school.'

They stood by the bed and looked at Opal, lying so still beneath the heavy bandages, intently watched by a nurse for any sign of change.

'I don't know where we're going to put all the flowers and cards which keep arriving,' the nurse said. 'As you can see, we've no more room in here, and still they come.'

Queenie sat down and took Opal's hand in her own.

'Dear Opal! She's never understood how much people admire her! In spite of all her success she never thinks well of herself as a person. She's a woman surrounded by love which she doesn't know how to accept.'

Sister came back into the room as Queenie was speaking.

'That's a pity,' she said. 'I have the feeling that if she could know of all these good wishes, this tremendous goodwill, it might help her. I've been talking with Mr Talbot. We wonder if there's anything at all you can think of which might arouse Mrs Carson? Something which might pierce an abyss, the depth of which we don't understand. What does she care for most in the world?'

Mary and Queenie looked at each other.

'Opal's store, and her children, Daniel and Emmeline,' Queenie said.

'Well we can't bring the store to her,' Sister said. 'But the children . . . Her son, of course, has been here a great deal. But the baby . . . she's four months old, isn't she? If Mrs Carson were to hear her baby cry . . . ? Of I dare say it's fanciful, but what have we to lose? A baby's cry of need for its mother. Who knows how deep that goes?'

'Perhaps you're right,' Mary said hesitantly. 'Perhaps that's why Emmeline's cried so much these last few days. Being taken so suddenly off the breast . . . missing her mother's presence, not just food.'

'I'll contact Mr Talbot,' Sister said.

'In the meantime I shall stay here a little longer,' Queenie said, 'But, Mary, I insist you go home and get some rest.'

'Your sister-in-law is right, Miss Derwent,' Sister said gently. 'You're going to need all your strength in the next few weeks.' Whichever way it goes, she thought.

'My car's outside,' Queenie said. 'Ask Freeman to take you home. And if Mr Talbot should want you to bring Emmeline in later, I'll fetch you both.'

Later that evening Queenie returned to the hospital, accompanied by Mary, carrying Emmeline who was fast asleep. As they entered Opal's room a weary-faced Daniel walked behind them.

'Daniel wanted to come,' Mary told Sister. 'He thought he might be able to help.'

Sister looked at the boy; a lanky fourteen-year-old, badly in need of sleep and rest which he could not get;

stony-faced in his effort to be brave, but unable to hide the despair and helplessness in his eyes as he looked towards the still form on the bed.

'I'm sure he will,' she said kindly. 'Perhaps it would be a good idea if Daniel were to sit by the bed and hold the baby, instead of you doing so, Miss Derwent.'

It would make no difference to the patient, she thought, but the boy might feel he was doing something. She watched as the aunt handed the baby to Daniel, noted the careful, loving way he took his sister and held her in his arms. We must fight for this patient, she told herself. We must save her for these two children.

'It's Emmeline's feed time,' Mary said. 'She should waken any time now.'

As if she knew what was expected of her the baby wakened, screwed up her face and began to cry; the lusty cry of a healthy, four-month-old baby demanding attention.

'No, don't try to soothe her, Daniel!' Sister said. 'However cruel it seems for the moment, let her cry.'

The baby's cries, raucous, angry at being ignored, rent the air in the small room. On and on. The three women and the boy watched the bruised, lacerated face of the woman on the bed. Tears streamed down Daniel's face and at last he could bear it no more. He leaned over the bed and his loud cry rang out above the noise from the baby in his arms.

'Mother! Mother, you must come back! It's Daniel! I want you!'

He collapsed, sobbing, continuing to cry out. Mary took the baby from him. Queenie knelt down and took him in her arms. Only Sister saw Opal open her eyes.

*   *   *

It was a slow recovery. A little each day, and there were days when she seemed to slip back, called by some dark country of the mind, then somehow rallied again. It was a month before those so carefully watching knew that she would live. Christmas came and went and the winter of nineteen-thirty-six gave way to spring and then to early summer before Opal left hospital.

'But she has a long way to go yet,' Mr Talbot warned. 'She needs rest and quiet for many months to come. No worries. No business affairs. You must be very strict with her.'

'I will be,' Mary promised.

'Allow me one meeting with my Store Manager,' Opal pleaded. 'Just so that I can be assured that all is going well.'

Mr Talbot shook his head. 'It's against my better judgement,' he said. 'But one very short meeting to set your mind at rest, and then nothing more until I allow it.' He would have a word with Miss Derwent, get her to ensure that everything went smoothly.

On a morning in July David Hessle came to Oak House. It was a hot day. Opal was lying on a *chaise longue* in the garden, in the shade of the giant oak from which the house took its name, when Mary brought him to her. She admired his composure on seeing her. She knew how awful she looked, though Mr Talbot said the scars would fade with time. Her hair, though it was now growing well, was much too short to be fashionable. There was grey in it, too, though she was not yet thirty-six.

'I'm glad to hear you're recovering well,' David said.

'I hope to be back in the store for the Christmas season,' Opal told him.

'Well, I've been warned that we must keep our meeting short and that I mustn't overtire you.'

'As if hearing about my store could ever tire me!' Opal said scornfully. 'But if your time is to be limited please tell me everything as quickly as you can. How is the July sale going? Is the restaurant making a good profit?'

She had a hundred questions. He answered them all.

'I'm very grateful to you for taking care of things,' she said. 'I think you should get yourself an assistant, someone who'll really be of help to you over the next few months, until I return.'

'Actually,' David said, 'I did so a few months ago. As you rightly say, it's too much for one person. I took Miss Nash, from Toys. She's shaping well.'

'Miss Nash?'

'She was a temporary assistant on Toys two Christmases ago. I don't suppose you'll remember her.'

She didn't. Too much had happened.

'Here's Mary coming to see me off!' David sounded relieved, jumped to his feet.

Mary crossed the lawn hand in hand with Emmeline who, at thirteen months, was walking well. It was David's first sight of the child. If he feels any emotion, Opal thought, he is not showing it. The smile on his face remained fixed and his eyes revealed nothing. She herself felt nothing beyond the pleasure which the sight of her little daughter always gave her.

The child started to run, tottered, and overbalanced by Opal's chair.

'She is exactly like you, Opal,' David said. 'Exactly!'

Mary picked up Emmeline and set her on her feet again.

'Yes, isn't she,' she said. 'There seems to be nothing of Edgar in her.'

Opal had thought often about Edgar in the long days of her convalescense, but it was not the affair with David, but the years before, which ate at her conscience. 'If it had been a loving marriage,' Edgar had said. He was right. She knew now, she had learned painfully over the last months, that it was the warmth of love and affection, given and received, which made life worth while. She knew she would have died but for the love which had surrounded her, which had refused to let her go. Well, wherever he was, perhaps Edgar had found someone who would give him the affection he needed. But she would like him to know she had come to understand, and that she was sorry.

She had thought, too, about Mrs Carson, and longed to make her peace with the woman who had been so good to her. In the end she spoke to Mary about it.

'I want you to ask Mrs Carson if she will come to see me. Try to persuade her.'

'It will only upset you,' Mary objected. 'You know the doctor says you're not to be worried.'

'I shall worry far more lying here, thinking about it,' Opal said.

Mrs Carson came, and the meeting which Opal had wanted, yet dreaded, proved easier than she (and probably her mother-in-law, she thought) had expected.

'We've a lot to forgive each other for,' Mrs Carson said. 'Let bygones be bygones.'

'I have something to tell you,' Opal said. 'I intend to try to trace Edgar. I shall put advertisements in the Canadian Press – Toronto – and deposit a letter for him at the newspaper office if they'll let me. Perhaps you could send a letter, too.'

'I can't write,' Mrs Carson said. 'Neither me nor Percy can write. Edgar knows that. But if I could just know where he was, even if I can't see him again, I'd be happy.'

Opal wrote that night – a short letter because she could not yet hold a pen well.

Dear Edgar, (she wrote) I have been thinking of you a great deal lately, realizing what I did to you. I am writing to ask you if you can find it in yourself to forgive me.

Daniel is well. He never forgets you. I would like it if we could be friends, for his sake. I saw your mother today. She longs to know where you are, as we all do. Please, if nothing else, let us know that.

She said nothing of Emmeline, or of her accident – which was why she signed and sealed the letter before telling Daniel what she had decided.

'Here it is,' she said. 'But you and Auntie Mary must see to the rest. I can't quite manage it.'

'I'll do *anything*!' Daniel said. 'Anything! Oh Mother, do you think he'll come back to us?'

'I doubt that,' Opal said. She was not sure that she wanted that. 'If we can establish contact with him, that's the most we should hope for.'

But as the months went by, as advertisement after advertisement appeared, with no word from Edgar, even that hope died in Opal. It never died in Daniel.

With each week that passed Opal grew stronger. But in spite of her pleas that she was as fit as a fiddle the doctor refused to let her go back to the store for the pre-Christmas season, or for the following January sales.

'If you progress as well as you are doing now, and if you behave yourself,' he promised her, 'you can start work at the beginning of February.'

With that she had to be content. Remembering a previous occasion when she had done so, she dare not mark off the days in her diary. But in her head she kept a count, and knew it would not be long now.

Chapter Thirteen

'What I want to do most of all, right away, is to walk around the store,' Opal said. 'See how everything's going, say hello to everyone. I've been looking forward to it so long.'

'Then I'll come with you,' David offered. 'Explain one or two changes and so on.'

'No. You know I've always liked to do this on my own.'

She was out of her office and hurrying down the stairs before he could reply. She made for the side door, intending to look at all the display windows before starting inside the store. She felt tremendously fit this morning, ready for anything. It was wonderful to be back.

But not ready for this, she thought, fifteen minutes later! What has happened? What has happened to my beautiful store?

At first she thought that it was just something wrong with the side windows, that they were still heaped with the sordid detritus of the January sales because the window dressers had been busy along the front. It was annoying, but she would quickly deal with it. But when she turned the corner to the windows which faced on to the main road it was exactly the same. The sale remnants – unsold skirts, jumpers, hats, tea-towels, gloves, materials, china – were still unattractively on show, though the sale was over. Not a single window had been cleared and the new season's display which custom said must begin just before the sale ended had not been started. In a fashion window two naked models had been left undraped, a vulgarity undreamt of in any decent store. Moreover, there was not a sign of a window dresser at work.

She marched swiftly into the store and made for the nearest telephone, on Haberdashery.

'Staff Office? Have someone find Mr Lambert and report to me at once! Ground floor, main entrance. Well if he's left send whoever's taken his place as Senior Window Dresser. *I* don't know where you'll find him. All I know is he's not where he should be!'

She turned from the telephone and saw a woman impatiently drumming her fingers on the counter. There was no assistant in sight.

'Could you find someone to serve me, Miss,' the woman said. 'I'll swear I've been waiting here ten minutes!'

'I'm sorry about that. I'm not quite sure what's happened but I'll be pleased to serve you myself. What can I get for you?' Opal was trying hard to control her feelings, to speak pleasantly.

'I want five yards of bias binding, navy, to match this.' She held out a piece of material.

'I'm sure we shall have that,' Opal said.

She opened the drawer marked 'bindings, bias'. True enough, there were some cards of binding in the drawer. There was also lace, tape, ribbons, and an odd card of grey darning wool. The ends of the bindings and laces had not been pinned after use and were coming adrift. She rummaged through the drawer.

'Ah! Here we are! But we seem to have only the one

233

shade of navy at the moment. Let's see if it matches.'
She placed it against the material.

'It doesn't really,' the customer said. 'It's too light.
More of a French navy.'

'You're quite right,' Opal agreed. 'It won't do! Were
you wanting to use it today?'

'Tomorrow at the latest. I'll try Miller's.'

'Oh, but I'm sure we can get it for you,' Opal said
quickly. 'If you like to leave you name and address we'll
do that today and we'll put it in the afternoon post to
you. We'll enclose a bill and you can pay next time you
come into the store. I dare say you come fairly often?'

'I used to,' the woman said. 'You wouldn't believe
what a good store this used to be.'

As the woman was leaving the haberdashery assistant
returned. She smiled happily at Opal.

'Ta! I had to go to powder my nose, so to speak.
Miss Titmarsh on ribbons said she'd keep an eye open,
but she seems to have disappeared.'

'You know the rules!' Opal snapped. 'No department
is ever to be left unattended. If Miss Titmarsh was not
free to relieve you, you should have remained at your
post until she was.'

'Here, I didn't know that was a rule!' the girl said.
'Come to that, I don't know who *you* are!'

'You soon will,' Opal said grimly. 'Where's your
buyer?'

'Miss Foster? Well she had a rotten cold on Saturday
so I reckon she must be tucked up in bed with a hot
water bottle.'

She looked again at Opal, saw, under the make-up,
the scar running down the left side of her face. 'Oh
Lord,' she wailed. 'You're not Miss Opal?'

But Opal had gone, walking swiftly away towards a

man in a brown overall who stood by the main entrance.

'Are you the Senior Window Dresser?' she asked sharply.

'Yes Miss. The thing is, Miss, no-one has given me the plans for the new displays. I can't dress windows until I know what's to go in them.'

'I want action, not excuses,' Opal interrupted. 'Go around to every buyer, tell them Miss Opal sent you and that they are to give you a selection of their new season's goods immediately. Tell them the theme is "Winter into Spring". We want plenty of yellow and green to brighten things up. And while you're doing that see to it that your assistants are cleaning the windows. They're filthy! I shall expect every window in the store to be cleaned and dressed today. If it means working overtime, then you must do that. Now get going!'

At first she told herself she had simply made a bad start, picked on two inefficient employees. But it was more than that. Everywhere was the same. As she progressed, her temper rising, her footsteps quickening as she marched from department to department, she saw all around her evidence of neglect such as she could never have dreamt of. Assistants chatting in corners, dirty showcases carelessly dressed, counters cluttered and, worst of all, customers unattended. She had been away less than two years. How could her wonderful store, which had run like clockwork, which had been a byword far beyond Leasfield for service and efficiency – how could it have come to this? This seemingly fourth-rate, run-down emporium?

She advanced into gowns, her high heels viciously

stabbing into the carpet. An assistant sat on a chair behind a counter.

'Are you ill? Or menstruating?' Opal demanded.

'No!' The girl looked startled.

'Then stand up!' Opal ordered. 'A chair is provided in each department for any assistant who is unwell, or unduly fatigued. You are not ill, and at ten-o-clock on a Monday morning, with not a customer in sight, you can hardly be fatigued. Where is Miss Baxter?'

'Gone to coffee.' the assistant said.

Opal walked around the department, examined the dresses on the rails, looked into the fitting rooms.

'Tell Miss Baxter that Miss Opal will see her later,' she said. 'In the meantime there are several gowns hanging in the fitting rooms. Get them back on the rails where they belong. They won't sell if they're out of sight! If there is a Junior, get her to clean the mirrors. If there isn't, then do it yourself.'

In the Fabric department she ordered that bolts of cloth be replaced on the shelves where they belonged. In Glass and China she demanded that the whole stock be dusted forthwith. She would have liked to have picked up the entire stock, piece by piece, and smashed it against the wall.

Last of all she went into the restaurant. By now she knew what to expect. Spotty tablecloths and messy cruets. My beautiful restuarant, she thought miserably. She sat at a table in the corner, which used to be reserved for her. She was trembling from head to foot with a mixture of rage and shock. She clenched her fists, took long, deep breaths to prevent herself breaking into angry tears.

'Why, Miss Opal! How nice to see you back! Shall I get you some coffee?'

She looked up into the bright, shining face of Kate Lewis, the waitress who always looked after her. Kate had worked in the store since opening day. At least *she* had not changed. She was as immaculate as ever in her black dress, snow-white apron, pleated cap threaded with velvet ribbon. And then, suddenly, Opal realized that nothing else around her had changed, either. The starched tablecloths were in pristine condition, there were posies of fresh flowers on each table, the cutlery and cruets gleamed. It was all exactly as it used to be, exactly as she had thought of it in the long time she had been away.

'I don't believe it,' she whispered, looking around her. 'I don't believe it. How can it be?'

The waitress looked at her with compassion.

'I can't pretend not to know what you're talking about, Miss Opal. I knew you had a shock coming to you, and as you walked into the restaurant I could see you'd had it. I just wish you'd come in here first. I'd have warned you.'

'Why *did* no-one warn me? Why did no-one say anything?'

Kate shrugged her shoulders. 'Ask me another! Of course we didn't know you were coming today, else it might not have been quite so bad.'

'No,' Opal said. 'No-one did. I'd arranged to start on Thursday but I changed my mind at the last minute, decided to come in earlier. I didn't tell anyone because I wanted it to be a surprise. Well, it was that all right!'

'It's a shame,' Kate said. 'Many's the time I've said to the girls "Miss Opal would be grieved to the heart if she could see what's happening." But you see *here* we have Mr Soames. That makes all the difference. *He* didn't change, even when the buyers' commission was cut, and his with it.'

'The buyers' commission cut?' Opal could not believe what she was hearing. It was like some bad dream.

'Well, everybody's commission, right through the store. But the buyers feel it most, don't they, because they've most to lose. But Mr Soames didn't let it make any difference to him and of course we still get our tips.'

Mr Soames. She had almost forgotten him, though she herself had engaged him to manage the new restaurant when it first opened.

'Mr Soames is a bit of a martinet,' Kate said. 'A bit like yourself if you'll excuse me saying so. It's what's needed. Oh he's always fair – like you were, Miss Opal. And he looks after us like you did. He's kindness itself when necessary. You might say he's the heart of this restaurant. But the heart went out of the store when you went, Miss Opal! I hear what customers say when they sit at my tables and I've heard them use those very words, more than once. Well, let's hope you've brought it back.'

'Oh I have,' Opal said slowly. 'I have!'

In the last hour she had felt that all the world's anger was contained in her; that it choked in her throat and soured in her stomach. Now, though the fury and the rage were still in her, they were combined with a fierce, grim determination.

'Let's say that you and Mr Soames have put new heart into me! Everything's going to be all right in the end, I promise you, Kate. Just you watch me!'

But to most of the people she had seen this morning it would seem, for some time to come, a heart of iron. She felt that she had a ball of iron where her heart

238

should be and that iron ran in her veins. And David
Hessle would be the first to suffer. She would gladly
kill him.

'Give Mr Soames my compliments,' she said to Kate.
'Tell him I'll see him tomorrow. I'm going to be very
busy the rest of today.'

Opal burst into David Hessle's office without knocking. He was comfortably seated behind his large desk.
A young woman with corn-blonde hair bent over the
desk beside him, their heads close together as they
studied a sheet of paper. They looked up as Opal
entered. David, half rising from his chair, was clearly
apprehensive, disconcerted. Not so the girl. The look
she gave Opal was defiant, self-satisfied. That something was going on Opal did not doubt, but it did not
concern her now. All that mattered was her store, that
here was the man to whom she had entrusted her
most precious possession, here was the man who had
wrecked it, perhaps beyond repair.

'You've not met Miss Nash,' David said nervously.

'Please leave us at once!' Opal did not look at the
girl as she spoke to her.

'You'd better go,' David said.

The door closed noisily behind her. Opal had not
taken her eyes off David.

'What have you done? How dare you do this to me?
How dare you?' She hurled the words at him; cold,
venomous, as if she would like to spit poison with them.

David sank back into his chair, raised his hands as
if to fend her off.

'Opal, don't fly off the handle! Let me explain.
Nothing has been easy these last two years. Business
hasn't been easy!'

'Business is never easy! Do you think I found it so?

239

You undertook the job – for which, incidentally, you were paid a higher rate than most people in the retail world – and you didn't do it! You cheated me, David, as certainly as if you'd embezzled my money.' Her voice was hoarse, trembling.

'That's a harsh judgement, Opal,' he said defensively. 'You don't know all the facts. I can explain them to you.'

'I've seen enough of the facts in front of me this morning. Filth, apathy, carelessness. An almost total lack of discipline. But worst of all, you've damaged what I hold most dear – my relationship I had with my customers, the confidence they had in me!'

'How can you possibly know that?' David demanded.

'I do know it. And you can't deny it. You've been totally incompetent. As for your dishonesty, I've yet to find out how far that has gone! But it's what you've done to my customers that I care about most.'

David leaned back in his chair. His abject air had vanished and the look he gave Opal now was insolent.

'Well now,' he sneered. 'You could never expect me to come up to Miss Opal, could you? Who could ever do that? Miss Opal, Queen of Storekeepers!'

'And I will be again!' Opal shouted. How dare he mock her! 'But not with your help! I'm giving you a month's notice from this minute. It being February it will mercifully be a short month. During that time you will have nothing whatever to do with the running of the store.'

Somewhere, deep underneath her anger, her heart ached that she should be saying these words to David Hessle. How could such a thing be? She had realized more than two years ago that in personal relationships he was weak; that the strength for which she had admired him had never been his. It was a quality with which she had endowed him because she had longed for a strong man in her life. But she had always thought, until today, that in business he was reliable, talented, trustworthy.

'You can't do that!' he objected.

'Can't I? It's my store. I can do what I like! There'll be a staff meeting tomorrow evening. You can attend if you wish, or you can leave me to announce your departure.'

'I'm sure you'll do it very well,' he said dryly. 'For the sake of your store you won't say anything cheap. Actually, you might find there are some people who quite like me, won't want me to go.'

'After you've cut their commission? Don't be absurd. You've cheated them as you've cheated me. But if anyone wants to leave with you, they're welcome. And now I'd like the Minutes of the last two years' Staff Meetings. Have them sent up to my office at once.'

She turned to leave. She could not bear to be with him a moment longer. He called out after her as she went towards the door.

'We haven't been having staff meetings. People have better things to do after work – but you wouldn't understand that.'

Over lunch, which Kate brought on a tray to her office, Opal studied the accounts. It did not surprise her to see in the figures concrete evidence of falling sales and diminished profits, but what worried her more was the large amount of money owing to suppliers. The total was appalling. On starting the store she had been grateful for the lengthy credit many of her suppliers had allowed her, and as soon as she was established she had repaid that trust, and ensured their further good service, by paying her bills promptly. Desperately, she checked the figures again. These bills must be paid or her supplies would be cut off. Somewhere, she was dreadfully sure, she would find letters saying just that. There were going to have to be so many economies in the store; streamlining; perhaps merging of departments; cutting down of staff. It would not be popular.

She looked up as Miss Carver, who ran the Staff Department, entered.

'Ah, Miss Carver! I know Miss Morton left when she married her young man in Accounts. I can't manage without a secretary but I don't want us to take on any more staff at the moment. Is there anyone in your office, or perhaps in Accounts, who could be spared to help me? It would mean her present job being shared out among the rest of you, but for the moment that's how it is.'

'Well,' Miss Carver said thoughtfully, 'I suppose you could borrow Mrs Sylvester. She's an older woman . . . a widow . . .'

'Has she got lots of common sense,' Opal interrupted. 'Is she a hard worker?'

'Yes to both those questions.'

'Then send her along. At once if you can. I've got several things for her to do.'

She liked the look and sound of Mrs Sylvester; plump, neat, grey-haired, with a quiet voice and a matter-of-fact manner.

'The first thing I want you to do' Opal said 'is to get a notice right around the store, to be read and initialled by everyone on every department, from the buyer to the Junior, about tomorrow's staff meeting. Six o'clock in the restaurant. Make it clear that I want a full attendance.'

'And the agenda?'

'There isn't one. What I have to say won't fit into nice, neat headings. And just before you start that will you phone Mr Hessle and ask him to send Miss Nash up with the Customer Relations file? You can use this phone.'

Mrs Sylvester looked up a moment later.

'Mr Hessle says he can't lay hands on it at the minute.'

Opal took the telephone from her.

'You will lay hands on it and send Miss Nash to my office with it inside fifteen minutes!' she told him.

When Miss Nash came, carrying the file, she wore an expression which Opal, without knowing where, recognized as one she had seen before. Silently brazen, as if she had a secret which pleased her and would anger Opal. And then Opal remembered. It was the look she had seen on the face of Connie Browning a long time ago. So her impression of Miss Nash and David had been correct.

'I'd like to speak to you in private,' Miss Nash said.

'You can say anything you have to say in front of Mrs Sylvester,' Opal said. 'Make it short. I'm busy.'

'Very well then. I hear that Mr David is leaving. If that's the case I'm afraid I can't stay.'

'I quite agree,' Opal said.

'So I'm giving in my notice.'

'Wrong!' Opal said. 'I've already spoken to Staff Office. Your cards and your wages in lieu of notice are ready for you. You'll leave now and pick up what's due to you on your way out.'

'But you can't do that!' Miss Nash protested.

'As I recently told Mr Hessle,' Opal said, 'in this place I can do as I like. Good day to you!'

She stayed late that evening, working out what she would say at the staff meeting next day. By the time she arrived home Emmeline had been in bed and asleep for two hours.

'You look exhausted,' Mary said.

'I am. Why didn't you tell me about the store, Mary?'

Mary reddened. 'I wanted to warn you,' she said. 'I didn't know what to do. I don't go into the store much, as you know, so I wasn't quite sure about things. But what I thought most important was that you shouldn't be worried. Queenie thought so too. We discussed it between us and came to that decision.

'I think it was the wrong one.'

'Perhaps it's not as bad as you think,' Mary suggested. 'You know what a perfectionist you are.'

'On the contrary, I dare say it's worse than I think,' Opal said. 'I'm pretty sure I haven't seen everything yet.'

Opal was encouraged to see that most of the staff were at the meeting. Whether they had turned up from a sense of duty or merely from curiosity hardly mattered at this stage. She was also pleased to see that David Hessle was not present.

Standing on the small platform which had been arranged for her so that, tiny of stature though she was, she could be seen by everyone, she fingered her opal pendant and waited for silence. When it came she began to speak.

'I can't tell you how glad I am to be back! I'd like

you to know that I'm totally fit and in good health. I've never felt better in my life.'

There was a round of polite applause.

'I want to thank those of you who have served me loyally while I've been away. But now that I am back I think the time has come to make changes in the store. I'm sure you will agree with me.'

She looked at the rows of expressionless faces, trying to read the thoughts behind them.

'First of all,' she continued, 'I have to tell you that Mr Hessle will be leaving us at the end of the month. Mr Hessle has been of untold help to me in the past, but now he is moving on. He is sorry he could not be here this evening to tell you this himself.'

In the small movements of heads and hands, the slight shifting of bodies, she detected the signs of uneasiness.

'And now' she said 'I'm going to come straight to the point. This store is not what it was when I left to have my daughter two years ago. It has deteriorated sadly. In some ways it has deteriorated almost beyond belief. Those of you who were with me then – and looking around I can see many of you, though others I had hoped to see on my return are missing – you will know that what I say is true. It is now my intention, without wasting any time, to make this store what it once was! And that I can only do with the help and co-operation of each one of you, from the most Senior Buyer to the most Junior Assistant. I need to know that I can count on you. So, if there is even one amongst you who cannot give me that co-operation, then it is better that I should know. Please come and tell me tomorrow.'

A man on the back row jumped to his feet.

'*We* thought we could count on our commission,' he shouted. 'But we were let down! We're expected to work hard, give everything we've got to Opal's store, but where are the incentives?'

Heads swerved round to look at him, nodded in agreement.

It was a sign of the times, a sign that jobs were at last a little more plentiful, Opal thought, that he should dare to speak so. She did not blame him.

'If you had not mentioned that, Mr Bell, I would have. I feel bound to say that it was not with my knowledge that your commissions were cut . . .'

'Not cut – cut *out*!' someone called.

'I've gone into the question carefully,' Opal continued. 'I'm happy to tell you that it is my intention to restore your commission from the end of this month!'

She interrupted the roar of approval which went around the meeting.

'Wait! Please let me finish. I must tell you that the figures I have seen yesterday and today do not warrant me taking this step. The profit margins are far too low. But I am taking a gamble. I am gambling, as I first did when I opened this store eight years ago, on the loyalty and co-operation of my staff.

'There can be no commission without sales, no sales without customers. And it is you as well as I who must bring back the customers. People have more money to spend than when I first started in business but there is also more competition. Prospects of success are brightest when what we offer – be it goods or services – are better than those offered by anyone else in the area. That is the way it was with Opal's store – and will be again!'

She definitely had the meeting in her hand now. She

could feel the power returning to her and she knew that, however difficult the going was over the next few months, she would get there in the end. She held up her hand to quell the chatter which had broken out.

'I want you and our customers to feel secure, to have a sense of continuity in the very special world of a well-appointed, well-run store. Remember, where the customer is concerned, that you are not only selling the goods. Whether it is a yard of elastic or a fur stole you are handing across the counter, you are selling Opal's store.

'I told you there must be changes if we are to become strong again. What these will be, when they will take place, we shall work out together.'

She sat down. The applause now went far beyond politeness. When the meeting broke up she went and stood at the door of the restaurant, shaking hands, receiving good wishes. She hoped that the same mood would be upon everyone tomorrow when she started visiting the departments, began the work of pulling everything into shape.

She beckoned to Mrs Sylvester.

'Would you find Mr Soames and ask him if he could spare me a few minutes in my office before he goes home?'

She had it in mind, had had since yesterday's visit to the restaurant, to offer Mr Soames David Hessle's job. She hoped he would accept it.

The most worrying thing she had come across so far was not the accounts, not David Hessle, not the state of the store, even, but the contents of the Customer Relations file. After the staff meeting she had taken it home with her to study it more carefully, hoping that on a second reading it would seem less disastrous. It did not. It bulged with complaints: of sub-standard goods, delays in deliveries, mistakes in almost every area, but most of all with complaints of poor service; of indifference, indolence and, occasionally, insolence on the part of her staff.

It was the most serious discovery of all because her customers were the reason for her store's existence. And because she knew that for every customer who took the trouble to write and complain, there would be a dozen who silently went elsewhere. What made it all so much worse was that, as far as she could see, not one of the complaints had been dealt with. This, she resolved, was something she must attend to personally.

'In the meantime,' she said to Mrs Sylvester on the morning after the meeting, 'I want you to write to each of these customers – just a short letter. Explain that I have only now seen their complaint, that I'm looking into it and I'll be in touch with them later. Say that if they wish they can come in and see me. I'll sign all the letters.'

One of the many good things Opal had already discovered about Mrs Sylvester was that she could write a good letter without every phrase being dictated by her boss.

'Very well,' Mrs Sylvester said. 'And before you go down into the store, Mrs David Hessle is waiting to see you. I put her in my office.'

Connie? Why? If it was to plead for her husband's job back it was no go.

'Mr Hessle isn't in this morning,' Mrs Sylvester said.

'I see. Well show her in.'

It was not only Connie who came into the office. She was accompanied by her small daughter. Opal gasped at the sight of her. The child was the image of David. The same red hair, clear skin, grey-green eyes, beautiful features. Though she never thought of Emmeline as having anything to do with David, she realized with a jolt that this was how her own daughter could have looked, instead of being a small replica of herself.

'Yes, little Dinah's the spit of her dad, isn't she? Connie said. 'Let's hope she doesn't take after him in character!'

'I won't beat about the bush,' she went on. 'David has hopped it. Packed up and went last night. Need I say who with?'

What have I *done*, Opal thought, what *have* I done?

'In case you're thinking of blaming yourself, don't bother,' Connie said. 'I've seen it coming. I knew he'd go sooner or later, if not with her then with someone else. I haven't come here to reproach you for sacking him. I've come to ask if there's any money due to him. I'm short.'

Opal hesitated. 'I'm not sure that I should . . .'

'Well you can't give it to him because you don't know where he is – though I happen to think he's gone to Manchester because that's where *she* comes from. So if you were to give me the cash to hand over to him – well, it's off your plate isn't it?'

'Very well,' Opal said. 'I'll give you a month's salary. 'Go into the restaurant and have some coffee while I have it made up for you. But how will you manage afterwards? I'd like to offer you a job here – you have some experience – but right now I'm not setting anyone on.'

'Oh don't you worry about me, love,' Connie said airily. 'What's sauce for the goose is sauce for the gander and I've got my friends, only too willing to step in when I say the word! Well, that's that then! Who would have thought it would come to this?'

As soon as Connie had left Opal rang Mr Soames and asked him to come to her office. When Kate Lewis had first mentioned George Soames yesterday morning Opal had hardly remembered what he looked like. Then, last evening, when he had come to her office she wondered how she could possibly have forgotten him. It was not that his appearance was in any way remarkable. He was a man of medium height, as dark as herself but, though a couple of years older than she, with no grey in his hair. The clear hazel eyes which looked directly into her own were kindly and honest. She felt an immediate trust in him. Kate had described him as a bit of a martinet, but it was not apparent in his manner. But then Kate had also described her as a martinet – which was absurd!

'Ah! Thank you for coming so soon,' she said. 'You already know how pleased I am that you've consented to be my Store Manager. Now I'm going to ask you if you could take over as quickly as possible. The very first minute your deputy in the restaurant can replace you. I hope it won't be long. There's so much to be done and I really do need you.'

Chapter Fourteen

'So you agree with me, now that Miss Tyler is leaving us, that Miss Foster should be asked to add Hosiery, Gloves and Trimmings to her present Haberdashery, Handkerchiefs and Scarves?' Opal said.

George Soames, sitting on the opposite side of the desk, nodded approval.

'Absolutely. As we've said before, the more we can amalgamate several departments under the one buyer, the better. It means lower expenses on buyers' trips to London, or Manchester. And of course it saves a salary.'

'Not quite,' Opal reminded him. 'A buyer who takes on extra departments must be paid more. Also, a buyer with several departments, even if they're small ones, must have an under-buyer – though that's a job which can be combined with First Sales. Most of our First Sales will be all the better for having the added responsibility. Like you, I'm a great believer in encouraging oeople to do more than they think they're capable of.'

'So will you see Miss Foster, or shall I?' he asked.

'I think jointly. I've always done it myself but I think now, when it's a question of senior posts, we should do it together.'

She picked up the telephone. 'Mrs Sylvester, will you ask Miss Foster if she can spare me a few minutes right away?'

Miss Foster was the first buyer to be asked to take on extra territory. After that Opal planned that Sports Equipment should be moved to the ground floor and placed under the wing of Mr Bell, of Menswear. Ladies Sportswear – swimsuits, hiking shorts and so on – would be amalgamated into skirts, jumpers and blouses in a department for which Opal still searched for the right name. These moves were part of a plan worked out by herself and George Soames soon after he had taken up his new post, but because of Opal's proviso that no buyer who wished to continue working for her, and was willing to work hard, should be either demoted or sacked, it was only now that the scheme could be started. When a buyer left, unless no other solution could be found, he or she was not to be replaced; at least not until better times.

Miss Foster knocked and entered. She was a large, regal-looking lady. Her black marocain dress strained over an impressive bosom. If appearance was anything to go by she should have been in charge of something very important, like fur coats or model millinery, rather than elastic and buttons. Opal put the proposition to her.

'We can't offer you any more staff,' she pointed out, 'but the departments are physically close together and I suggest that you train your staff to keep an eye on each other's counters as well as on their own. I would like them, as soon as you can manage it, to get to know the stock on each counter, so that they are really interchangeable. It's a policy we intend to follow right through the store. I'm sure you'll be an excellent person to show us the way.'

'Well I'll try,' Miss Foster said. 'But there's one thing I would like.'

'What's that?'

'I'd like to have Miss Singleton as my under-buyer.'

'Miss Singleton?' Opal said. 'Are you sure?' Miss Singleton was the young woman who had been missing from her counter on Opal's first morning back.

'Quite sure, Miss Opal. She made a somewhat frivolous start, but in the last few months she's improved enormously. She's a good saleswoman – she had experience before she came to us – she knows her stock thoroughly now, and she's particularly good with customers.'

'Well?' Opal looked at her Store Manager.

'If Miss Foster believes her to be the right person, then we should give her a chance,' he said. 'She knows the young lady better than you or I do.'

'Very well then,' Opal said.

'Do I sense, George,' Opal said when Miss Foster had left them, 'that you think our buyers should have more say in choosing their assistants – moving them around, promoting them and so on?'

'I do. I think they should have much more part in it, right from the first interview. As it is, we engage them and the first the buyer sees of the new assistant is on the Monday morning when she arrives on the department.'

'Well, you could be right. But you don't mean I shouldn't see the staff we engage?'

'No. But you could take less part in it. Your job is policy, not detail. And your overriding job is Customer Relations. No-one can do that as well as you can. Look how marvellously you dealt with all those complaints.'

'Well, however you flatter me,' Opal said, smiling, 'there's one job you'll never take from me. Nothing will stop me doing my walk-around. When I do that I just pick up the whole spirit of the place. I can feel at once how everything's going, both with staff *and* customers. And I must say, over the last few months the change is unbelievable. I have a lot to thank you for, George.'

He rose, ready to leave.

'You're the one who's done it, Opal. I've been privileged to help, but you're the one who's been the inspiration to just about everyone. Not really having seen you in action before, I wouldn't have believed it possible!'

'I reckoned from the beginning that my employees would be loyal to me,' Opal said thoughtfully. 'And with a few exceptions they were. I think it helped that I decided not to look back at what had happened, but just to push forward, make a fresh start. But I couldn't have put my ideas into practice without you.'

And now, she thought as he left, he's coming up with ideas of his own, which is good. He's showing me that there's another point of view, that I'm not right all the time. She blessed the day he had taken on the job. Not only was he her right hand, he was accepted throughout the store as a manager who was firm, who would stand no nonsense, but who was fair. It was as if David Hessle had never existed.

Though not for me, Opal thought. She doubted that she would ever see him again but it was impossible that she should ever quite forget him. And there had been good times as well as bad. The last she had heard of him was that Connie was suing him for divorce.

But however pleasing it was that matters were going so well in the store, that the place was once more its clean, attractive, efficient self, that relationships between staff and customers seemed as good as they had ever been, she knew, and so did George, that there were still serious financial problems to be overcome. She did not like to confide them to her staff, other than to exert them to make every economy, and to sell, sell, sell. It would not do for the public, for her customers, to know how difficult it was proving to pay the bills which had been run up in her absence. Sales had increased steadily over the last six months but she had needed ready money for staff commissions and, most importantly, to buy up the two bankrupt stocks which had given them a good July sale. From now until autumn was the quietest time yet she desperately needed money to pay her suppliers so that they would let her have all the goods she needed for a bumper Christmas season. On that she depended to make her solvent for nineteen-thirty-eight.

There was a knock on her door and Daniel came in. When the school year ended she had given him a job in the Packing Department, since he needed to earn pocket money for a trip to Scotland he was taking with Queenie and her family. His cousin, Robert Derwent, was his closest friend. Almost his only friend. He was a solitary boy.

'I know I'm not supposed to invade the Big Chief's office from my humble bench in Packing, but I forgot to tell you that I won't be coming home with you this evening. I'm going to see Robert about the holiday.'

At sixteen he was taller than ever, but too thin, she thought. His voice had long ago settled down to something uncannily like Edgar's. and he had already started to shave. He was like Edgar in manner, too: quiet, reserved, and sometimes just as obstinate.

'Well, give my love to Aunt Queenie and Uncle Mark,' she said. 'Don't be too late home.'

He had, with unconcealed delight, left his boarding school in July and was looking forward to taking his place in the Art school. She was sure that most of his time in Scotland would be devoted to painting and that the pittance he earned in Packing would be spent on paints and brushes. He seemed happy enough most of the time this vacation, except that he still longed for his father. It had grown to be an obsession with him and there was nothing she could do about it. As if reading her thoughts he said:

'If you were to hear from Father while I am in Scotland you would let me know right away?'

She sighed. 'My dear, of course I would. But I don't expect to hear from him. All this time – all the efforts we've made. Daniel, I hate to say it, but wouldn't it be easier for you if you resigned yourself to the facts?'

'You mean give up hope?'

The forward thrust of his chin, the way he spoke, were so like Edgar.

'Do you mean you've given up hope?' he asked.

'Almost,' Opal said quietly. Yet it seemed impossible to her, too, that they would not see Edgar again. He was more alive to her now than David Hessle would ever be.

'I'll never give up hope!' Daniel said passionately. 'And neither should you. Never! When I've finished my art training I shall go to look for him. I don't know where I'll get the money, but I'll get it somehow, and I'll go.'

'Canada is a big place,' Opal said.

'I know. It might take me a long time. But I *shall* go. Perhaps you can give me a whole year's job in Packing or somewhere, so that I can earn the money.'

'I won't condemn you to a whole year in Packing,'

Opal said. 'But when you've finished Art School you can take your proper place in the store, learn all the departments.'

'Mother,' he said patiently, 'I've already told you, and I mean it – I don't want to come into the store with you. Not as a career. It isn't that I hate it. I just don't want to be caught up in it. I want to be a painter. Why can't you resign yourself to that?'

'The store's given you a great deal,' Opal pointed out. 'Almost everything.'

'I know that. I appreciate it. But please don't pretend that you've done it all for me. The store is your world, Mother. It could never be mine. Why can't you accept me for what I am?'

As, perhaps, she had never accepted Edgar. She had not wanted to shut him out but she had wanted him to be part of her world; she had never been prepared to enter his. And now she was doing the same thing with Daniel.

'I'm sorry, Mother!'

'No, don't be,' she said quickly. 'Perhaps it's I who should be sorry. Oddly enough it's the second time today I've been shown that I can't have all my own way! Well, perhaps I'm old enough to accept it now – but if I'd done so when I was younger I wouldn't have had my career. In a way you're really doing what I did then, fighting for what you want. But perhaps you won't hurt as many people on the way.'

'Perhaps I won't need to. Perhaps it will be easier for me than it was for you.'

He leaned across the desk and kissed her on the cheek. It was a rare gesture from her undemonstrative son. It gave her great pleasure.

'Get along with you,' she said, 'or Mr Beecham will

complain that you're not pulling your weight and I shall have to sack you!'

At the end of the first week in November the enlarged Toy Department, its extra territory grabbed from the reluctant buyers of other departments, was ready for the Christmas season. The Wonderland Grotto, to which it led, would in a day or two's time be fit to receive Santa Claus when he arrived, ostensibly from some far-off, cold country.

No-one would ever know, Opal thought, what effort it had cost, what juggling of accounts, what pleading with suppliers, to present this splendid display of toys, games, annuals, puzzles – everything that a child could wish for. Nor how difficult it had been to furnish the Grotto more spectacularly than ever before. Its nurseryland figures, its fairy lights and glitter, its dark, exciting corners and air of magic as well as its sacks of ninepenny parcels to be handed out to the children, had arisen only after a great effort, with small resources, by the staff of the Display Department, and much juggling of finance by Opal and George Soames. Her credit was now stretched to the limit and the bank would allow no further increase in her overdraft. Everything now depended upon the Christmas season.

It was Santa Claus himself who now presented the problem. He hailed, not from the Arctic regions but from the main entrance, where for ten-and-a-half months of the year he was the commissionaire, resplendent in uniform, with medals from the wars in South Africa and France.

'It's hopeless!' George Soames said. 'He's the worse for wear again this afternoon. He sneaks across to the Black Swan at dinner-time and people buy him drinks because he's an old soldier. Potter simply can't be Santa Claus!'

'I know,' Opal agreed miserably. 'Yet I hate to tell him. He so looks forward to it. Well, I'll see to this myself. I've known Sam a long time.'

Sam Potter, sent for, stood to attention in front of Opal's desk and saluted.

'Sit down, Sam,' Opal said. 'You know why you're here, don't you?'

'Of course I do, Miss Opal! Santa Claus time again!'

He was steady enough, but his over-careful enunciation and the powerful smell of whisky which hung around him left no doubt that he was, if only slightly, drunk.

'But not for you, I'm afraid,' Opal said. 'Sam, you must know what I'm talking about. You've been drinking again. It's by no means the first time. And now I have to tell you that you can't be Santa Claus this year. I can't have you breathing whisky all over the children. Their parents would object most strongly.'

She felt terrible, watching this man so proud in his uniform struggle for words to express his shock.

'It's only a little drop I take,' he mumbled. 'Just to keep out the cold. It's a chilly job standing in that entrance.'

'I know,' she said, 'but you can't risk warming yourself up with whisky. I can't prevent you spending your dinner hour in the Black Swan but I have to warn you, Sam, that if you don't put a stop to it then Santa Claus won't be the only job I'll have to take from you.'

He rose to his feet. He was unsteady now and swayed towards her.

'Are you threatening me with the sack?' he demanded.

'Threatening isn't a word I like,' Opal said. 'I'm advising you for your own good.'

He leaned across the desk, his face close to hers so that his drink-laden breath almost choked her.

'You'll be sorry for this,' he said thickly. 'I know all your customers, all the posh people, every one of them. They like me. You'll be sorry for this!'

'And so will you if you don't behave yourself,' Opal said firmly. 'Now take the rest of the day off. Go home, and come back sober in the morning.'

'And if I do, can I have the Santa Claus job?'

'No,' Opal said. 'I'm sorry, I can't risk it.'

In the event a young man from the Stockroom became Santa Claus. He does it very well, Opal thought, watching him, head bent down to a small child confiding its secret wishes. She noted with satisfaction the long queue which wound, caterpillar-like, through the Grotto and out into the Toy Department. It had been like this every minute since Santa had arrived last Saturday, riding through the streets of Leasfield on the back of an elephant which had been hired from a circus in winter quarters on the outskirts of the town. He had left his sledge, he explained to clever children who asked too many questions, with the circus owner.

She walked through the Grotto several times a day since the staircase to her office was at the far end of it. Apart from the business it was bringing in, she enjoyed seeing the children. She must get Mary to bring Emmeline, which would not be difficult for since George Soames had become Store Manager Mary, for one reason or another, visited the store far more often.

Sam Potter had not changed his ways. He was never very drunk but, in the afternoons, never quite sober.

She had put it to him that an indoor job in the Stockroom or in Packing might suit him better but he had refused on the grounds that he would not be able to wear his uniform.

'He'll have to go,' she said to George Soames, 'but it's not something I can do before Christmas. It would be too cruel.'

Working late in her office that evening she thought again about Sam Potter, wished she could do something for him. He was too young to be pensioned off but too old to find another job. He had muttered more threats at her but that did not worry her. He was in no position to do her any harm.

She looked at her watch. Nine o'clock. She must go home. She put on her hat and coat, drew on her gloves, took the car keys out of her handbag, opened her office door – and almost choked.

The narrow staircase was filled with smoke; thick, acrid. It filled her lungs and she coughed and spluttered, tried to hold her breath and could not. Beyond the bottom of the staircase, where a screen divided it from the Grotto, the smoke thickened and glowed red. She was trapped!

She ran back into her office, closed the door, picked up the telephone and rang the Fire Brigade. Then she climbed on to the desk and from there she opened the high window and climbed out on to the steep, frost-covered roof. How long would it be, she wondered, shivering in the night air, trying to keep her footing on the icy slates, before the flames reached her office and licked through to the roof?

'Granted that the Grotto and most of the Toy Department is a write-off,' George Soames said, 'I still say you were lucky. You were fortunate to be rescued in time!'

They were sitting in his office, which she must now share since the fire had burnt out the bottom half of the staircase leading to her own.

'Which is more than can be said for Sam Potter,' Opal said. 'Though thank goodness he *will* recover.'

'To face a charge of arson,' George said. 'There isn't any doubt that he started the fire and if the firemen hadn't come across him quickly he'd have died in it. As might you,' he added soberly, 'had you not decided to go home when you did!'

She was glad to be alive. Every hour since she had been rescued from that icy roof had been like a gift to her. But the joy of living when she might have perished did nothing to solve the problem of what she must do next.

'I'd staked everything on the Grotto and the Toy Department in these six weeks before Christmas,' she reminded George. 'You know that. Now only five weeks to go and nothing left to sell except the fairy cycles and toy motor cars which were at the far end of the department.'

There would be the insurance, of course, when it came through, but she knew she was under-insured and had been for some time. And her credit everywhere was stretched to the limit.

'Even if we had the money,' George Soames said, 'we don't have the time.'

'You're wrong there,' Opal said vehemently. 'If we had the money quickly, we could do it in the time. I know my people. They've already proved themselves. I know they'd work night and day to put everything right. But that's no good unless we have new stock. What can we do, George? What can we do?'

She beat her hands against her head as if she would force some sort of solution from her brain.

George shook his head.

'I have a few hundred pounds, perhaps a thousand. Not being married I've been able to save a bit. It's yours if you want it but it won't go far.'

She looked up quickly, her face suddenly glowing, her eyes alight.

'George, you're a genius! You're an absolute genius!'

'I've only offered you a few hundred pounds,' he said, nonplussed. 'There's nothing especially wonderful about that.'

'Yes there is,' she cried. 'Because it's shown me what I must do! I must do exactly as I did when I needed money to start my store. I went to my richest customer, my darling Miss Taylor, and I asked her to lend me the money.'

She had also asked Queenie but it would not be fair to do that again. Queenie and Mark now had a large family to bring up and educate.

'That's what I shall do,' Opal said. She felt excited, hopeful. 'I shall write to the customers I know best, who know me and, I hope, trust me. I shall tell them the position – they know the kind of year I've had, putting the store to rights again – and I shall frankly ask each one of them for a loan – large or small, according to their means, as long as it's immediate. I shall offer them a good rate of repayment and if I must – if I absolutely must – I'll offer them a share in Opal's. I don't want to go so far, and I'd only do it for a very substantial loan, but if it's the only way then I'll take it.'

'It's impossible!' George protested. 'You can't write and ask customers to lend you money.'

'Yes I can. I'm a woman in trouble, asking for help

263

from my fellow women. I believe I shall get it, at least in some cases. Besides, what's the alternative?'

She rang for her secretary.

'Mrs Sylvester, I have to write a number of letters. No, I don't want them typed. I shall write them in my own hand. But I don't want any interruptions. All these letters must go in today's post. And before I can begin I want the ledgers of all our account customers. It doesn't matter if Accounts Department is working on them; tell them I have to have them.'

While waiting for the ledgers to arrive she drafted out what she would say, writing and re-writing, discarding one attempt after another.

'How will this do?' she said to George at last.

'Dear Mrs So-and-so,

You will doubtless have read of the dreadful fire which destroyed the Wonderland Grotto and most of the Toy Department in Opal's store. Mercifully there was no loss of life and the one person injured is now recovering in hospital. What faces me now is the speedy restoration of those areas, partly because of the great pleasure which they give to the children of Leasfield and beyond, partly – I will be quite frank with you – for the successful continuance of my business.

As you are a regular and valued customer I need not tell you that since my return from my two-year enforced absence I have been fighting a battle to make my store what it once was. That battle was almost over. Had it not been for the fire we should have won through by Christmas. Now we cannot possibly do so without the help of our well-wishers and friends.

I am taking the bold but necessary step of asking you if you would be willing to help me, and Opal's store, by making me a loan. Large or small, it will be welcome, but I need it quickly. I have already been offered several hundred pounds but I need more, much more.

If you are able and willing to help I shall be at your disposal to discuss terms. If you cannot or do not wish to do so I hope that I shall still continue to have your much appreciated custom in my store. Yours sincerely, Opal Carson.

'What do you think, George?'

'Fine, if you think it'll work,' George said doubtfully. 'What can I do to help?'

'Leave me alone to write. Nothing more just now.'

Two days later the replies began to arrive. There were few letters which did not contain money, sometimes in surprisingly large amounts. But even before the letters, on the very day on which they had received the appeal, the customers came in person. Of those who came thus, no-one arrived without an offering of some kind. But from first to last it was not the offer of money which moved Opal most; it was the wealth of good wishes which accompanied it. Mrs Sylvester found her sitting behind a desk spread with letters, tears streaming down her face.

'I can't help it,' she apologized. 'I just had no idea! I had no idea what people thought of us!'

'Of you,' Mrs Sylvester corrected.

'It sounds a terrible thing to say, but it was almost worth having a fire to have this happen!'

She dried her eyes and began to collect the letters together. 'I shall never part with these as long as I live,' she said. 'Now we have to show what we can do with the money. First of all, Mrs Sylvester, I want you to call a special staff meeting. I'm going to need everyone's help.'

Within ten days the Grotto had been rebuilt and the Toy Department was usable again. The display staff, joined by members of the sales staff and office workers who declared themselves handy with paint brushes, hammers and nails, buckets and brooms, had worked around the clock in shifts. Volunteer drivers collected toys from suppliers far and wide; helpers from several departments gave up their lunch hours to price and label them and put them on display.

'It's a miracle,' Opal said when it was finished. 'But no more than I expected!'

'All we want now is the customers,' George Soames said.

'They'll come,' Opal said. 'You watch. They'll come more than ever now, just to see what we've accomplished.'

She was right. When the Toy Department and the Wonderland Grotto re-opened, the smell of smoke still hanging in the air, the crowds of Christmas shoppers flocked in – and continued to do so every day until Christmas.

At closing time on Christmas Eve Opal went to every department in the store, exchanging good wishes, collecting the sales sheets. When the last late customer had left, the last cover been draped over its counter, the last assistant gone home for Christmas, she walked back through the deserted store to George Soames's office.

'You should go home, Opal,' he said. 'You look all in.'

'Not until I've checked the sales sheets,' Opal said. 'Will you give me a hand?'

Long before they had reached the last of the sheets she looked up, smiling. Her eyes were bright, in spite of the fatigue which she knew must soon overwhelm her.

'George, it's far and away the best Christmas we've ever had! We've broken all records and we still have four more departments to check!'

Not long afterwards, the job completed, she took her coat from the closet and he helped her into it.

'Don't be late for Christmas dinner tomorrow,' she said.

'I won't,' he promised. 'I'm looking forward to it. It's a long time since I spent Christmas with a family.'

Chapter Fifteen

The Christmas of nineteen-thirty-seven, as well as being the best ever in the store, was for the most part a happy one at Oak House. When Opal arrived home on Christmas Eve, coming in from the frosty darkness outside to the bright warmth of the hall, Daniel and her father were putting the last touches to the six-foot-tall Christmas tree. Benjamin Derwent stepped back to view the effect.

'I think that's a bit of all right!' he declared. 'Though I say it myself as shouldn't. What do you think, Opal love?'

'It's beautiful,' Opal agreed. 'You two have been really busy.'

She wished, with a pang of remembrance, that Miss Taylor could see her house now. She would surely approve.

'And another thing, our Opal,' her father said, 'I've sawed up enough logs to see us right through Christmas. Now if we had a great big fireplace like your Grandpa Derwent's on the farm we could have a real yule log, big enough to last until New Year.'

Opal shook her head. 'You do too much, Dad. You know you shouldn't overtire yourself.'

'Nay lass, I haven't,' he assured her. 'I'm a very fit man, nowadays, for my age.'

Opal laid a hand on his arm. 'I know you are, love. And now I'll just go up to Emmeline. I wanted to be home before she fell asleep.'

'You are,' Daniel said. 'The little monkey's too excited to sleep.'

As Opal entered the bedroom Emmeline darted back under the bedclothes, bright eyes wide open, determined not to miss a moment of this exciting day. On either side of her a teddy bear, a stuffed elephant and two dolls shared the bed.

'Hey, Miss! You're supposed to be asleep!' Opal said. 'Do you know what time it is?'

'I'm not a bit tired!' Emmeline protested. 'Will it soon be Christmas Day, Mummy?'

'After you've been to sleep. Now you lie still and I'll tell you the Christmas story again, and then you must try to sleep. What if Santa Claus came and found you awake?'

Sitting beside the bed, Opal had hardly begun the story before Emmeline's eyes closed and she was fast asleep. Opal tucked the blankets around the child's shoulders and went back downstairs.

'She was worn out,' she said, laughing. 'But quite determined to stay awake. She'll sleep until morning now.'

On Christmas Day Emmeline delighted, and was delighted by, everyone. In her wonder at the tall tree with its glass baubles, tinsel and fairy lights, in her excited cries as she tore the wrapping from her presents, revealing the spinning top, the toy piano, the dolls, the sweets, they all took pleasure. Benjamin, in particular, watched her with loving eyes.

'Little 'uns are what make Christmas,' he said.

Though he tried not to show it and would never have admitted it, Opal was sure that Emmeline was her father's favourite grandchild.

269

'Well I must get on,' Mary said, picking up the wrapping paper, smoothing it out to be used again. 'What time do you suppose George will arrive?'

'He said he'd be here at twelve noon,' Opal answered. 'Mary can't you slow down? You've hardly given yourself time to look at your presents!' Her sister was flushed this morning, though whether it was from the heat of the kitchen or from the thought of George Soames's presence at such an intimate family gathering, Opal was not certain.

'Nonsense! I'm thrilled by my presents,' Mary said. 'But I've still got lots to do. The dinner won't cook itself. And I want everything to be just right.'

'I'll help you,' Opal offered.

'Indeed you won't!' Mary retorted. 'If anyone needs a rest it's you!'

In the event, George Soames arrived early, laden with presents.

'I thought if I came in good time I could give a hand,' he said.

'Well if you really mean it you can help me with the table,' Mary said. 'Come along. I'll show you what's to be done.'

With mixed feelings Opal watched the two of them disappear into the dining-room. In the last few months she had sometimes caught herself wondering whether she and George might not come together, make a go of it. In spite of her success in the store she felt herself incomplete, felt, from time to time, an indefinable sadness, an inner loneliness, especially when the day's work was over.

She admired and respected George and she was confident that he was fond of her. It was a good basis for marriage and more might be added to it. But when she observed the meeting between George and her sister on that Christmas morning she knew it was not to be. Mary lit a flame in him so bright and clear that no-one, seeing them together, could miss it. It was a flame she could never have kindled.

After the huge Christmas dinner, when they had pushed back their chairs and George and Mary had gone into the kitchen to make coffee, Opal said, 'I'm going to put Emmeline to bed for a while. She's tired out.'

'I think I'll have a lie down,' her father said. 'I don't want any coffee.' When Opal came down again Daniel was on his own. Sitting at the table, his head in his hands, he did not hear her enter. She put an arm around his shoulders, stroked his hair.

'I know' she whispered. 'I know!'

'If there'd only been a word from him,' he said. 'I thought at Christmas there'd be a word.'

On Boxing Day the word came. Opal and Daniel drove over to Mr and Mrs Carson's to take presents.

'But are you otherwise happier, now?' Opal asked as they sat in the car.

'Of course I am,' he replied. 'I've had a great term at college, doing what I actually want to do. And the new easel you've given me for Christmas is perfect. I'm going to feel really professional using it. I think I shall paint your portrait.' He hesitated. 'It's just . . . well, you know!'

'Let's go by way of Acer Street,' Opal said on an impulse.

It was the first time she had been near the street since they had left to go to Madame Dora's. It was narrower than she remembered it, the houses even smaller. The stonework was still soot black but the net curtains which hung at every window had been newly laundered for Christmas and all along the street the front doors had been painted and glossily varnished in a light oak colour. The mill was doing better now. Most of the families in Acer Street would be in work.

'Do you remember this, Daniel?' she asked.

'Of course I do,' he said. 'I was five when we left here. I didn't want to go.'

She drove slowly down the street. She had passionately wanted to leave it, never to see the place again, but now she could admit that not every day in Acer Street had been a bad one. The first year with Edgar, when Daniel was a small baby, had been happy enough. It was poverty which had changed everything. Though had it not been for poverty, which had relentlessly compelled her to find something better, she would not now be driving along the street (too ostentatiously she thought) in this expensive car.

At the end of the street she turned right into William Street. Her parents-in-law no longer ran the bakery. Percy Carson had been ailing for some years and they had sold the business and moved into a small terraced house near by. By the time Opal stopped the car Mrs Carson was at the front door, waving an envelope.

'It's for you, Daniel love!' she cried. 'It was delivered to the bakery in the Christmas post and they brought it down here this morning. One for me as well. From Montreal!'

'Montreal?'

Daniel tore open the envelope, took out the card, read it while his mother and grandmother watched.

'What does he say?' the old lady asked impatiently. 'Does he give an address?'

Opal knew the answer, read it in the sick disappointment in her son's face.

'I'm afraid not,' he said slowly. 'He just says "Merry Christmas, Son. Merry Christmas to your mother." Nothing more.'

'Aye, that's about all mine says, except that he's well. I hoped he might have let us know where he is.'

Mrs Carson's voice was flat with dejection. Daniel put an arm around her shoulders. Opal looked at the two of them and could hardly bear the sadness in their eyes.

Daniel handed her the Christmas card. The familiarity of the angular handwriting was like a presence. She had not seen it since before she was married, in the days when, between visits, Edgar used to write surprisingly fluent letters to her at Highcliffe. The Christmas card was the first time in three years that he had mentioned her. Did it mean she was forgiven? Perhaps that was reading too much into it, but she would like to think they were no longer enemies.

'Come and see me more often, lad,' Mrs Carson said to Daniel when they were leaving. 'It does me good to see you.'

'I will,' Daniel promised.

The first half of nineteen-thirty-eight brought so much work with it that Opal, except occasionally, had no time for the loneliness she had felt at Christmas. Daniel, though she noticed that he visited his grandmother more often, worked hard and said little. No word came from Edgar.

In the store it was the busiest time Opal had ever known. New housing estates were going up in and around Leasfield – semi-detached houses for a few

273

hundred pounds. As young couples paid the deposit and moved into them, so the demand came for furniture; three-piece suites, kitchen cabinets, curtains – everything (especially if it could be had on hire purchase) to make the new home a palace. Opal quickly had the cellars under the store cleared out and decorated, bright lighting installed, and opened up a basement entirely devoted to everything which could possibly be needed to furnish a home in the latest style.

'Do you realize' she said to George Soames as the store closed on Easter Saturday 'that we've done so well this spring, not only with the new departments but with fashion too, that we're now on an even keel with our suppliers? It even looks as though by the end of the year I'll have repaid most of the loans to my customers.'

'I do realize,' George answered. 'I've sometimes felt this last few weeks that the whole of Leasfield is putting up new curtains and refurnishing! But you deserve the success, Opal. Once again you were quick off the mark.'

And now it was June, and Emmeline's third birthday, and since it was a perfect summer Sunday she and the children were in the garden. George had taken Mary and her father for a drive to Ilkley, promising to be back in time for the birthday tea. Daniel was gently pushing his sister on the swing. From the seat where she watched them Opal smelt the spicy clove scent of the border pinks and the more heady perfume of the roses. The roses, old-fashioned ones which bloomed profusely now and by next month would be gone, had been planted by Miss Taylor.

She watched Daniel. He was so good with

Emmeline, so caring; as if, at seventeen years old, knowing his own loss, he was trying to be the father the little girl did not have. How very much she loved her children! They were the mainspring of her life, more to her than anything in the world, and she wanted the world to be perfect for them.

But people were saying that war would come, that it was inevitable. When she went to the cinema, as she sometimes did with Daniel or her father, the films were full of music and romance but the newsreels showed uniformed men marching across Europe. If war came, what about Daniel? The thought came unbidden and unwelcome into her mind, as it did all too often these days. She pushed it away. It had no place in this perfect June day.

From time to time she closed her eyes, trying to banish all thought, letting the heat soak into her body; sliding towards sleep, so that when the man came towards her she did not see him, or hear his footsteps on the grass. It was only when his shadow blocked out the sun that she opened her eyes and looked up – and believed that she must, in fact, have fallen asleep and be dreaming.

'Edgar!' She managed no more than a whisper.

At the same time as she jumped to her feet, Daniel saw his father. He cried out, and bounded across the lawn, leaving Emmeline to fend for herself. The two men – automatically Opal noticed that Daniel was taller than his father – were locked in an embrace. She stood awkwardly by, not knowing how to act, confused thoughts crowding in on her. It was too sudden. Why had he not warned them?

Emmeline climbed down from the swing, ran across the lawn and took her mother's hand, examining the strange man with a quizzical look. Edgar and Daniel turned to face Opal and she felt herself deeply moved by the luminous joy in her son's face. Edgar made no move towards her, not even holding out his hand. He looked at her with a hard, direct gaze and then from her to the little girl at her side.

'So this is Emmeline,' he said quietly. 'I've seen my mother and she told me about Emmeline. Well, she's a beautiful child, Opal. And the image of you.'

'I was never beautiful,' Opal said nervously. How stupid she sounded, but she could not think of the right words, if there were any for an occasion like this.

'You don't appear to have changed much,' he said. She could not say that Edgar had not changed. It was not only that he looked older; he was thinner; held himself straighter, like a man who could face the world and take it on. Perhaps the greatest visible change in him was the air of strength, which had nothing to do with physique. It was in his eyes, clear and unafraid; in the firmer line of his mouth, in the confident way he held himself. Here was a man who was in charge of himself and of his life, Opal thought. He had not returned to her cap in hand, she was sure of that. He was as strong as she was.

'I'm sure I *have* changed,' she replied. 'Though perhaps not in looks.' And then she remembered, as she still occasionally did, and lifted her hand to touch the scar which ran down her cheek.

'I heard about your accident from my mother today,' Edgar said. 'I'm sorry. I'd have come back if I'd known.'

'I'm completely recovered,' Opal said. 'What brought you . . . ?' She was interrupted by Daniel.

'This is your new daddy, Emmeline,' he said happily. 'Say hello to your new daddy!'

Opal's eyes, meeting Edgar's, flashed a warning. Don't spoil it for him. For his sake, not yours or mine, don't spoil this moment. She tried to will him to understand but his eyes gave nothing away. She was terrified of what he would say. It seemed an age before he spoke, turning to Emmeline, holding out his hand.

'Would you like me to push you on the swing?' he asked.

The evening, it seemed to Opal, went on for ever, the long northern daylight lingering in the summer sky. She was ill at ease, wanting to be alone with Edgar, knowing that there were things which must be said – yet not wanting to be. She was glad of Daniel's presence long after Emmeline had gone to bed, yet uneasy because of it. Mary and her father, embarrassingly tactful, had gone off to their rooms early, as soon as George had left. In the end Daniel, too, had wished his parents a reluctant 'good night'.

'But you'll be staying, won't you?' he asked his father anxiously.

'I have to go back to your grandmother's,' Edgar said. 'I dare say I'll have to stay there quite a while. Grandad's very ill, you know. But I'll see you tomorrow.'

Opal was grateful for his tact. She felt herself surrounded by people who now saw her future miraculously bright, all problems solved. Daniel saw it that way from ignorance; Mary and her father, she supposed, because they wanted a happy ending. Mary, in the throes of a love which had come suddenly and late, wanted everyone else as amicably settled as she herself would soon be. But it was not so simple, Opal thought. The future was not at all clear to her. It was all too soon. Even if she could sort out her own feelings – which she could not – she had no idea of Edgar's.

One thing was certain, he was not the man who had left her. He was a new man. It seemed impossible that in three years he could have changed so much, but the evidence was there before her and had been constantly reaffirmed in the hours since his arrival. Was it possible that but for the years of unemployment, followed by the third-rate job which he had hated, he would in any case have emerged like this? What part had her own success, at the very time when he saw himself as a failure, played in keeping down this man? She didn't know the answer to that one.

But the success he had won for himself, without help from anyone, had made him into a different person. Whether she would like this new person or not she didn't yet know. Nor could she guess at his feelings for her. The talk over the last few hours, in the presence of the rest of the family, had been general. He had treated her with no more familiarity than he had shown to Mary, and he had shown no eagerness to be alone with her.

When Daniel had finally gone to bed Edgar said, 'Let's go outside again. We don't get midsummer nights like this in Canada. It's one of the things I've dreamed about.'

They walked around the garden. With the setting of the sun the scents of the garden had intensified. The flowers seemed all one pale shade of cream, starkly outlined in the dusk. It was a romantic atmosphere, the last thing she wanted.

'You haven't *really* said what made you decide to come back. I know you never had my letter.'

'No. But then as I've told you, I was never in Toronto after the first year.'

Once in Canada he had quickly found a job, in a new insurance company just starting up. He had done well, grown with the Company, until in three years he had become a senior manager. It had meant, though, that he must move about the country, finding new business, opening new branches.

Was it possible, Opal wondered suddenly, that he had met someone in Canada? A woman he wanted to marry. Had he come to ask her for a divorce?

'I came back because there's going to be a war,' Edgar said. 'I didn't want to talk about it in front of your family, not today. But I reckon it's a certainty. I couldn't stay in Canada with my family in England when there was a war on. At Daniel's age he'll soon be called up. Apart from anything I can do in the war, I had to be here to see Daniel!'

Why must everyone be so sure about war, Opal thought? Did men make war inevitable by accepting it as inevitable? But could she, by refusing to think of it, make it go away?

'You're thirty-nine,' she said. 'Won't you be too old to fight?'

'I didn't come back just to fight,' Edgar said. 'And I have a job here if I want one. My company are only too eager for me to start up here. I may have to fight, of course, though I shall hate it. That's been my trouble. Even for something that meant most in the world to me – you, Daniel – I wouldn't fight. I gave in, ran away. It's not a mistake I shall make again. *You* fought for what you wanted.'

'Is that why you fought for your new company?' Opal asked. 'For your place with them?'

'I didn't fight for the company. I fought for me. For my own self-respect. I had something to prove and I proved it. I assure you, the world looks a very different place to me now! But I also discovered you usually wound someone. I hurt Daniel.'

'Yes you did,' Opal agreed. 'As much by your silence as by your leaving. But Daniel will be all right. He's never doubted that he'd find you again one day, and now he has. Right now, Daniel's world is complete!'

How long it would stay complete if she and Edgar were not to come together was another matter. But Daniel was almost grown up and she must give him credit for understanding. His parents could not build their future on what would please him. Not even Emmeline, she thought, can claim that from me – though my debt to her is greater and will take longer to discharge.

'And you and me?' Edgar asked. 'What did I do to us?'

'We did it to each other. But it appears not to have been all loss for either of us. You found strength and independence. You found that you could survive without me.'

'And what did you find?' he asked.

'Oh quite a lot. Including my weaknesses. I'd been arrogant enough to think that I could run my world single-handed, needing no-one. I was wrong. I've needed – and been given – the help of so many people. I couldn't have survived otherwise.'

It was dark now. The last vestige of colour had faded from the garden and a breeze was beginning to blow.

'I love Emmeline dearly,' Opal said, apropos, it seemed, of nothing.

'And her father?'

'David? I never think of him as Emmeline's father. He's only set eyes on her once, for a few minutes – far less time than you have. He never will again.'

'Where is he?'

'Who knows? Wherever he is I doubt if he'll stay there long. He, at least, is someone I don't have to think about. But Emmeline is another matter.'

They were silent for a while. Then Edgar said, 'She's *your* child. More important, she's a person in her own right. Emmeline shouldn't be punished.'

'And never will be,' Opal said fiercely. 'I wouldn't allow it. As I've told you, I love her dearly.'

'If war comes,' she said after a while, 'Daniel will be involved in no time at all. He'll join the Air Force or something silly like that.'

'We shall all be involved,' Edgar said. 'It will be that kind of war. But Daniel will make out. He has his own strengths. I can see that.'

Opal shivered. 'It's getting quite cool,' she said.

'Yes. And I must be leaving.'

'Would you like a nightcap before you go?'

They went into the house. Watching him as he sipped his drink Opal thought that he was an attractive man. He always had been, but now the bitterness of those years in the 'twenties had left him. He was a man at peace with himself. At peace, but not necessarily acquiescent.

He raised his head, caught her watching him.

'There is the question of you and me, Opal.'

'Not now . . .' she began.

'I agree,' he said. 'It's early days. That was what I was going to say.'

'Unless' Opal said quickly 'there is someone else involved. Someone I don't know about.'

'There's no-one else. There was, but it's over. But you and I are two different people, Opal. We have to get to know each other again. It won't be like it was before.'

'I know.' She knew, too, that if there was to be a relationship between them it would not be on her terms alone. 'We have to be certain,' she said.

'Nothing is certain,' Edgar said. 'But at least let's try to be honest with each other.'

By mutual, unspoken consent, they dropped the subject. It would come up again in its own good time. Neither of them would force it.

'What shall *I* do if war comes?' Opal speculated, turning the conversation. 'Though I refuse to take it for granted that it will. I suppose I'll go on as usual. They say there'd be conscription for women as well as for men so I expect half my staff would be taken. There'd be shortages, rules, regulations – goodness knows what other difficulties. I'd have my battles all right. But the country can't do without retailers so I suppose I'd come through!'

'Oh I know you would,' Edgar assured her. 'I can't see Opal's store going under! I can't see you ever giving up!'

He stood up, ready to leave.

'I'll see you tomorrow, then?' he said.

'Yes,' Opal replied. She was surprised how the thought pleased her.

THE END